THE SWEETNESS BETWEEN US

sarah winifred searle

First Second
New York

For my sweet.

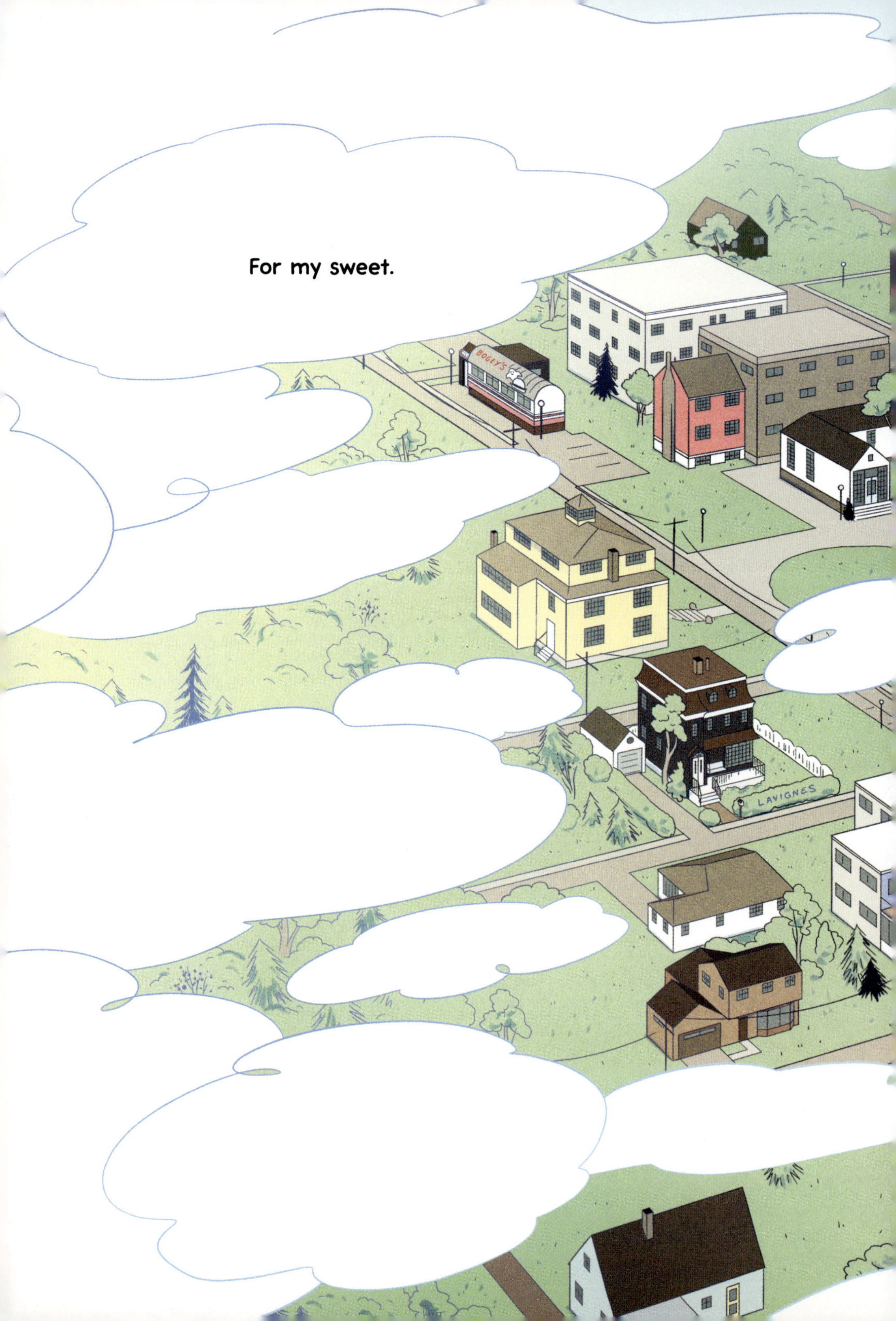
BOGEY'S
LAVIGNES

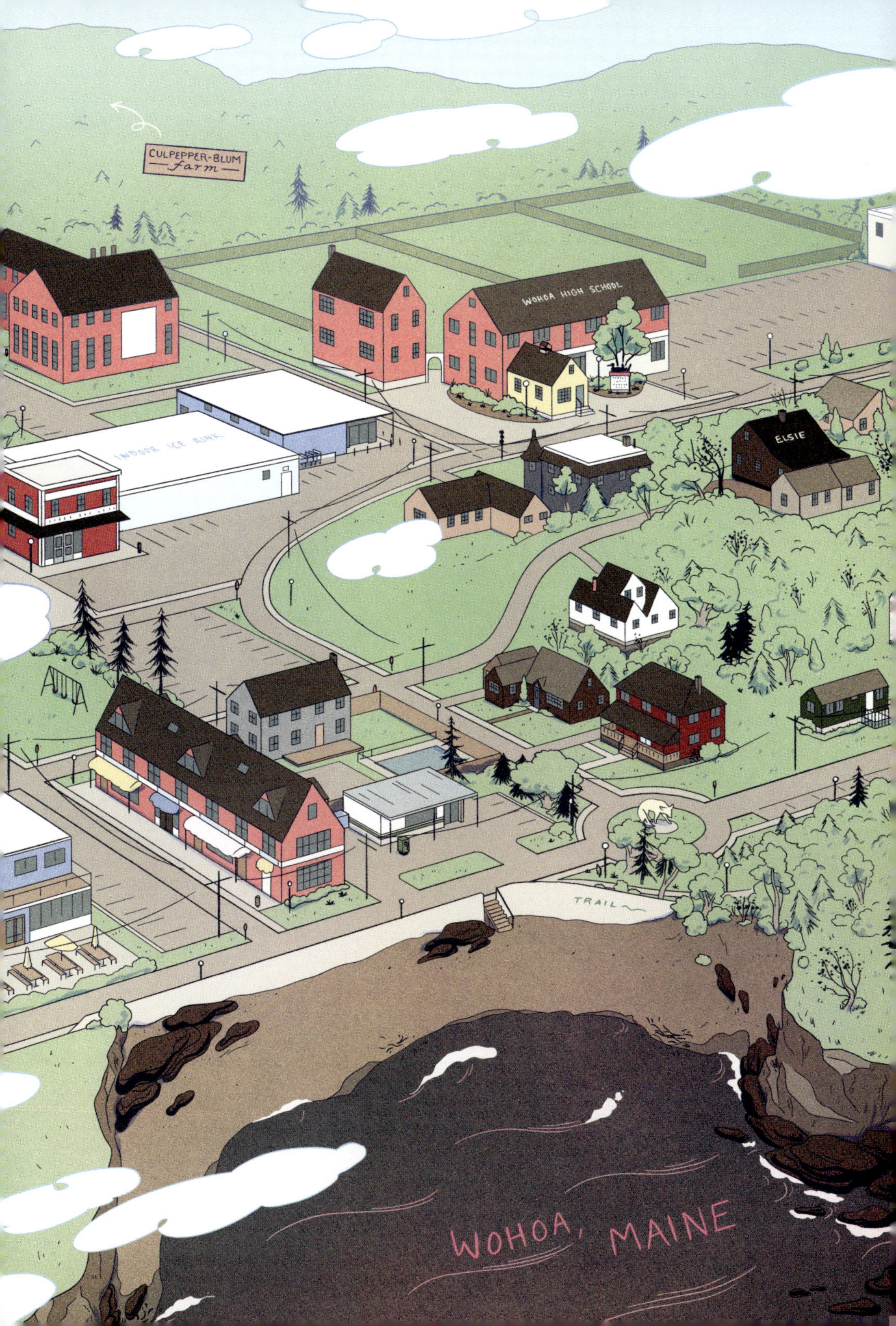
CULPEPPER-BLUM farm
WOHOA HIGH SCHOOL
INDOOR ICE RINK
ELSIE
TRAIL
WOHOA, MAINE

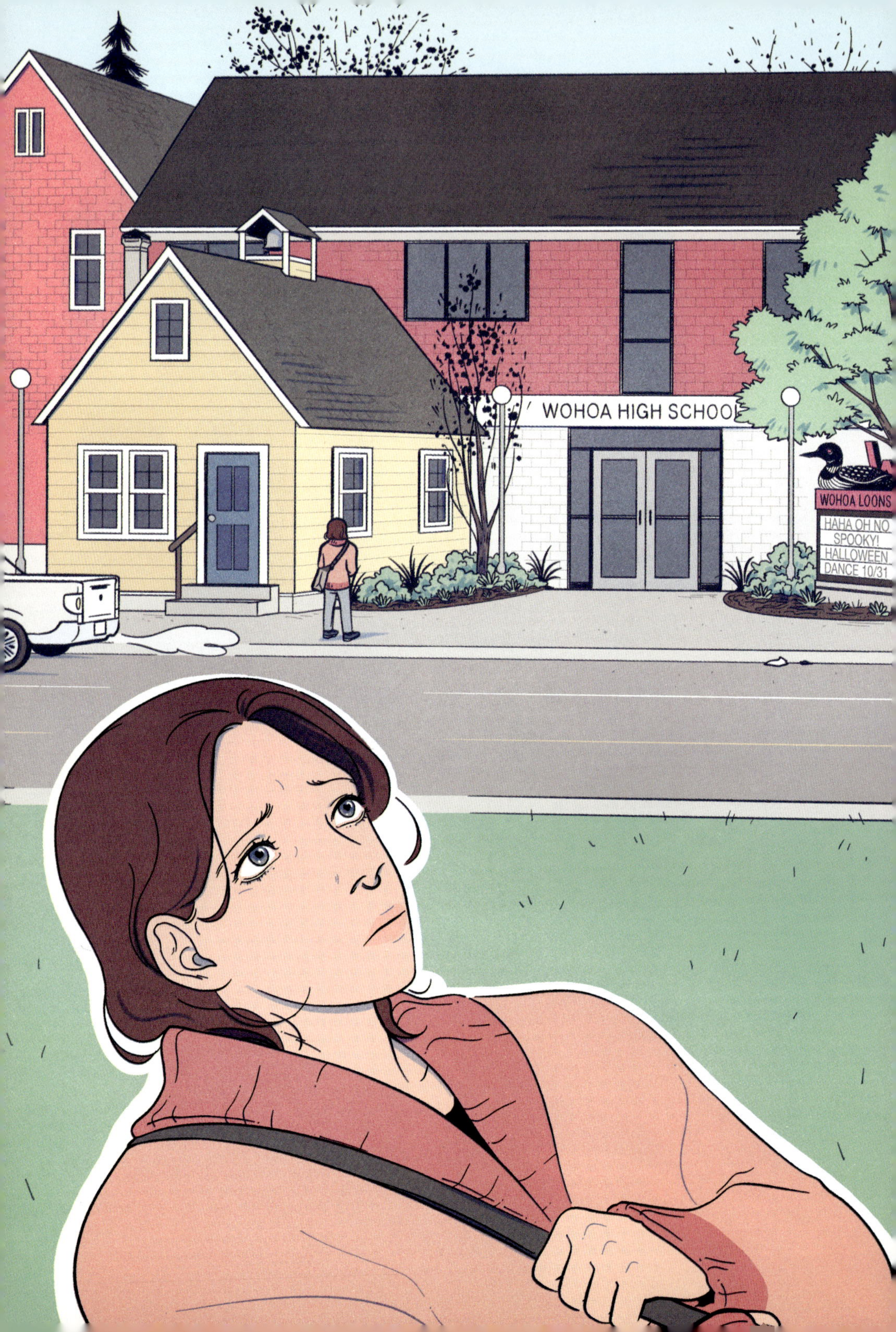
WOHOA HIGH SCHOOL
WOHOA LOONS
HAHA OH NO
SPOOKY!
HALLOWEEN
DANCE 10/31

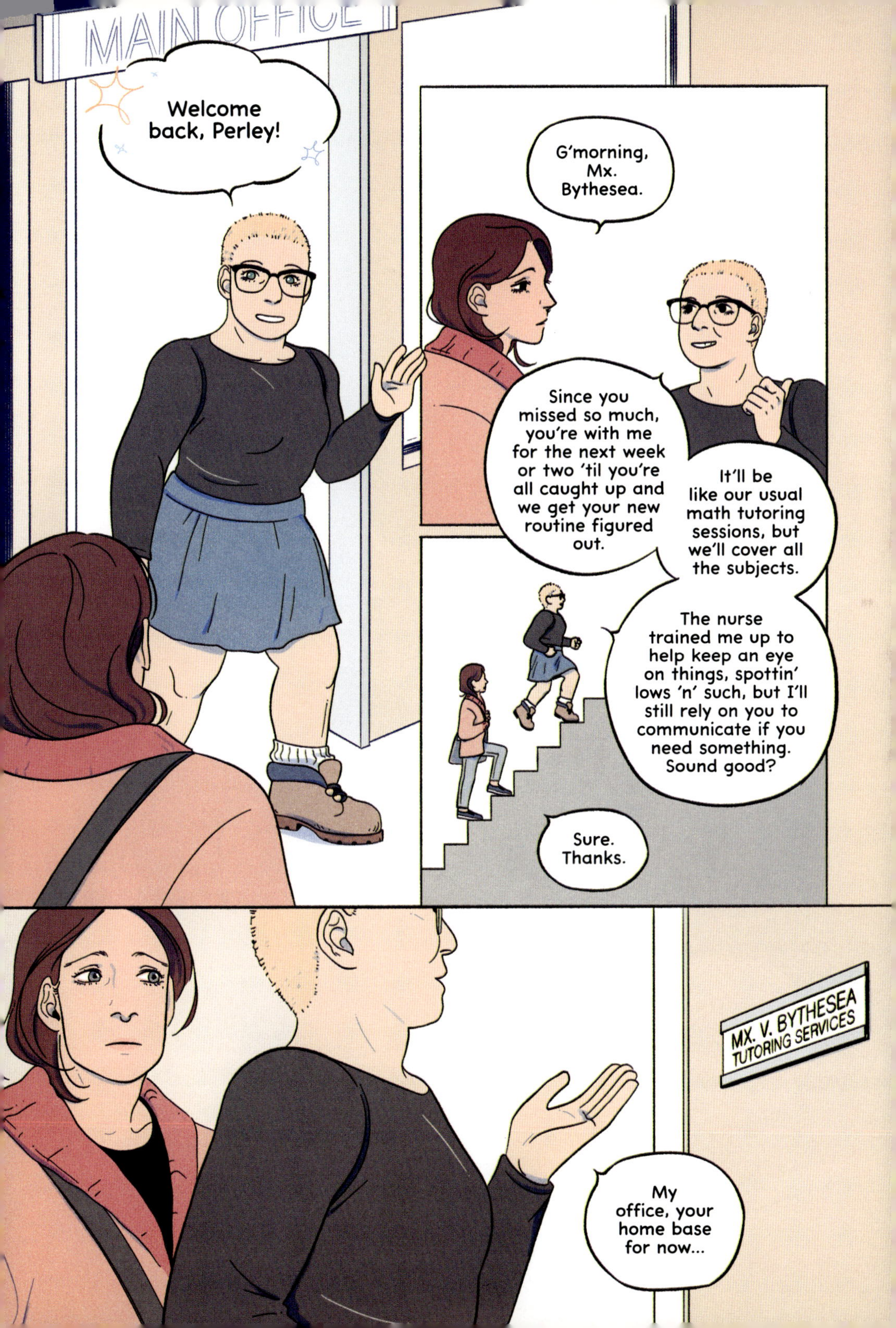
MAIN OFFICE
Welcome back, Perley!
G'morning, Mx. Bythesea.
Since you missed so much, you're with me for the next week or two 'til you're all caught up and we get your new routine figured out.
It'll be like our usual math tutoring sessions, but we'll cover all the subjects.
The nurse trained me up to help keep an eye on things, spottin' lows 'n' such, but I'll still rely on you to communicate if you need something. Sound good?
Sure. Thanks.
MX. V. BYTHESEA
TUTORING SERVICES
My office, your home base for now...

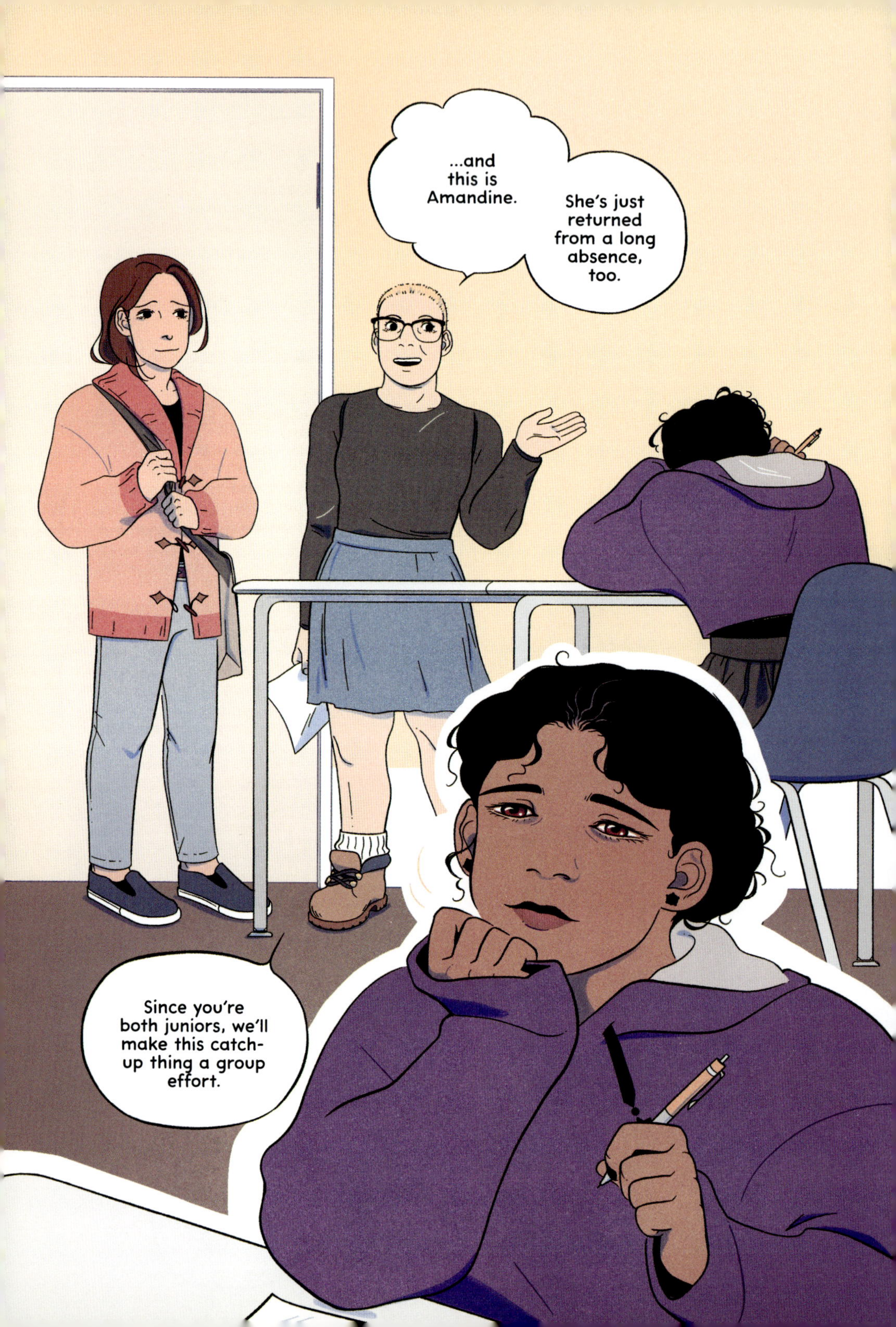
...and this is Amandine.
She's just returned from a long absence, too.
Since you're both juniors, we'll make this catch-up thing a group effort.

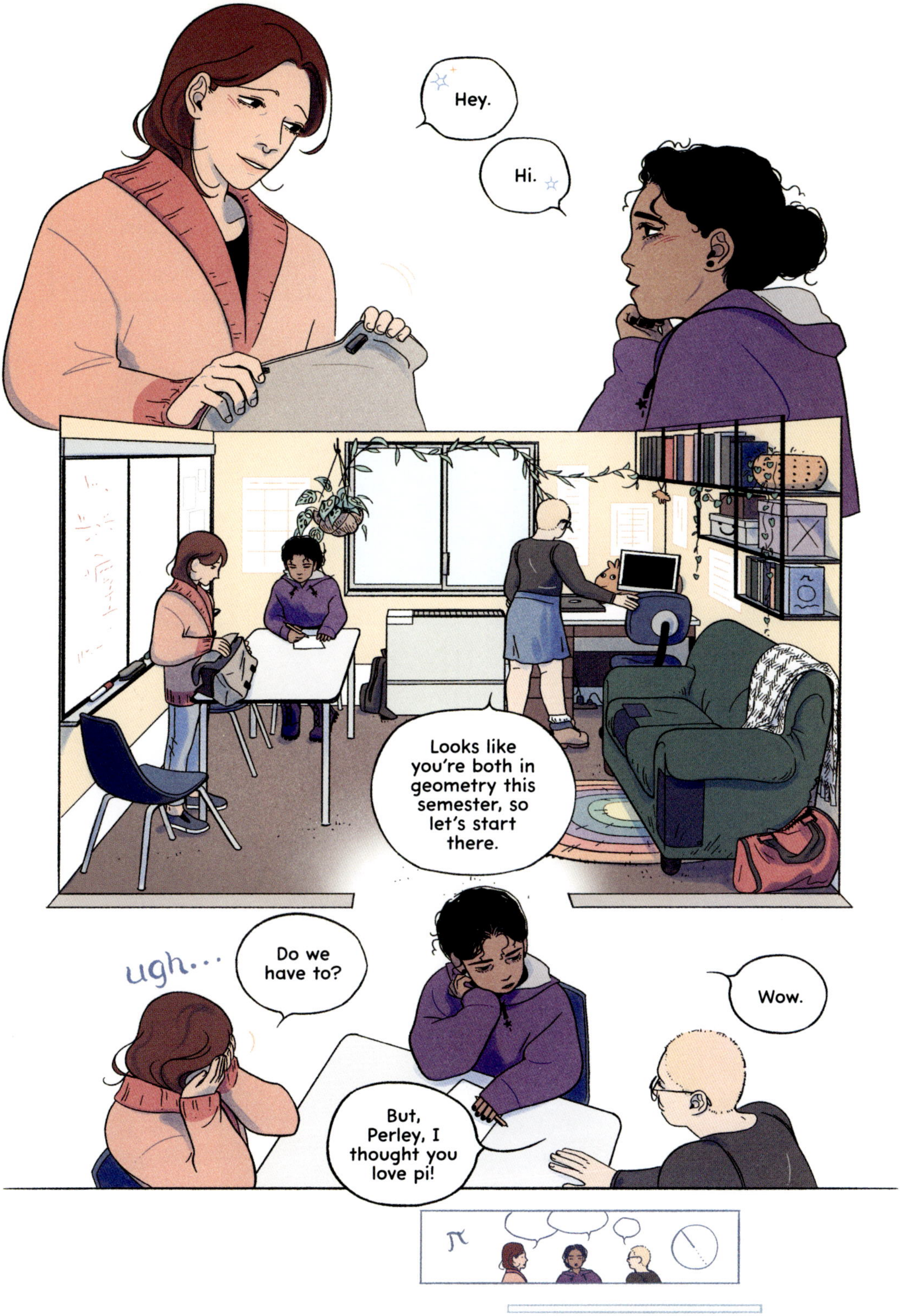
Hey.
Hi.
Looks like you're both in geometry this semester, so let's start there.
ugh...
Do we have to?
Wow.
But, Perley, I thought you love pi!
π

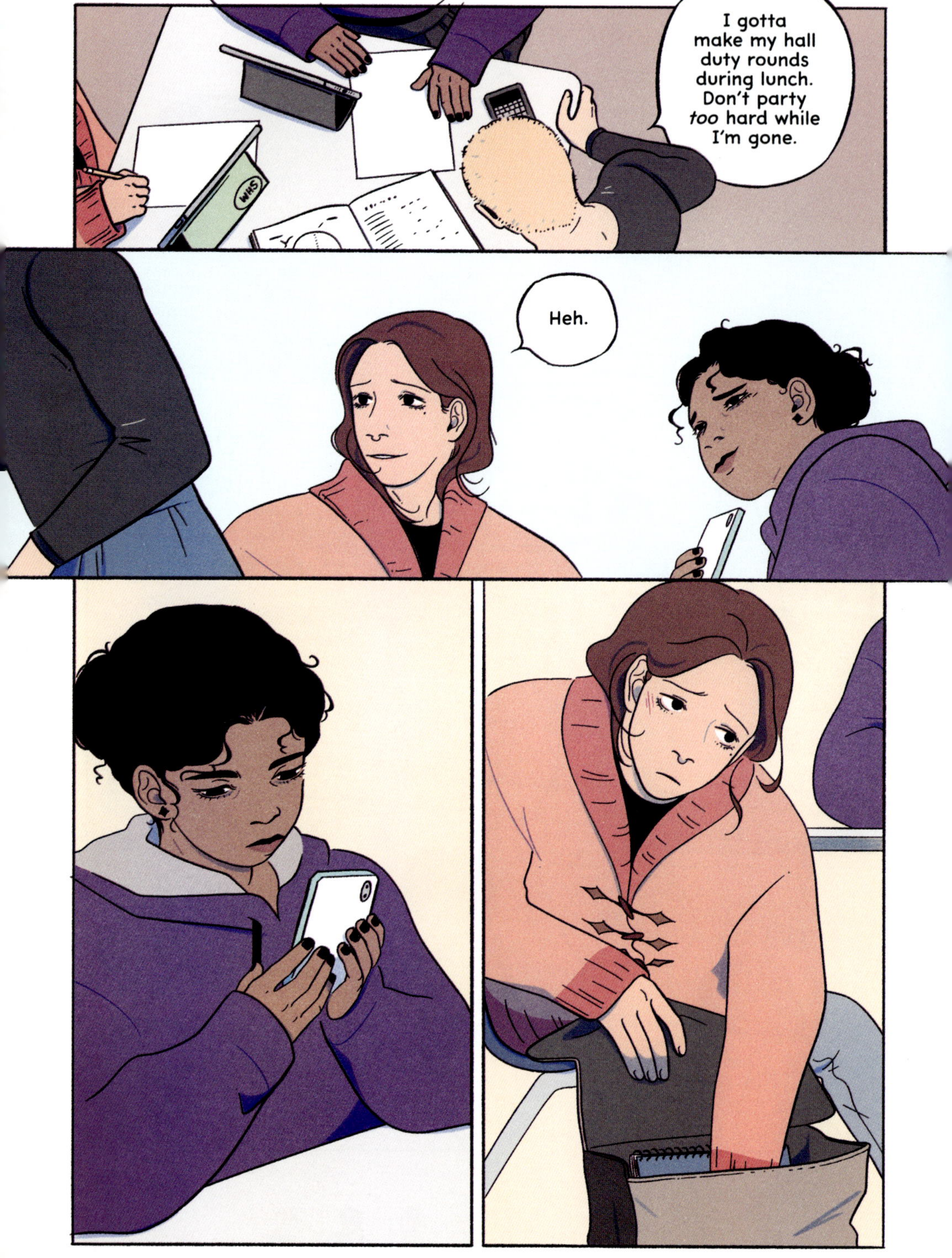
I gotta make my hall duty rounds during lunch. Don't party *too* hard while I'm gone.
Heh.

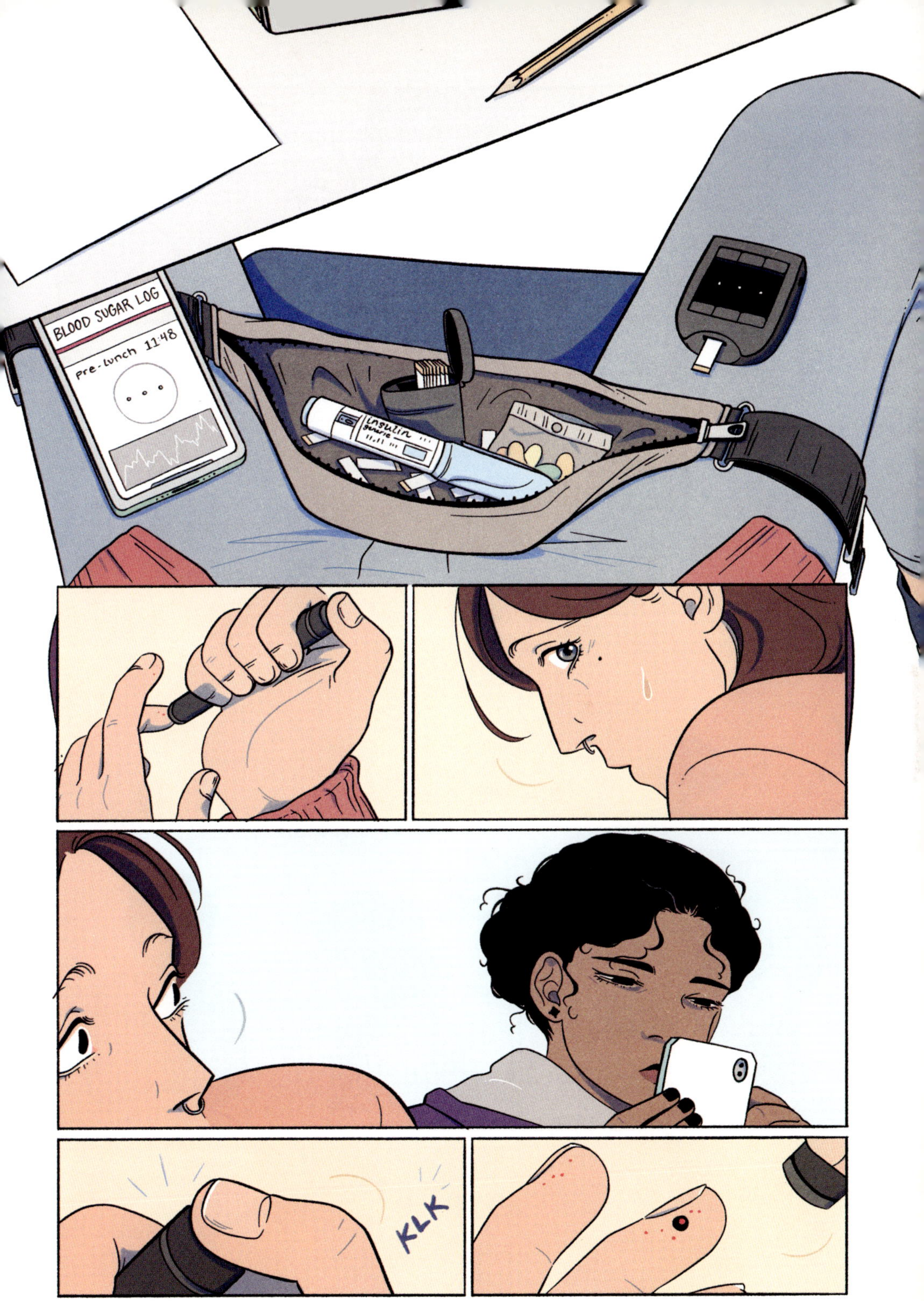
BLOOD SUGAR LOG
Pre-lunch 11:48
insulin
KLK

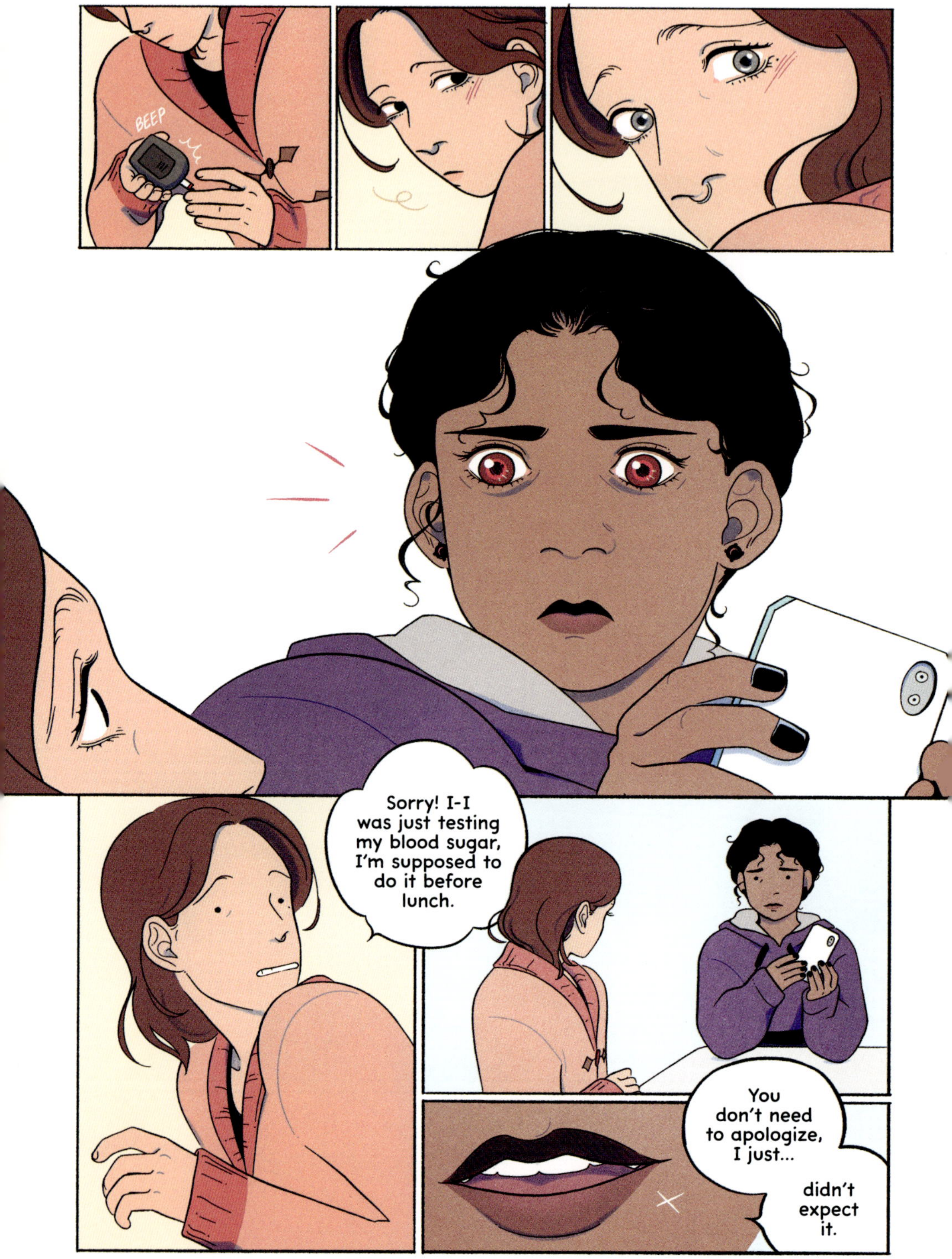
BEEP
Sorry! I-I was just testing my blood sugar, I'm supposed to do it before lunch.
You don't need to apologize, I just...
didn't expect it.

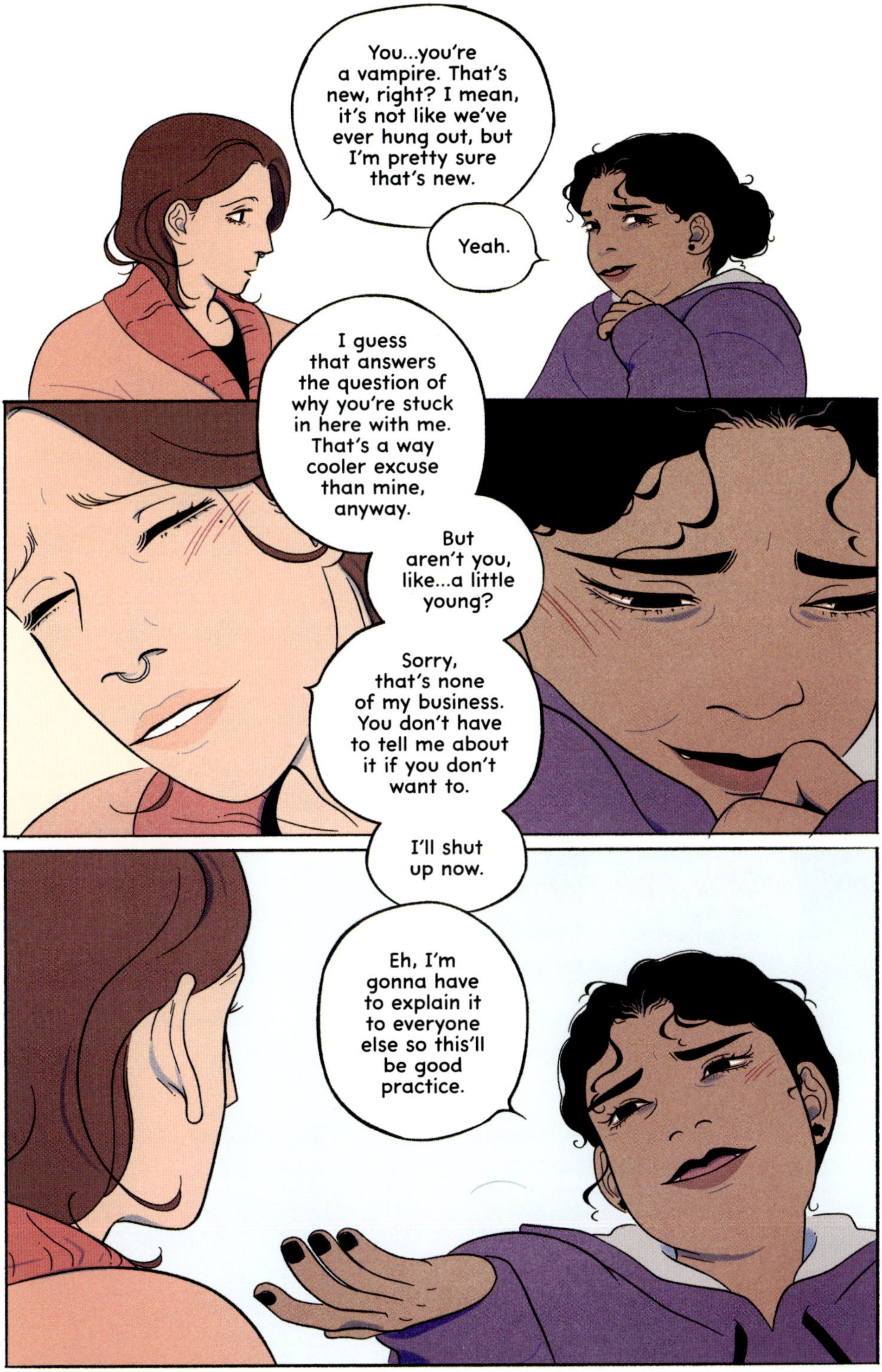
You...you're a vampire. That's new, right? I mean, it's not like we've ever hung out, but I'm pretty sure that's new.
Yeah.
I guess that answers the question of why you're stuck in here with me. That's a way cooler excuse than mine, anyway.
But aren't you, like...a little young?
Sorry, that's none of my business. You don't have to tell me about it if you don't want to.
I'll shut up now.
Eh, I'm gonna have to explain it to everyone else so this'll be good practice.

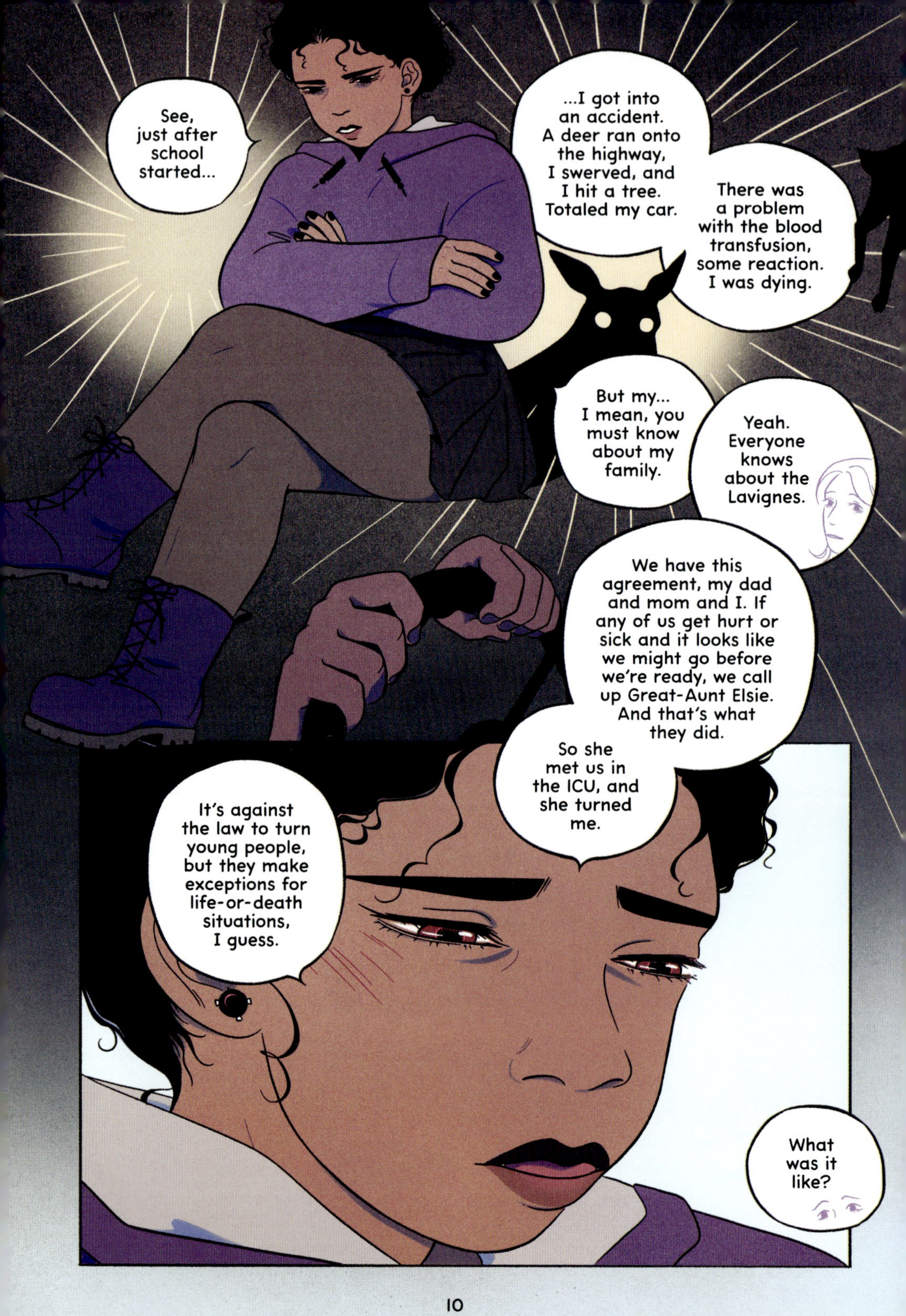
See, just after school started...
...I got into an accident. A deer ran onto the highway, I swerved, and I hit a tree. Totaled my car.
There was a problem with the blood transfusion, some reaction. I was dying.
But my... I mean, you must know about my family.
Yeah. Everyone knows about the Lavignes.
We have this agreement, my dad and mom and I. If any of us get hurt or sick and it looks like we might go before we're ready, we call up Great-Aunt Elsie. And that's what they did.
So she met us in the ICU, and she turned me.
It's against the law to turn young people, but they make exceptions for life-or-death situations, I guess.
What was it like?

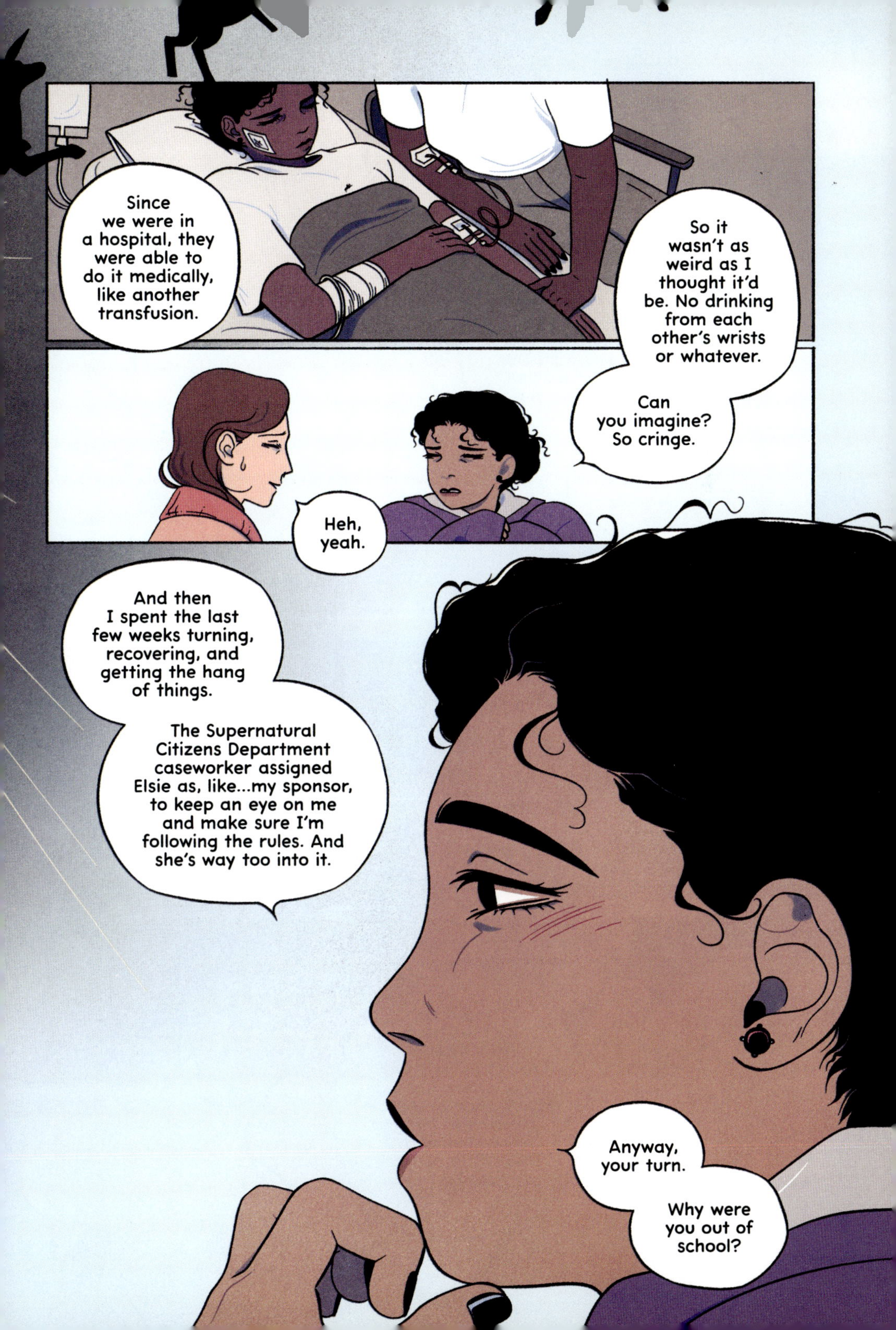
Since we were in a hospital, they were able to do it medically, like another transfusion.
So it wasn't as weird as I thought it'd be. No drinking from each other's wrists or whatever.
Can you imagine? So cringe.
Heh, yeah.
And then I spent the last few weeks turning, recovering, and getting the hang of things.
The Supernatural Citizens Department caseworker assigned Elsie as, like...my sponsor, to keep an eye on me and make sure I'm following the rules. And she's way too into it.
Anyway, your turn.
Why were you out of school?

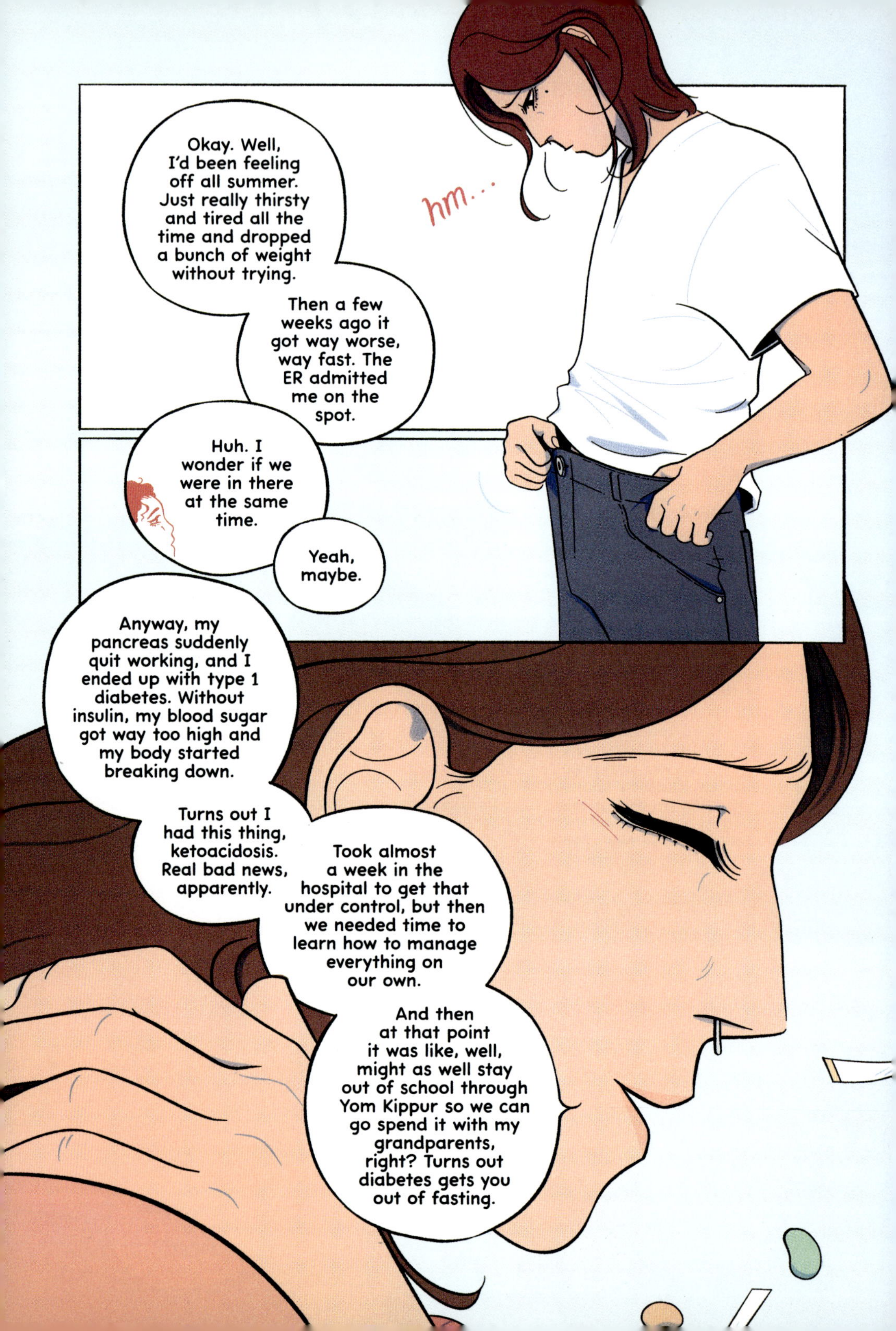
Okay. Well, I'd been feeling off all summer. Just really thirsty and tired all the time and dropped a bunch of weight without trying.
hm...
Then a few weeks ago it got way worse, way fast. The ER admitted me on the spot.
Huh. I wonder if we were in there at the same time.
Yeah, maybe.
Anyway, my pancreas suddenly quit working, and I ended up with type 1 diabetes. Without insulin, my blood sugar got way too high and my body started breaking down.
Turns out I had this thing, ketoacidosis. Real bad news, apparently.
Took almost a week in the hospital to get that under control, but then we needed time to learn how to manage everything on our own.
And then at that point it was like, well, might as well stay out of school through Yom Kippur so we can go spend it with my grandparents, right? Turns out diabetes gets you out of fasting.

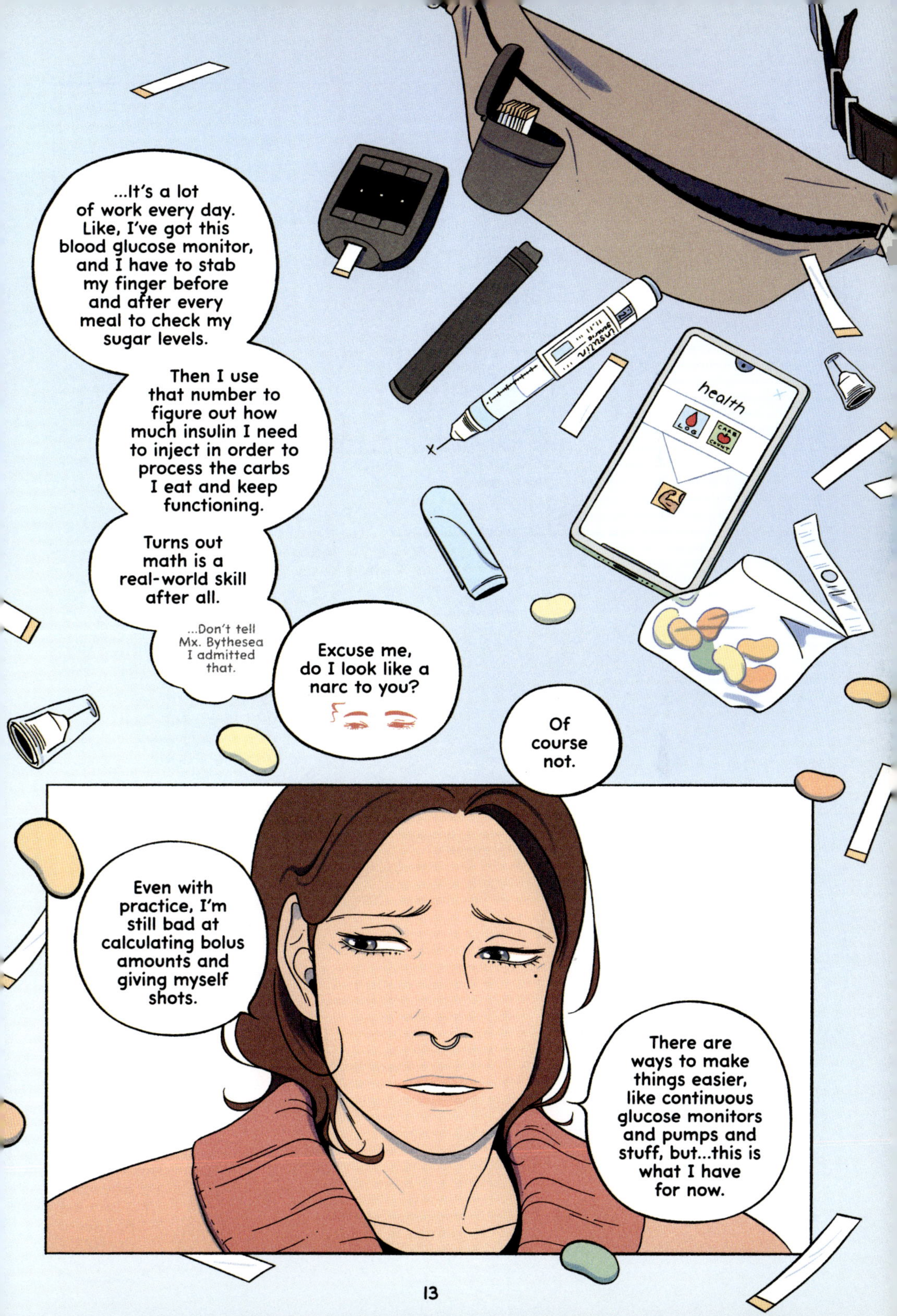
...It's a lot of work every day. Like, I've got this blood glucose monitor, and I have to stab my finger before and after every meal to check my sugar levels.
Then I use that number to figure out how much insulin I need to inject in order to process the carbs I eat and keep functioning.
Turns out math is a real-world skill after all.
...Don't tell Mx. Bythesea I admitted that.
Excuse me, do I look like a narc to you?
Of course not.
health
LOG
CARB COUNT
Even with practice, I'm still bad at calculating bolus amounts and giving myself shots.
There are ways to make things easier, like continuous glucose monitors and pumps and stuff, but...this is what I have for now.

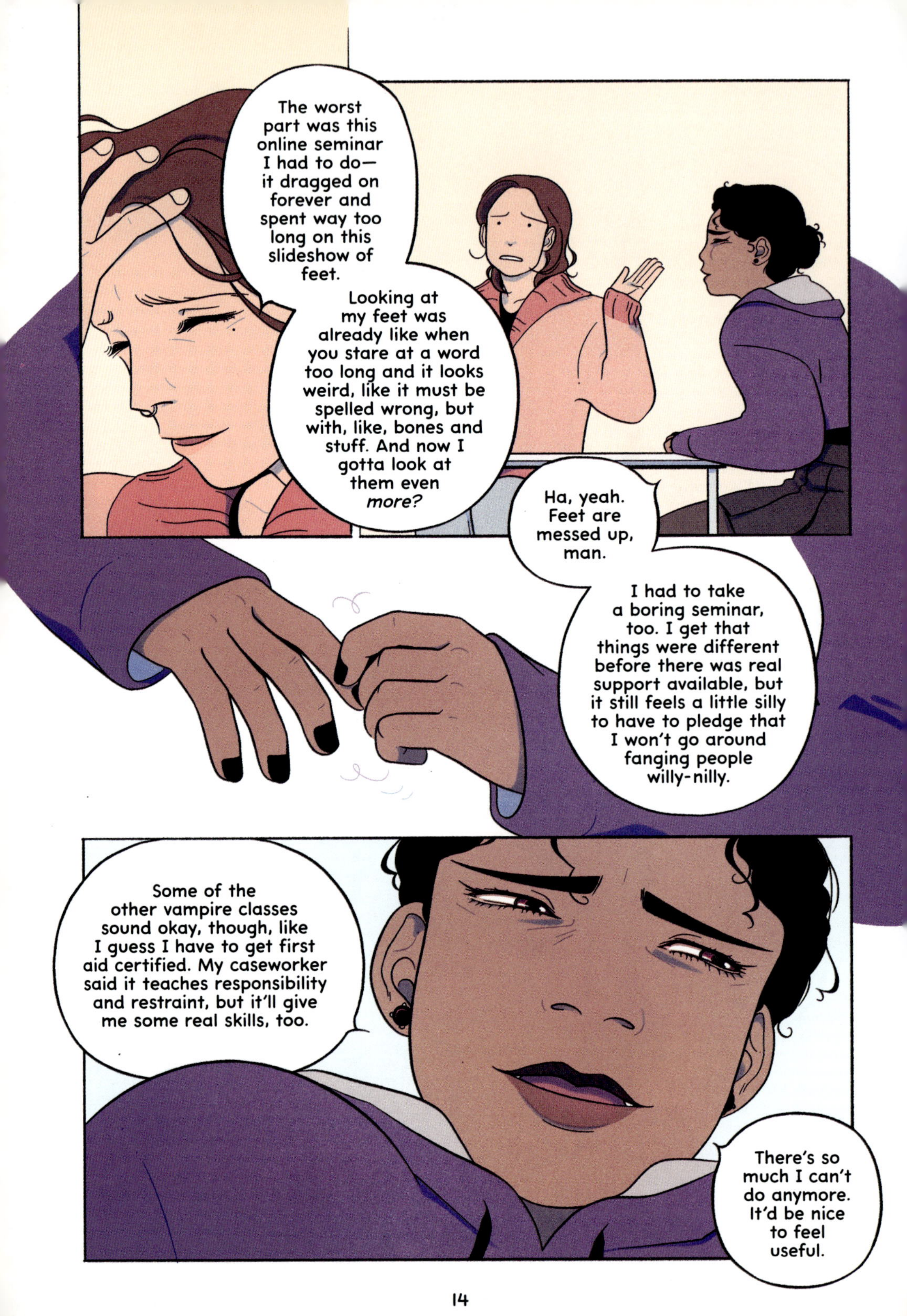
The worst part was this online seminar I had to do— it dragged on forever and spent way too long on this slideshow of feet.
Looking at my feet was already like when you stare at a word too long and it looks weird, like it must be spelled wrong, but with, like, bones and stuff. And now I gotta look at them even *more?*
Ha, yeah. Feet are messed up, man.
I had to take a boring seminar, too. I get that things were different before there was real support available, but it still feels a little silly to have to pledge that I won't go around fanging people willy-nilly.
Some of the other vampire classes sound okay, though, like I guess I have to get first aid certified. My caseworker said it teaches responsibility and restraint, but it'll give me some real skills, too.
There's so much I can't do anymore. It'd be nice to feel useful.

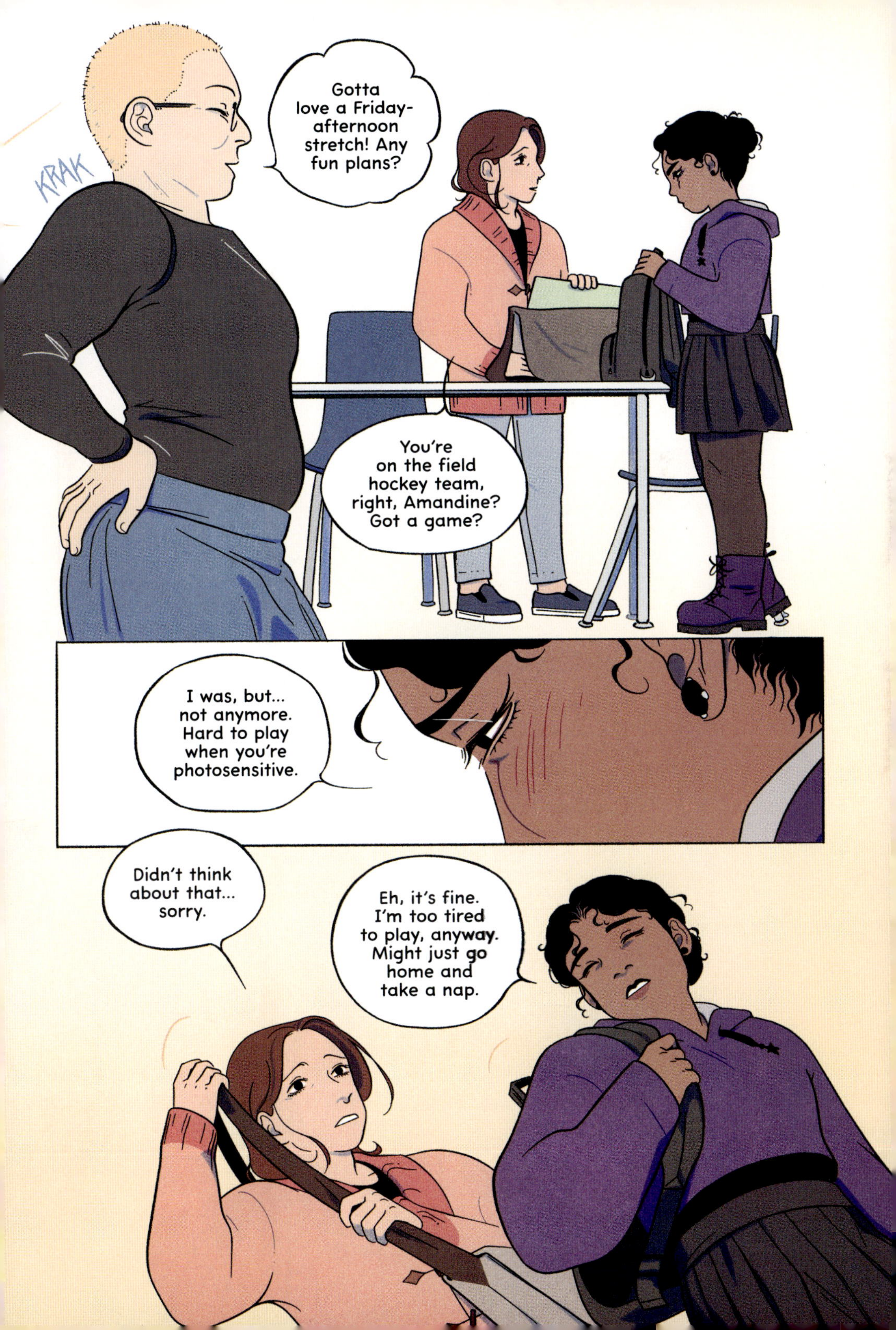
KRAK
Gotta love a Friday-afternoon stretch! Any fun plans?
You're on the field hockey team, right, Amandine? Got a game?
I was, but... not anymore. Hard to play when you're photosensitive.
Didn't think about that... sorry.
Eh, it's fine. I'm too tired to play, anyway. Might just go home and take a nap.

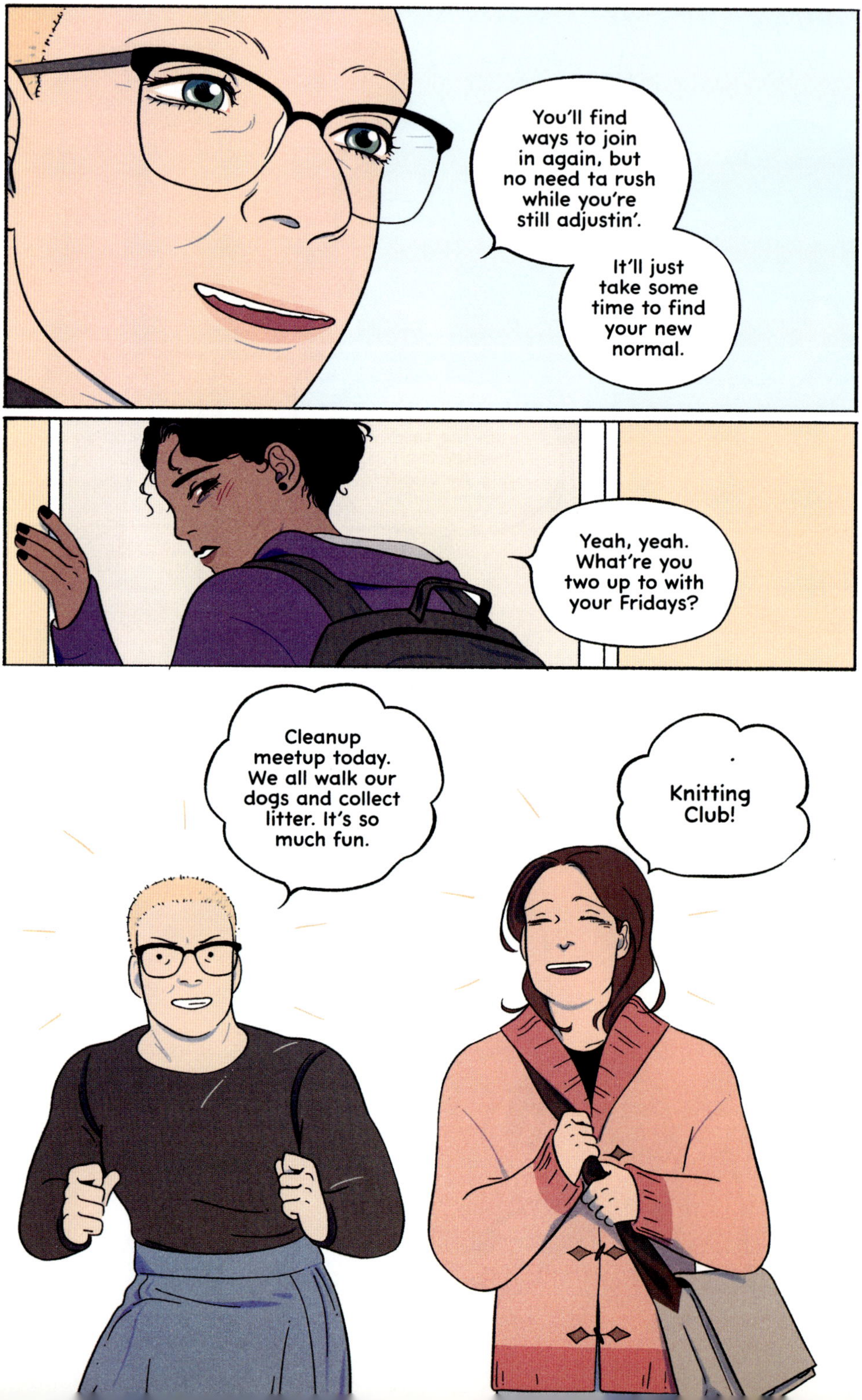
You'll find ways to join in again, but no need ta rush while you're still adjustin'.
It'll just take some time to find your new normal.
Yeah, yeah. What're you two up to with your Fridays?
Cleanup meetup today. We all walk our dogs and collect litter. It's so much fun.
Knitting Club!

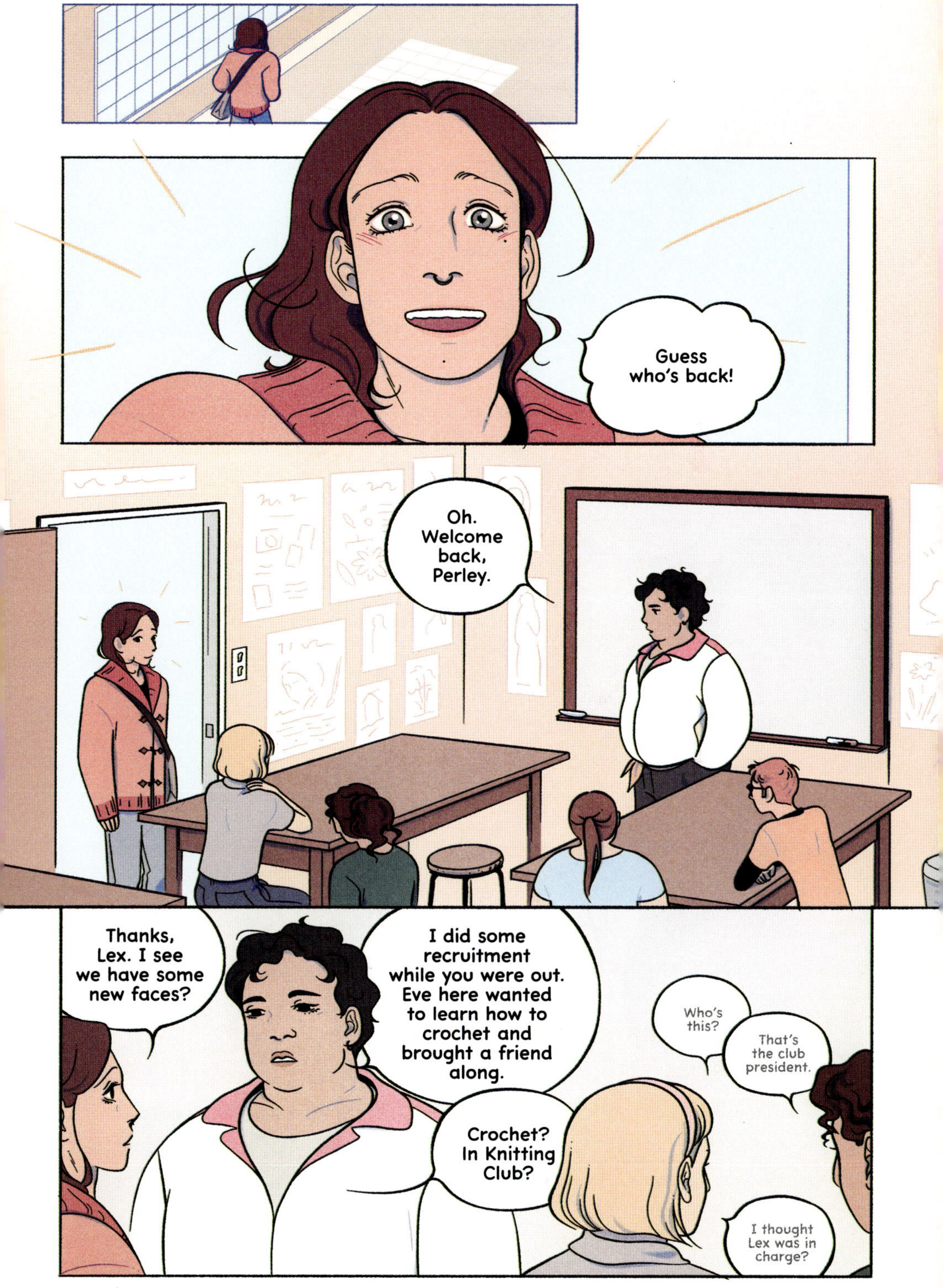
Guess who's back!
Oh. Welcome back, Perley.
Thanks, Lex. I see we have some new faces?
I did some recruitment while you were out. Eve here wanted to learn how to crochet and brought a friend along.
Who's this?
That's the club president.
Crochet? In Knitting Club?
I thought Lex was in charge?

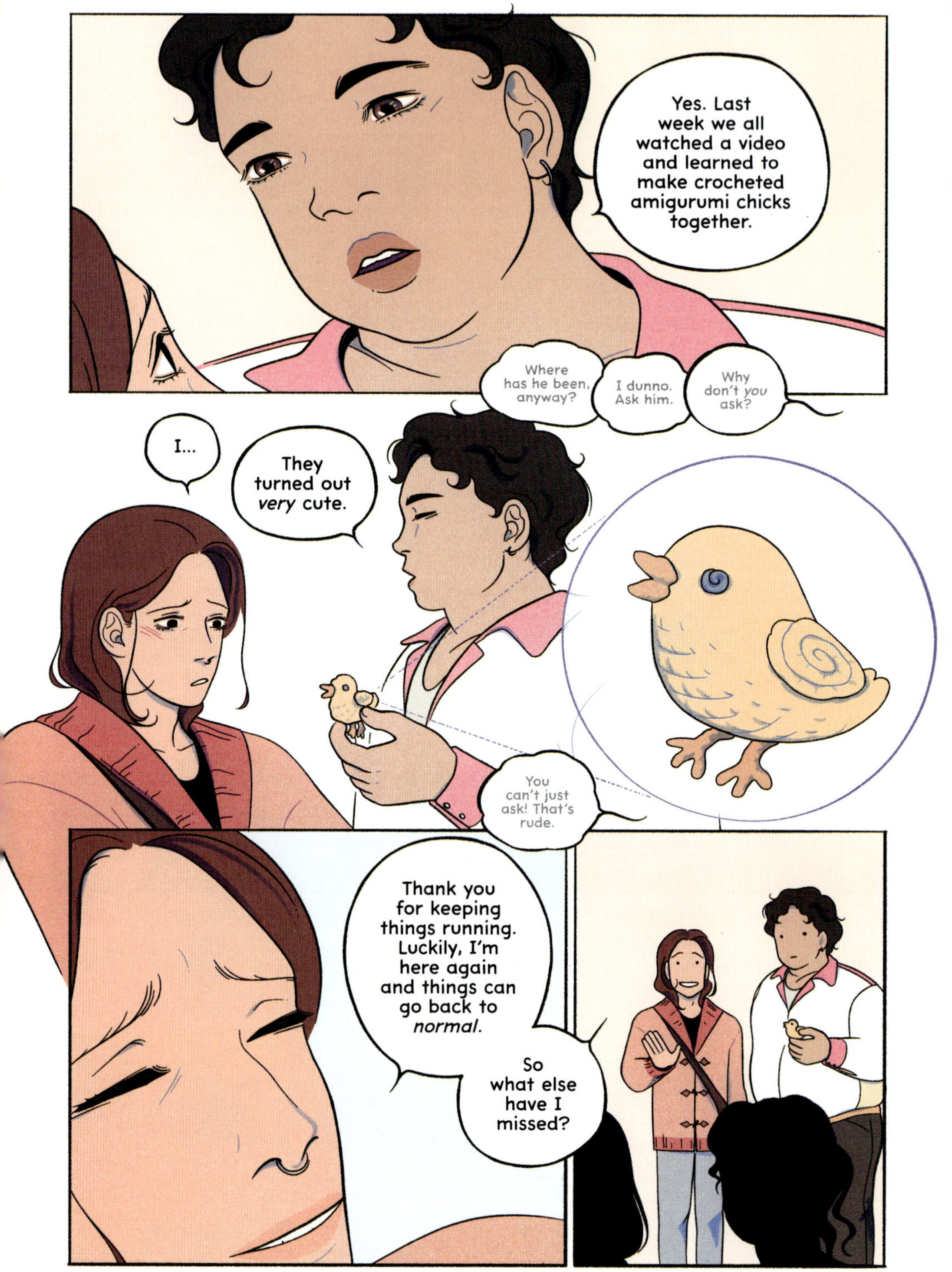
Yes. Last week we all watched a video and learned to make crocheted amigurumi chicks together.
Where has he been, anyway?
I dunno. Ask him.
Why don't *you* ask?
I...
They turned out *very* cute.
You can't just ask! That's rude.
Thank you for keeping things running. Luckily, I'm here again and things can go back to *normal*.
So what else have I missed?

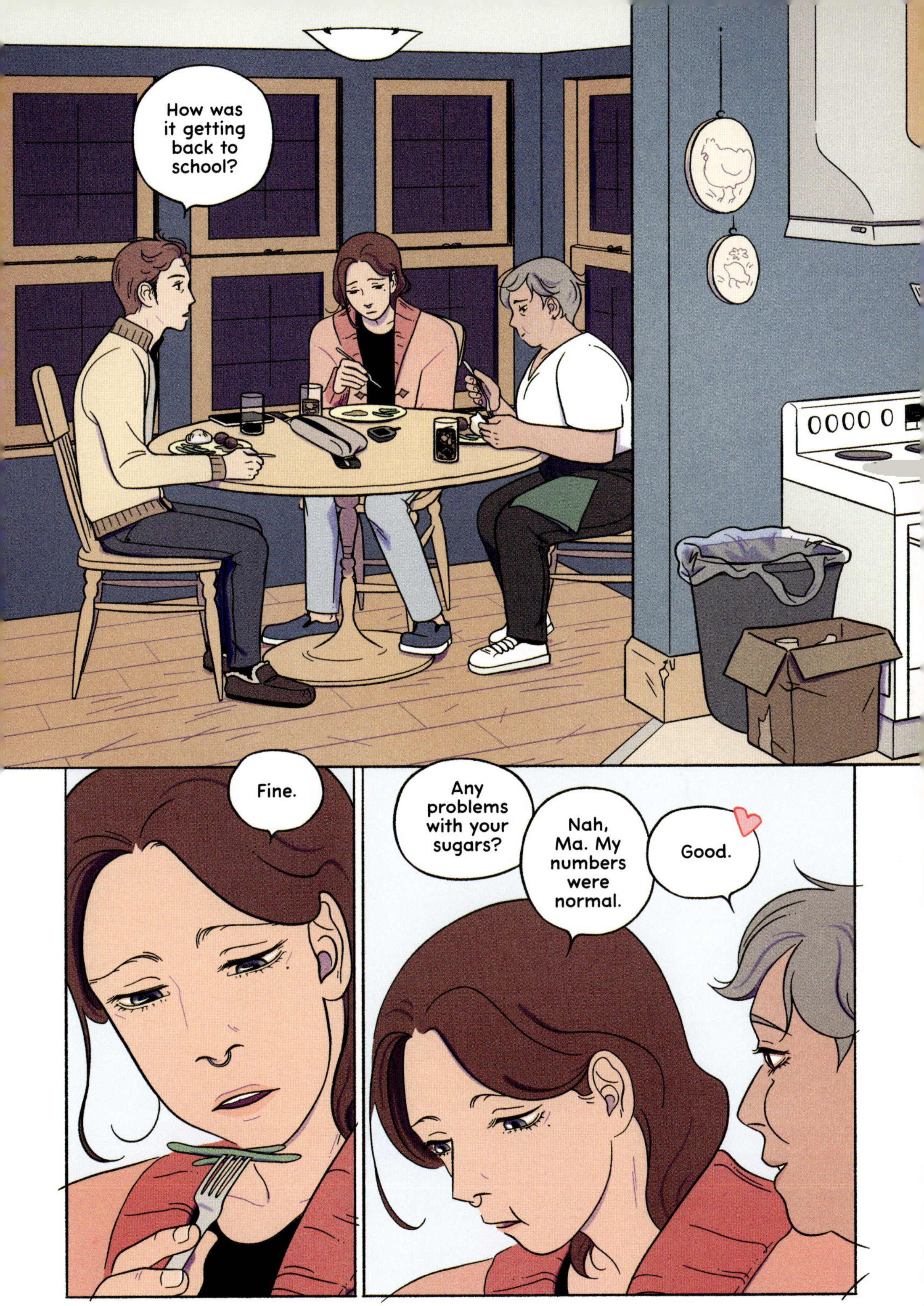
How was it getting back to school?
Fine.
Any problems with your sugars?
Nah, Ma. My numbers were normal.
Good.

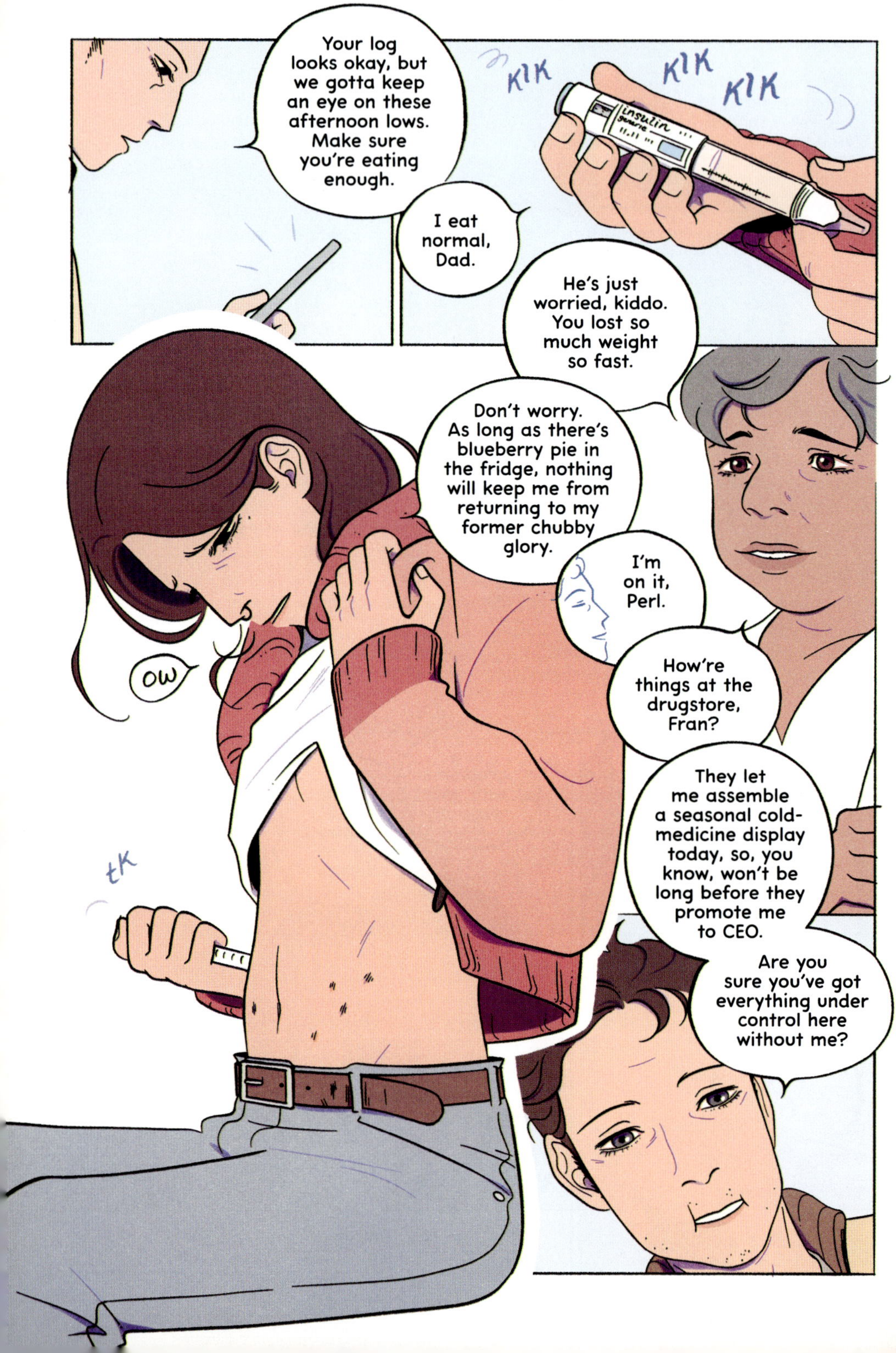
Your log looks okay, but we gotta keep an eye on these afternoon lows. Make sure you're eating enough.
KIK
KIK
KIK
I eat normal, Dad.
He's just worried, kiddo. You lost so much weight so fast.
Don't worry. As long as there's blueberry pie in the fridge, nothing will keep me from returning to my former chubby glory.
I'm on it, Perl.
OW
How're things at the drugstore, Fran?
tK
They let me assemble a seasonal cold-medicine display today, so, you know, won't be long before they promote me to CEO.
Are you sure you've got everything under control here without me?

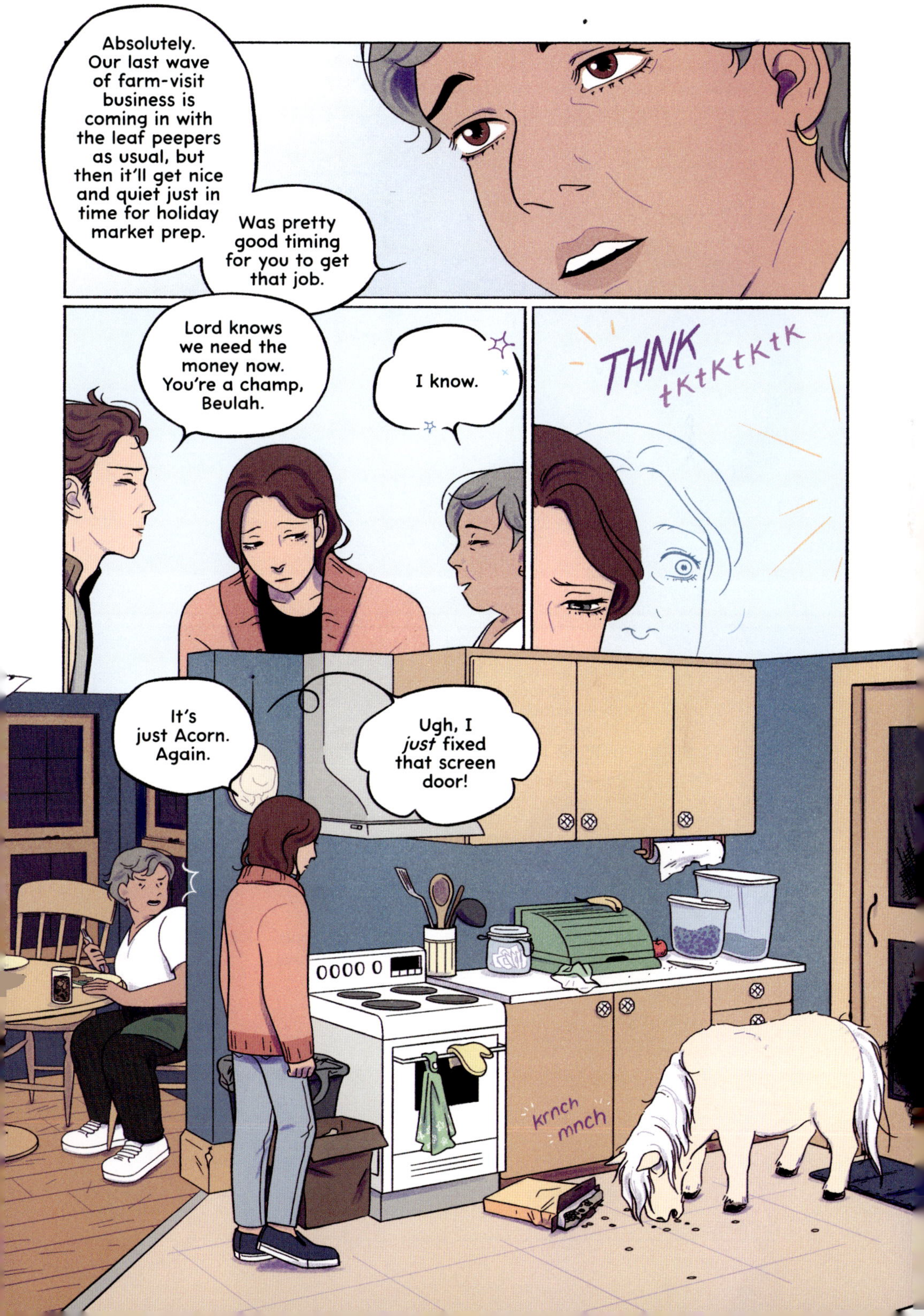
Absolutely. Our last wave of farm-visit business is coming in with the leaf peepers as usual, but then it'll get nice and quiet just in time for holiday market prep.
Was pretty good timing for you to get that job.
Lord knows we need the money now. You're a champ, Beulah.
I know.
THNK
tKtKtKtK
It's just Acorn. Again.
Ugh, I *just* fixed that screen door!
krnch mnch

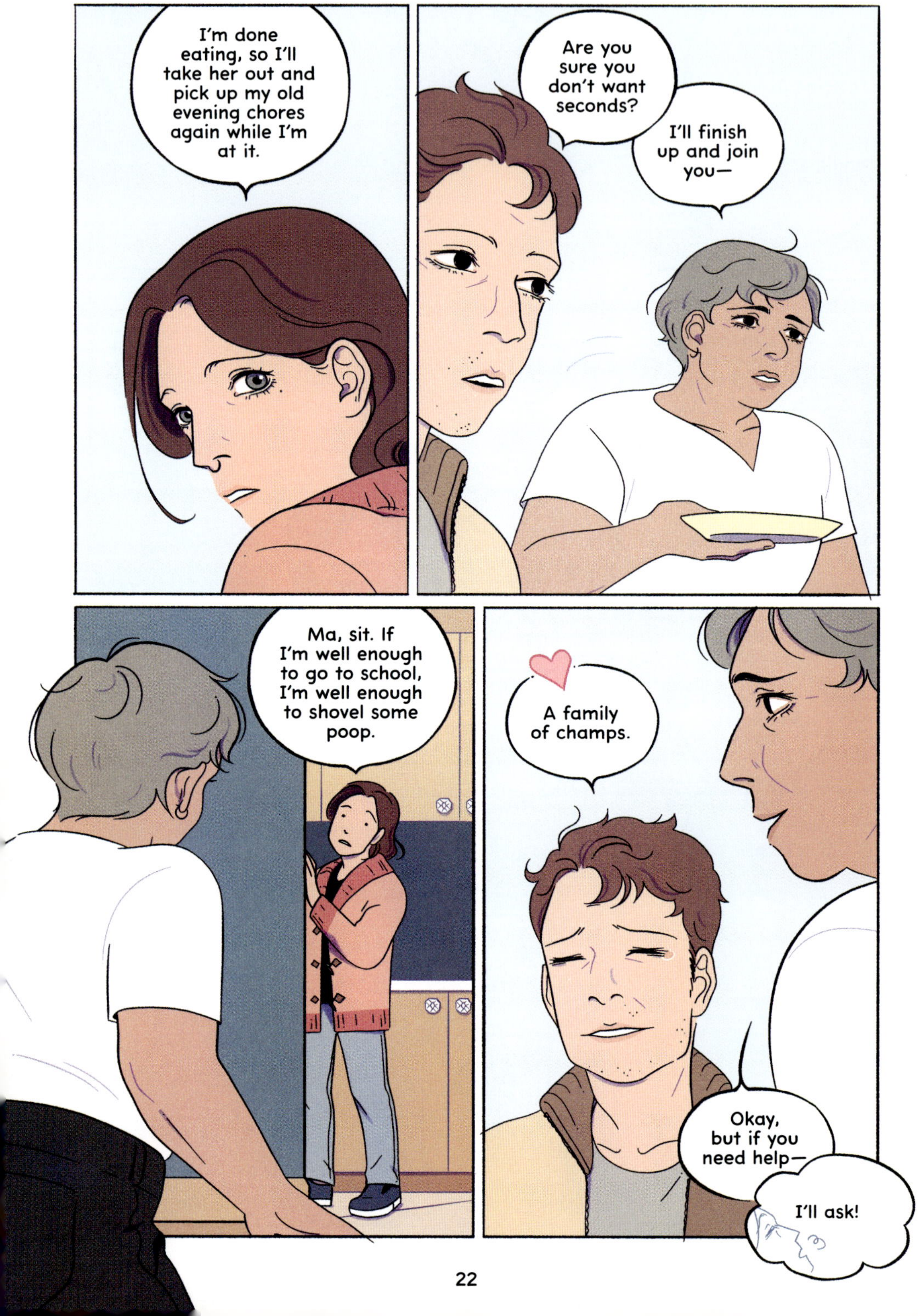
I'm done eating, so I'll take her out and pick up my old evening chores again while I'm at it.
Are you sure you don't want seconds?
I'll finish up and join you—
Ma, sit. If I'm well enough to go to school, I'm well enough to shovel some poop.
A family of champs.
Okay, but if you need help—
I'll ask!

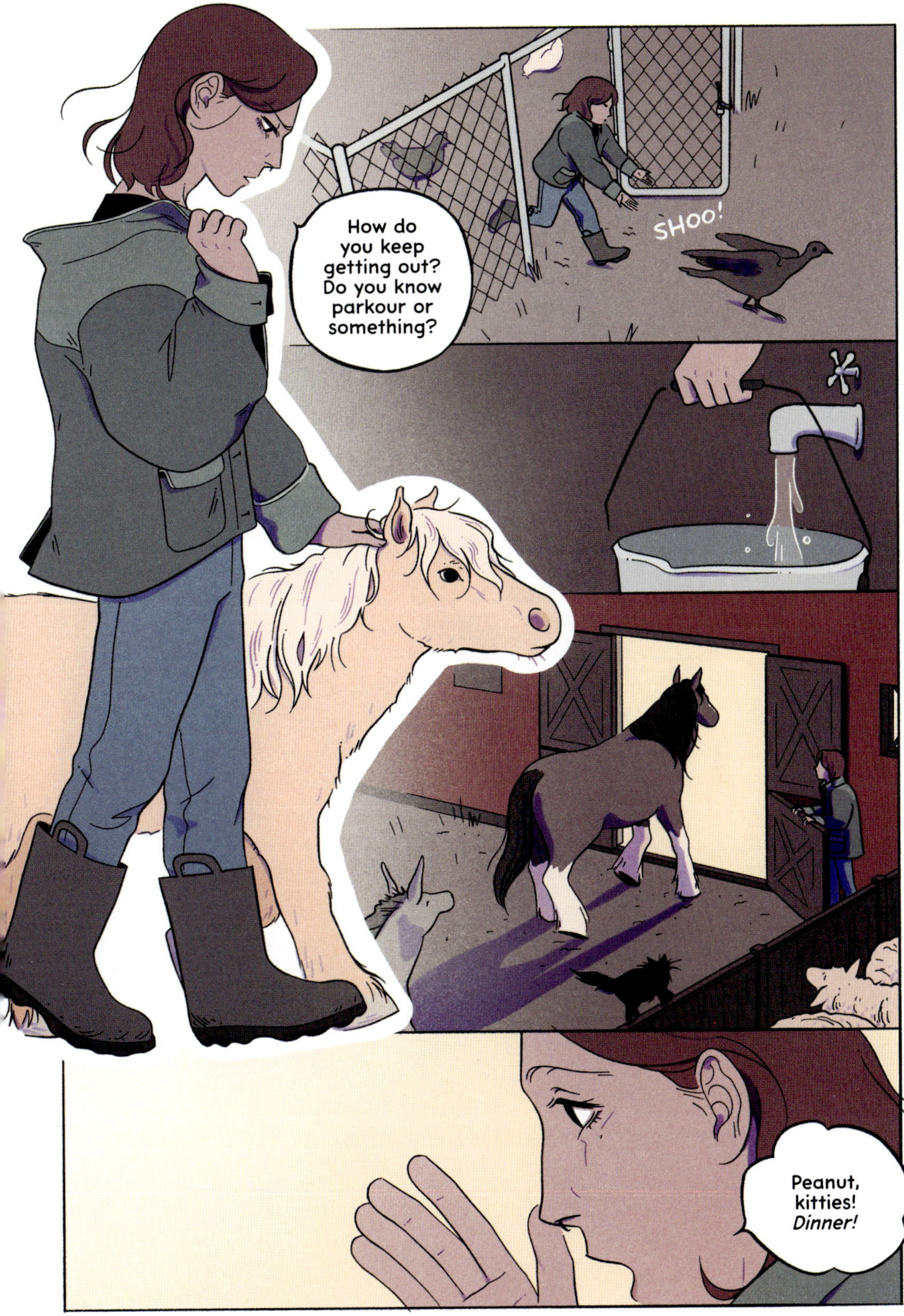
How do you keep getting out? Do you know parkour or something?
SHOO!
Peanut, kitties! *Dinner!*

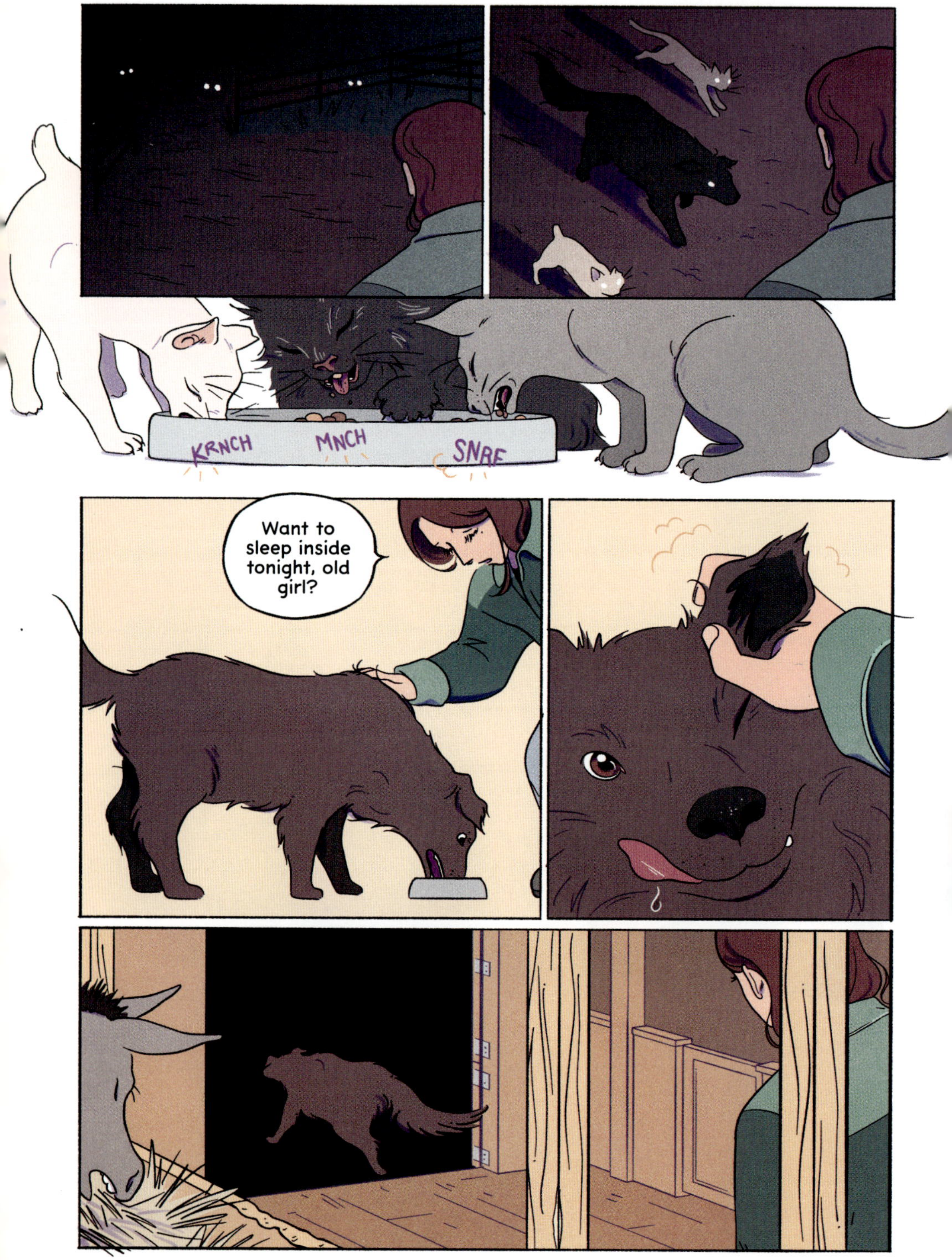
KRNCH
MNCH
SNRF
Want to sleep inside tonight, old girl?

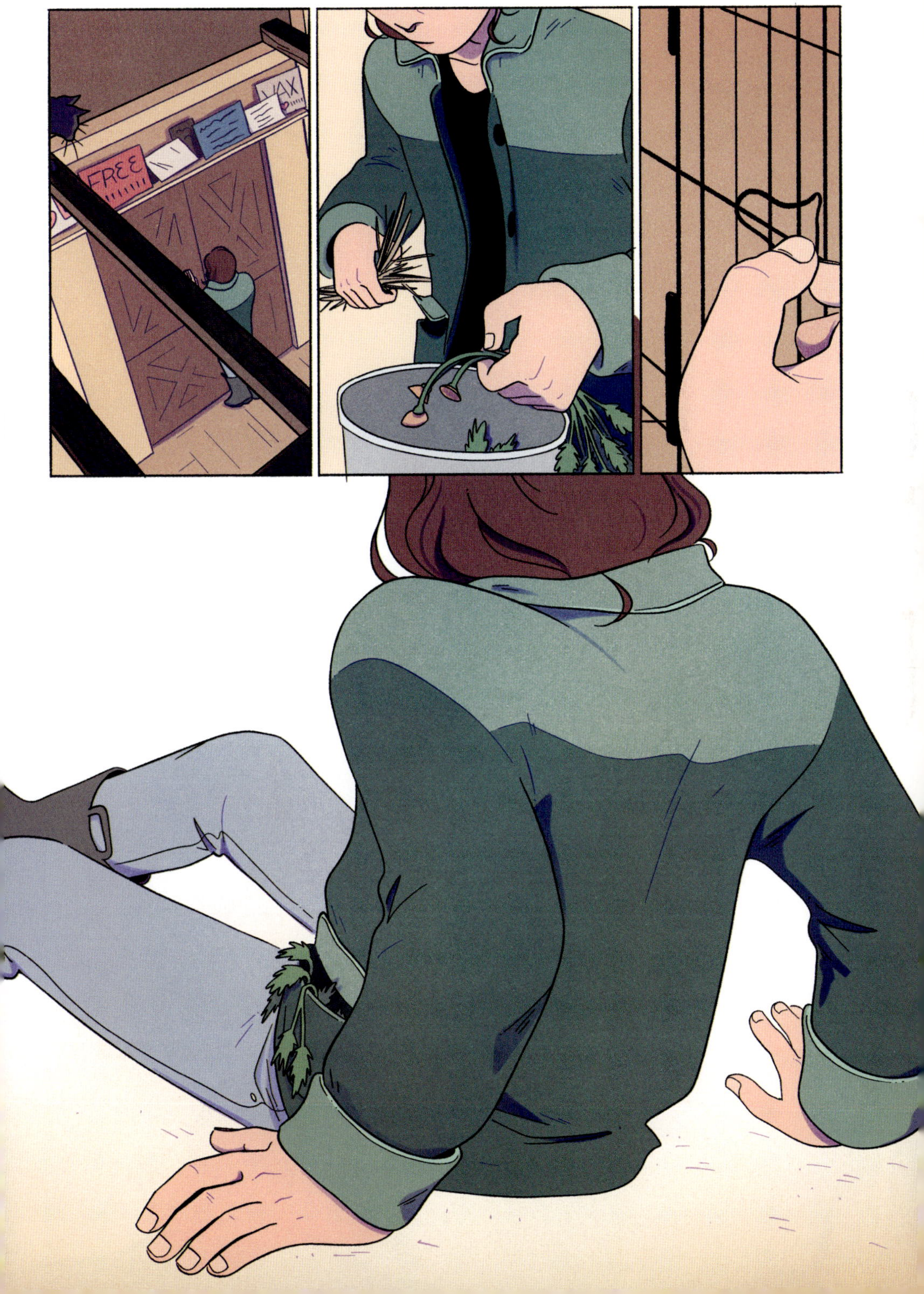
FREE

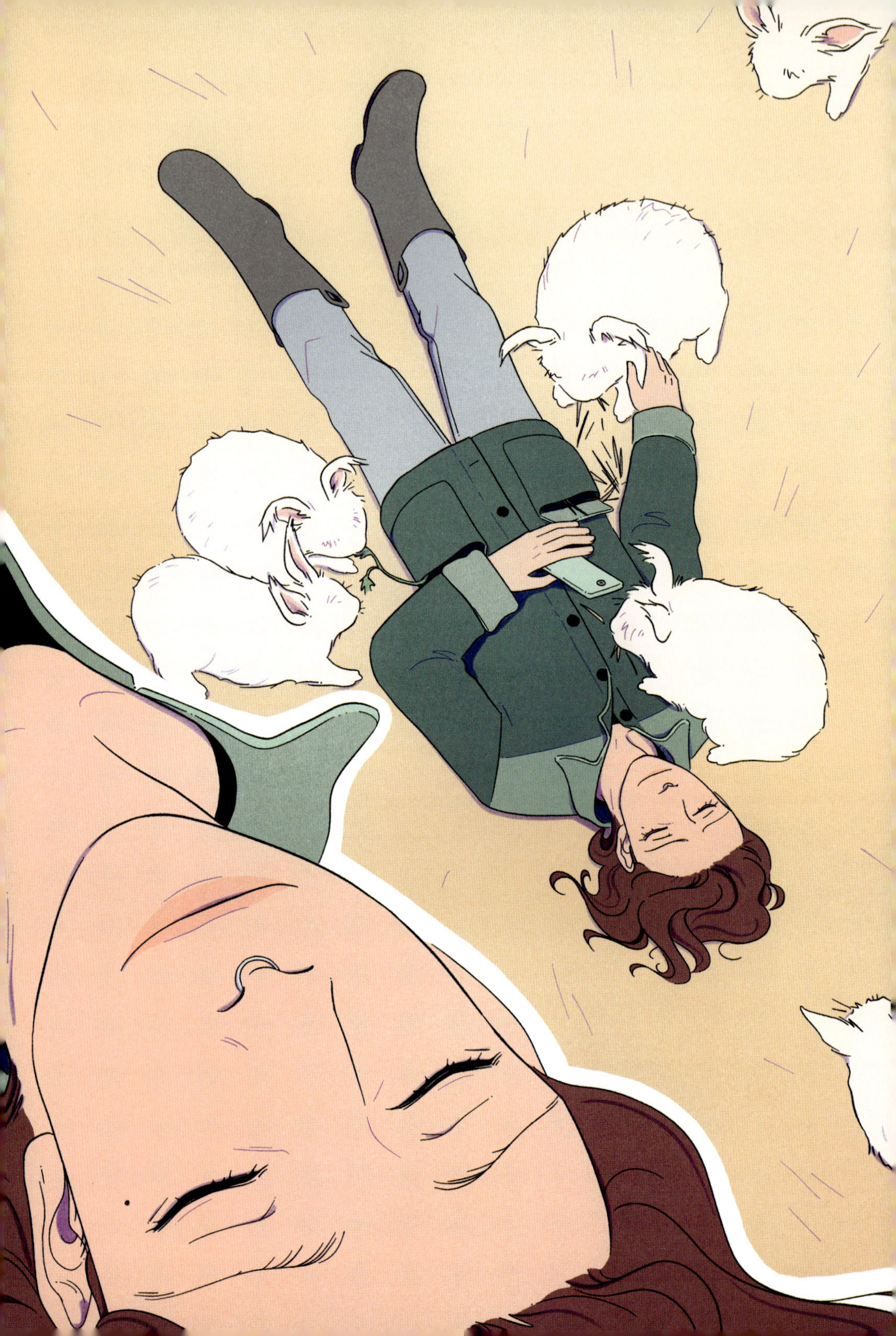

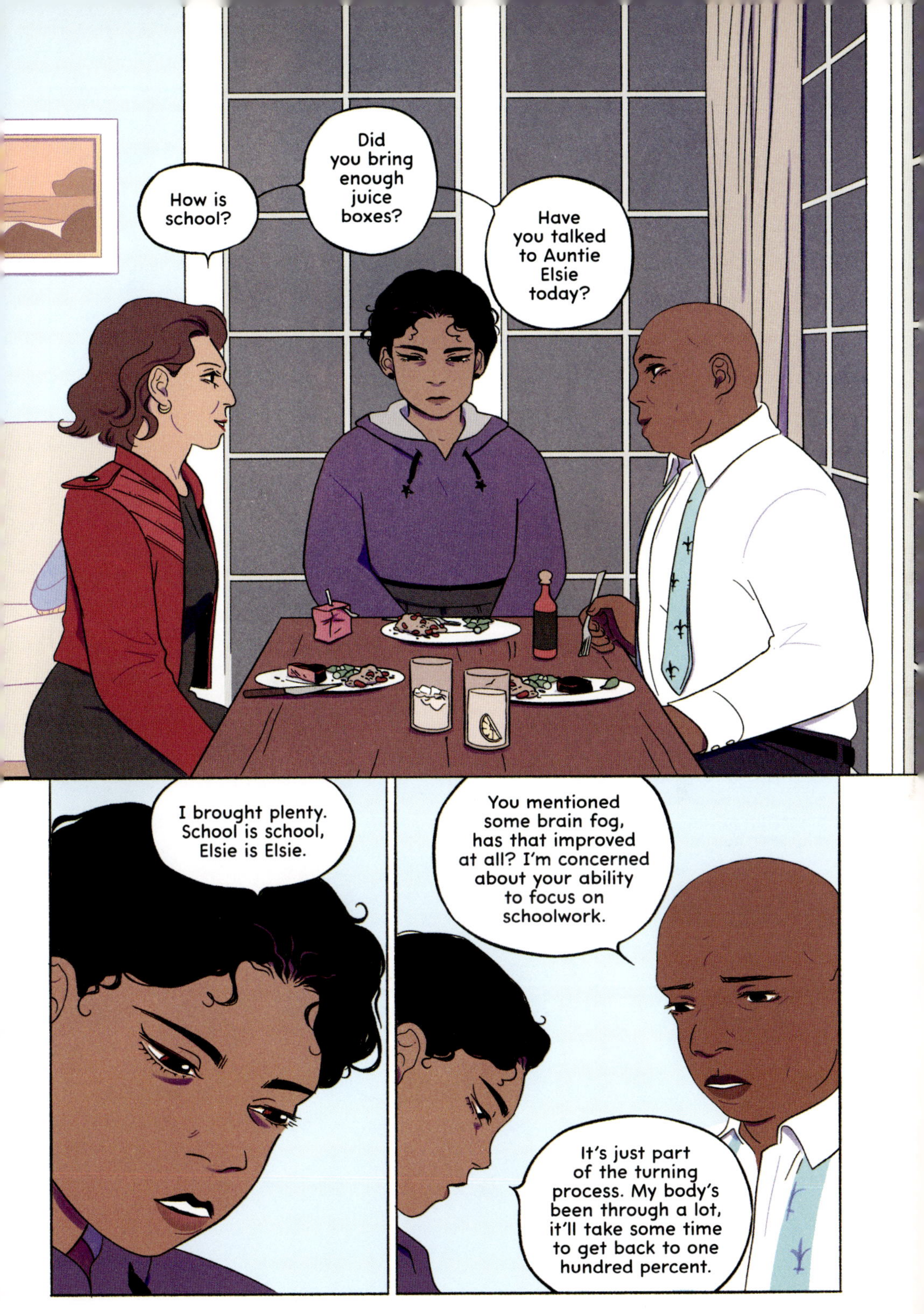
How is school?
Did you bring enough juice boxes?
Have you talked to Auntie Elsie today?
I brought plenty. School is school, Elsie is Elsie.
You mentioned some brain fog, has that improved at all? I'm concerned about your ability to focus on schoolwork.
It's just part of the turning process. My body's been through a lot, it'll take some time to get back to one hundred percent.

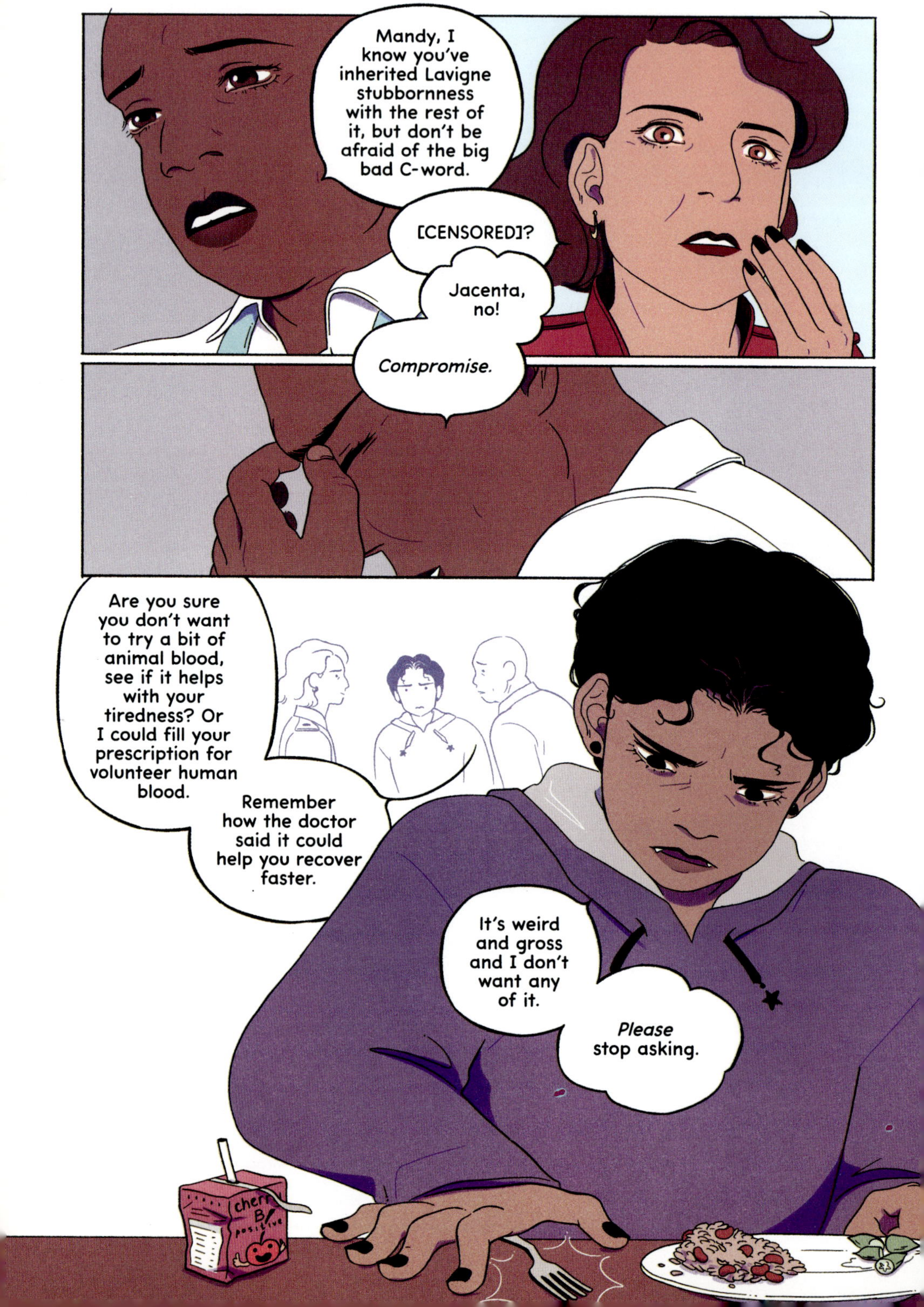
Mandy, I know you've inherited Lavigne stubbornness with the rest of it, but don't be afraid of the big bad C-word.
[CENSORED]?
Jacenta, no!
Compromise.
Are you sure you don't want to try a bit of animal blood, see if it helps with your tiredness? Or I could fill your prescription for volunteer human blood.
Remember how the doctor said it could help you recover faster.
It's weird and gross and I don't want any of it.
Please stop asking.
cherry B positive

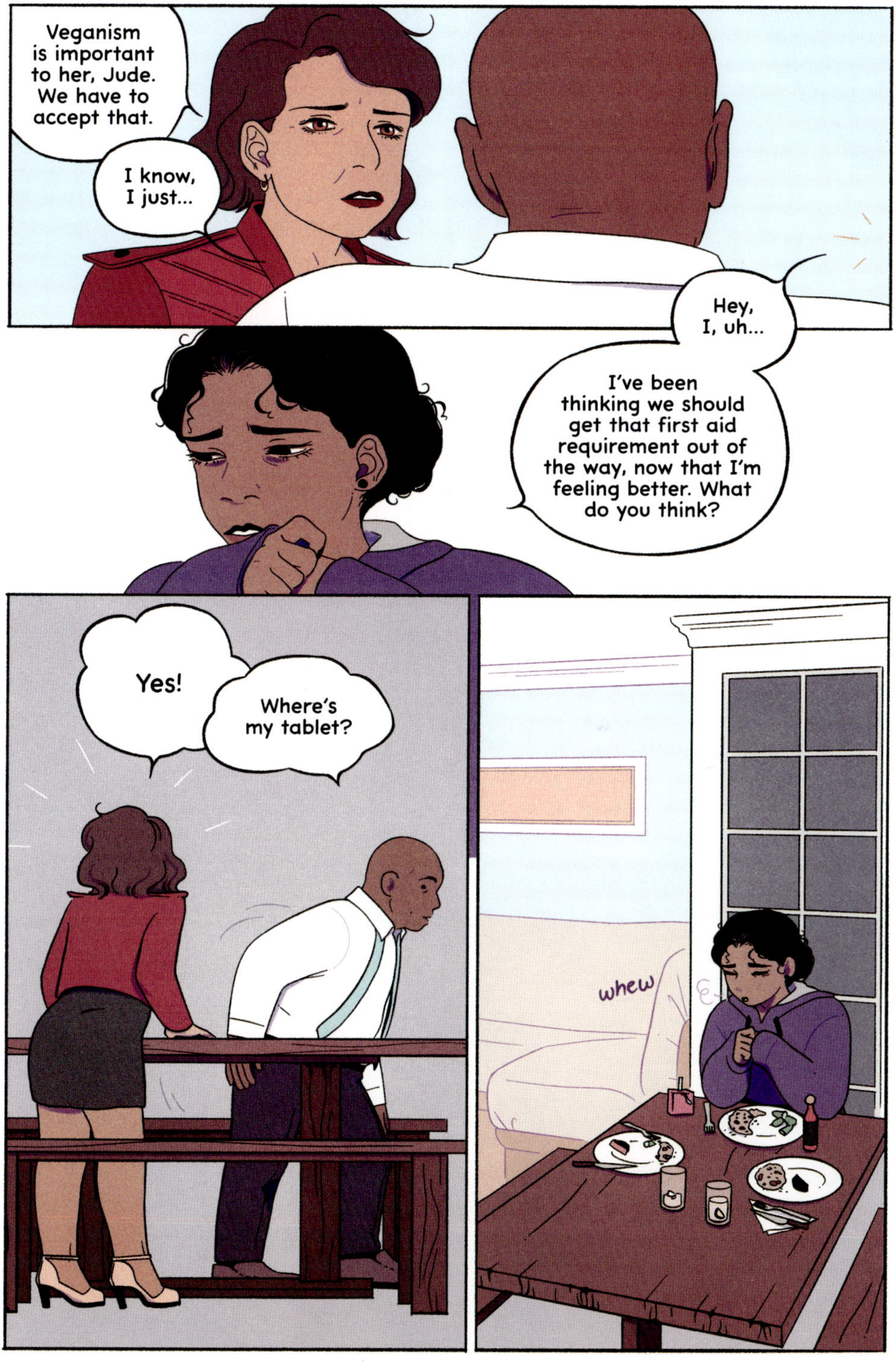
Veganism is important to her, Jude. We have to accept that.
I know, I just...
Hey, I, uh...
I've been thinking we should get that first aid requirement out of the way, now that I'm feeling better. What do you think?
Yes!
Where's my tablet?
whew

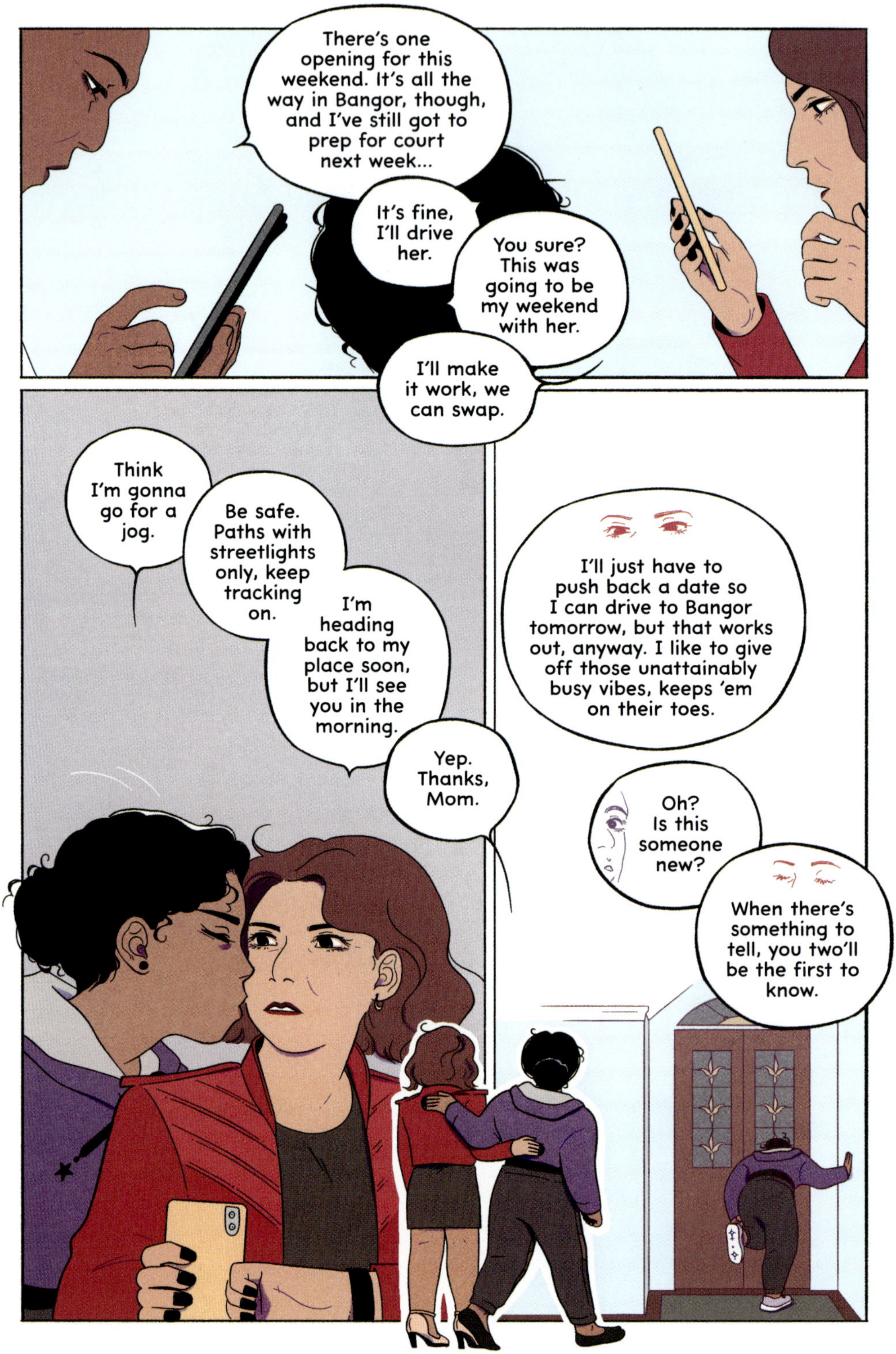

There's one opening for this weekend. It's all the way in Bangor, though, and I've still got to prep for court next week...
It's fine, I'll drive her.
You sure? This was going to be my weekend with her.
I'll make it work, we can swap.
Think I'm gonna go for a jog.
Be safe. Paths with streetlights only, keep tracking on.
I'm heading back to my place soon, but I'll see you in the morning.
Yep. Thanks, Mom.
I'll just have to push back a date so I can drive to Bangor tomorrow, but that works out, anyway. I like to give off those unattainably busy vibes, keeps 'em on their toes.
Oh? Is this someone new?
When there's something to tell, you two'll be the first to know.

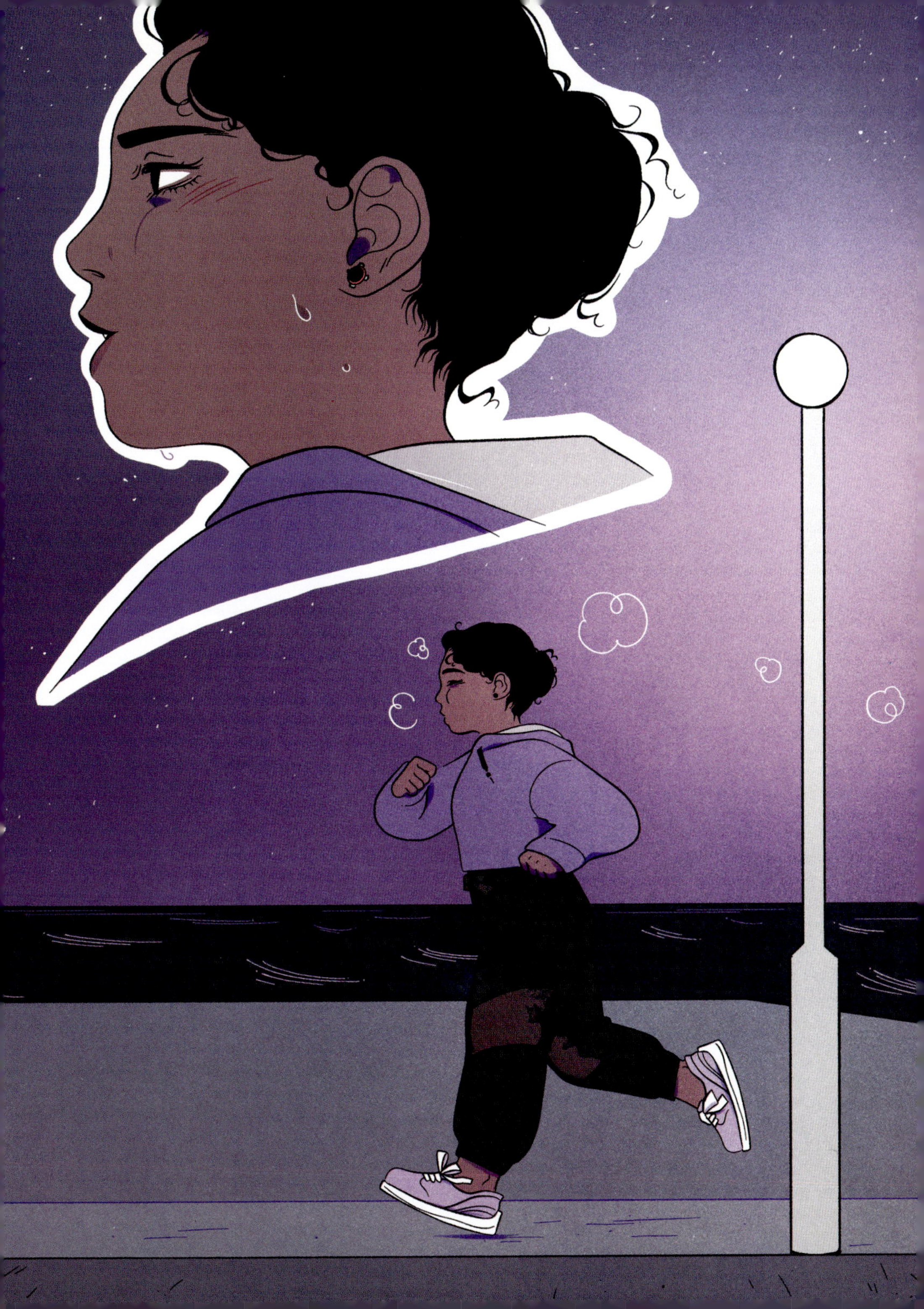

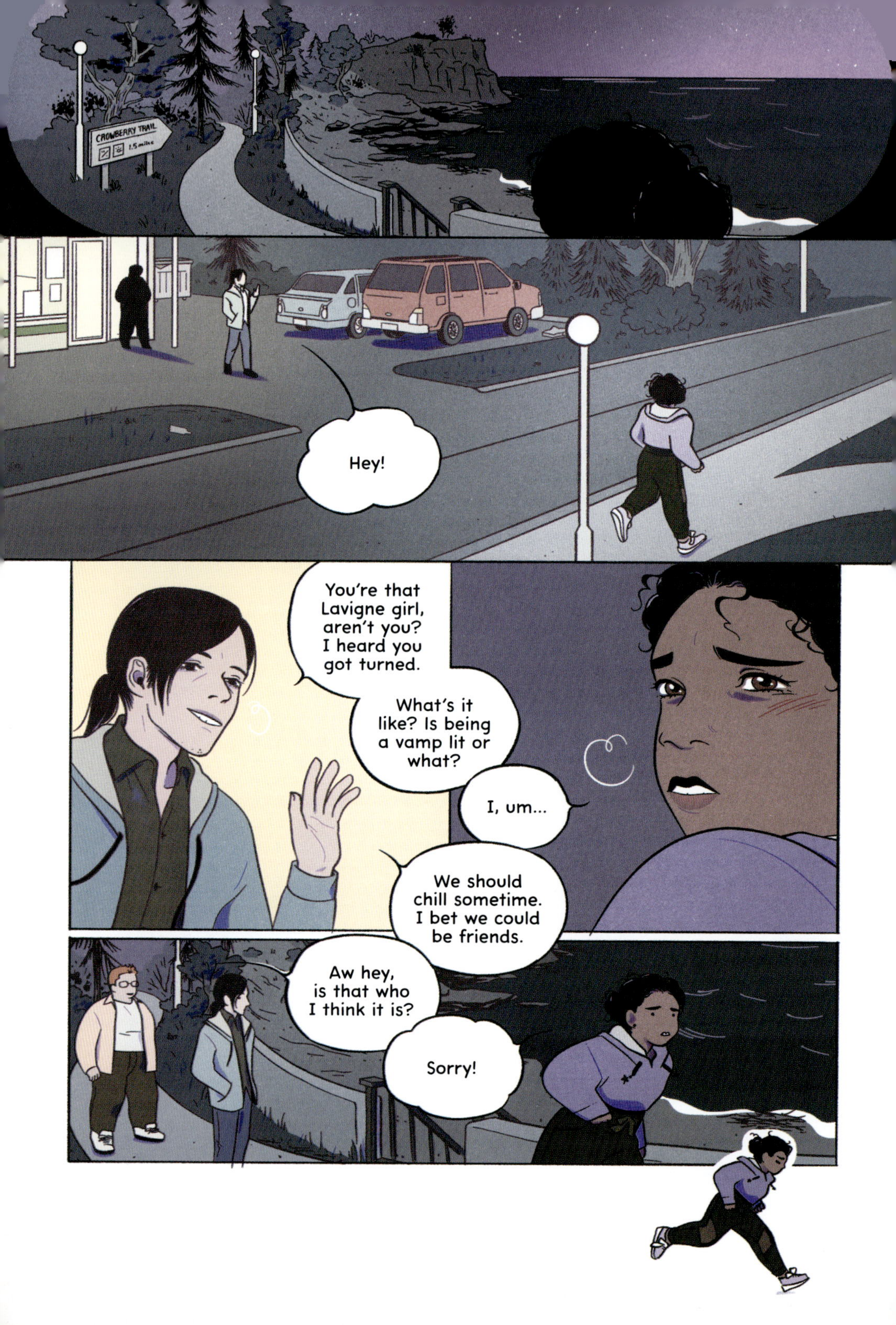
CROWBERRY TRAIL
1.5 miles
Hey!
You're that Lavigne girl, aren't you? I heard you got turned.
What's it like? Is being a vamp lit or what?
I, um...
We should chill sometime. I bet we could be friends.
Aw hey, is that who I think it is?
Sorry!

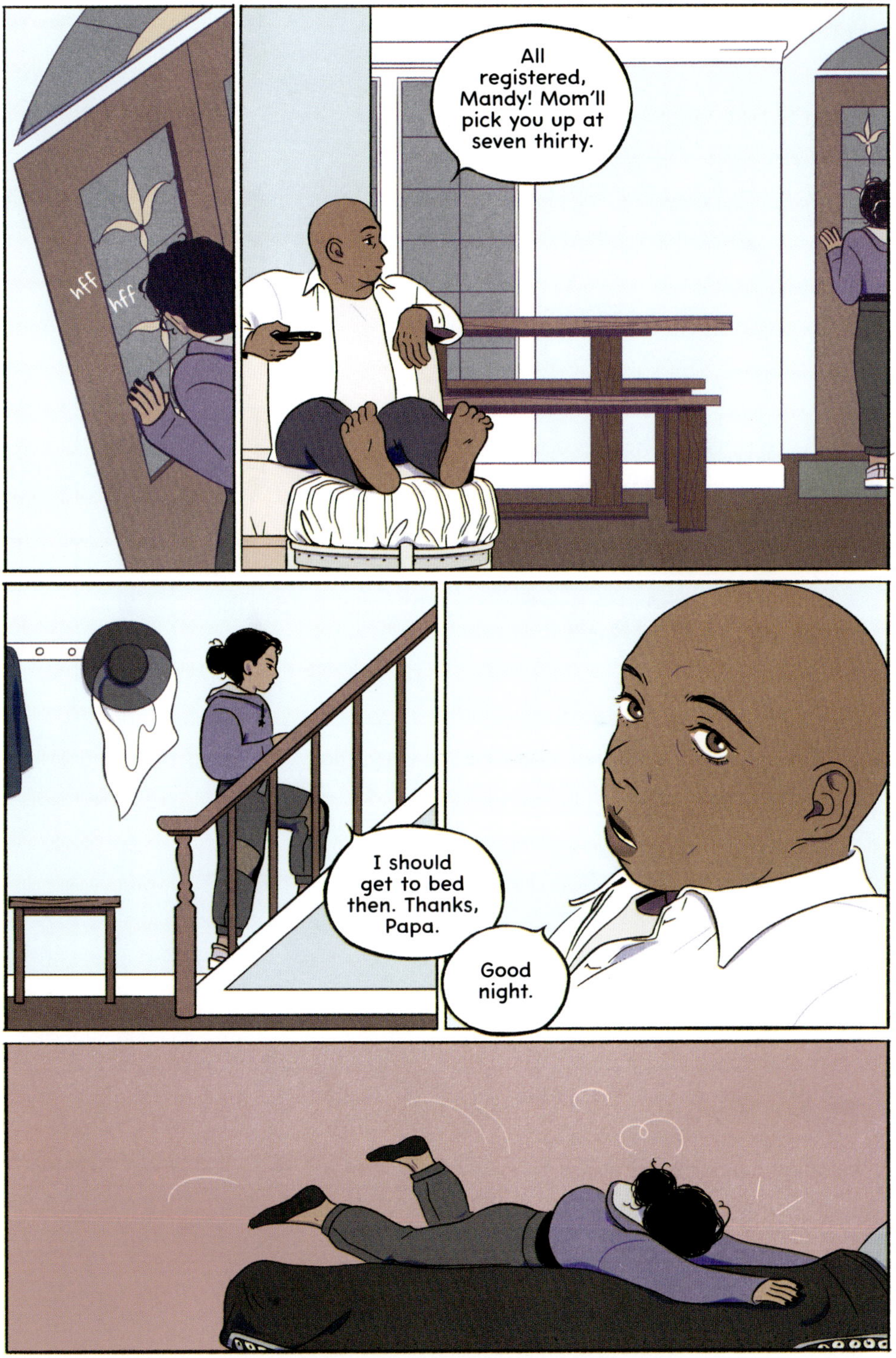
hff
hff
All registered, Mandy! Mom'll pick you up at seven thirty.
I should get to bed then. Thanks, Papa.
Good night.

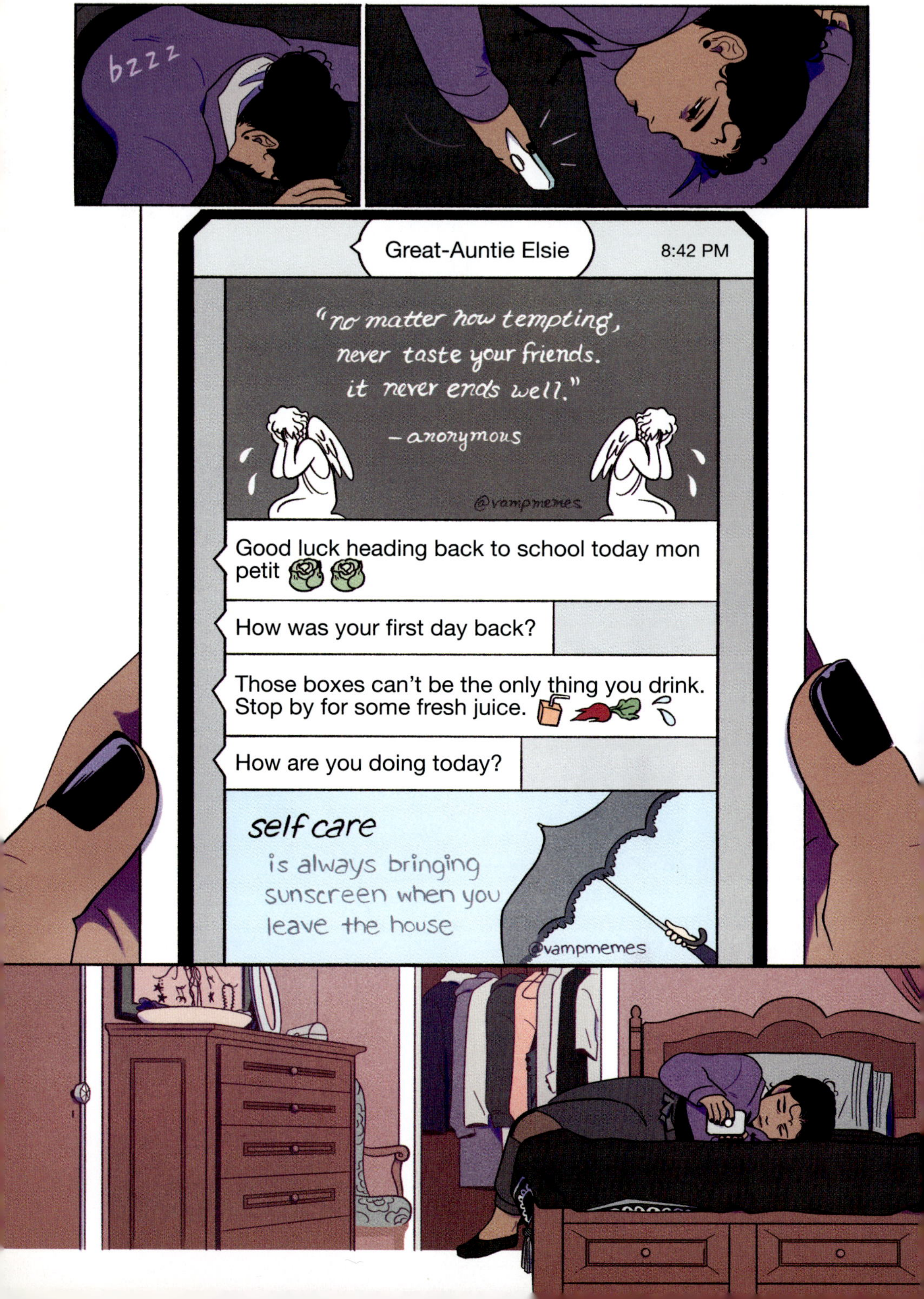
bzzz
Great-Auntie Elsie
8:42 PM
"no matter how tempting, never taste your friends. it never ends well."
- anonymous
@vampmemes
Good luck heading back to school today mon petit
How was your first day back?
Those boxes can't be the only thing you drink. Stop by for some fresh juice.
How are you doing today?
self care
is always bringing sunscreen when you leave the house
@vampmemes

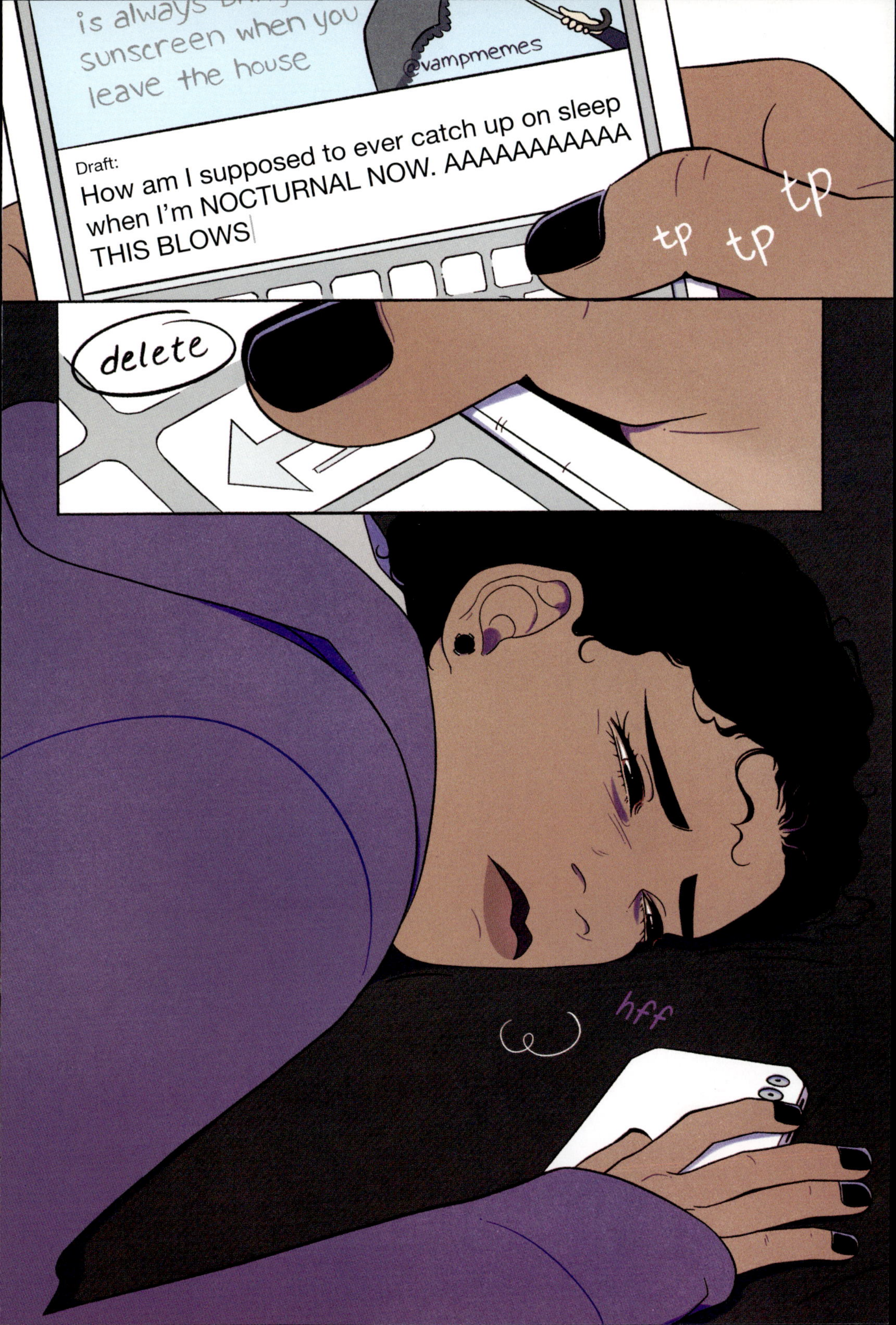
sunscreen when you leave the house
@vampmemes
Draft:
How am I supposed to ever catch up on sleep when I'm NOCTURNAL NOW. AAAAAAAAAAA THIS BLOWS
tp tp tp
delete
hff

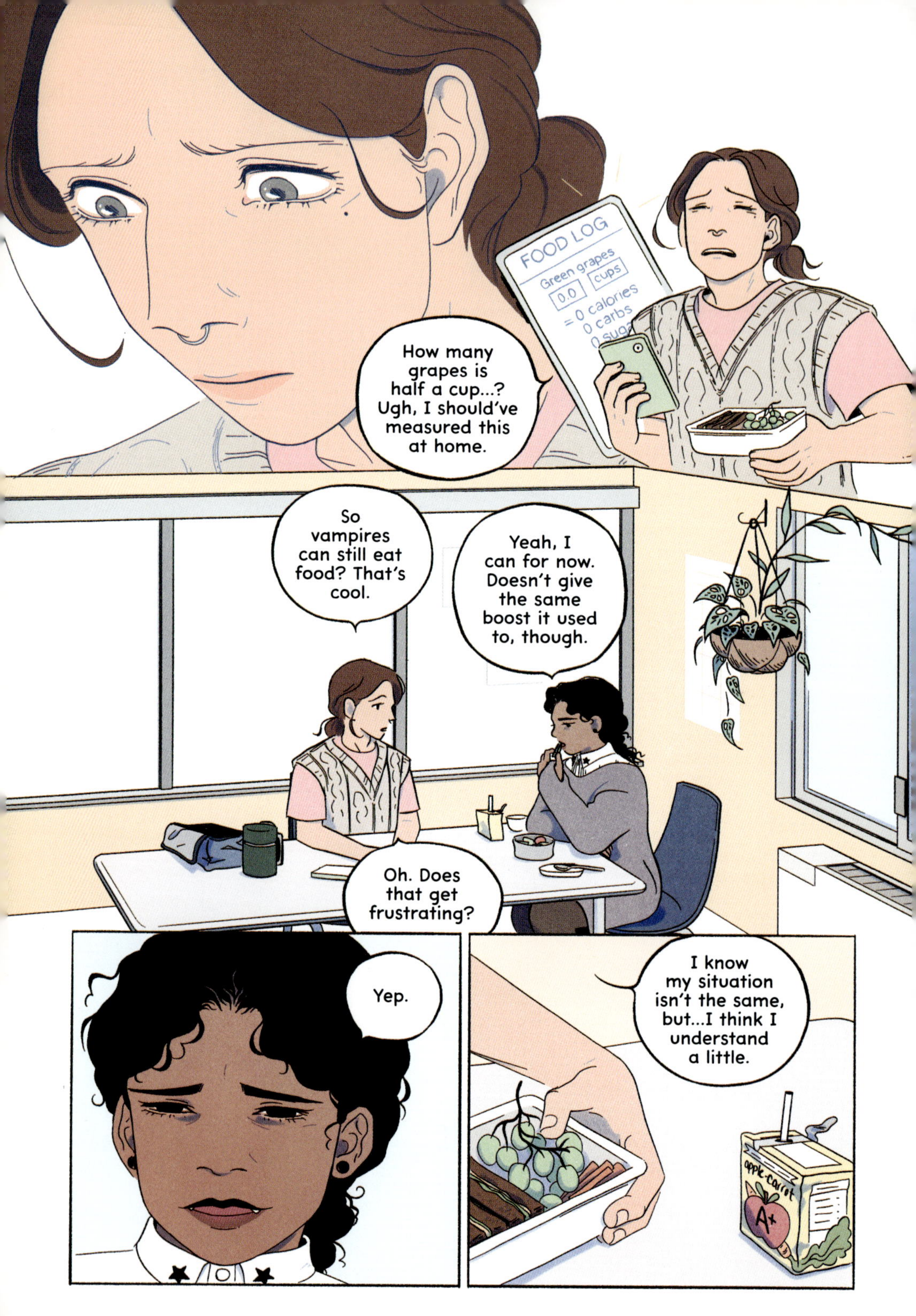
FOOD LOG
Green grapes
0.0 cups
= 0 calories
0 carbs
How many grapes is half a cup...? Ugh, I should've measured this at home.
So vampires can still eat food? That's cool.
Yeah, I can for now. Doesn't give the same boost it used to, though.
Oh. Does that get frustrating?
Yep.
I know my situation isn't the same, but...I think I understand a little.
apple-carrot
A+

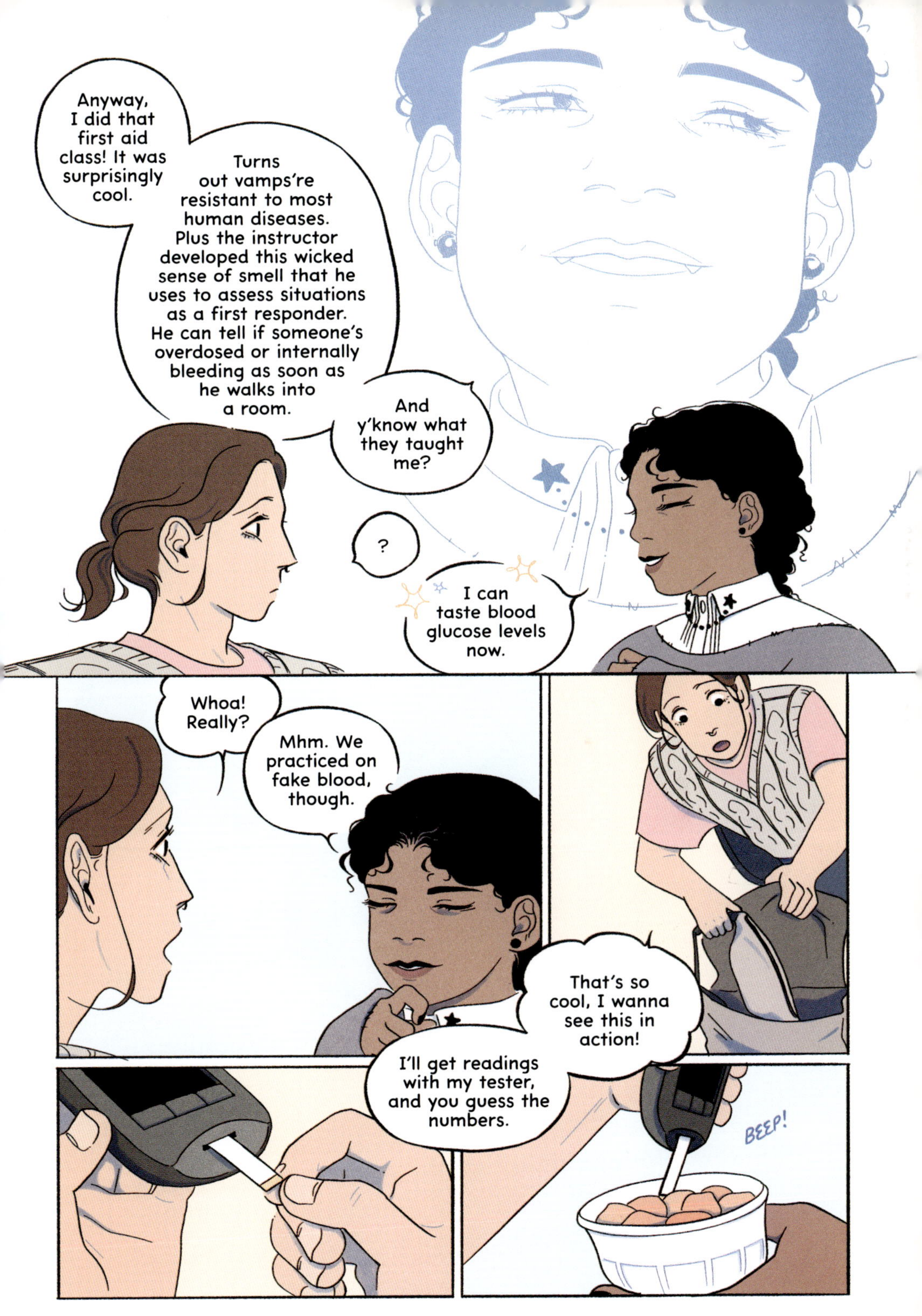

Anyway, I did that first aid class! It was surprisingly cool.
Turns out vamps're resistant to most human diseases. Plus the instructor developed this wicked sense of smell that he uses to assess situations as a first responder. He can tell if someone's overdosed or internally bleeding as soon as he walks into a room.
And y'know what they taught me?
?
I can taste blood glucose levels now.
Whoa! Really?
Mhm. We practiced on fake blood, though.
That's so cool, I wanna see this in action!
I'll get readings with my tester, and you guess the numbers.
BEEP!

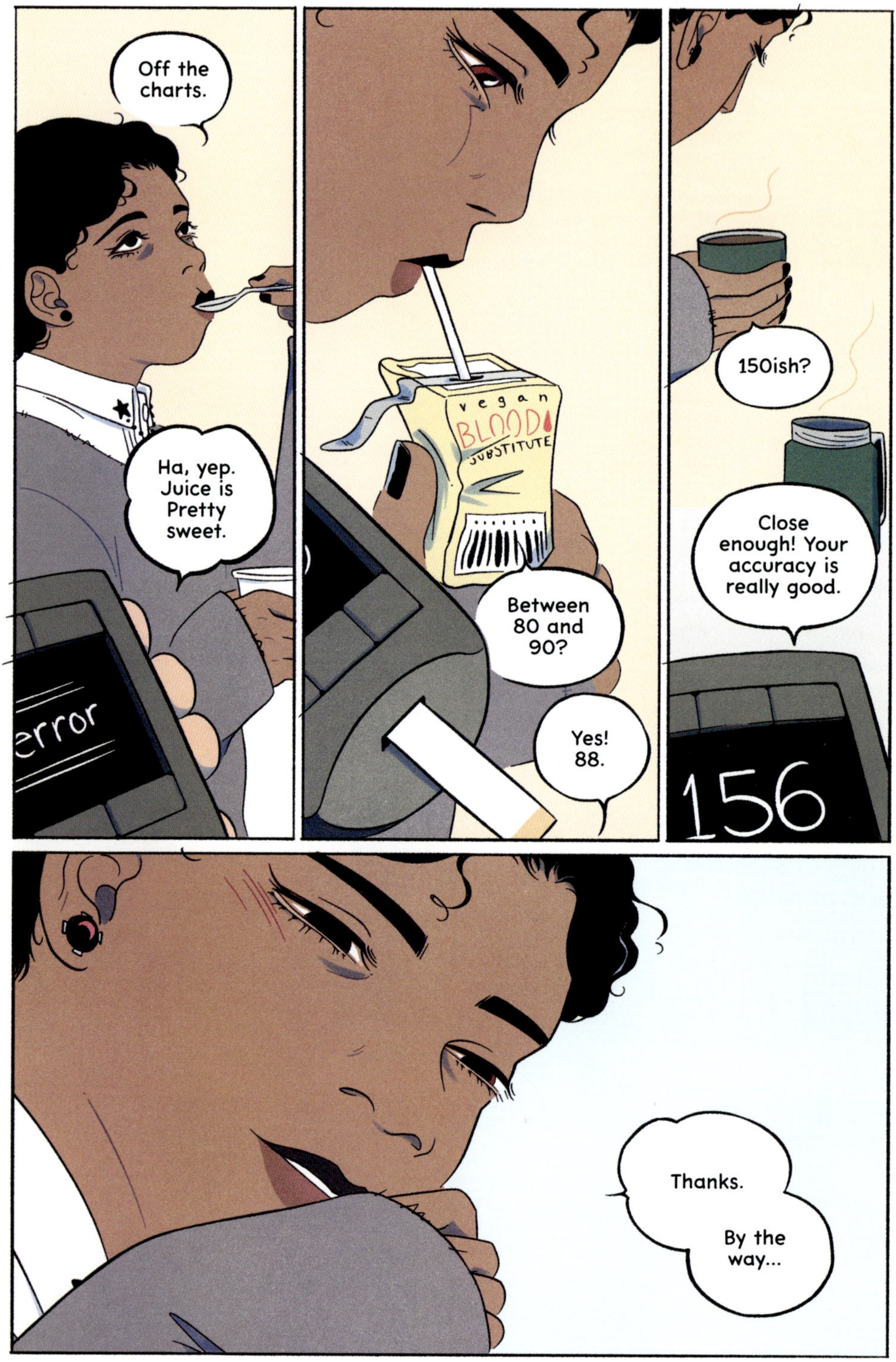
Off the charts.
Ha, yep. Juice is Pretty sweet.
error
vegan BLOOD SUBSTITUTE
Between 80 and 90?
Yes! 88.
150ish?
Close enough! Your accuracy is really good.
156
Thanks.
By the way...

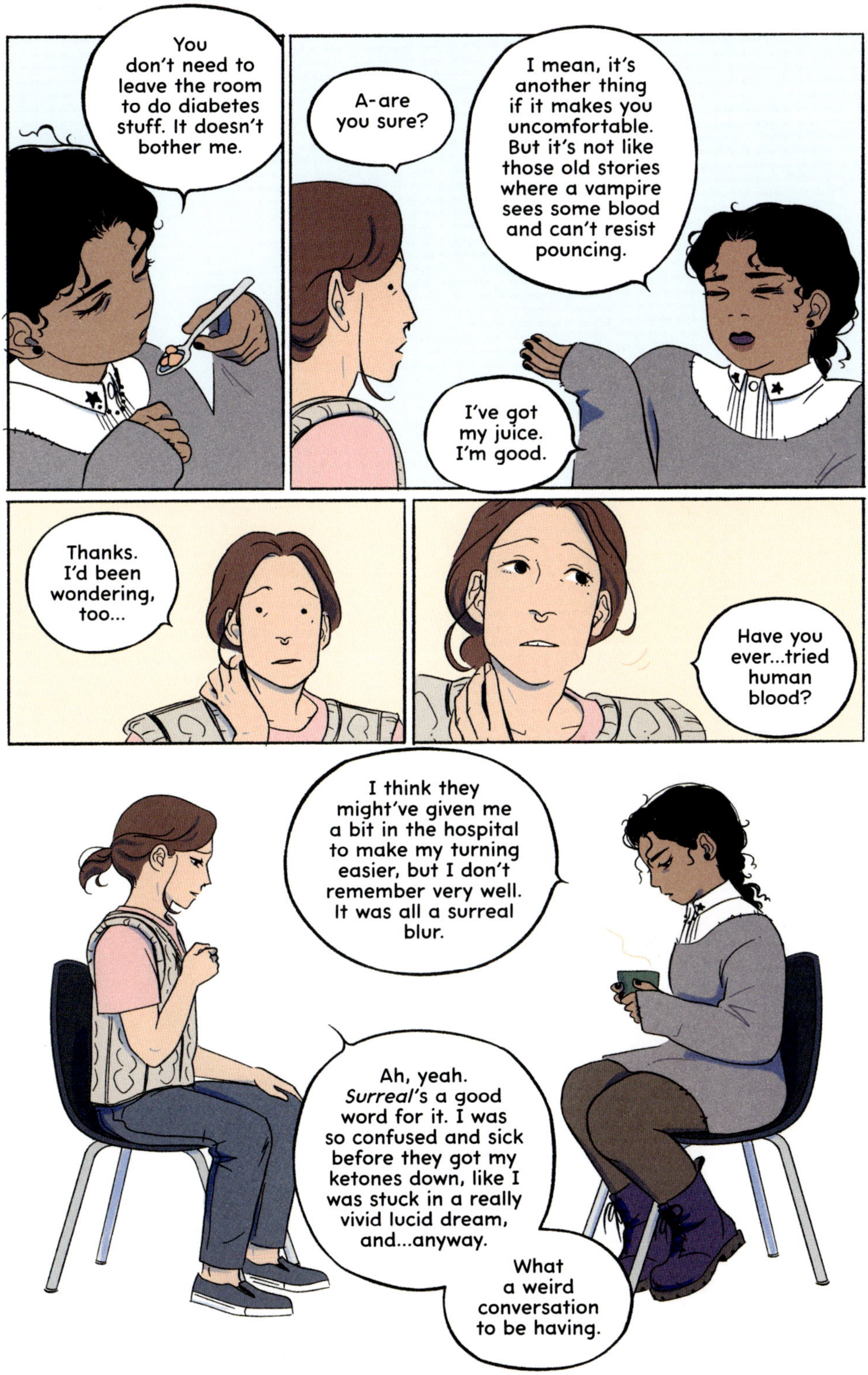
You don't need to leave the room to do diabetes stuff. It doesn't bother me.
A-are you sure?
I mean, it's another thing if it makes you uncomfortable. But it's not like those old stories where a vampire sees some blood and can't resist pouncing.
I've got my juice. I'm good.
Thanks. I'd been wondering, too...
Have you ever...tried human blood?
I think they might've given me a bit in the hospital to make my turning easier, but I don't remember very well. It was all a surreal blur.
Ah, yeah. *Surreal*'s a good word for it. I was so confused and sick before they got my ketones down, like I was stuck in a really vivid lucid dream, and...anyway.
What a weird conversation to be having.

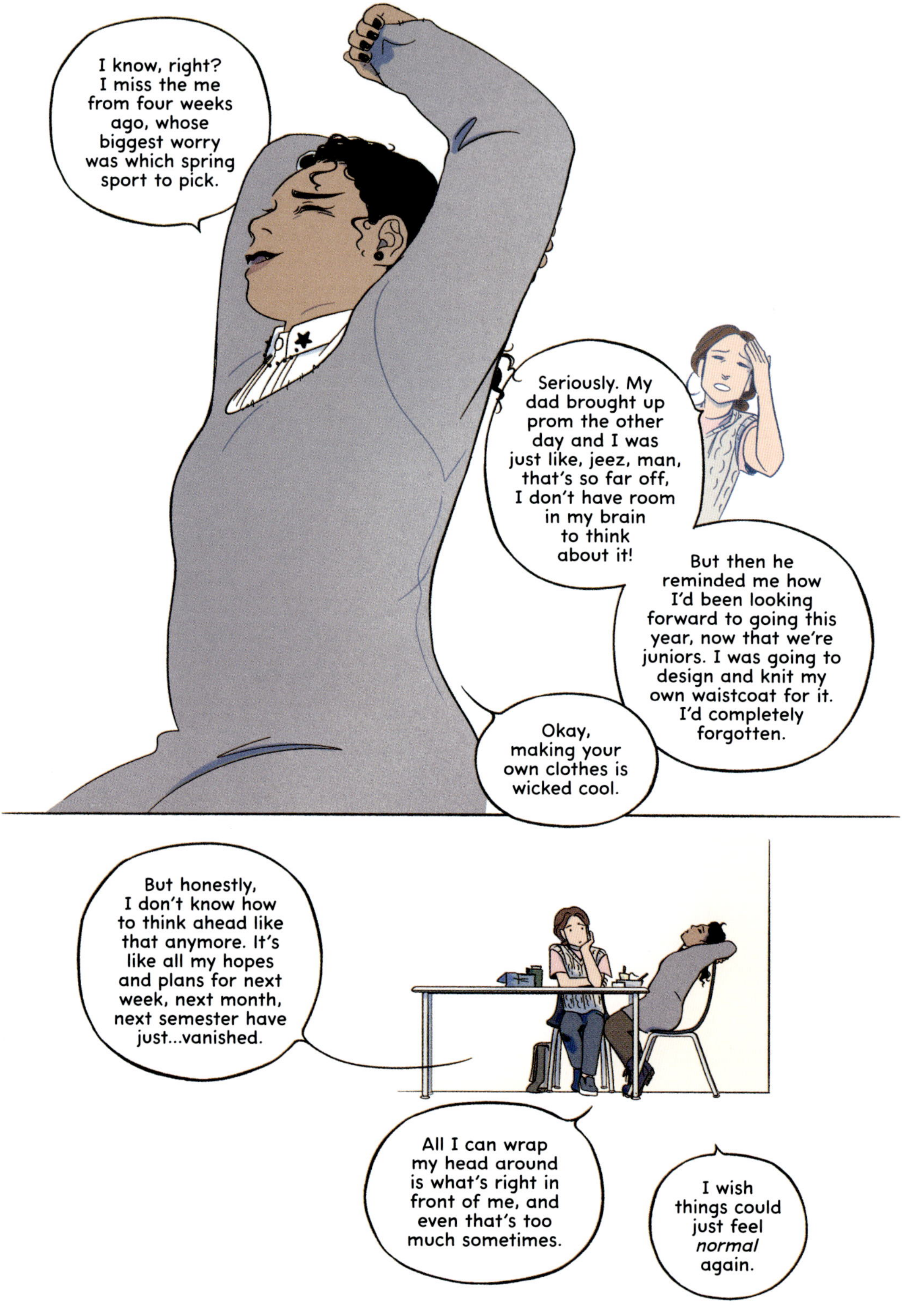
I know, right? I miss the me from four weeks ago, whose biggest worry was which spring sport to pick.
Seriously. My dad brought up prom the other day and I was just like, jeez, man, that's so far off, I don't have room in my brain to think about it!
But then he reminded me how I'd been looking forward to going this year, now that we're juniors. I was going to design and knit my own waistcoat for it. I'd completely forgotten.
Okay, making your own clothes is wicked cool.
But honestly, I don't know how to think ahead like that anymore. It's like all my hopes and plans for next week, next month, next semester have just...vanished.
All I can wrap my head around is what's right in front of me, and even that's too much sometimes.
I wish things could just feel *normal* again.

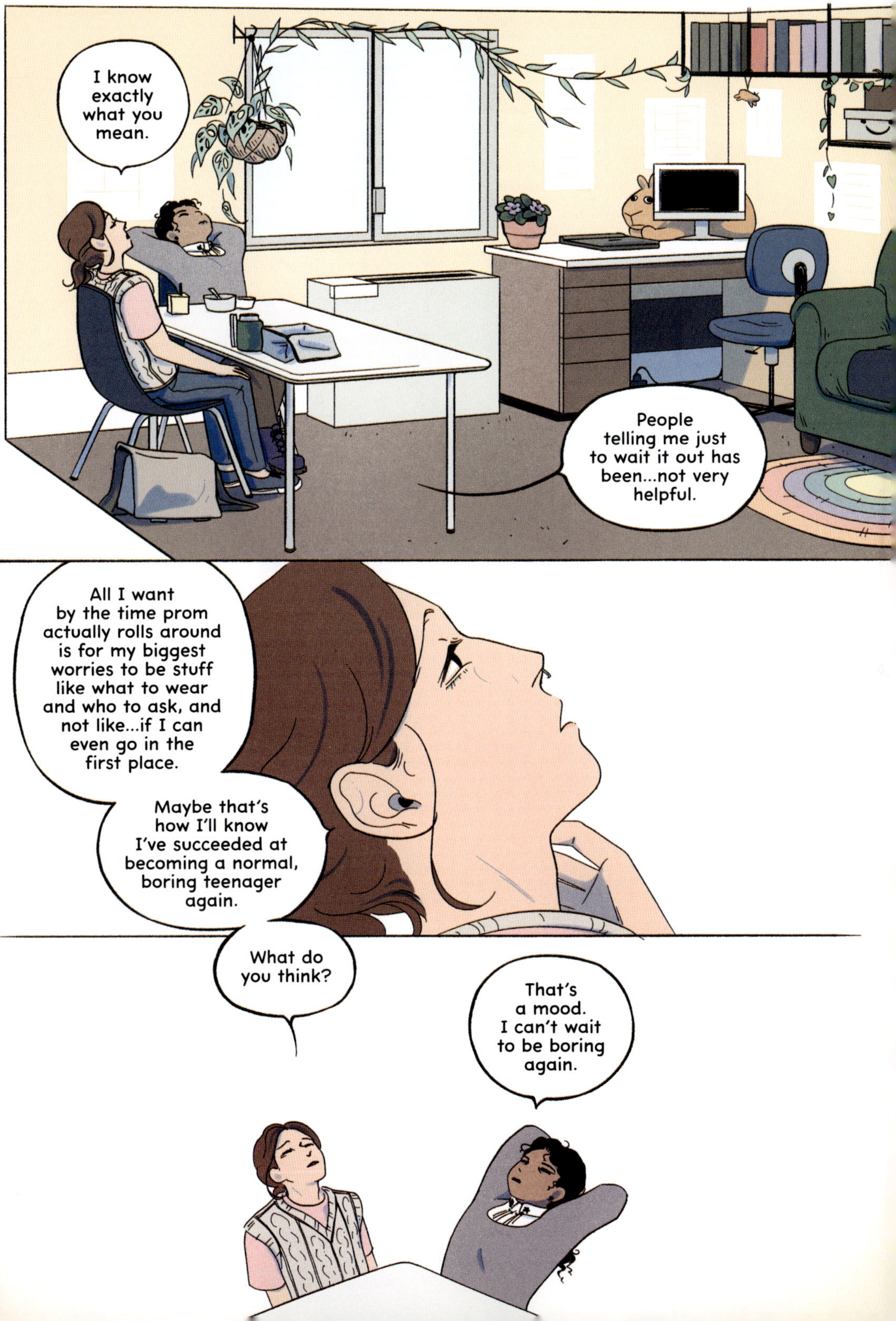
I know exactly what you mean.
People telling me just to wait it out has been...not very helpful.
All I want by the time prom actually rolls around is for my biggest worries to be stuff like what to wear and who to ask, and not like...if I can even go in the first place.
Maybe that's how I'll know I've succeeded at becoming a normal, boring teenager again.
What do you think?
That's a mood. I can't wait to be boring again.

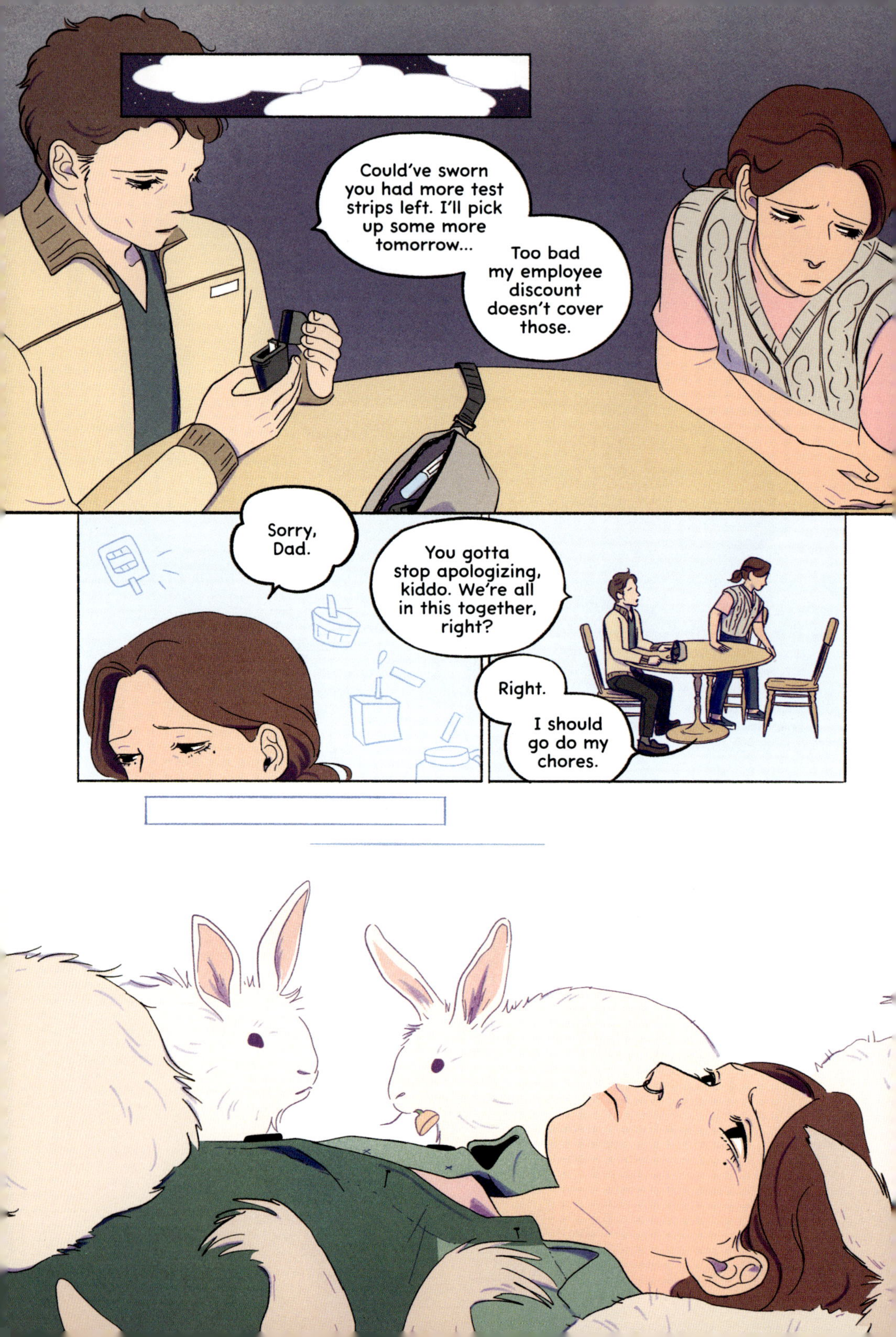

Could've sworn you had more test strips left. I'll pick up some more tomorrow...
Too bad my employee discount doesn't cover those.
Sorry, Dad.
You gotta stop apologizing, kiddo. We're all in this together, right?
Right.
I should go do my chores.

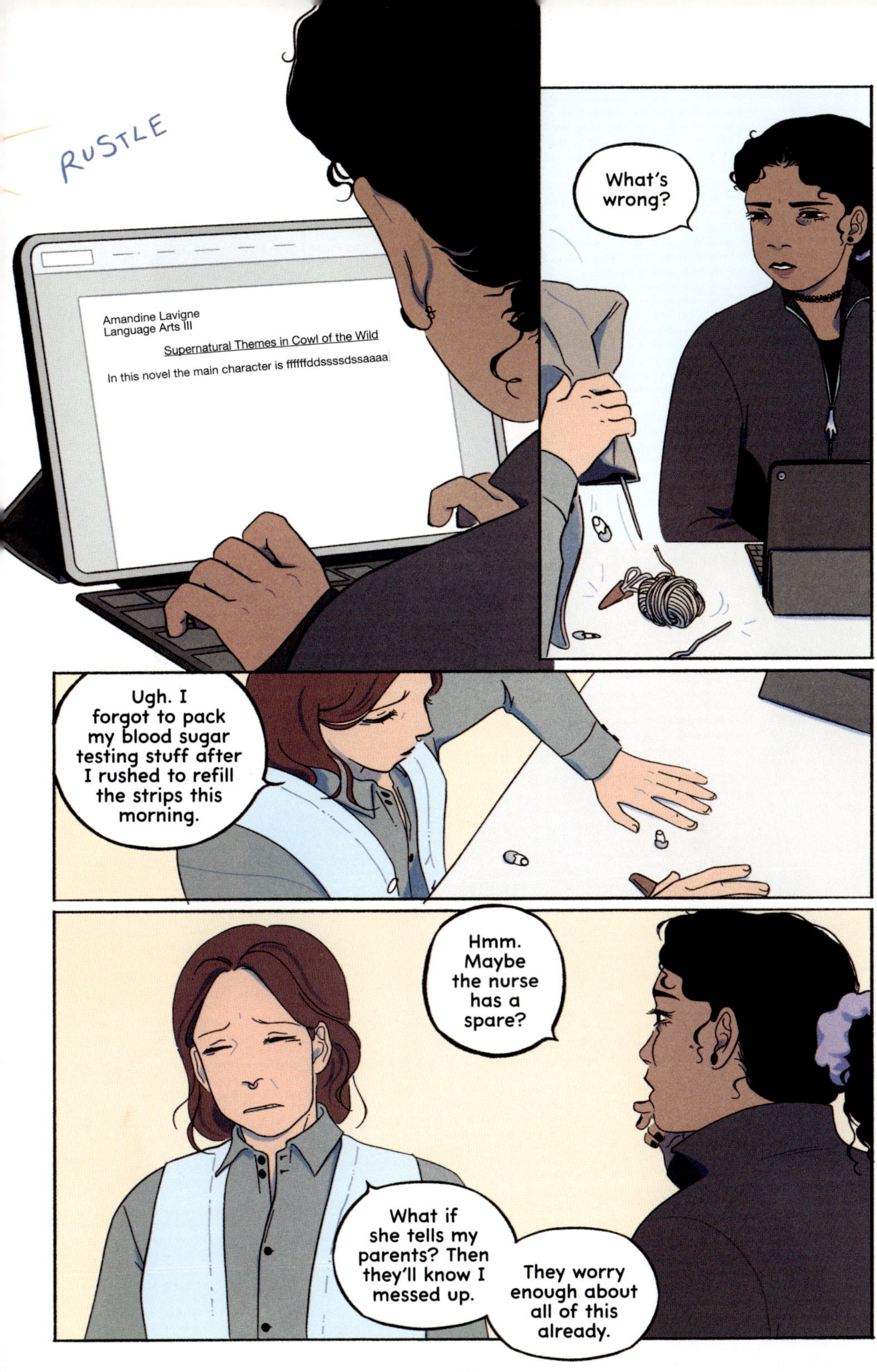
RUSTLE
Amandine Lavigne
Language Arts III
Supernatural Themes in Cowl of the Wild
In this novel the main character is ffffffddssssdssaaaa
What's wrong?
Ugh. I forgot to pack my blood sugar testing stuff after I rushed to refill the strips this morning.
Hmm. Maybe the nurse has a spare?
What if she tells my parents? Then they'll know I messed up.
They worry enough about all of this already.

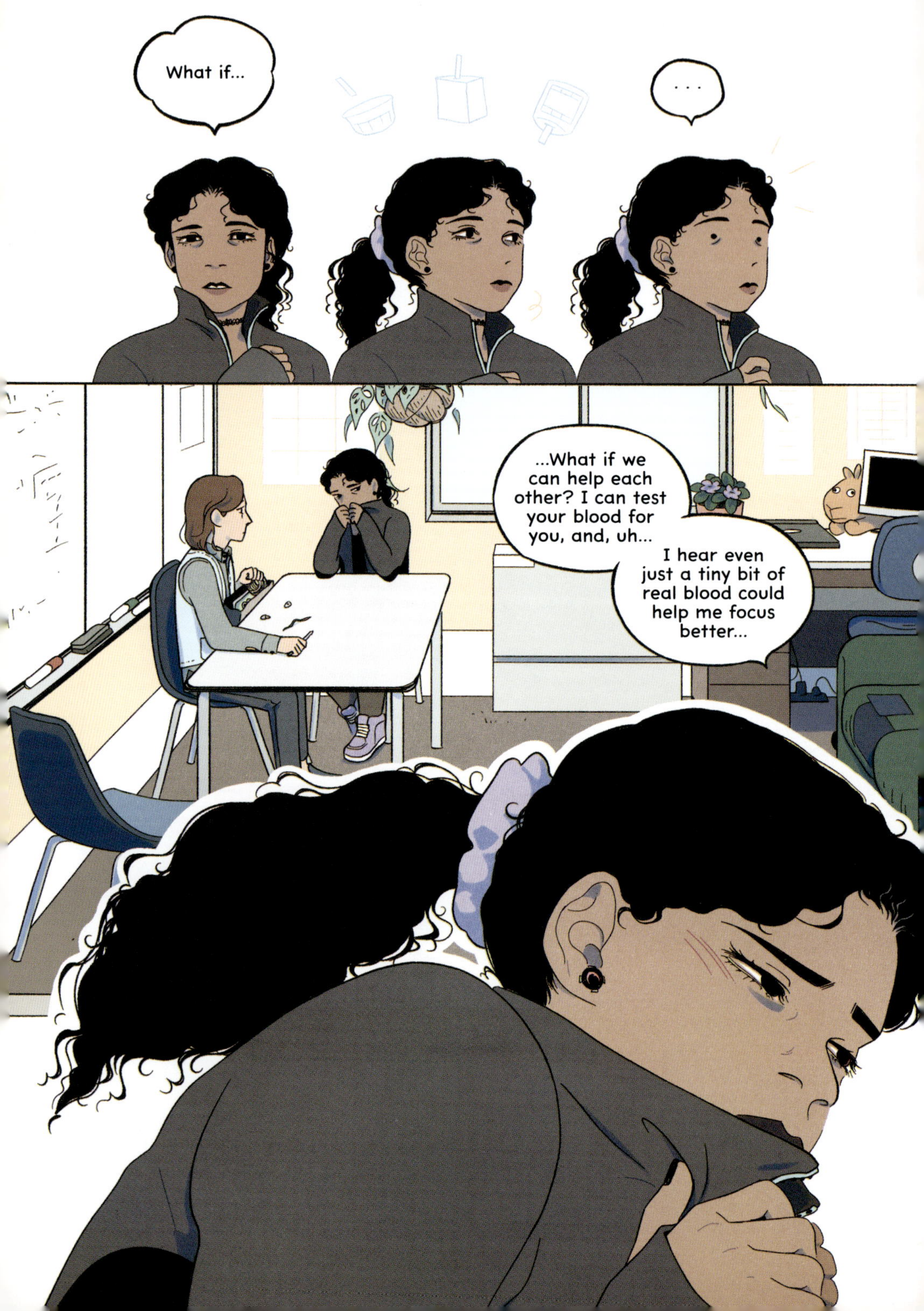
What if...
...
...What if we can help each other? I can test your blood for you, and, uh...
I hear even just a tiny bit of real blood could help me focus better...

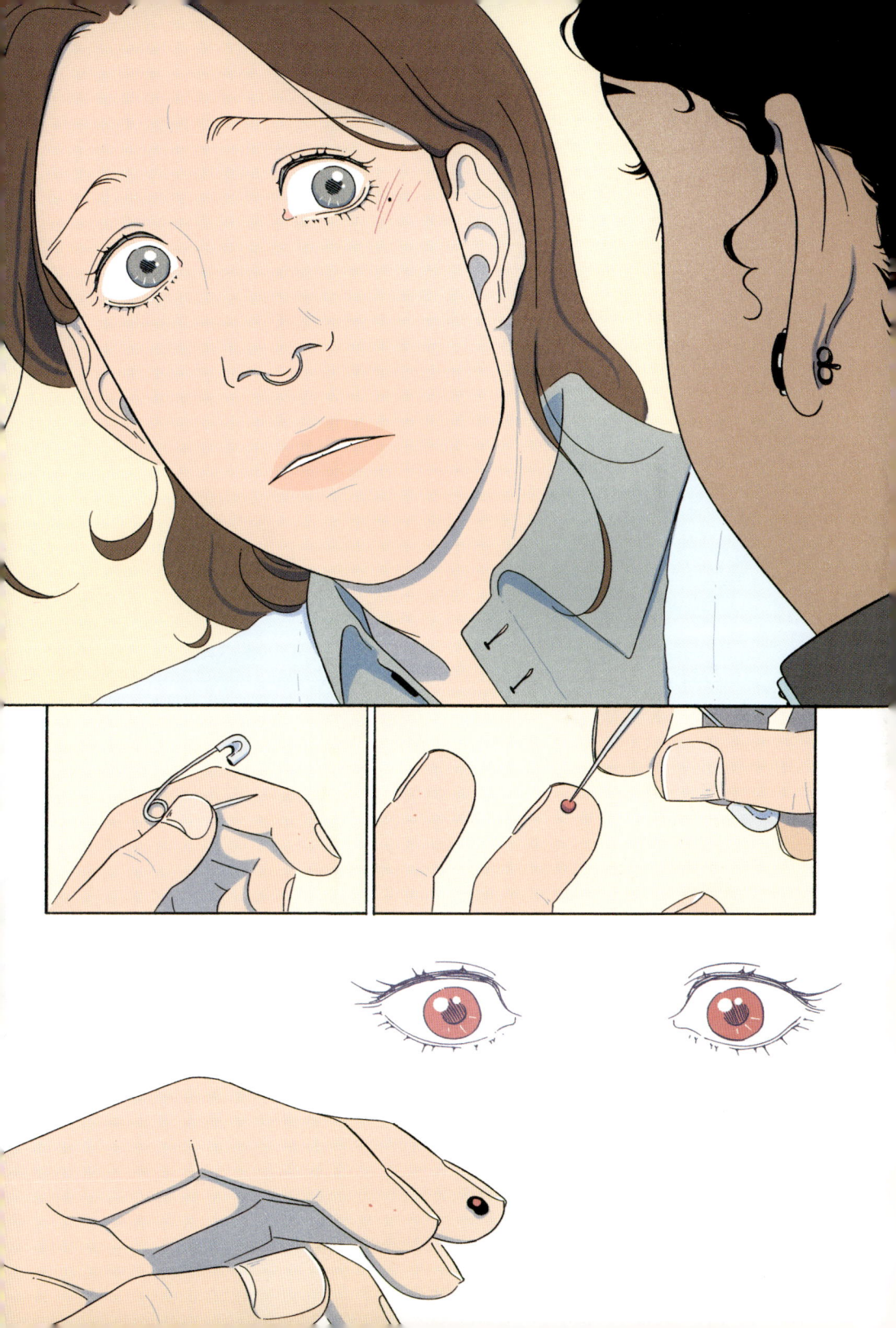

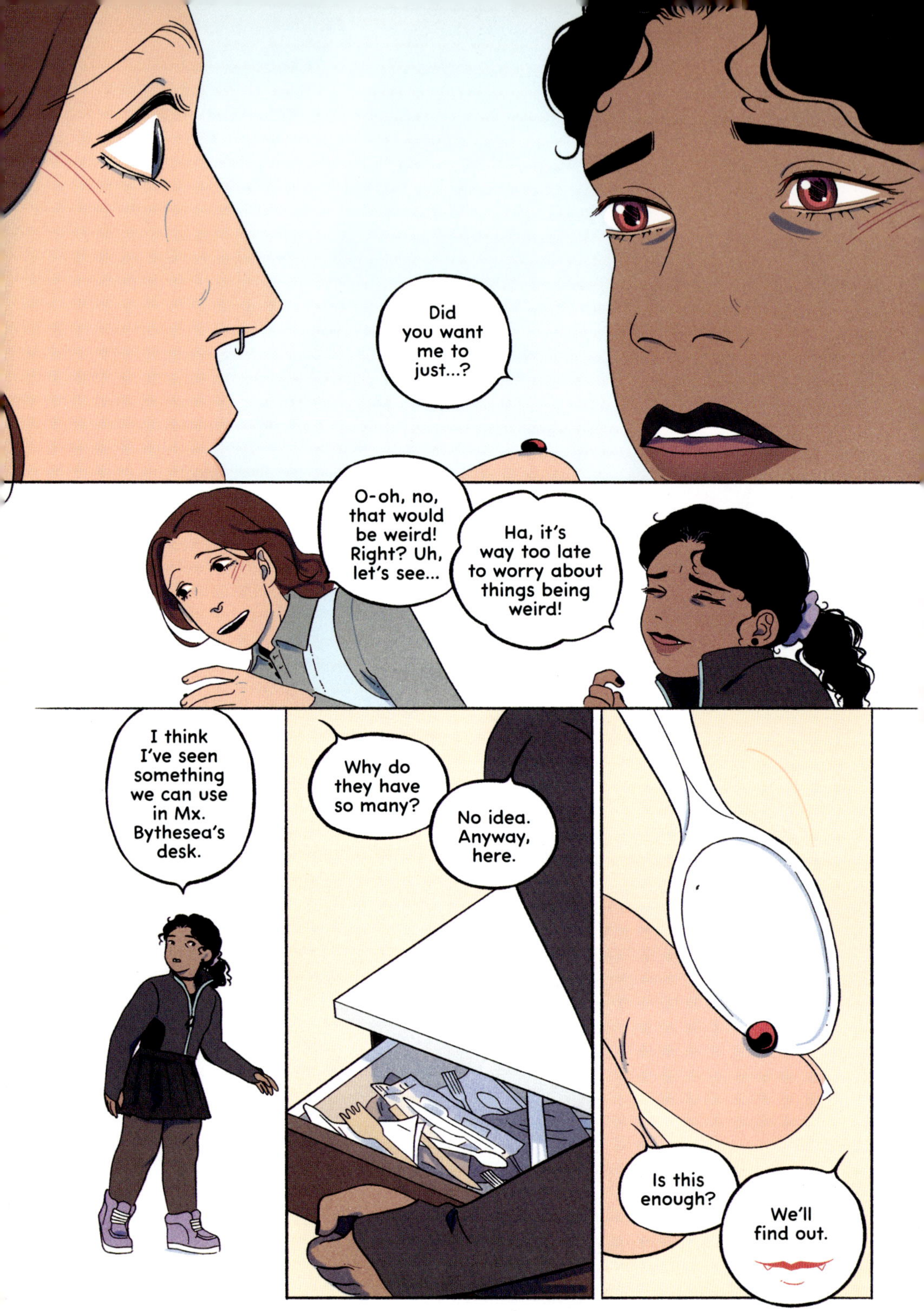
Did you want me to just...?
O-oh, no, that would be weird! Right? Uh, let's see...
Ha, it's way too late to worry about things being weird!
I think I've seen something we can use in Mx. Bythesea's desk.
Why do they have so many?
No idea. Anyway, here.
Is this enough?
We'll find out.

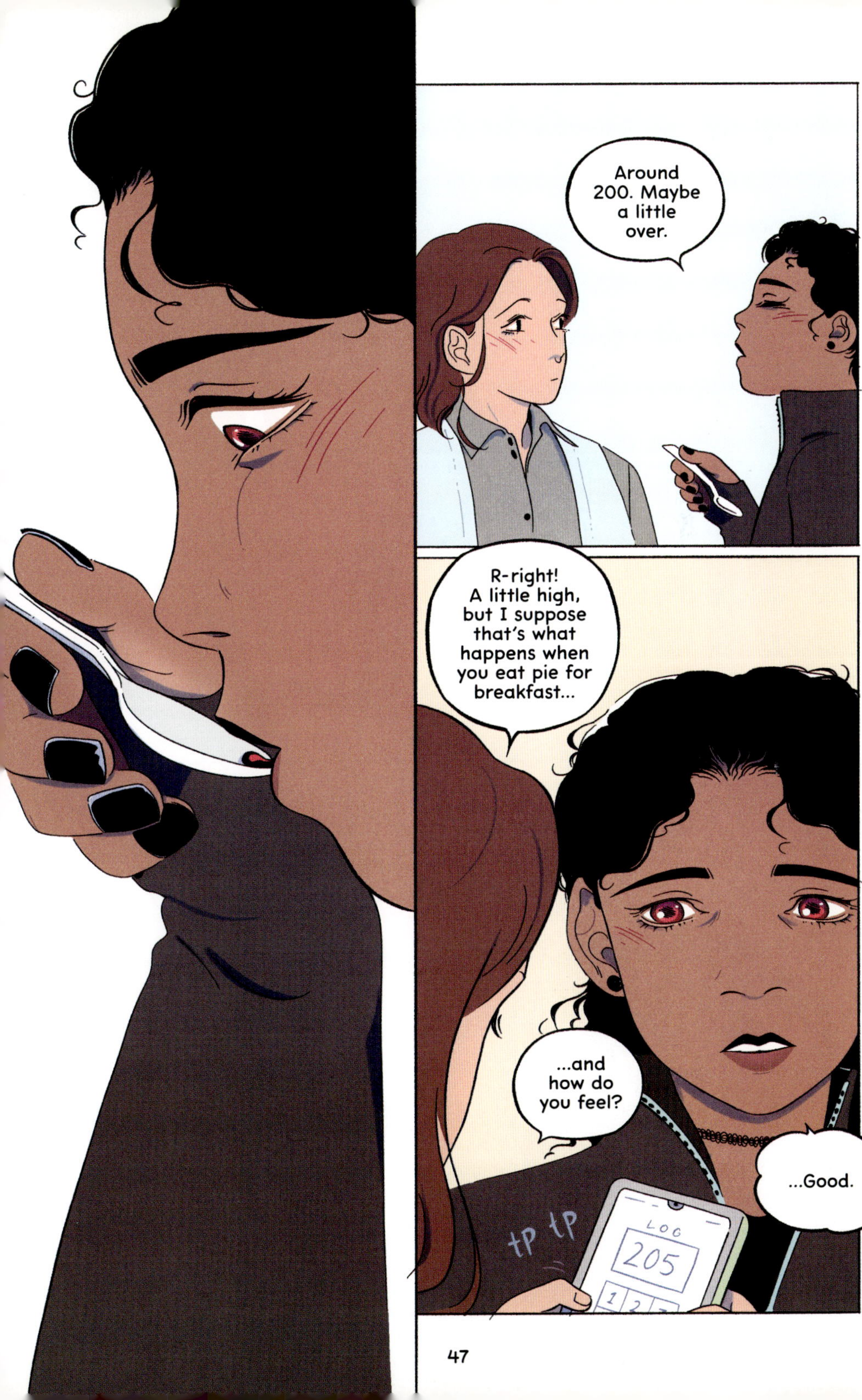
Around 200. Maybe a little over.
R-right! A little high, but I suppose that's what happens when you eat pie for breakfast...
...and how do you feel?
...Good.
tp tp
LOG
205

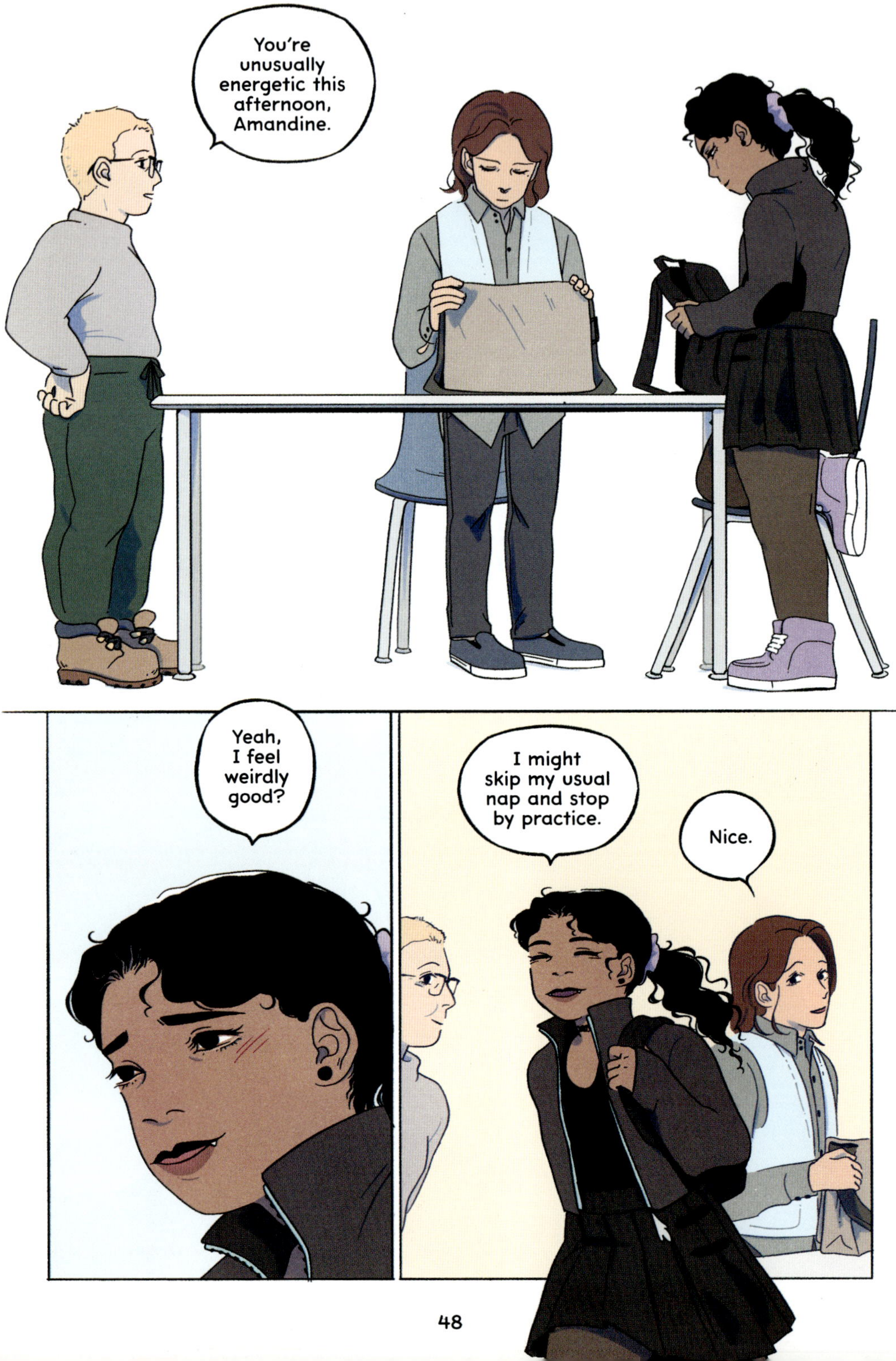
You're unusually energetic this afternoon, Amandine.
Yeah, I feel weirdly good?
I might skip my usual nap and stop by practice.
Nice.

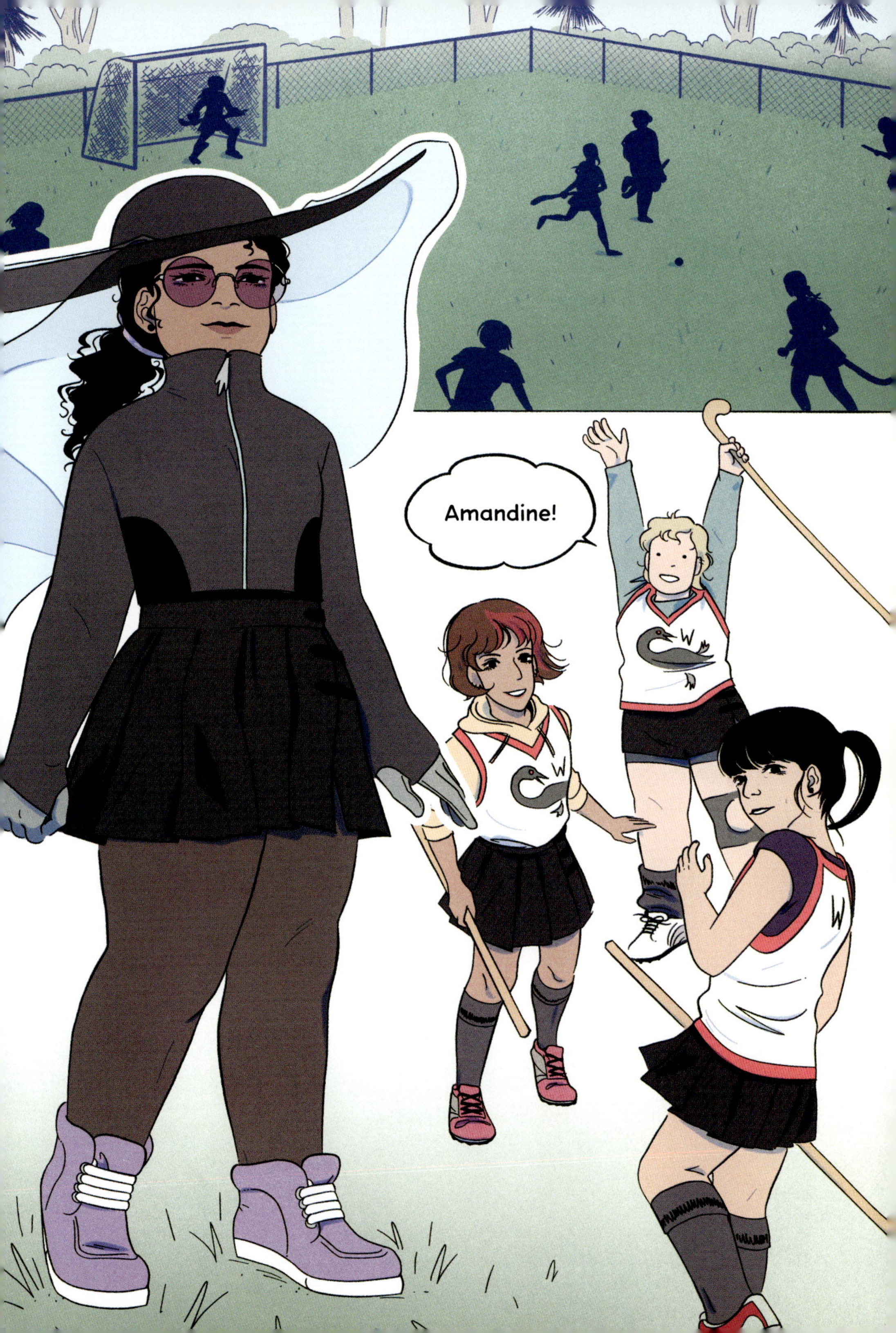
Amandine!

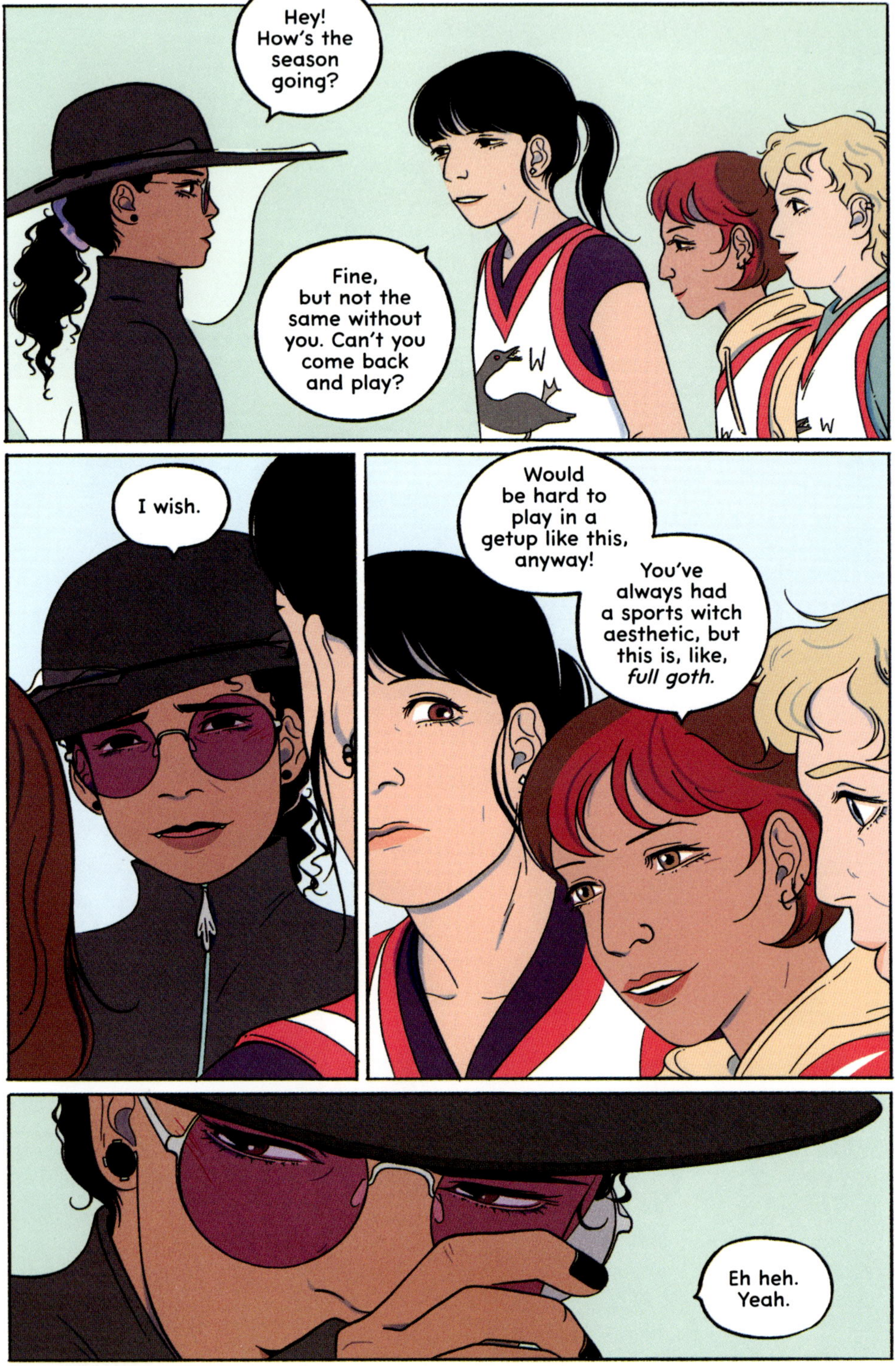
Hey! How's the season going?
Fine, but not the same without you. Can't you come back and play?
I wish.
Would be hard to play in a getup like this, anyway!
You've always had a sports witch aesthetic, but this is, like, *full goth.*
Eh heh. Yeah.

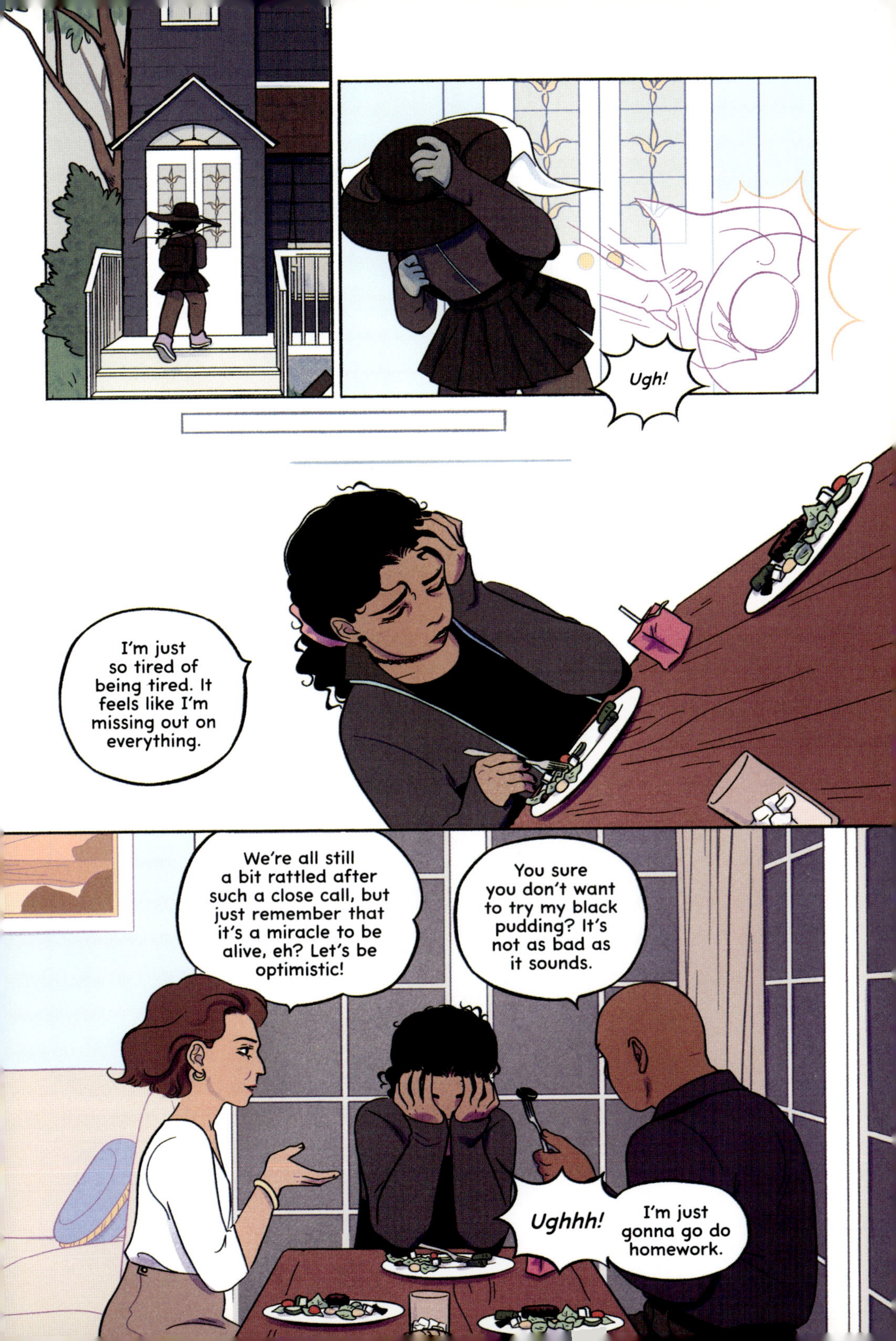
Ugh!
I'm just so tired of being tired. It feels like I'm missing out on everything.
We're all still a bit rattled after such a close call, but just remember that it's a miracle to be alive, eh? Let's be optimistic!
You sure you don't want to try my black pudding? It's not as bad as it sounds.
Ughhh!
I'm just gonna go do homework.

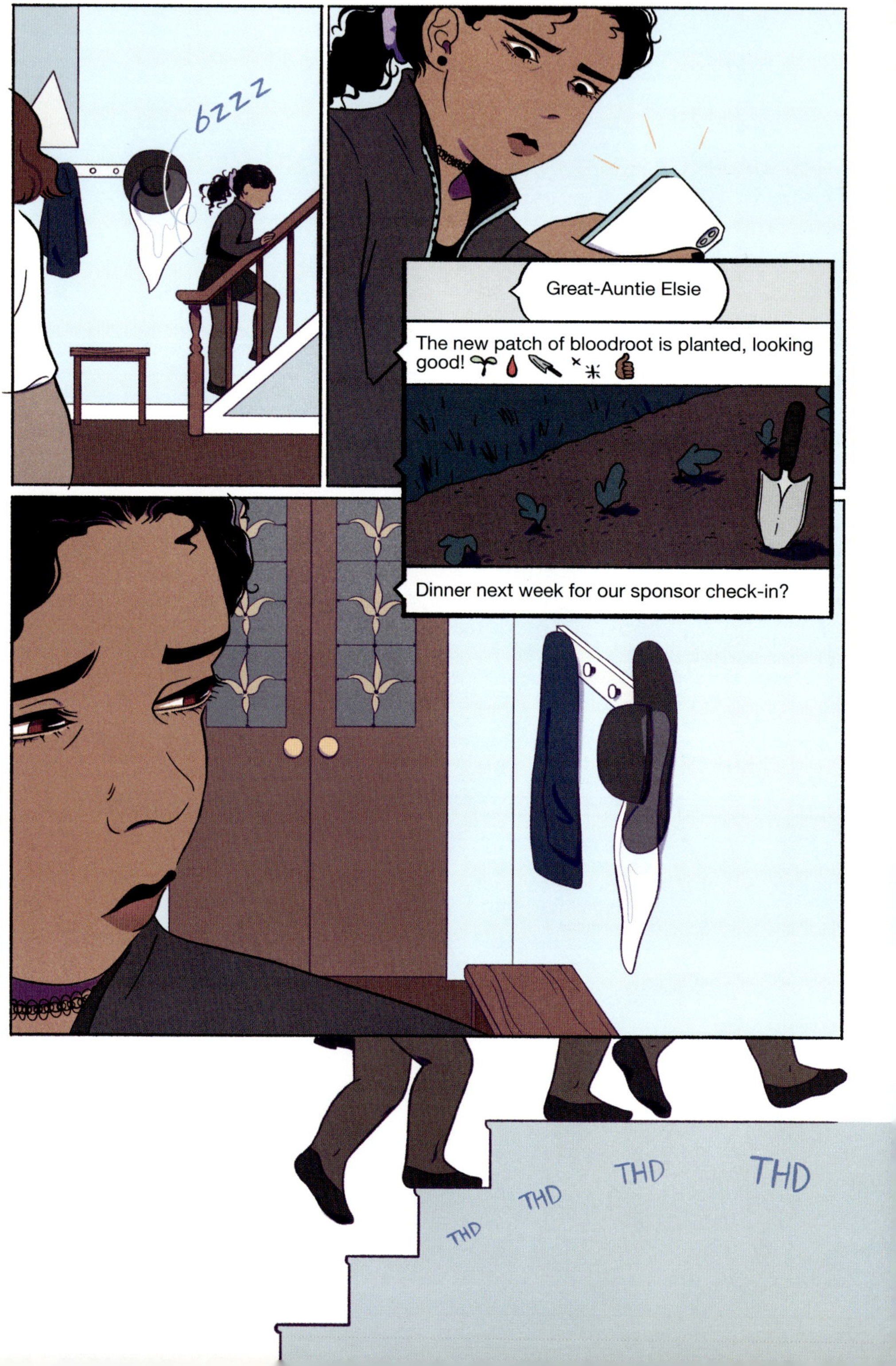
bzzz
Great-Auntie Elsie
The new patch of bloodroot is planted, looking good!
Dinner next week for our sponsor check-in?
THD
THD
THD
THD

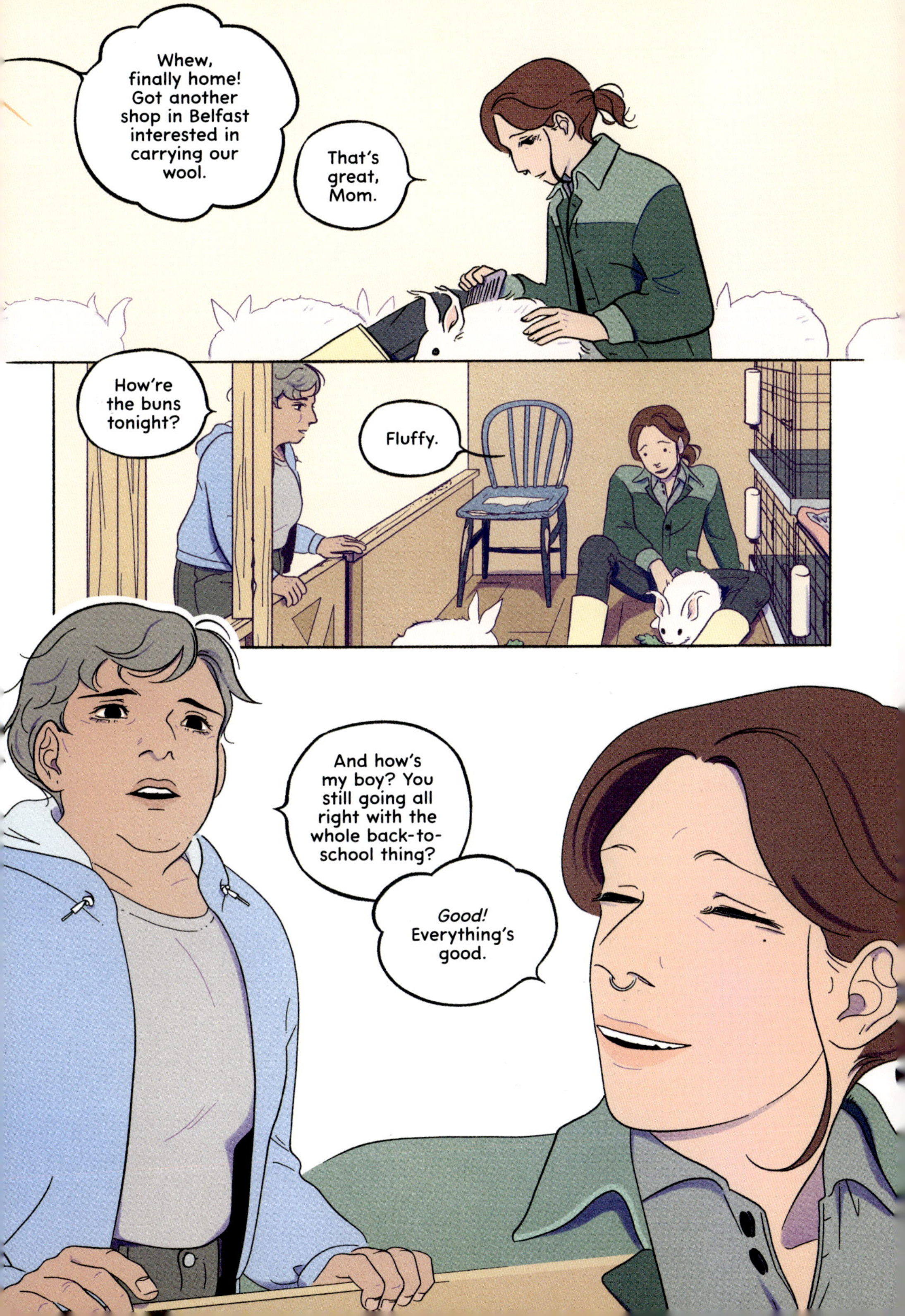
Whew, finally home! Got another shop in Belfast interested in carrying our wool.
That's great, Mom.
How're the buns tonight?
Fluffy.
And how's my boy? You still going all right with the whole back-to-school thing?
Good! Everything's good.

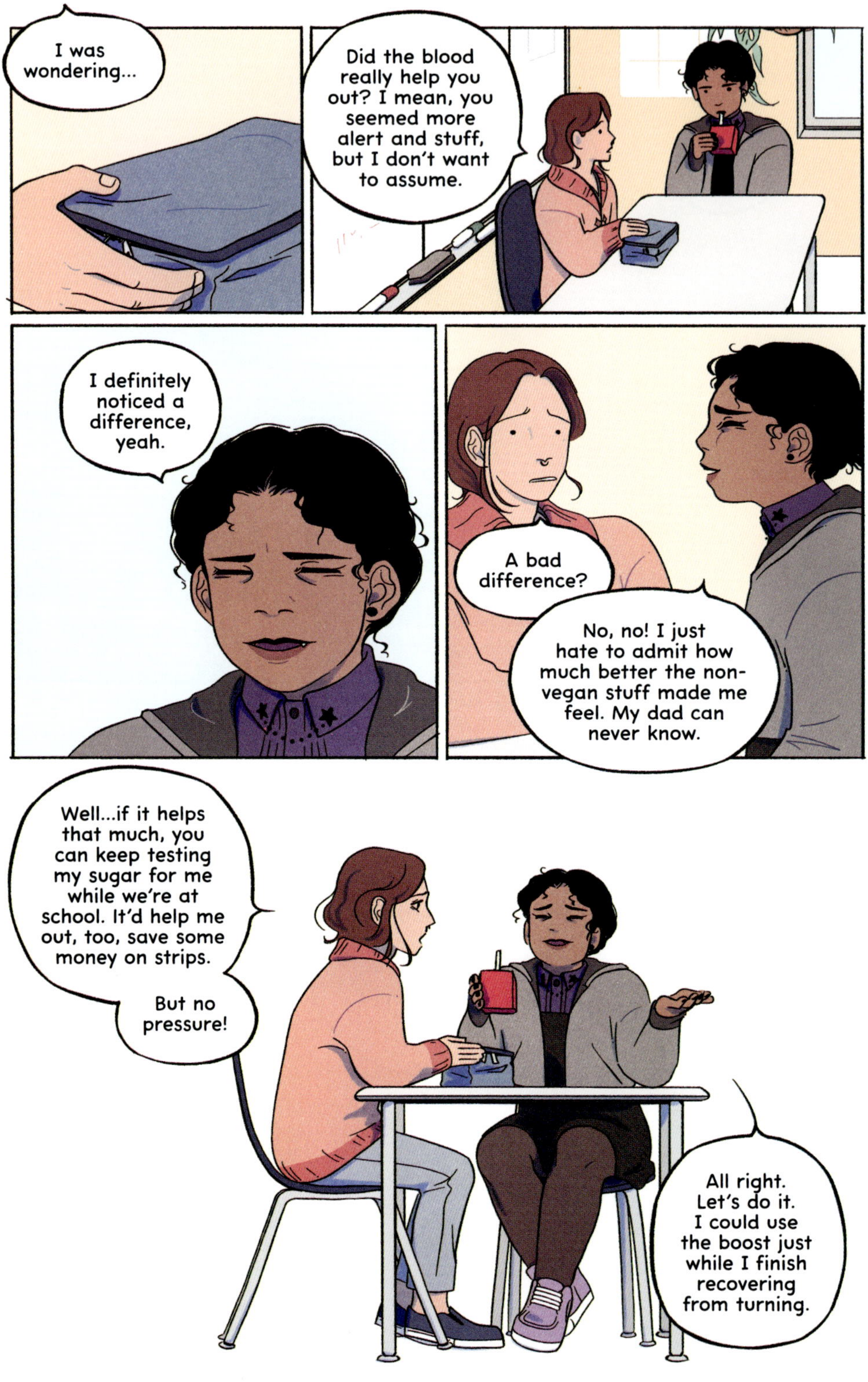
I was wondering...
Did the blood really help you out? I mean, you seemed more alert and stuff, but I don't want to assume.
I definitely noticed a difference, yeah.
A bad difference?
No, no! I just hate to admit how much better the non-vegan stuff made me feel. My dad can never know.
Well...if it helps that much, you can keep testing my sugar for me while we're at school. It'd help me out, too, save some money on strips.
But no pressure!
All right. Let's do it. I could use the boost just while I finish recovering from turning.

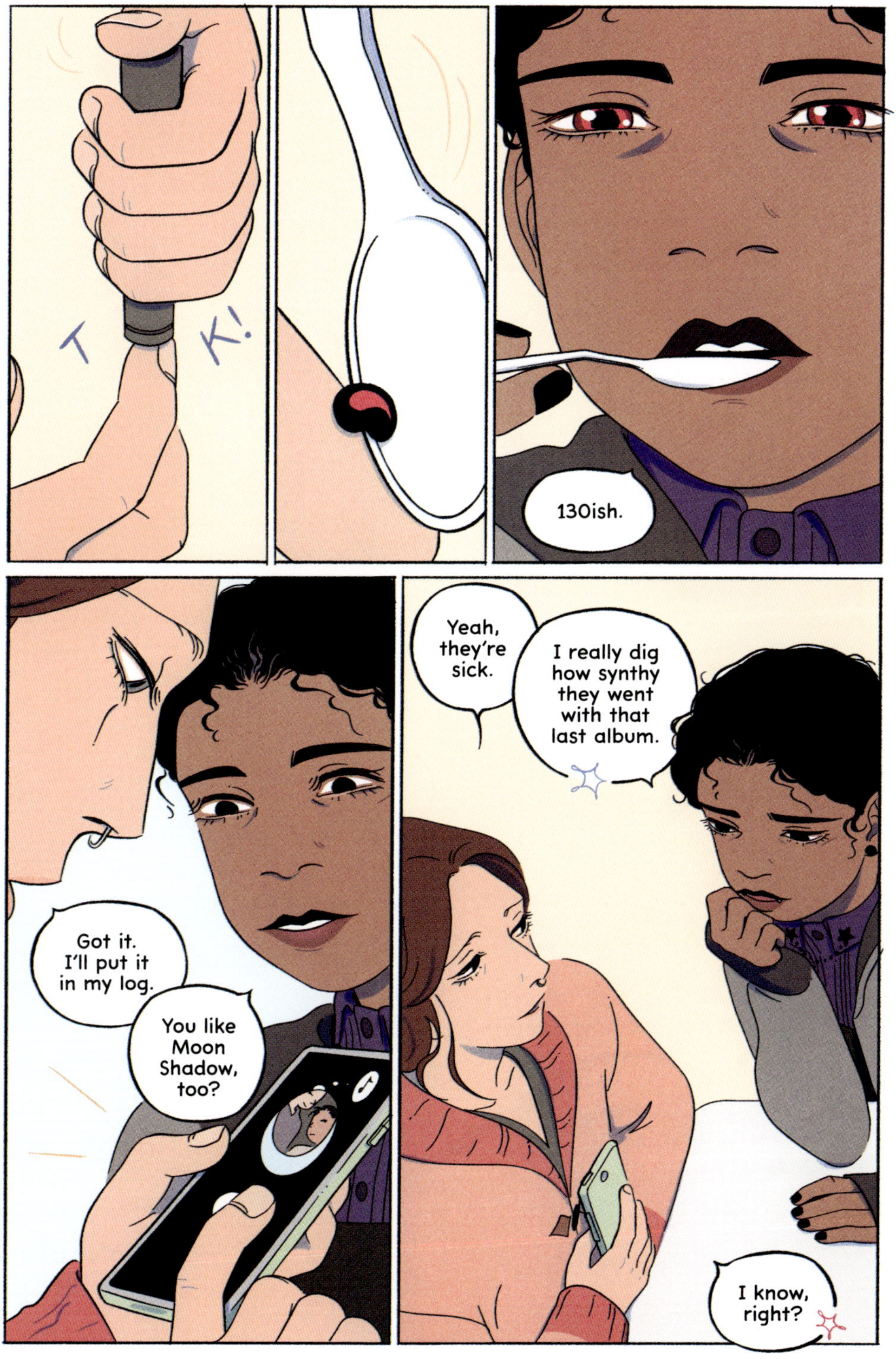
T K!
130ish.
Got it. I'll put it in my log.
You like Moon Shadow, too?
Yeah, they're sick.
I really dig how synthy they went with that last album.
I know, right?

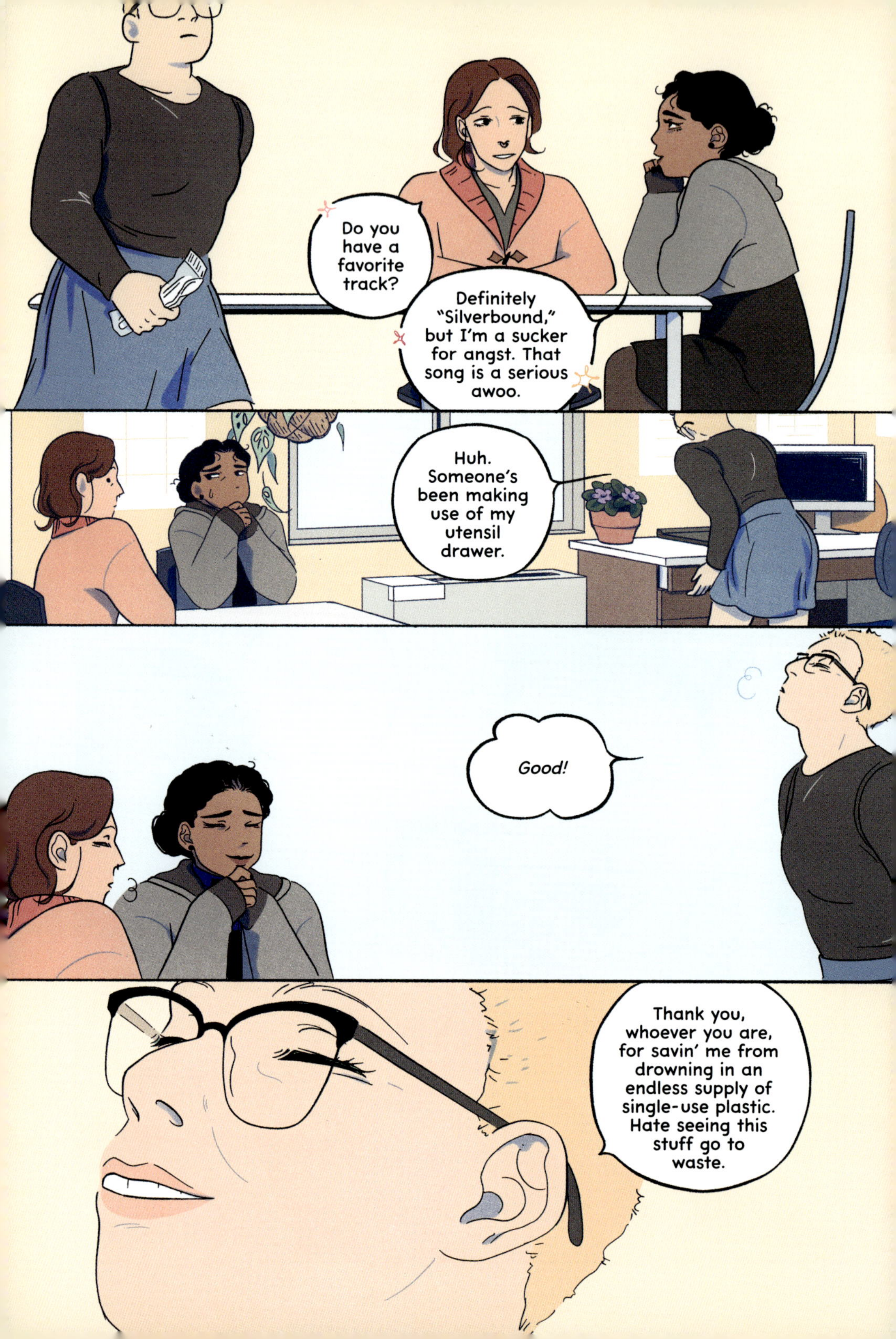

Do you have a favorite track?
Definitely "Silverbound," but I'm a sucker for angst. That song is a serious awoo.
Huh. Someone's been making use of my utensil drawer.
Good!
Thank you, whoever you are, for savin' me from drowning in an endless supply of single-use plastic. Hate seeing this stuff go to waste.

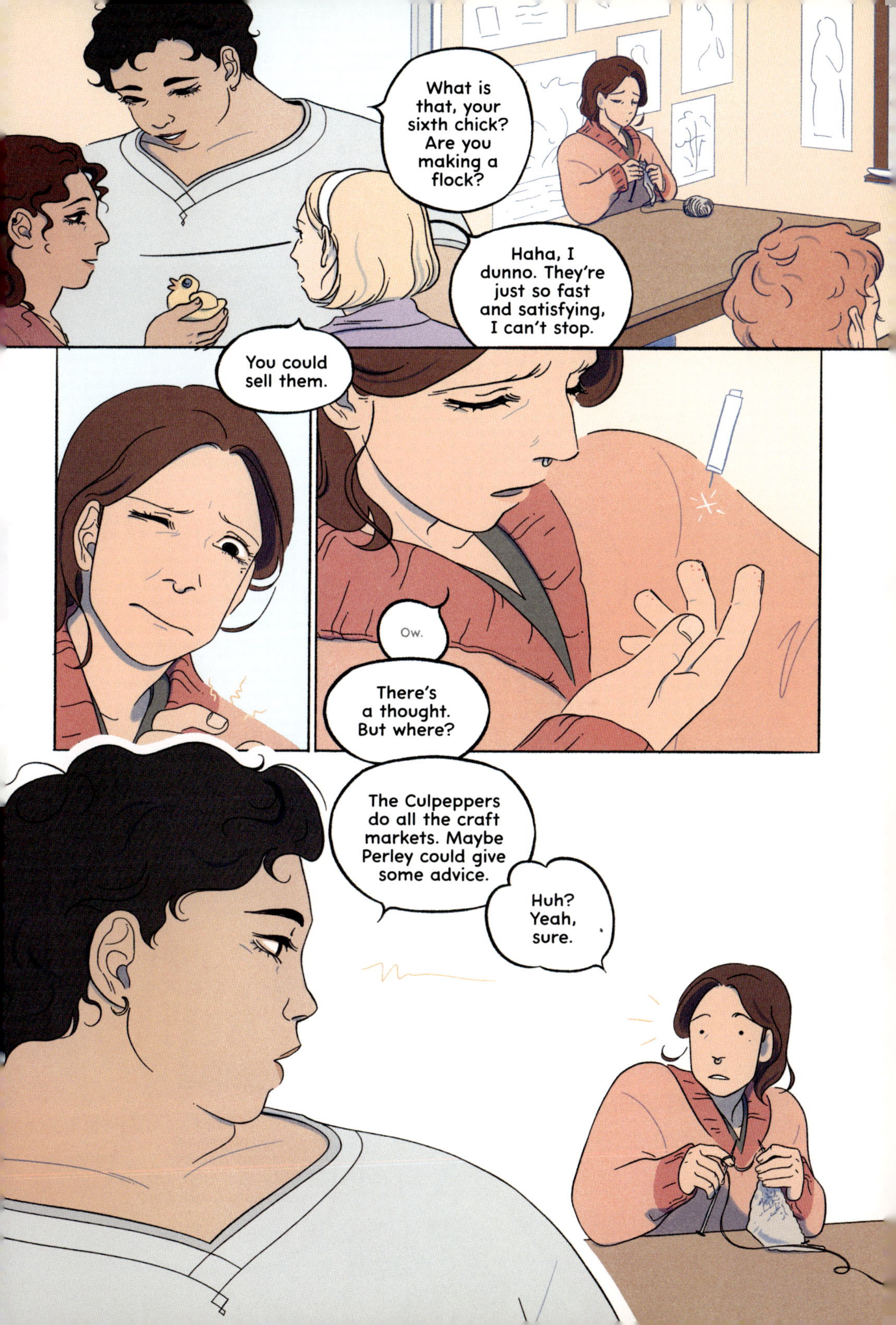
What is that, your sixth chick? Are you making a flock?
Haha, I dunno. They're just so fast and satisfying, I can't stop.
You could sell them.
Ow.
There's a thought. But where?
The Culpeppers do all the craft markets. Maybe Perley could give some advice.
Huh? Yeah, sure.

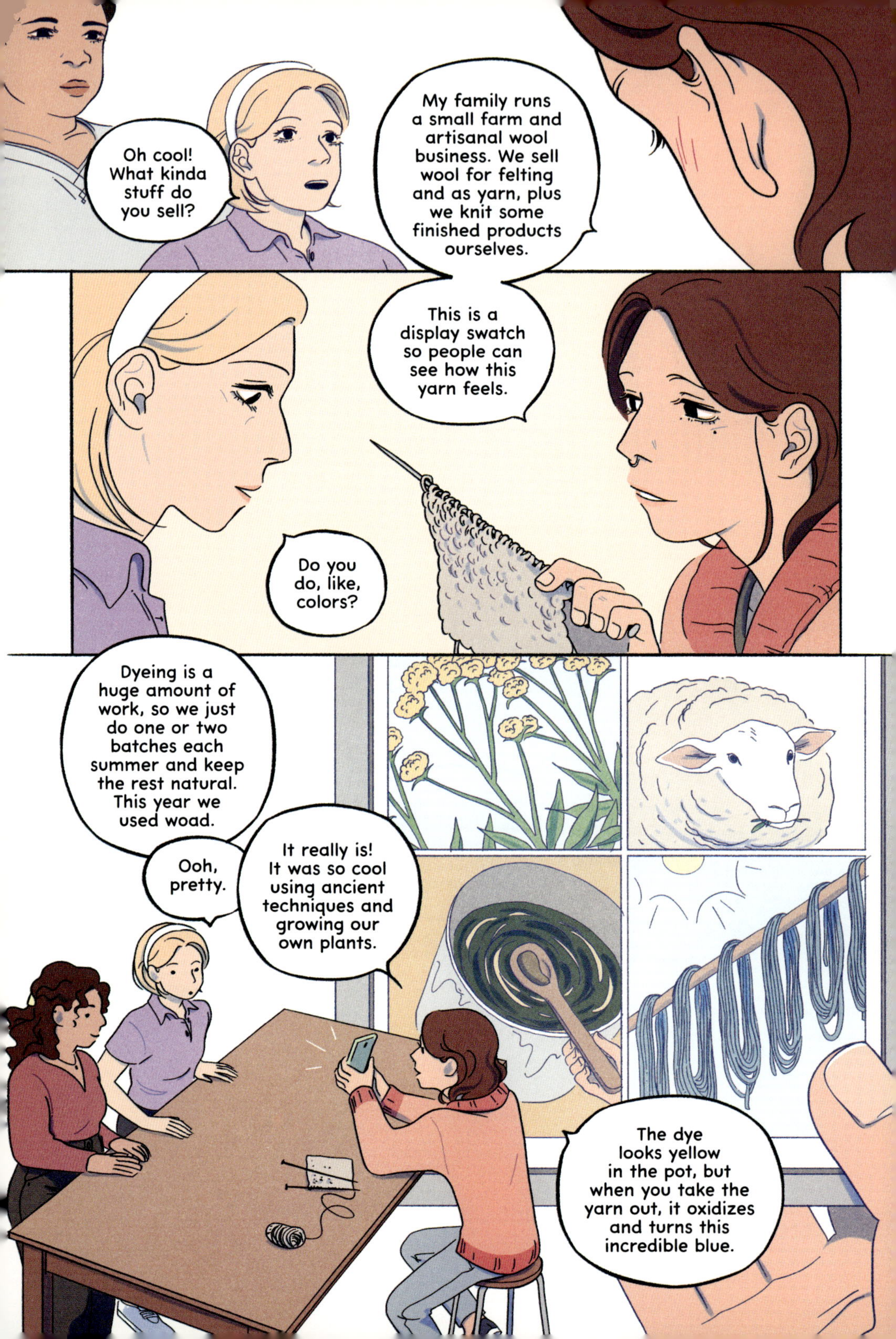
Oh cool! What kinda stuff do you sell?
My family runs a small farm and artisanal wool business. We sell wool for felting and as yarn, plus we knit some finished products ourselves.
This is a display swatch so people can see how this yarn feels.
Do you do, like, colors?
Dyeing is a huge amount of work, so we just do one or two batches each summer and keep the rest natural. This year we used woad.
Ooh, pretty.
It really is! It was so cool using ancient techniques and growing our own plants.
The dye looks yellow in the pot, but when you take the yarn out, it oxidizes and turns this incredible blue.

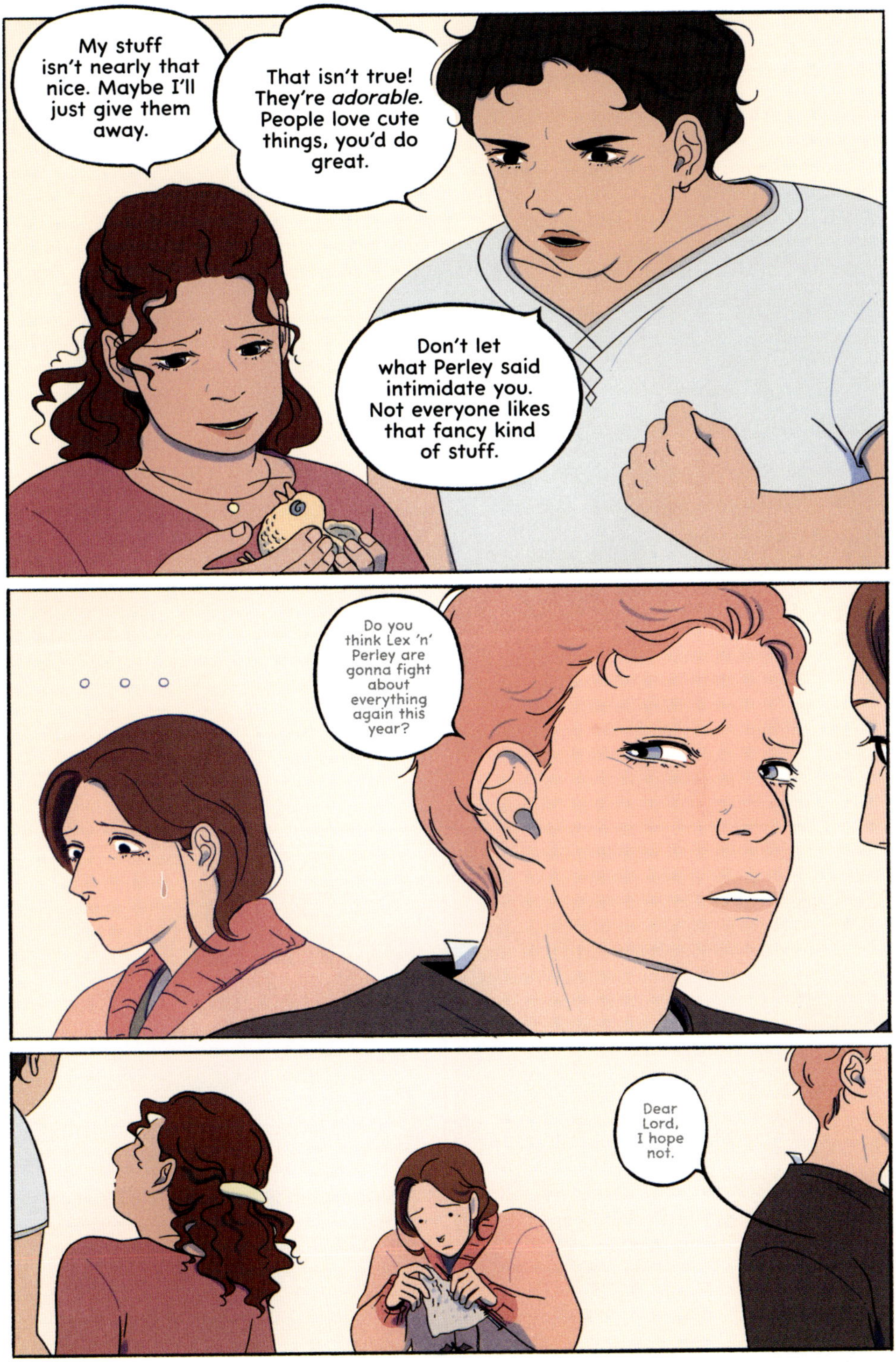
My stuff isn't nearly that nice. Maybe I'll just give them away.
That isn't true! They're *adorable.* People love cute things, you'd do great.
Don't let what Perley said intimidate you. Not everyone likes that fancy kind of stuff.
...
Do you think Lex 'n' Perley are gonna fight about everything again this year?
Dear Lord, I hope not.

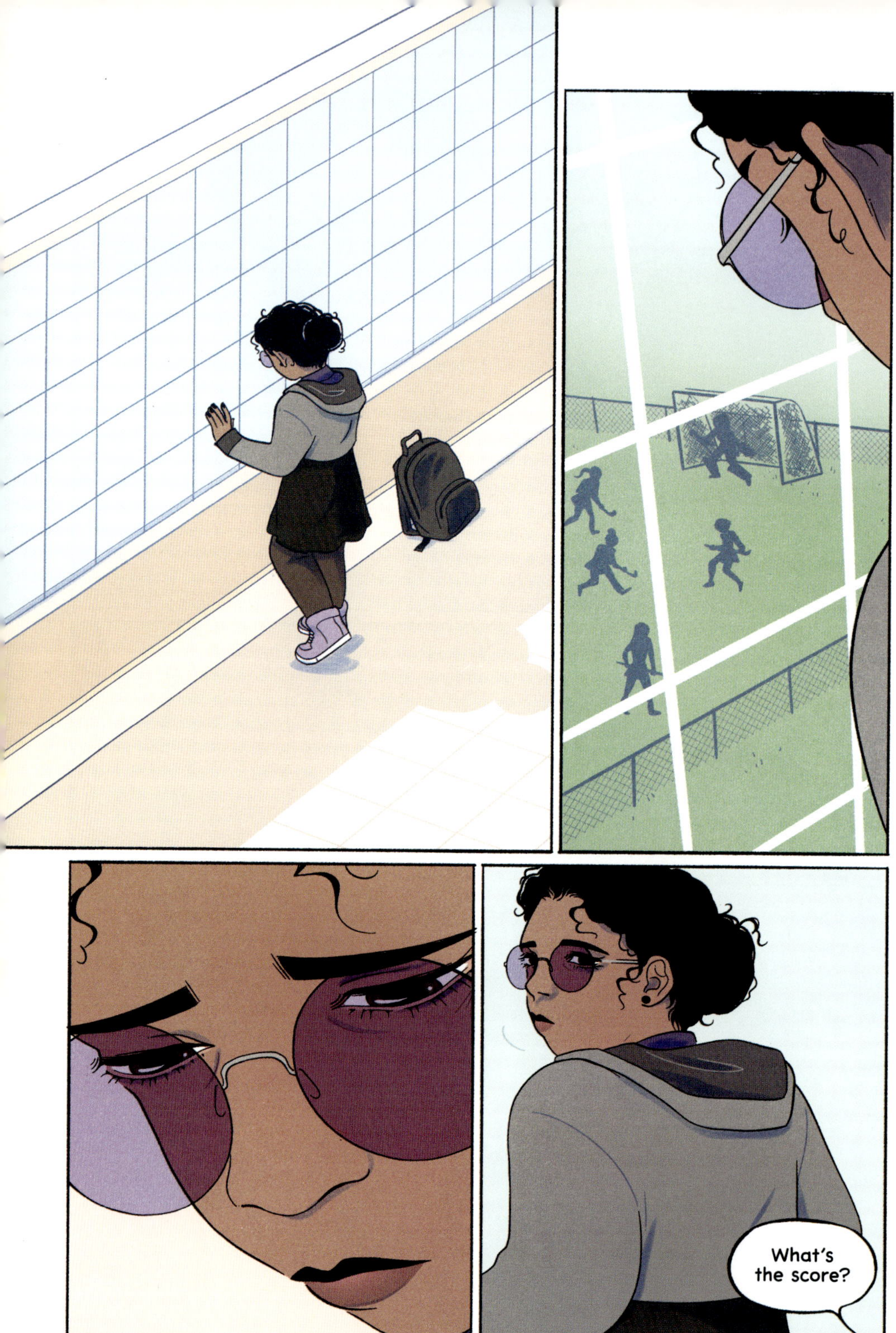
What's
the score?

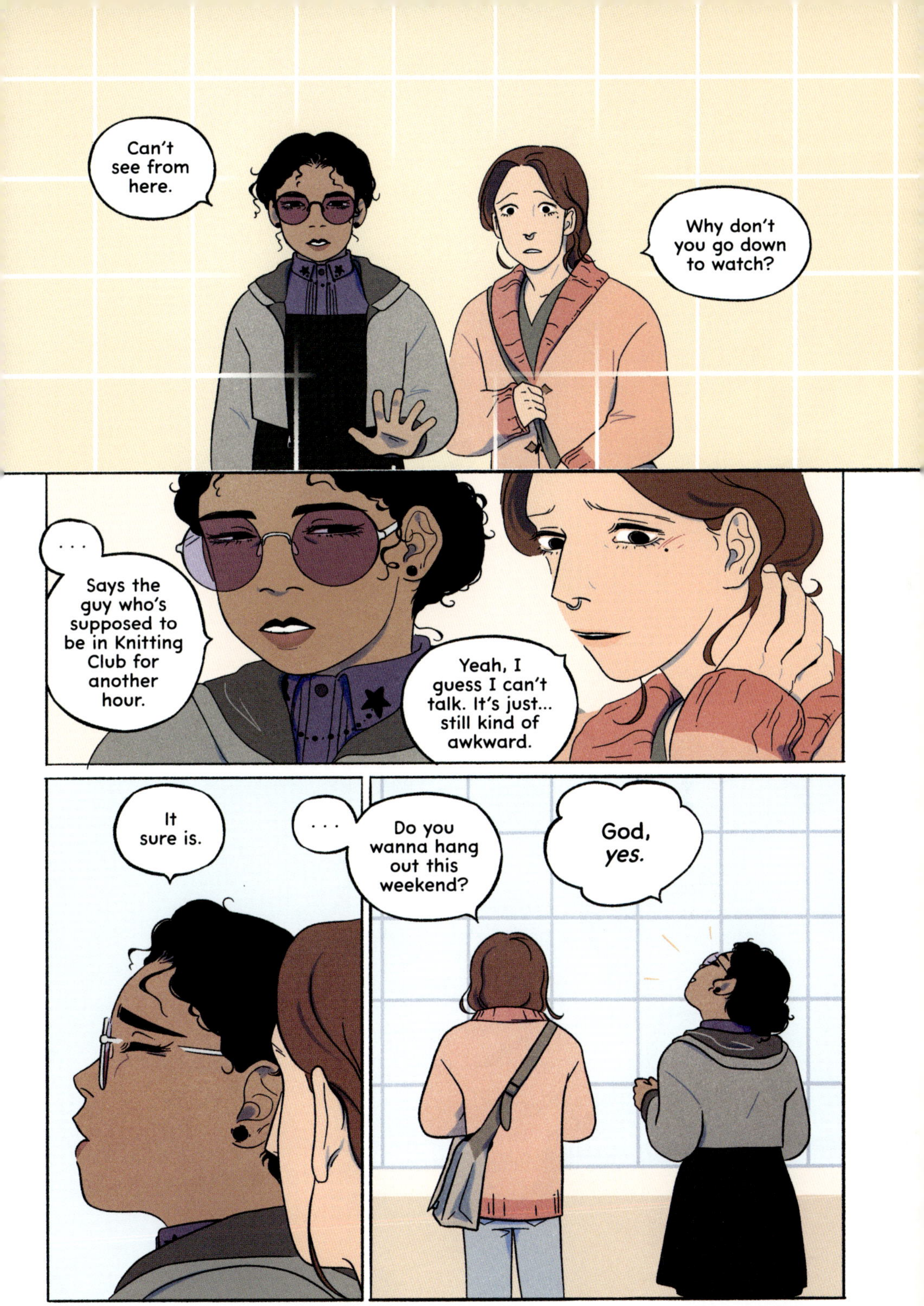
Can't see from here.
Why don't you go down to watch?
. . .
Says the guy who's supposed to be in Knitting Club for another hour.
Yeah, I guess I can't talk. It's just... still kind of awkward.
It sure is.
. . .
Do you wanna hang out this weekend?
God, *yes.*

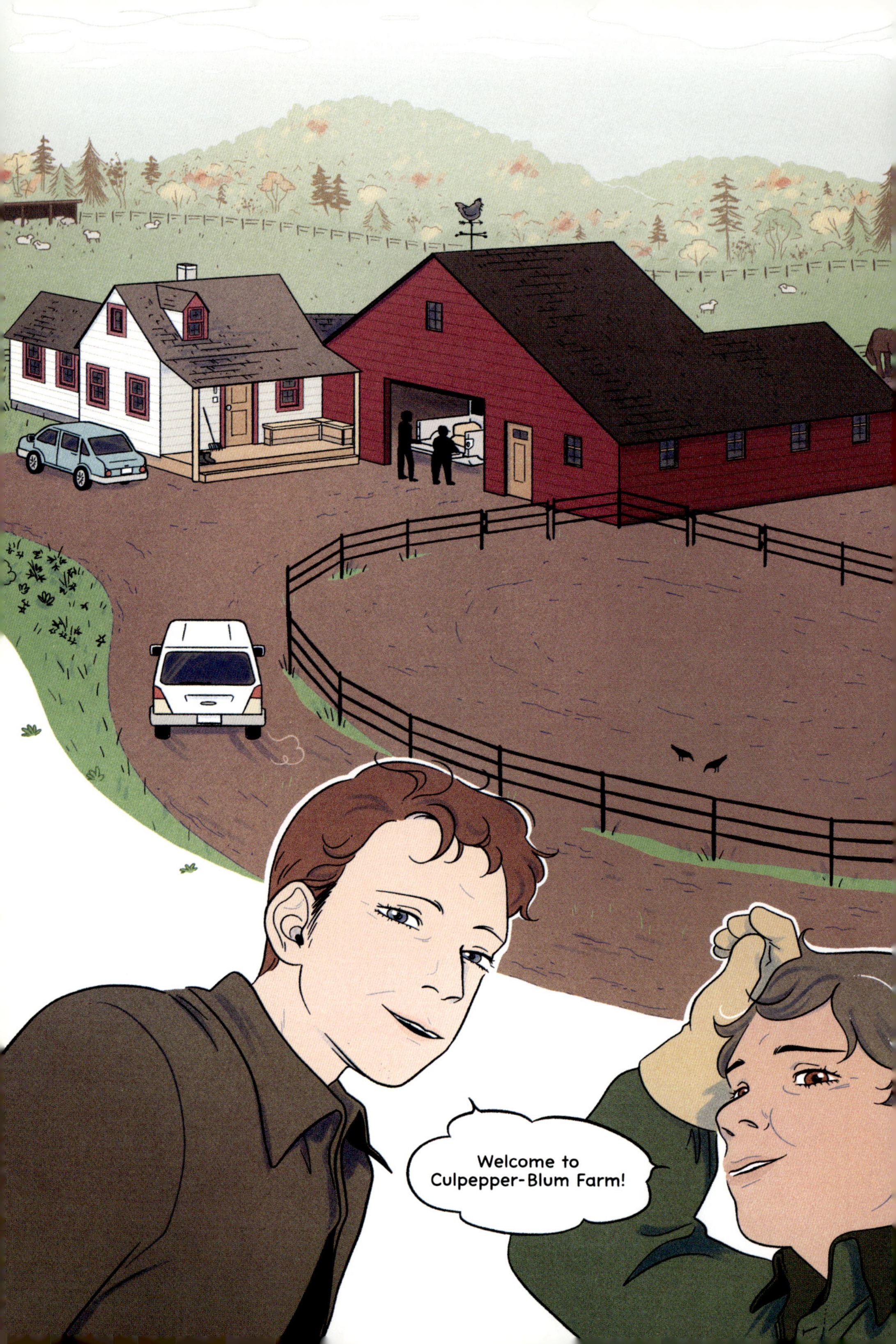
Welcome to
Culpepper-Blum Farm!

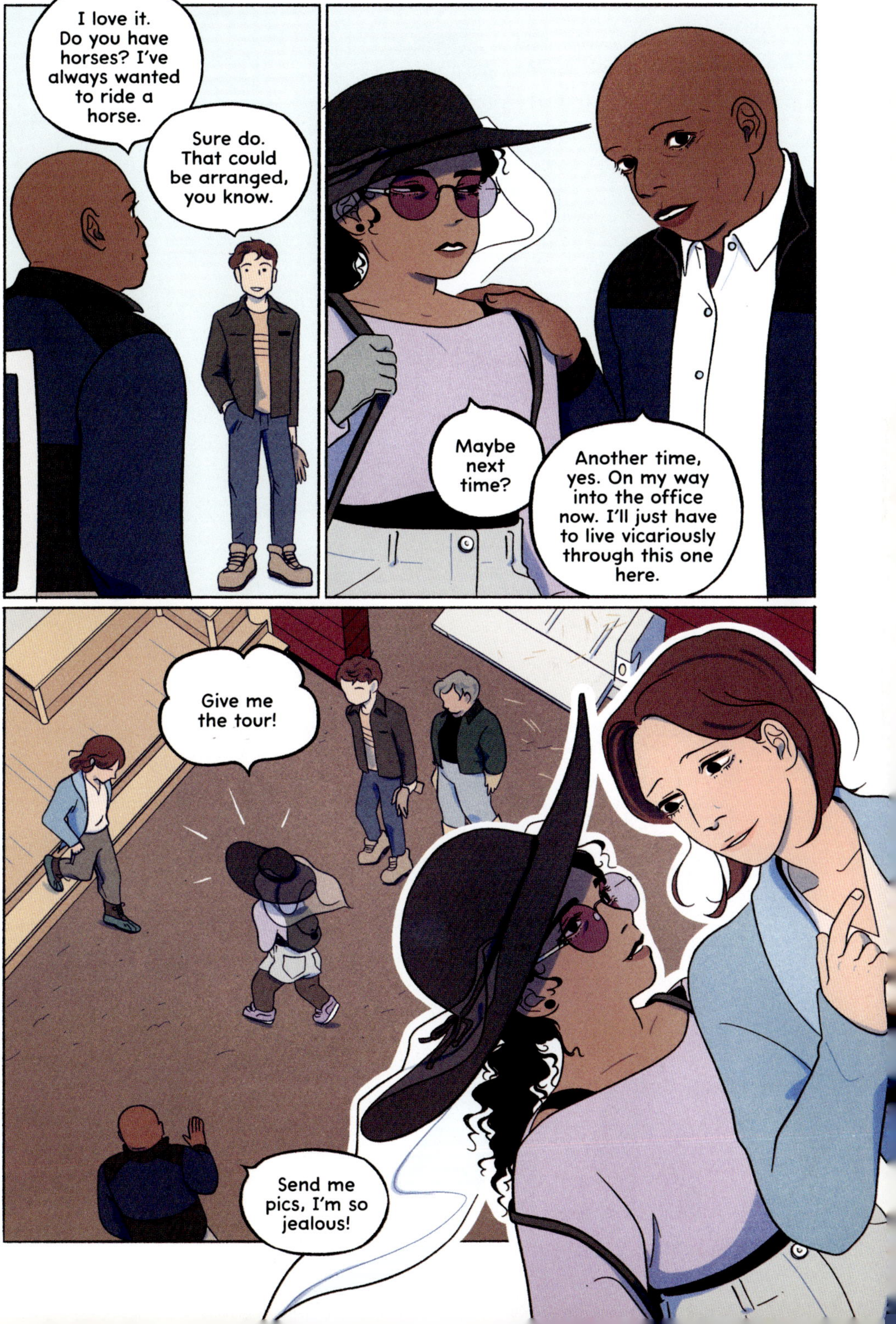
I love it. Do you have horses? I've always wanted to ride a horse.
Sure do. That could be arranged, you know.
Maybe next time?
Another time, yes. On my way into the office now. I'll just have to live vicariously through this one here.
Give me the tour!
Send me pics, I'm so jealous!

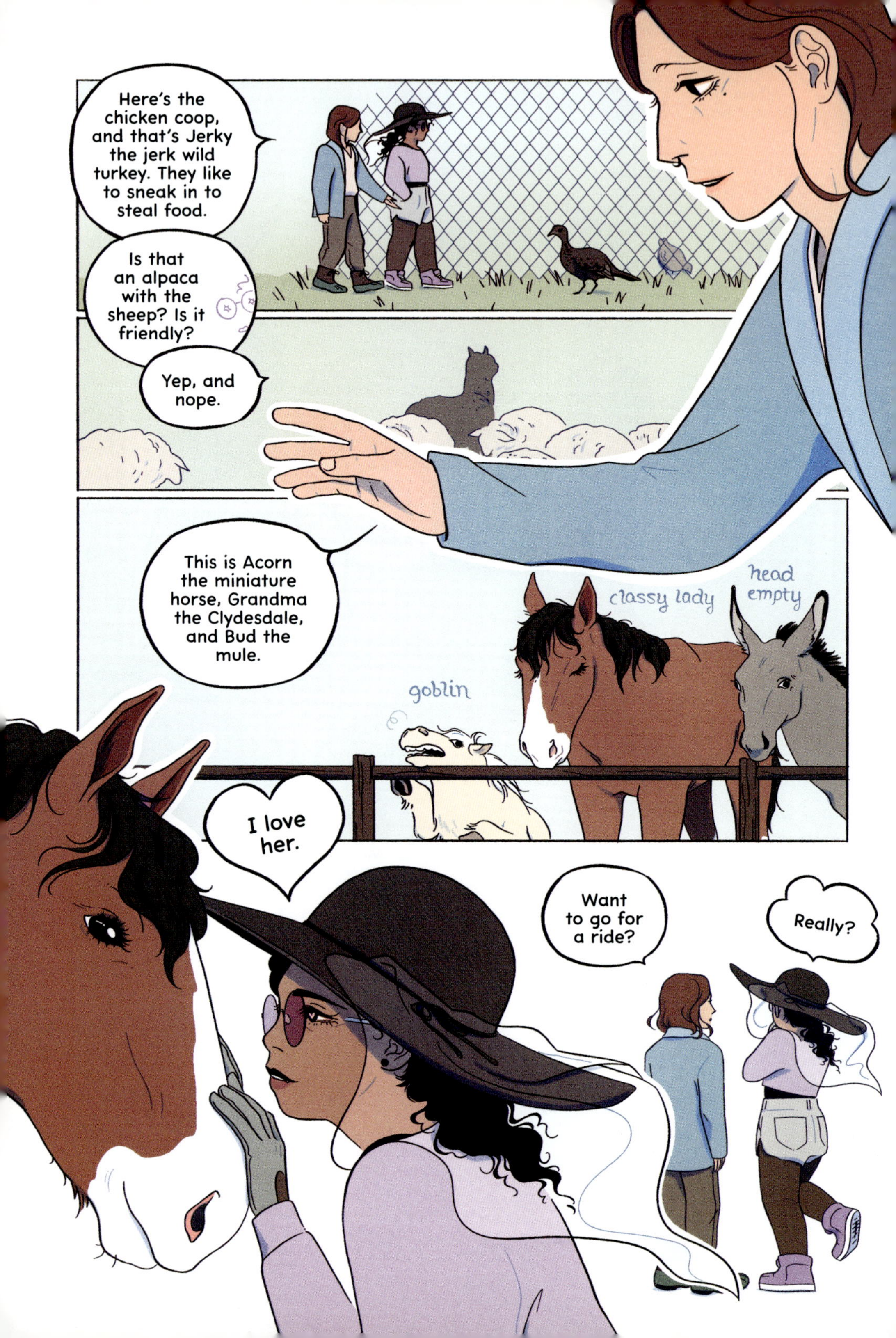
Here's the chicken coop, and that's Jerky the jerk wild turkey. They like to sneak in to steal food.
Is that an alpaca with the sheep? Is it friendly?
Yep, and nope.
This is Acorn the miniature horse, Grandma the Clydesdale, and Bud the mule.
classy lady
head empty
goblin
I love her.
Want to go for a ride?
Really?

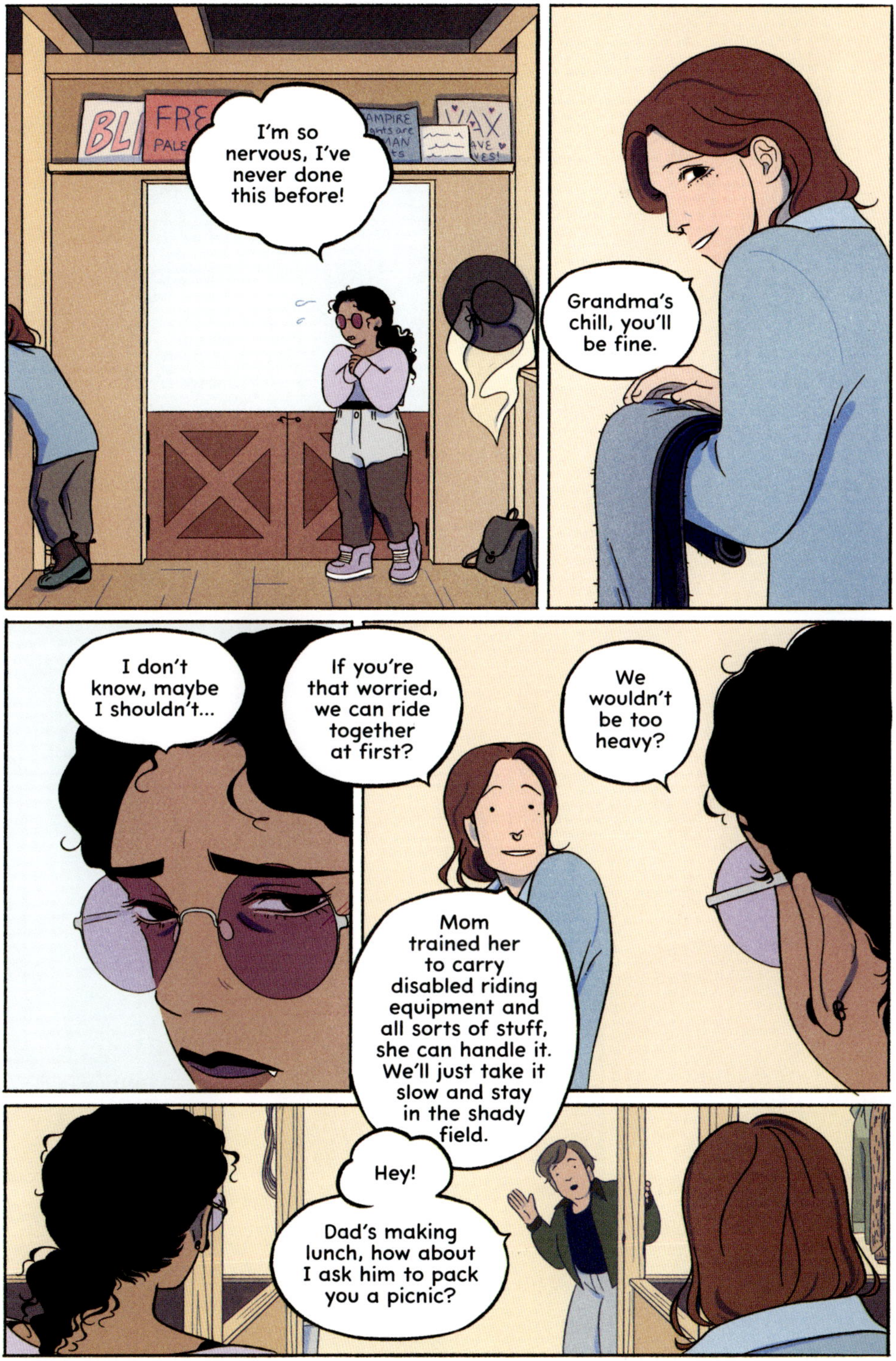
I'm so nervous, I've never done this before!
Grandma's chill, you'll be fine.
I don't know, maybe I shouldn't...
If you're that worried, we can ride together at first?
We wouldn't be too heavy?
Mom trained her to carry disabled riding equipment and all sorts of stuff, she can handle it. We'll just take it slow and stay in the shady field.
Hey!
Dad's making lunch, how about I ask him to pack you a picnic?

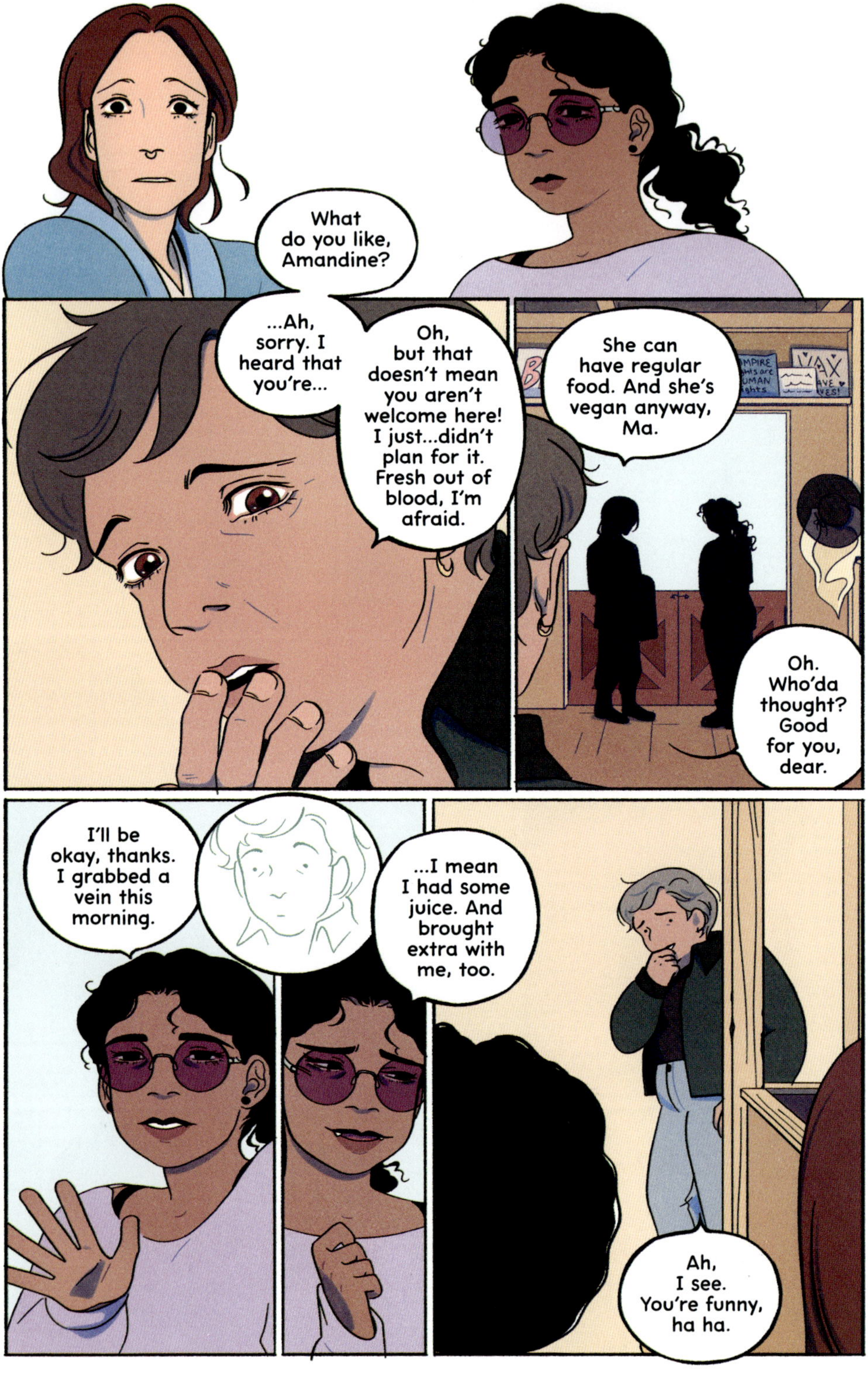
What do you like, Amandine?
...Ah, sorry. I heard that you're...
Oh, but that doesn't mean you aren't welcome here! I just...didn't plan for it. Fresh out of blood, I'm afraid.
She can have regular food. And she's vegan anyway, Ma.
Oh. Who'da thought? Good for you, dear.
I'll be okay, thanks. I grabbed a vein this morning.
...I mean I had some juice. And brought extra with me, too.
Ah, I see. You're funny, ha ha.

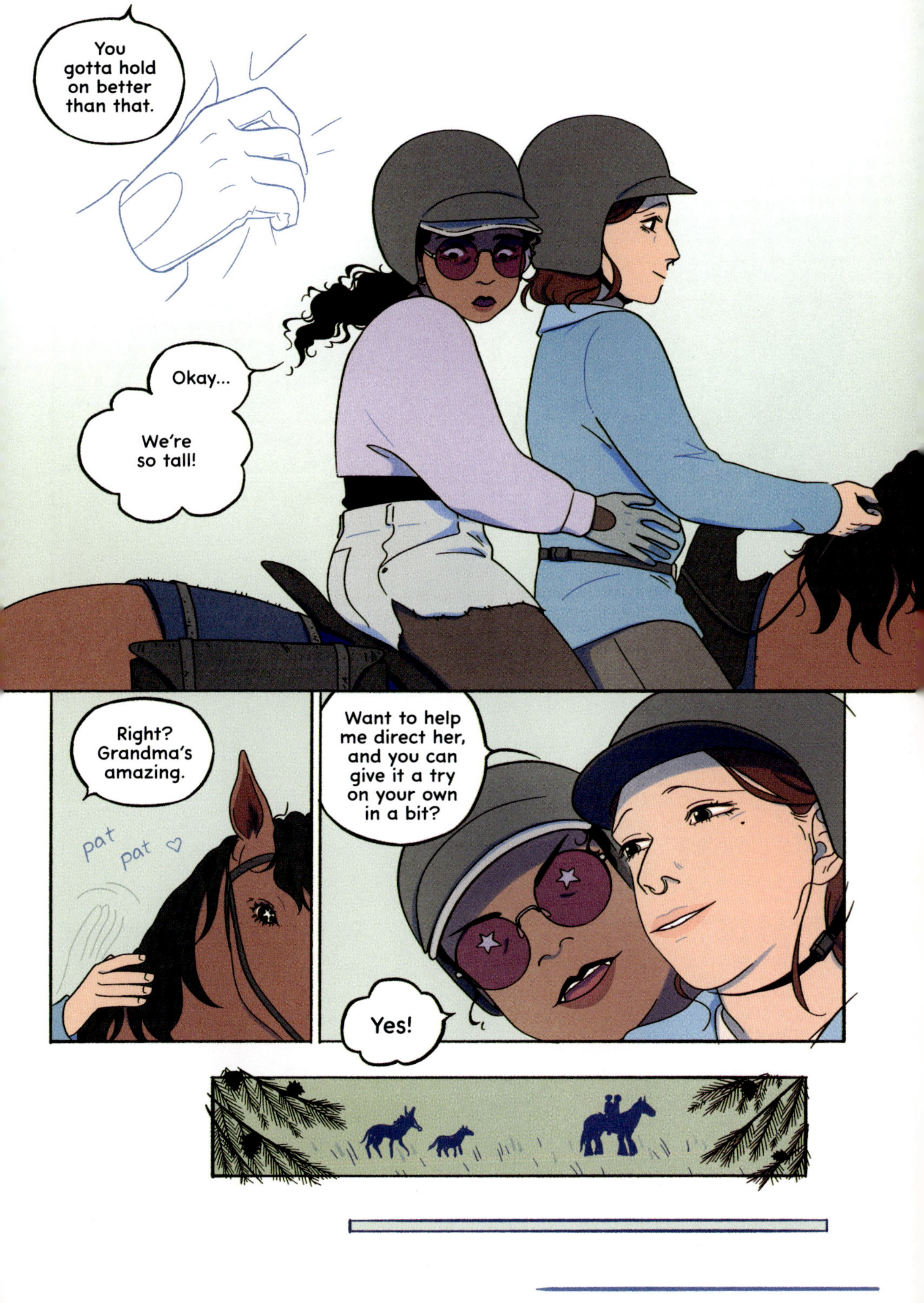
You gotta hold on better than that.
Okay...
We're so tall!
Right? Grandma's amazing.
pat pat ♡
Want to help me direct her, and you can give it a try on your own in a bit?
Yes!

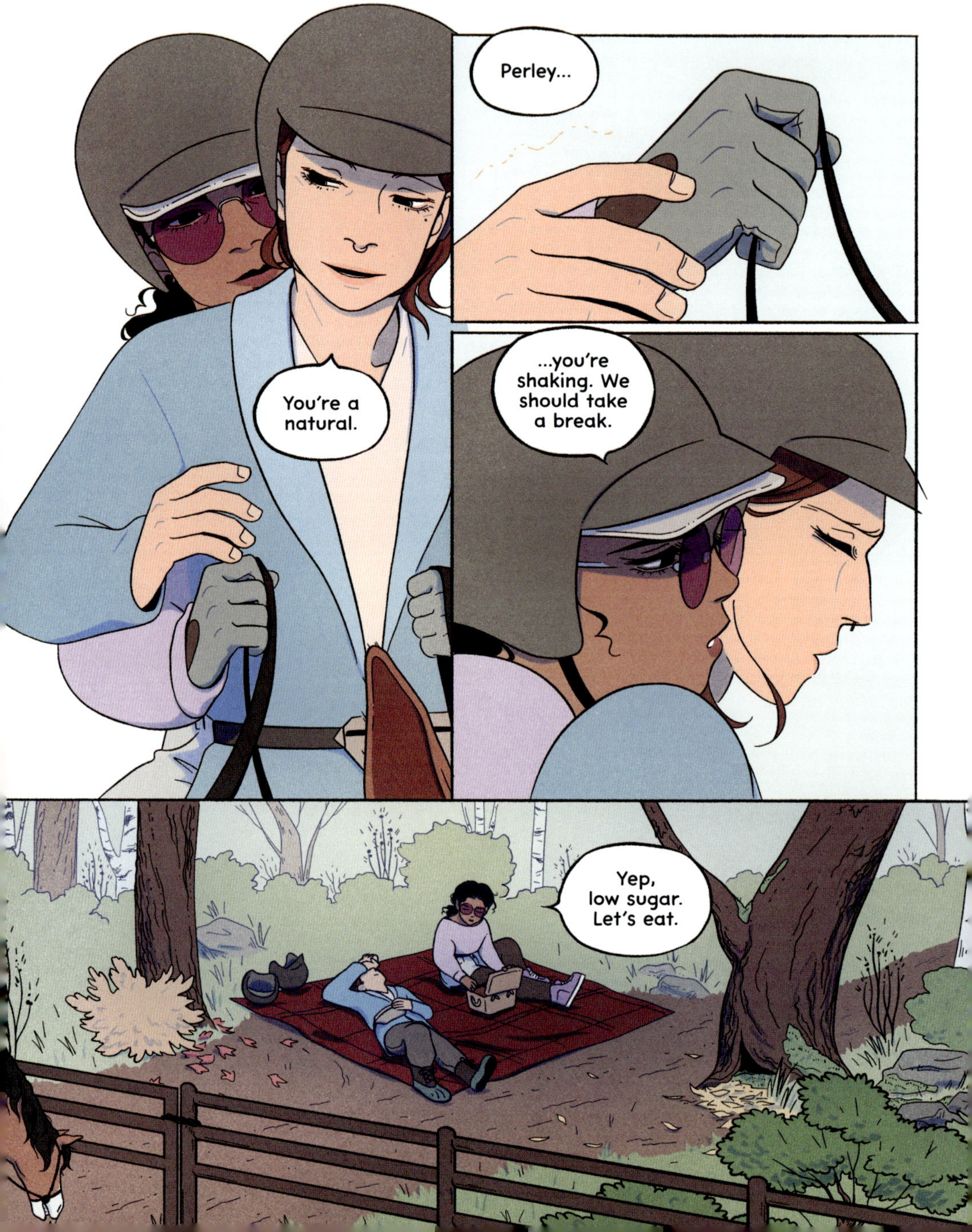
Perley...
You're a natural.
...you're shaking. We should take a break.
Yep, low sugar. Let's eat.

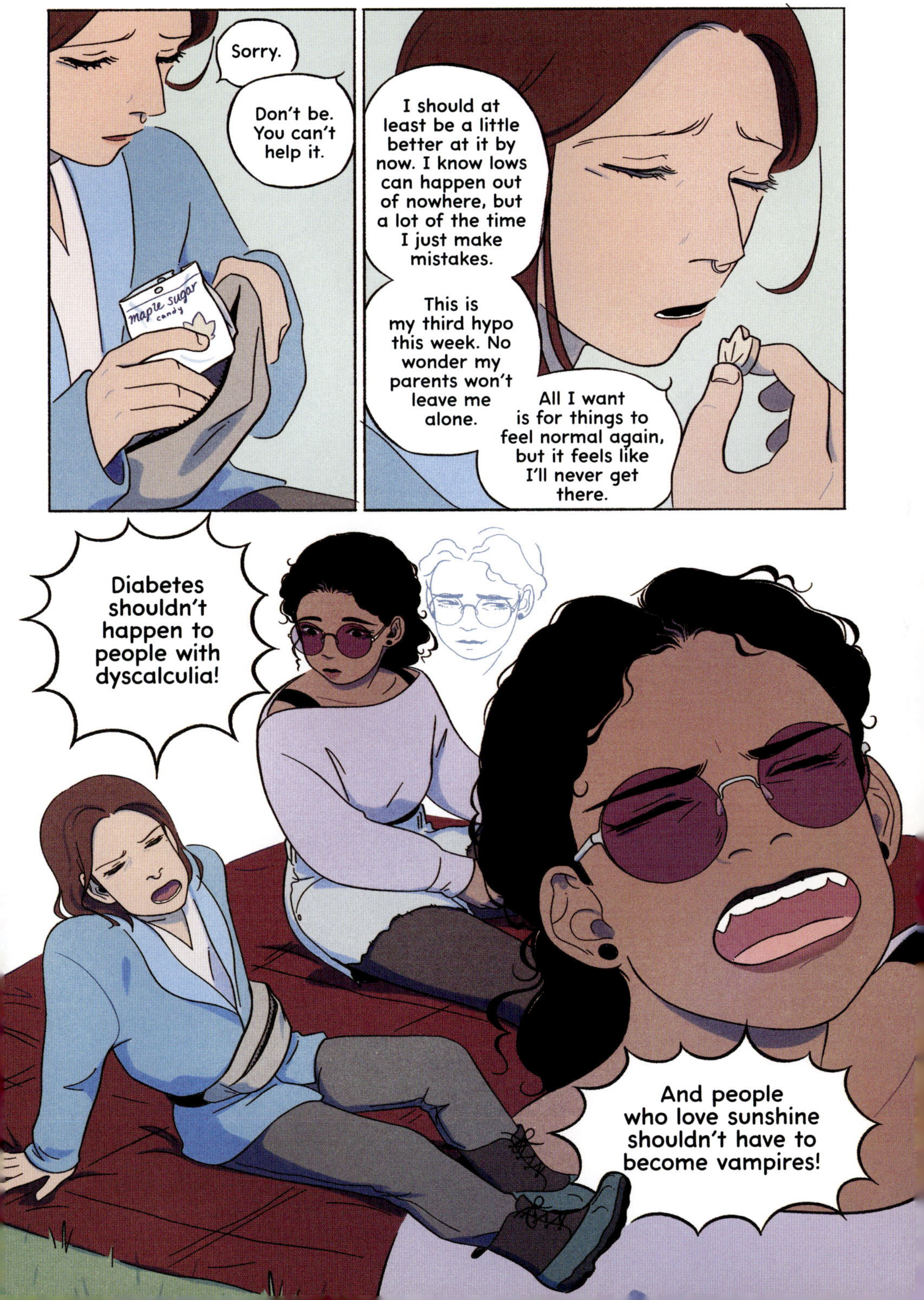
Sorry.
Don't be. You can't help it.
maple sugar candy
I should at least be a little better at it by now. I know lows can happen out of nowhere, but a lot of the time I just make mistakes.
This is my third hypo this week. No wonder my parents won't leave me alone.
All I want is for things to feel normal again, but it feels like I'll never get there.
Diabetes shouldn't happen to people with dyscalculia!
And people who love sunshine shouldn't have to become vampires!

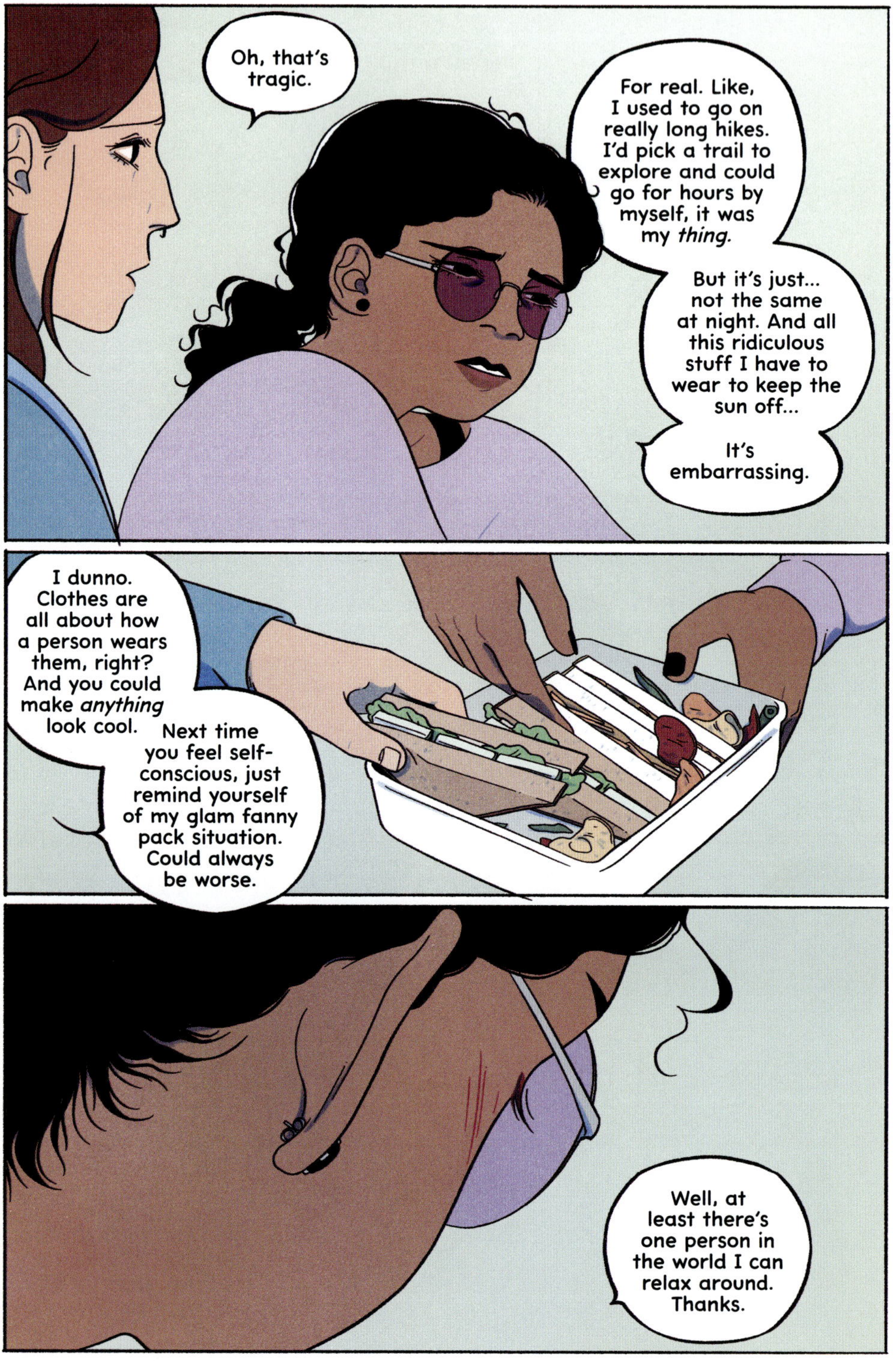
Oh, that's tragic.
For real. Like, I used to go on really long hikes. I'd pick a trail to explore and could go for hours by myself, it was my *thing.*
But it's just... not the same at night. And all this ridiculous stuff I have to wear to keep the sun off...
It's embarrassing.
I dunno. Clothes are all about how a person wears them, right? And you could make *anything* look cool.
Next time you feel self-conscious, just remind yourself of my glam fanny pack situation. Could always be worse.
Well, at least there's one person in the world I can relax around. Thanks.

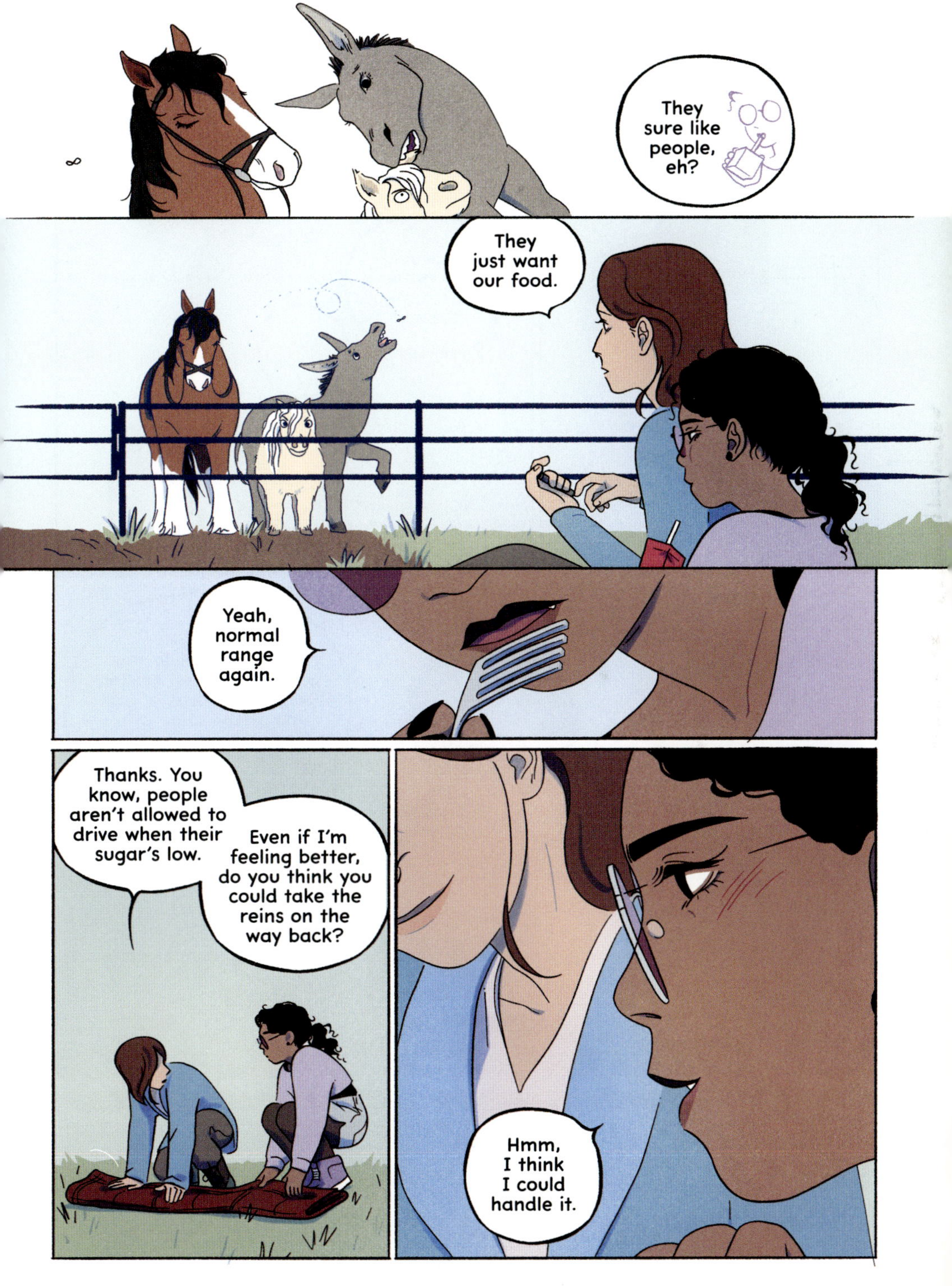
They sure like people, eh?
They just want our food.
Yeah, normal range again.
Thanks. You know, people aren't allowed to drive when their sugar's low.
Even if I'm feeling better, do you think you could take the reins on the way back?
Hmm, I think I could handle it.

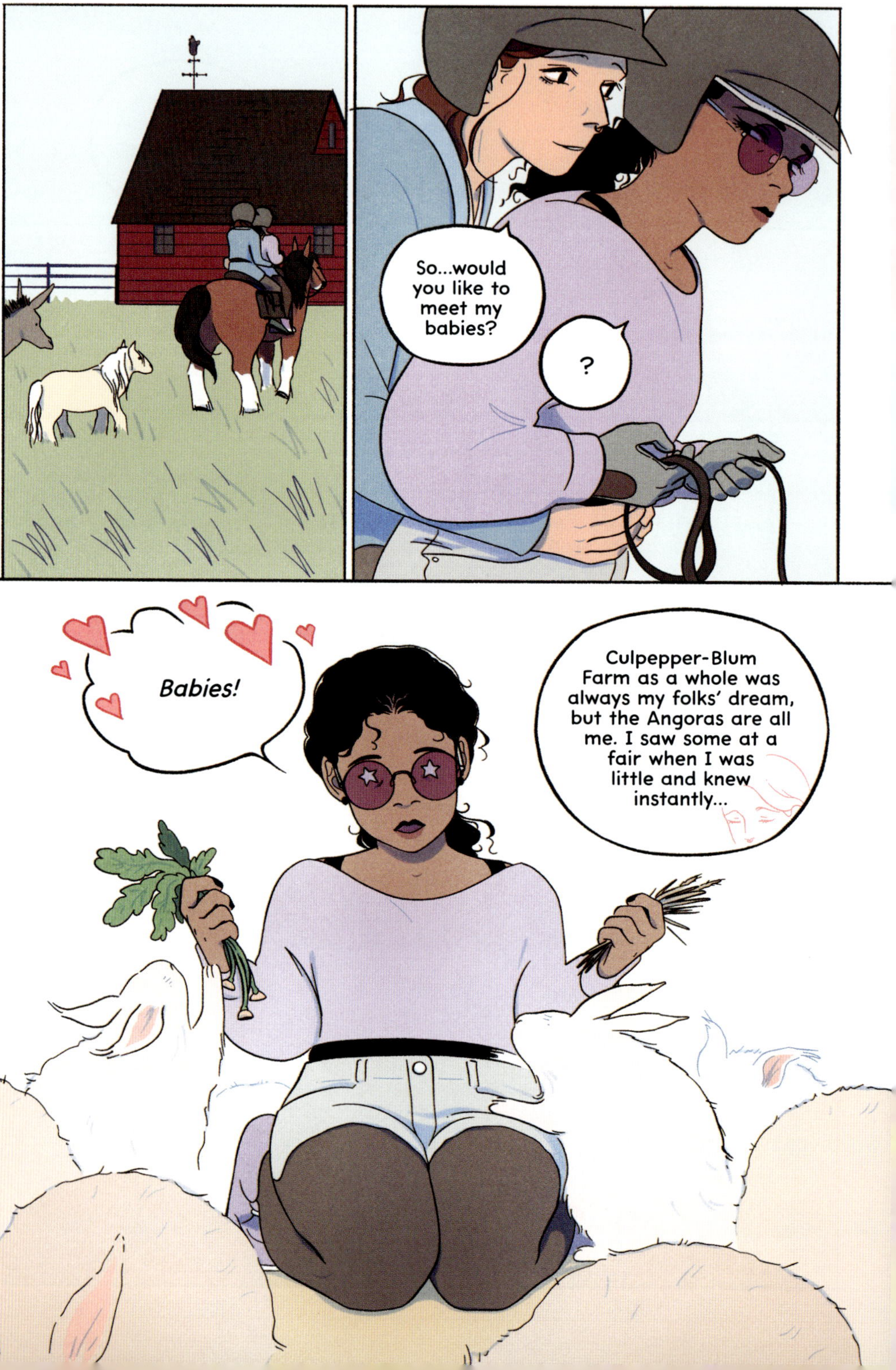
So...would you like to meet my babies?
?
Babies!
Culpepper-Blum Farm as a whole was always my folks' dream, but the Angoras are all me. I saw some at a fair when I was little and knew instantly...

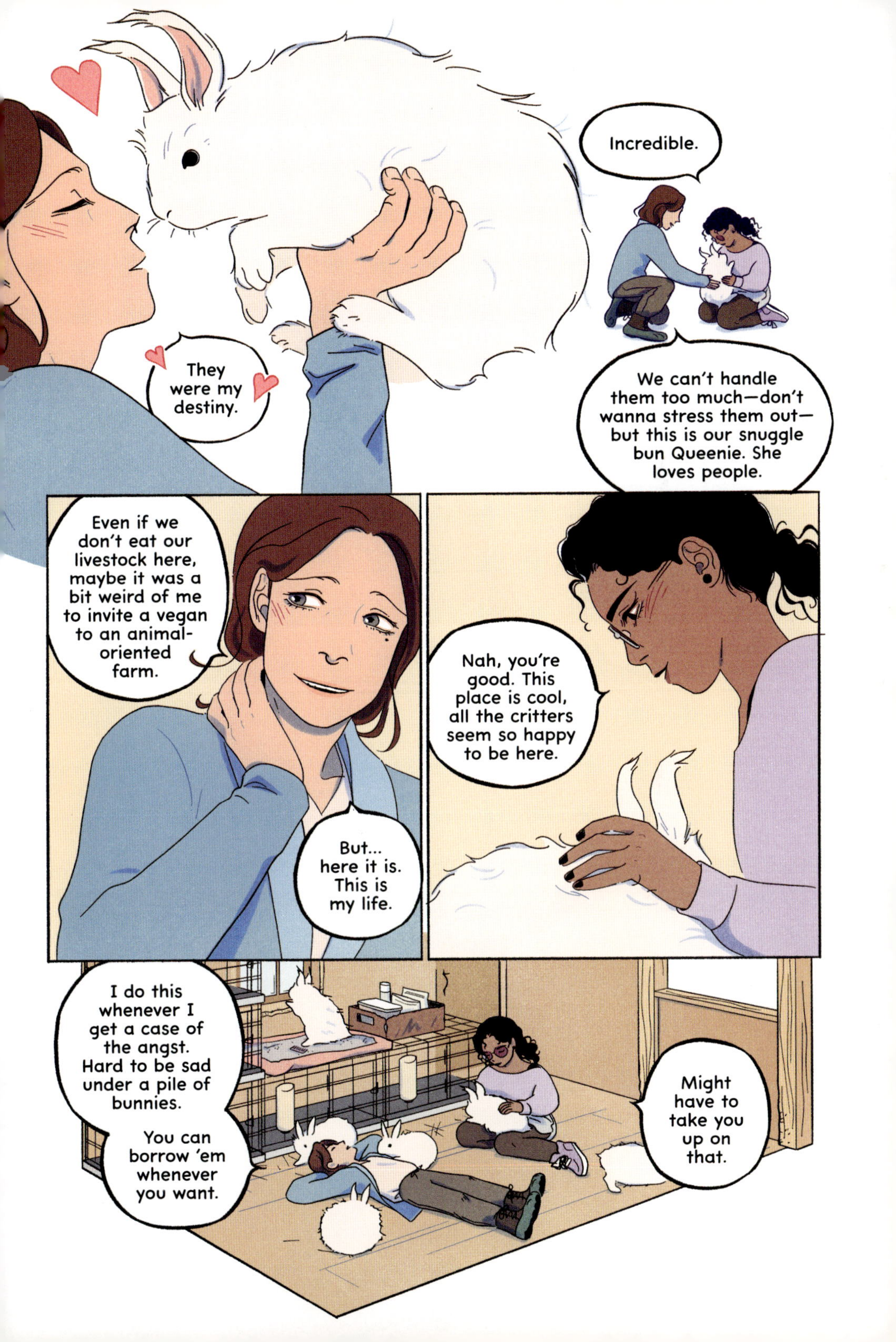
They were my destiny.
Incredible.
We can't handle them too much—don't wanna stress them out—but this is our snuggle bun Queenie. She loves people.
Even if we don't eat our livestock here, maybe it was a bit weird of me to invite a vegan to an animal-oriented farm.
But... here it is. This is my life.
Nah, you're good. This place is cool, all the critters seem so happy to be here.
I do this whenever I get a case of the angst. Hard to be sad under a pile of bunnies.
You can borrow 'em whenever you want.
Might have to take you up on that.

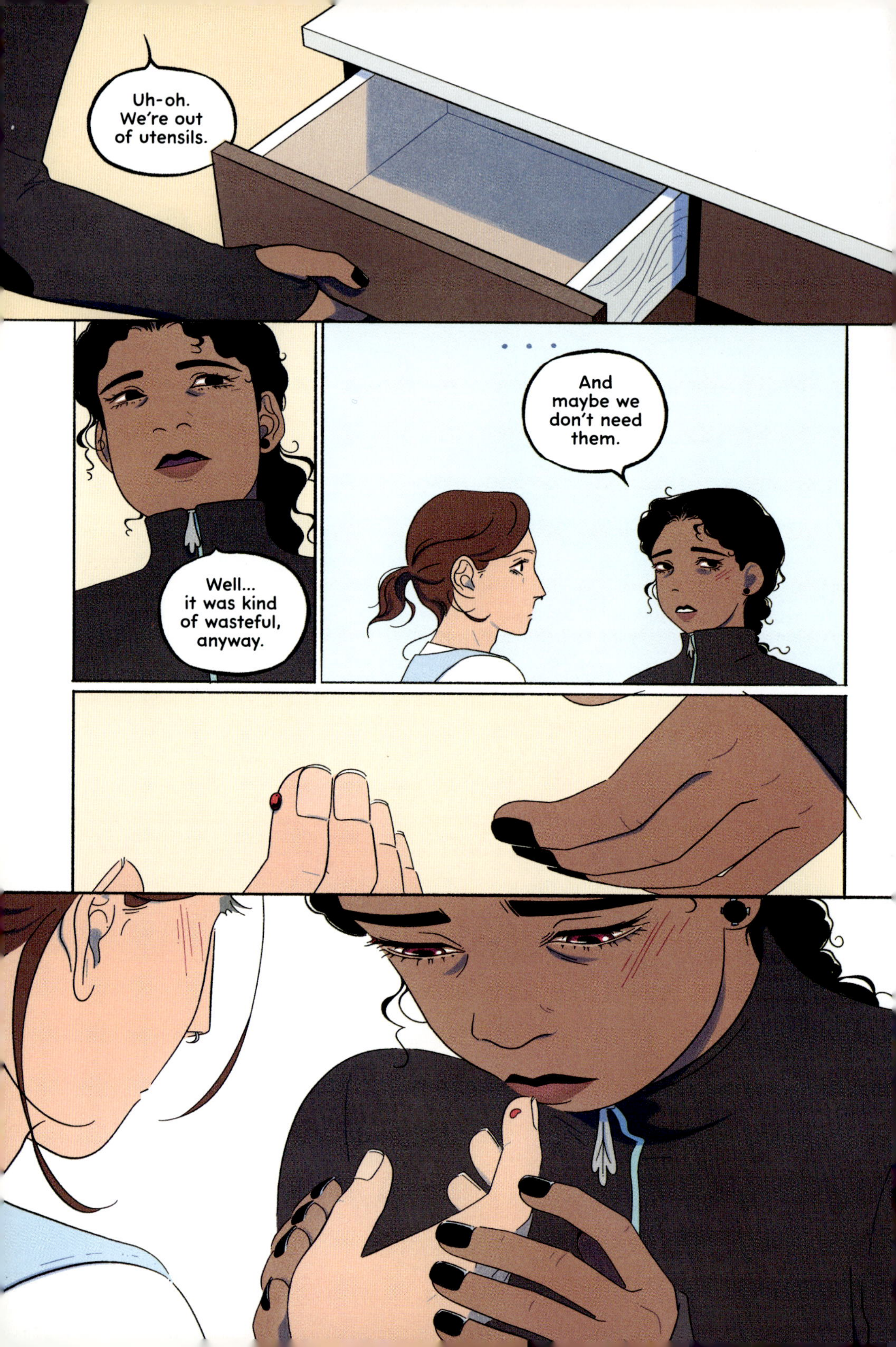
Uh-oh.
We're out of utensils.
Well... it was kind of wasteful, anyway.
...
And maybe we don't need them.

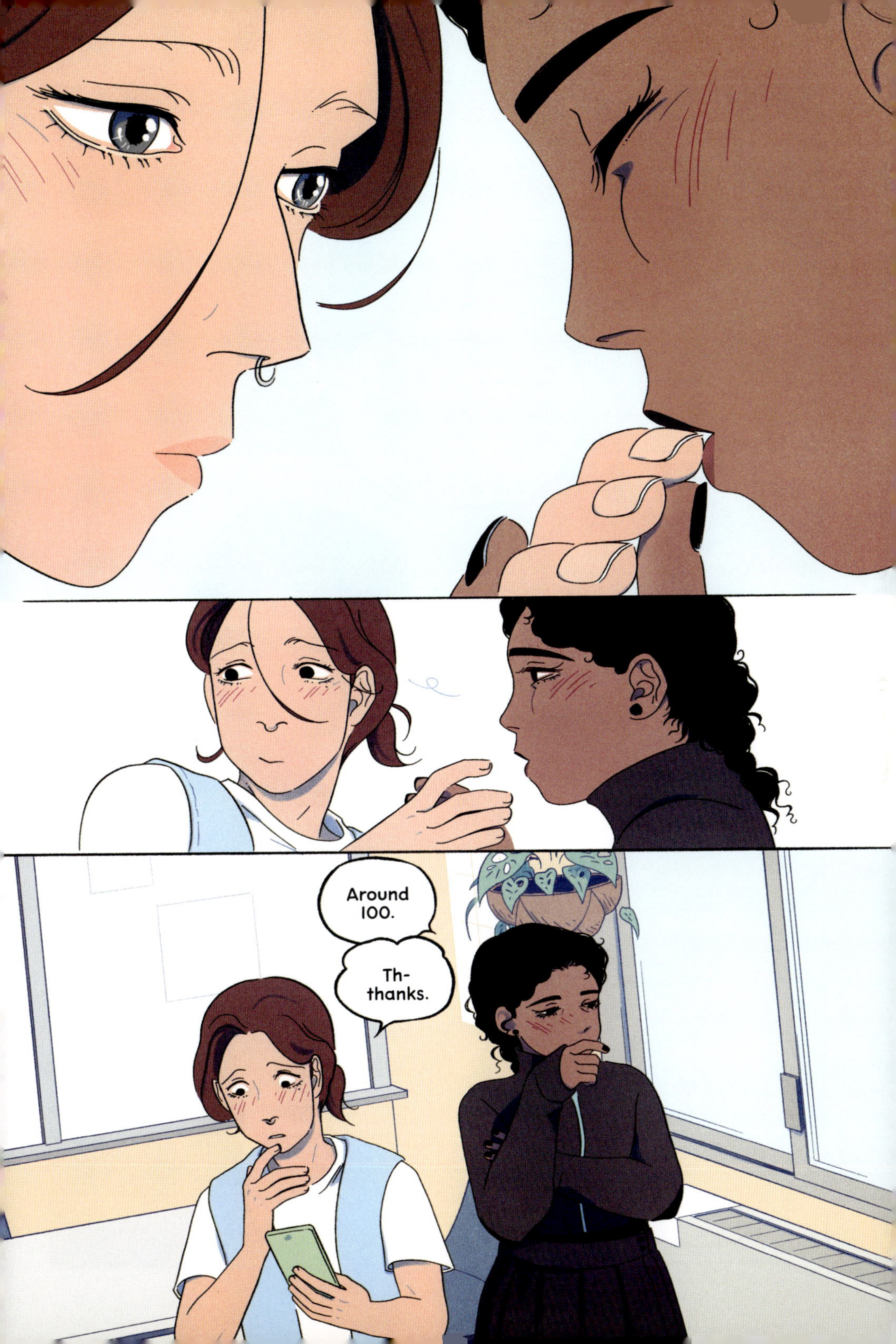
Around 100.
Th- thanks.

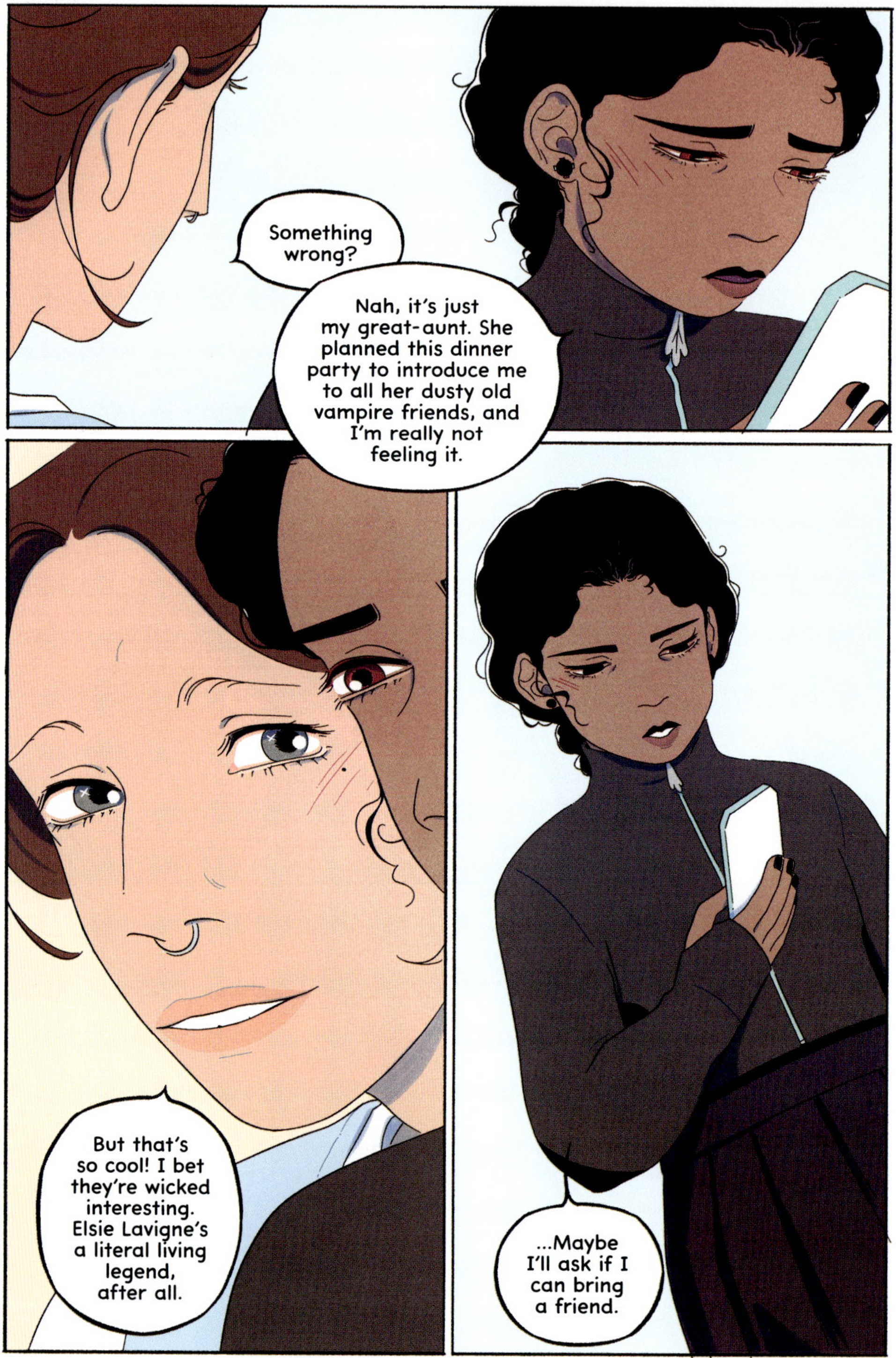
Something wrong?
Nah, it's just my great-aunt. She planned this dinner party to introduce me to all her dusty old vampire friends, and I'm really not feeling it.
But that's so cool! I bet they're wicked interesting. Elsie Lavigne's a literal living legend, after all.
...Maybe I'll ask if I can bring a friend.

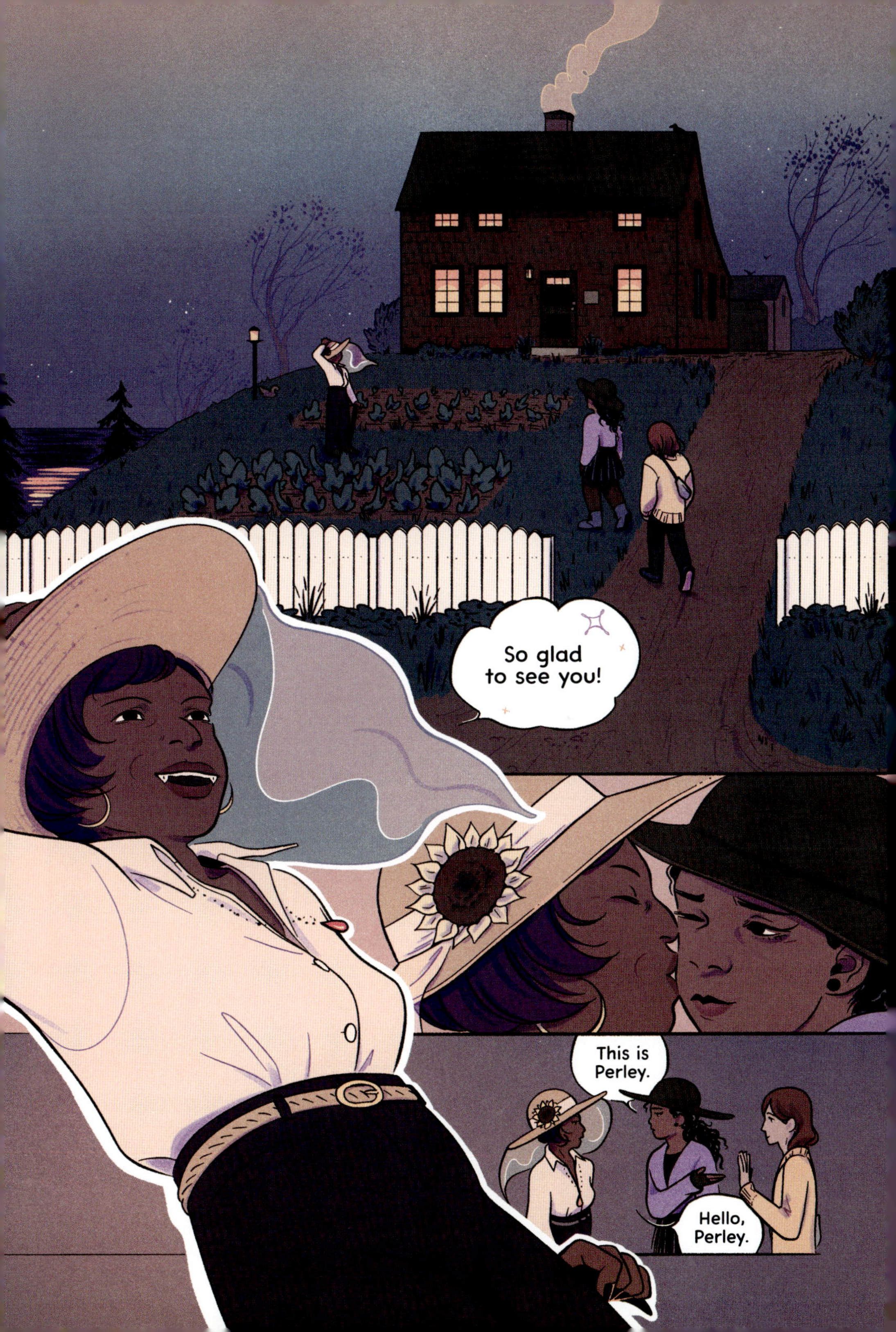
So glad to see you!
This is Perley.
Hello, Perley.

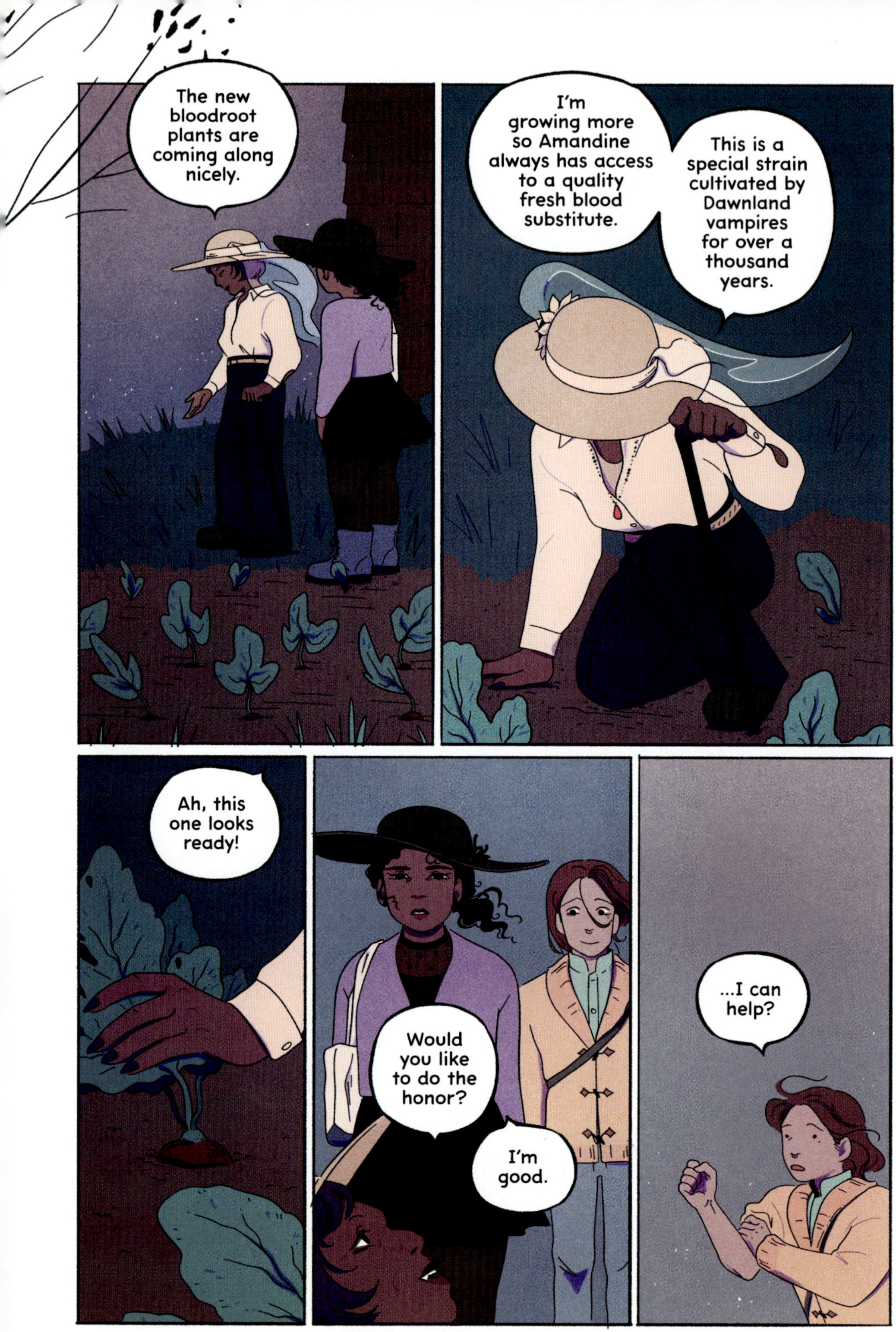
The new bloodroot plants are coming along nicely.
I'm growing more so Amandine always has access to a quality fresh blood substitute.
This is a special strain cultivated by Dawnland vampires for over a thousand years.
Ah, this one looks ready!
Would you like to do the honor?
I'm good.
...I can help?

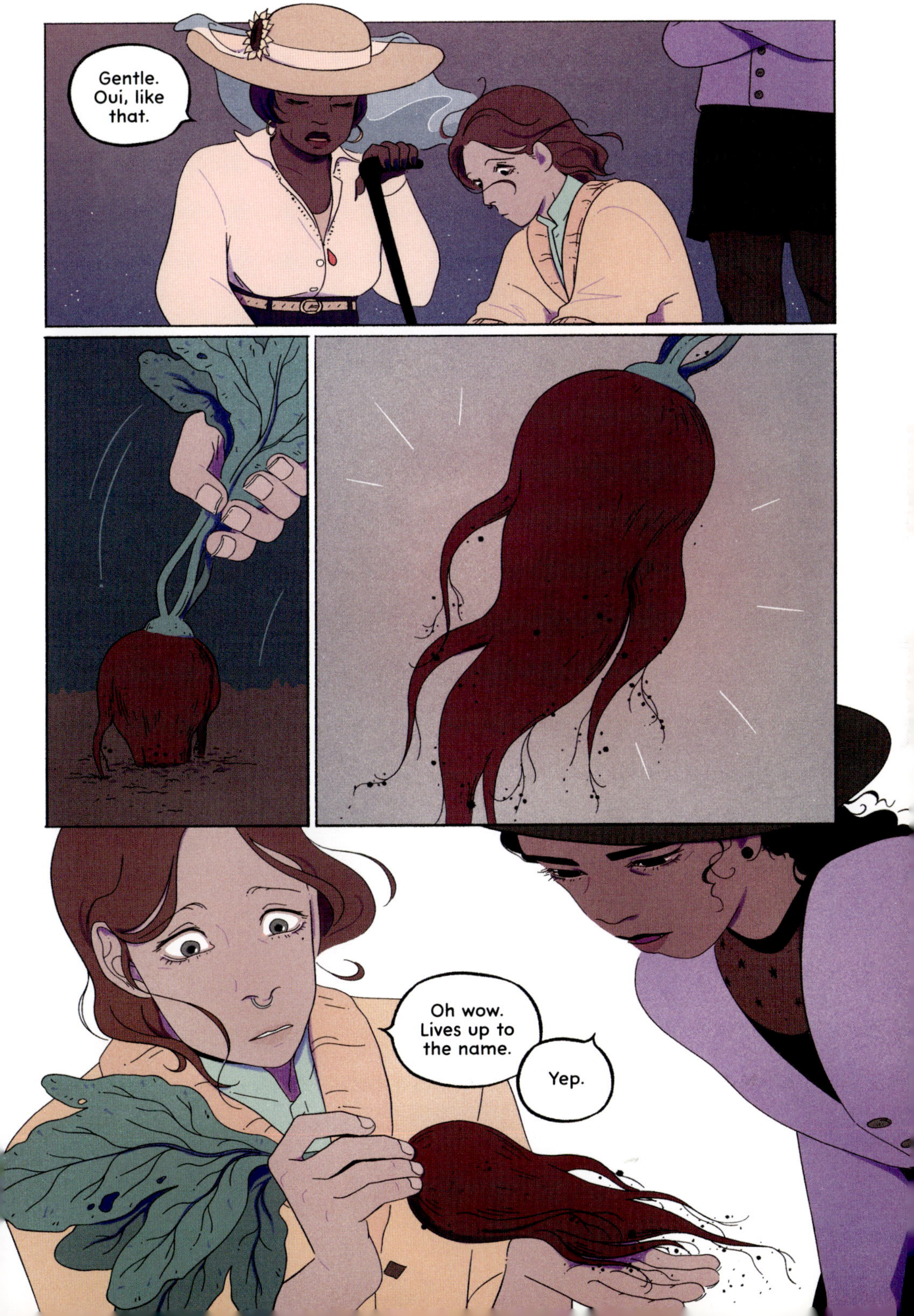
Gentle. Oui, like that.
Oh wow. Lives up to the name.
Yep.

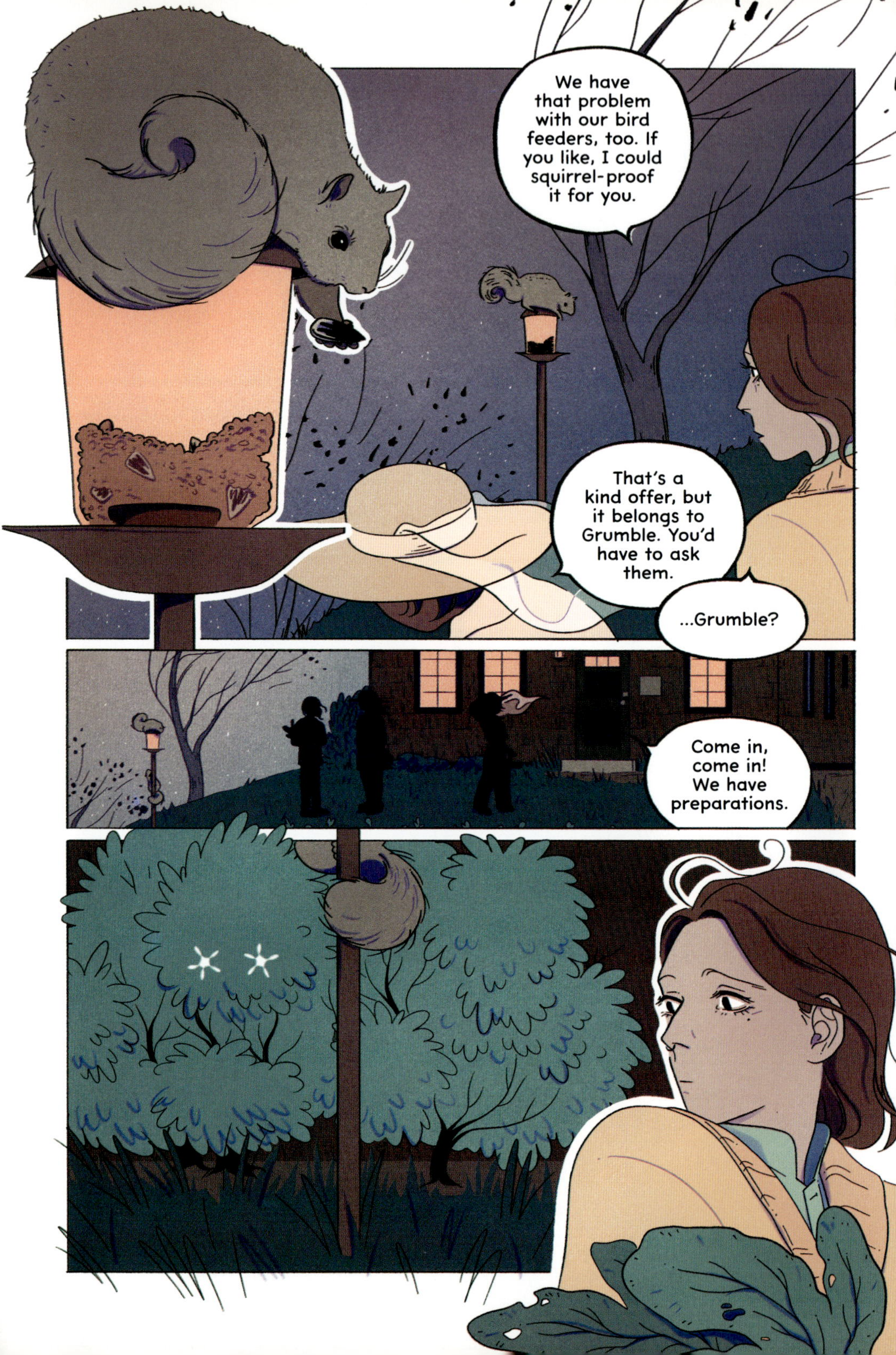
We have that problem with our bird feeders, too. If you like, I could squirrel-proof it for you.
That's a kind offer, but it belongs to Grumble. You'd have to ask them.
...Grumble?
Come in, come in! We have preparations.

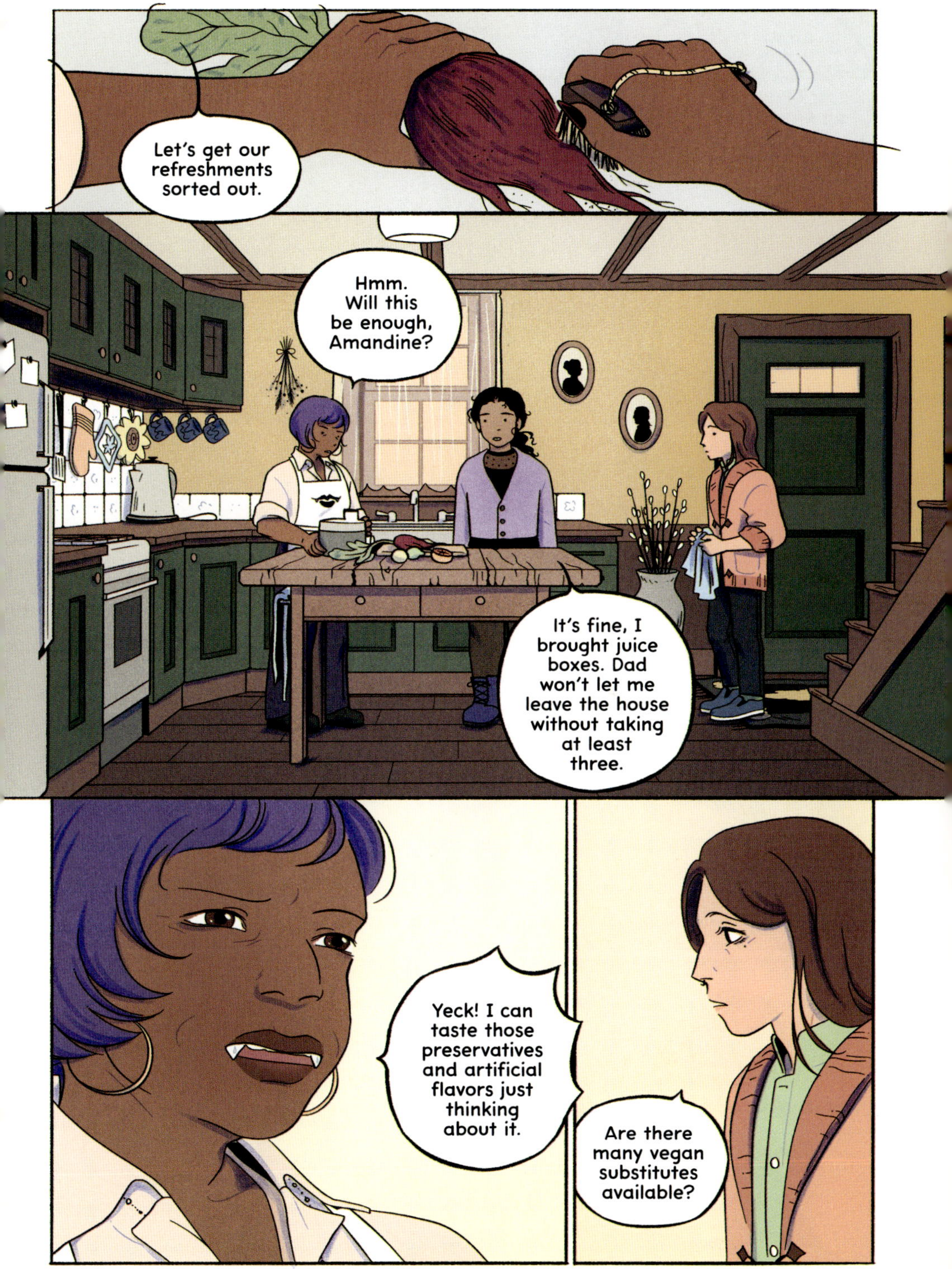

Let's get our refreshments sorted out.
Hmm. Will this be enough, Amandine?
It's fine, I brought juice boxes. Dad won't let me leave the house without taking at least three.
Yeck! I can taste those preservatives and artificial flavors just thinking about it.
Are there many vegan substitutes available?

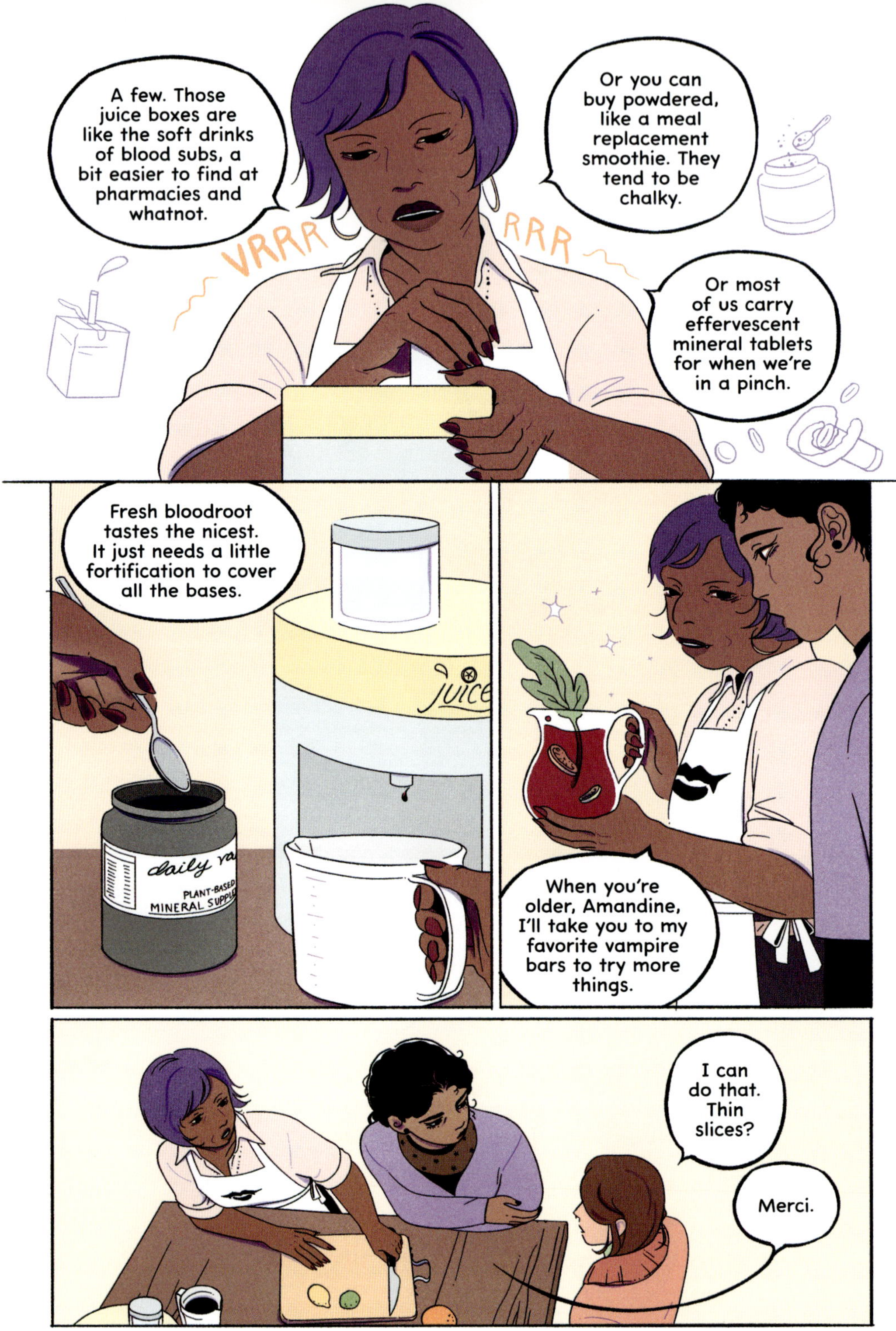
A few. Those juice boxes are like the soft drinks of blood subs, a bit easier to find at pharmacies and whatnot.
VRRR RRR
Or you can buy powdered, like a meal replacement smoothie. They tend to be chalky.
Or most of us carry effervescent mineral tablets for when we're in a pinch.
Fresh bloodroot tastes the nicest. It just needs a little fortification to cover all the bases.
juice
daily va
PLANT-BASED
MINERAL SUPPL
When you're older, Amandine, I'll take you to my favorite vampire bars to try more things.
I can do that. Thin slices?
Merci.

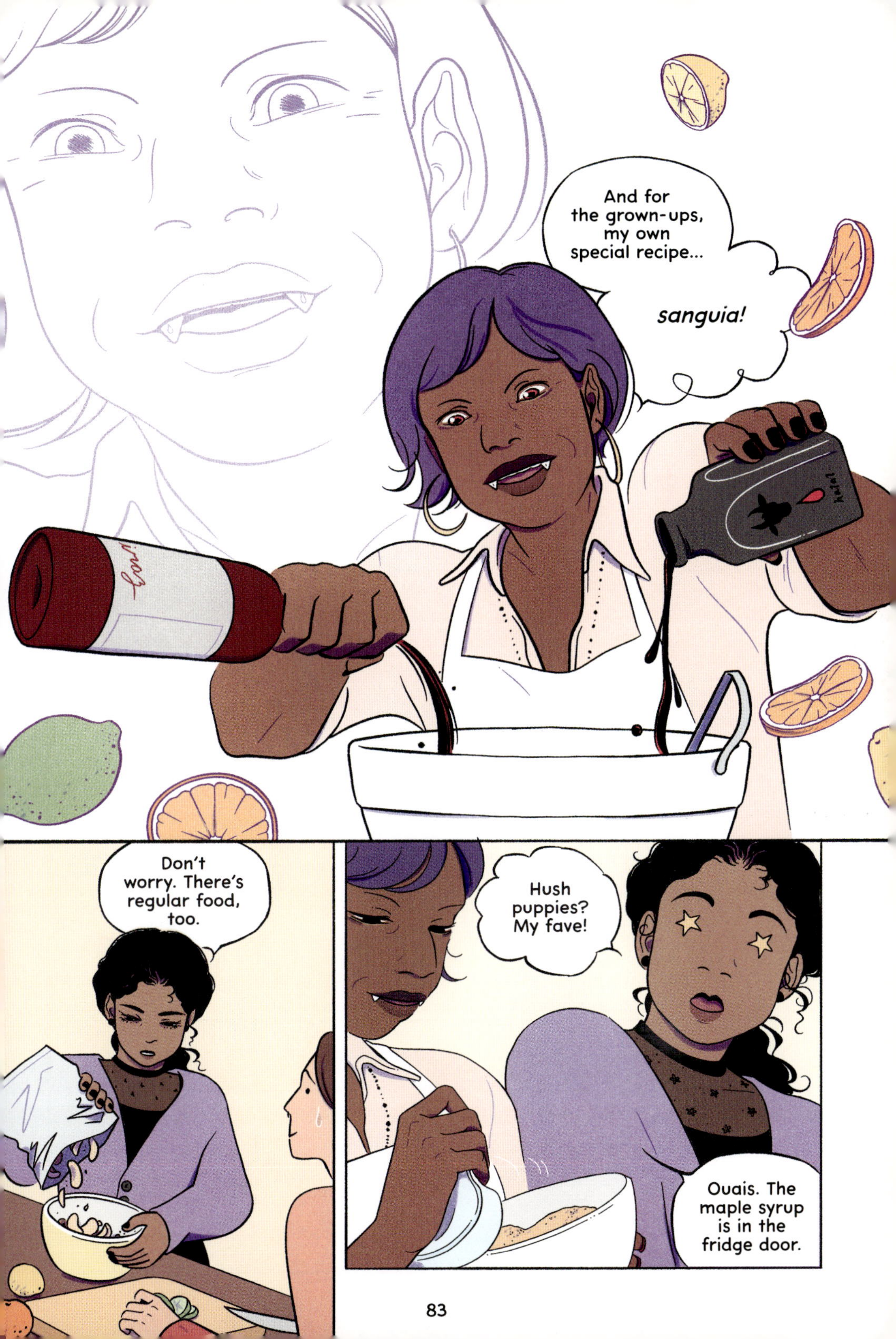
And for the grown-ups, my own special recipe...
sanguia!
Don't worry. There's regular food, too.
Hush puppies? My fave!
Ouais. The maple syrup is in the fridge door.

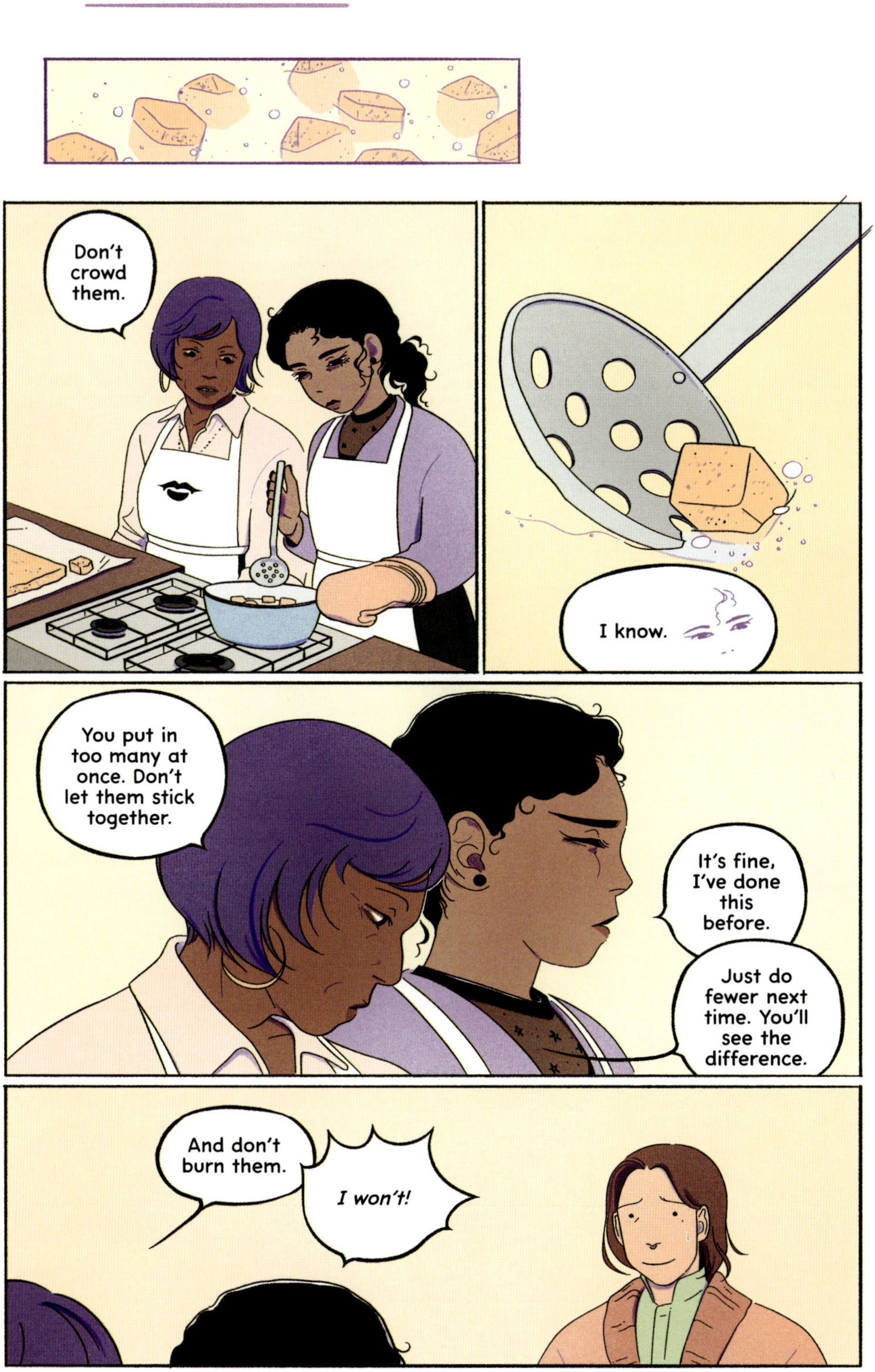
Don't crowd them.
I know.
You put in too many at once. Don't let them stick together.
It's fine, I've done this before.
Just do fewer next time. You'll see the difference.
And don't burn them.
I won't!

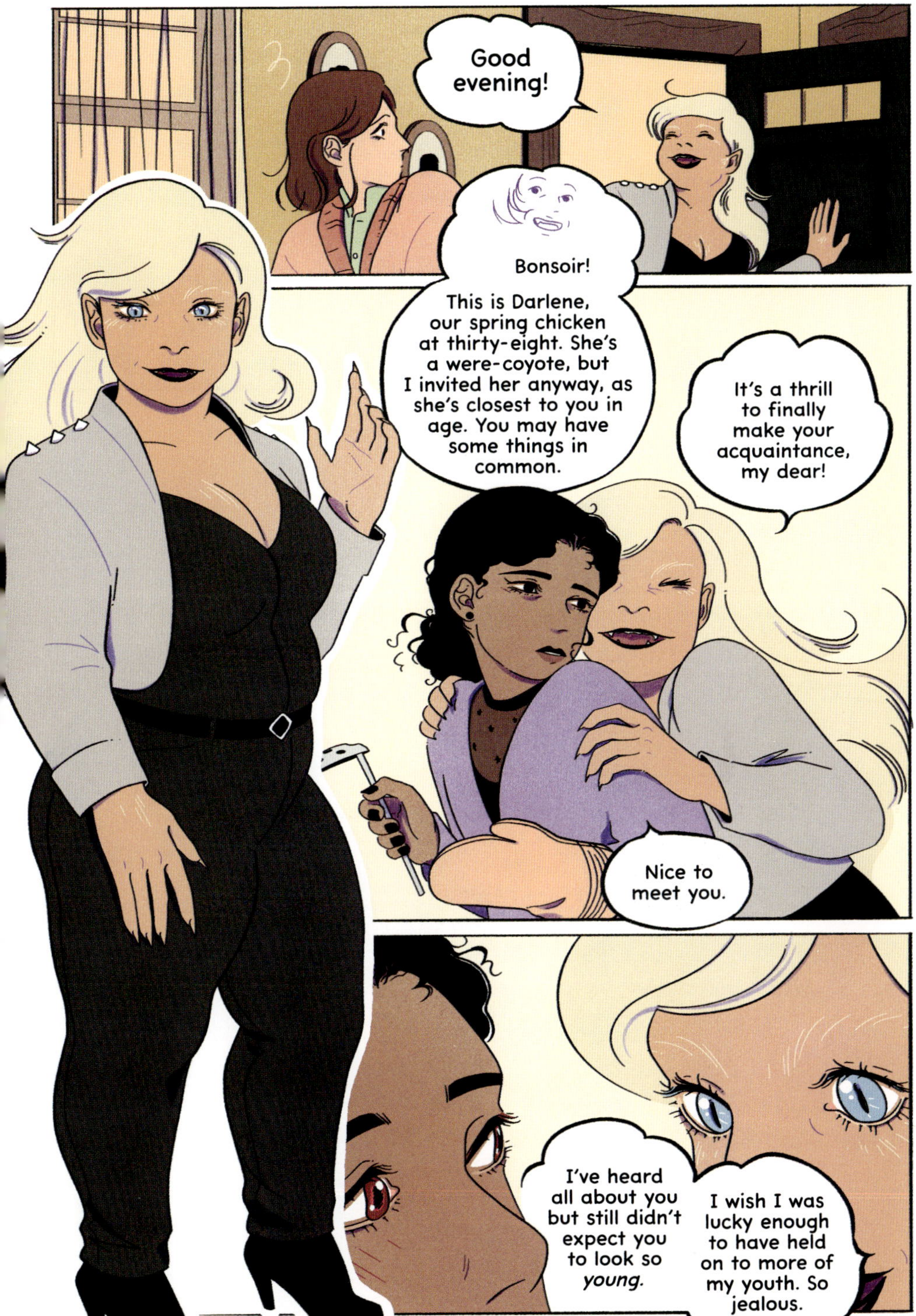
Good evening!
Bonsoir!
This is Darlene, our spring chicken at thirty-eight. She's a were-coyote, but I invited her anyway, as she's closest to you in age. You may have some things in common.
It's a thrill to finally make your acquaintance, my dear!
Nice to meet you.
I've heard all about you but still didn't expect you to look so *young.*
I wish I was lucky enough to have held on to more of my youth. So jealous.

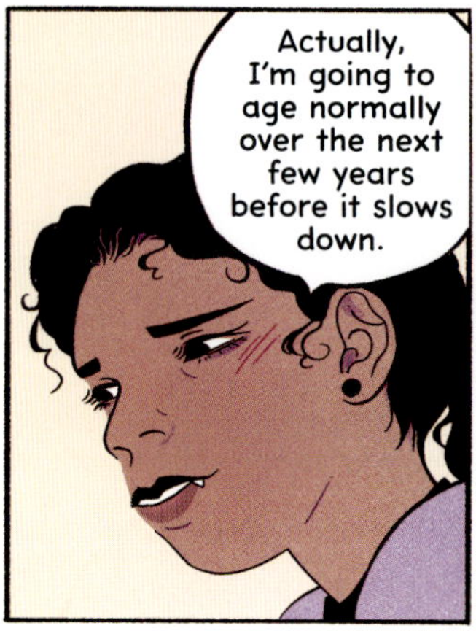
Actually, I'm going to age normally over the next few years before it slows down.

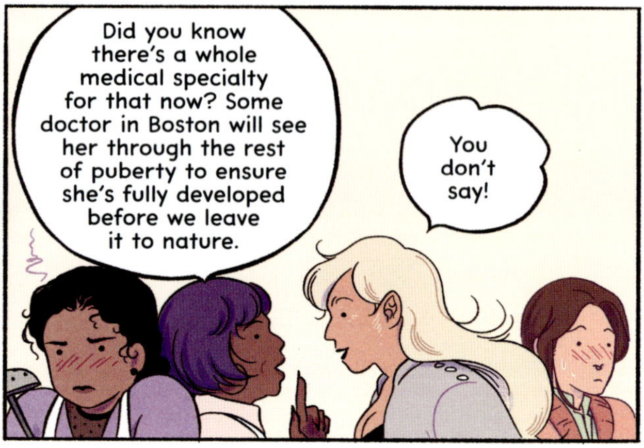
Did you know there's a whole medical specialty for that now? Some doctor in Boston will see her through the rest of puberty to ensure she's fully developed before we leave it to nature.
You don't say!

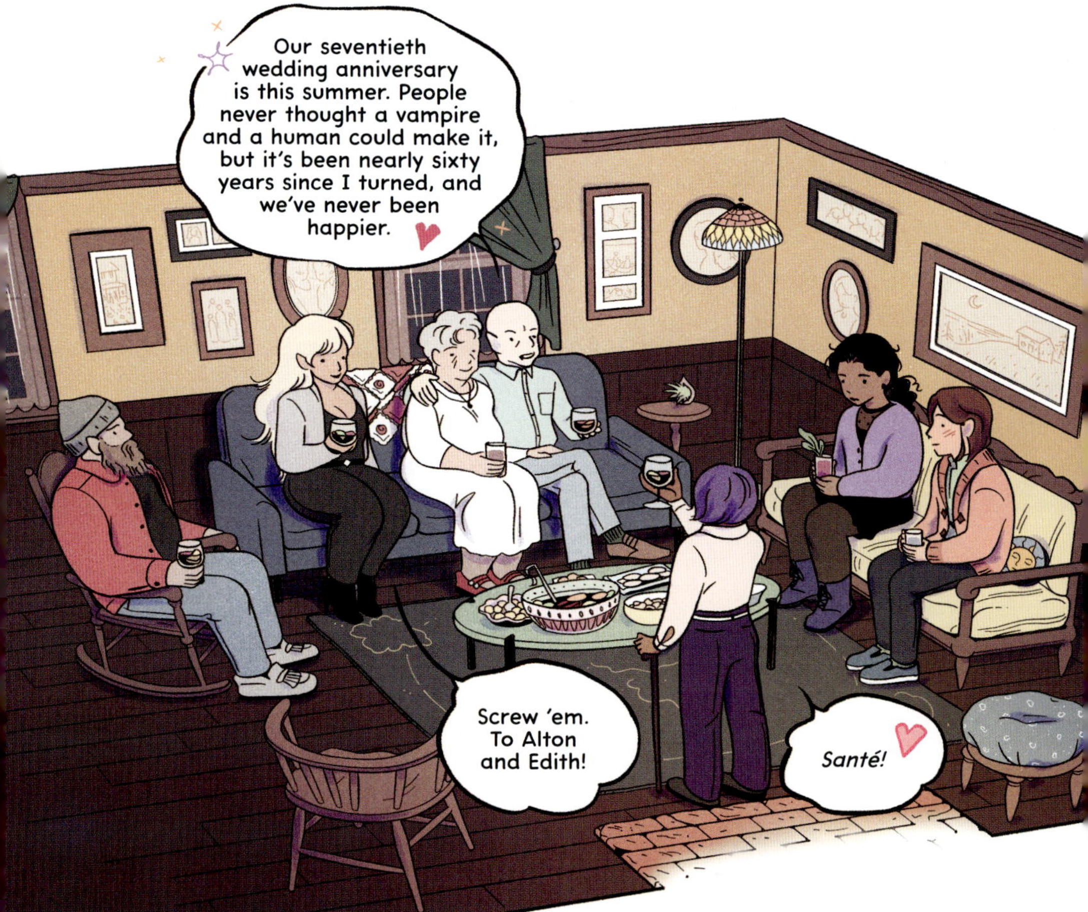
Our seventieth wedding anniversary is this summer. People never thought a vampire and a human could make it, but it's been nearly sixty years since I turned, and we've never been happier.
Screw 'em. To Alton and Edith!
Santé!

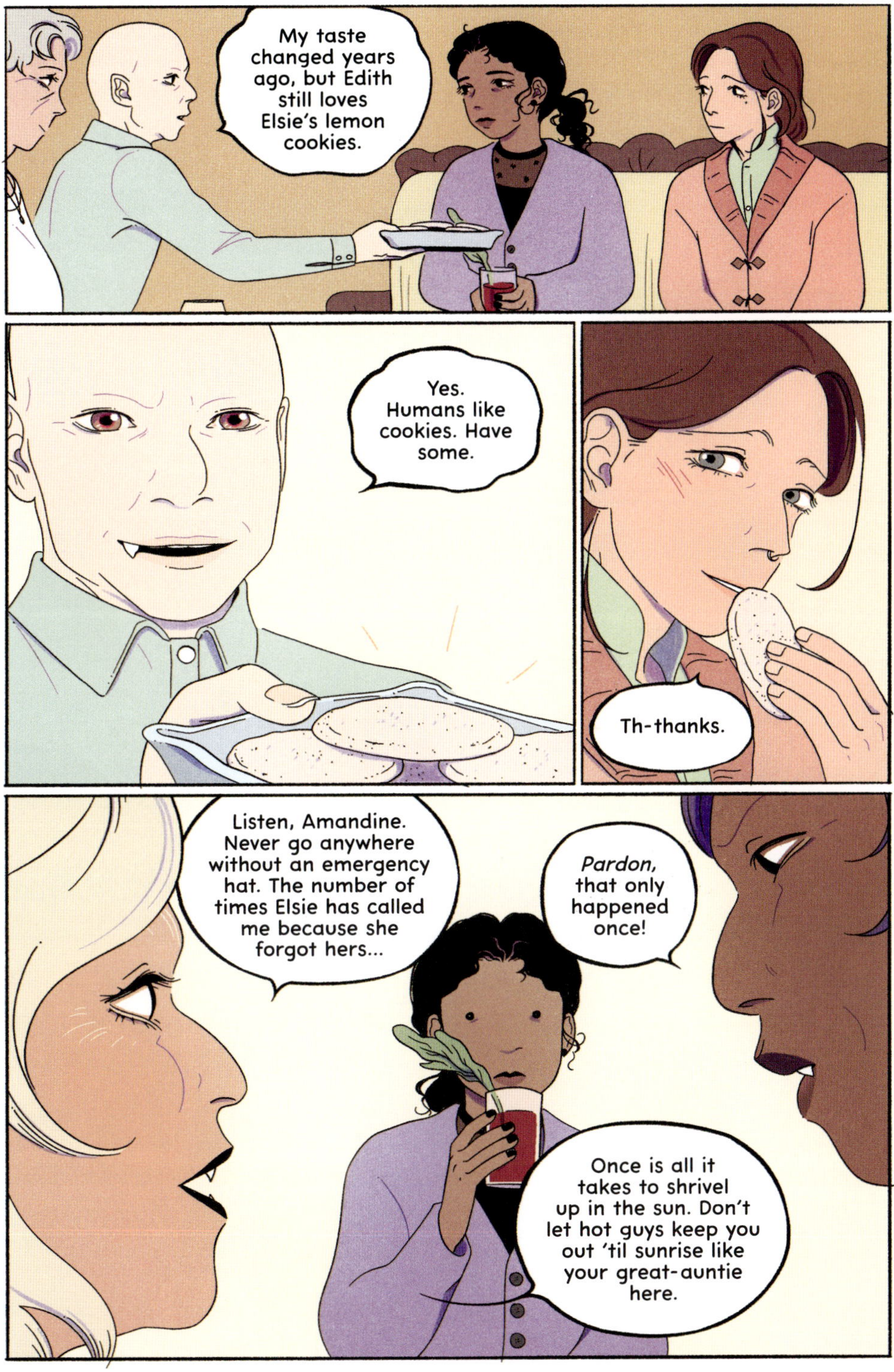
My taste changed years ago, but Edith still loves Elsie's lemon cookies.
Yes. Humans like cookies. Have some.
Th-thanks.
Listen, Amandine. Never go anywhere without an emergency hat. The number of times Elsie has called me because she forgot hers...
Pardon, that only happened once!
Once is all it takes to shrivel up in the sun. Don't let hot guys keep you out 'til sunrise like your great-auntie here.

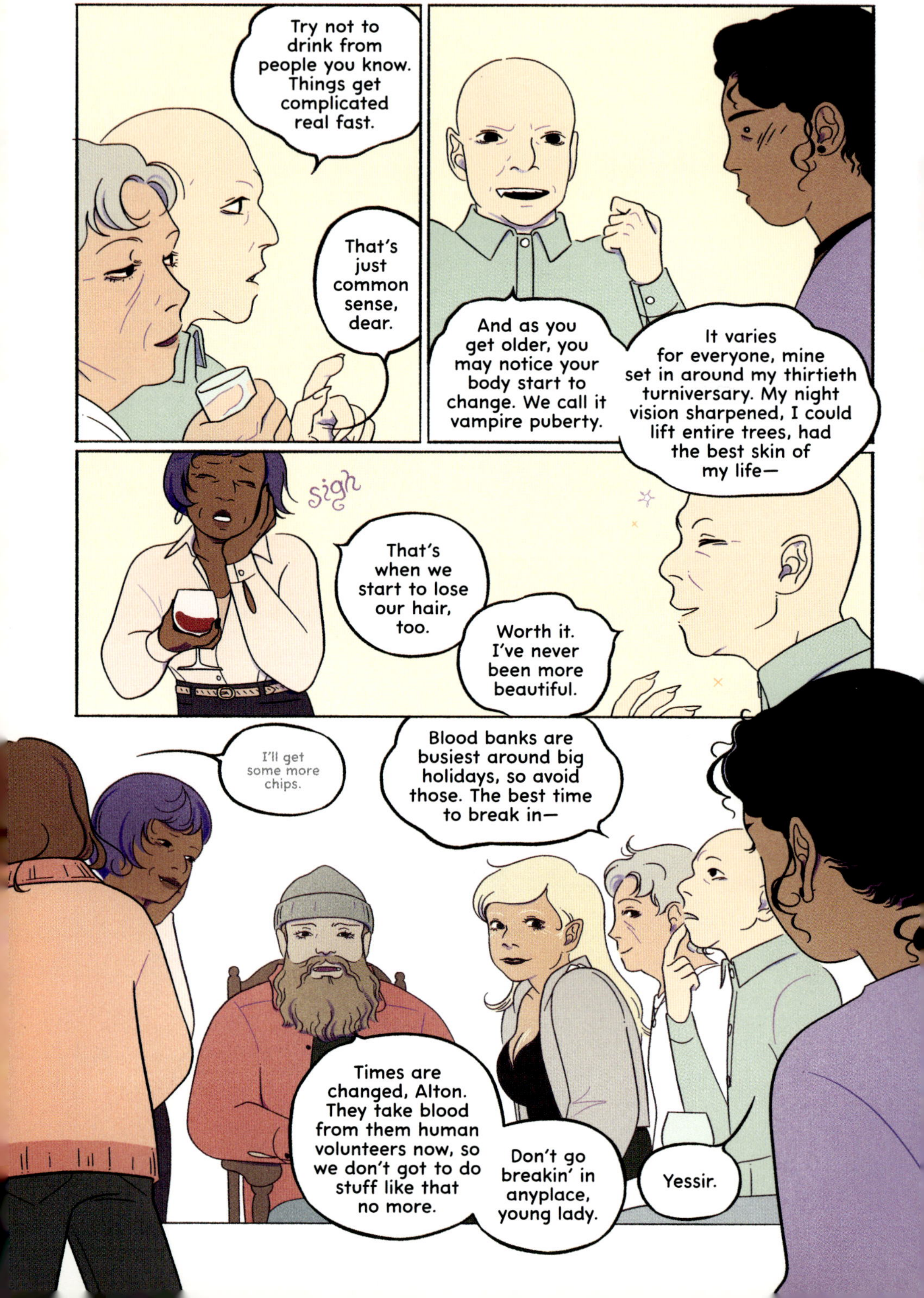
Try not to drink from people you know. Things get complicated real fast.
That's just common sense, dear.
And as you get older, you may notice your body start to change. We call it vampire puberty.
It varies for everyone, mine set in around my thirtieth turniversary. My night vision sharpened, I could lift entire trees, had the best skin of my life—
sigh
That's when we start to lose our hair, too.
Worth it. I've never been more beautiful.
I'll get some more chips.
Blood banks are busiest around big holidays, so avoid those. The best time to break in—
Times are changed, Alton. They take blood from them human volunteers now, so we don't got to do stuff like that no more.
Don't go breakin' in anyplace, young lady.
Yessir.

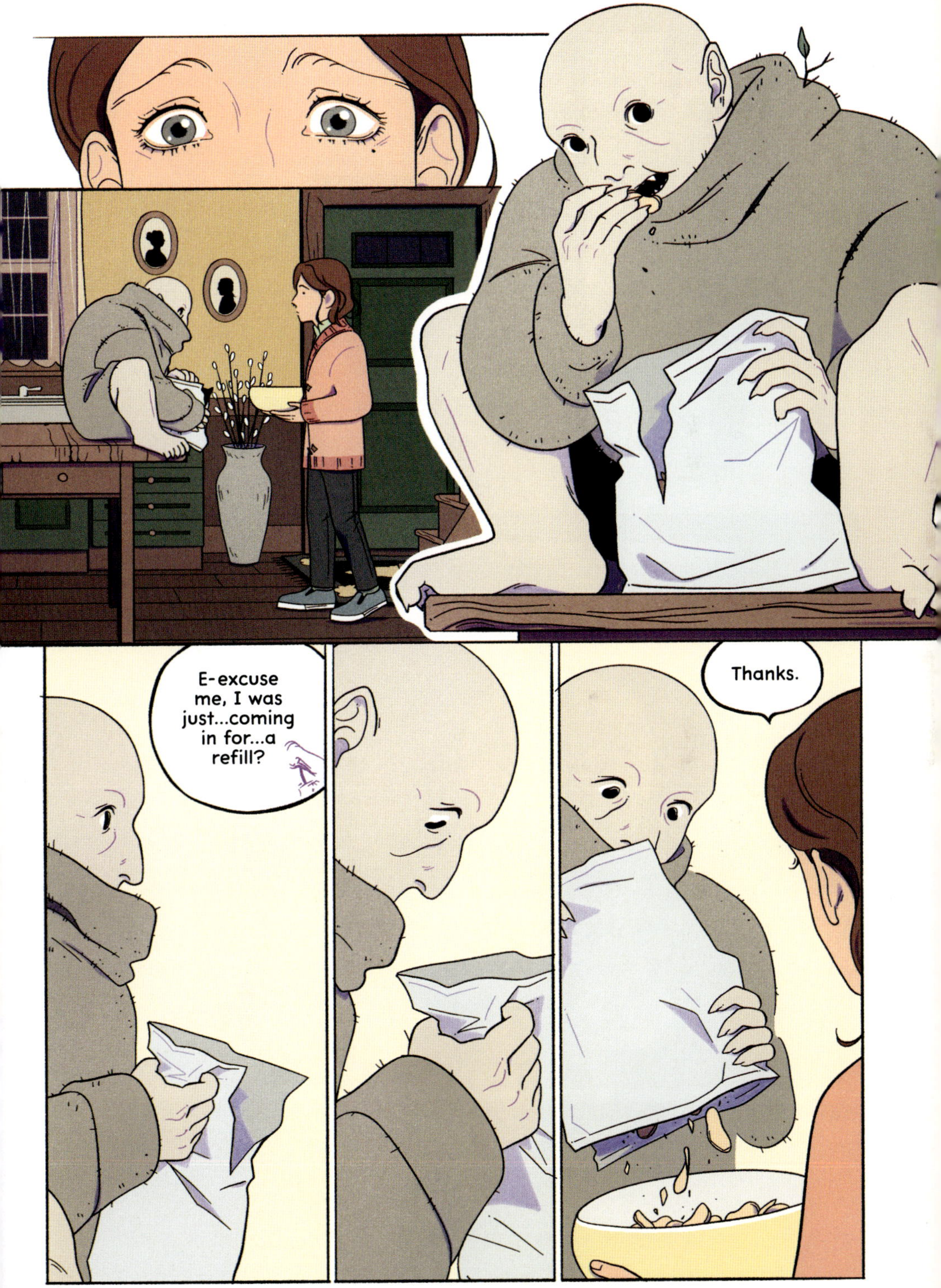
E-excuse me, I was just...coming in for...a refill?
Thanks.

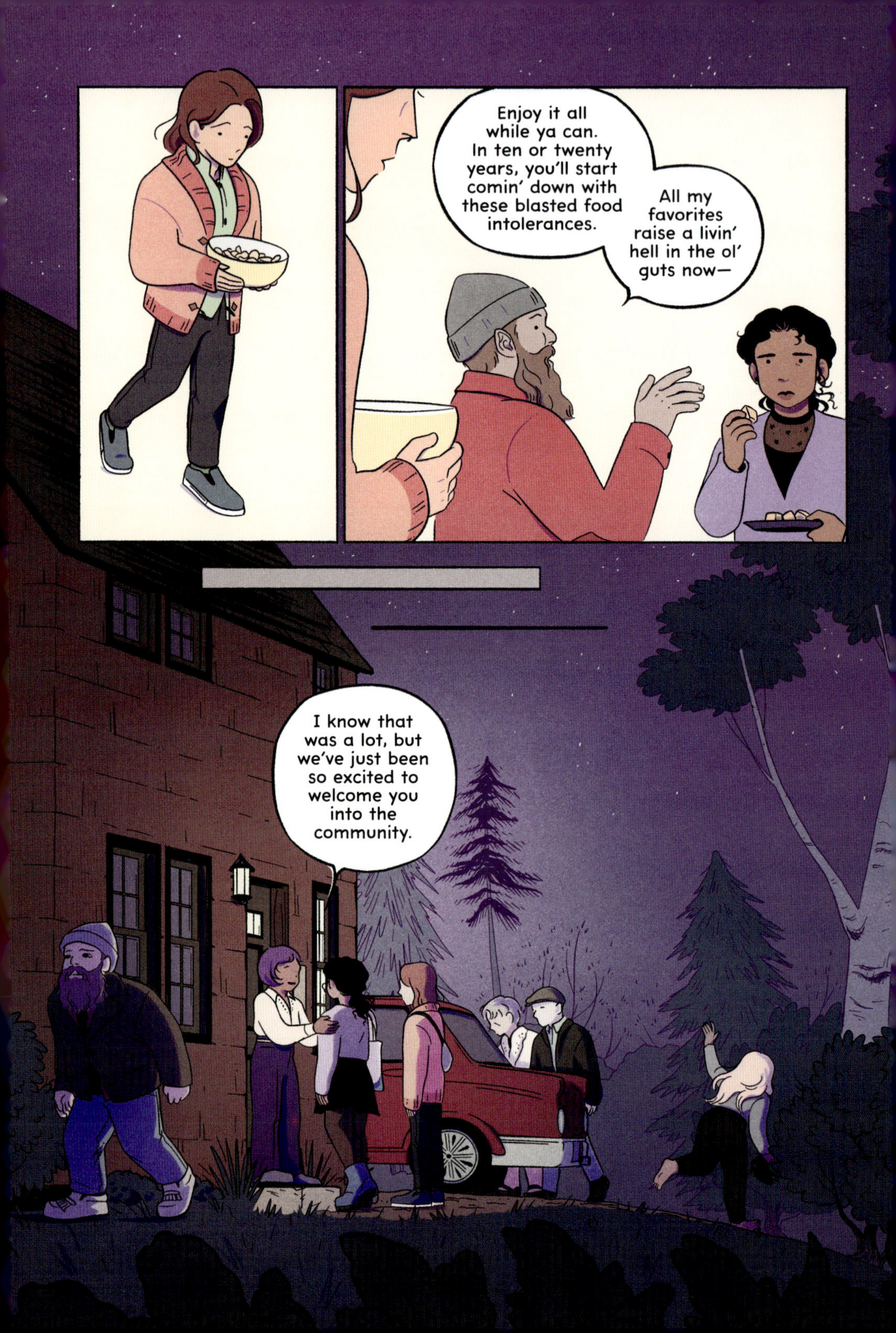
Enjoy it all while ya can. In ten or twenty years, you'll start comin' down with these blasted food intolerances.
All my favorites raise a livin' hell in the ol' guts now—
I know that was a lot, but we've just been so excited to welcome you into the community.

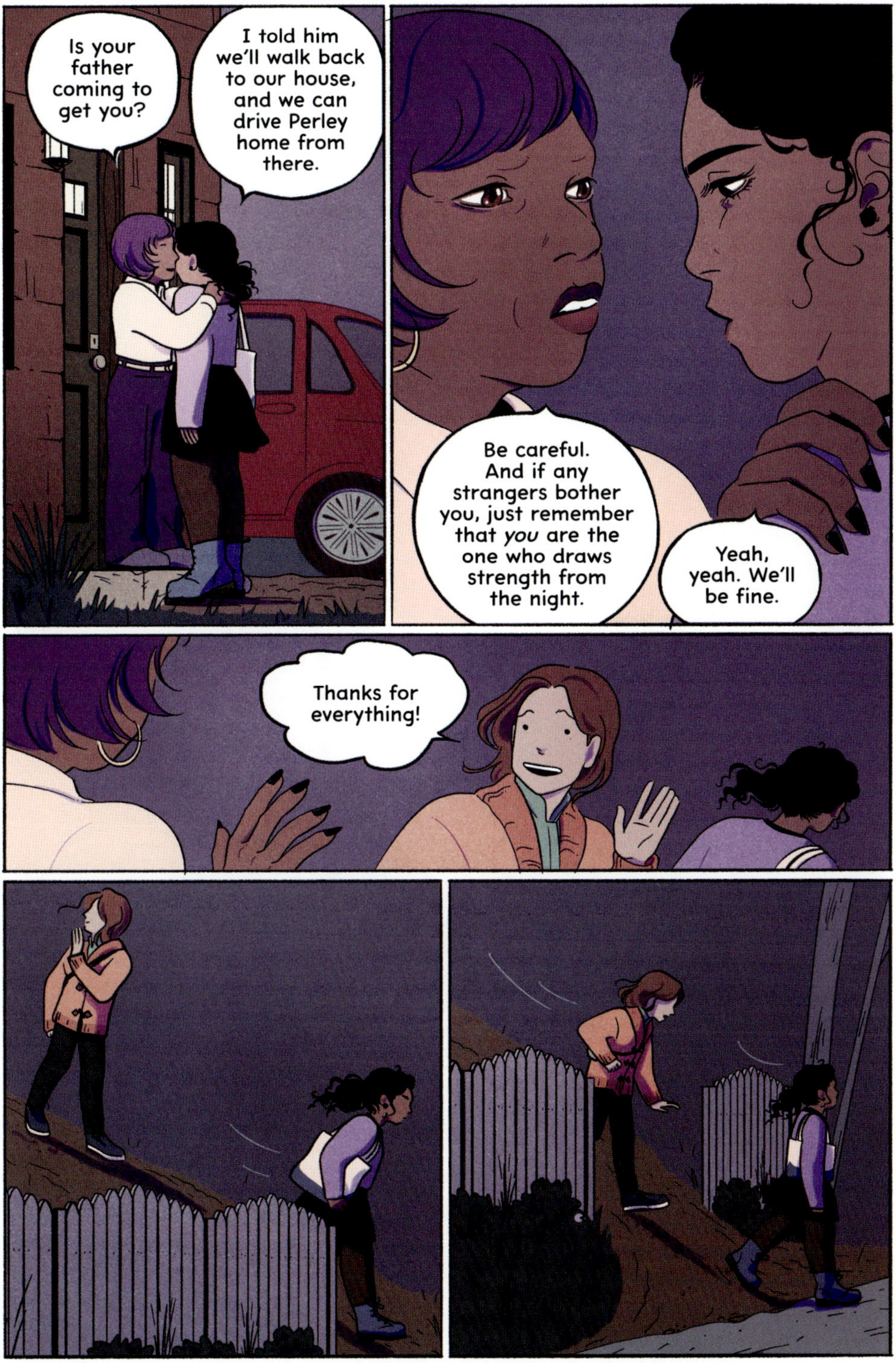
Is your father coming to get you?
I told him we'll walk back to our house, and we can drive Perley home from there.
Be careful. And if any strangers bother you, just remember that *you* are the one who draws strength from the night.
Yeah, yeah. We'll be fine.
Thanks for everything!

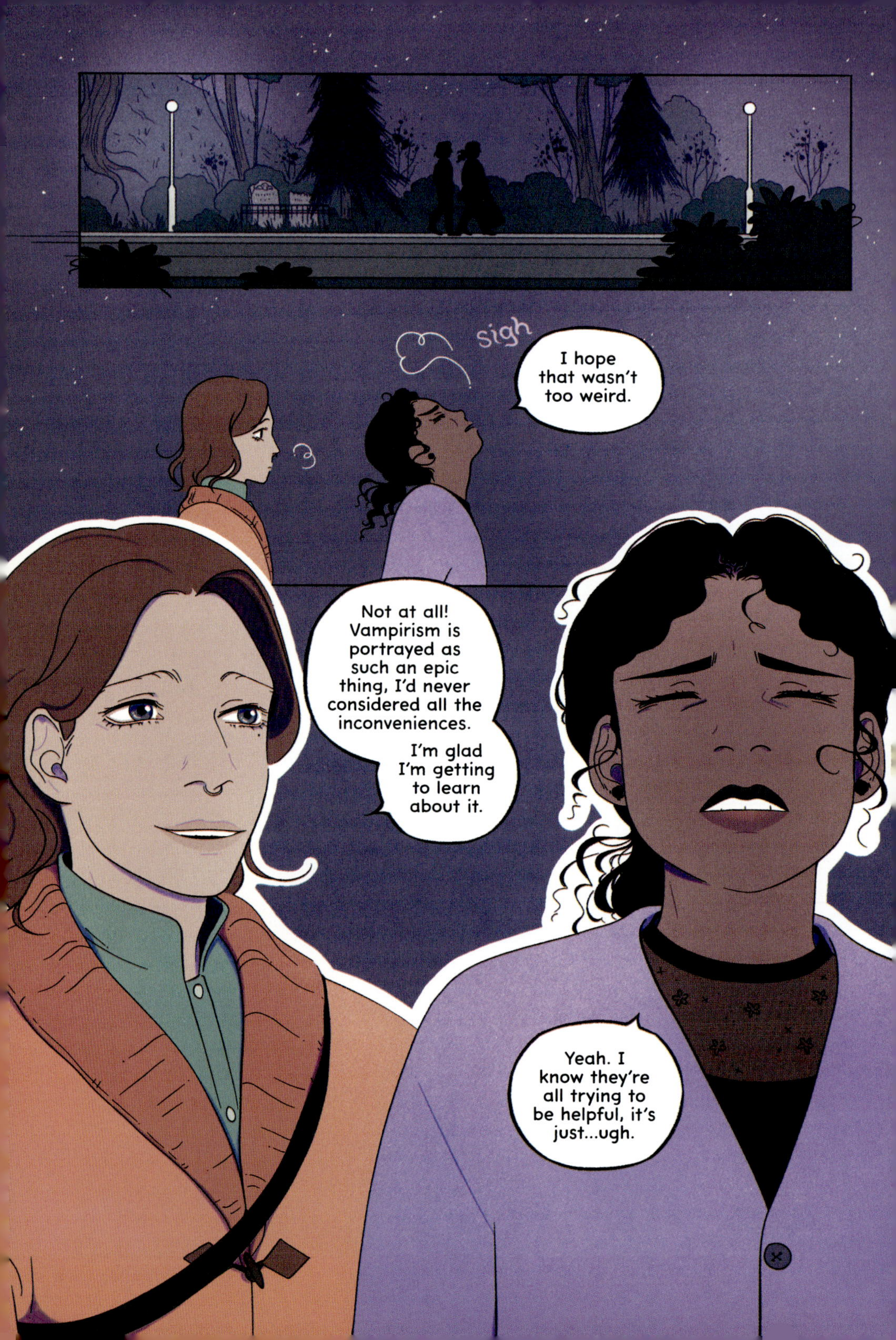
sigh
I hope that wasn't too weird.
Not at all! Vampirism is portrayed as such an epic thing, I'd never considered all the inconveniences.
I'm glad I'm getting to learn about it.
Yeah. I know they're all trying to be helpful, it's just...ugh.

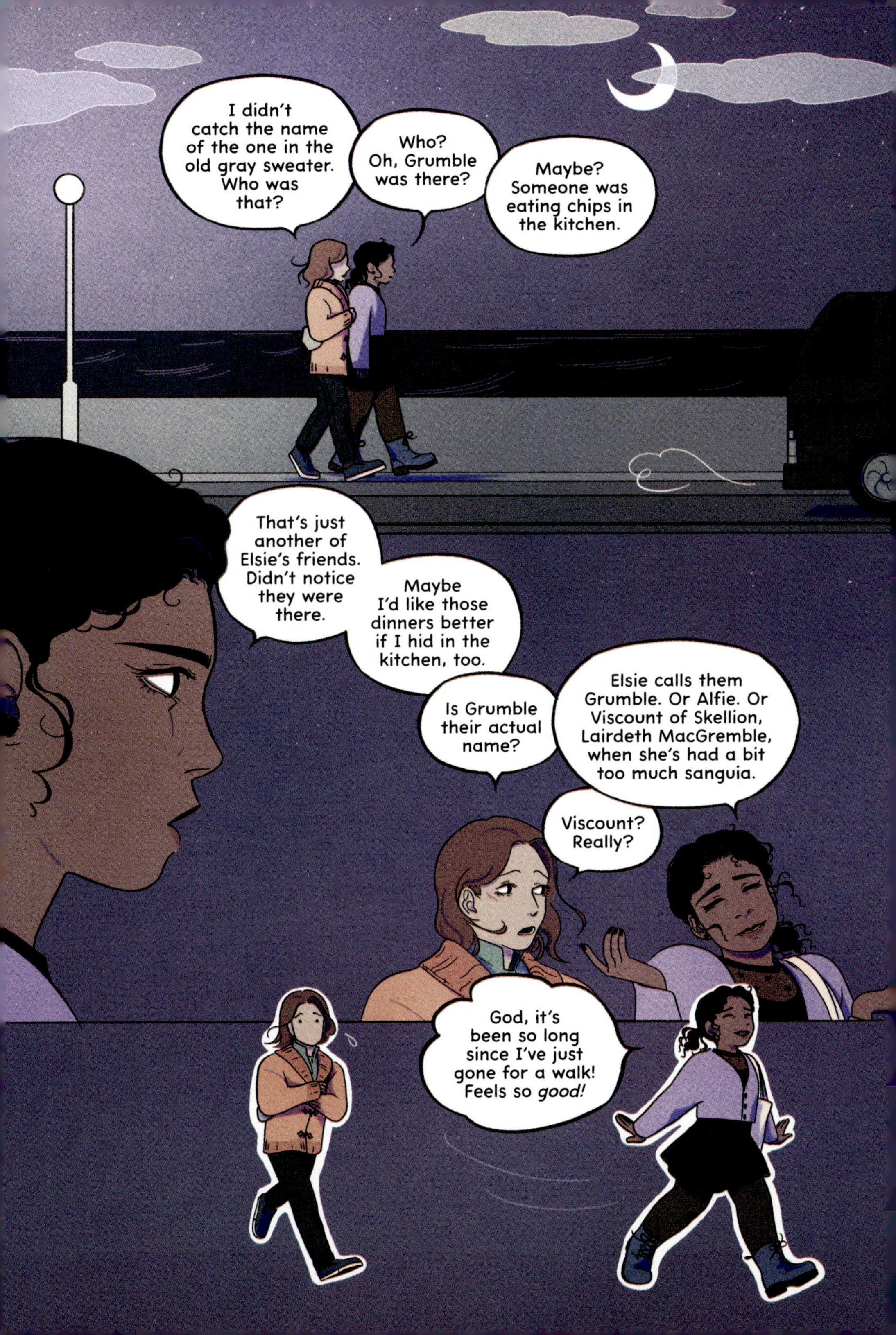
I didn't catch the name of the one in the old gray sweater. Who was that?
Who? Oh, Grumble was there?
Maybe? Someone was eating chips in the kitchen.
That's just another of Elsie's friends. Didn't notice they were there.
Maybe I'd like those dinners better if I hid in the kitchen, too.
Is Grumble their actual name?
Elsie calls them Grumble. Or Alfie. Or Viscount of Skellion, Lairdeth MacGremble, when she's had a bit too much sanguia.
Viscount? Really?
God, it's been so long since I've just gone for a walk! Feels so *good!*

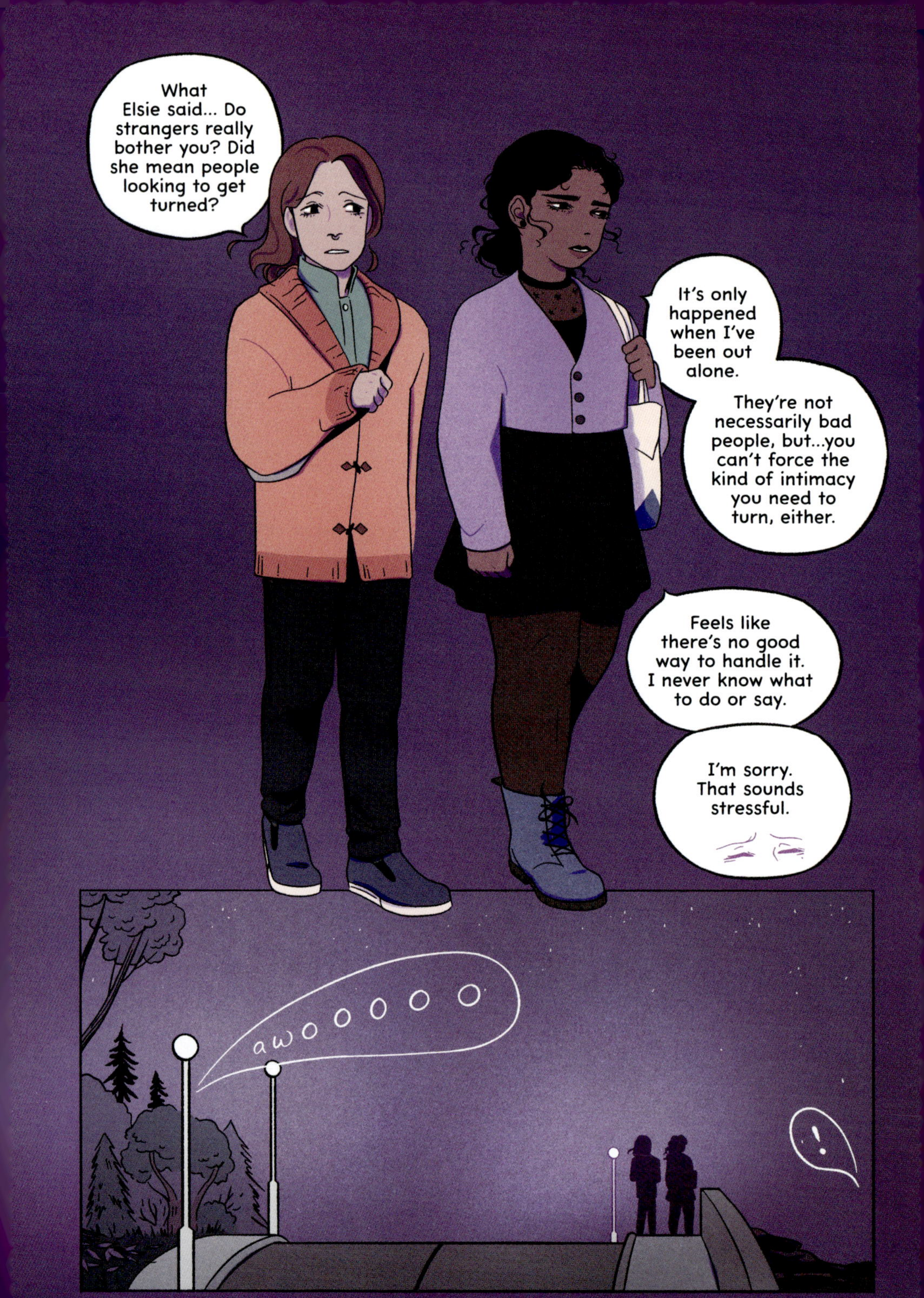
What Elsie said... Do strangers really bother you? Did she mean people looking to get turned?
It's only happened when I've been out alone.
They're not necessarily bad people, but...you can't force the kind of intimacy you need to turn, either.
Feels like there's no good way to handle it. I never know what to do or say.
I'm sorry. That sounds stressful.
awooooo
!

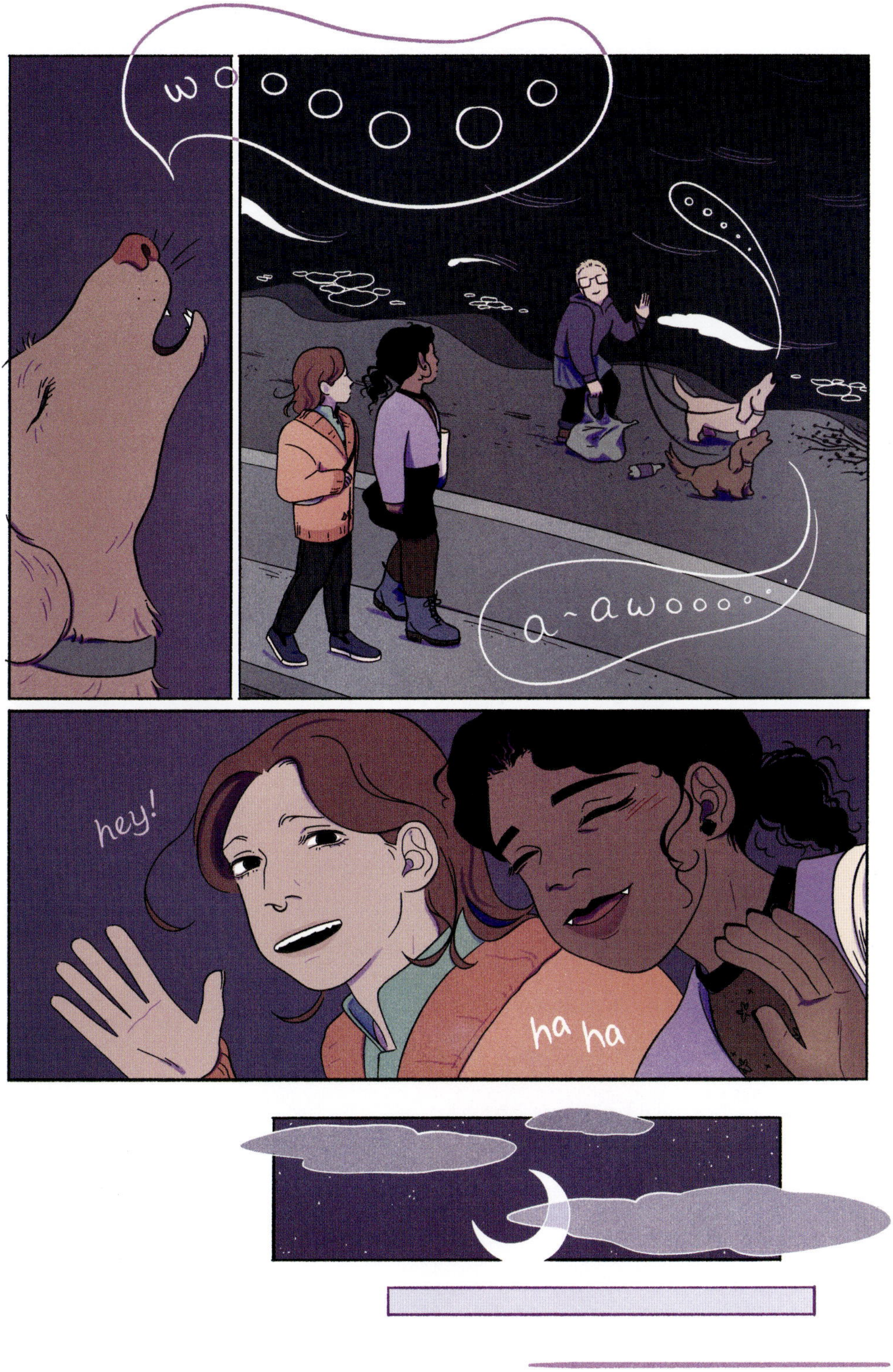
wooooooo
ooooo
a-awoooo
hey!
ha ha

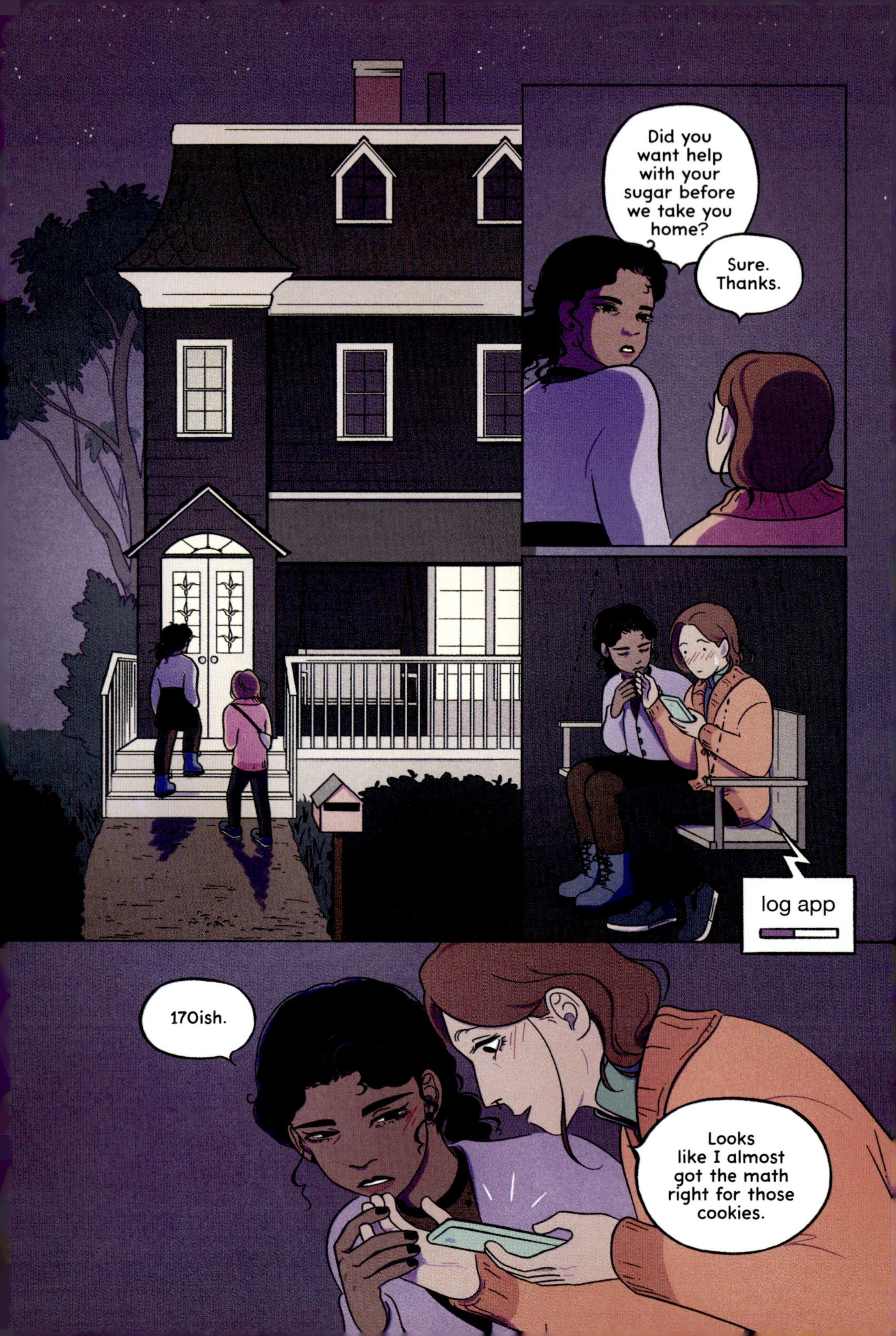
Did you want help with your sugar before we take you home?
Sure. Thanks.
log app
170ish.
Looks like I almost got the math right for those cookies.

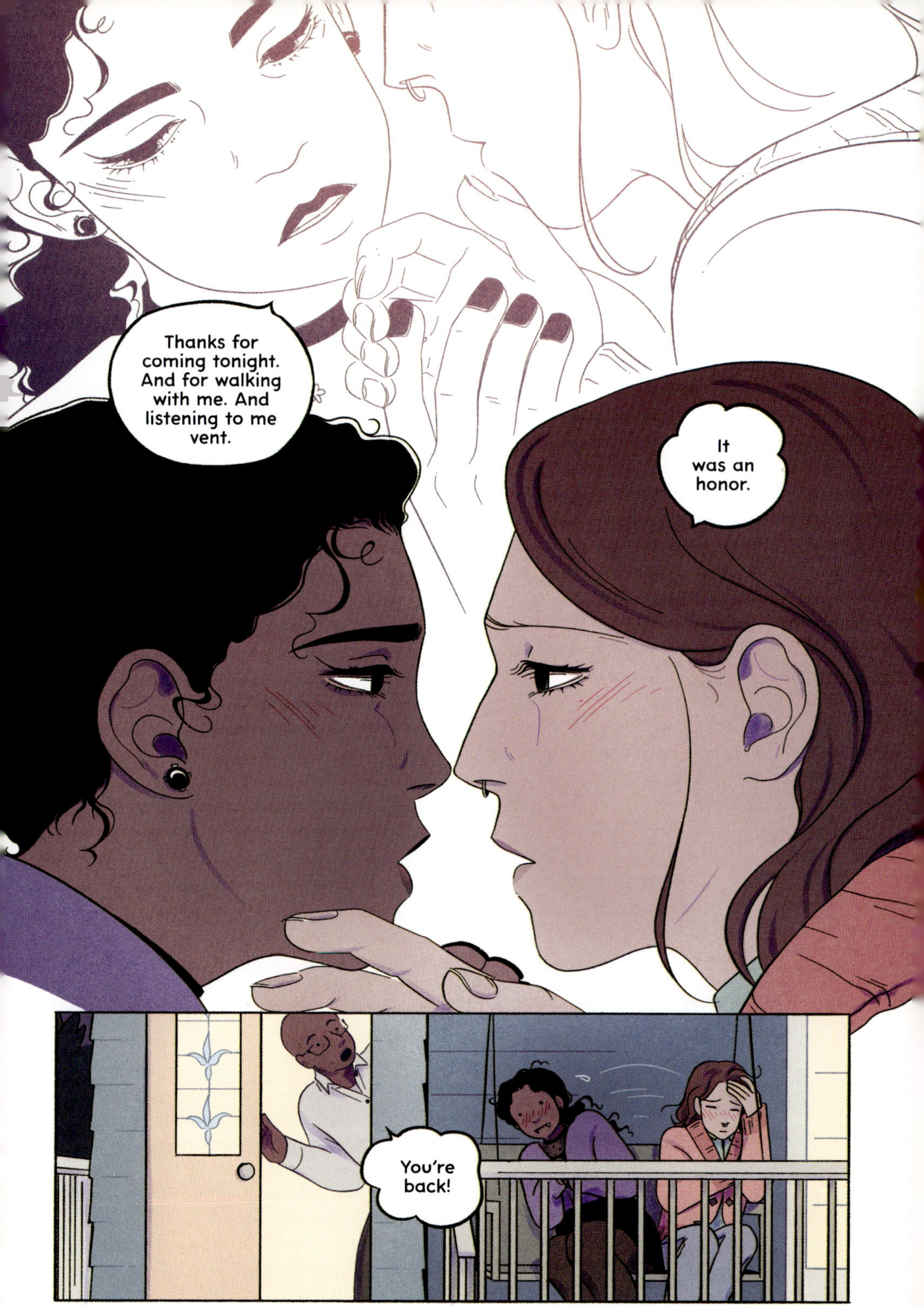
Thanks for coming tonight. And for walking with me. And listening to me vent.
It was an honor.
You're back!

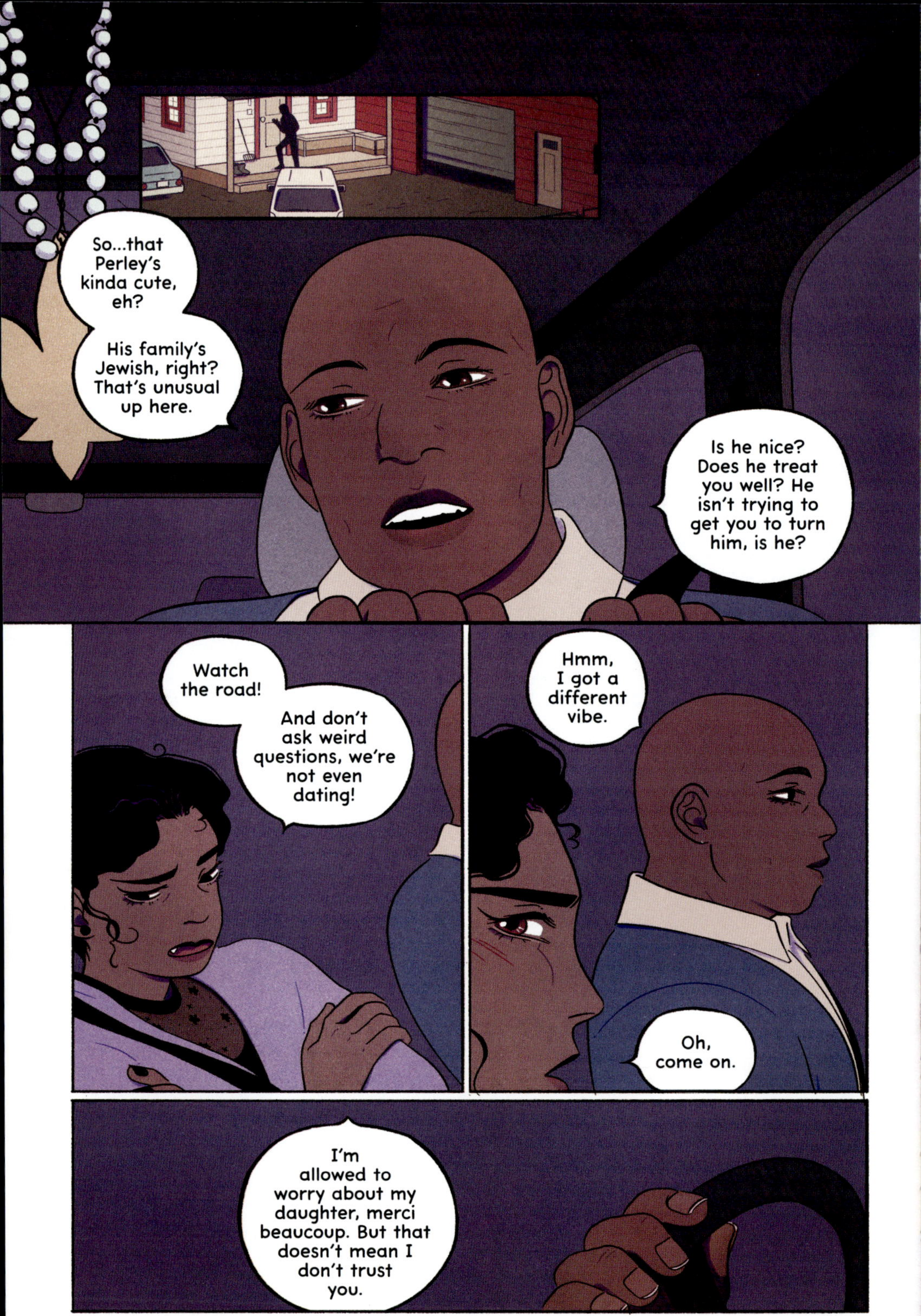
So...that Perley's kinda cute, eh?
His family's Jewish, right? That's unusual up here.
Is he nice? Does he treat you well? He isn't trying to get you to turn him, is he?
Watch the road!
And don't ask weird questions, we're not even dating!
Hmm, I got a different vibe.
Oh, come on.
I'm allowed to worry about my daughter, merci beaucoup. But that doesn't mean I don't trust you.

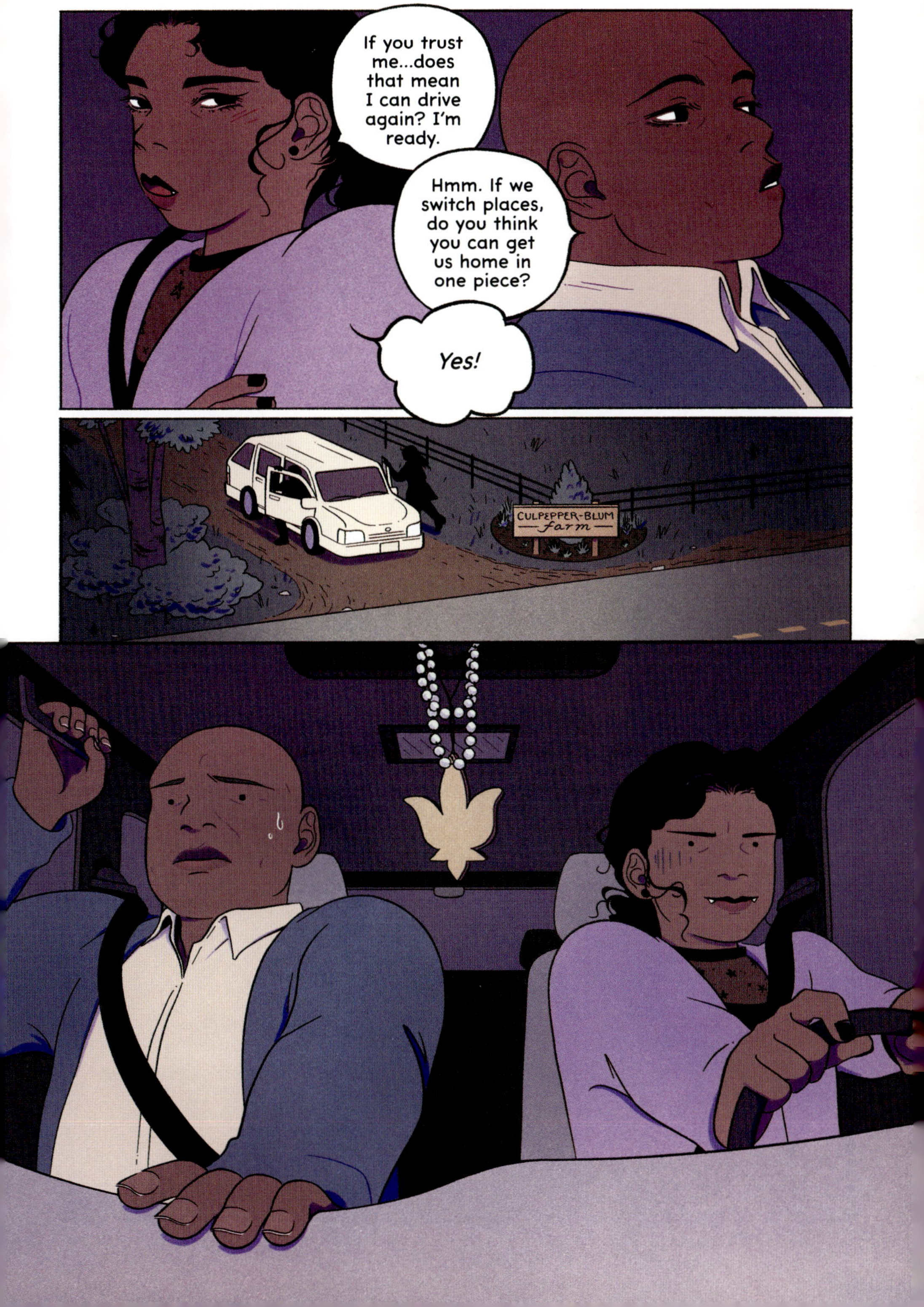
If you trust me...does that mean I can drive again? I'm ready.
Hmm. If we switch places, do you think you can get us home in one piece?
Yes!
CULPEPPER-BLUM farm

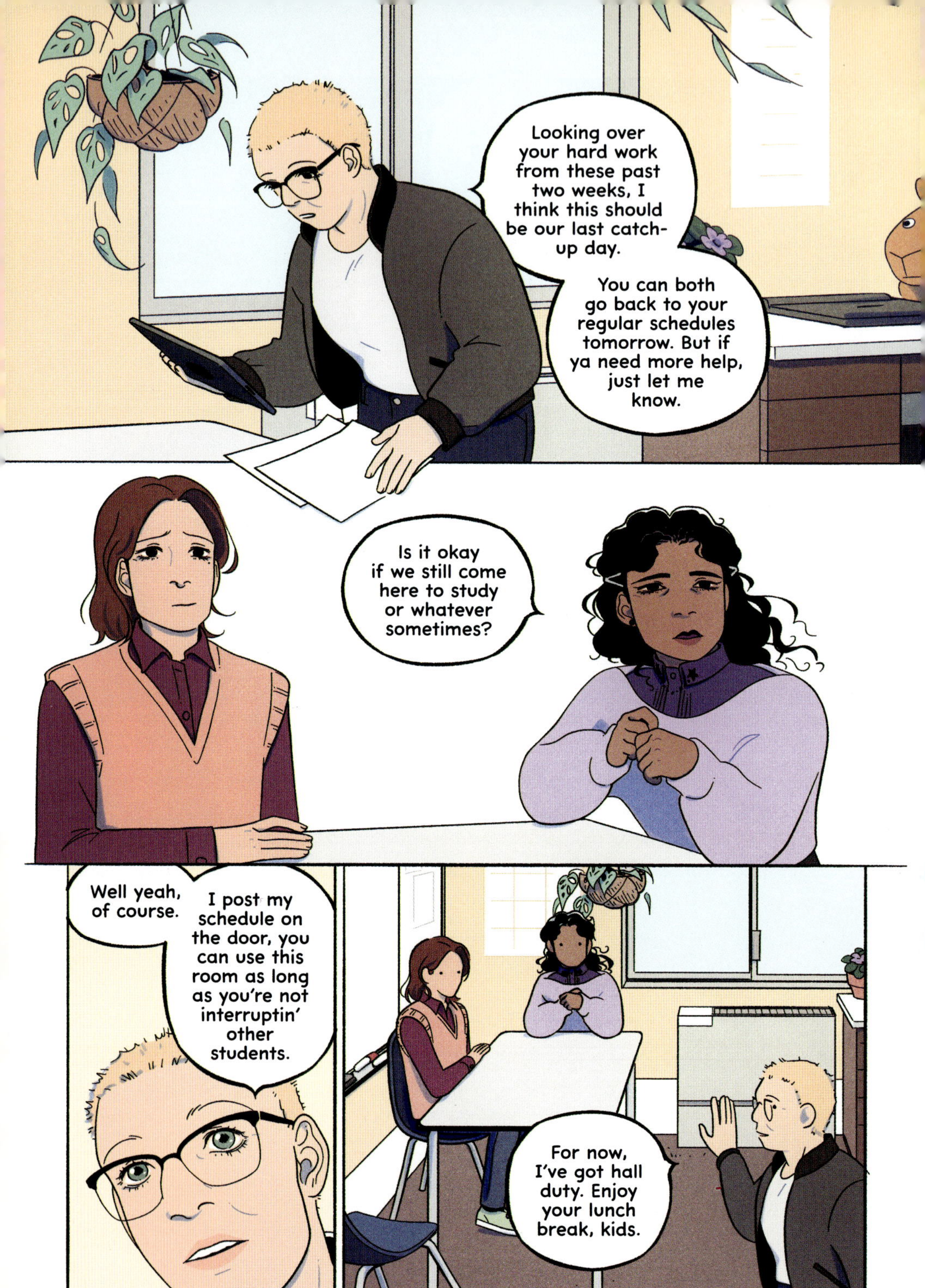

Looking over your hard work from these past two weeks, I think this should be our last catch-up day.
You can both go back to your regular schedules tomorrow. But if ya need more help, just let me know.
Is it okay if we still come here to study or whatever sometimes?
Well yeah, of course.
I post my schedule on the door, you can use this room as long as you're not interruptin' other students.
For now, I've got hall duty. Enjoy your lunch break, kids.

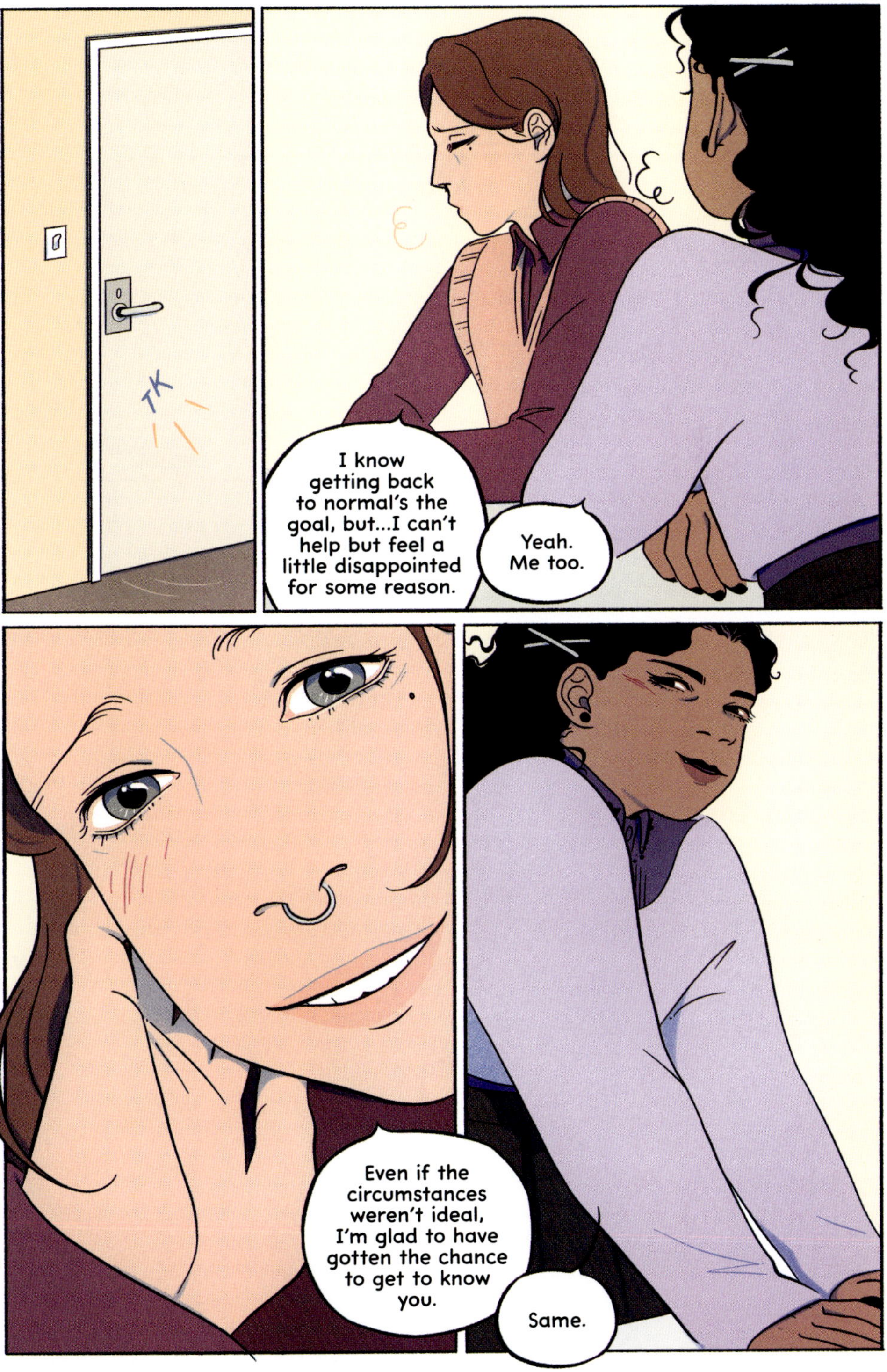
TK
I know getting back to normal's the goal, but...I can't help but feel a little disappointed for some reason.
Yeah. Me too.
Even if the circumstances weren't ideal, I'm glad to have gotten the chance to get to know you.
Same.

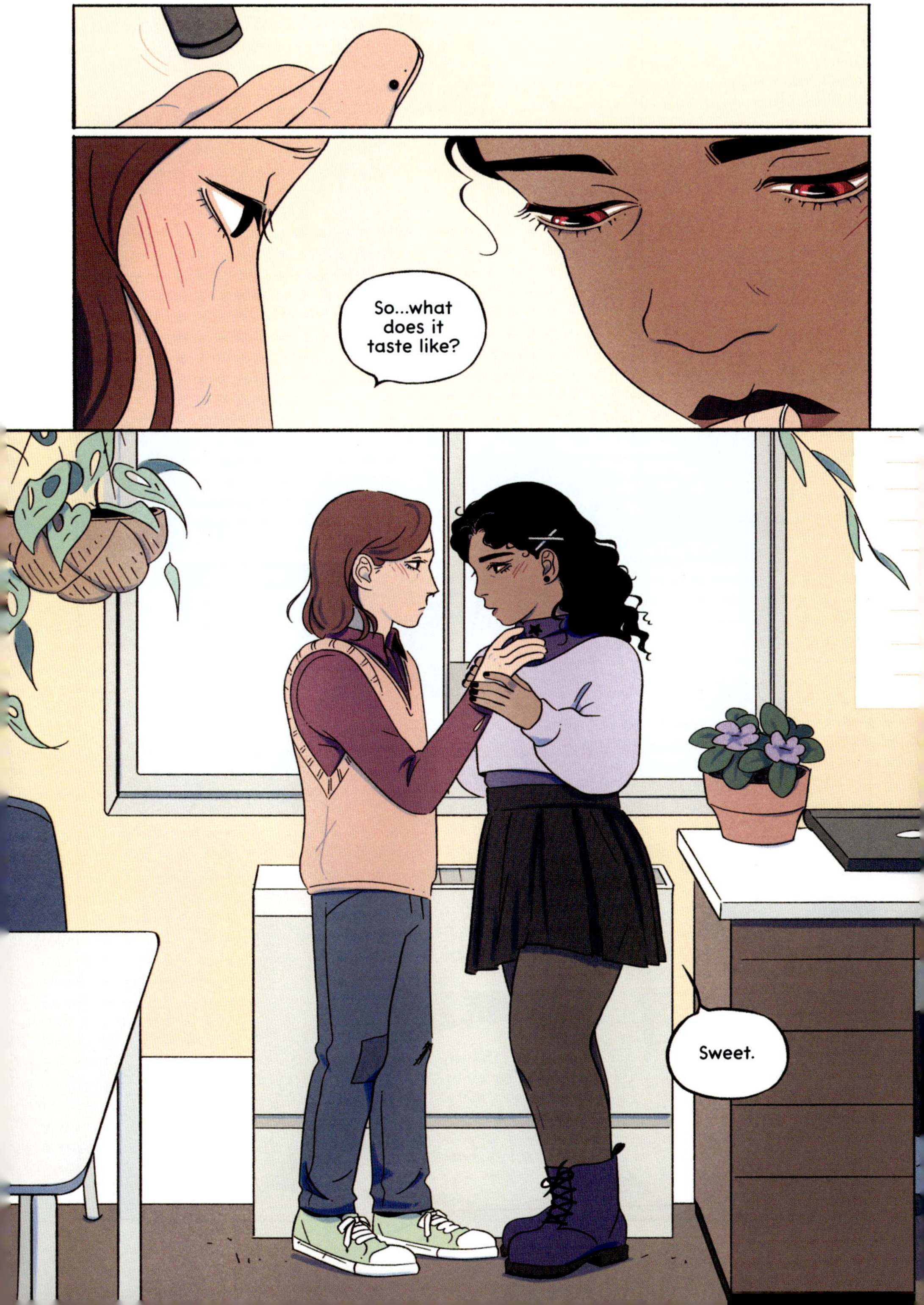
So...what does it taste like?
Sweet.

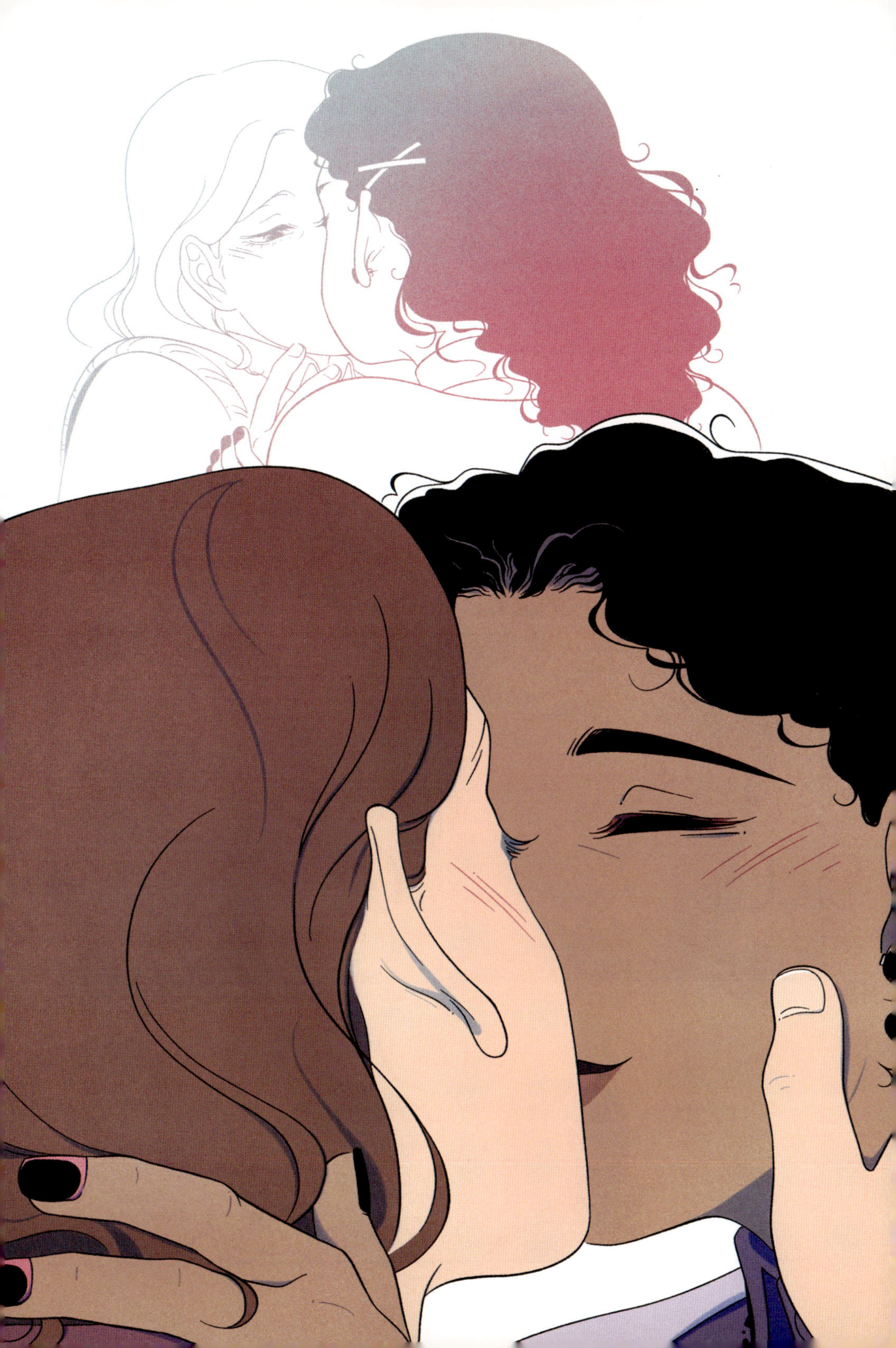

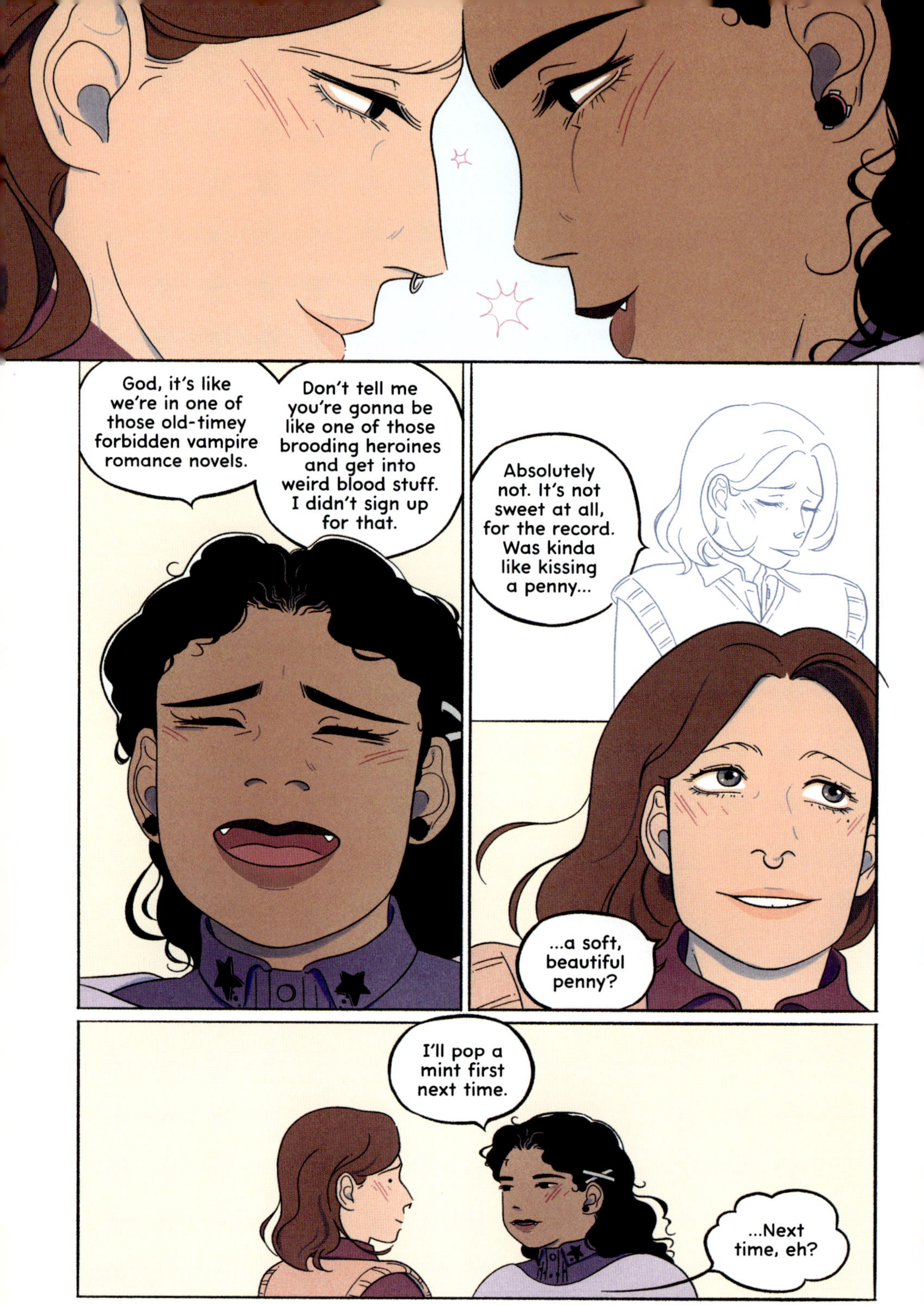
God, it's like we're in one of those old-timey forbidden vampire romance novels.
Don't tell me you're gonna be like one of those brooding heroines and get into weird blood stuff. I didn't sign up for that.
Absolutely not. It's not sweet at all, for the record. Was kinda like kissing a penny...
...a soft, beautiful penny?
I'll pop a mint first next time.
...Next time, eh?

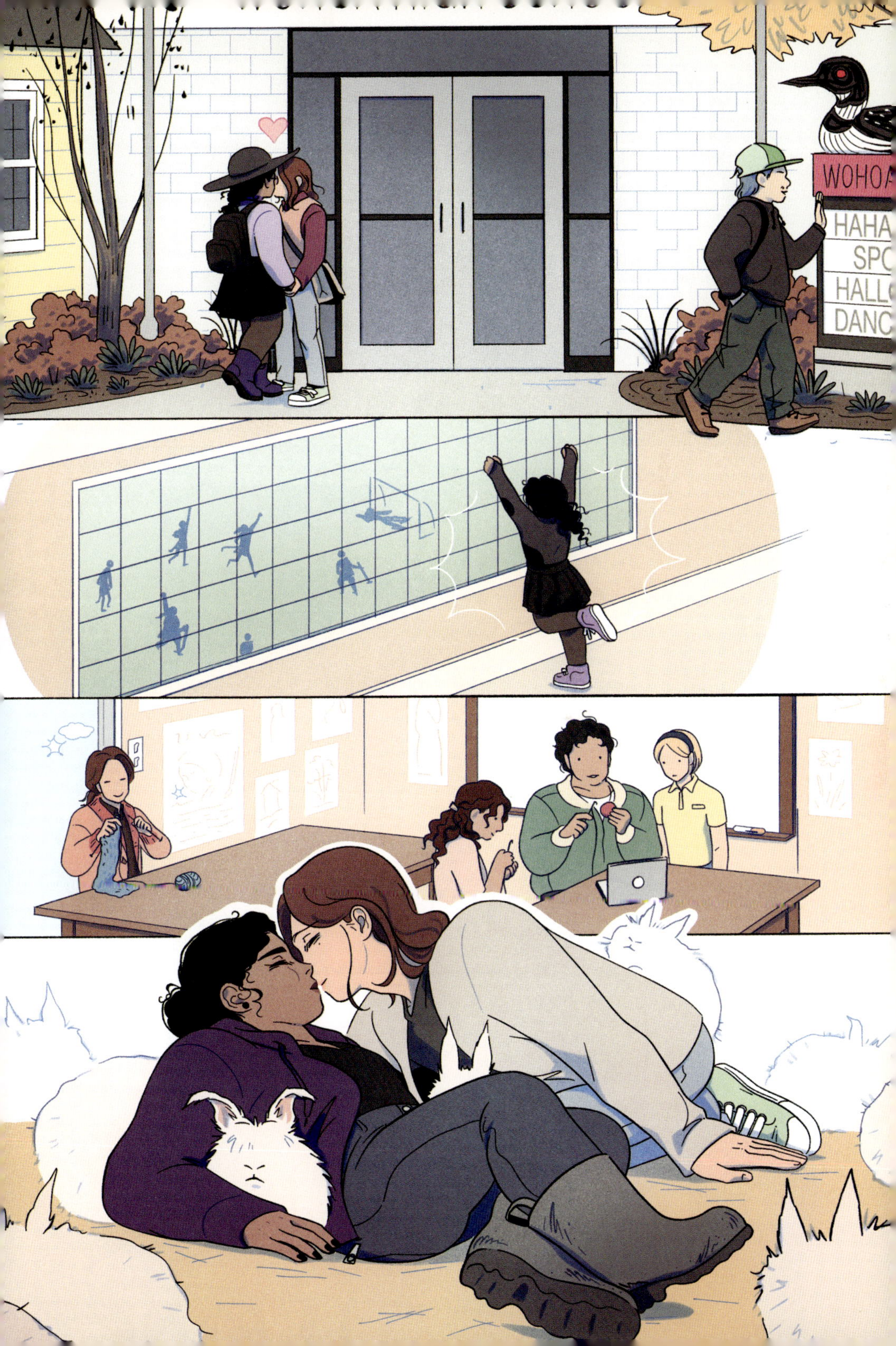
WOHOA
HAHA
SPO
HALL
DANC

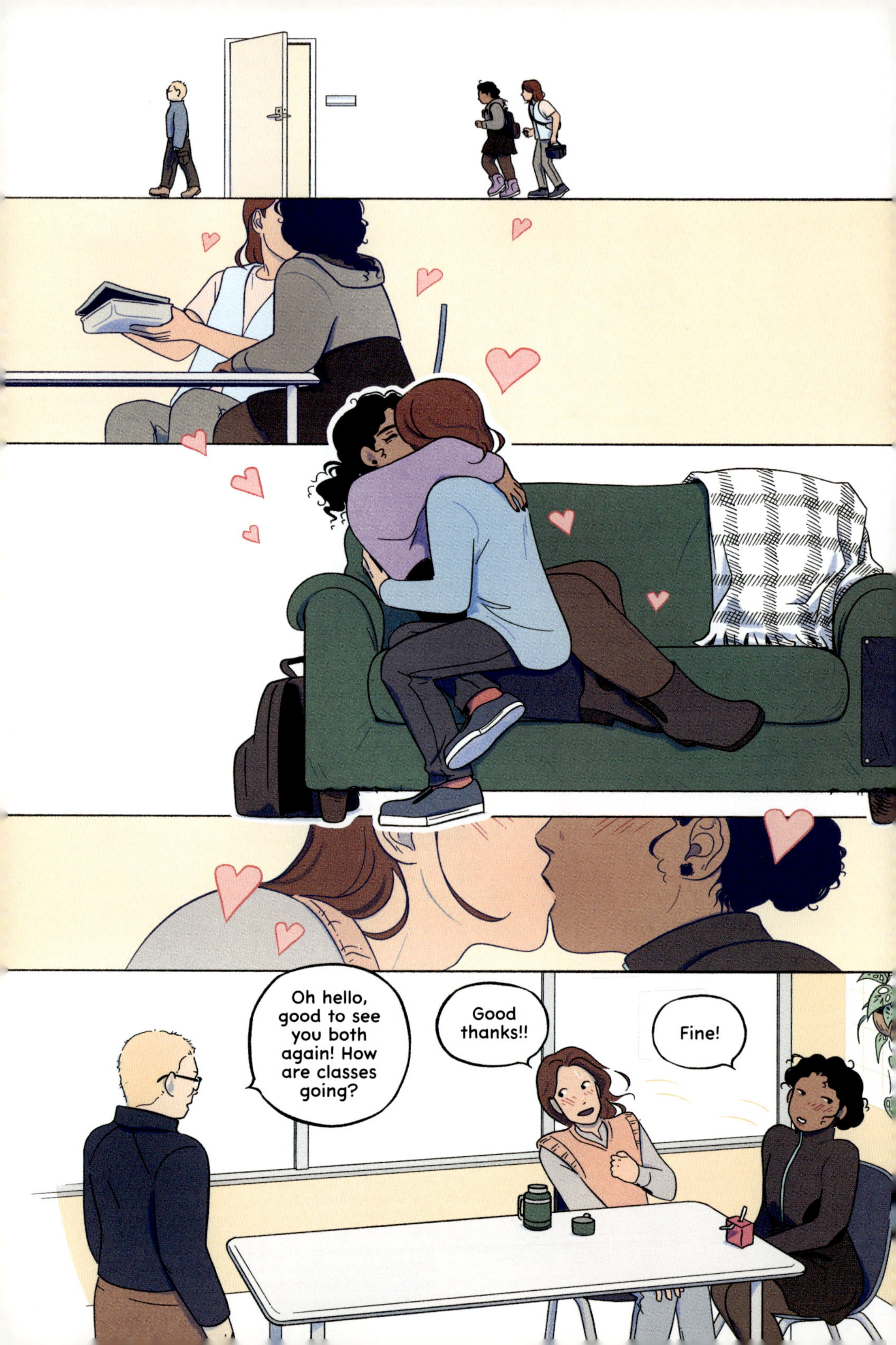
Oh hello, good to see you both again! How are classes going?
Good thanks!!
Fine!

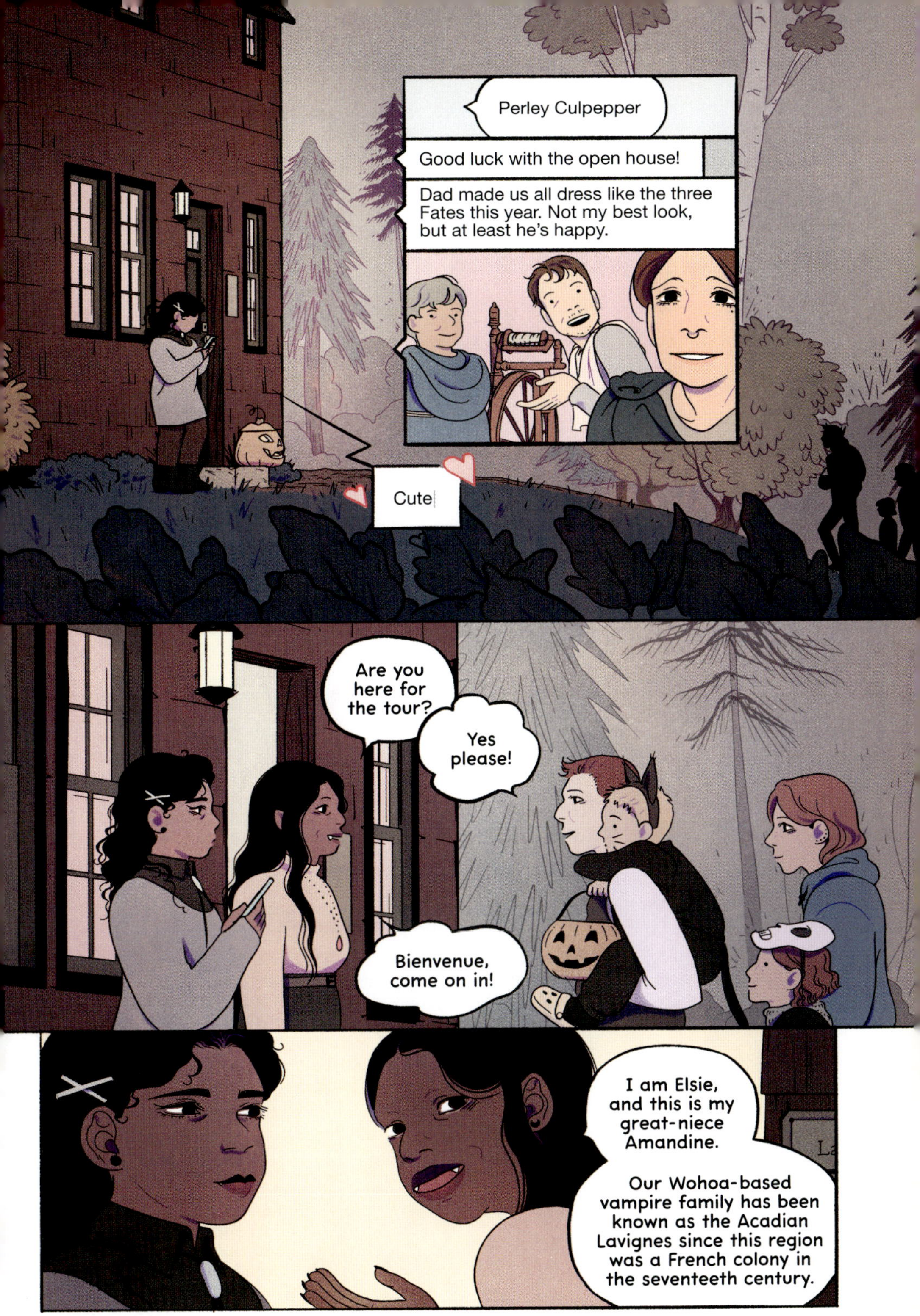
Perley Culpepper
Good luck with the open house!
Dad made us all dress like the three Fates this year. Not my best look, but at least he's happy.
Cute
Are you here for the tour?
Yes please!
Bienvenue, come on in!
I am Elsie, and this is my great-niece Amandine.
Our Wohoa-based vampire family has been known as the Acadian Lavignes since this region was a French colony in the seventeeth century.

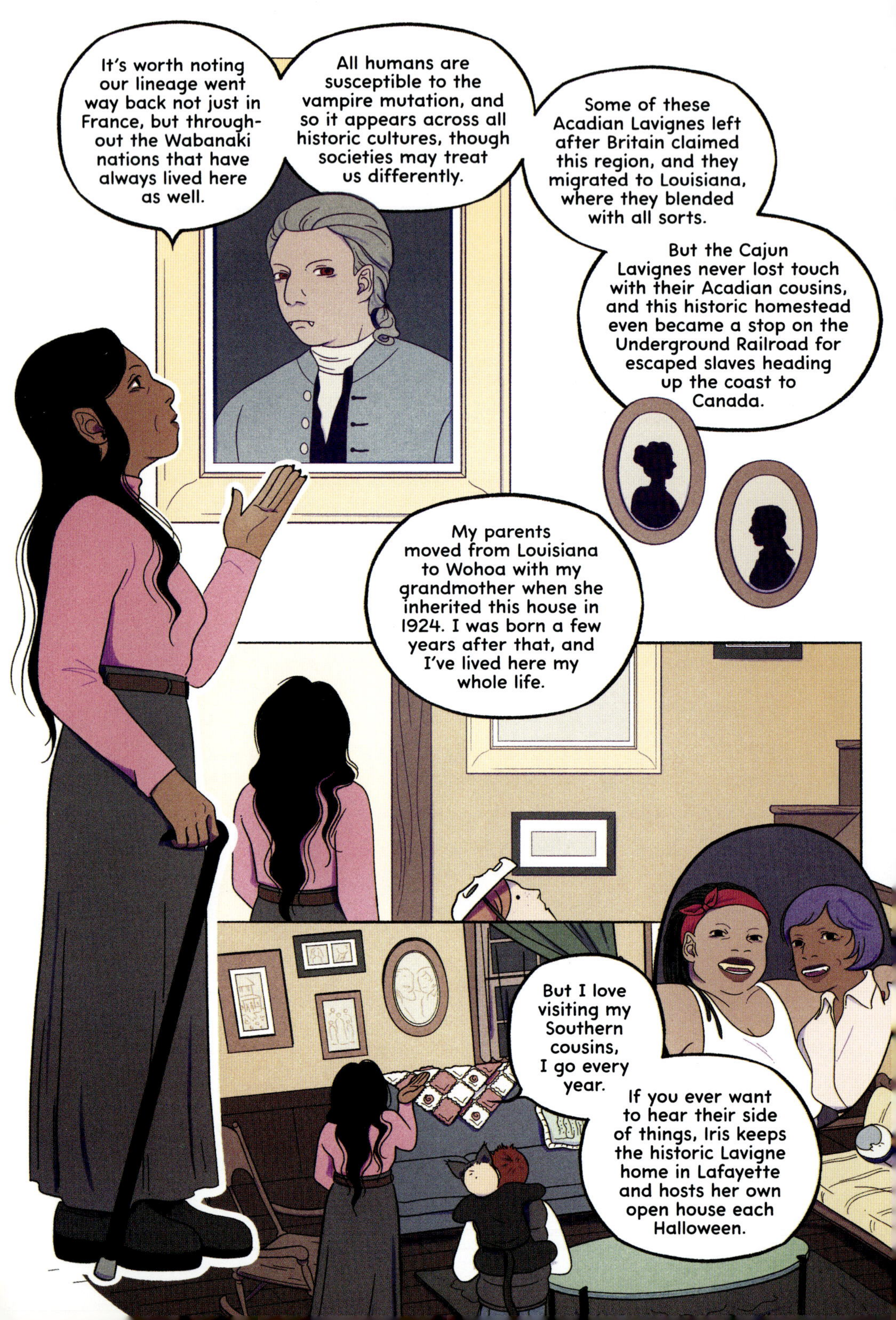
It's worth noting our lineage went way back not just in France, but throughout the Wabanaki nations that have always lived here as well.
All humans are susceptible to the vampire mutation, and so it appears across all historic cultures, though societies may treat us differently.
Some of these Acadian Lavignes left after Britain claimed this region, and they migrated to Louisiana, where they blended with all sorts.
But the Cajun Lavignes never lost touch with their Acadian cousins, and this historic homestead even became a stop on the Underground Railroad for escaped slaves heading up the coast to Canada.
My parents moved from Louisiana to Wohoa with my grandmother when she inherited this house in 1924. I was born a few years after that, and I've lived here my whole life.
But I love visiting my Southern cousins, I go every year.
If you ever want to hear their side of things, Iris keeps the historic Lavigne home in Lafayette and hosts her own open house each Halloween.

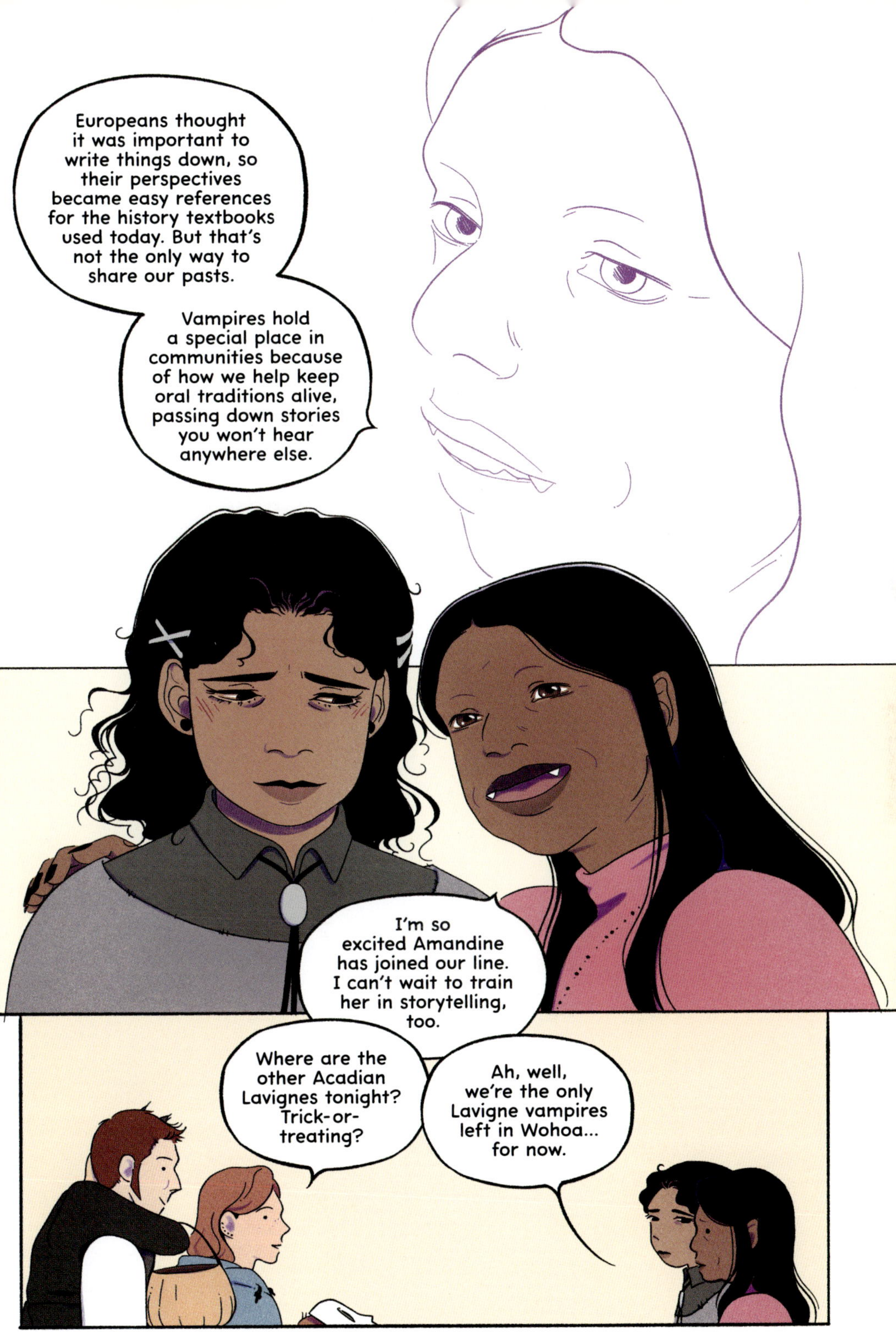
Europeans thought it was important to write things down, so their perspectives became easy references for the history textbooks used today. But that's not the only way to share our pasts.
Vampires hold a special place in communities because of how we help keep oral traditions alive, passing down stories you won't hear anywhere else.
I'm so excited Amandine has joined our line. I can't wait to train her in storytelling, too.
Where are the other Acadian Lavignes tonight? Trick-or-treating?
Ah, well, we're the only Lavigne vampires left in Wohoa... for now.

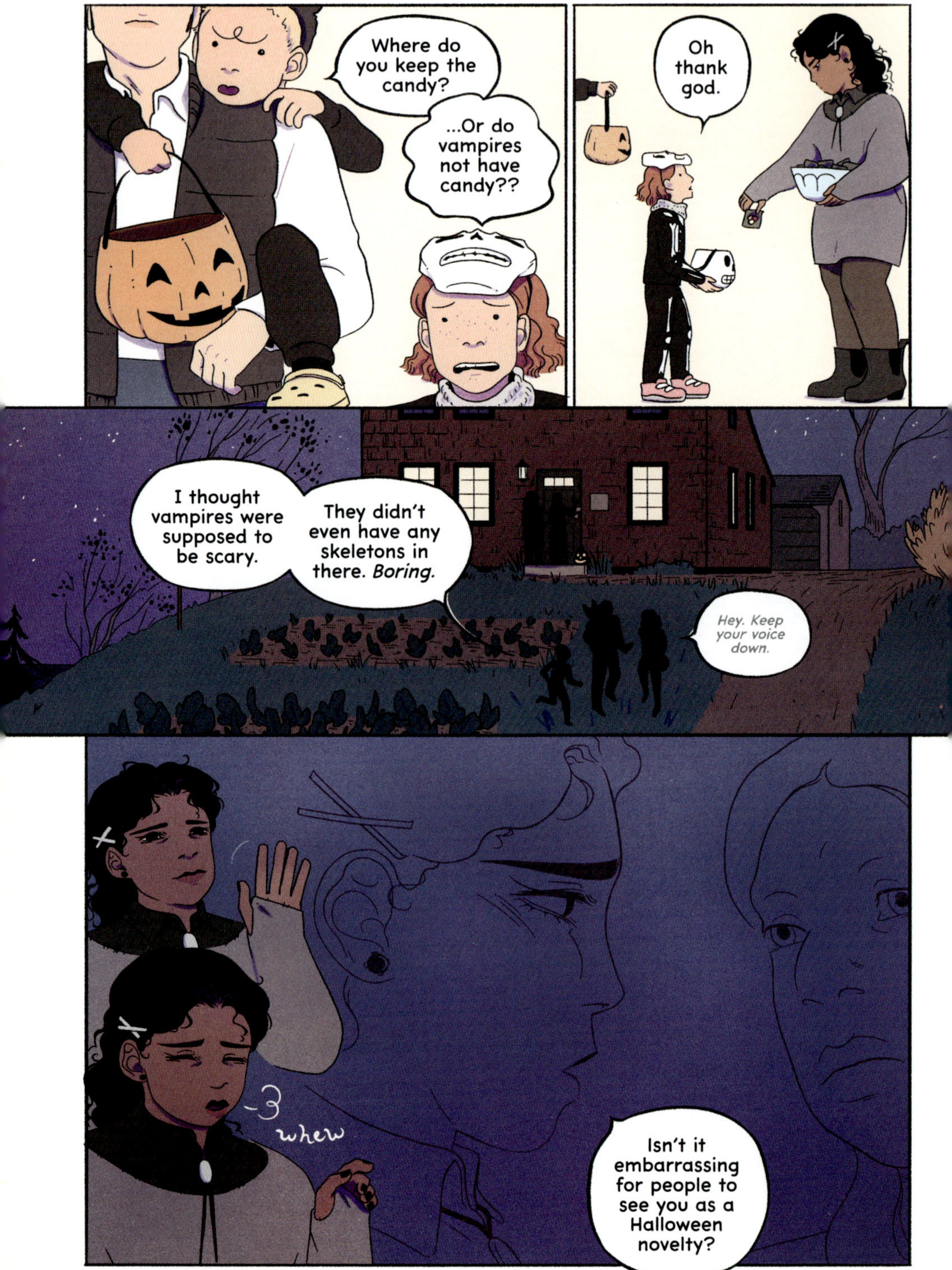
Where do you keep the candy?
...Or do vampires not have candy??
Oh thank god.
I thought vampires were supposed to be scary.
They didn't even have any skeletons in there. *Boring.*
Hey. Keep your voice down.
whew
Isn't it embarrassing for people to see you as a Halloween novelty?

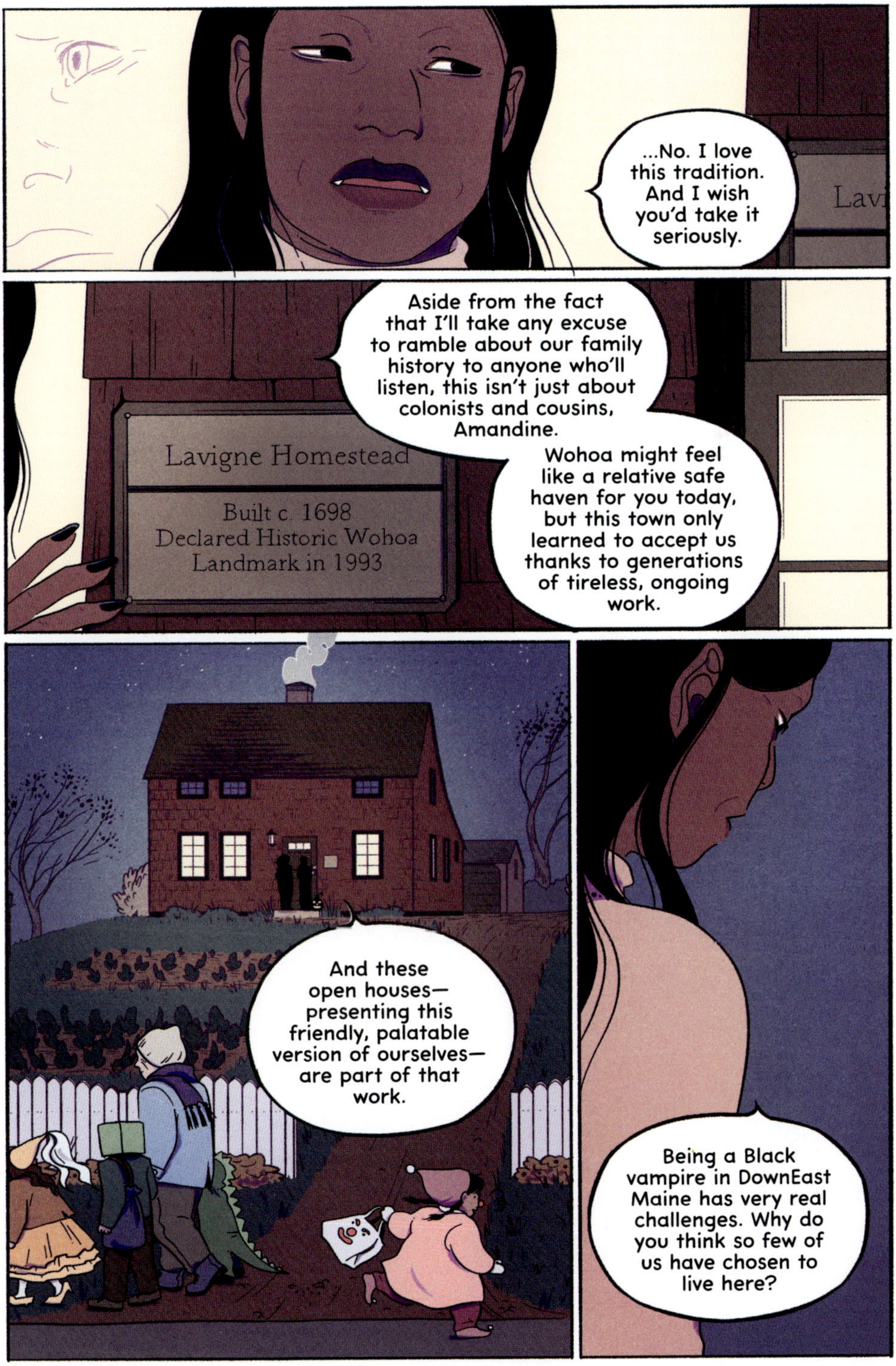
...No. I love this tradition. And I wish you'd take it seriously.
Lavi
Aside from the fact that I'll take any excuse to ramble about our family history to anyone who'll listen, this isn't just about colonists and cousins, Amandine.
Lavigne Homestead
Built c. 1698
Declared Historic Wohoa Landmark in 1993
Wohoa might feel like a relative safe haven for you today, but this town only learned to accept us thanks to generations of tireless, ongoing work.
And these open houses—presenting this friendly, palatable version of ourselves—are part of that work.
Being a Black vampire in DownEast Maine has very real challenges. Why do you think so few of us have chosen to live here?

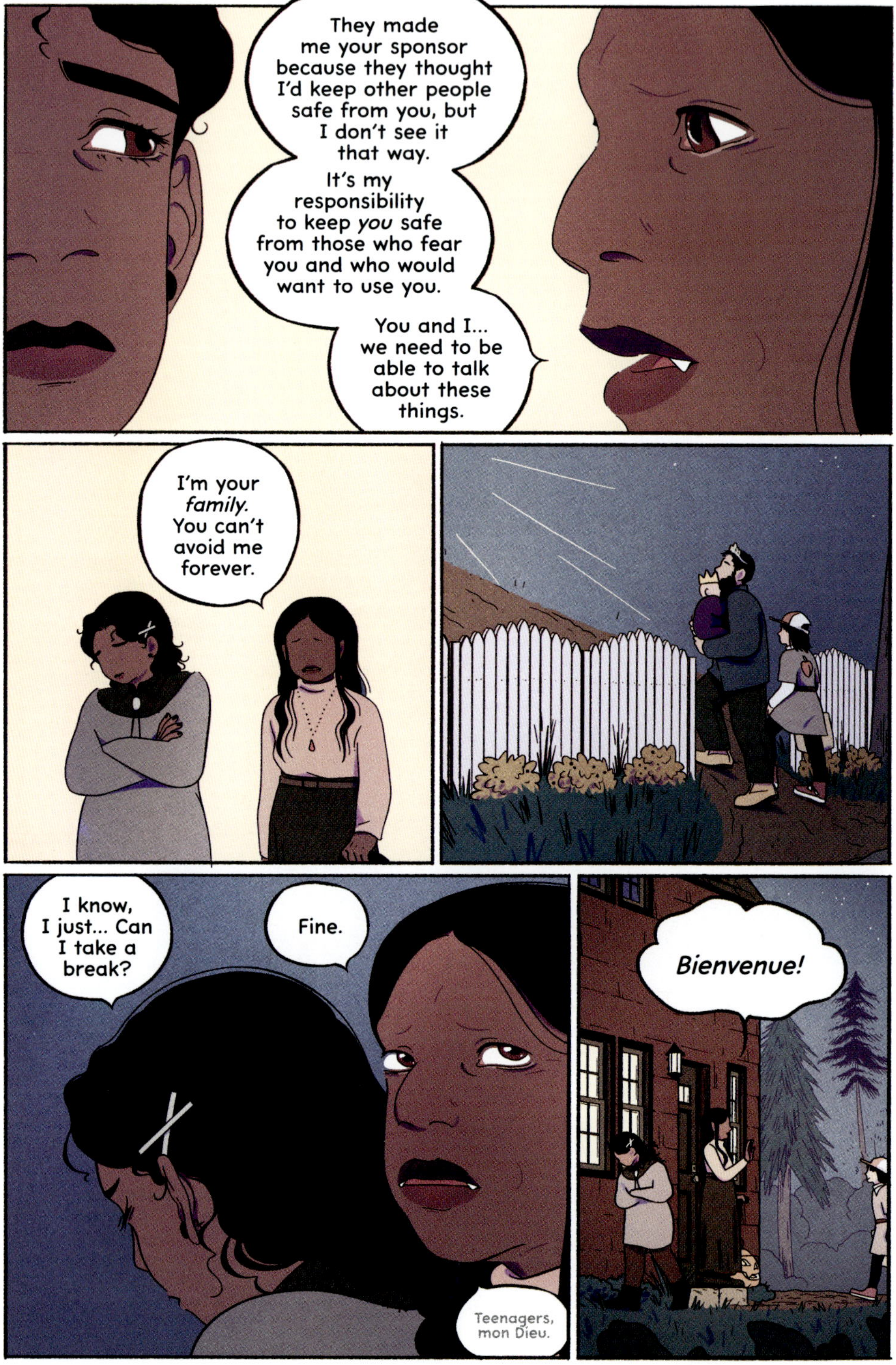
They made me your sponsor because they thought I'd keep other people safe from you, but I don't see it that way.
It's my responsibility to keep *you* safe from those who fear you and who would want to use you.
You and I... we need to be able to talk about these things.
I'm your *family.* You can't avoid me forever.
I know, I just... Can I take a break?
Fine.
Teenagers, mon Dieu.
Bienvenue!

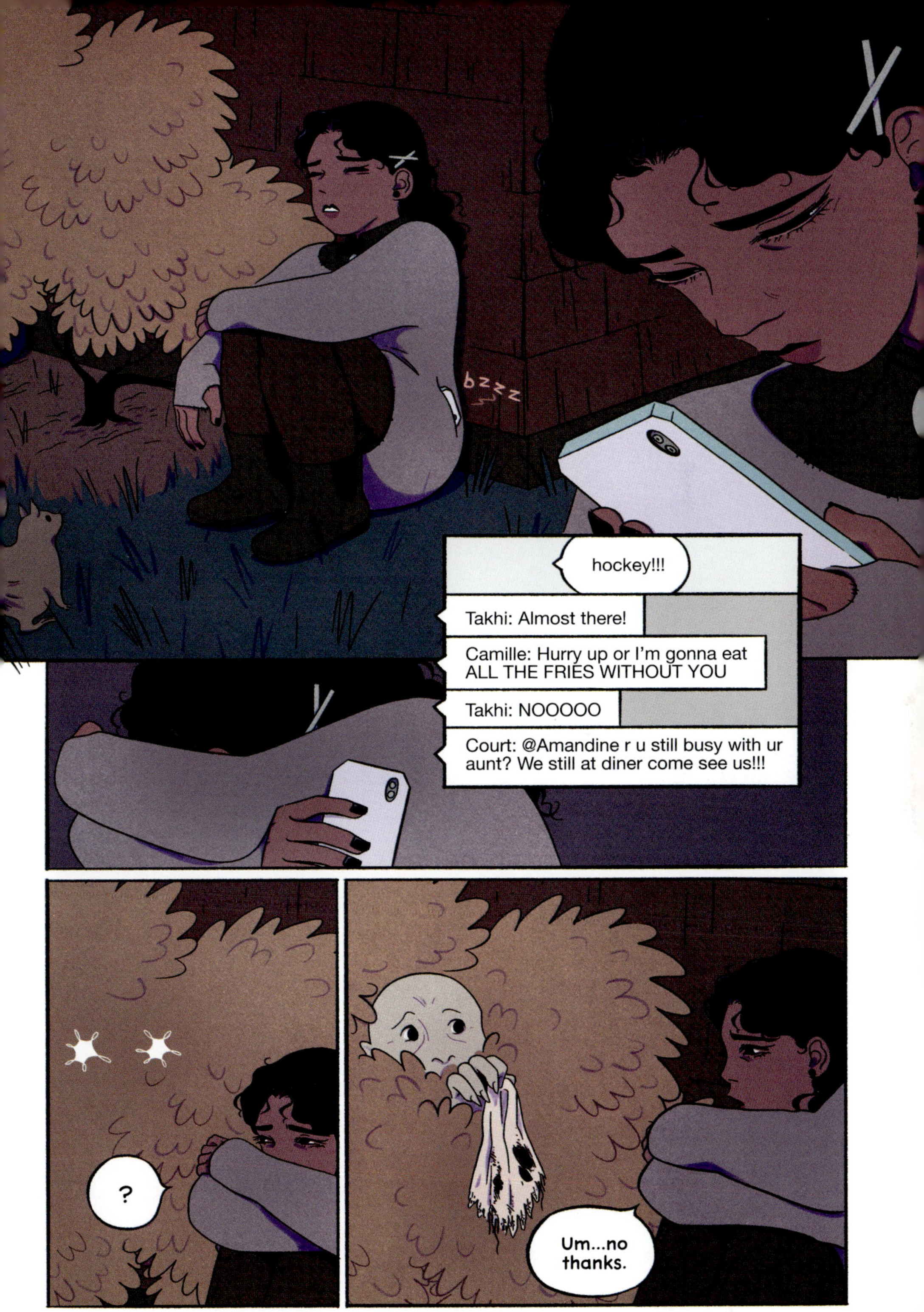
bzzz
hockey!!!
Takhi: Almost there!
Camille: Hurry up or I'm gonna eat ALL THE FRIES WITHOUT YOU
Takhi: NOOOOO
Court: @Amandine r u still busy with ur aunt? We still at diner come see us!!!
?
Um...no thanks.

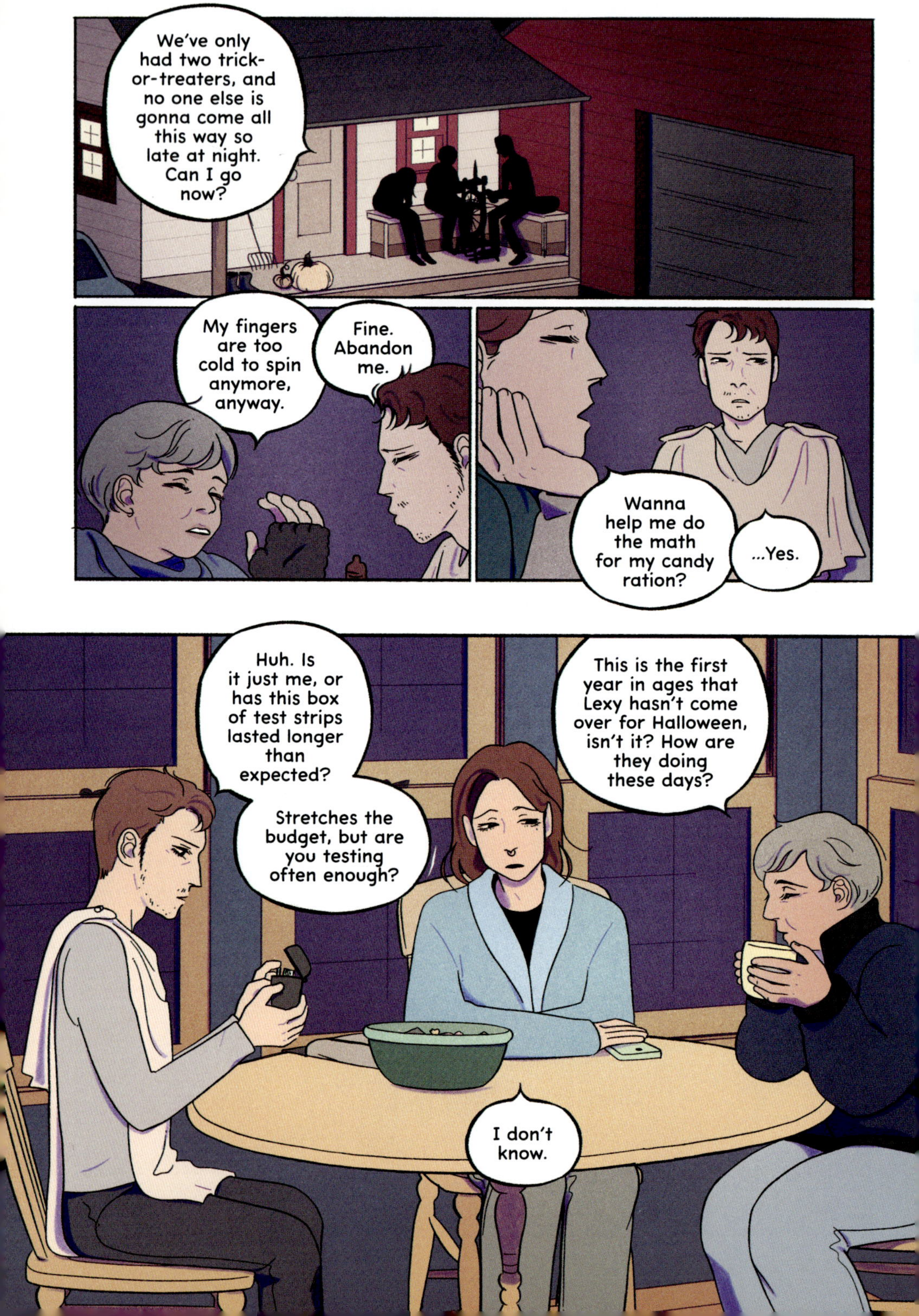
We've only had two trick-or-treaters, and no one else is gonna come all this way so late at night. Can I go now?
My fingers are too cold to spin anymore, anyway.
Fine. Abandon me.
Wanna help me do the math for my candy ration?
...Yes.
Huh. Is it just me, or has this box of test strips lasted longer than expected?
Stretches the budget, but are you testing often enough?
This is the first year in ages that Lexy hasn't come over for Halloween, isn't it? How are they doing these days?
I don't know.

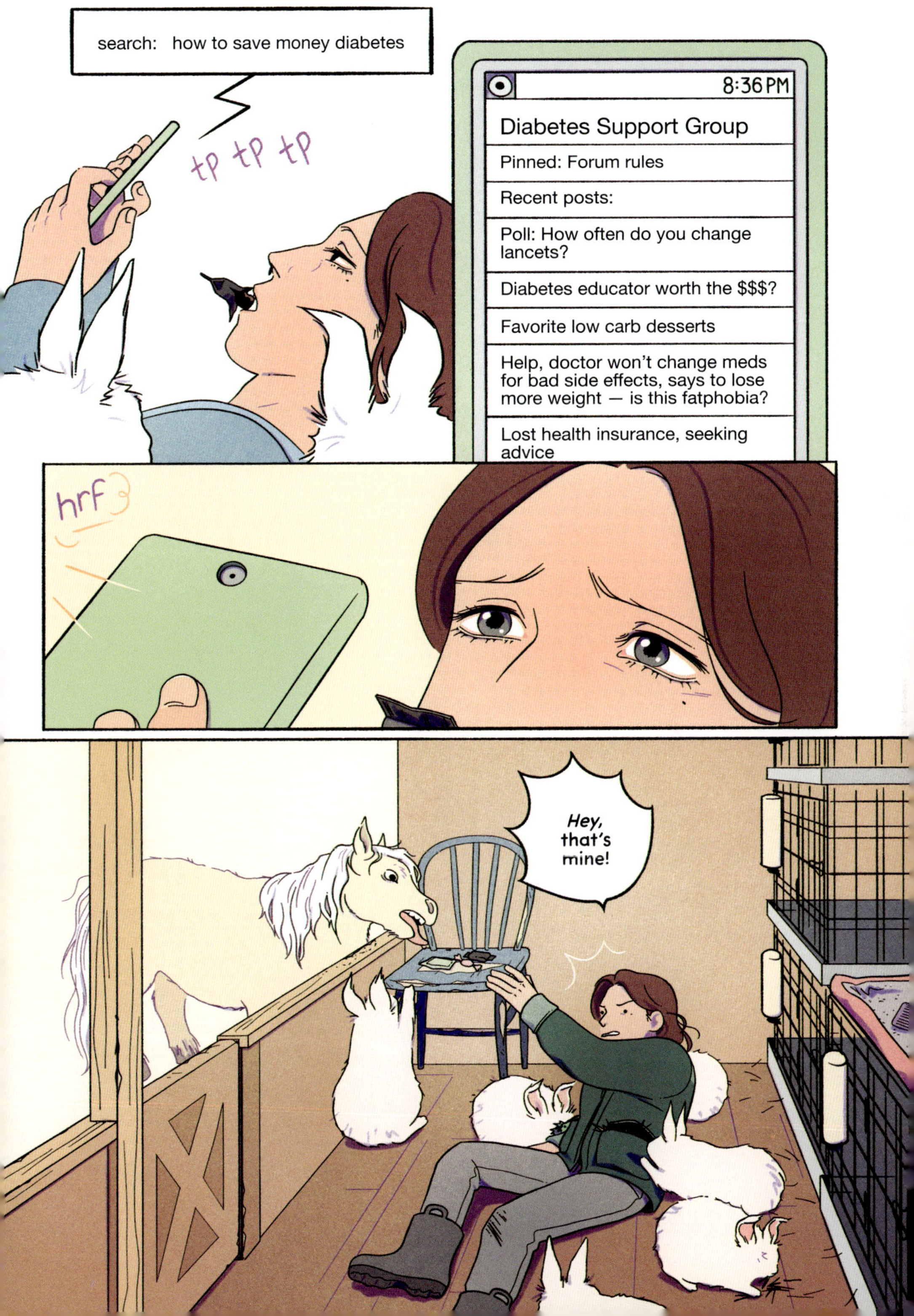
search: how to save money diabetes
tp tp tp
8:36 PM
Diabetes Support Group
Pinned: Forum rules
Recent posts:
Poll: How often do you change lancets?
Diabetes educator worth the $$$?
Favorite low carb desserts
Help, doctor won't change meds for bad side effects, says to lose more weight — is this fatphobia?
Lost health insurance, seeking advice
hrf
Hey, that's mine!

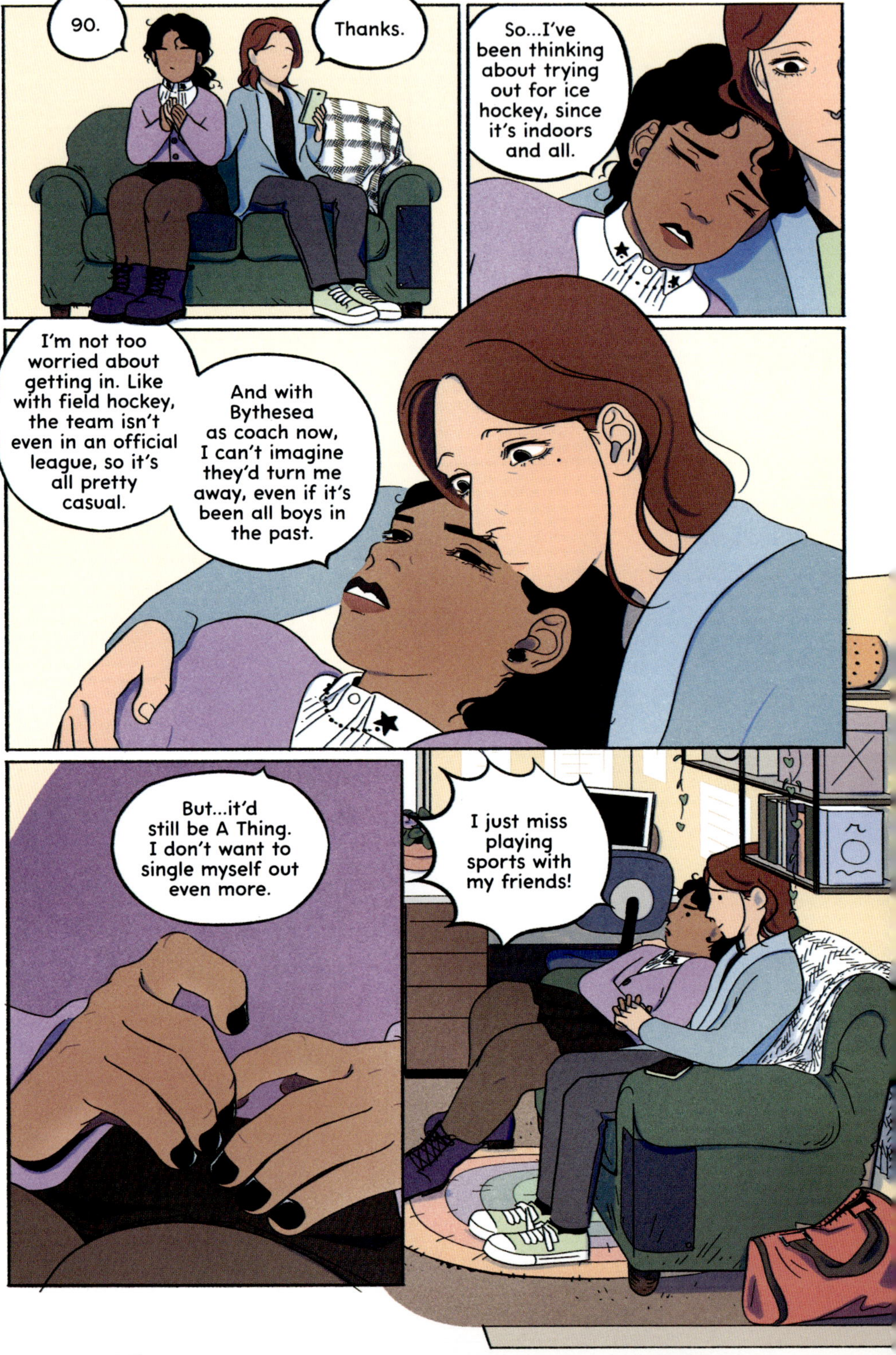
90.
Thanks.
So...I've been thinking about trying out for ice hockey, since it's indoors and all.
I'm not too worried about getting in. Like with field hockey, the team isn't even in an official league, so it's all pretty casual.
And with Bythesea as coach now, I can't imagine they'd turn me away, even if it's been all boys in the past.
But...it'd still be A Thing. I don't want to single myself out even more.
I just miss playing sports with my friends!

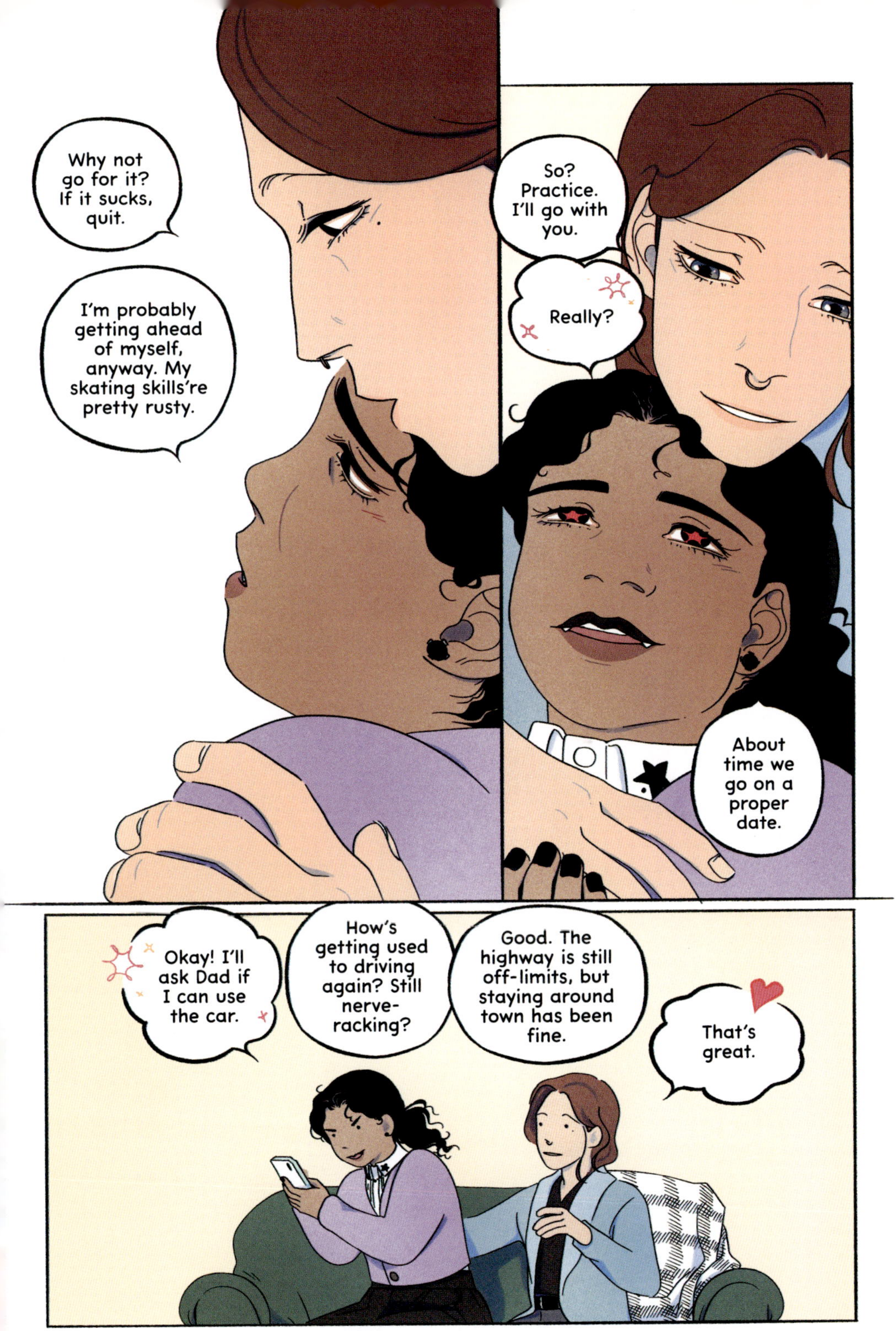
Why not go for it? If it sucks, quit.
I'm probably getting ahead of myself, anyway. My skating skills're pretty rusty.
So? Practice. I'll go with you.
Really?
About time we go on a proper date.
Okay! I'll ask Dad if I can use the car.
How's getting used to driving again? Still nerve-racking?
Good. The highway is still off-limits, but staying around town has been fine.
That's great.

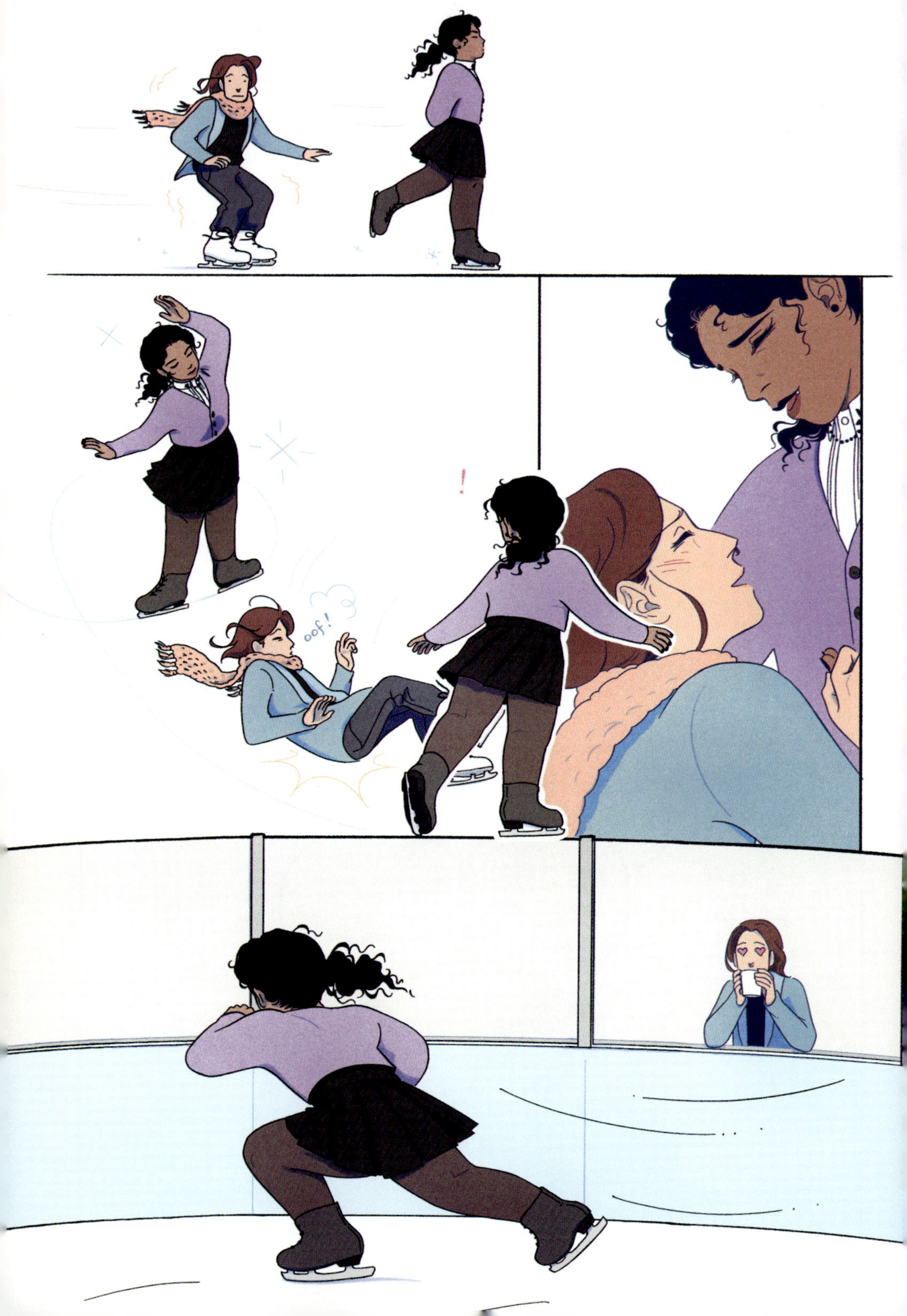
!
oof!

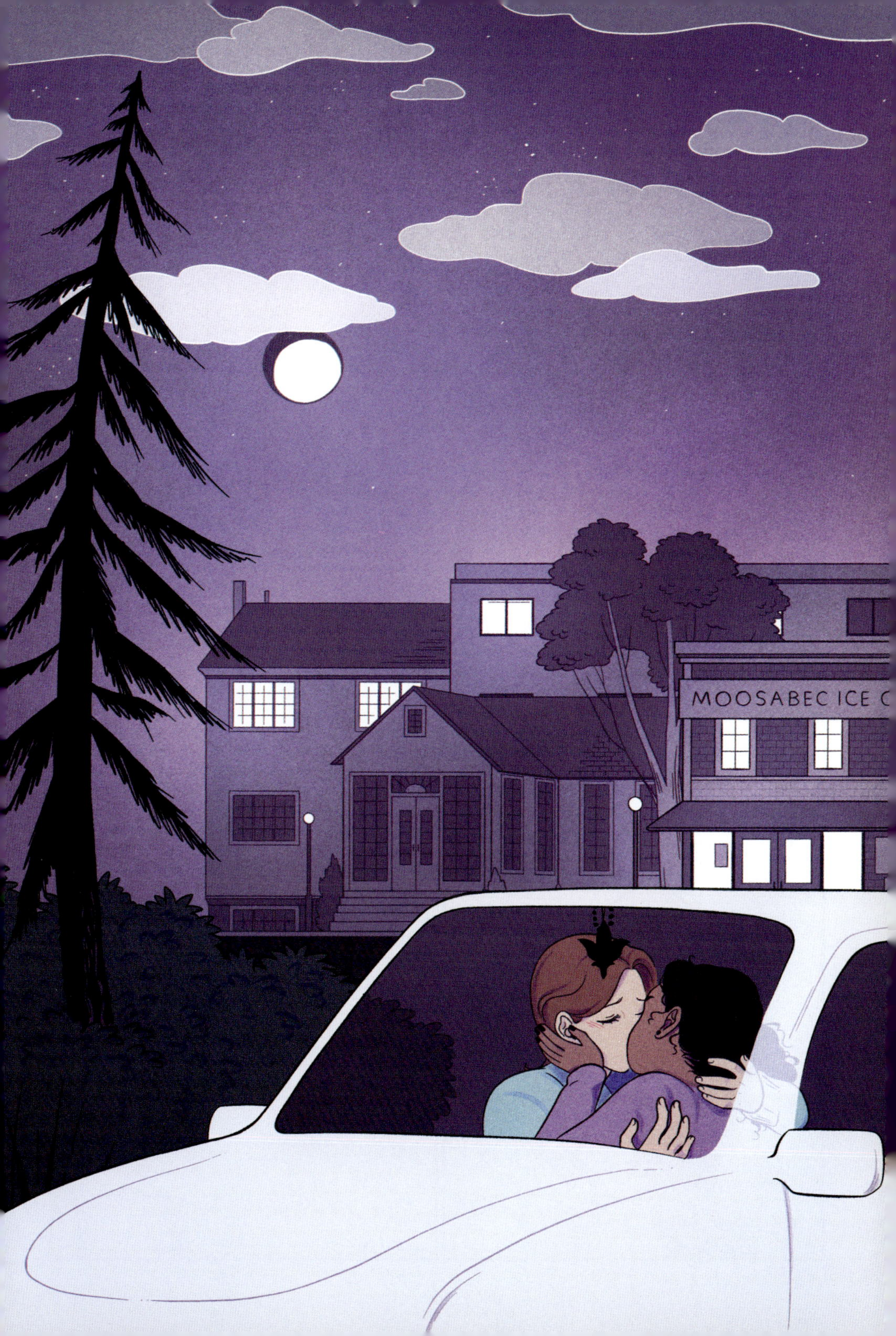
MOOSABEC ICE C

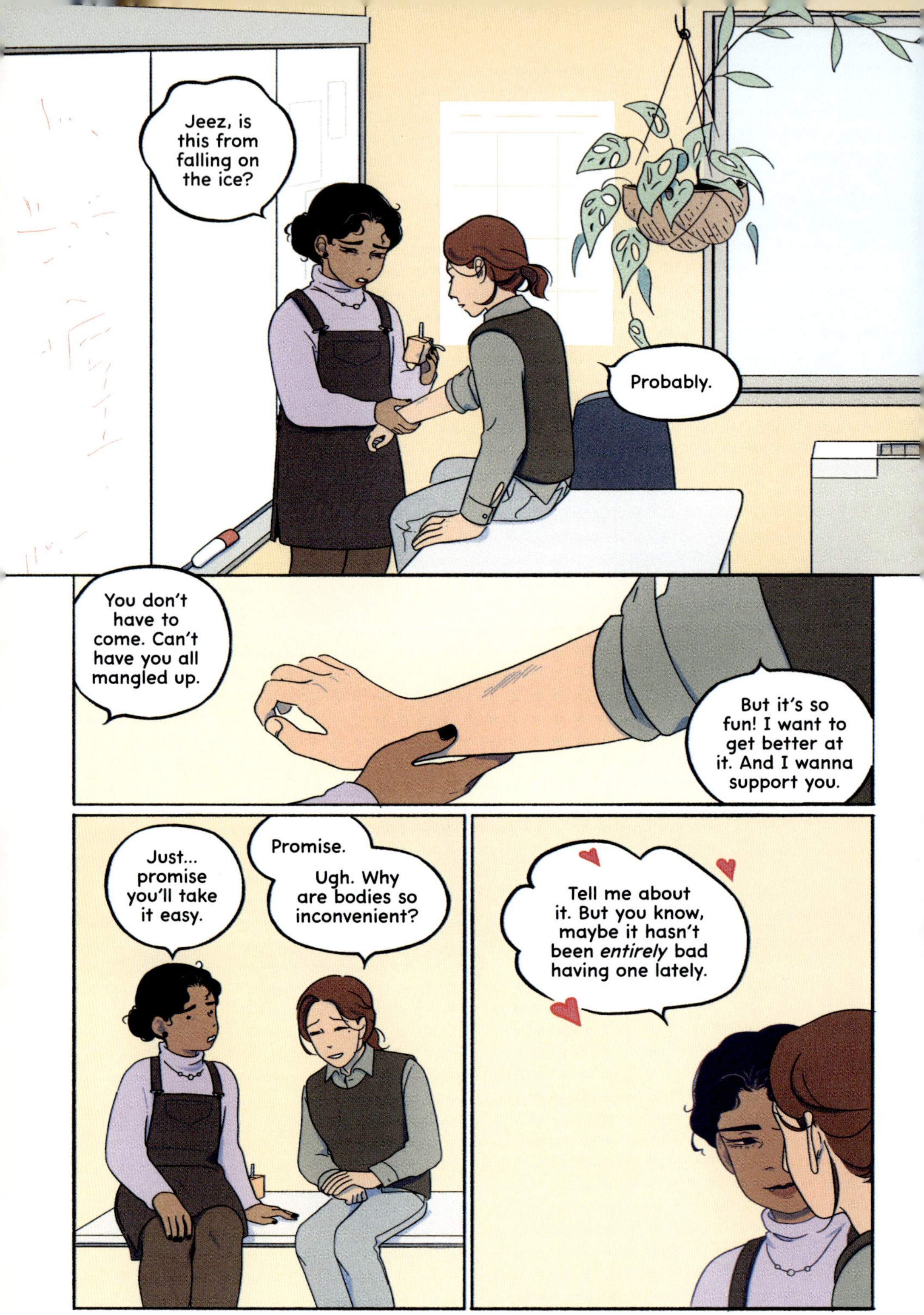
Jeez, is this from falling on the ice?
Probably.
You don't have to come. Can't have you all mangled up.
But it's so fun! I want to get better at it. And I wanna support you.
Just... promise you'll take it easy.
Promise.
Ugh. Why are bodies so inconvenient?
Tell me about it. But you know, maybe it hasn't been *entirely* bad having one lately.

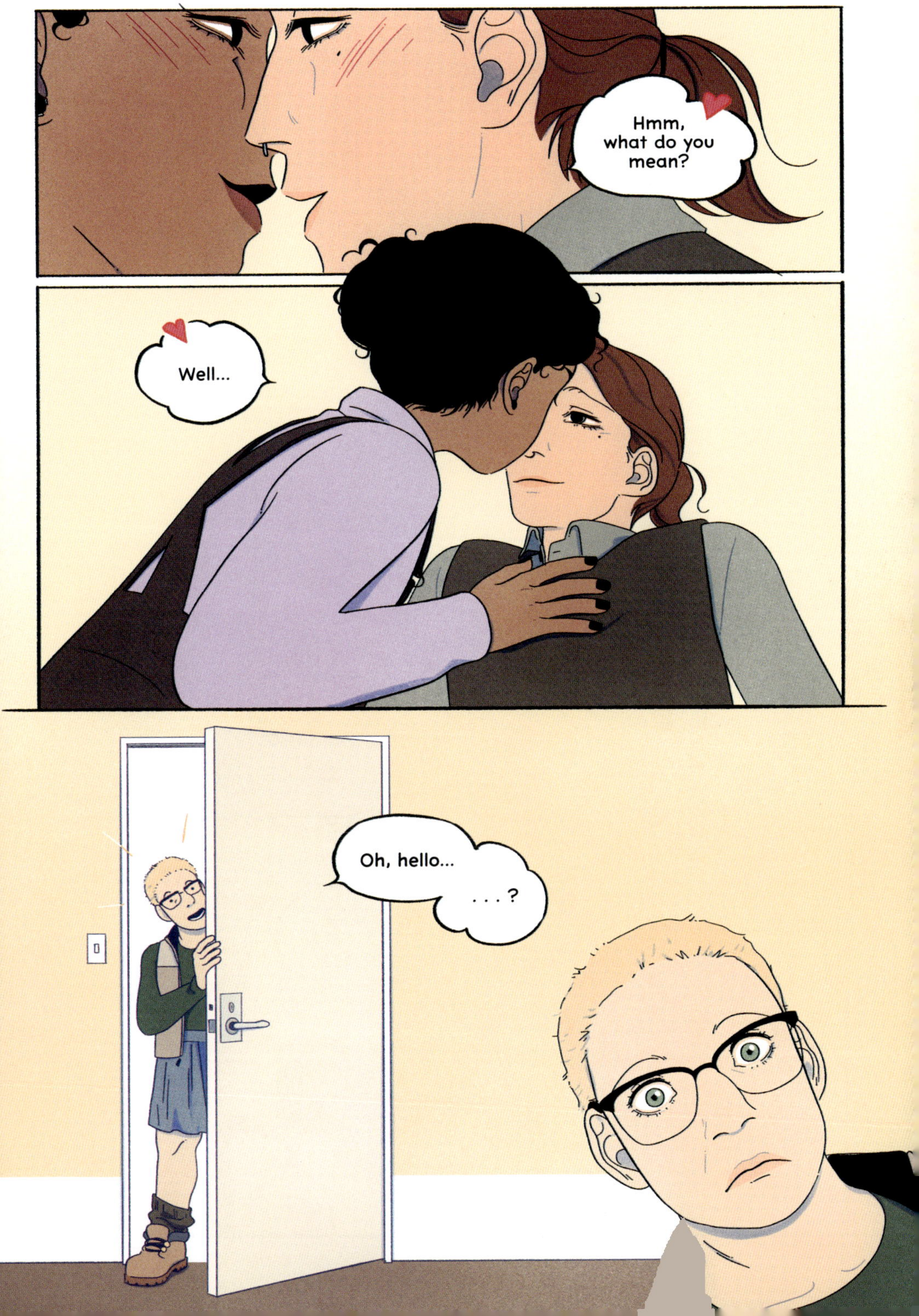
Hmm, what do you mean?
Well...
Oh, hello...
. . . ?

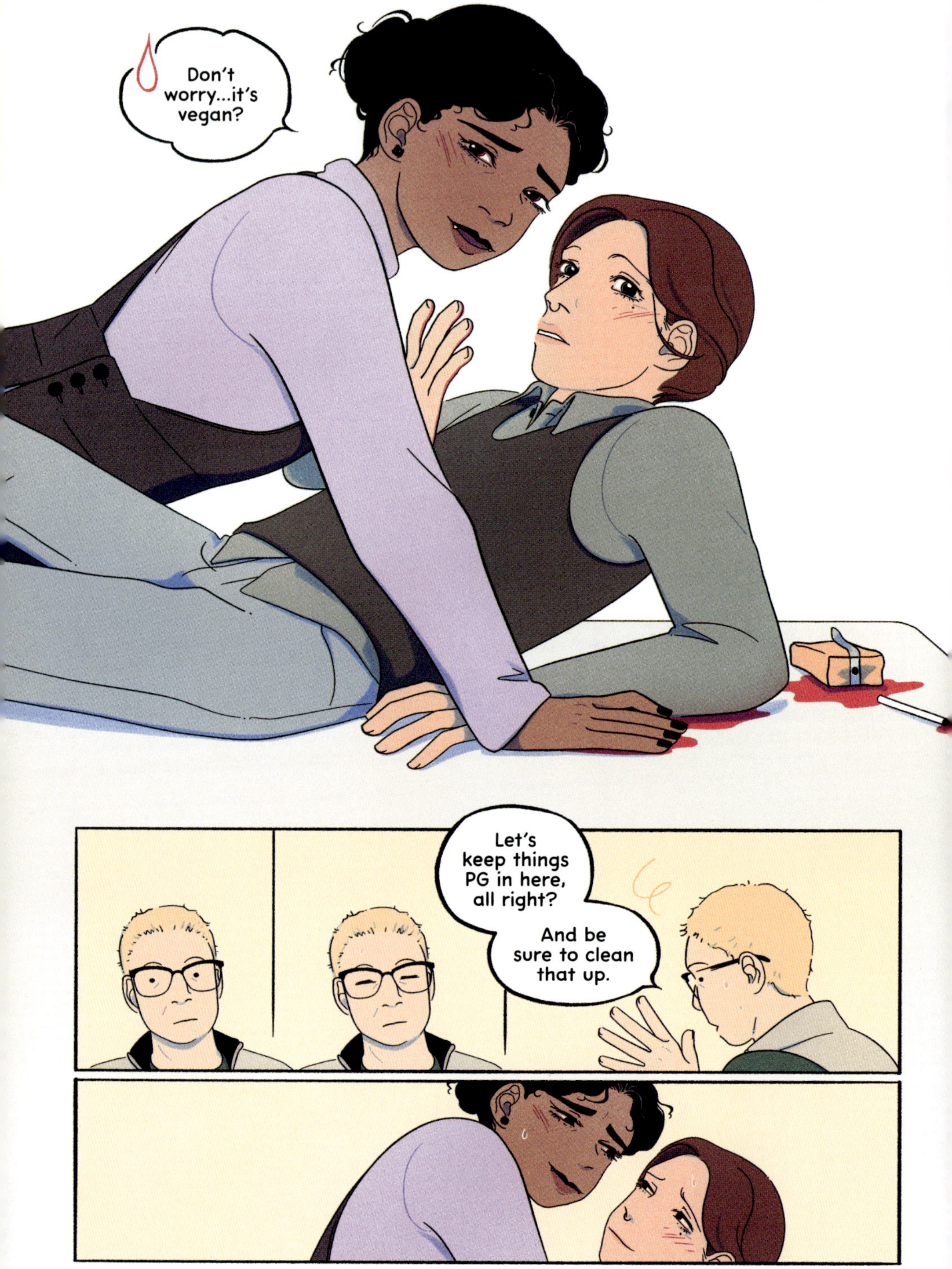
Don't worry...it's vegan?
Let's keep things PG in here, all right?
And be sure to clean that up.

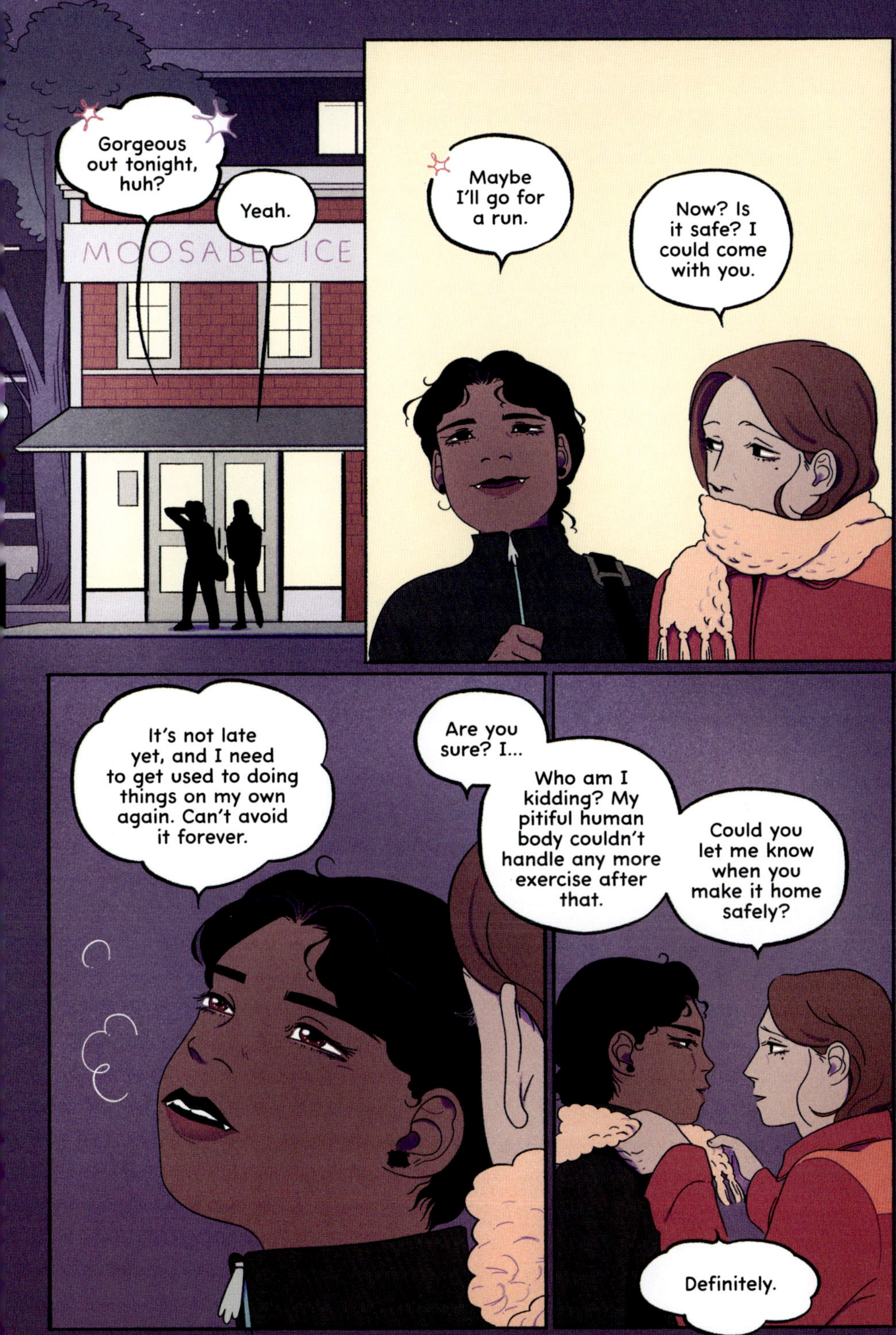
MOOSABEC ICE
Gorgeous out tonight, huh?
Yeah.
Maybe I'll go for a run.
Now? Is it safe? I could come with you.
It's not late yet, and I need to get used to doing things on my own again. Can't avoid it forever.
Are you sure? I...
Who am I kidding? My pitiful human body couldn't handle any more exercise after that.
Could you let me know when you make it home safely?
Definitely.

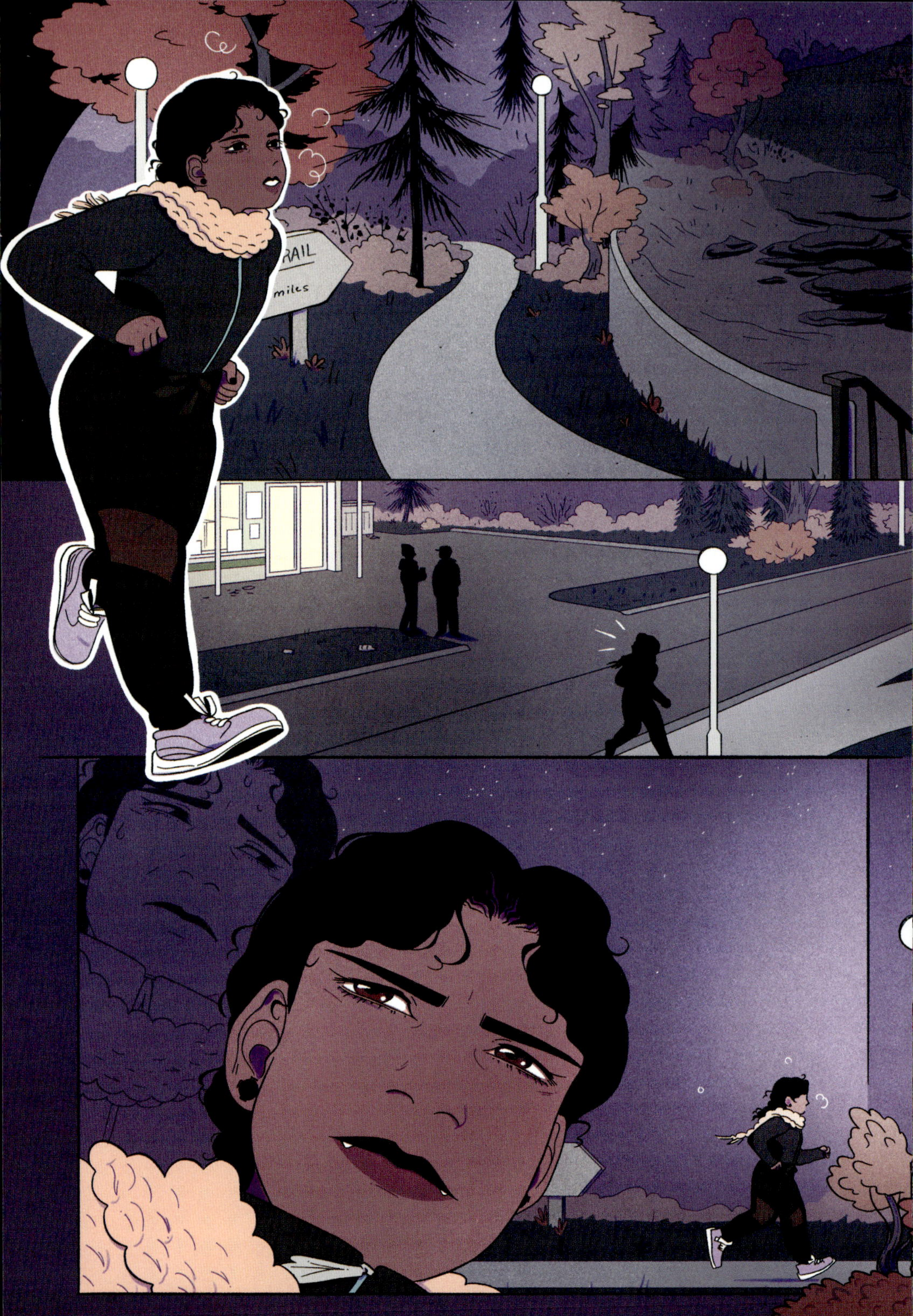
RAIL
miles

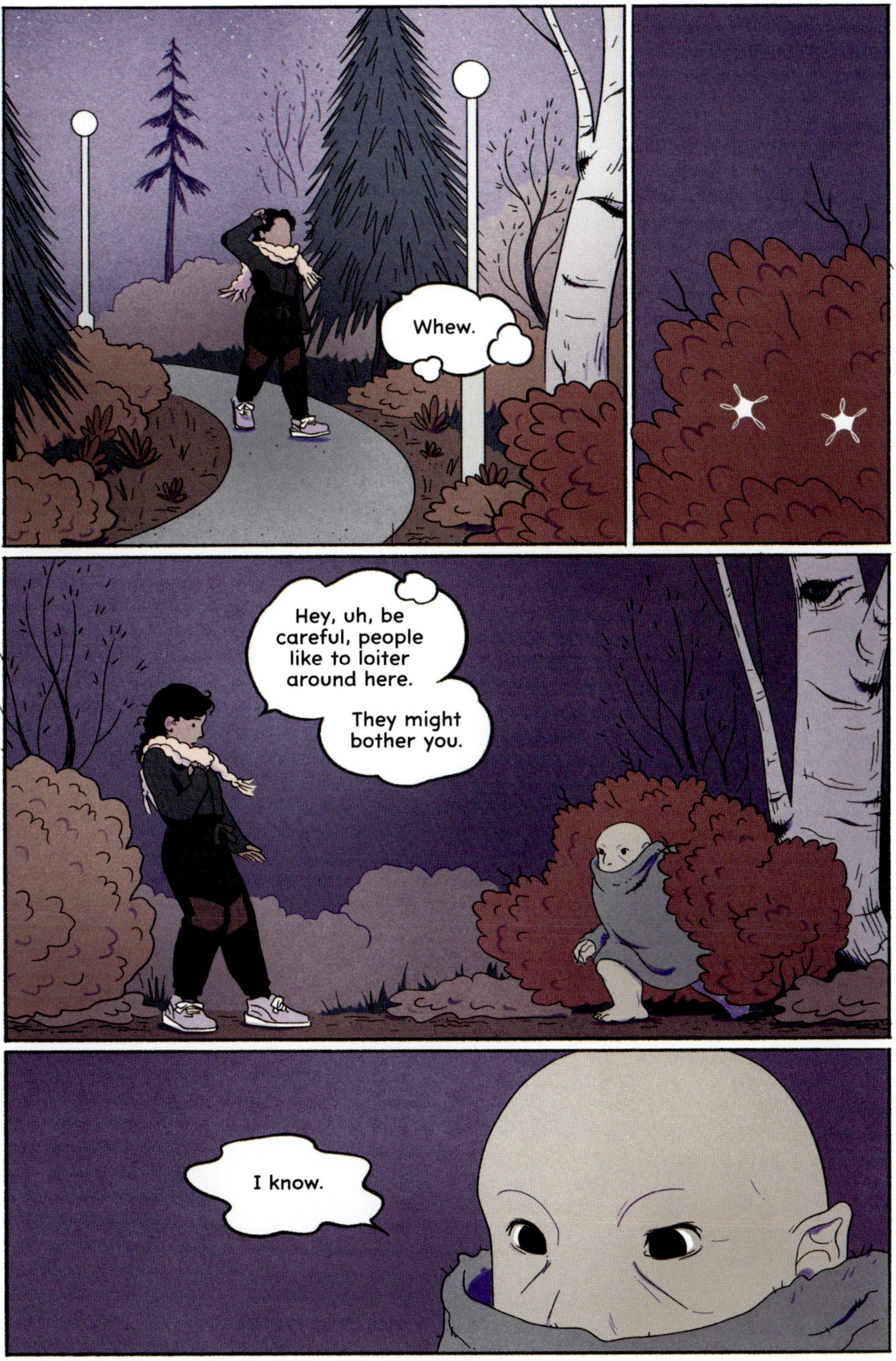
Whew.
Hey, uh, be careful, people like to loiter around here.
They might bother you.
I know.

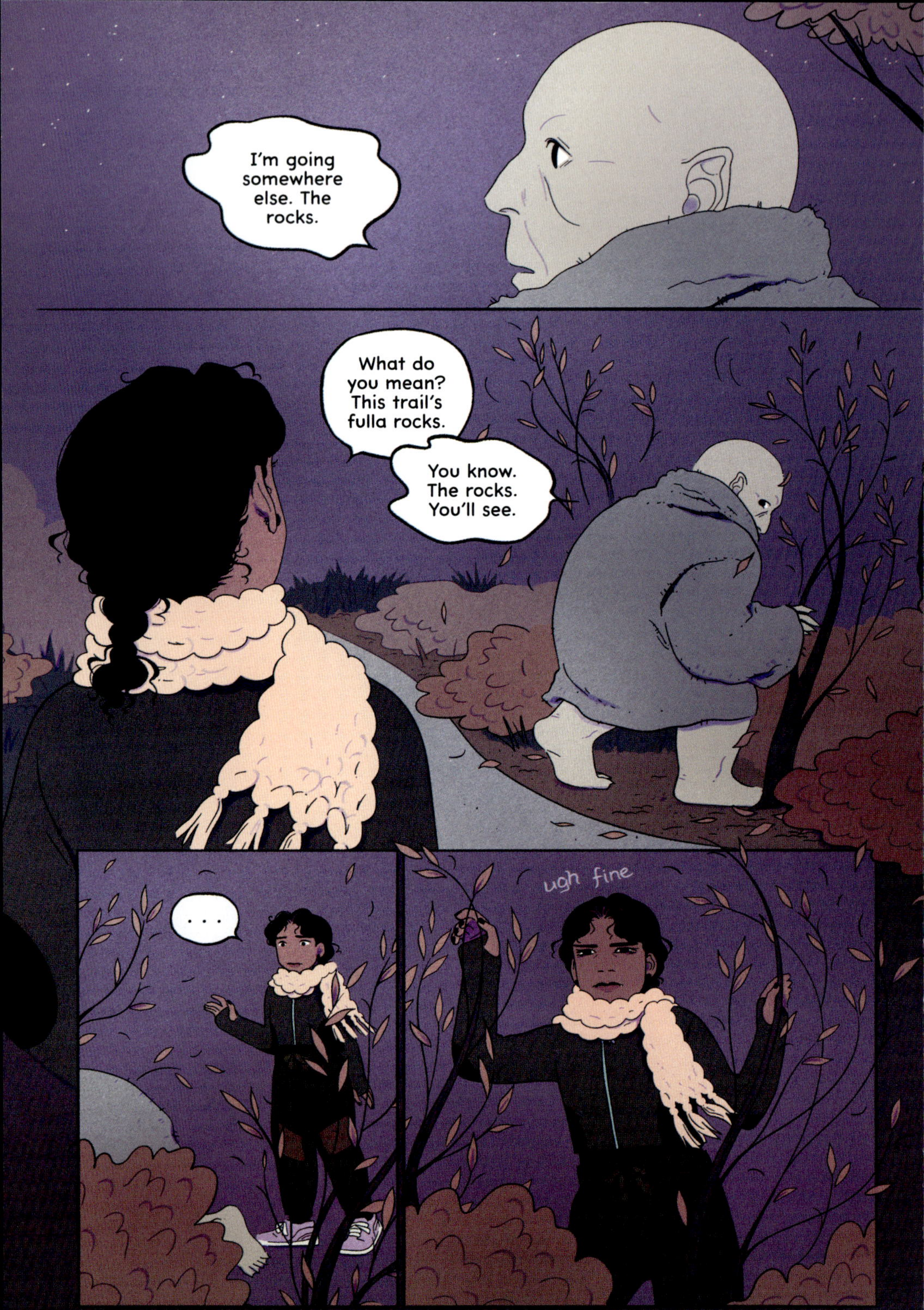

I'm going somewhere else. The rocks.
What do you mean? This trail's fulla rocks.
You know. The rocks. You'll see.
. . .
ugh fine

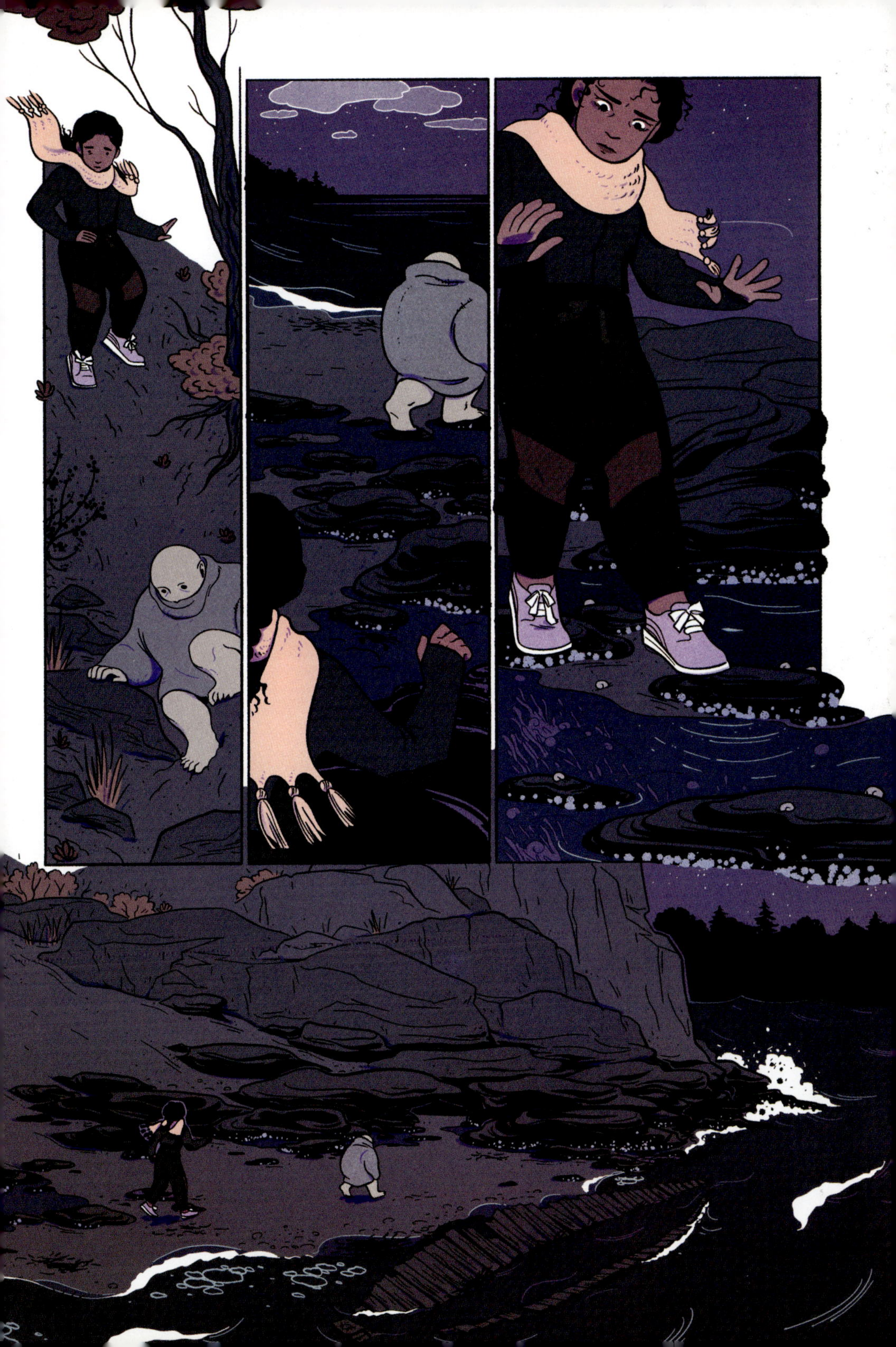

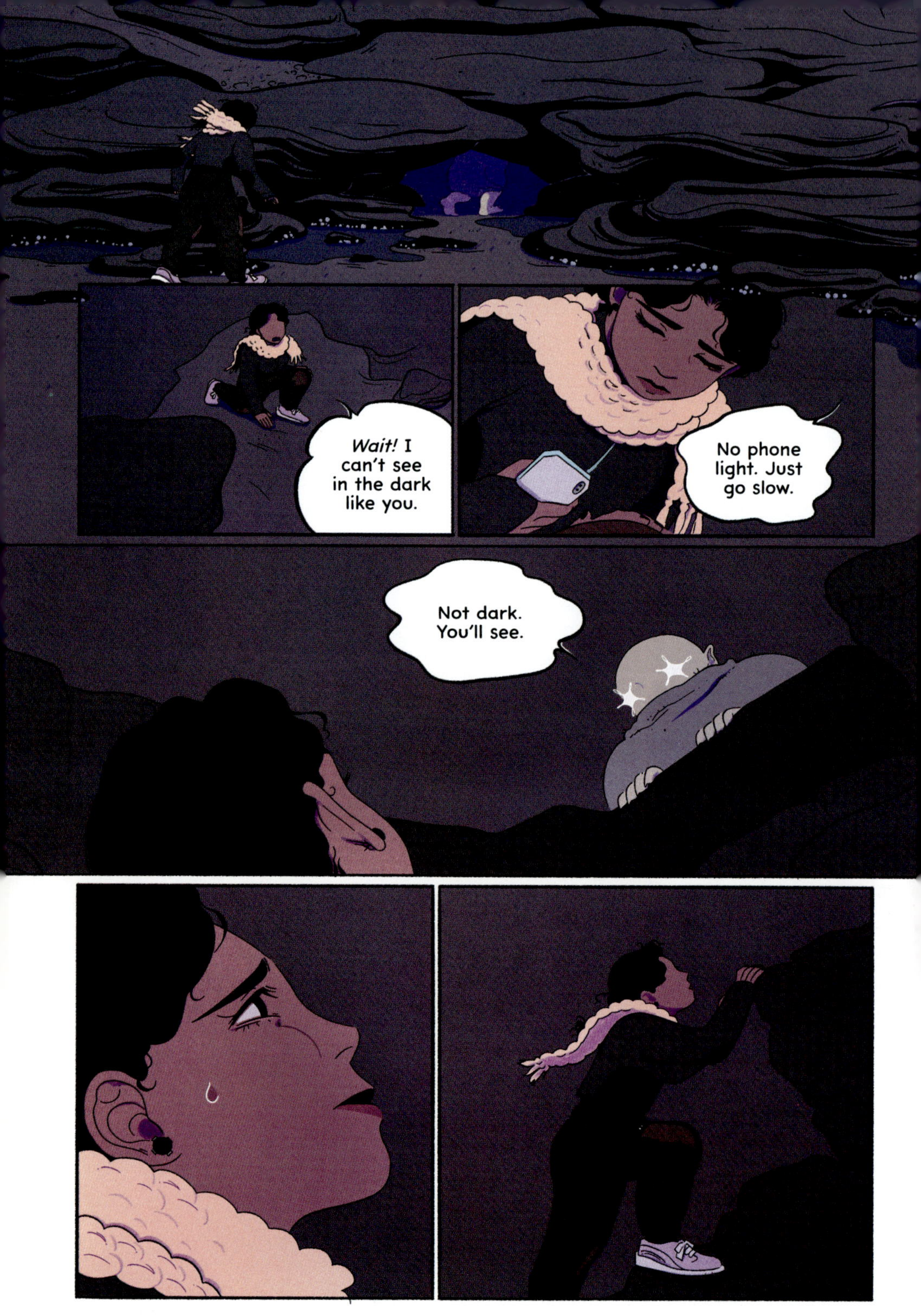

Wait! I can't see in the dark like you.
No phone light. Just go slow.
Not dark. You'll see.

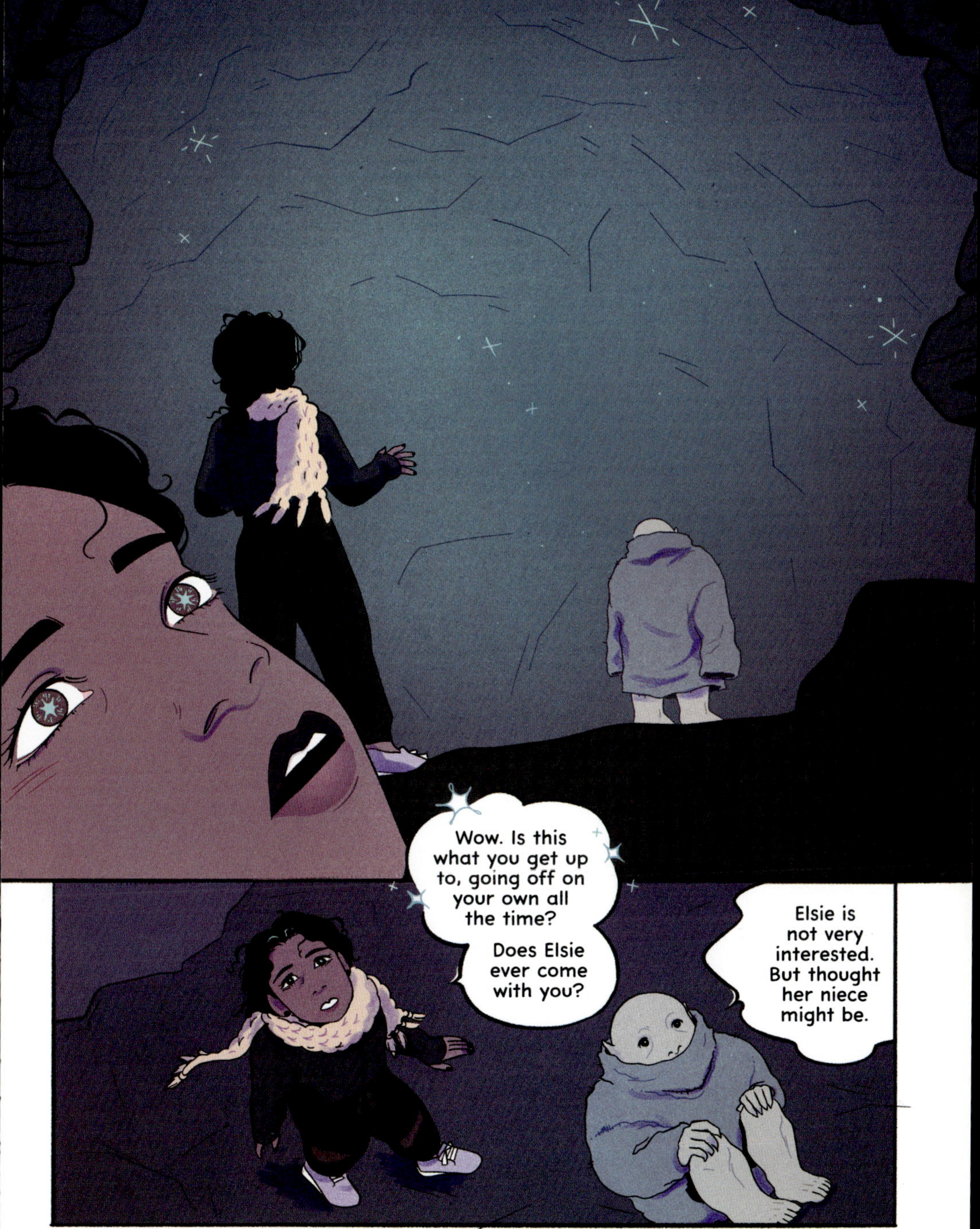
Wow. Is this what you get up to, going off on your own all the time?
Does Elsie ever come with you?
Elsie is not very interested. But thought her niece might be.

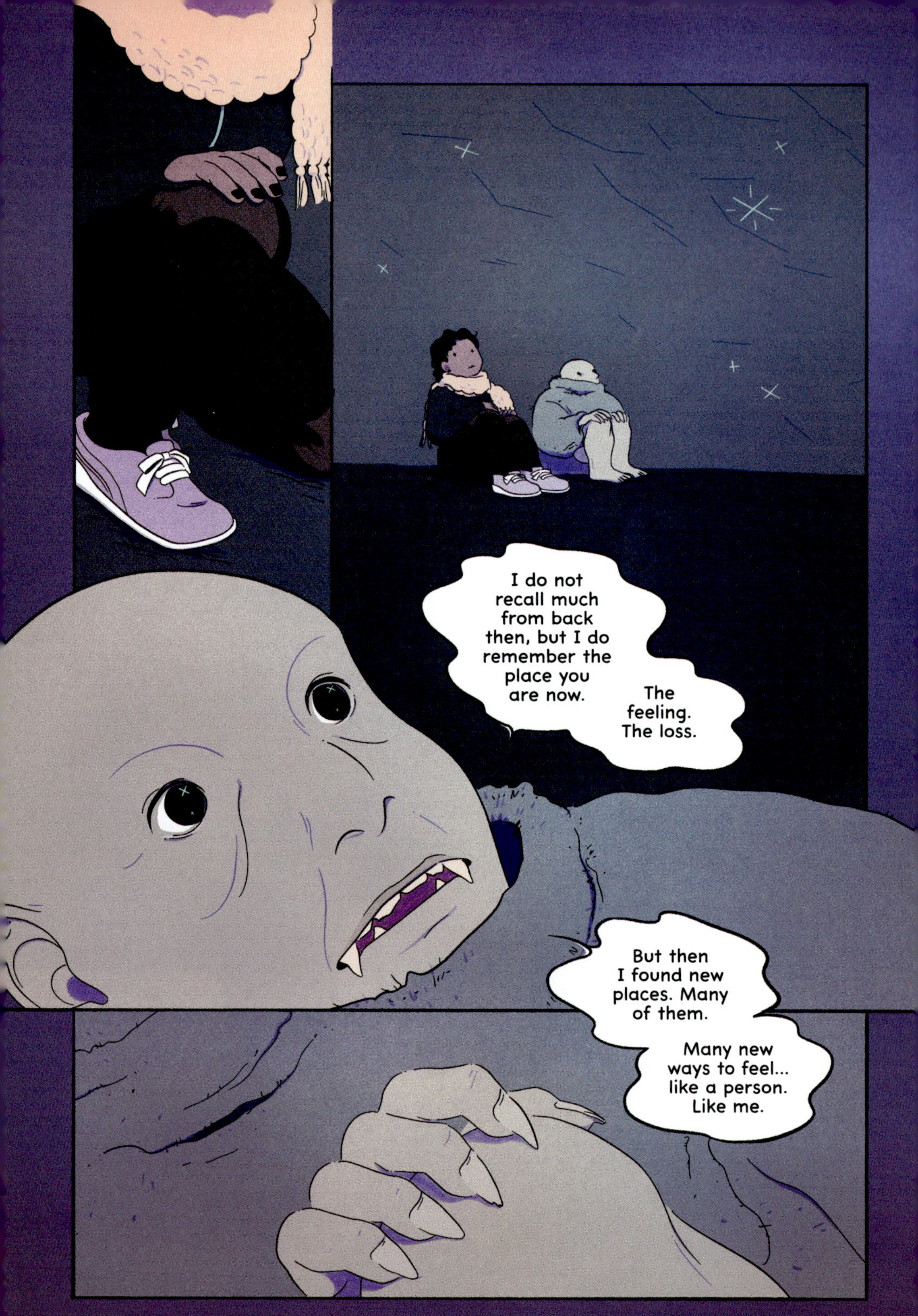
I do not recall much from back then, but I do remember the place you are now.
The feeling. The loss.
But then I found new places. Many of them.
Many new ways to feel... like a person. Like me.

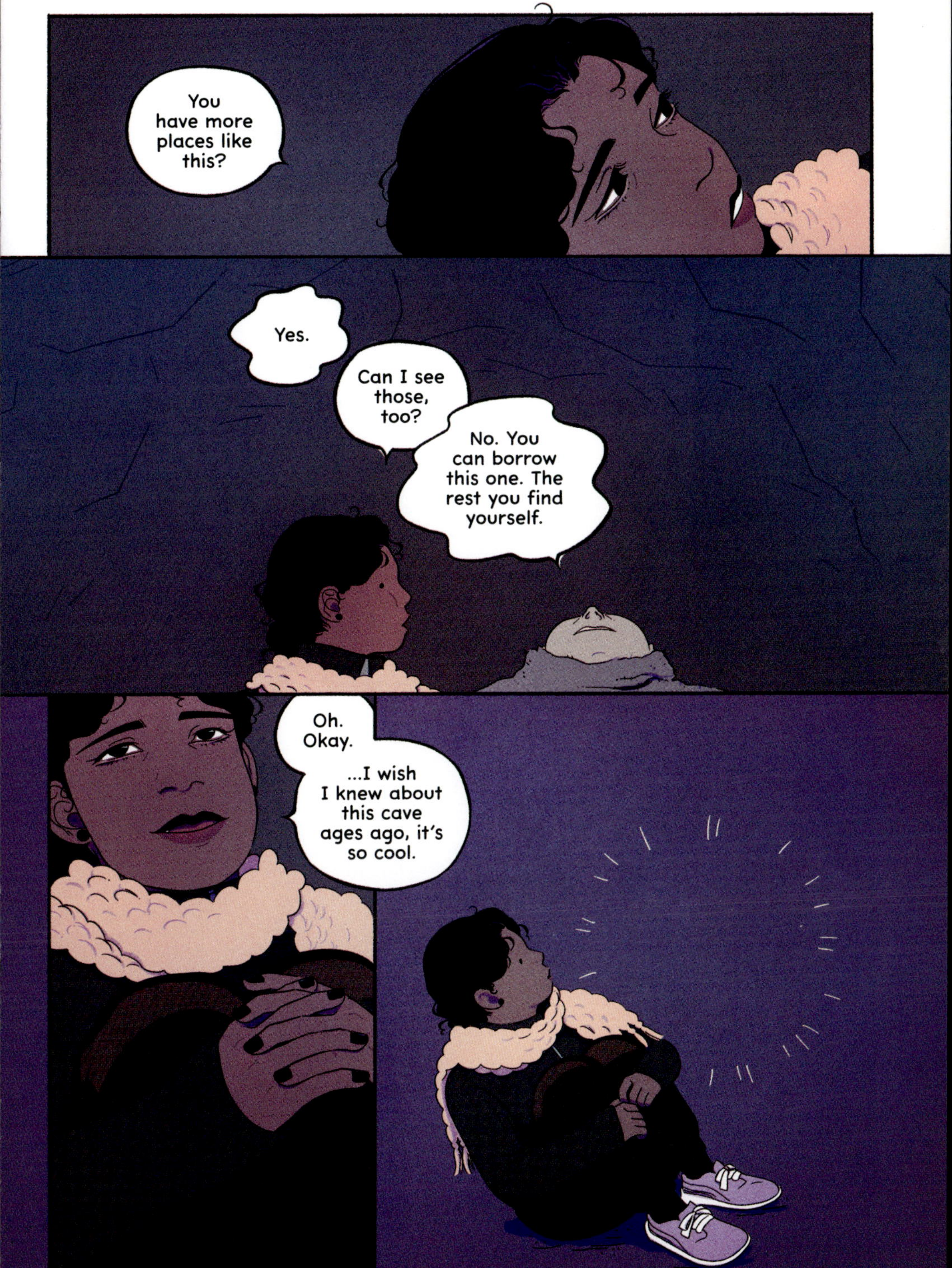
You have more places like this?
Yes.
Can I see those, too?
No. You can borrow this one. The rest you find yourself.
Oh. Okay.
...I wish I knew about this cave ages ago, it's so cool.

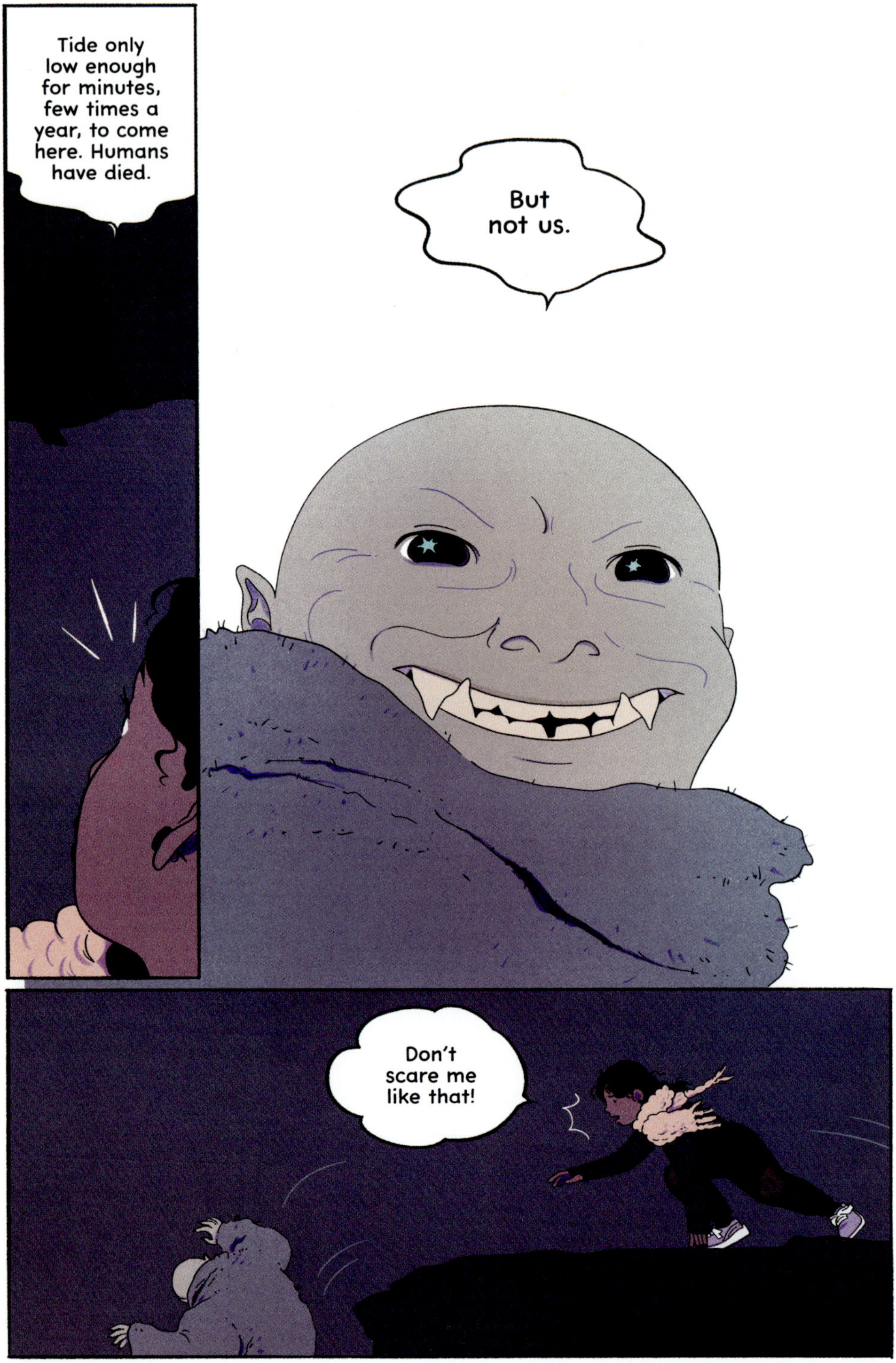
Tide only low enough for minutes, few times a year, to come here. Humans have died.
But not us.
Don't scare me like that!

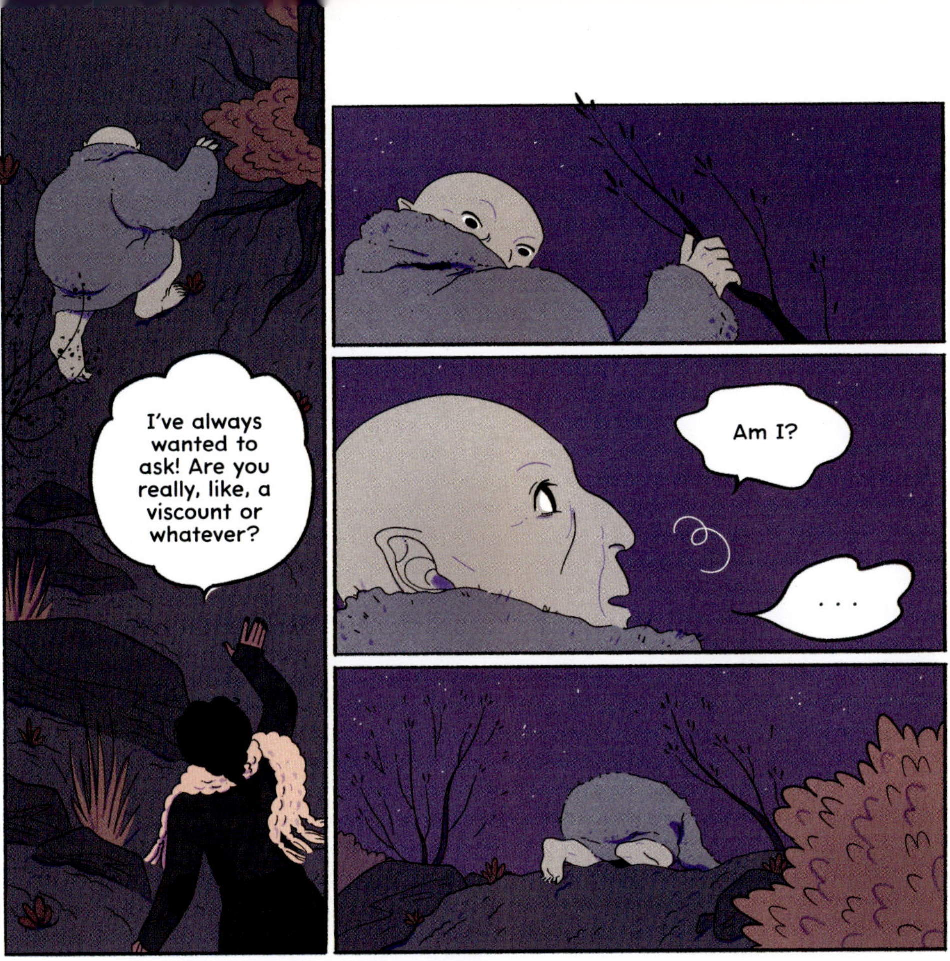
I've always wanted to ask! Are you really, like, a viscount or whatever?
Am I?
. . .

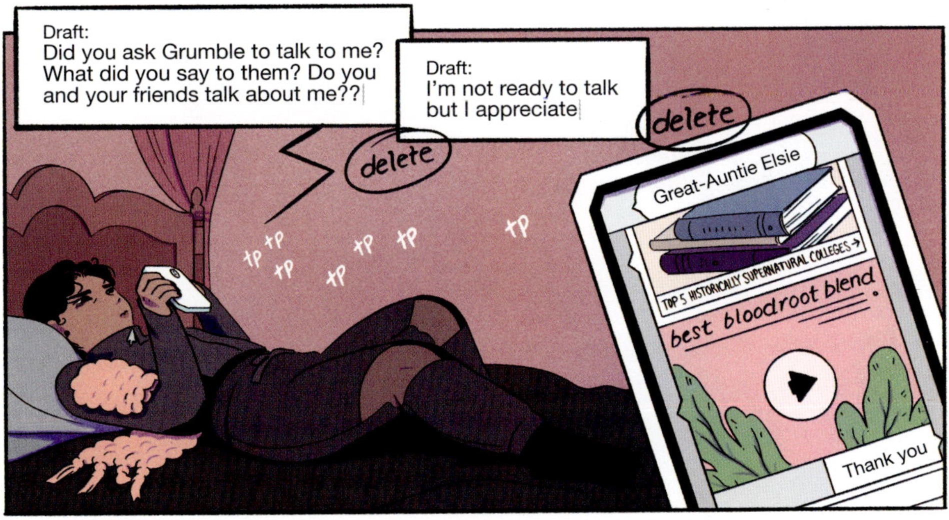
Draft:
Did you ask Grumble to talk to me? What did you say to them? Do you and your friends talk about me??
delete
Draft:
I'm not ready to talk but I appreciate
delete
tp tp tp tp tp tp tp
Great-Auntie Elsie
TOP 5 HISTORICALLY SUPERNATURAL COLLEGES →
best bloodroot blend
Thank you

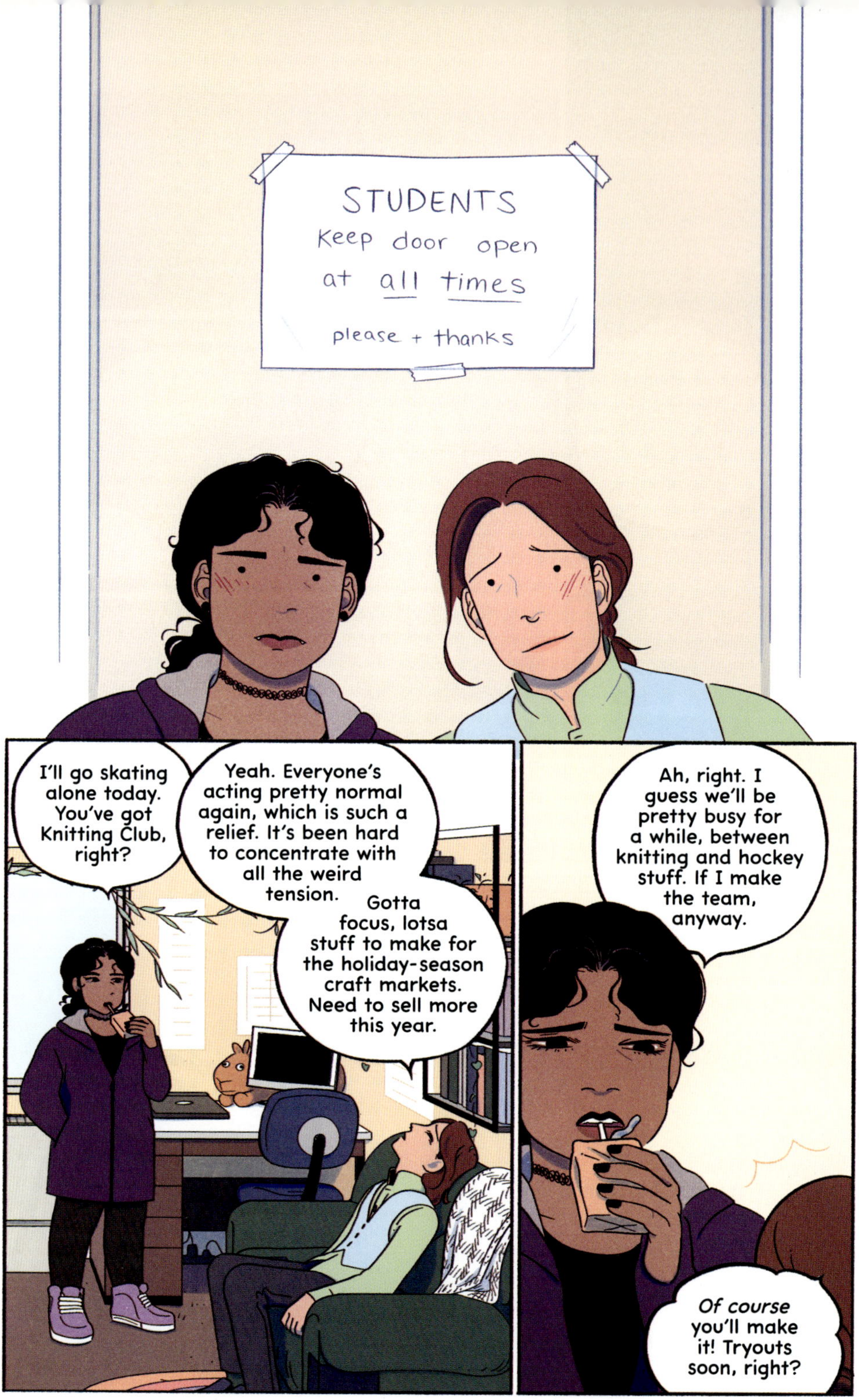
STUDENTS
keep door open
at all times
please + thanks
I'll go skating alone today. You've got Knitting Club, right?
Yeah. Everyone's acting pretty normal again, which is such a relief. It's been hard to concentrate with all the weird tension.
Gotta focus, lotsa stuff to make for the holiday-season craft markets. Need to sell more this year.
Ah, right. I guess we'll be pretty busy for a while, between knitting and hockey stuff. If I make the team, anyway.
Of course you'll make it! Tryouts soon, right?

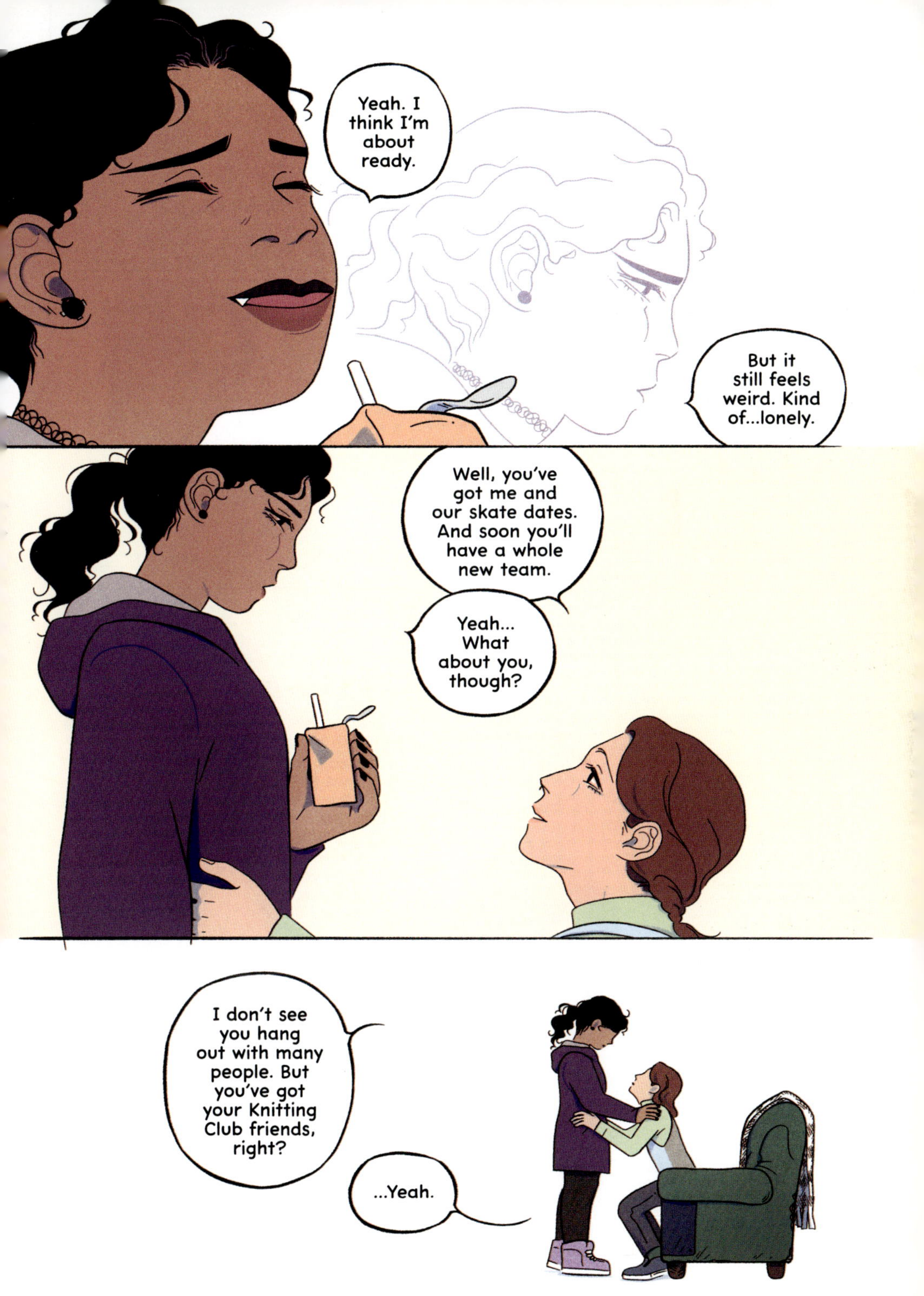
Yeah. I think I'm about ready.
But it still feels weird. Kind of...lonely.
Well, you've got me and our skate dates. And soon you'll have a whole new team.
Yeah... What about you, though?
I don't see you hang out with many people. But you've got your Knitting Club friends, right?
...Yeah.

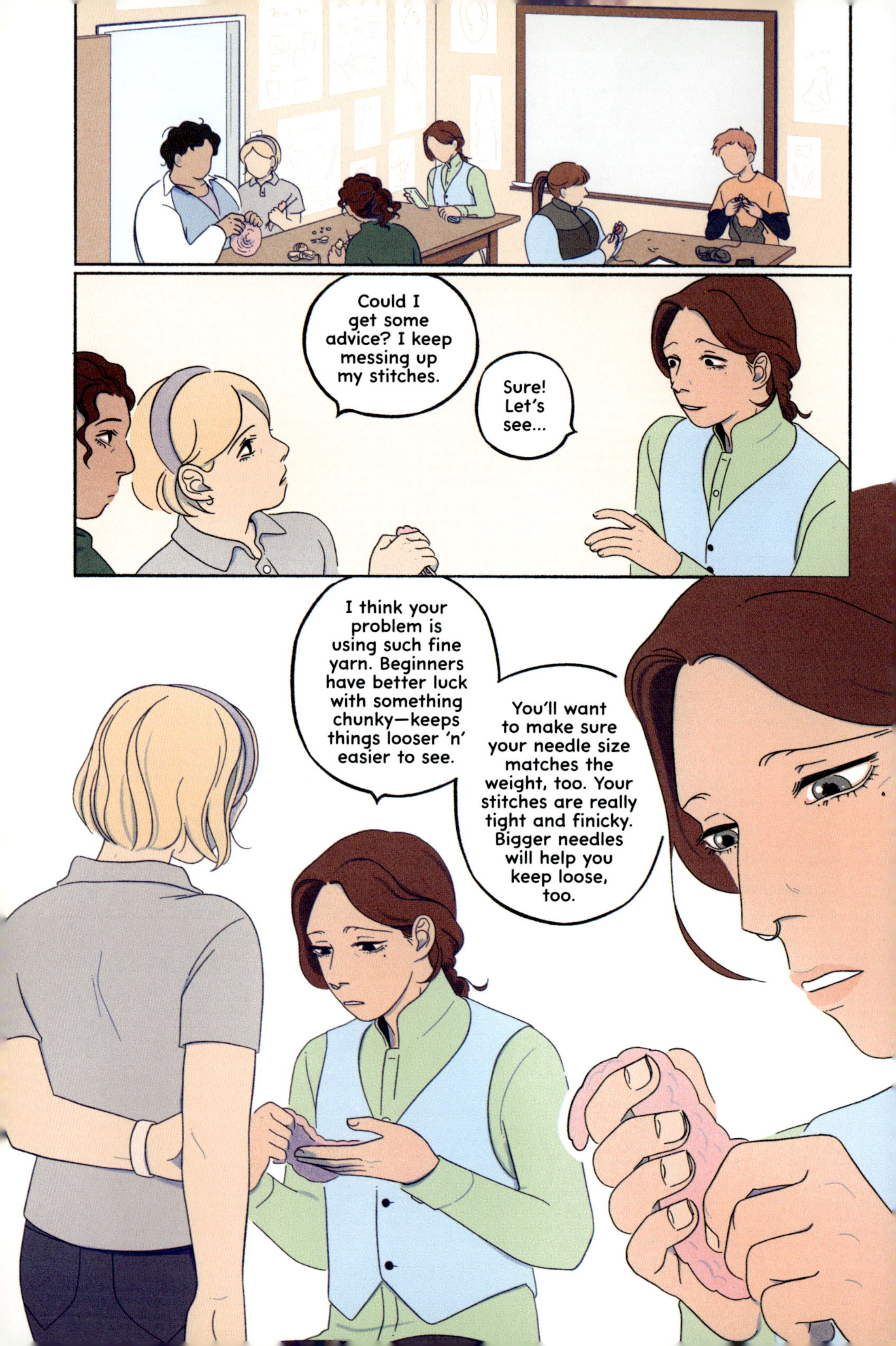
Could I get some advice? I keep messing up my stitches.
Sure! Let's see...
I think your problem is using such fine yarn. Beginners have better luck with something chunky—keeps things looser 'n' easier to see.
You'll want to make sure your needle size matches the weight, too. Your stitches are really tight and finicky. Bigger needles will help you keep loose, too.

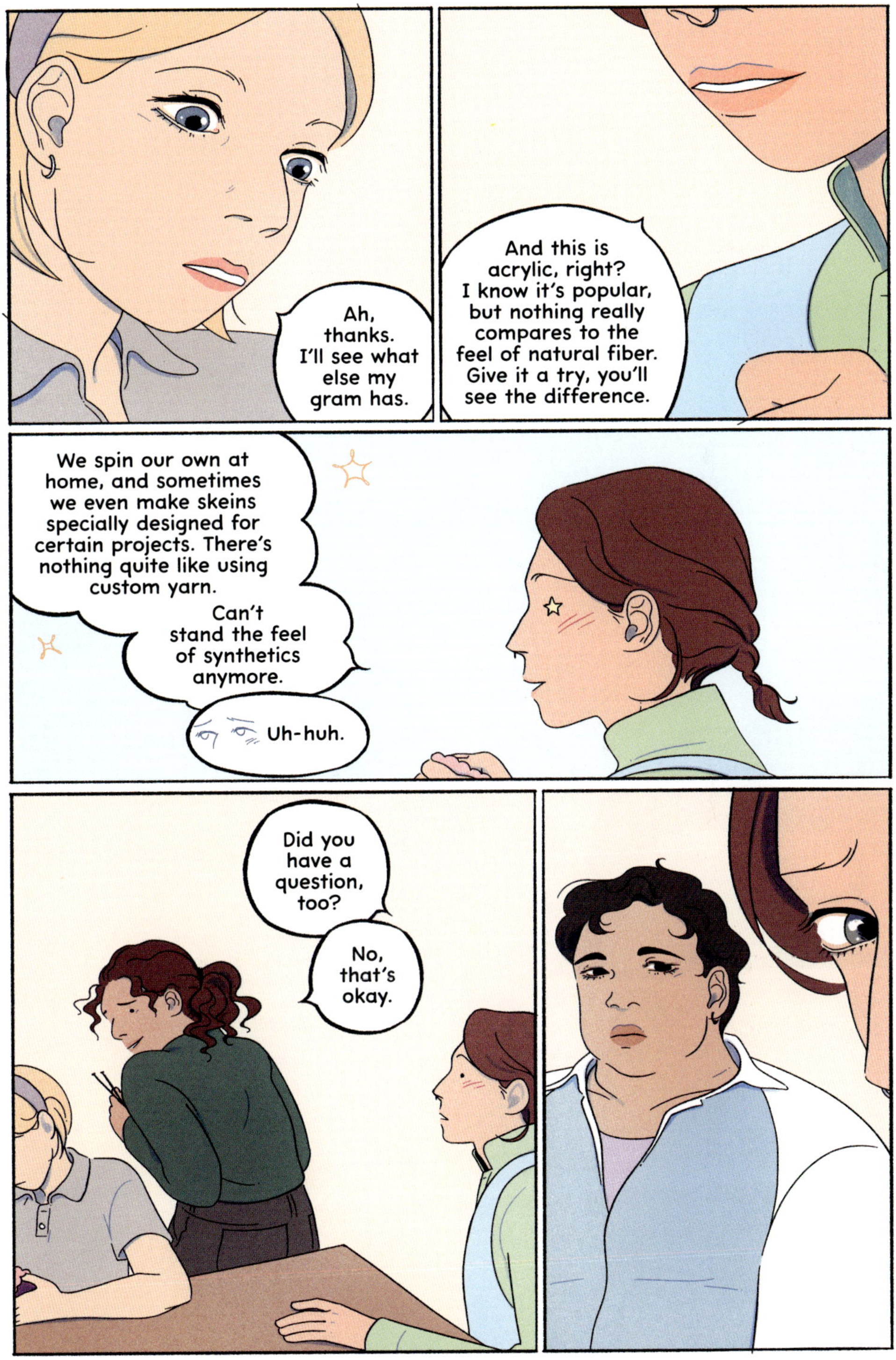
Ah, thanks. I'll see what else my gram has.
And this is acrylic, right? I know it's popular, but nothing really compares to the feel of natural fiber. Give it a try, you'll see the difference.
We spin our own at home, and sometimes we even make skeins specially designed for certain projects. There's nothing quite like using custom yarn.
Can't stand the feel of synthetics anymore.
Uh-huh.
Did you have a question, too?
No, that's okay.

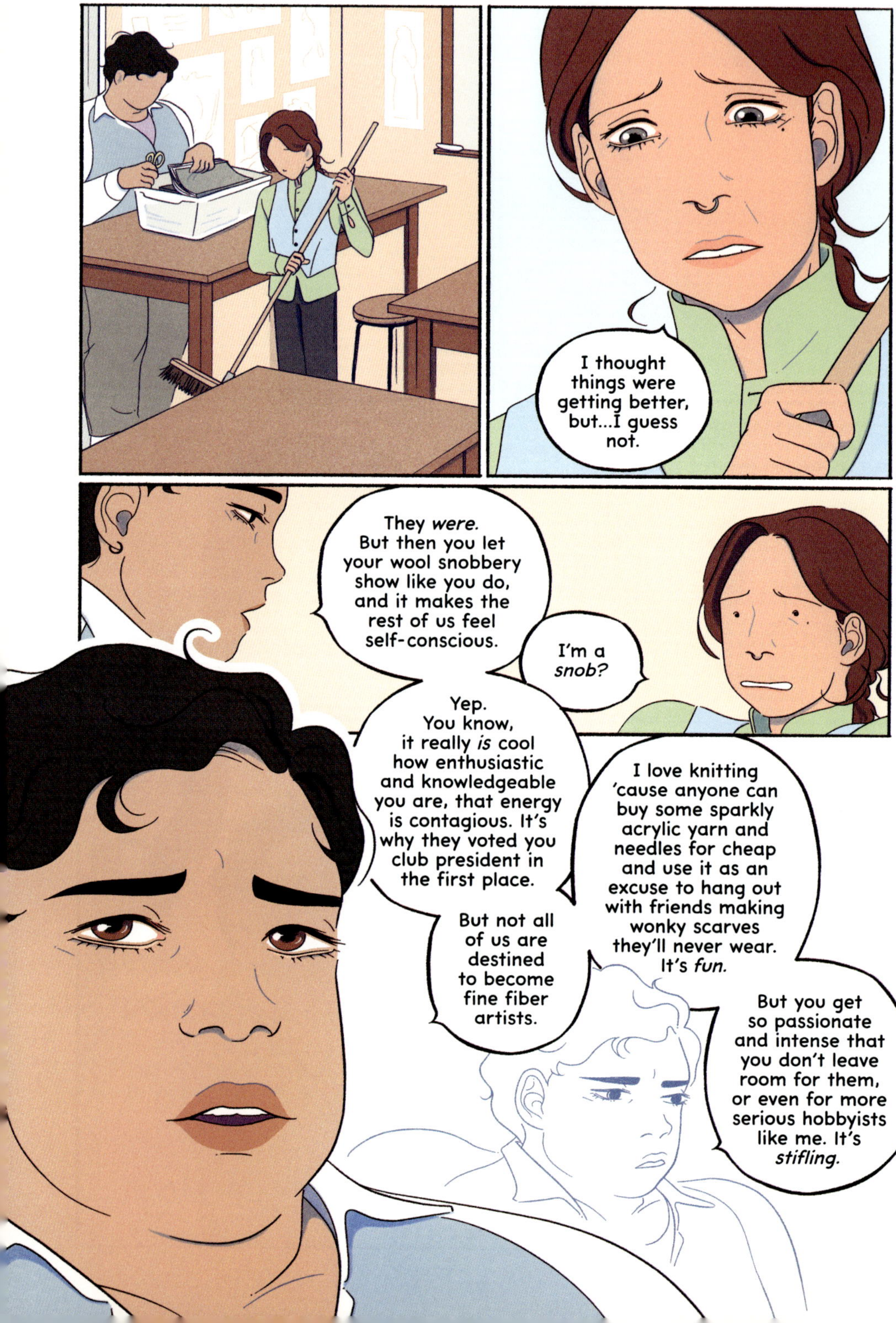
I thought things were getting better, but...I guess not.
They *were.* But then you let your wool snobbery show like you do, and it makes the rest of us feel self-conscious.
I'm a *snob?*
Yep. You know, it really *is* cool how enthusiastic and knowledgeable you are, that energy is contagious. It's why they voted you club president in the first place.
But not all of us are destined to become fine fiber artists.
I love knitting 'cause anyone can buy some sparkly acrylic yarn and needles for cheap and use it as an excuse to hang out with friends making wonky scarves they'll never wear. It's *fun.*
But you get so passionate and intense that you don't leave room for them, or even for more serious hobbyists like me. It's *stifling.*

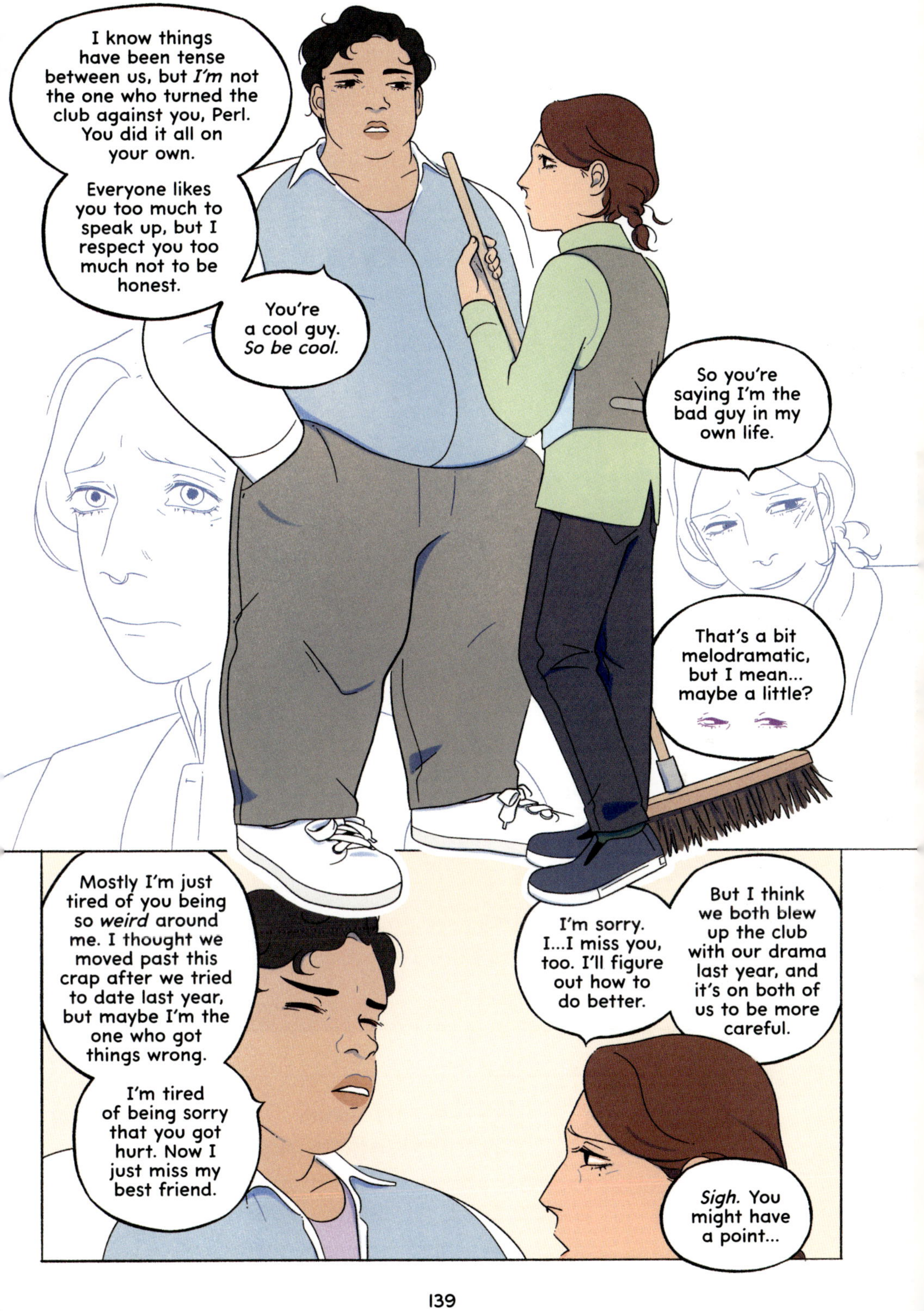
I know things have been tense between us, but *I'm* not the one who turned the club against you, Perl. You did it all on your own.
Everyone likes you too much to speak up, but I respect you too much not to be honest.
You're a cool guy. *So be cool.*
So you're saying I'm the bad guy in my own life.
That's a bit melodramatic, but I mean... maybe a little?
Mostly I'm just tired of you being so *weird* around me. I thought we moved past this crap after we tried to date last year, but maybe I'm the one who got things wrong.
I'm tired of being sorry that you got hurt. Now I just miss my best friend.
I'm sorry. I...I miss you, too. I'll figure out how to do better.
But I think we both blew up the club with our drama last year, and it's on both of us to be more careful.
Sigh. You might have a point...

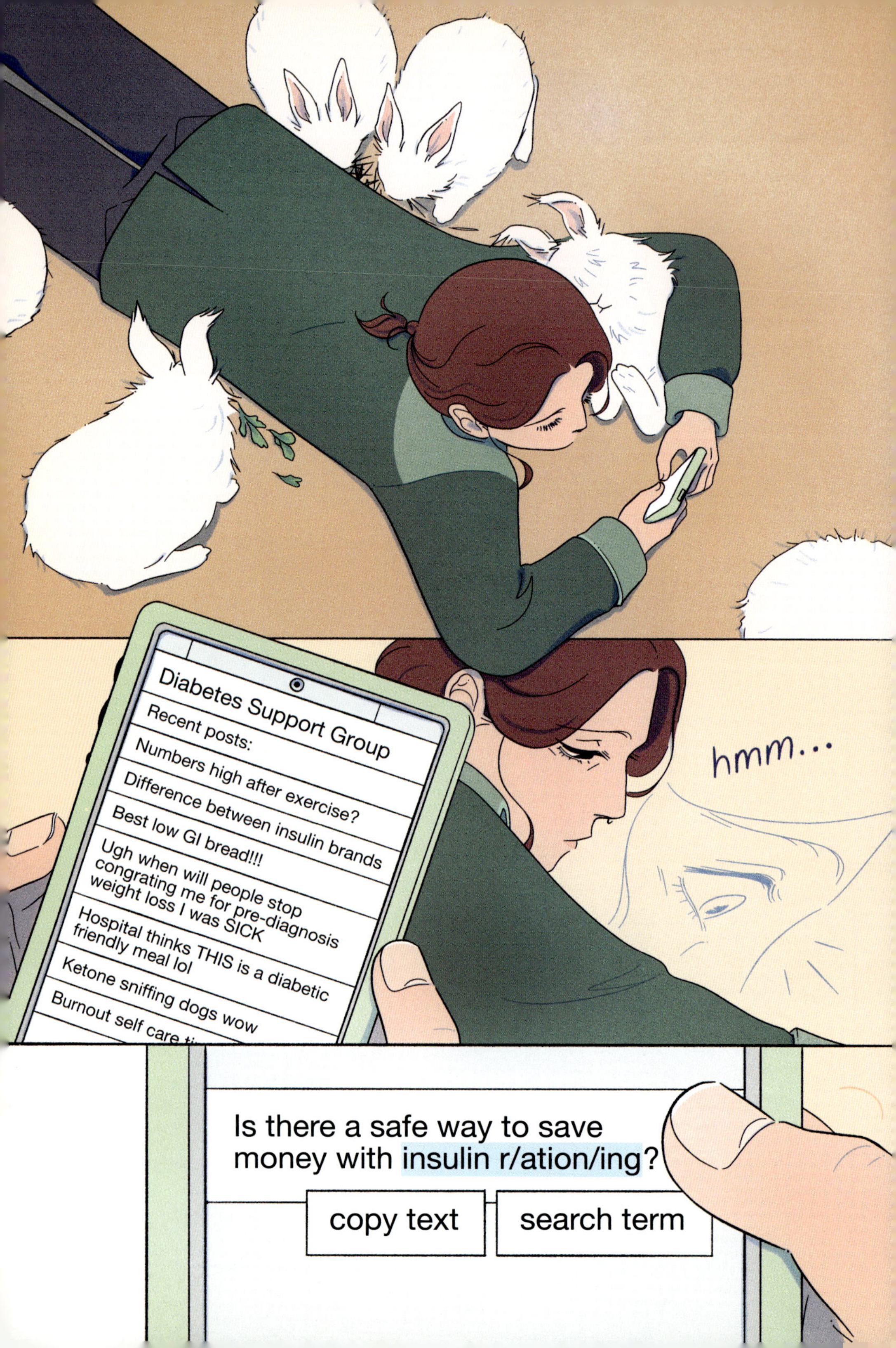
Diabetes Support Group
Recent posts:
Numbers high after exercise?
Difference between insulin brands
Best low GI bread!!!
Ugh when will people stop congrating me for pre-diagnosis weight loss I was SICK
Hospital thinks THIS is a diabetic friendly meal lol
Ketone sniffing dogs wow
hmm...
Is there a safe way to save money with insulin r/ation/ing?
copy text
search term

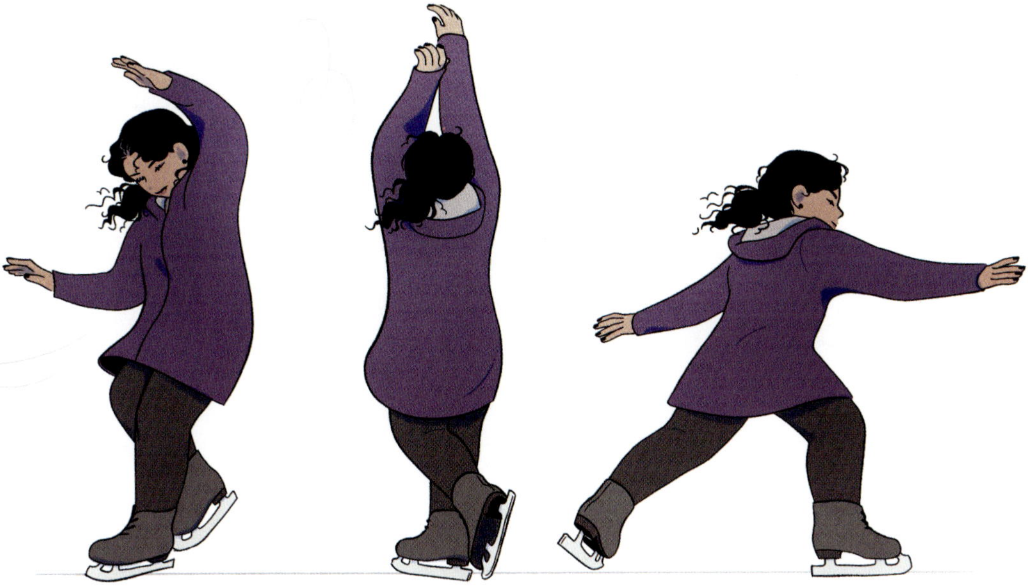

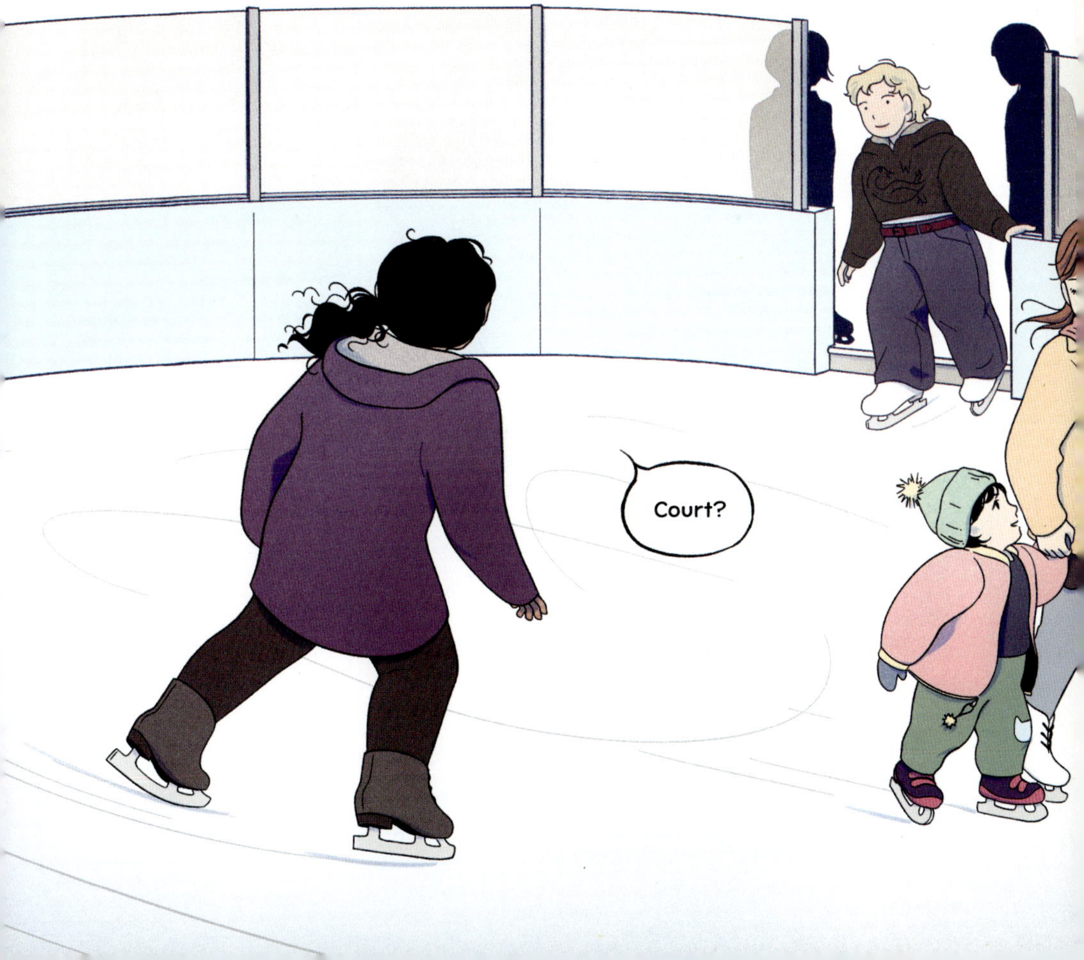
Court?

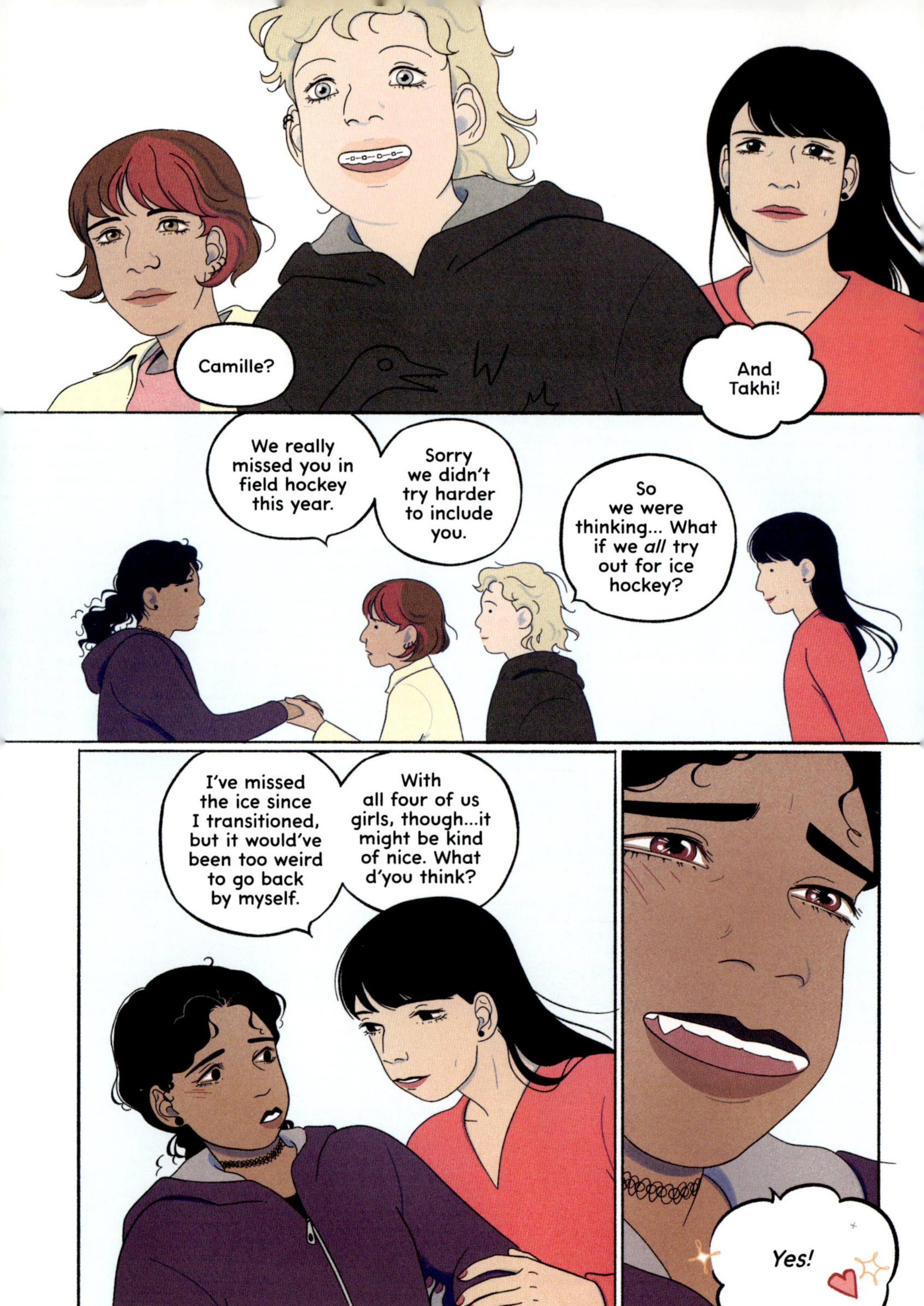
Camille?
And Takhi!
We really missed you in field hockey this year.
Sorry we didn't try harder to include you.
So we were thinking... What if we *all* try out for ice hockey?
I've missed the ice since I transitioned, but it would've been too weird to go back by myself.
With all four of us girls, though...it might be kind of nice. What d'you think?
Yes!

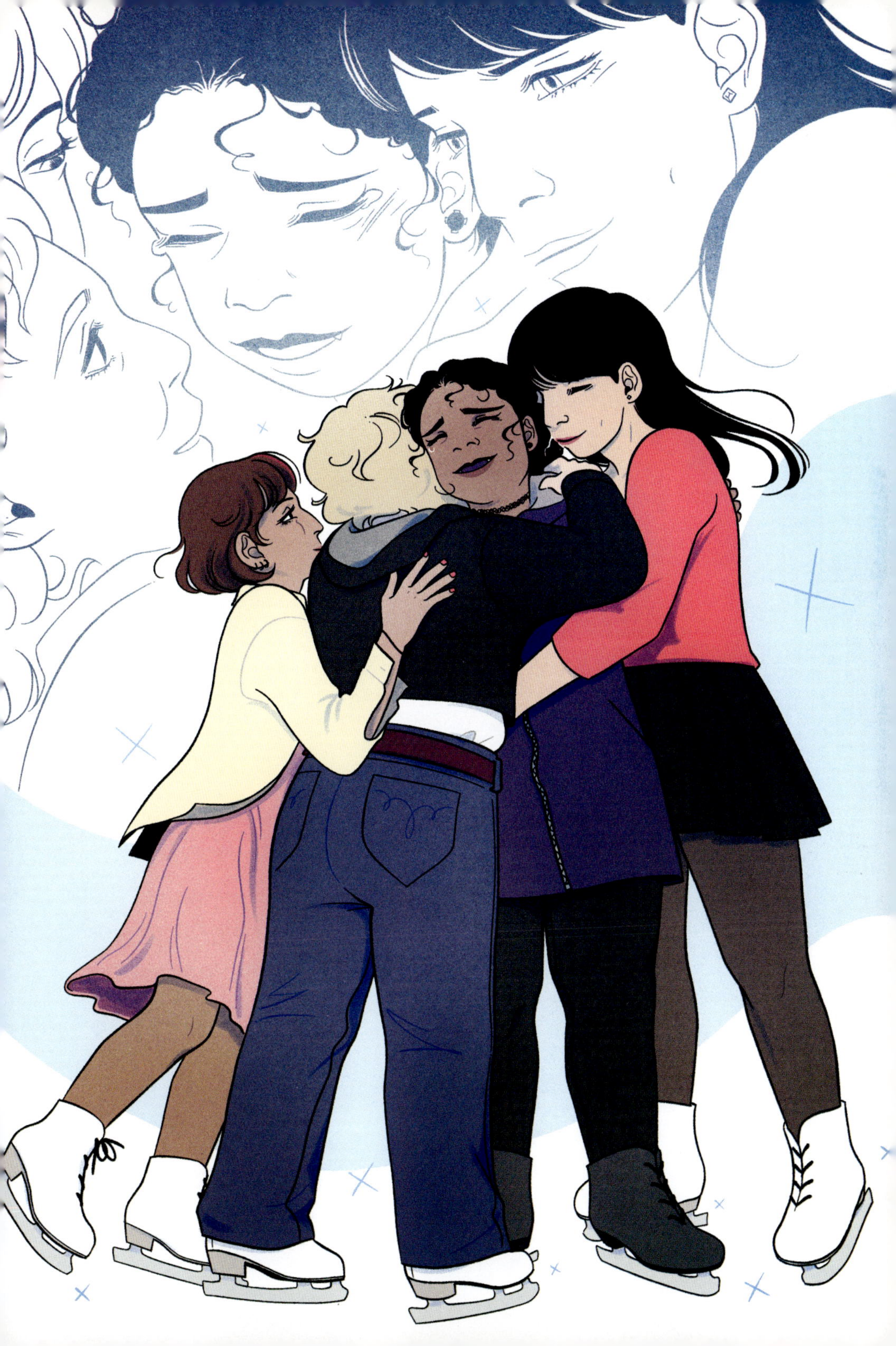

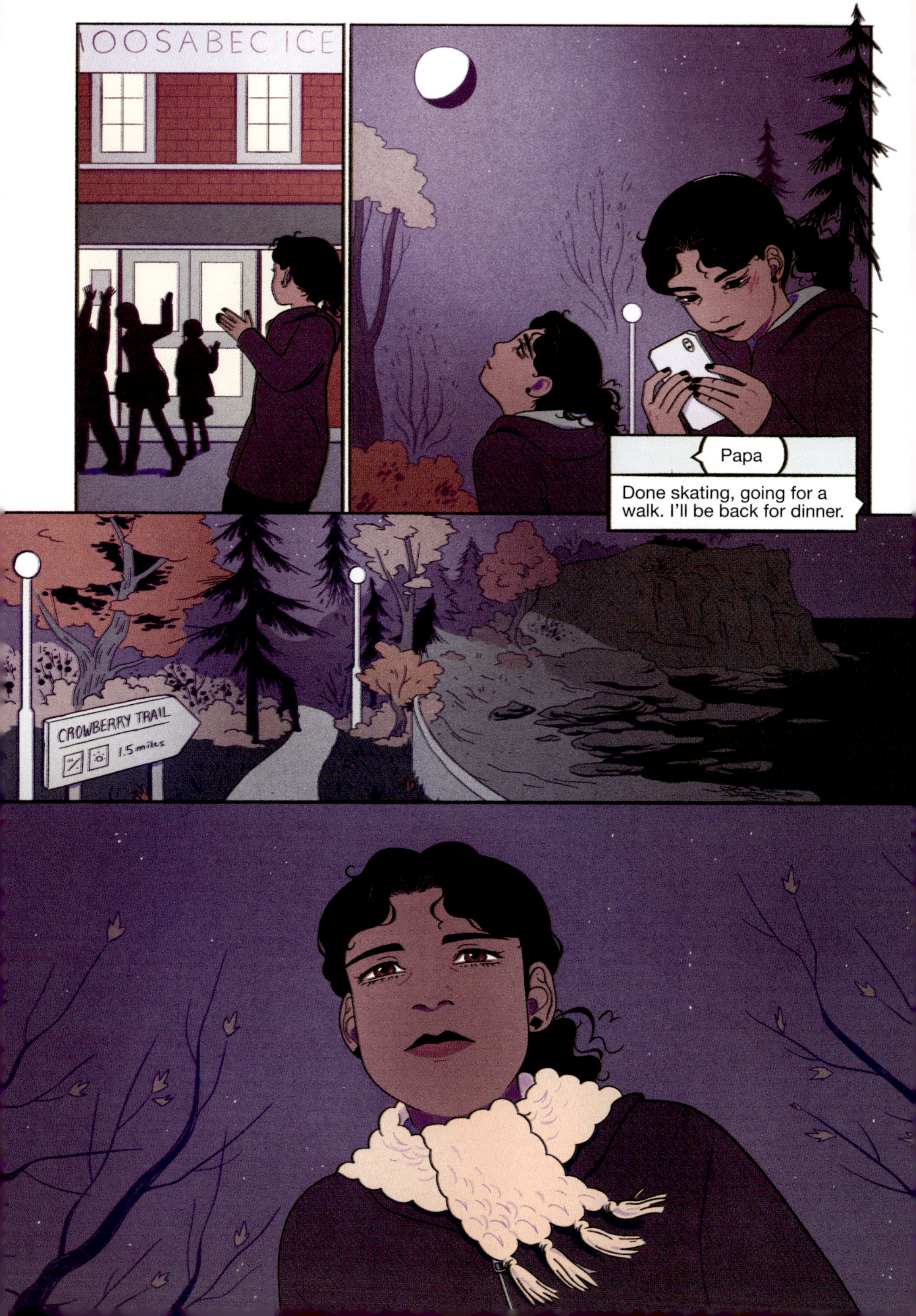
OOSABEC ICE
Papa
Done skating, going for a walk. I'll be back for dinner.
CROWBERRY TRAIL
1.5 miles

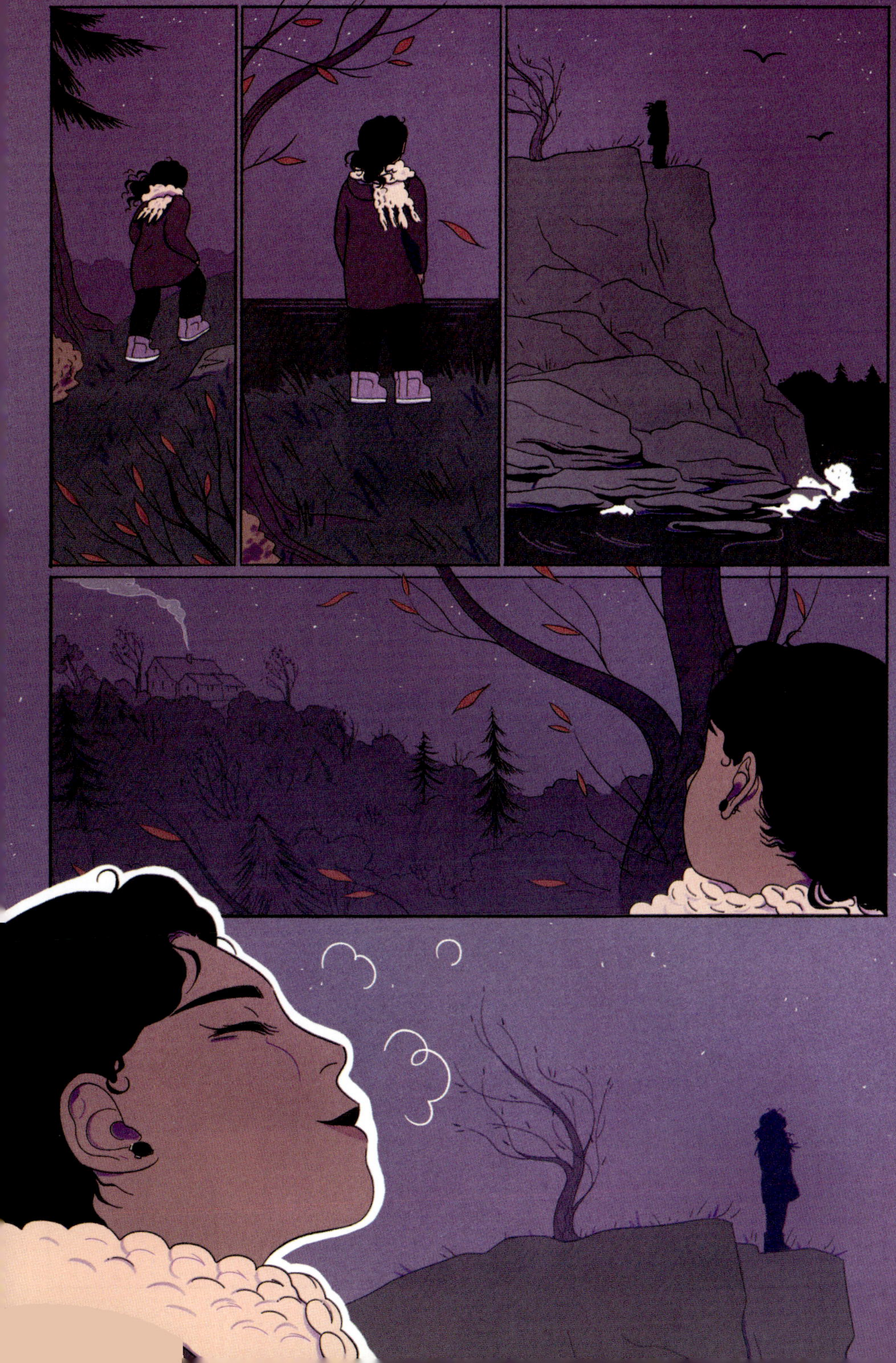

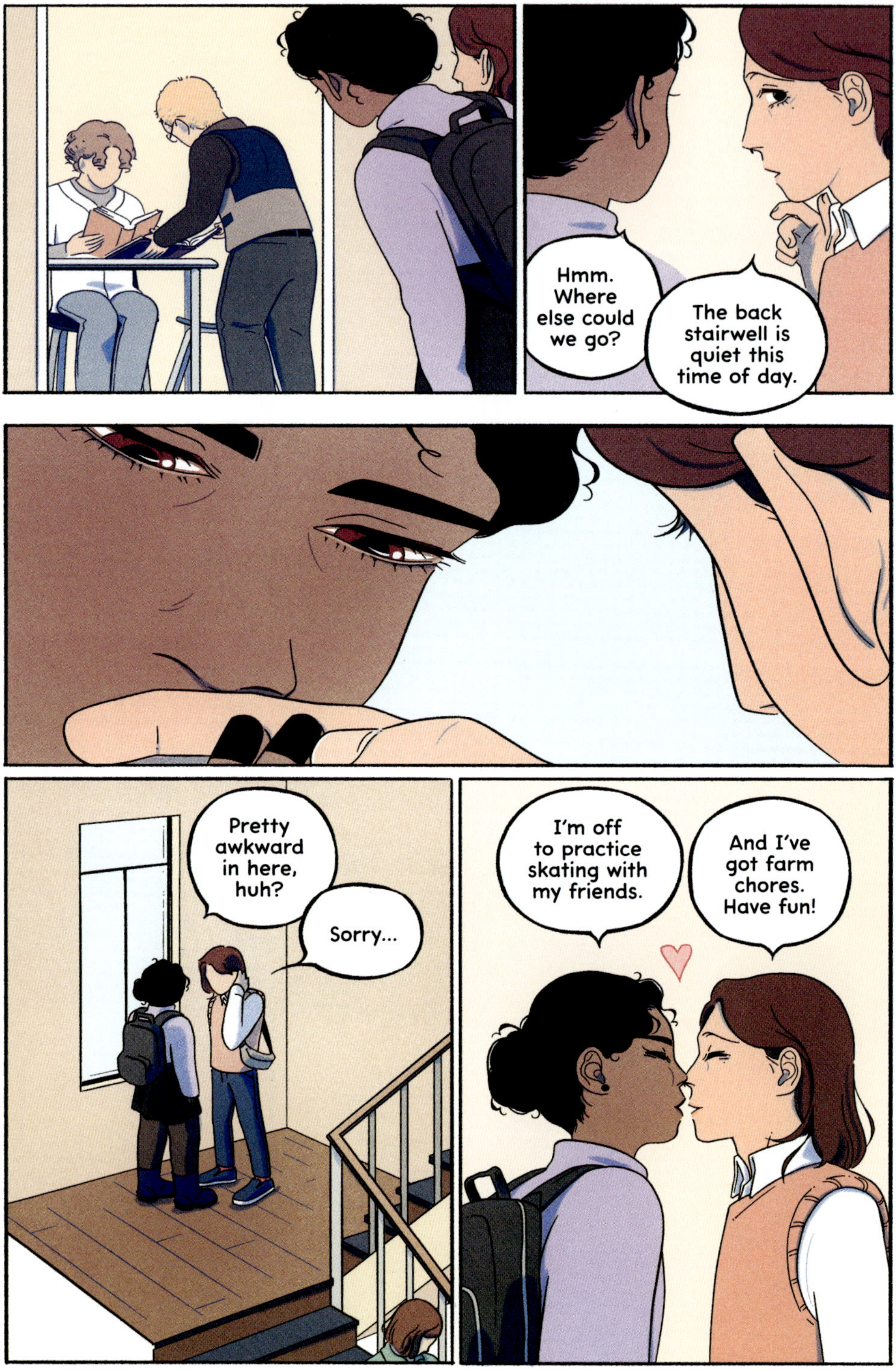
Hmm. Where else could we go?
The back stairwell is quiet this time of day.
Pretty awkward in here, huh?
Sorry...
I'm off to practice skating with my friends.
And I've got farm chores. Have fun!

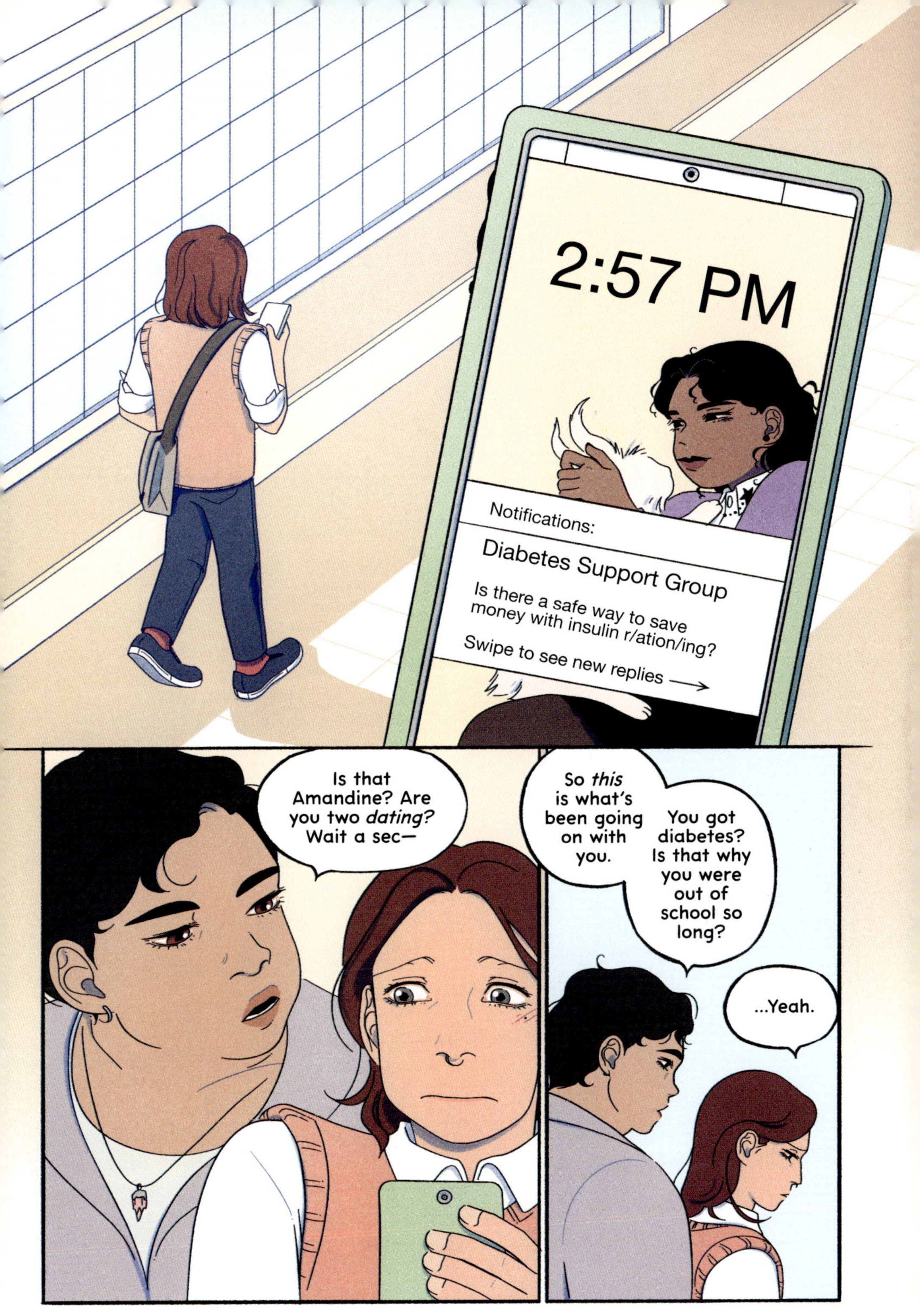
2:57 PM
Notifications:
Diabetes Support Group
Is there a safe way to save money with insulin r/ation/ing?
Swipe to see new replies →
Is that Amandine? Are you two *dating*? Wait a sec—
So *this* is what's been going on with you.
You got diabetes? Is that why you were out of school so long?
...Yeah.

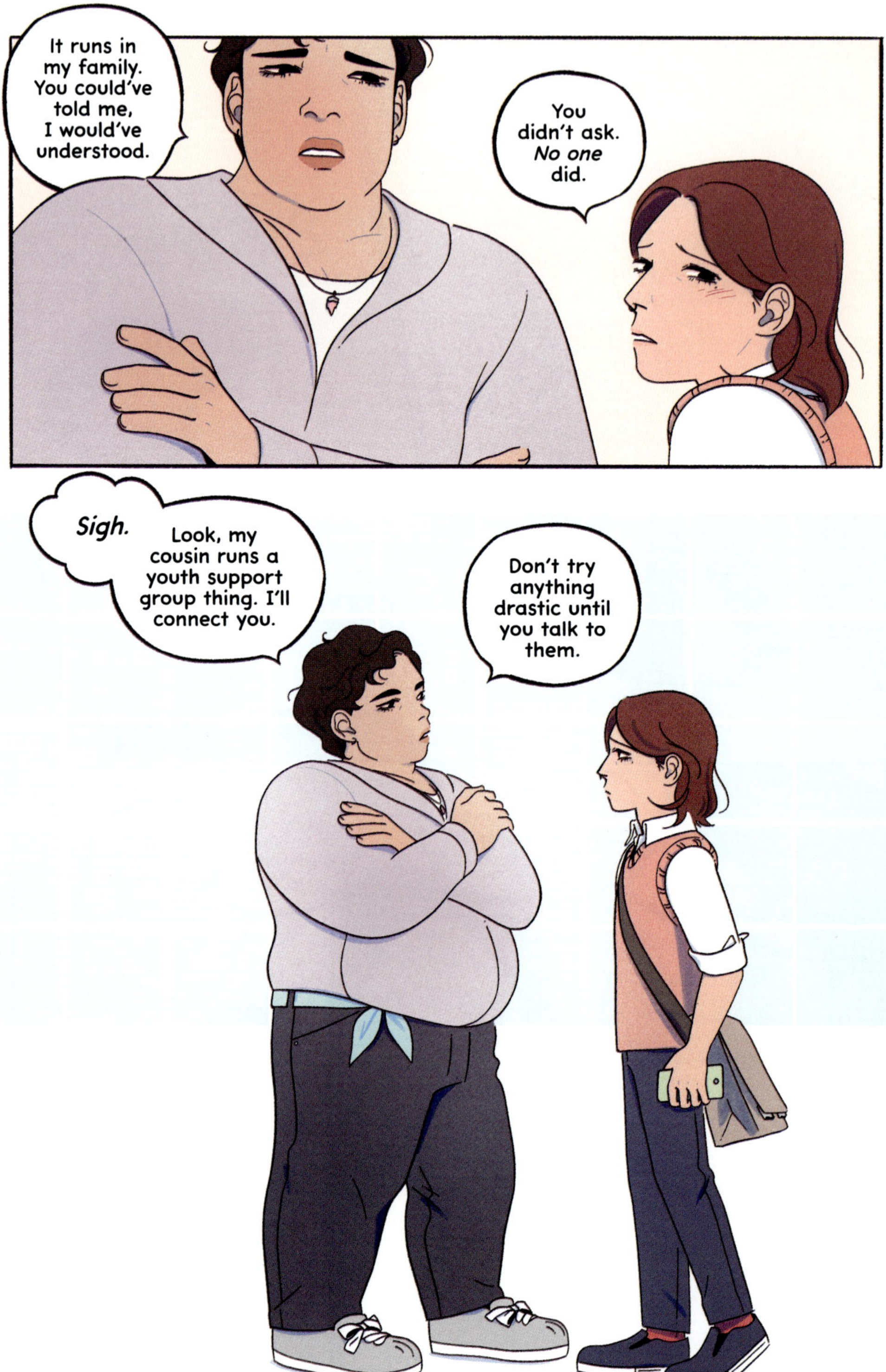
It runs in my family. You could've told me, I would've understood.
You didn't ask. *No one* did.
Sigh.
Look, my cousin runs a youth support group thing. I'll connect you.
Don't try anything drastic until you talk to them.

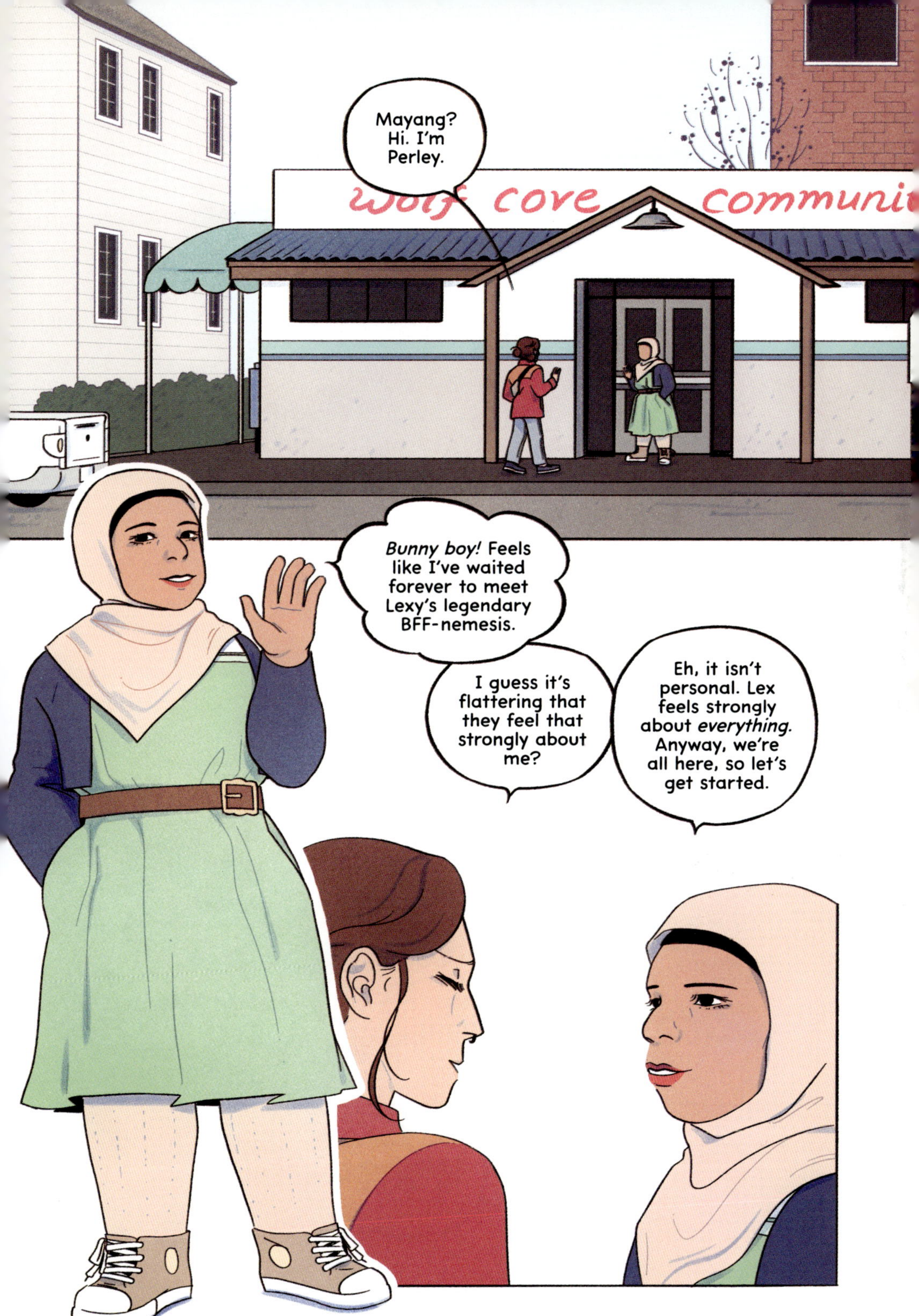
WOLF COVE COMMUNI
Mayang? Hi. I'm Perley.
Bunny boy! Feels like I've waited forever to meet Lexy's legendary BFF-nemesis.
I guess it's flattering that they feel that strongly about me?
Eh, it isn't personal. Lex feels strongly about *everything.* Anyway, we're all here, so let's get started.

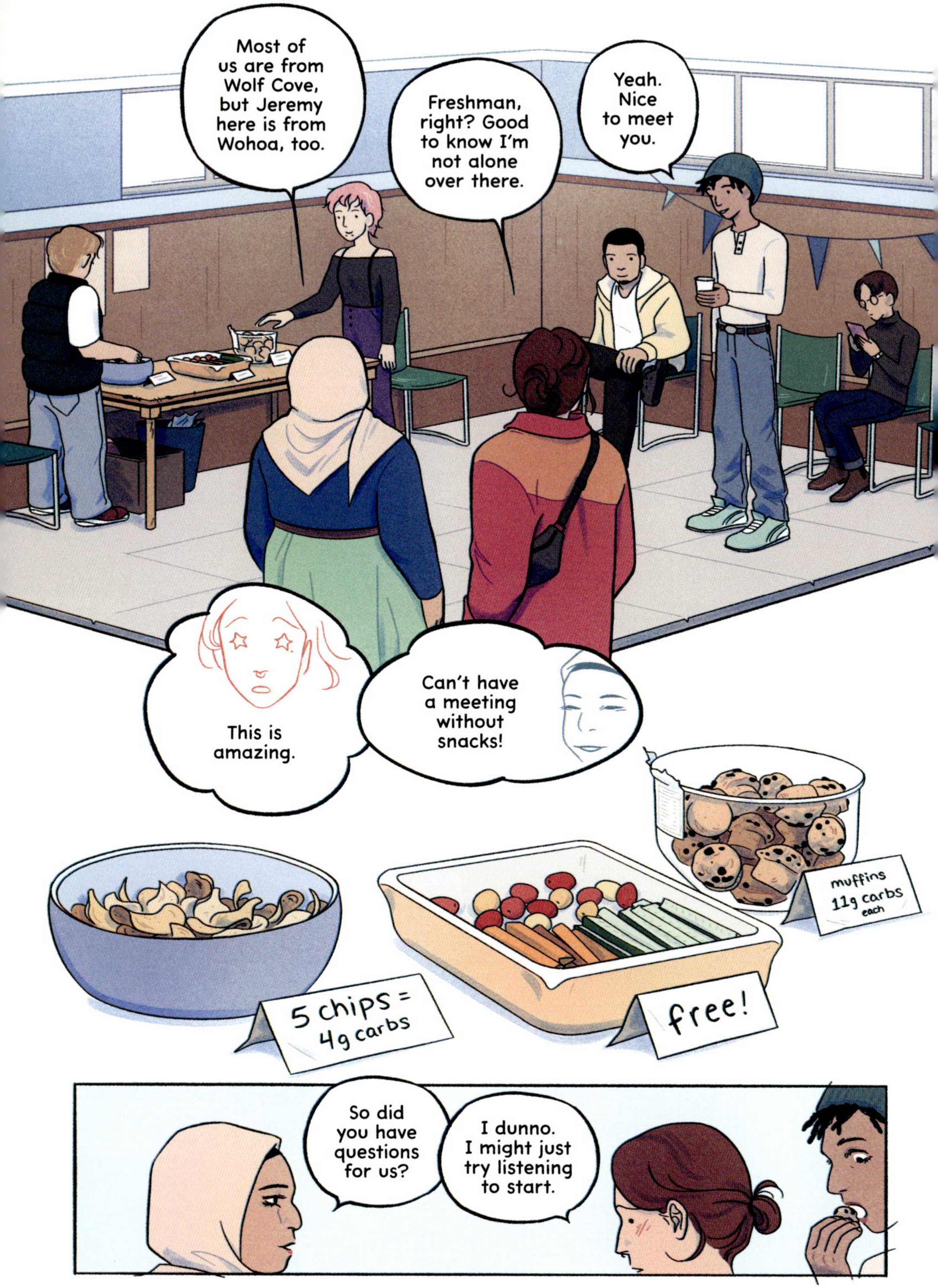
Most of us are from Wolf Cove, but Jeremy here is from Wohoa, too.
Freshman, right? Good to know I'm not alone over there.
Yeah. Nice to meet you.
This is amazing.
Can't have a meeting without snacks!
muffins 11g carbs each
5 chips = 4g carbs
free!
So did you have questions for us?
I dunno. I might just try listening to start.

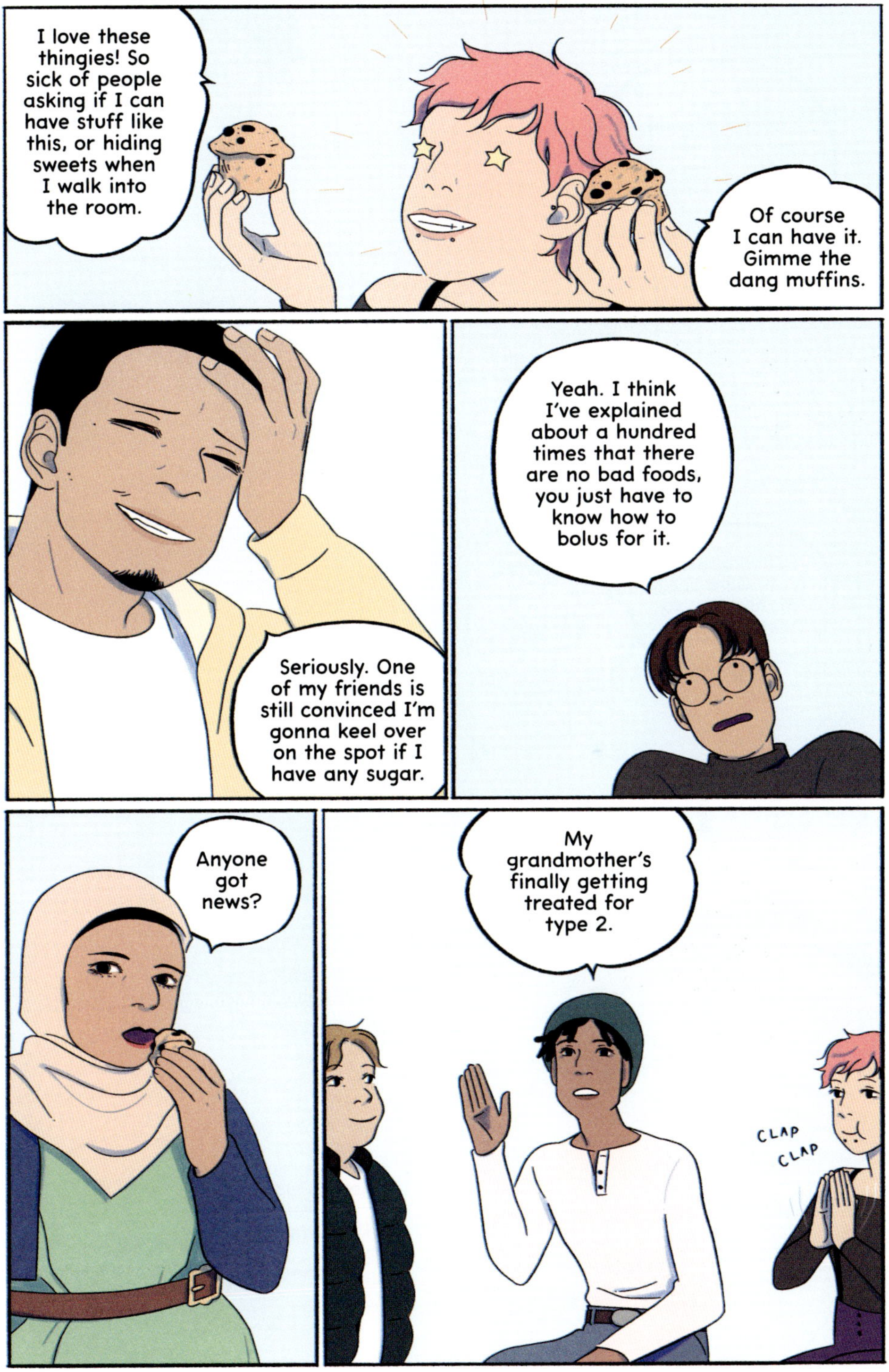
I love these thingies! So sick of people asking if I can have stuff like this, or hiding sweets when I walk into the room.
Of course I can have it. Gimme the dang muffins.
Seriously. One of my friends is still convinced I'm gonna keel over on the spot if I have any sugar.
Yeah. I think I've explained about a hundred times that there are no bad foods, you just have to know how to bolus for it.
Anyone got news?
My grandmother's finally getting treated for type 2.
CLAP
CLAP

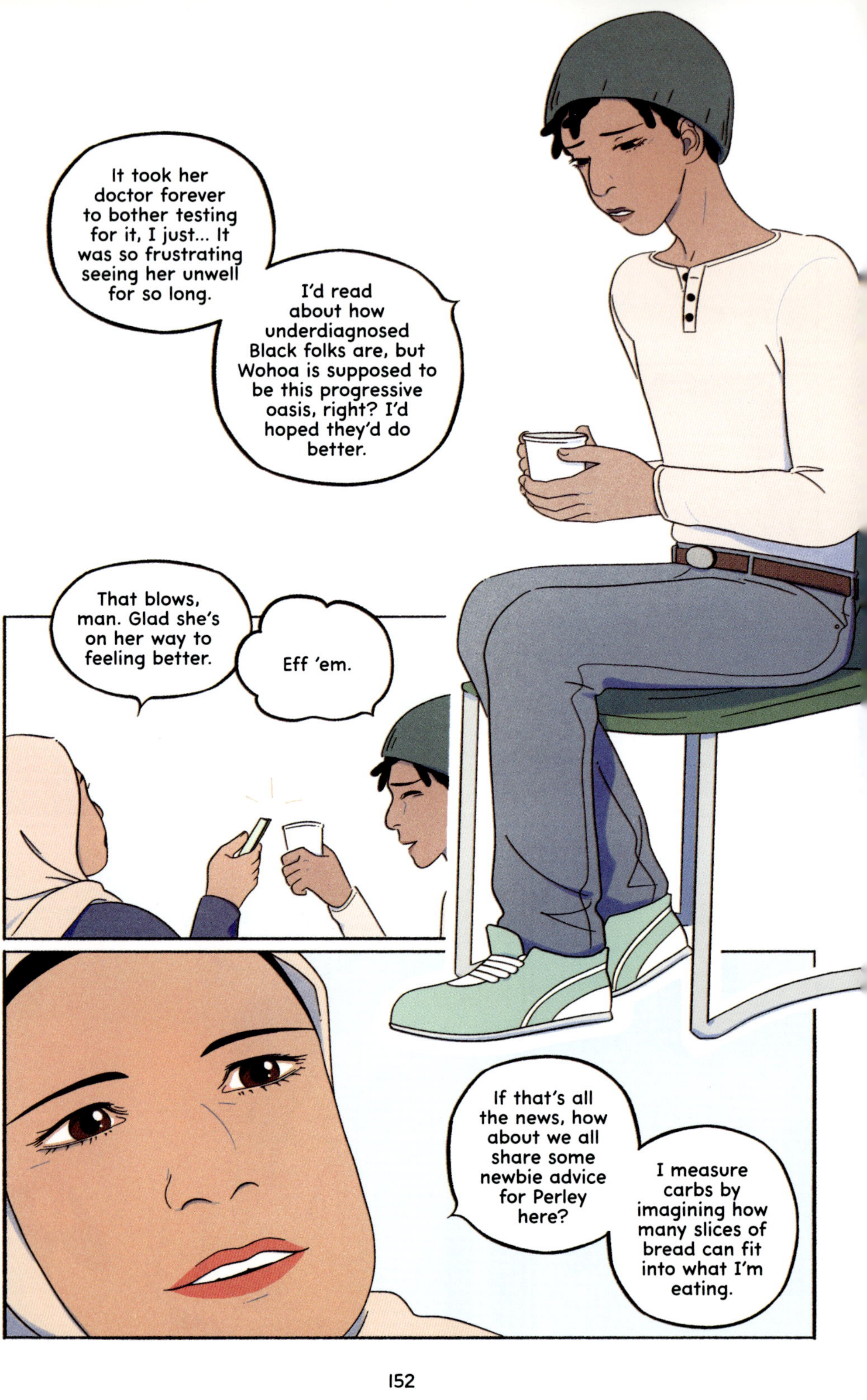

It took her doctor forever to bother testing for it, I just... It was so frustrating seeing her unwell for so long.
I'd read about how underdiagnosed Black folks are, but Wohoa is supposed to be this progressive oasis, right? I'd hoped they'd do better.
That blows, man. Glad she's on her way to feeling better.
Eff 'em.
If that's all the news, how about we all share some newbie advice for Perley here?
I measure carbs by imagining how many slices of bread can fit into what I'm eating.

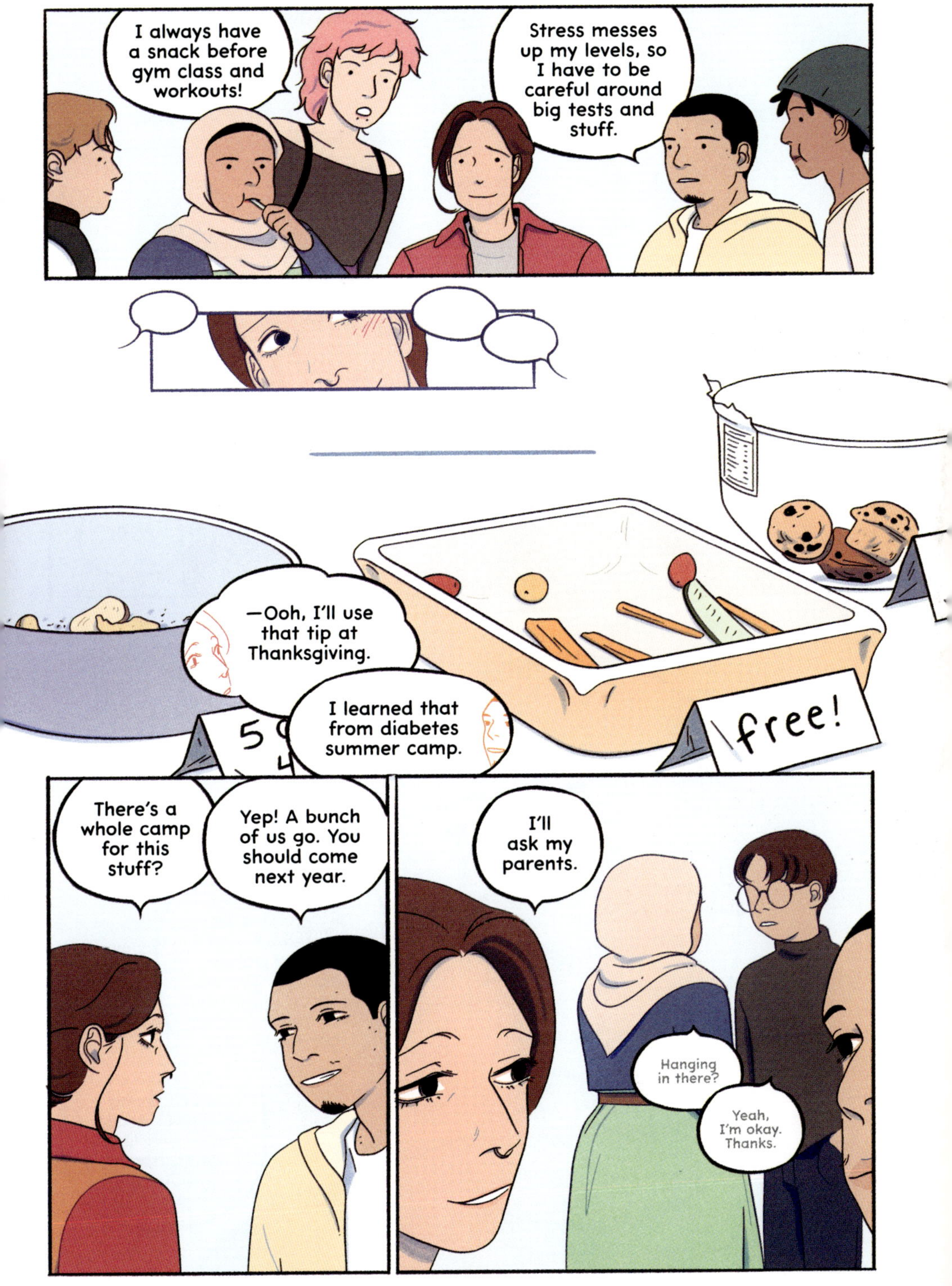
I always have a snack before gym class and workouts!
Stress messes up my levels, so I have to be careful around big tests and stuff.
—Ooh, I'll use that tip at Thanksgiving.
I learned that from diabetes summer camp.
free!
There's a whole camp for this stuff?
Yep! A bunch of us go. You should come next year.
I'll ask my parents.
Hanging in there?
Yeah, I'm okay. Thanks.

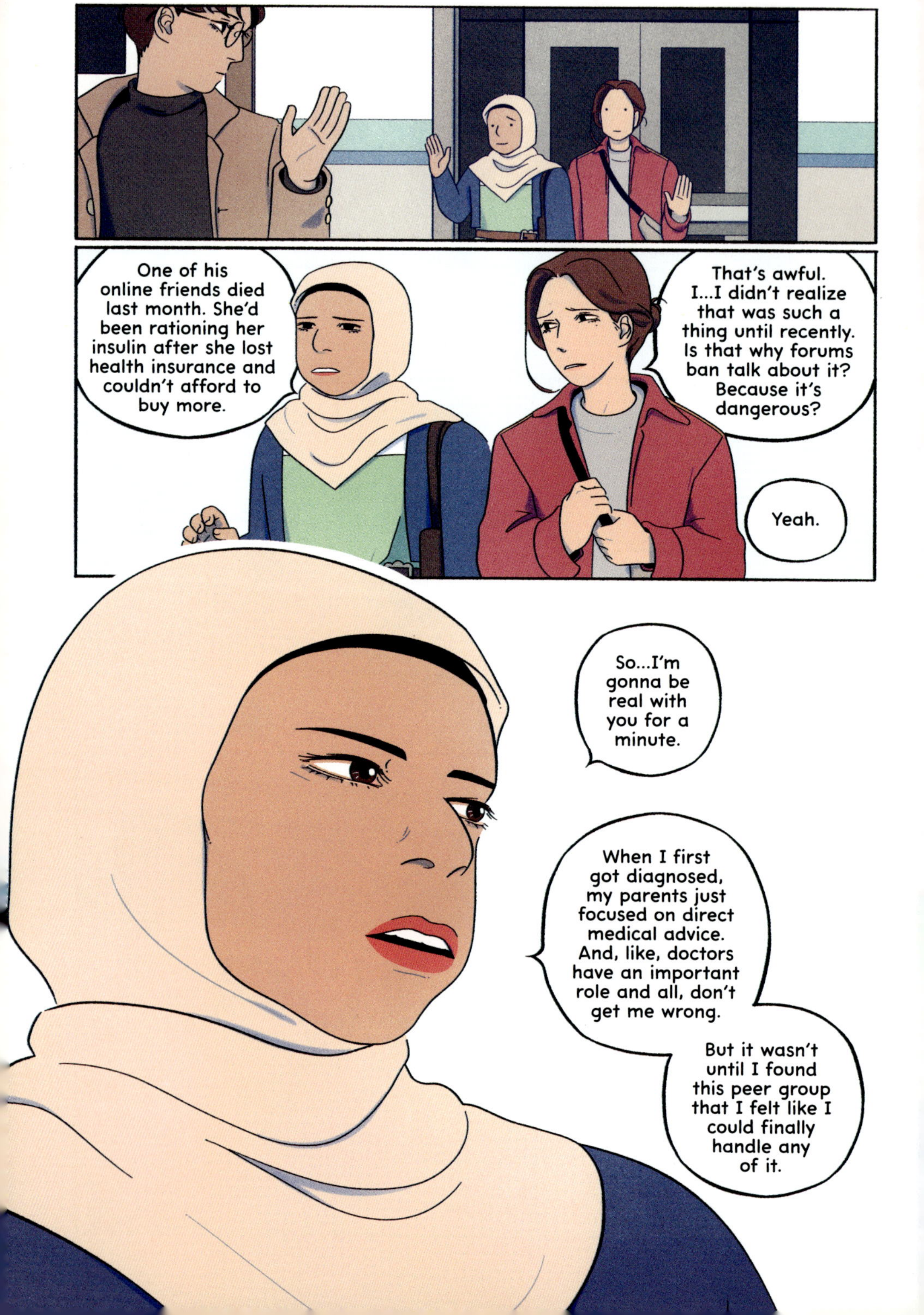
One of his online friends died last month. She'd been rationing her insulin after she lost health insurance and couldn't afford to buy more.
That's awful. I...I didn't realize that was such a thing until recently. Is that why forums ban talk about it? Because it's dangerous?
Yeah.
So...I'm gonna be real with you for a minute.
When I first got diagnosed, my parents just focused on direct medical advice. And, like, doctors have an important role and all, don't get me wrong.
But it wasn't until I found this peer group that I felt like I could finally handle any of it.

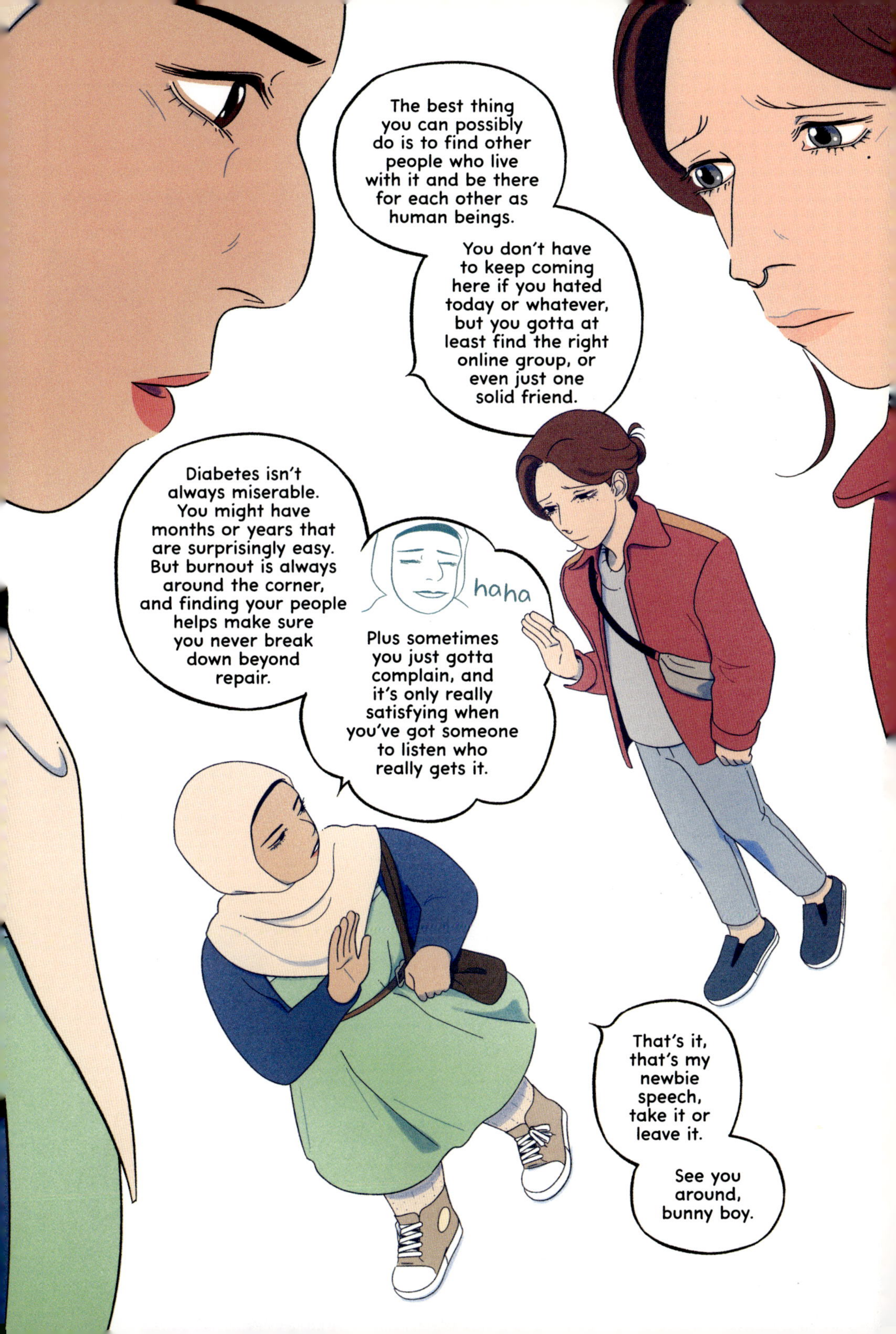
The best thing you can possibly do is to find other people who live with it and be there for each other as human beings.
You don't have to keep coming here if you hated today or whatever, but you gotta at least find the right online group, or even just one solid friend.
Diabetes isn't always miserable. You might have months or years that are surprisingly easy. But burnout is always around the corner, and finding your people helps make sure you never break down beyond repair.
haha
Plus sometimes you just gotta complain, and it's only really satisfying when you've got someone to listen who really gets it.
That's it, that's my newbie speech, take it or leave it.
See you around, bunny boy.

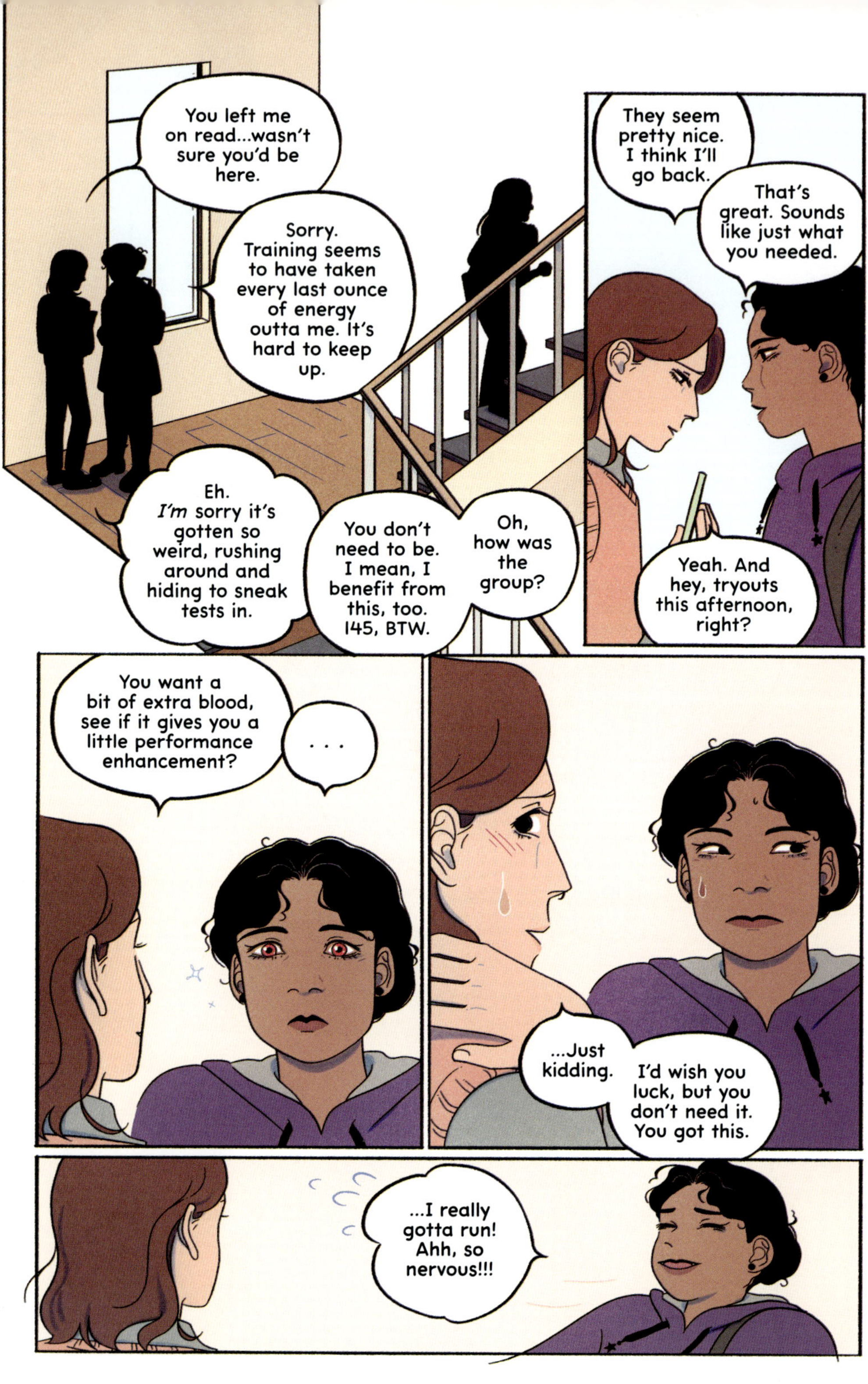
You left me on read...wasn't sure you'd be here.
Sorry. Training seems to have taken every last ounce of energy outta me. It's hard to keep up.
Eh. *I'm* sorry it's gotten so weird, rushing around and hiding to sneak tests in.
You don't need to be. I mean, I benefit from this, too. 145, BTW.
Oh, how was the group?
They seem pretty nice. I think I'll go back.
That's great. Sounds like just what you needed.
Yeah. And hey, tryouts this afternoon, right?
You want a bit of extra blood, see if it gives you a little performance enhancement?
. . .
...Just kidding.
I'd wish you luck, but you don't need it. You got this.
...I really gotta run! Ahh, so nervous!!!

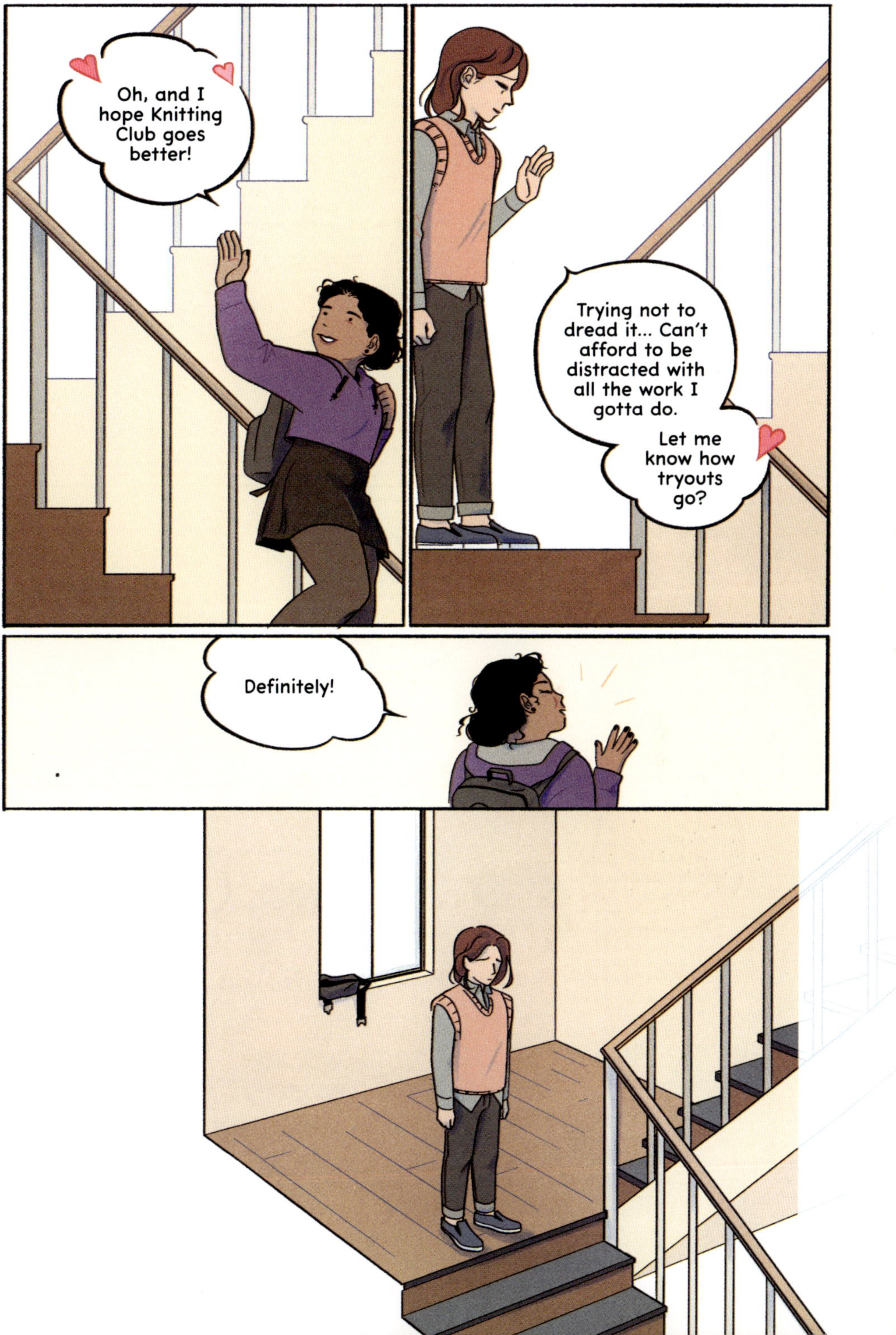
Oh, and I hope Knitting Club goes better!
Trying not to dread it... Can't afford to be distracted with all the work I gotta do.
Let me know how tryouts go?
Definitely!

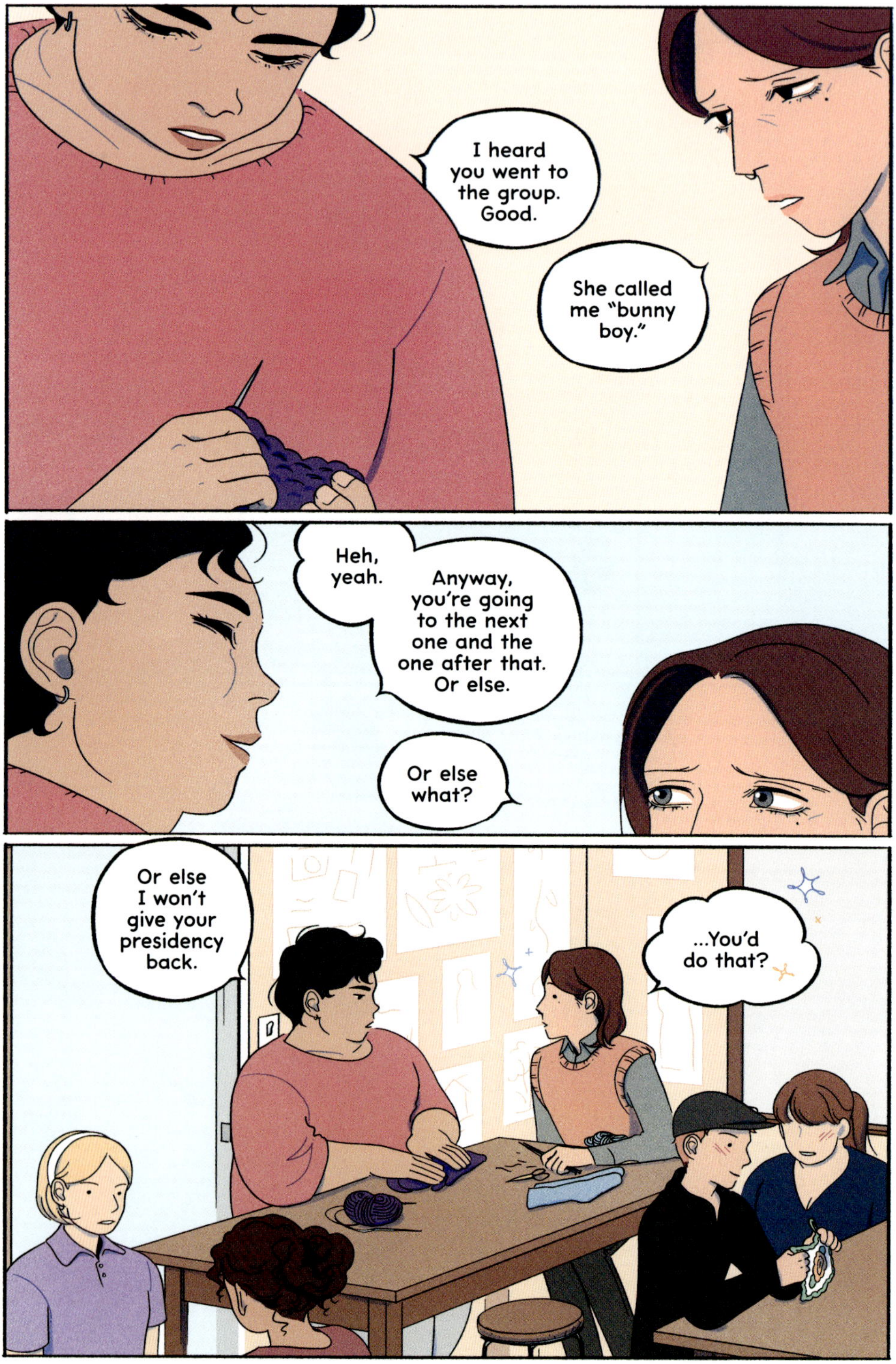
I heard you went to the group. Good.
She called me "bunny boy."
Heh, yeah.
Anyway, you're going to the next one and the one after that. Or else.
Or else what?
Or else I won't give your presidency back.
...You'd do that?

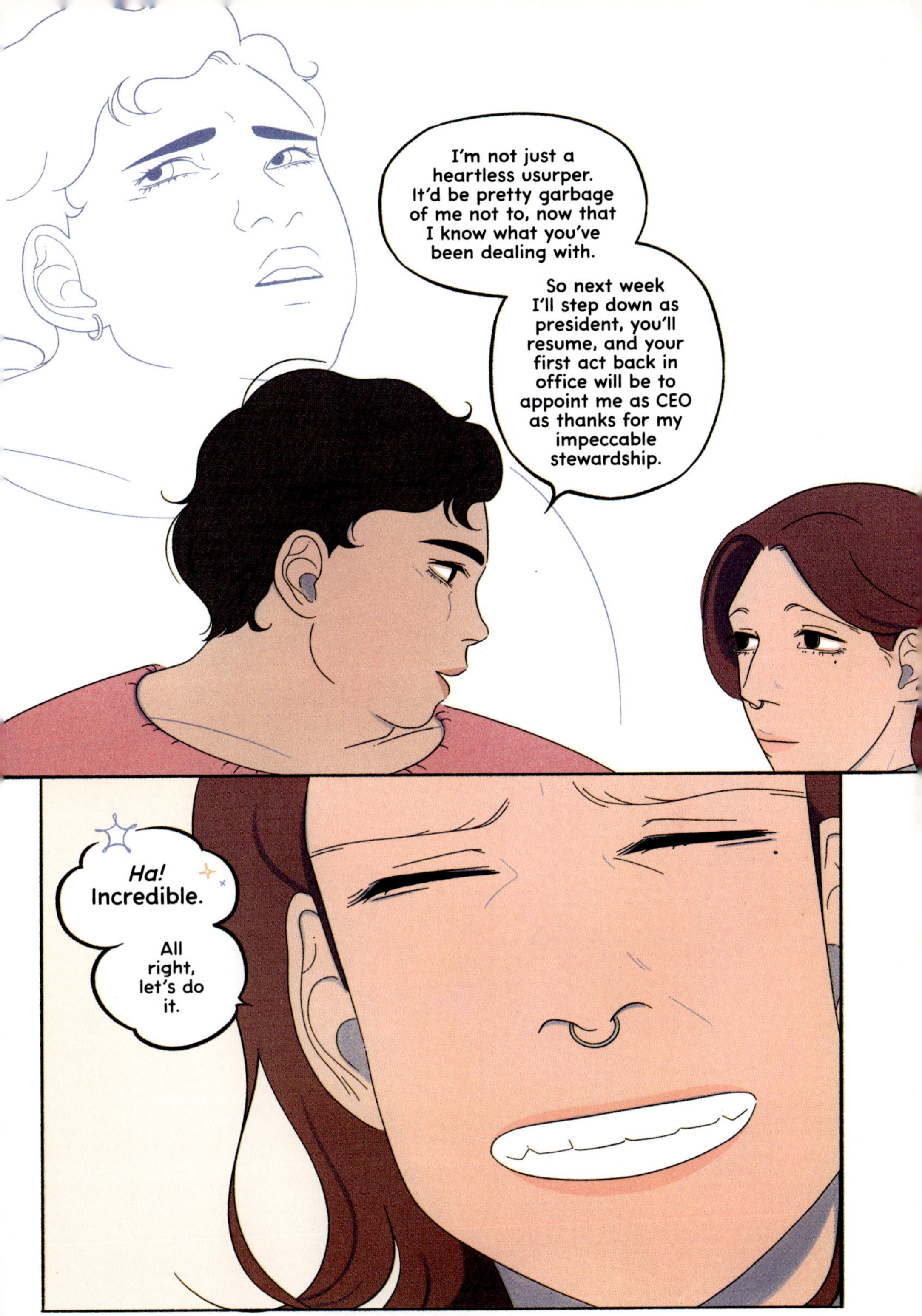
I'm not just a heartless usurper. It'd be pretty garbage of me not to, now that I know what you've been dealing with.
So next week I'll step down as president, you'll resume, and your first act back in office will be to appoint me as CEO as thanks for my impeccable stewardship.
Ha! Incredible.
All right, let's do it.

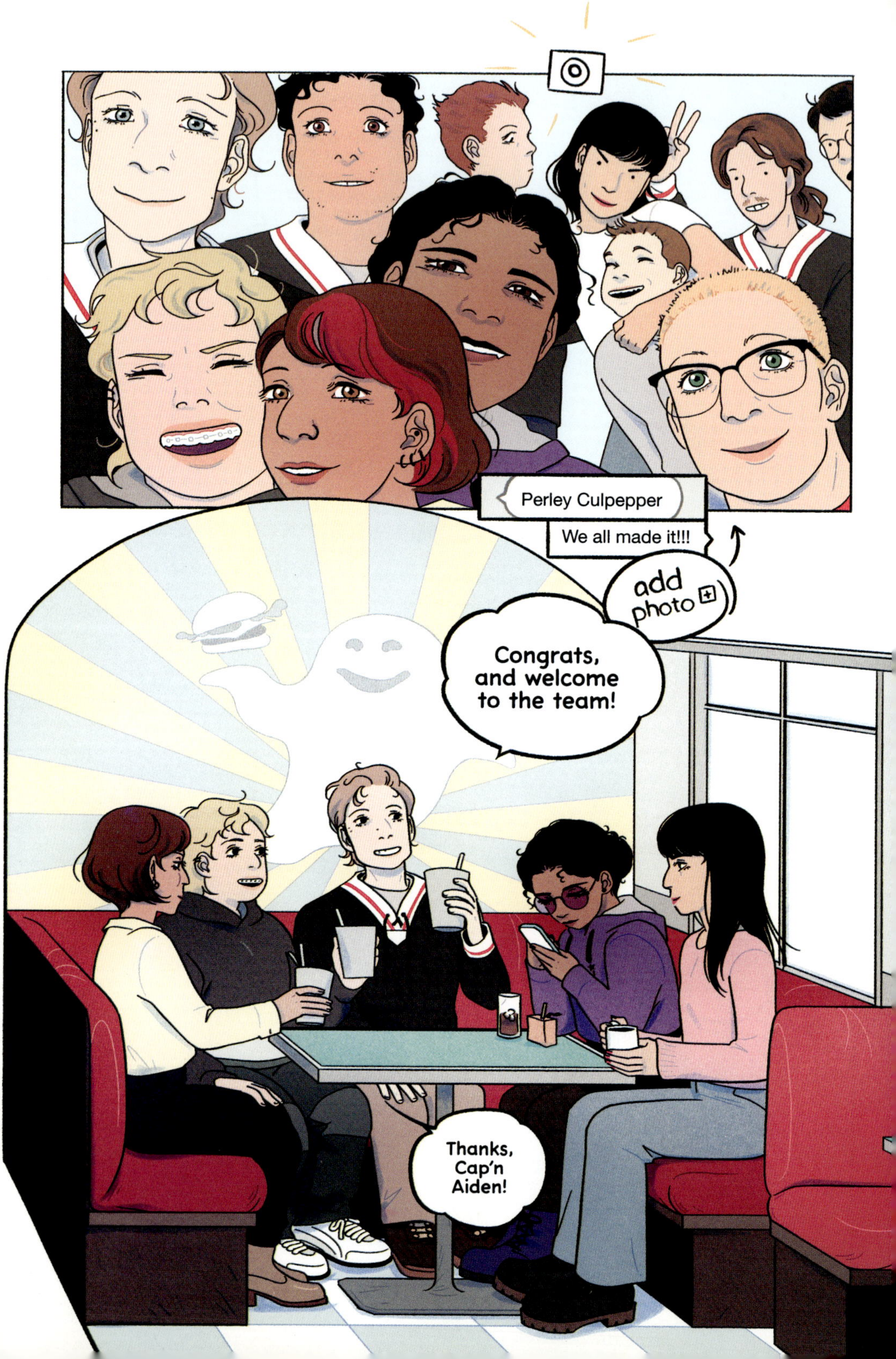
Perley Culpepper
We all made it!!!
add photo
Congrats, and welcome to the team!
Thanks, Cap'n Aiden!

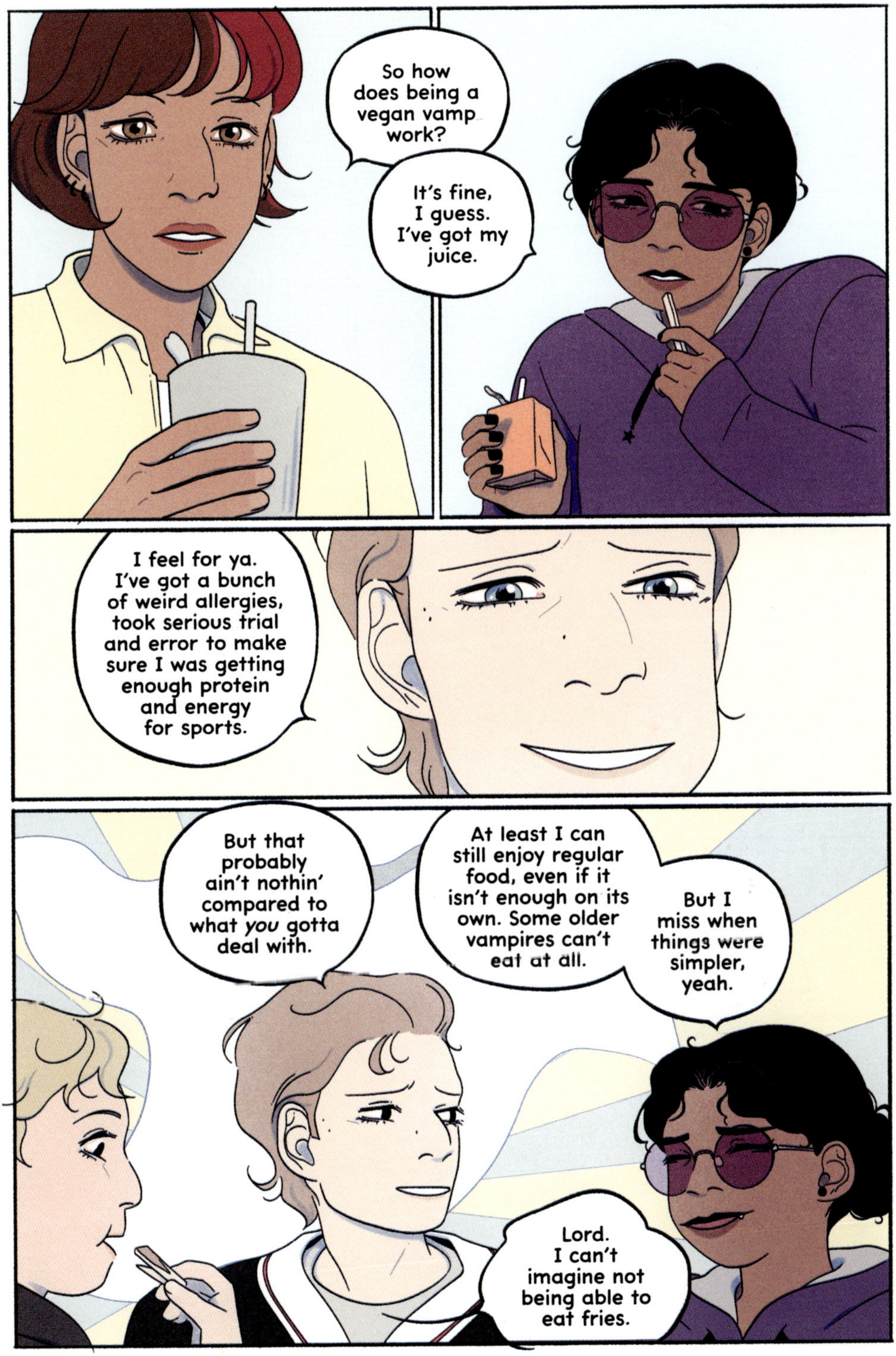
So how does being a vegan vamp work?
It's fine, I guess. I've got my juice.
I feel for ya. I've got a bunch of weird allergies, took serious trial and error to make sure I was getting enough protein and energy for sports.
But that probably ain't nothin' compared to what *you* gotta deal with.
At least I can still enjoy regular food, even if it isn't enough on its own. Some older vampires can't eat at all.
But I miss when things were simpler, yeah.
Lord. I can't imagine not being able to eat fries.

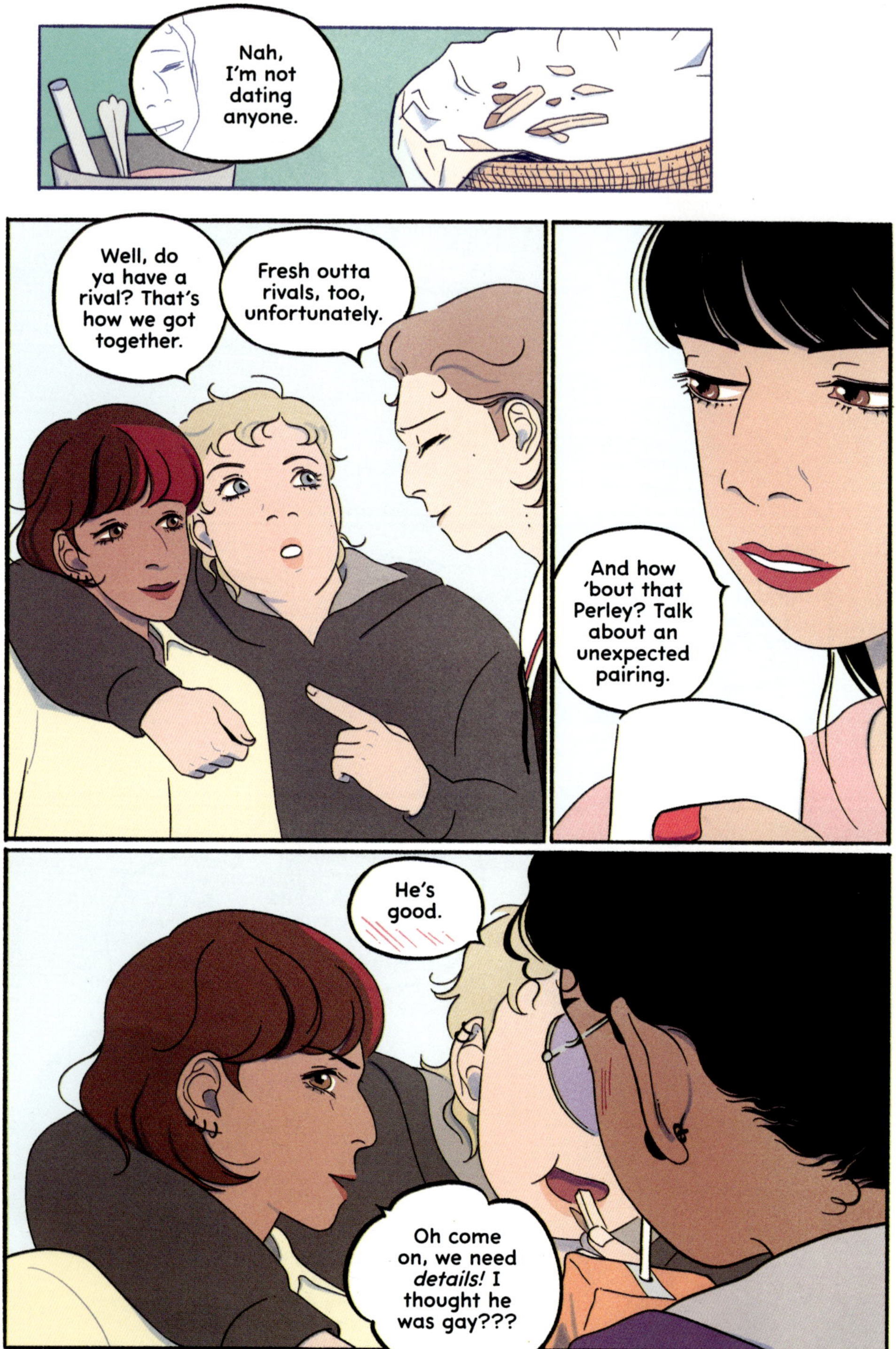
Nah, I'm not dating anyone.
Well, do ya have a rival? That's how we got together.
Fresh outta rivals, too, unfortunately.
And how 'bout that Perley? Talk about an unexpected pairing.
He's good.
Oh come on, we need *details!* I thought he was gay???

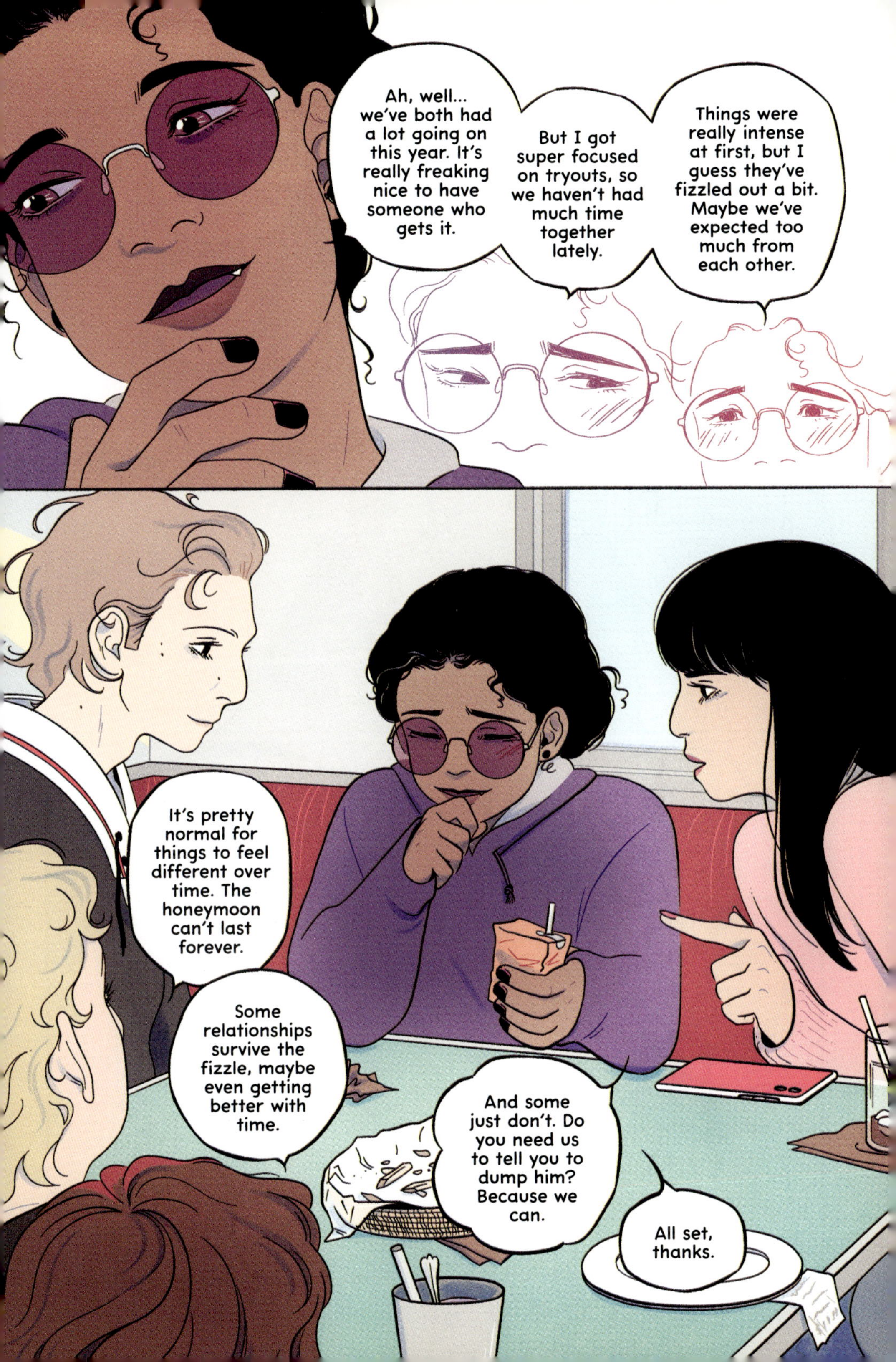
Ah, well... we've both had a lot going on this year. It's really freaking nice to have someone who gets it.
But I got super focused on tryouts, so we haven't had much time together lately.
Things were really intense at first, but I guess they've fizzled out a bit. Maybe we've expected too much from each other.
It's pretty normal for things to feel different over time. The honeymoon can't last forever.
Some relationships survive the fizzle, maybe even getting better with time.
And some just don't. Do you need us to tell you to dump him? Because we can.
All set, thanks.

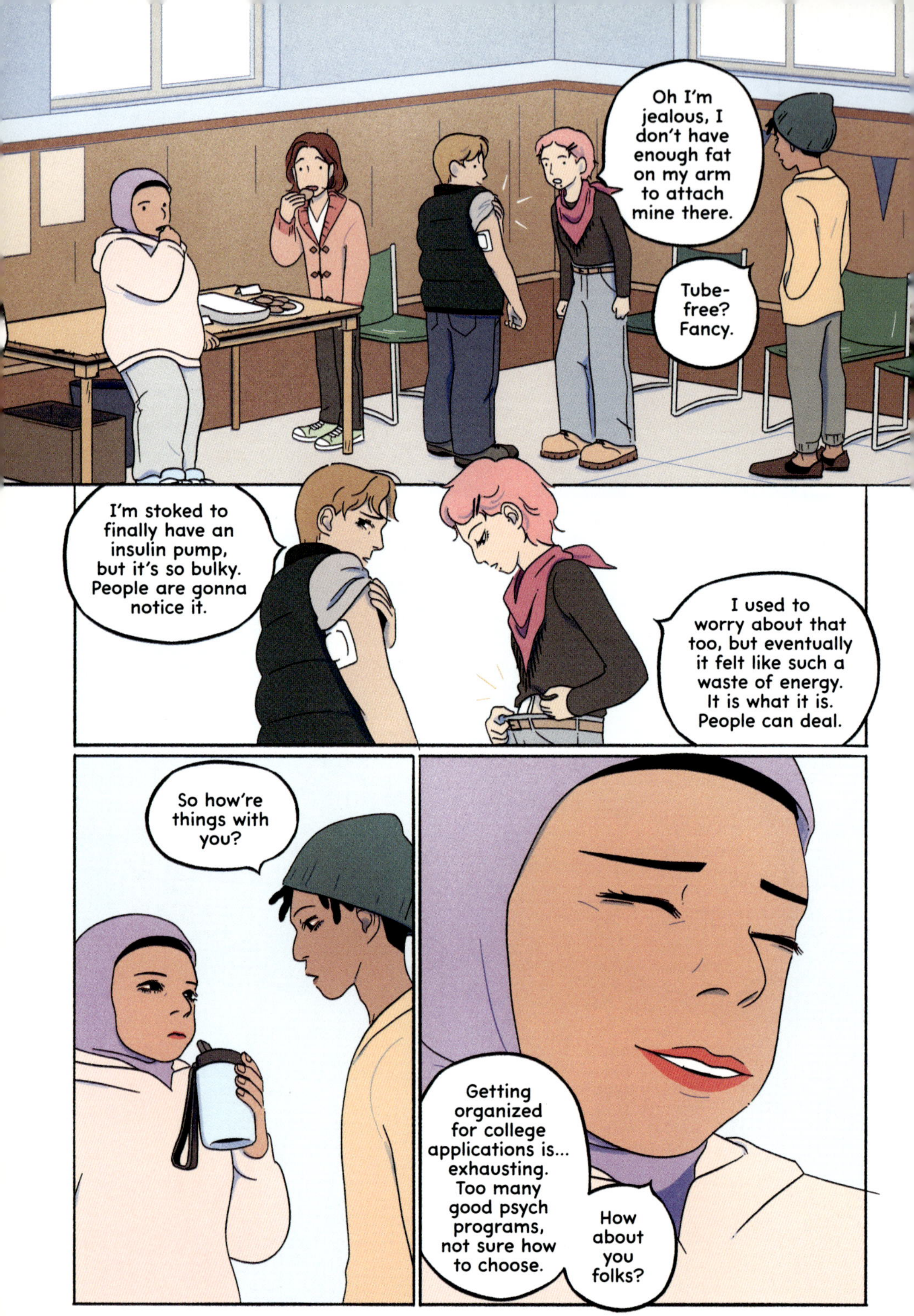

Oh I'm jealous, I don't have enough fat on my arm to attach mine there.
Tube-free? Fancy.
I'm stoked to finally have an insulin pump, but it's so bulky. People are gonna notice it.
I used to worry about that too, but eventually it felt like such a waste of energy. It is what it is. People can deal.
So how're things with you?
Getting organized for college applications is... exhausting. Too many good psych programs, not sure how to choose.
How about you folks?

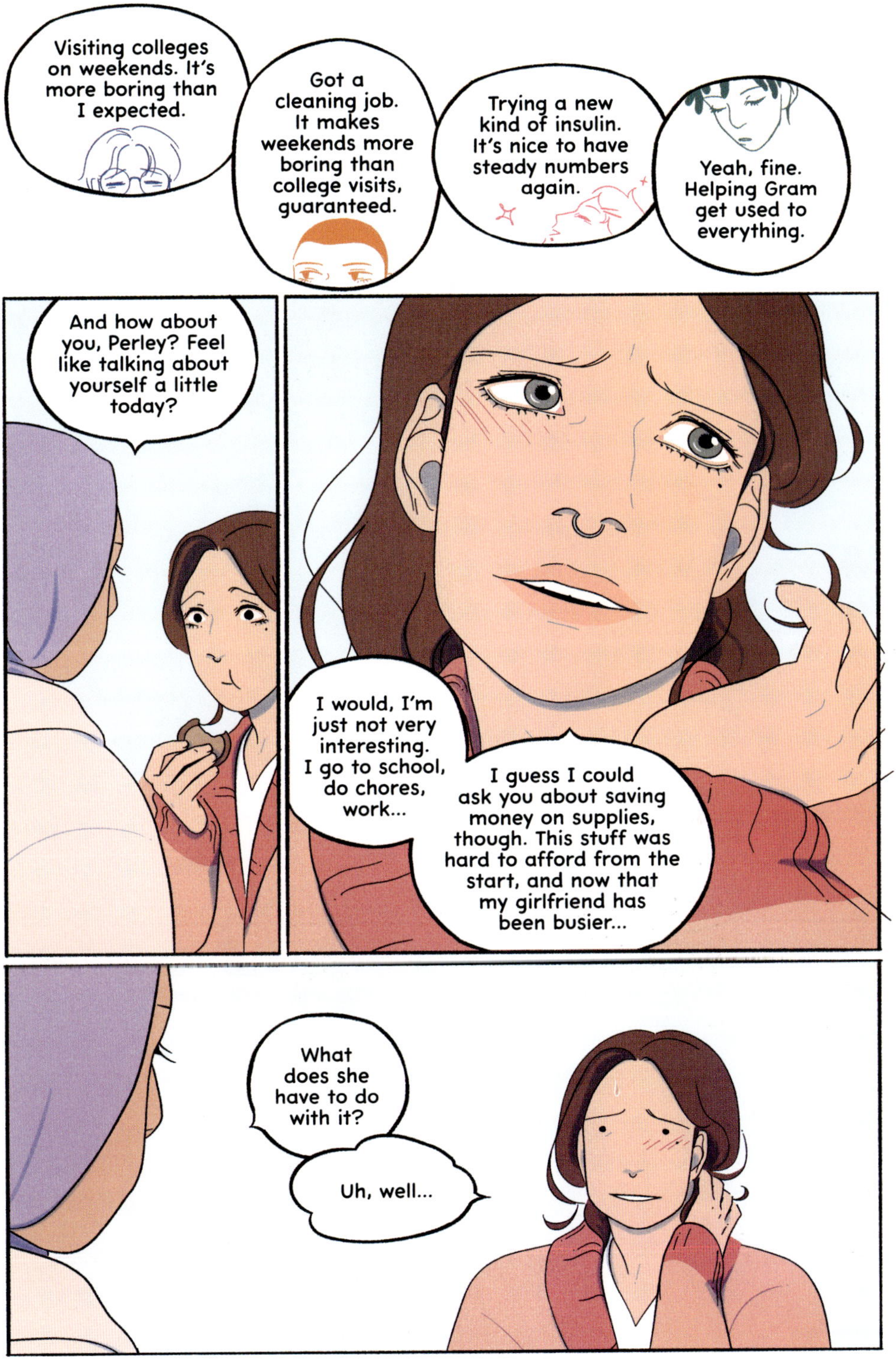
Visiting colleges on weekends. It's more boring than I expected.
Got a cleaning job. It makes weekends more boring than college visits, guaranteed.
Trying a new kind of insulin. It's nice to have steady numbers again.
Yeah, fine. Helping Gram get used to everything.
And how about you, Perley? Feel like talking about yourself a little today?
I would, I'm just not very interesting. I go to school, do chores, work...
I guess I could ask you about saving money on supplies, though. This stuff was hard to afford from the start, and now that my girlfriend has been busier...
What does she have to do with it?
Uh, well...

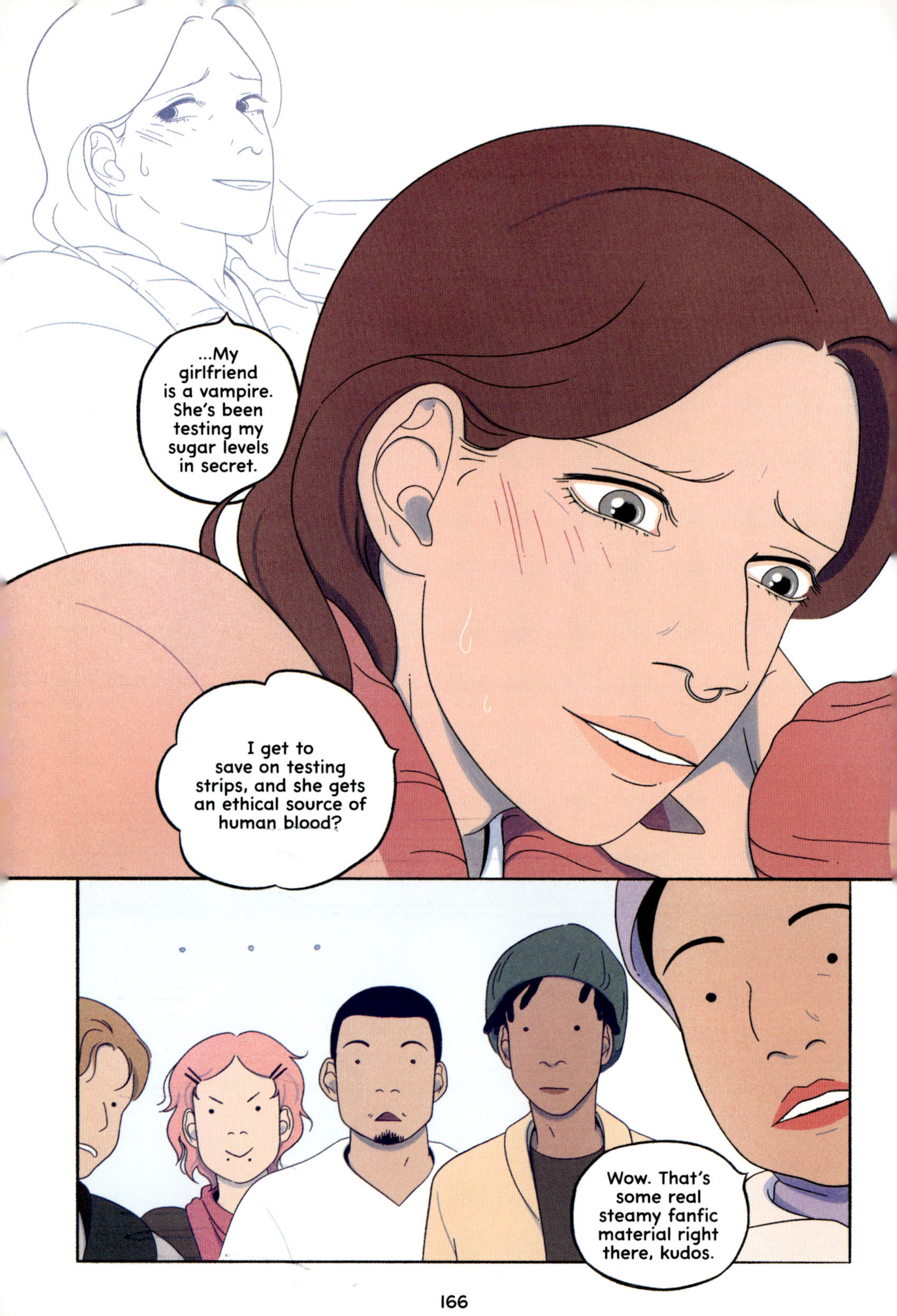
...My girlfriend is a vampire. She's been testing my sugar levels in secret.
I get to save on testing strips, and she gets an ethical source of human blood?
Wow. That's some real steamy fanfic material right there, kudos.

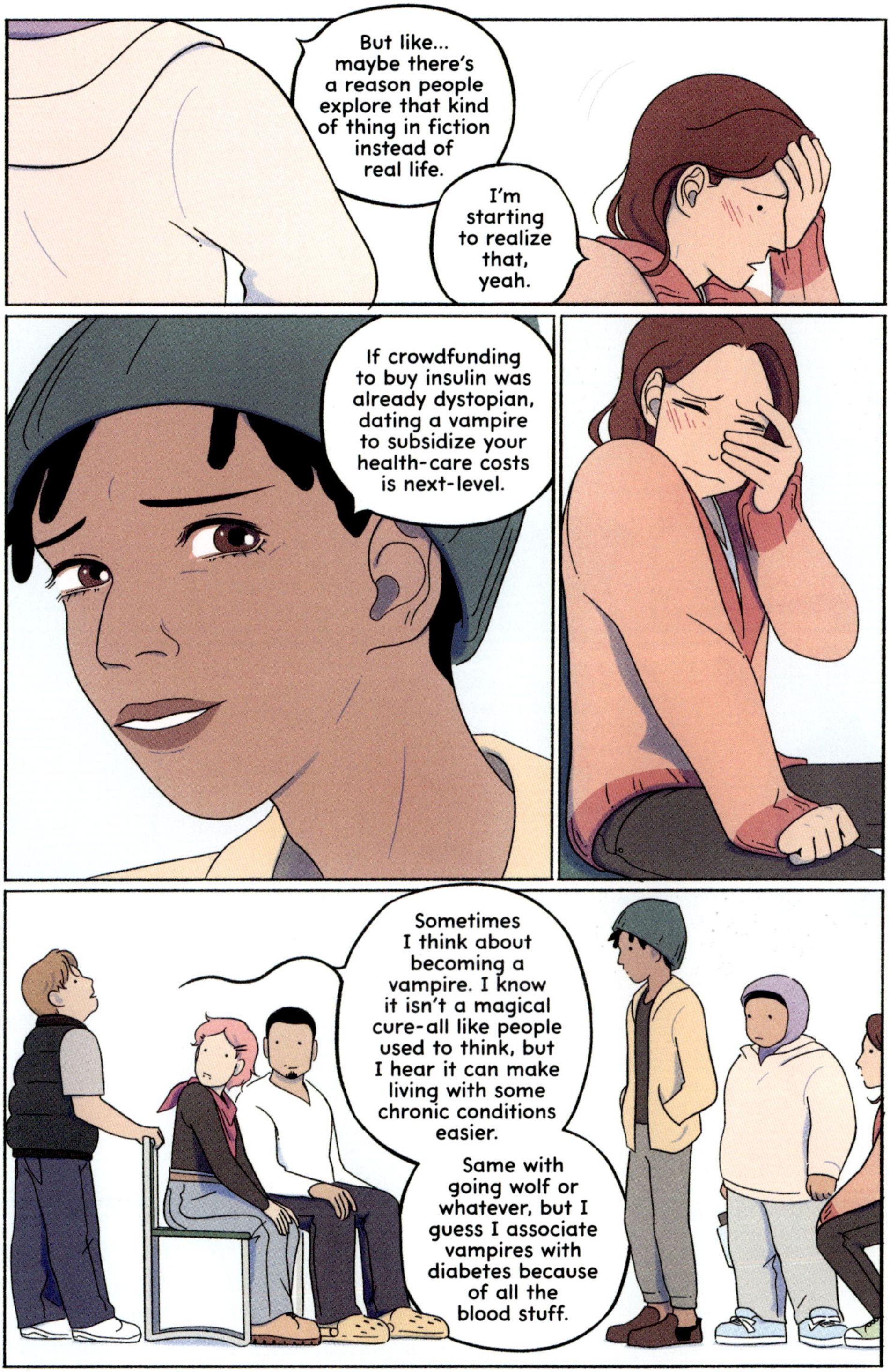
But like... maybe there's a reason people explore that kind of thing in fiction instead of real life.
I'm starting to realize that, yeah.
If crowdfunding to buy insulin was already dystopian, dating a vampire to subsidize your health-care costs is next-level.
Sometimes I think about becoming a vampire. I know it isn't a magical cure-all like people used to think, but I hear it can make living with some chronic conditions easier.
Same with going wolf or whatever, but I guess I associate vampires with diabetes because of all the blood stuff.

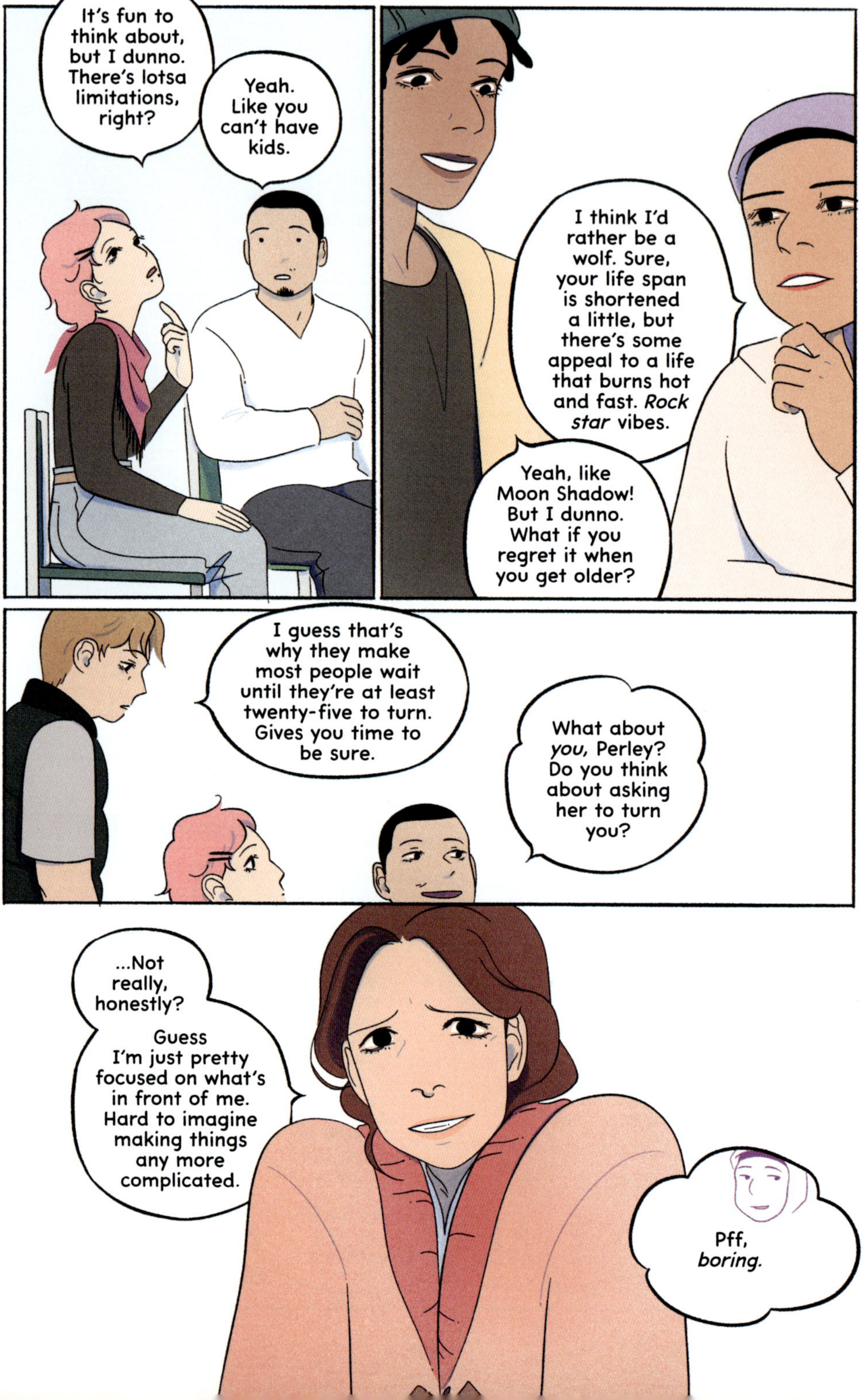
It's fun to think about, but I dunno. There's lotsa limitations, right?
Yeah. Like you can't have kids.
I think I'd rather be a wolf. Sure, your life span is shortened a little, but there's some appeal to a life that burns hot and fast. *Rock star* vibes.
Yeah, like Moon Shadow! But I dunno. What if you regret it when you get older?
I guess that's why they make most people wait until they're at least twenty-five to turn. Gives you time to be sure.
What about *you,* Perley? Do you think about asking her to turn you?
...Not really, honestly?
Guess I'm just pretty focused on what's in front of me. Hard to imagine making things any more complicated.
Pff, *boring.*

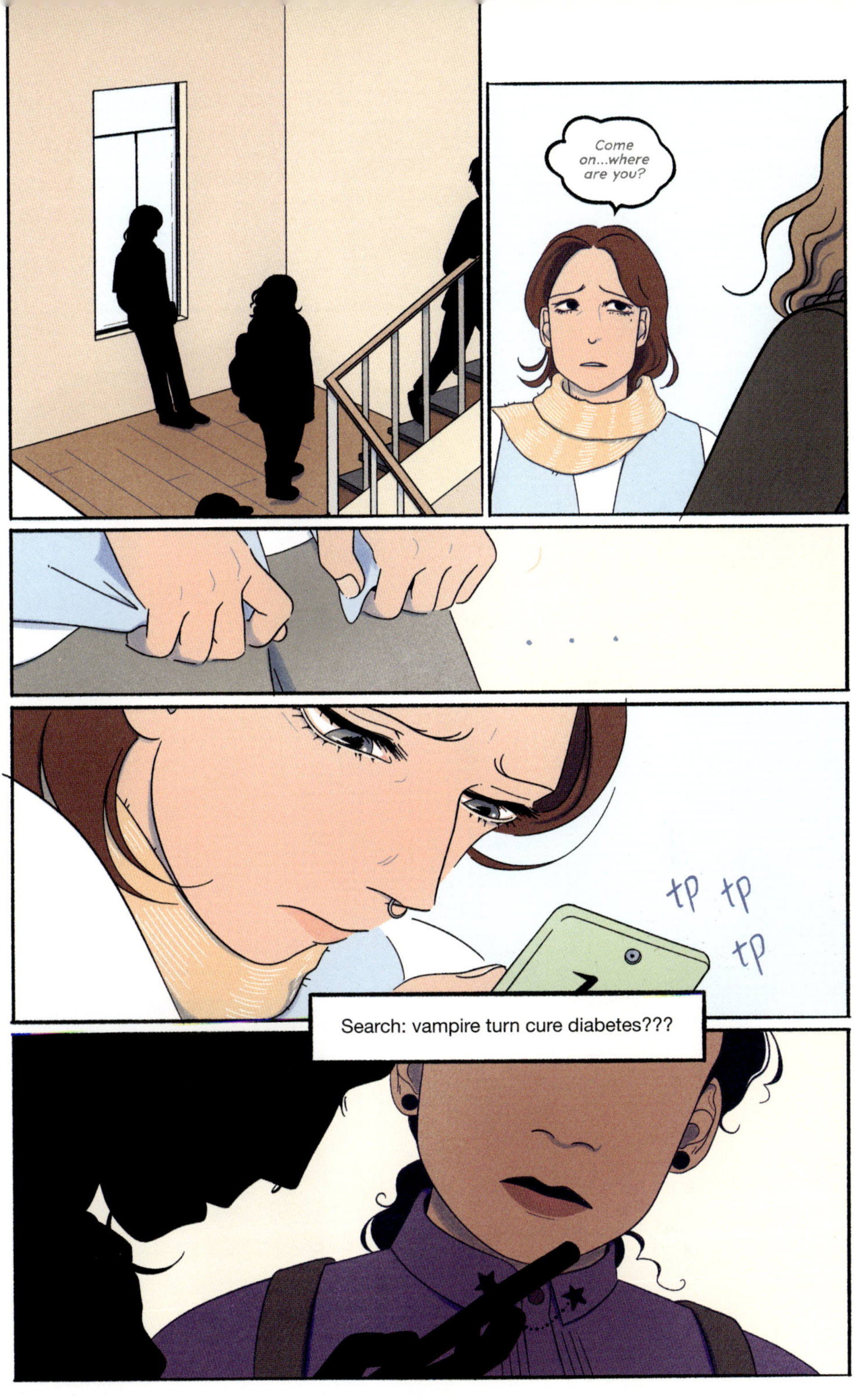
Come on...where are you?
. . .
tp tp
tp
Search: vampire turn cure diabetes???

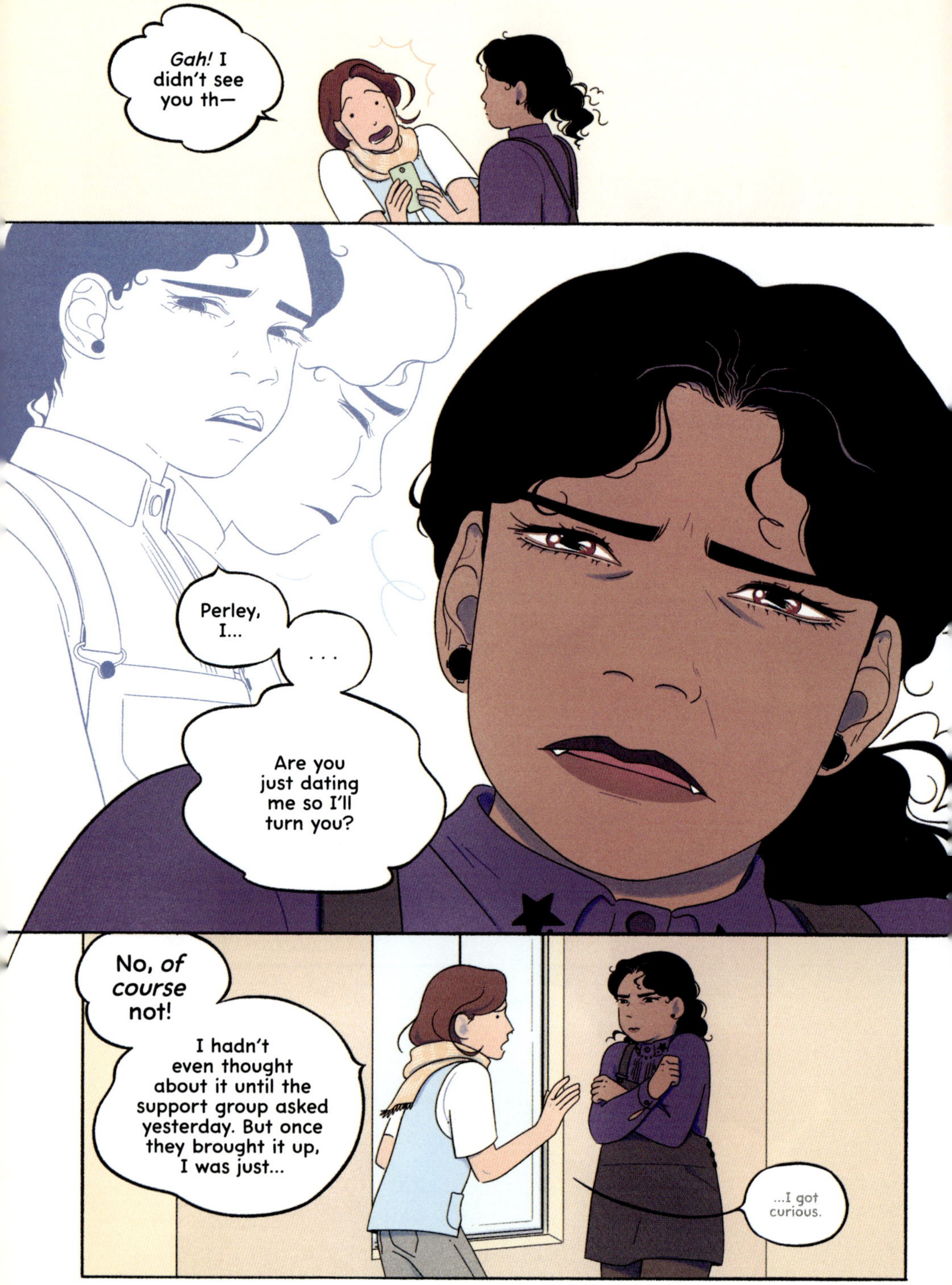
Gah! I didn't see you th—
Perley, I...
. . .
Are you just dating me so I'll turn you?
No, of course not!
I hadn't even thought about it until the support group asked yesterday. But once they brought it up, I was just...
...I got curious.

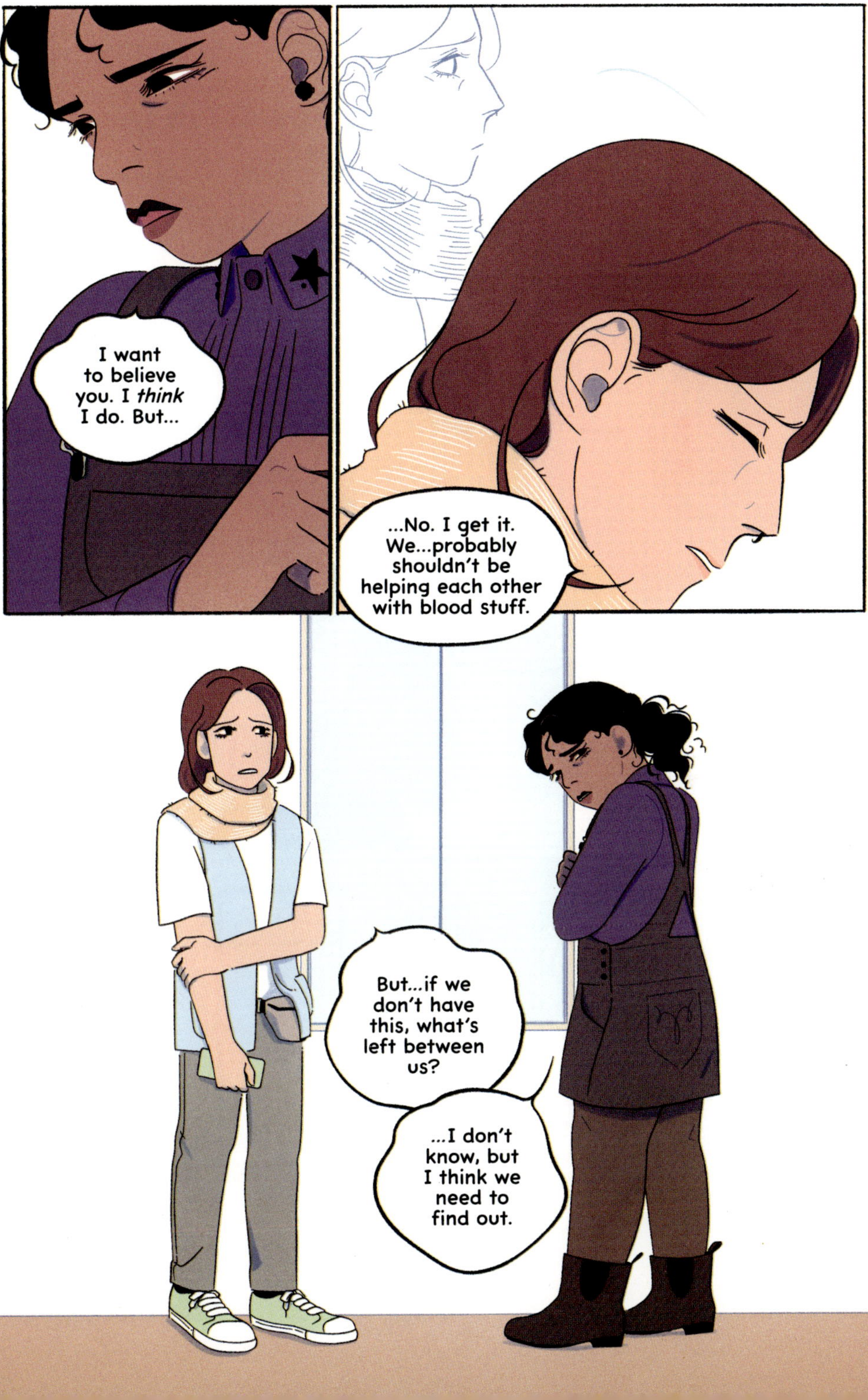
I want to believe you. I *think* I do. But...
...No. I get it. We...probably shouldn't be helping each other with blood stuff.
But...if we don't have this, what's left between us?
...I don't know, but I think we need to find out.

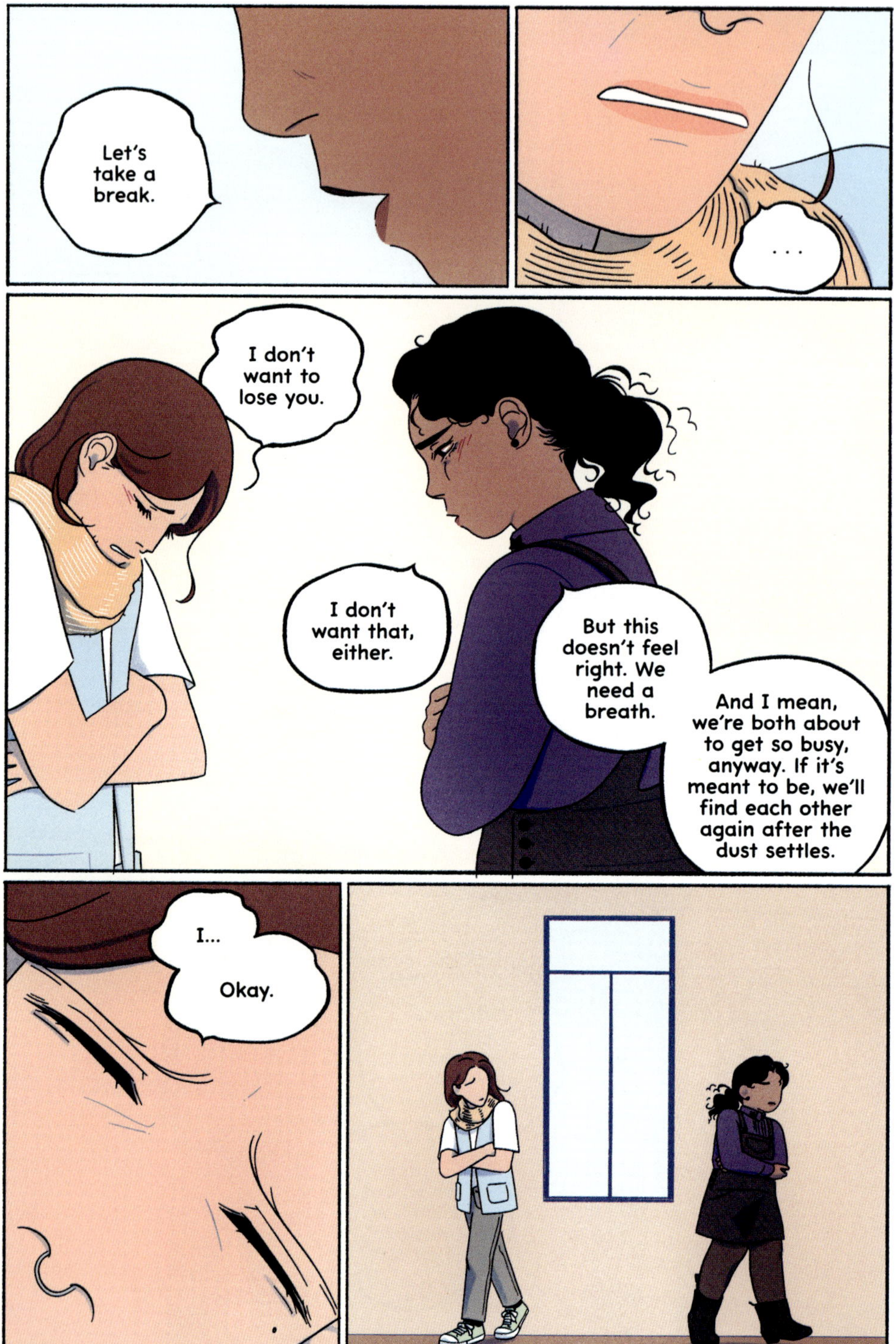
Let's take a break.
. . .
I don't want to lose you.
I don't want that, either.
But this doesn't feel right. We need a breath.
And I mean, we're both about to get so busy, anyway. If it's meant to be, we'll find each other again after the dust settles.
I...
Okay.

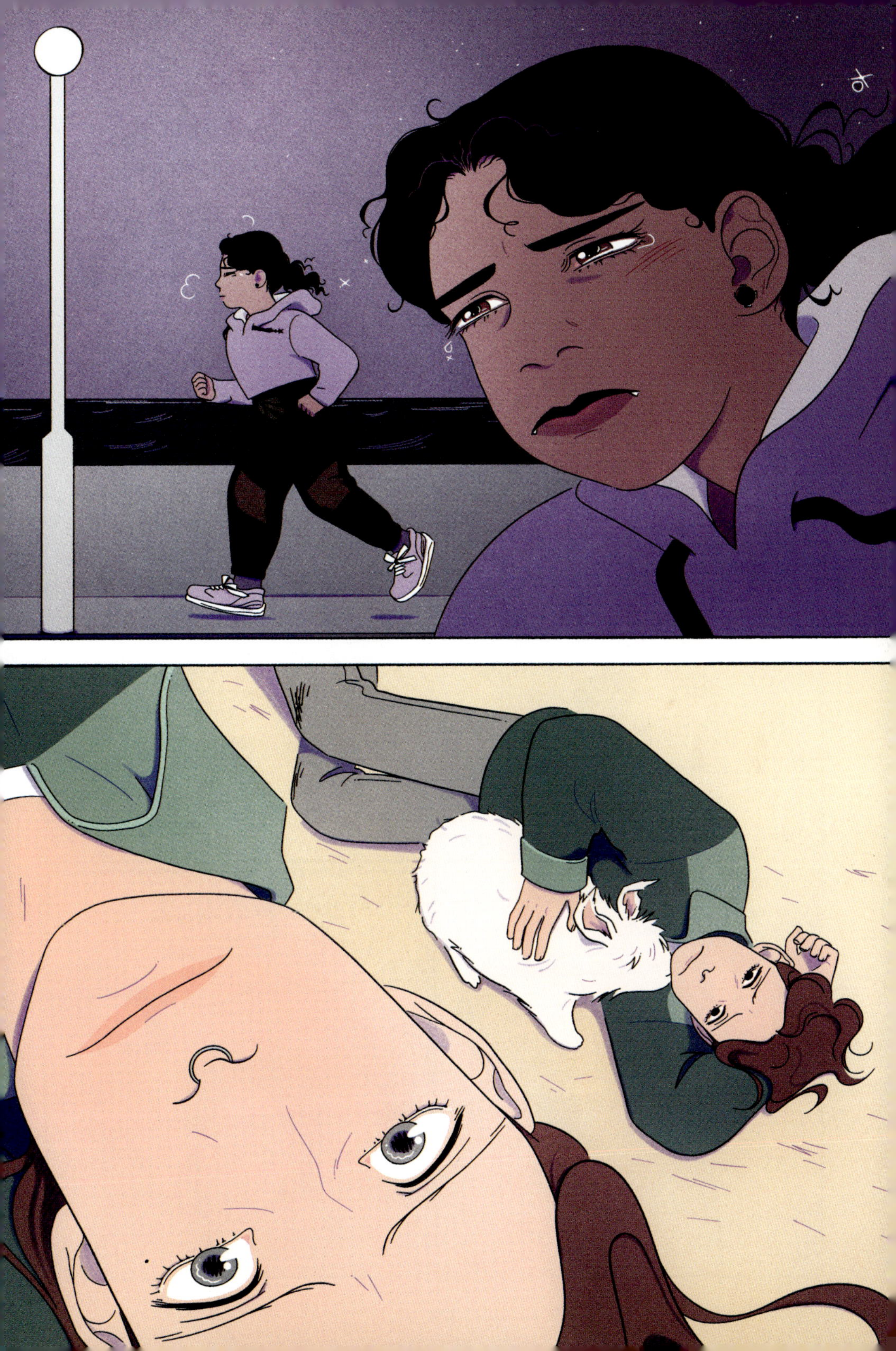

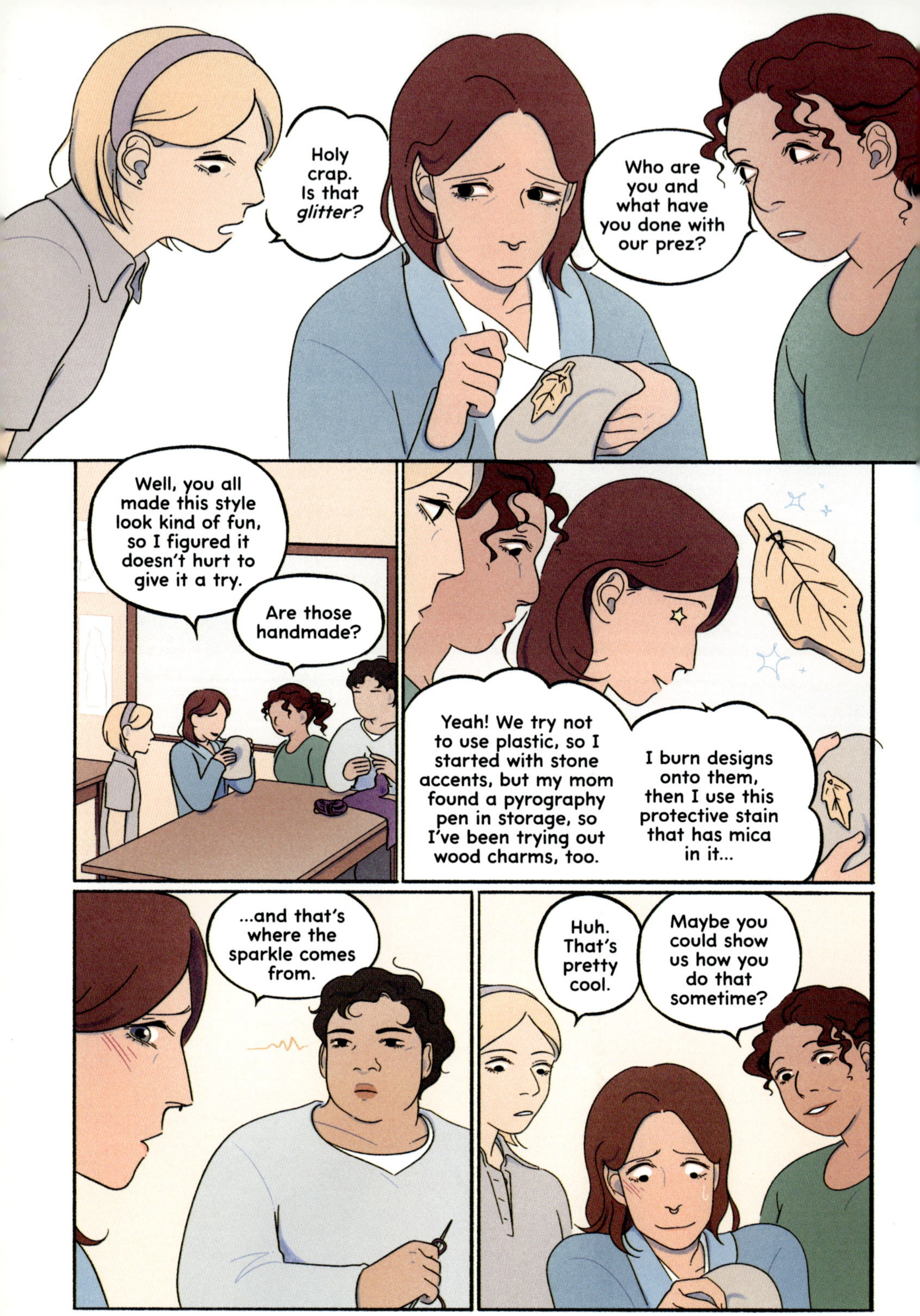
Holy crap. Is that *glitter*?
Who are you and what have you done with our prez?
Well, you all made this style look kind of fun, so I figured it doesn't hurt to give it a try.
Are those handmade?
Yeah! We try not to use plastic, so I started with stone accents, but my mom found a pyrography pen in storage, so I've been trying out wood charms, too.
I burn designs onto them, then I use this protective stain that has mica in it...
...and that's where the sparkle comes from.
Huh. That's pretty cool.
Maybe you could show us how you do that sometime?

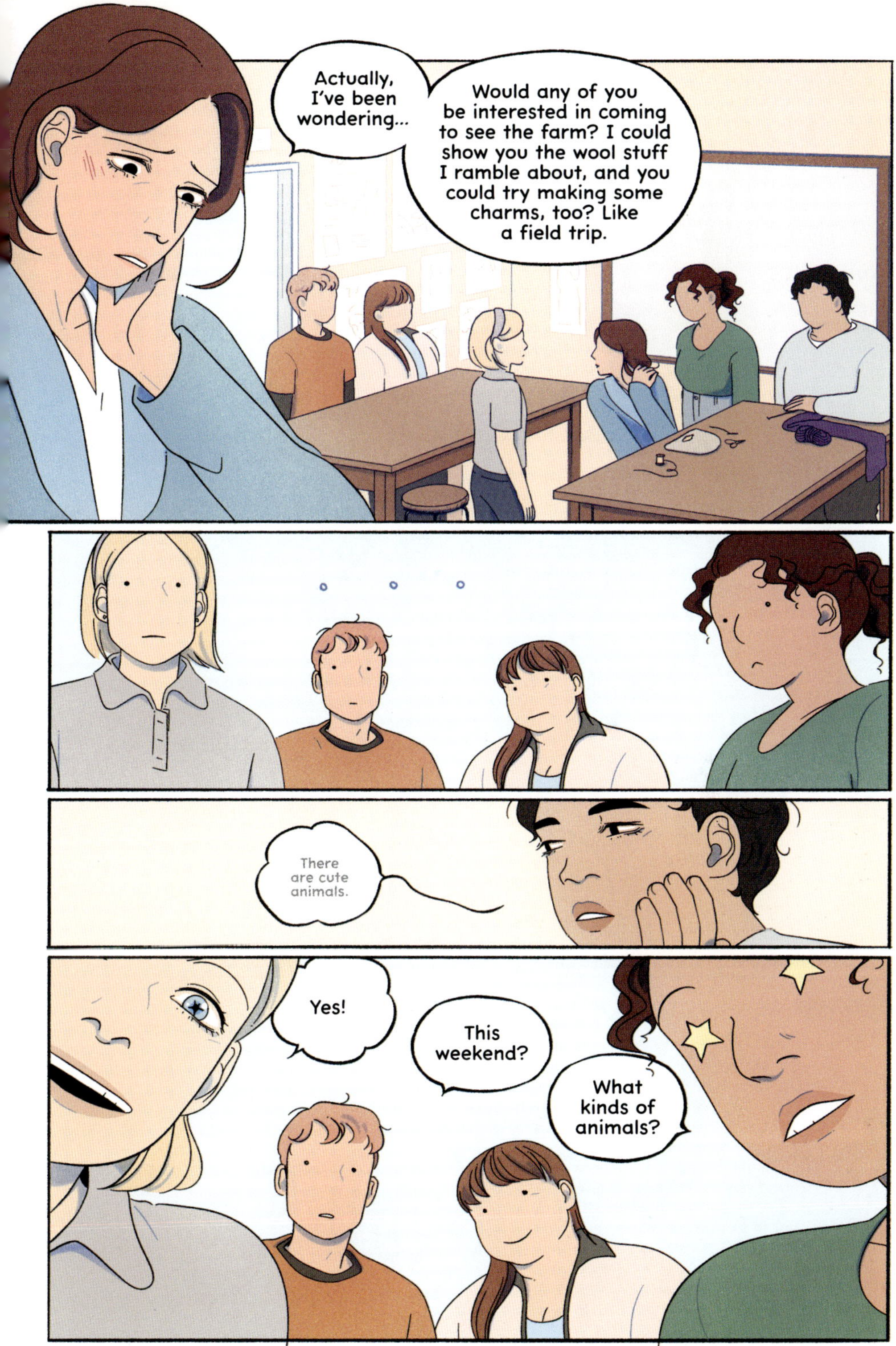
Actually, I've been wondering...
Would any of you be interested in coming to see the farm? I could show you the wool stuff I ramble about, and you could try making some charms, too? Like a field trip.
There are cute animals.
Yes!
This weekend?
What kinds of animals?

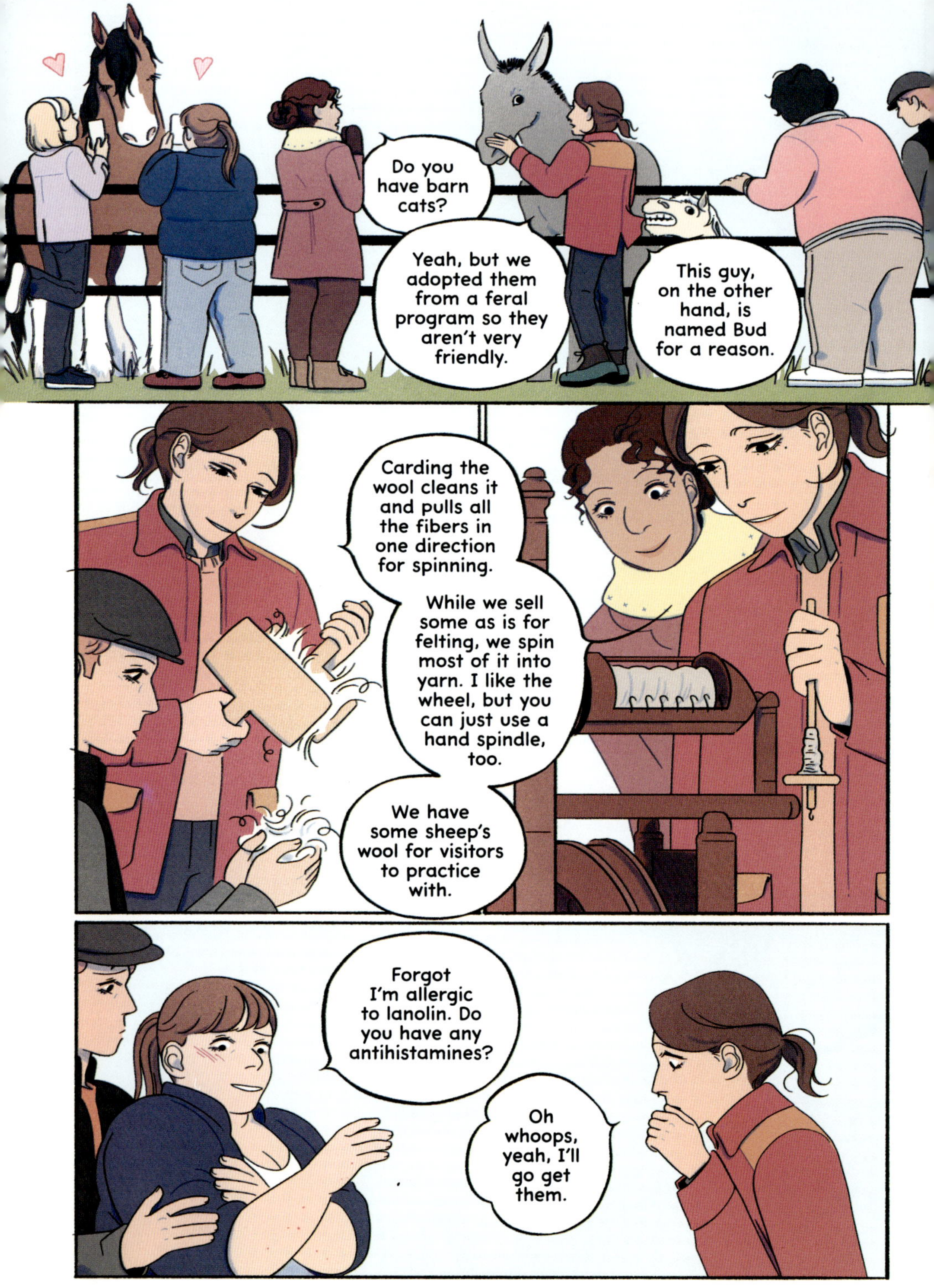
Do you have barn cats?
Yeah, but we adopted them from a feral program so they aren't very friendly.
This guy, on the other hand, is named Bud for a reason.
Carding the wool cleans it and pulls all the fibers in one direction for spinning.
While we sell some as is for felting, we spin most of it into yarn. I like the wheel, but you can just use a hand spindle, too.
We have some sheep's wool for visitors to practice with.
Forgot I'm allergic to lanolin. Do you have any antihistamines?
Oh whoops, yeah, I'll go get them.

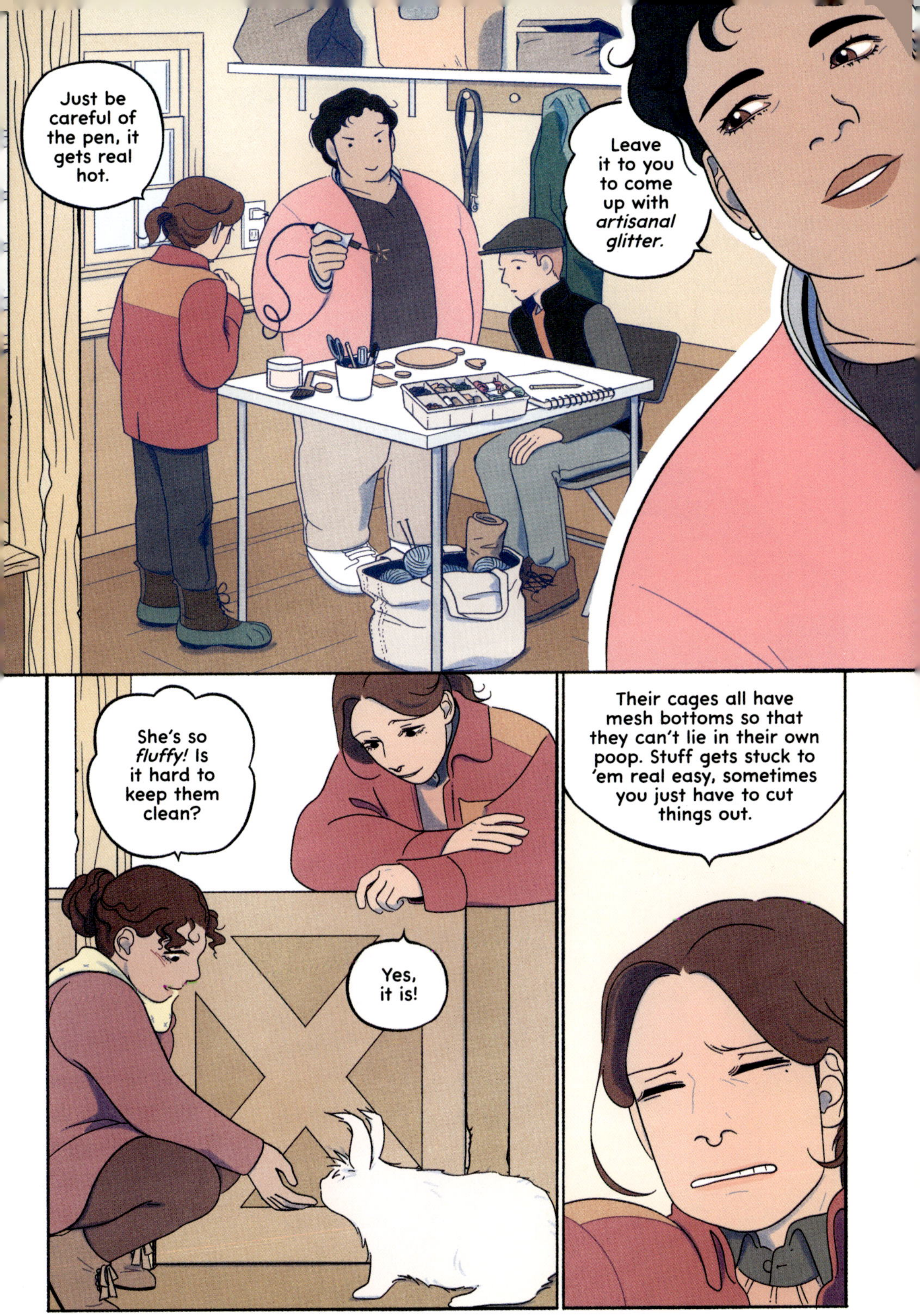

Just be careful of the pen, it gets real hot.
Leave it to you to come up with *artisanal glitter.*
She's so *fluffy!* Is it hard to keep them clean?
Yes, it is!
Their cages all have mesh bottoms so that they can't lie in their own poop. Stuff gets stuck to 'em real easy, sometimes you just have to cut things out.

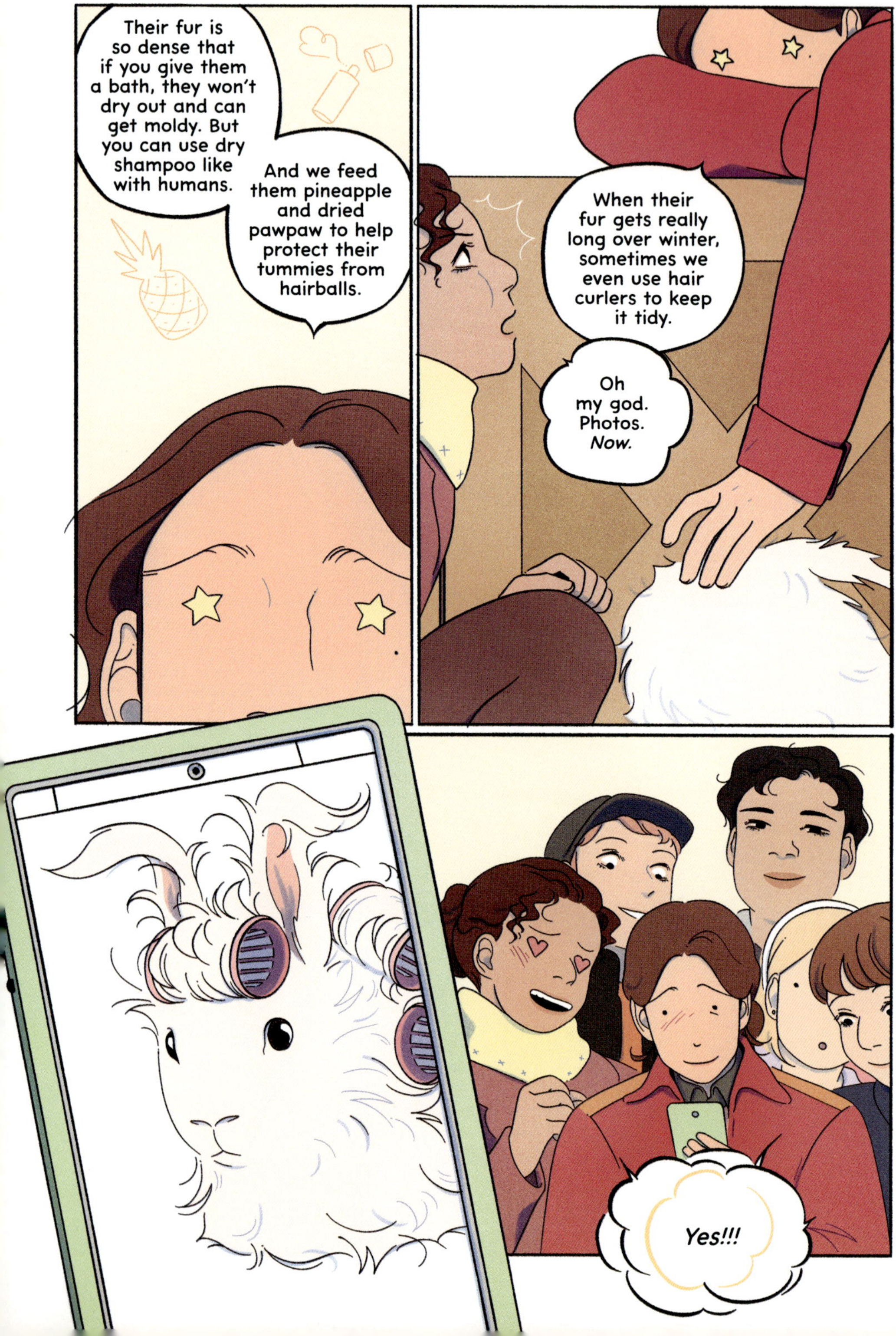
Their fur is so dense that if you give them a bath, they won't dry out and can get moldy. But you can use dry shampoo like with humans.
And we feed them pineapple and dried pawpaw to help protect their tummies from hairballs.
When their fur gets really long over winter, sometimes we even use hair curlers to keep it tidy.
Oh my god. Photos. *Now.*
Yes!!!

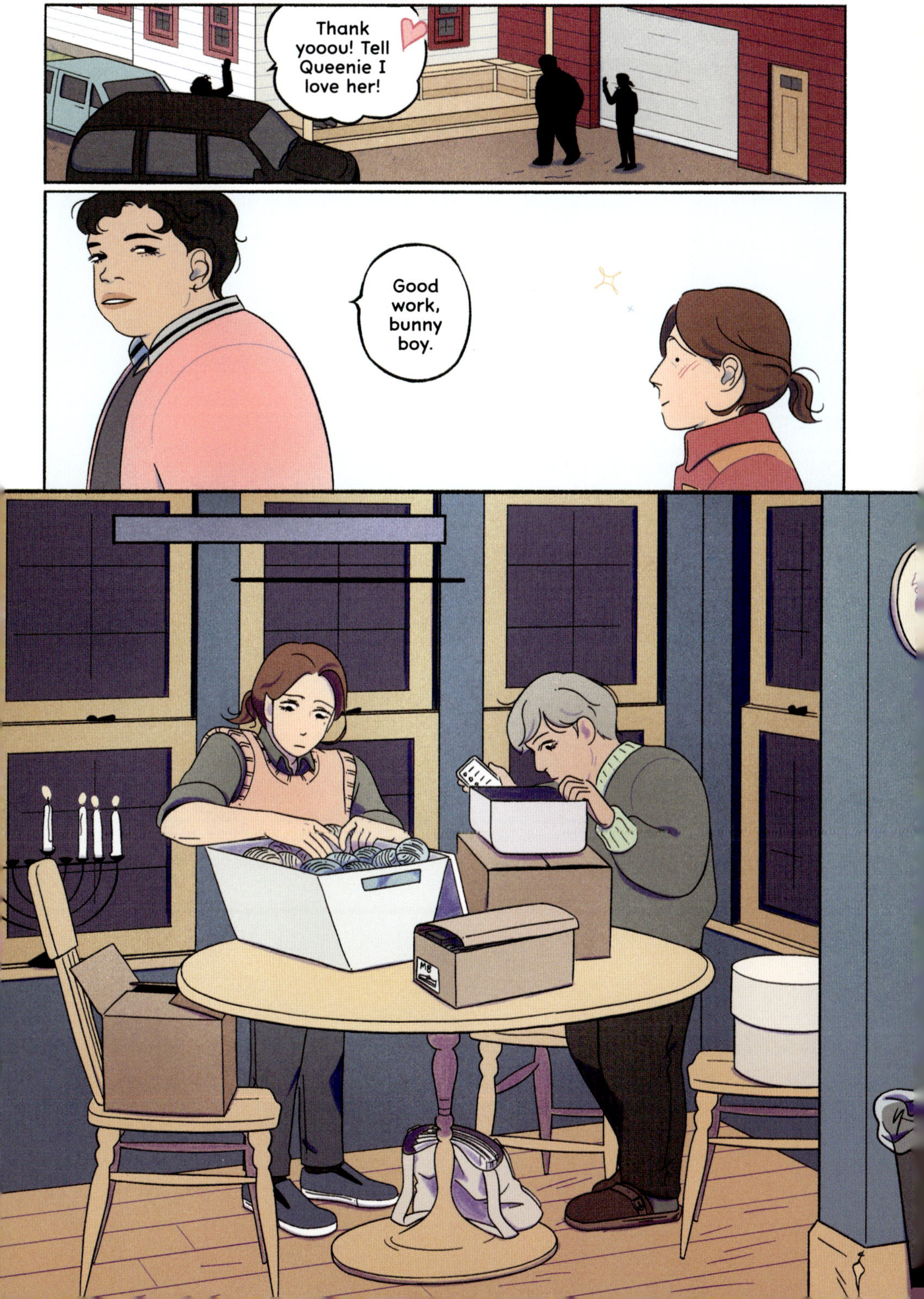
Thank yooou! Tell Queenie I love her!
Good work, bunny boy.
MB

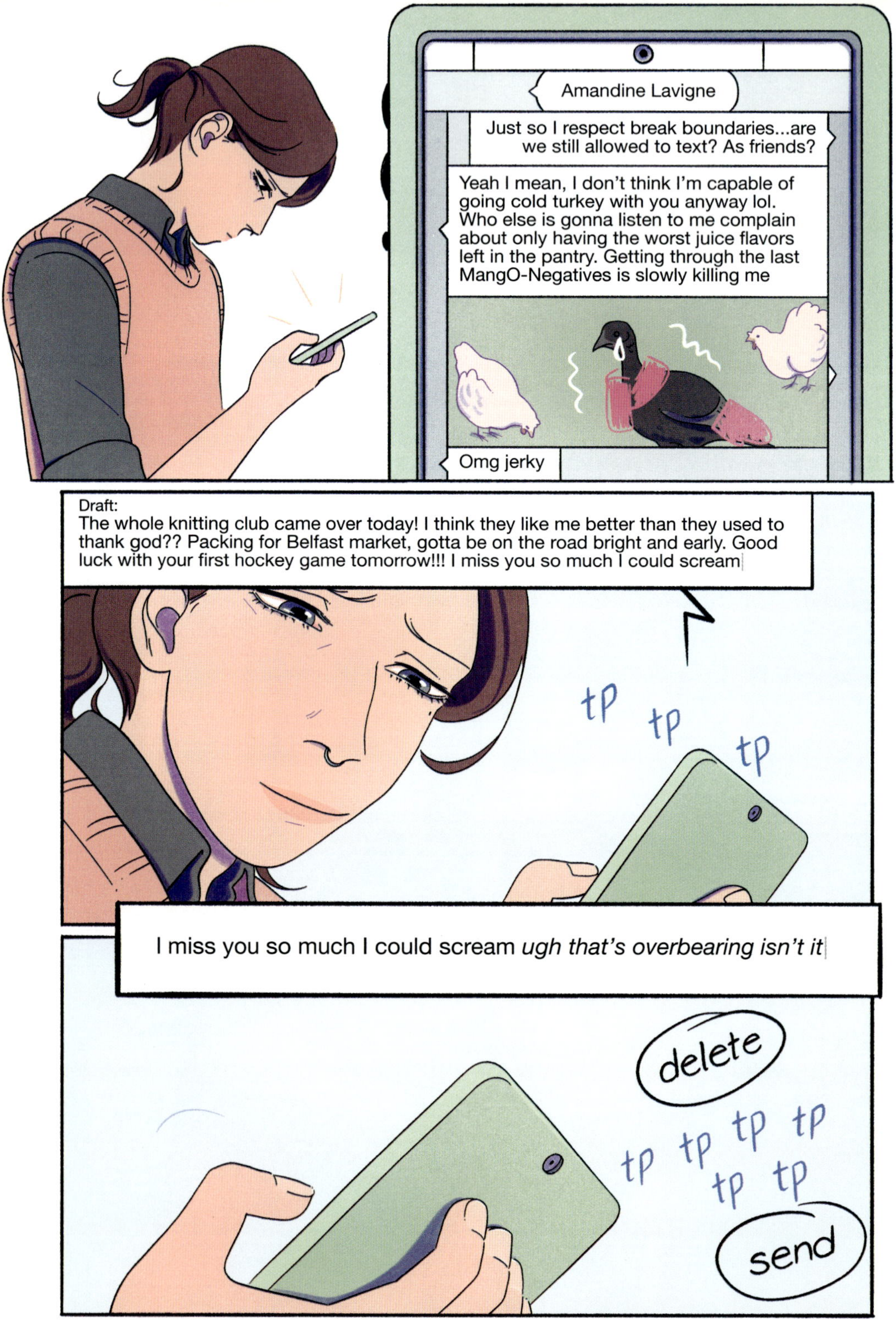

Amandine Lavigne
Just so I respect break boundaries...are we still allowed to text? As friends?
Yeah I mean, I don't think I'm capable of going cold turkey with you anyway lol. Who else is gonna listen to me complain about only having the worst juice flavors left in the pantry. Getting through the last MangO-Negatives is slowly killing me
Omg jerky
Draft:
The whole knitting club came over today! I think they like me better than they used to thank god?? Packing for Belfast market, gotta be on the road bright and early. Good luck with your first hockey game tomorrow!!! I miss you so much I could scream
tp tp tp
I miss you so much I could scream *ugh that's overbearing isn't it*
delete
tp tp tp tp tp tp
send

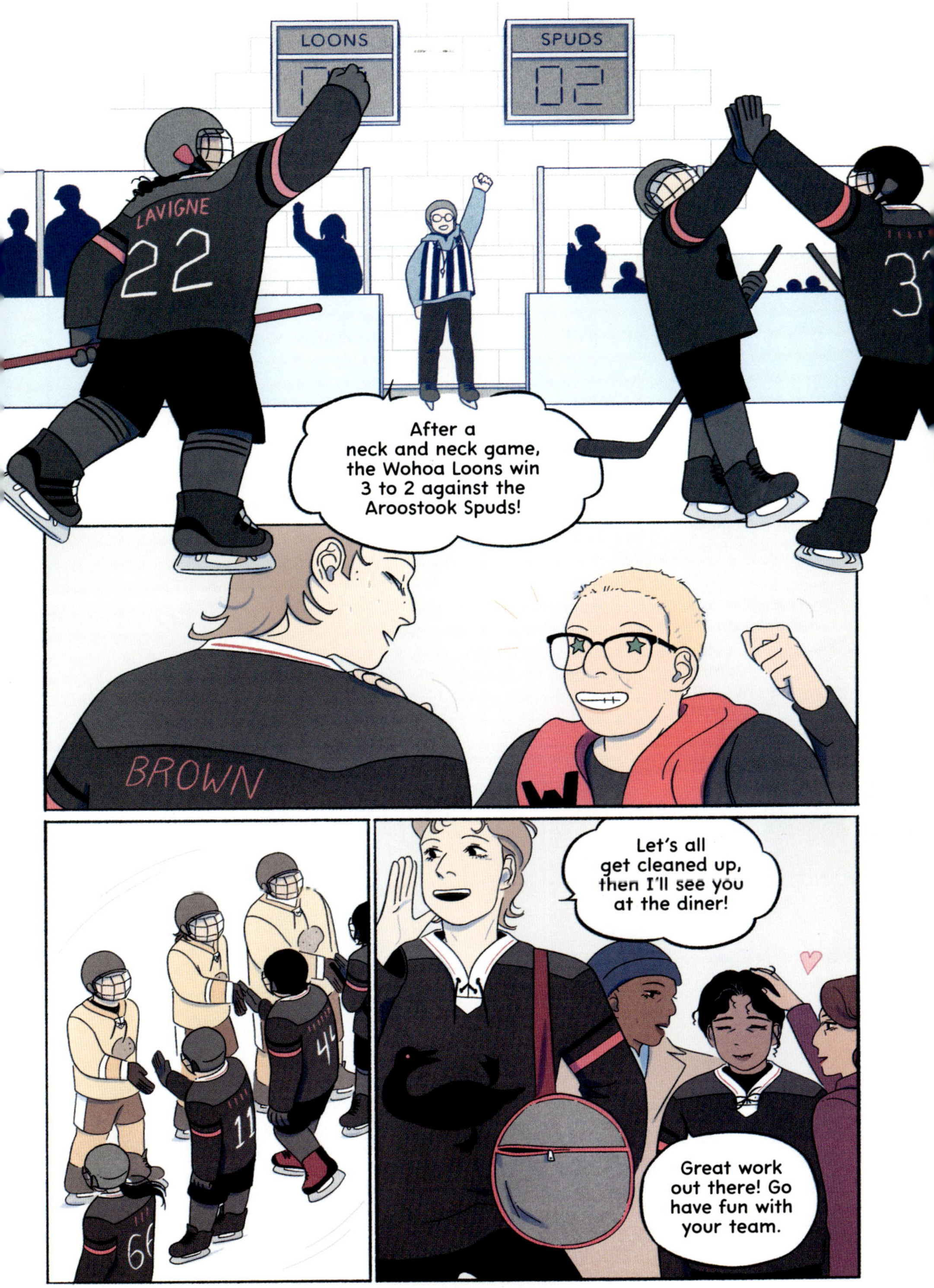
LOONS
SPUDS
02
LAVIGNE
After a neck and neck game, the Wohoa Loons win 3 to 2 against the Aroostook Spuds!
BROWN
Let's all get cleaned up, then I'll see you at the diner!
Great work out there! Go have fun with your team.

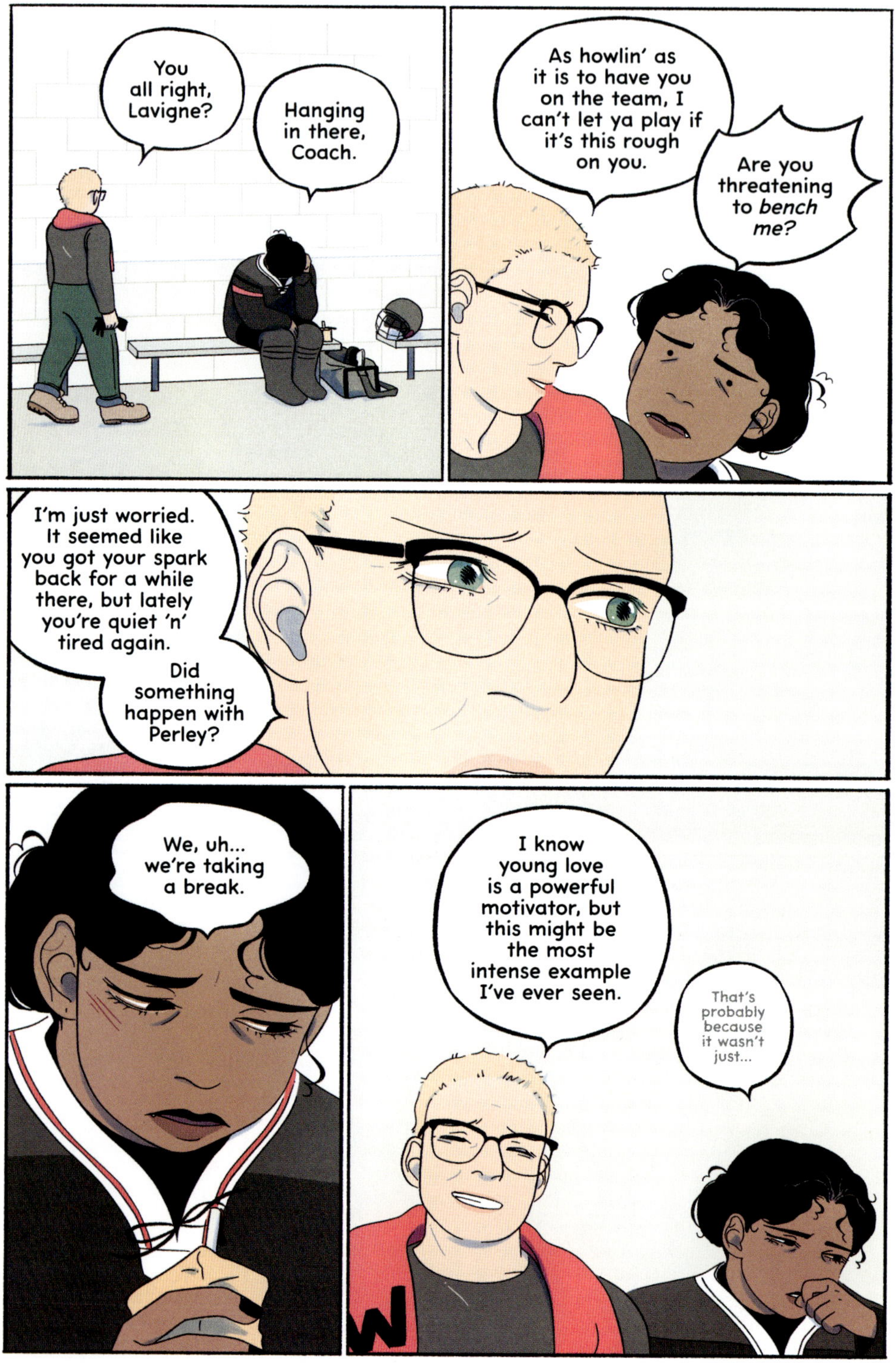
You all right, Lavigne?
Hanging in there, Coach.
As howlin' as it is to have you on the team, I can't let ya play if it's this rough on you.
Are you threatening to *bench* me?
I'm just worried. It seemed like you got your spark back for a while there, but lately you're quiet 'n' tired again.
Did something happen with Perley?
We, uh... we're taking a break.
I know young love is a powerful motivator, but this might be the most intense example I've ever seen.
That's probably because it wasn't just...

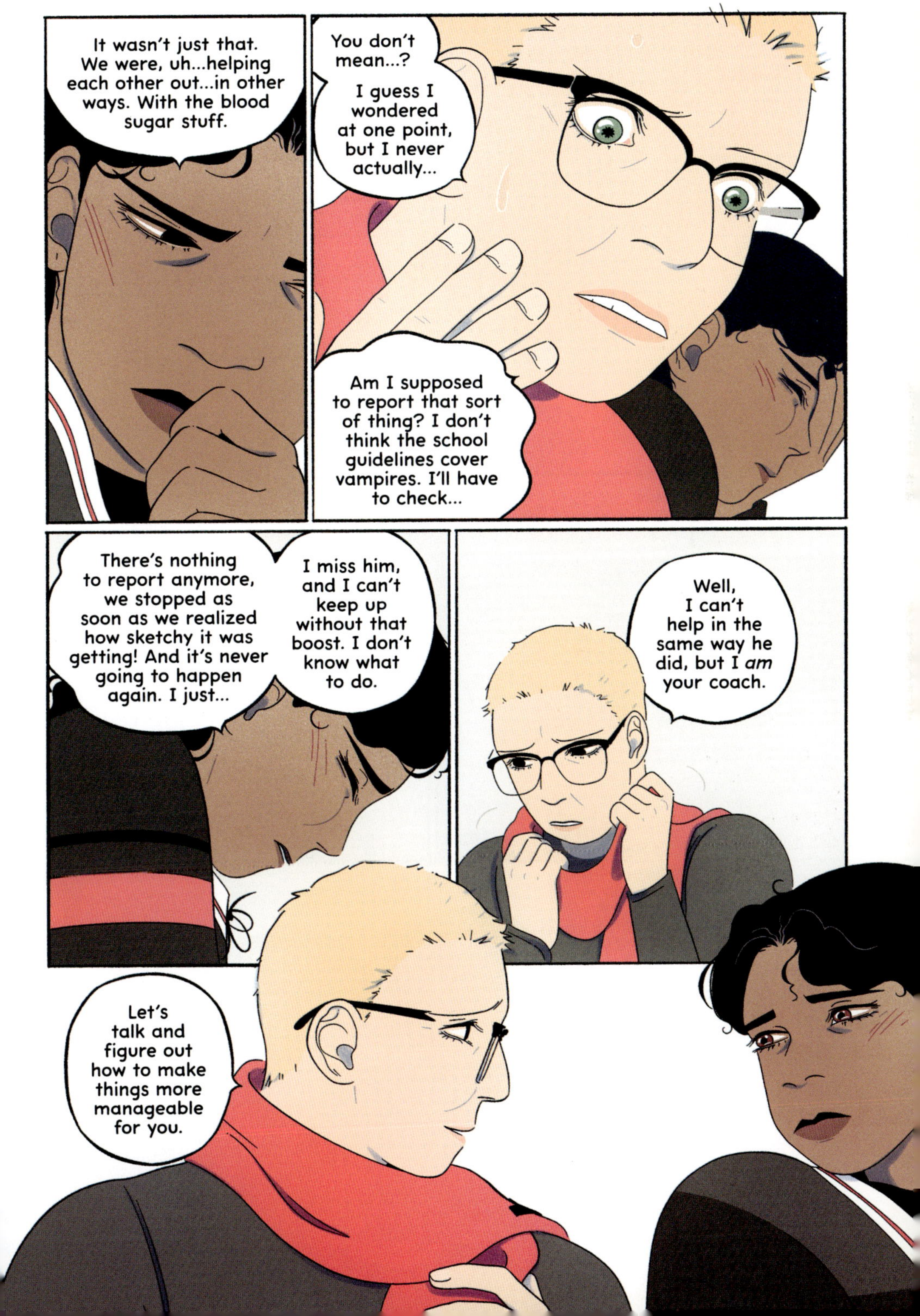
It wasn't just that. We were, uh...helping each other out...in other ways. With the blood sugar stuff.
You don't mean...?
I guess I wondered at one point, but I never actually...
Am I supposed to report that sort of thing? I don't think the school guidelines cover vampires. I'll have to check...
There's nothing to report anymore, we stopped as soon as we realized how sketchy it was getting! And it's never going to happen again. I just...
I miss him, and I can't keep up without that boost. I don't know what to do.
Well, I can't help in the same way he did, but I *am* your coach.
Let's talk and figure out how to make things more manageable for you.

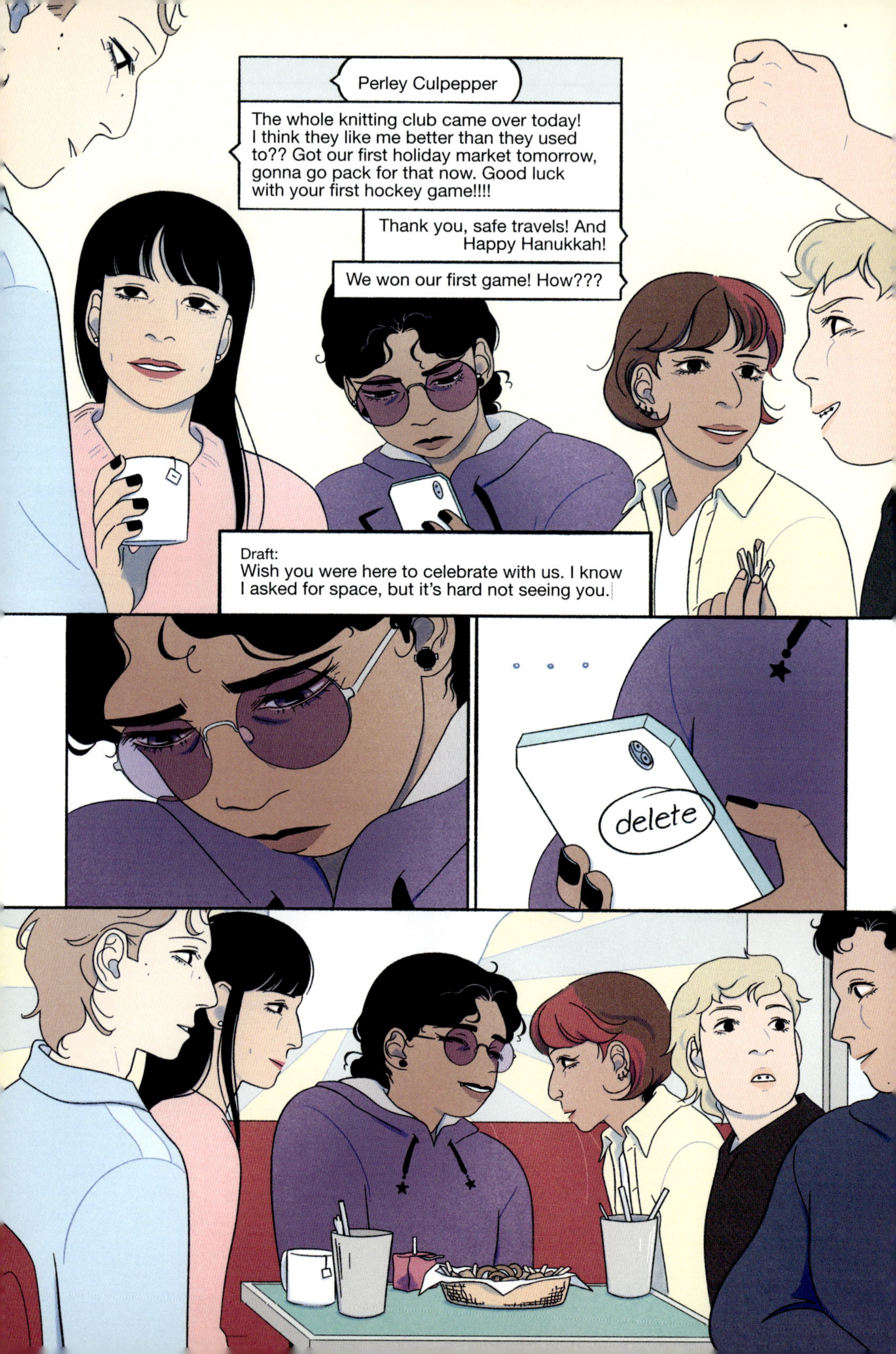
Perley Culpepper
The whole knitting club came over today! I think they like me better than they used to?? Got our first holiday market tomorrow, gonna go pack for that now. Good luck with your first hockey game!!!!
Thank you, safe travels! And Happy Hanukkah!
We won our first game! How???
Draft:
Wish you were here to celebrate with us. I know I asked for space, but it's hard not seeing you.
delete

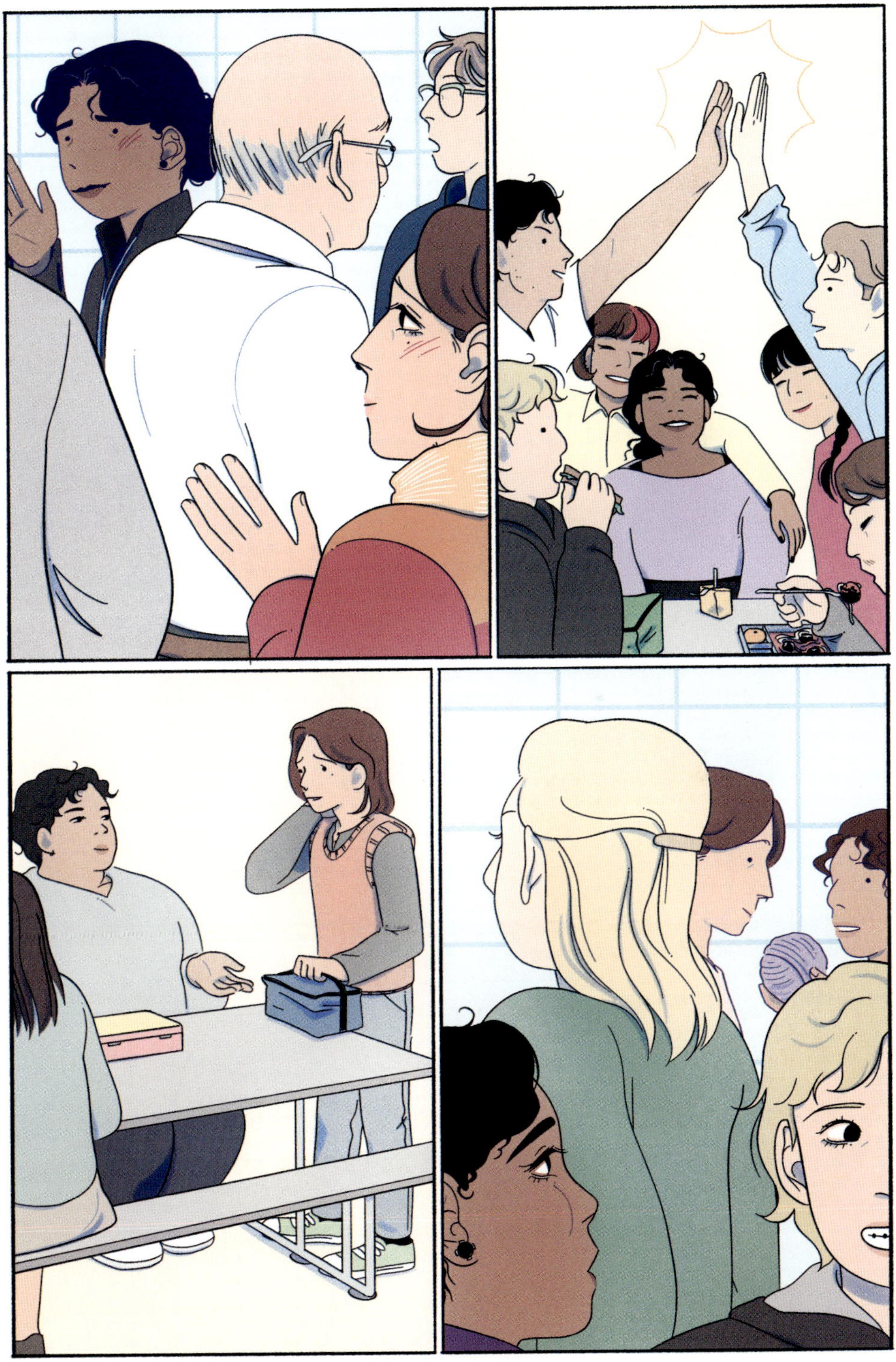

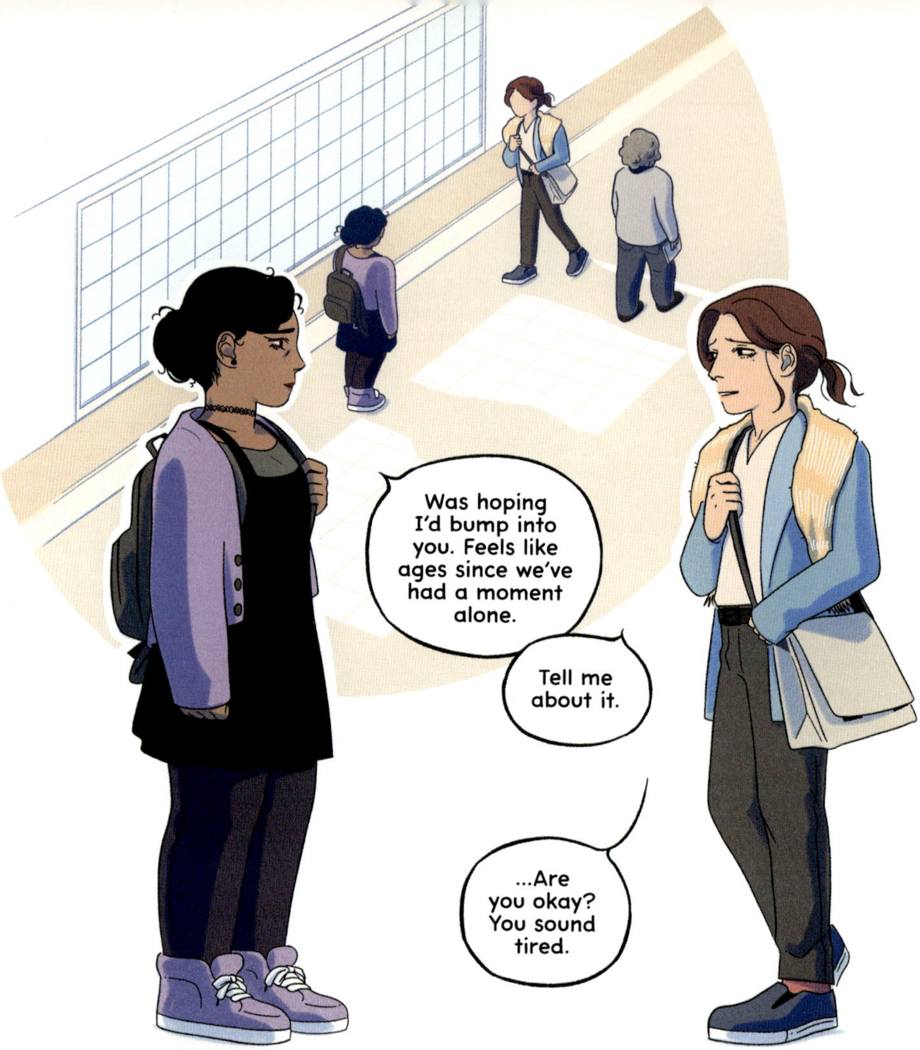
Was hoping I'd bump into you. Feels like ages since we've had a moment alone.
Tell me about it.
...Are you okay? You sound tired.

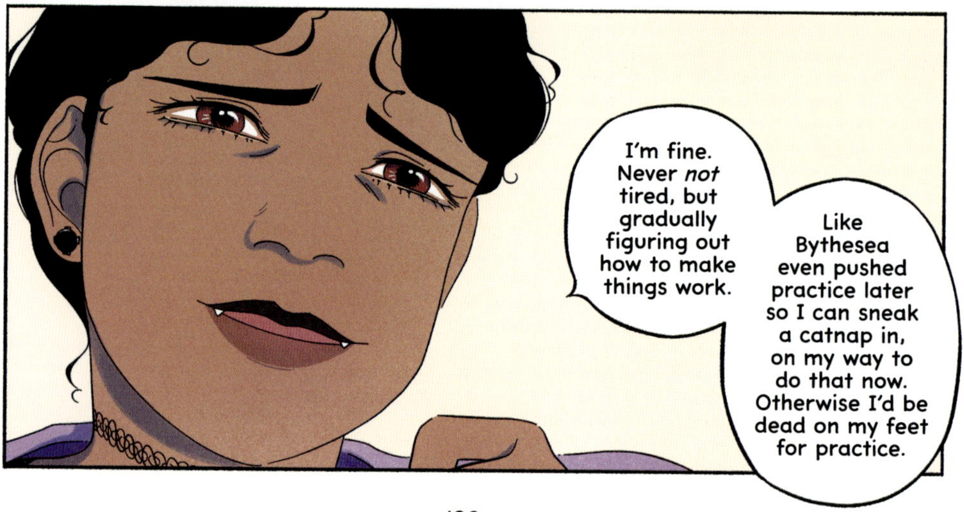
I'm fine. Never *not* tired, but gradually figuring out how to make things work.
Like Bythesea even pushed practice later so I can sneak a catnap in, on my way to do that now. Otherwise I'd be dead on my feet for practice.

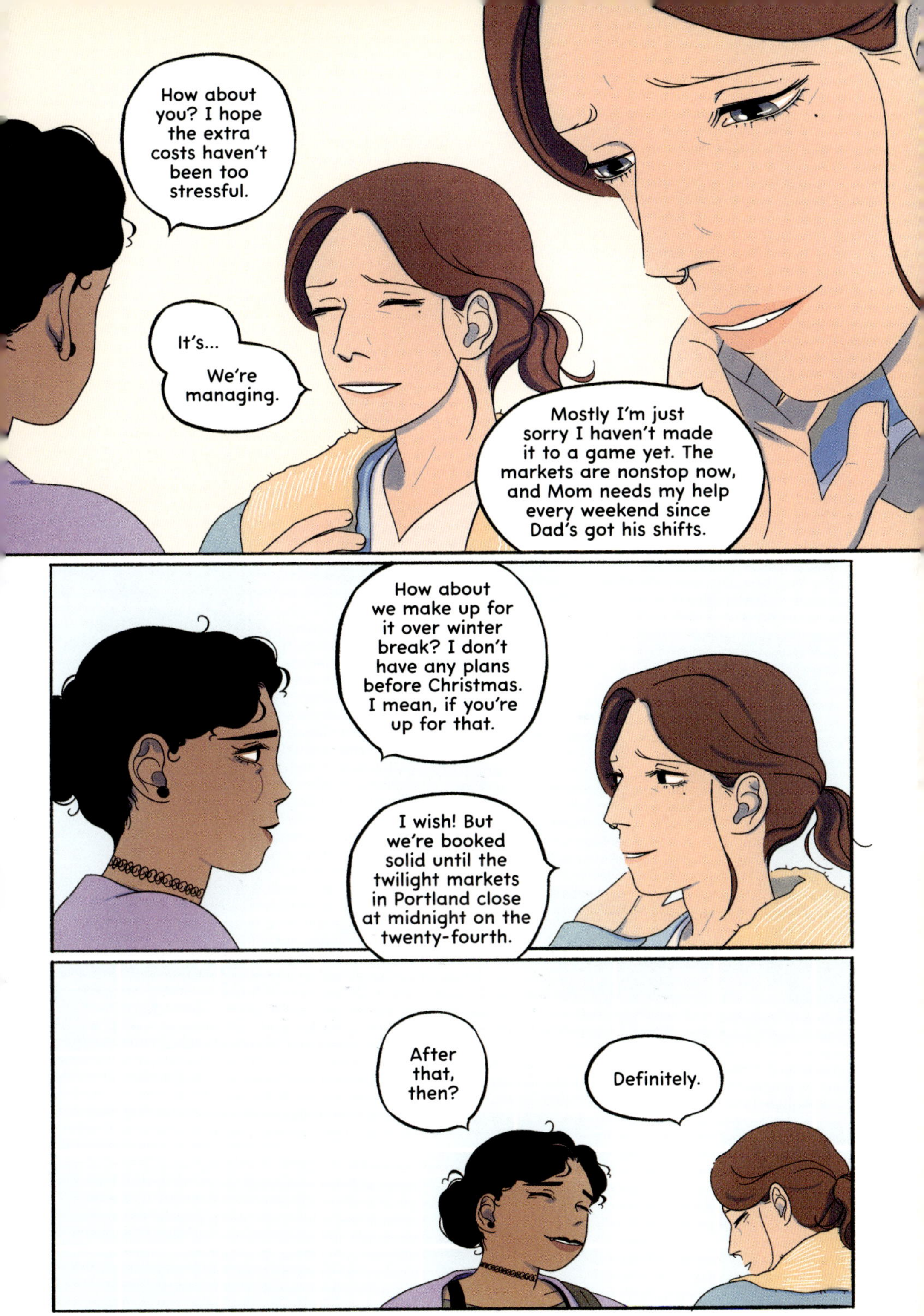
How about you? I hope the extra costs haven't been too stressful.
It's...
We're managing.
Mostly I'm just sorry I haven't made it to a game yet. The markets are nonstop now, and Mom needs my help every weekend since Dad's got his shifts.
How about we make up for it over winter break? I don't have any plans before Christmas. I mean, if you're up for that.
I wish! But we're booked solid until the twilight markets in Portland close at midnight on the twenty-fourth.
After that, then?
Definitely.

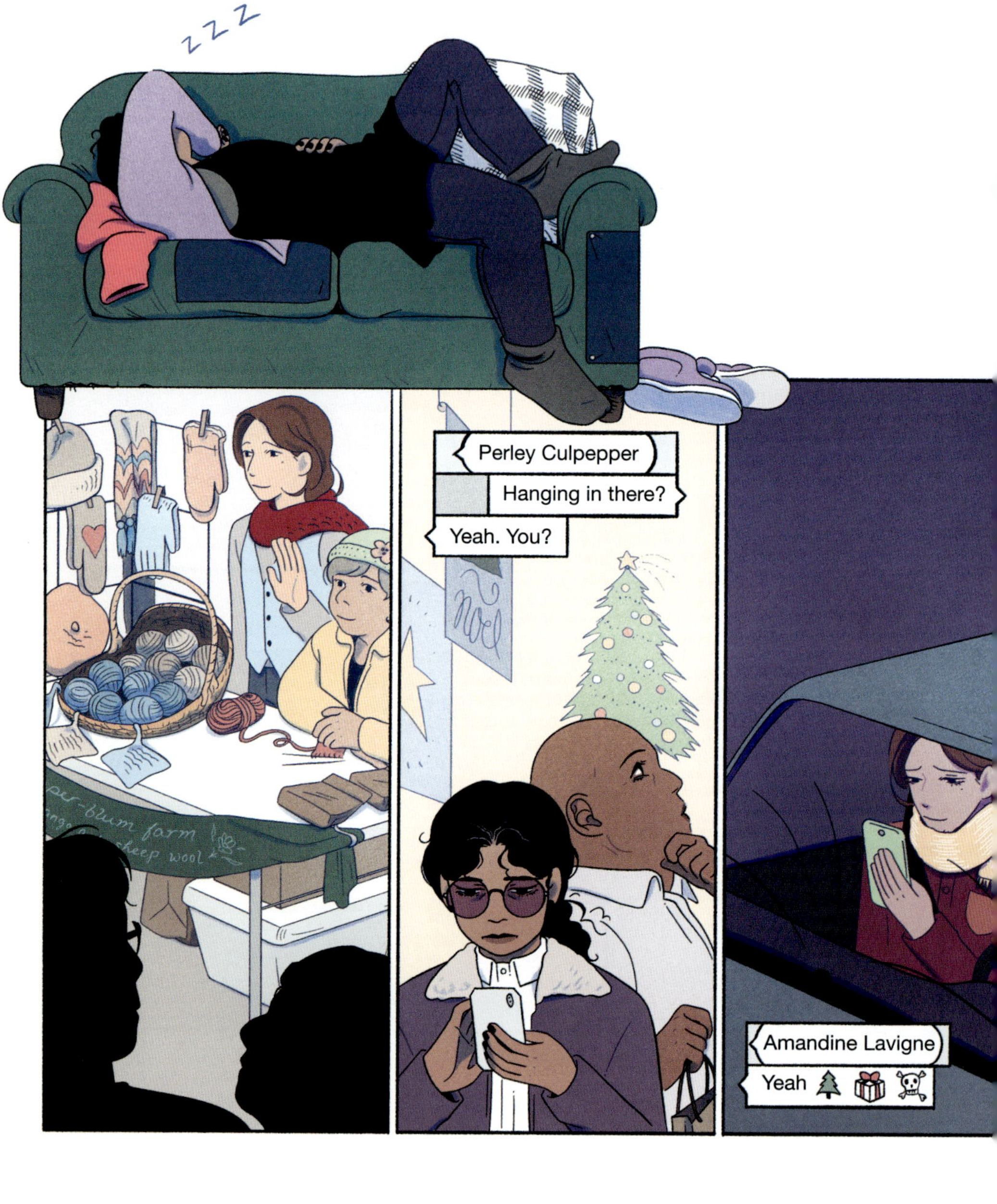
ZZZ
Perley Culpepper
Hanging in there?
Yeah. You?
Amandine Lavigne
Yeah

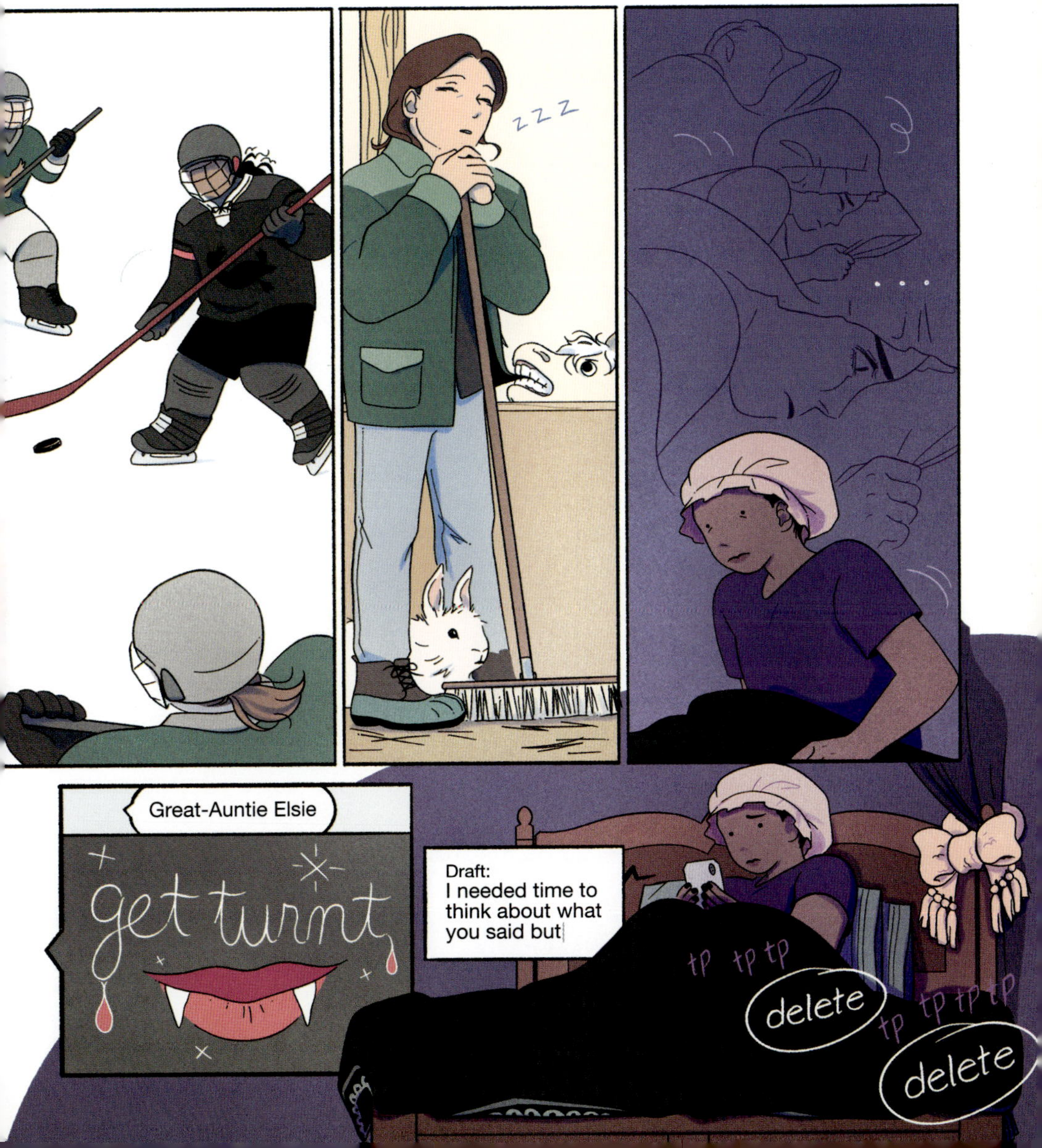

Z Z Z
...
Great-Auntie Elsie
get turnt
Draft:
I needed time to think about what you said but
tp tp tp
delete
tp tp tp tp
delete

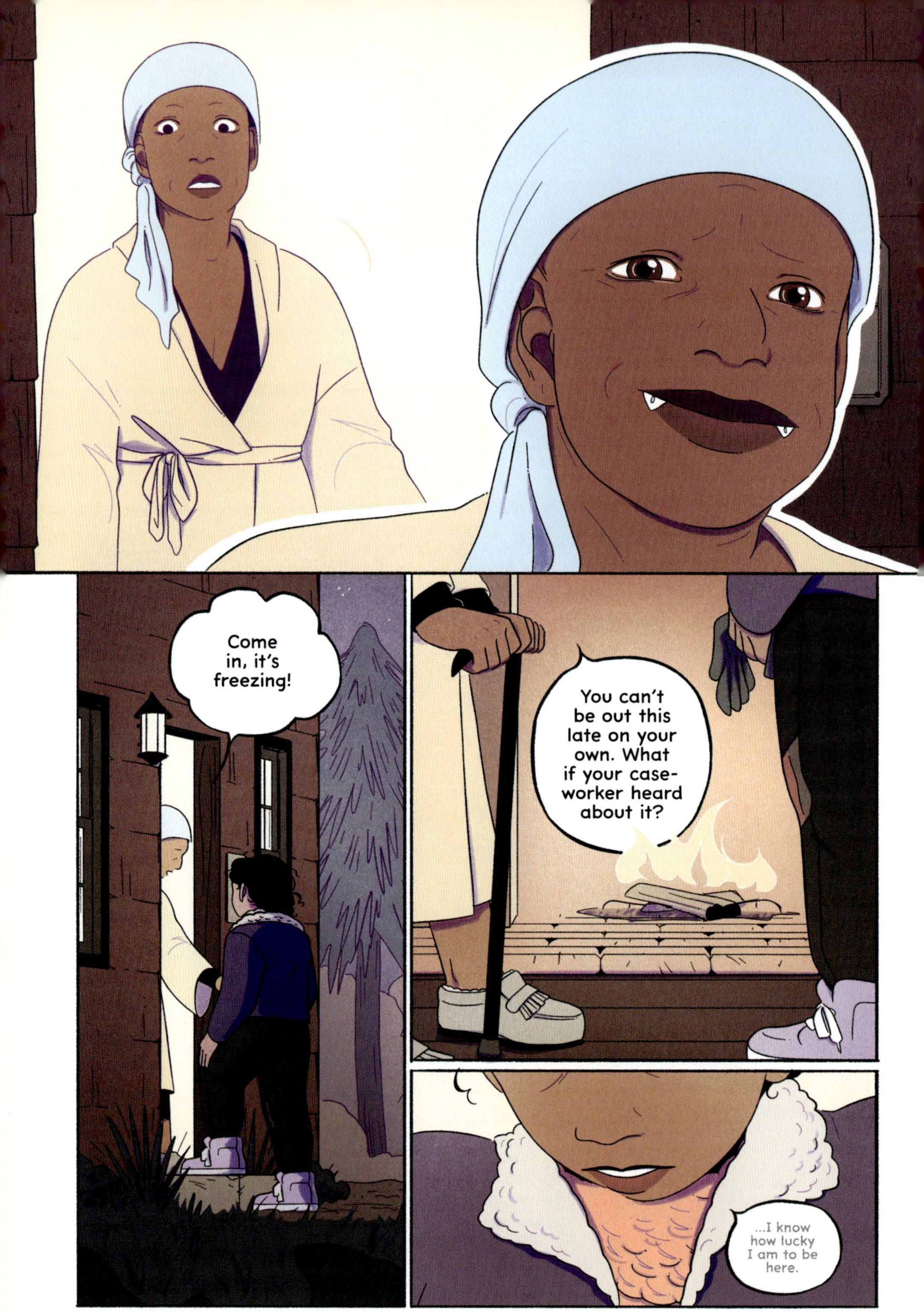

Come in, it's freezing!
You can't be out this late on your own. What if your case-worker heard about it?
...I know how lucky I am to be here.

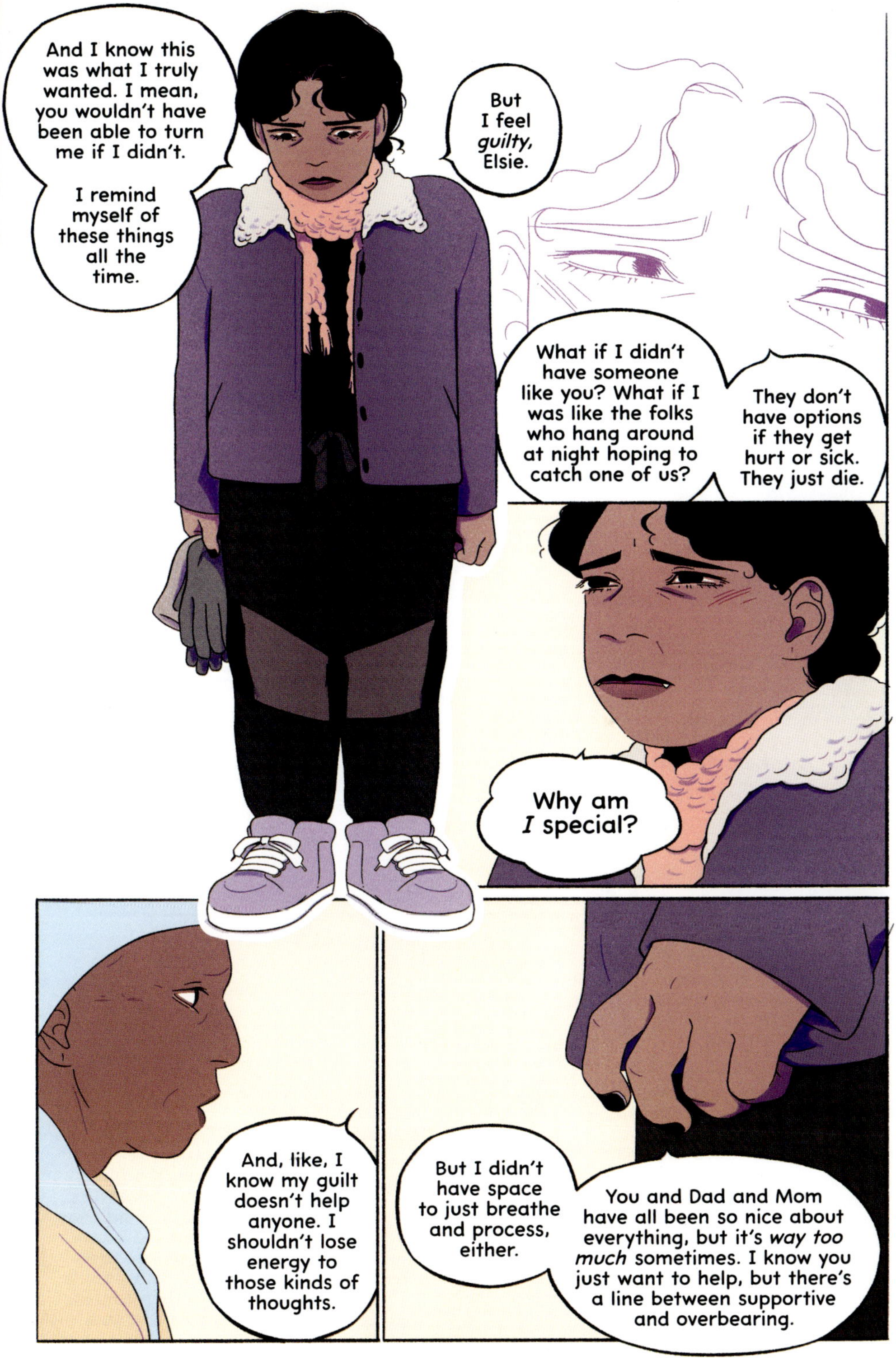
And I know this was what I truly wanted. I mean, you wouldn't have been able to turn me if I didn't.
I remind myself of these things all the time.
But I feel *guilty,* Elsie.
What if I didn't have someone like you? What if I was like the folks who hang around at night hoping to catch one of us?
They don't have options if they get hurt or sick. They just die.
Why am *I* special?
And, like, I know my guilt doesn't help anyone. I shouldn't lose energy to those kinds of thoughts.
But I didn't have space to just breathe and process, either.
You and Dad and Mom have all been so nice about everything, but it's *way too much* sometimes. I know you just want to help, but there's a line between supportive and overbearing.

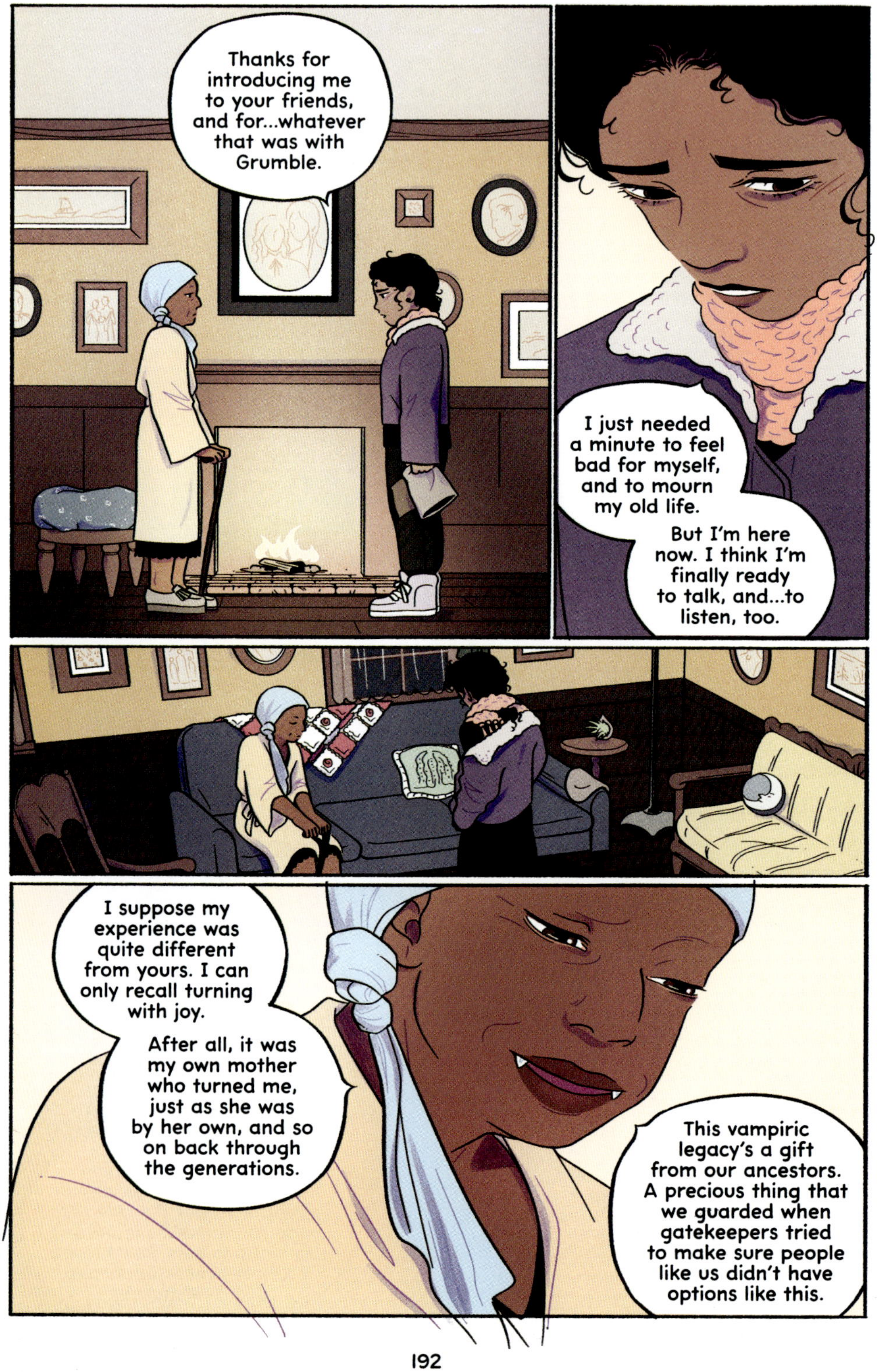
Thanks for introducing me to your friends, and for...whatever that was with Grumble.
I just needed a minute to feel bad for myself, and to mourn my old life.
But I'm here now. I think I'm finally ready to talk, and...to listen, too.
I suppose my experience was quite different from yours. I can only recall turning with joy.
After all, it was my own mother who turned me, just as she was by her own, and so on back through the generations.
This vampiric legacy's a gift from our ancestors. A precious thing that we guarded when gatekeepers tried to make sure people like us didn't have options like this.

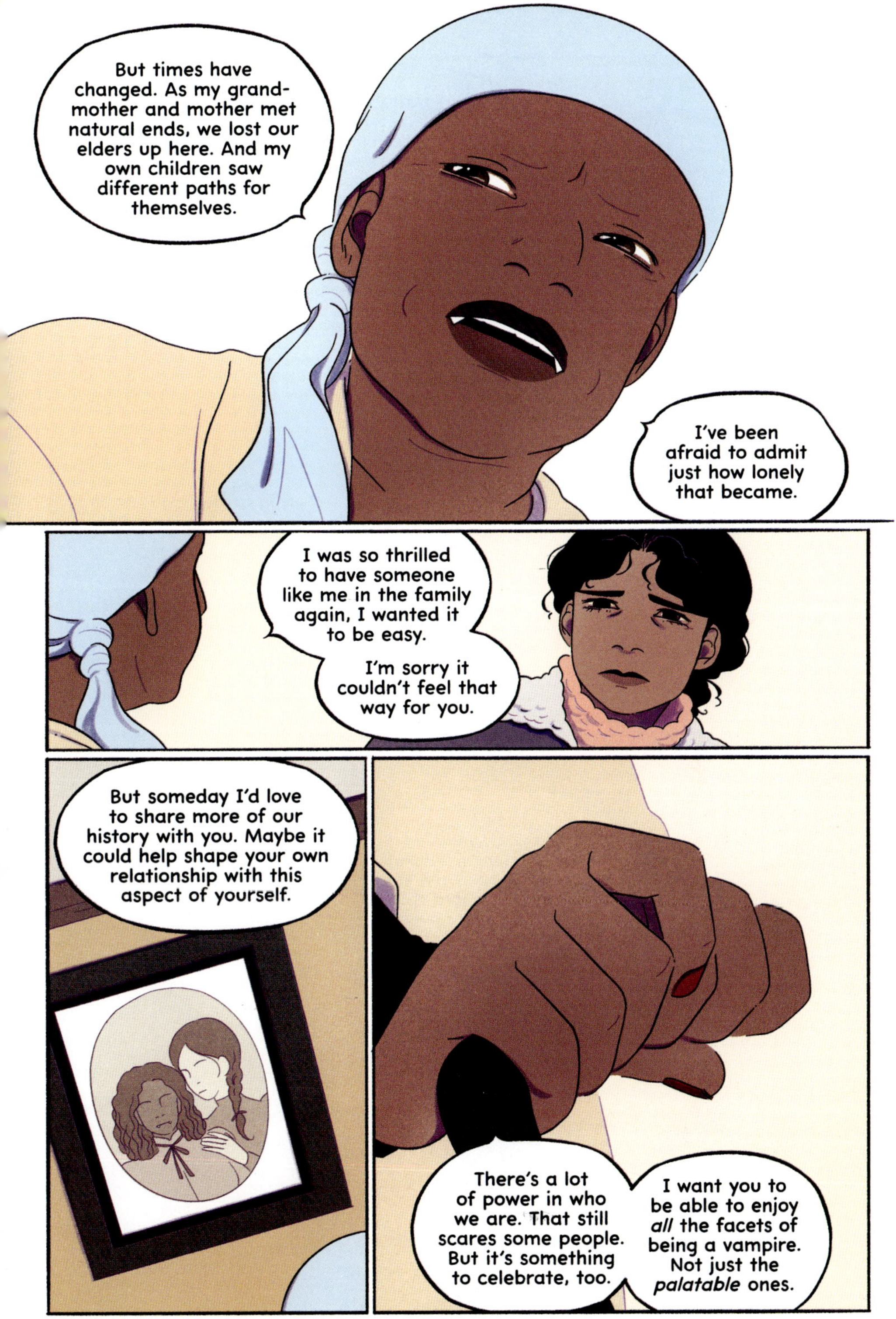
But times have changed. As my grand-mother and mother met natural ends, we lost our elders up here. And my own children saw different paths for themselves.
I've been afraid to admit just how lonely that became.
I was so thrilled to have someone like me in the family again, I wanted it to be easy.
I'm sorry it couldn't feel that way for you.
But someday I'd love to share more of our history with you. Maybe it could help shape your own relationship with this aspect of yourself.
There's a lot of power in who we are. That still scares some people. But it's something to celebrate, too.
I want you to be able to enjoy *all* the facets of being a vampire. Not just the *palatable* ones.

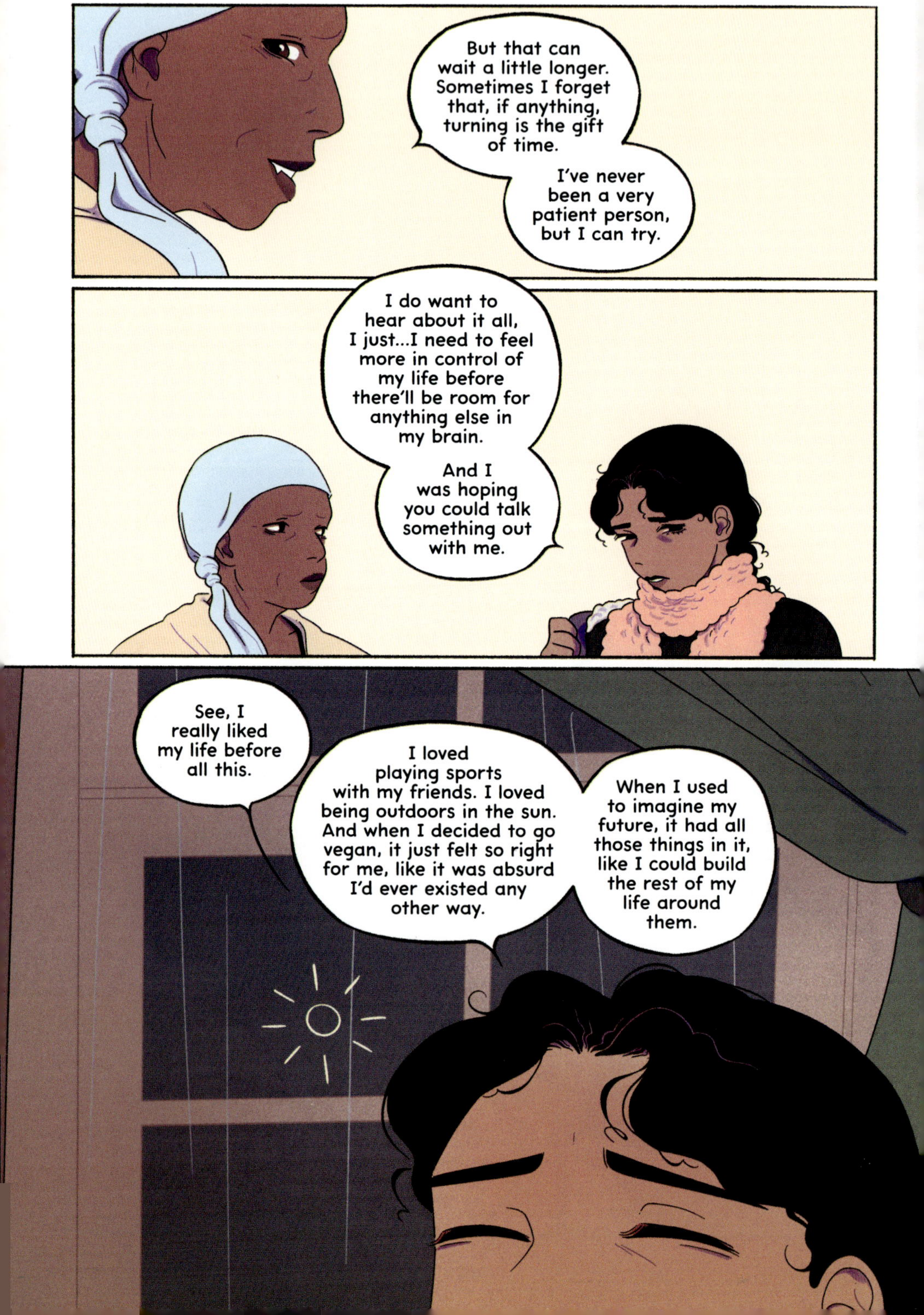

But that can wait a little longer. Sometimes I forget that, if anything, turning is the gift of time.
I've never been a very patient person, but I can try.
I do want to hear about it all, I just...I need to feel more in control of my life before there'll be room for anything else in my brain.
And I was hoping you could talk something out with me.
See, I really liked my life before all this.
I loved playing sports with my friends. I loved being outdoors in the sun. And when I decided to go vegan, it just felt so right for me, like it was absurd I'd ever existed any other way.
When I used to imagine my future, it had all those things in it, like I could build the rest of my life around them.

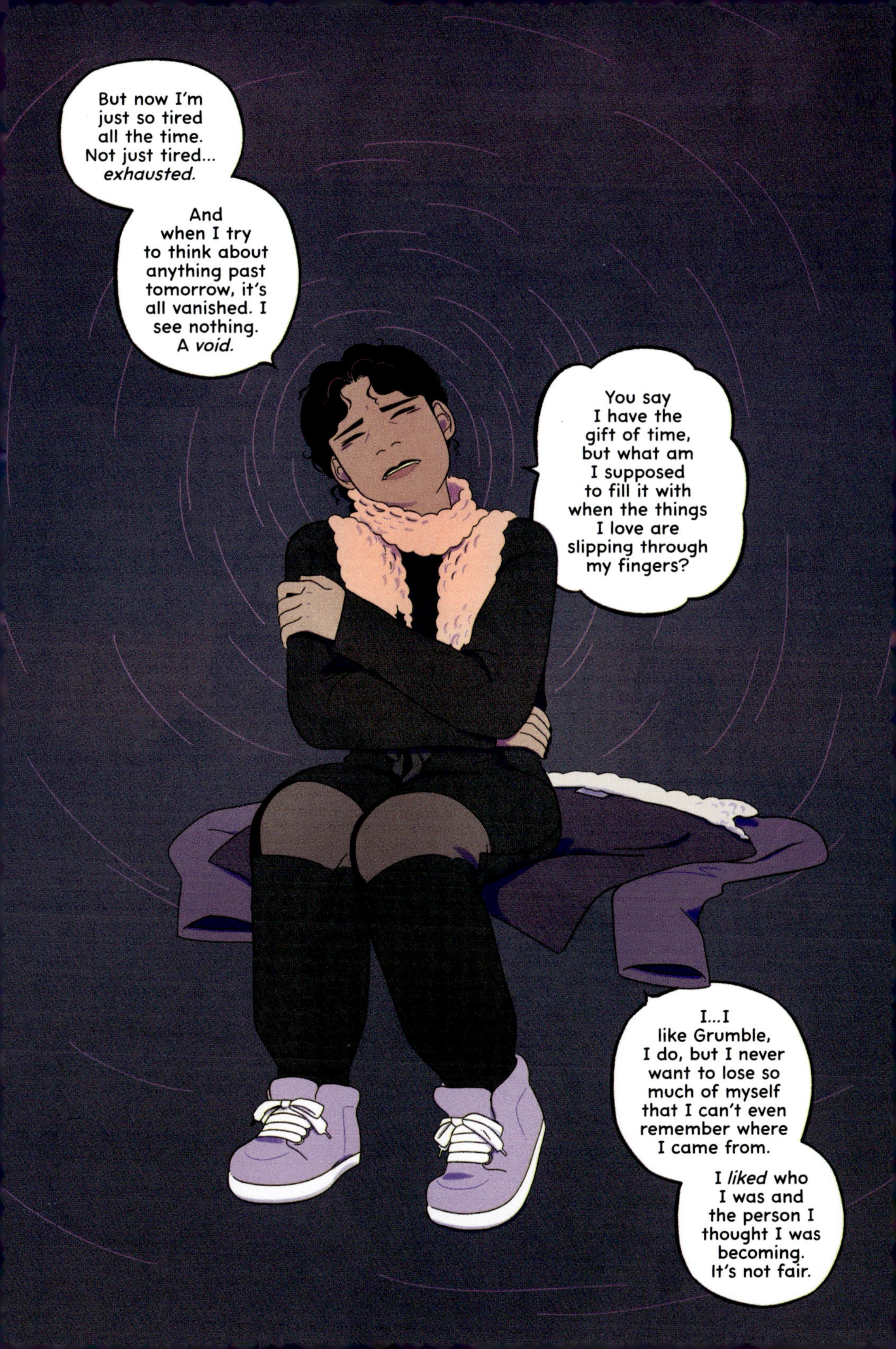

But now I'm just so tired all the time. Not just tired... *exhausted.*
And when I try to think about anything past tomorrow, it's all vanished. I see nothing. A *void.*
You say I have the gift of time, but what am I supposed to fill it with when the things I love are slipping through my fingers?
I...I like Grumble, I do, but I never want to lose so much of myself that I can't even remember where I came from.
I *liked* who I was and the person I thought I was becoming. It's not fair.

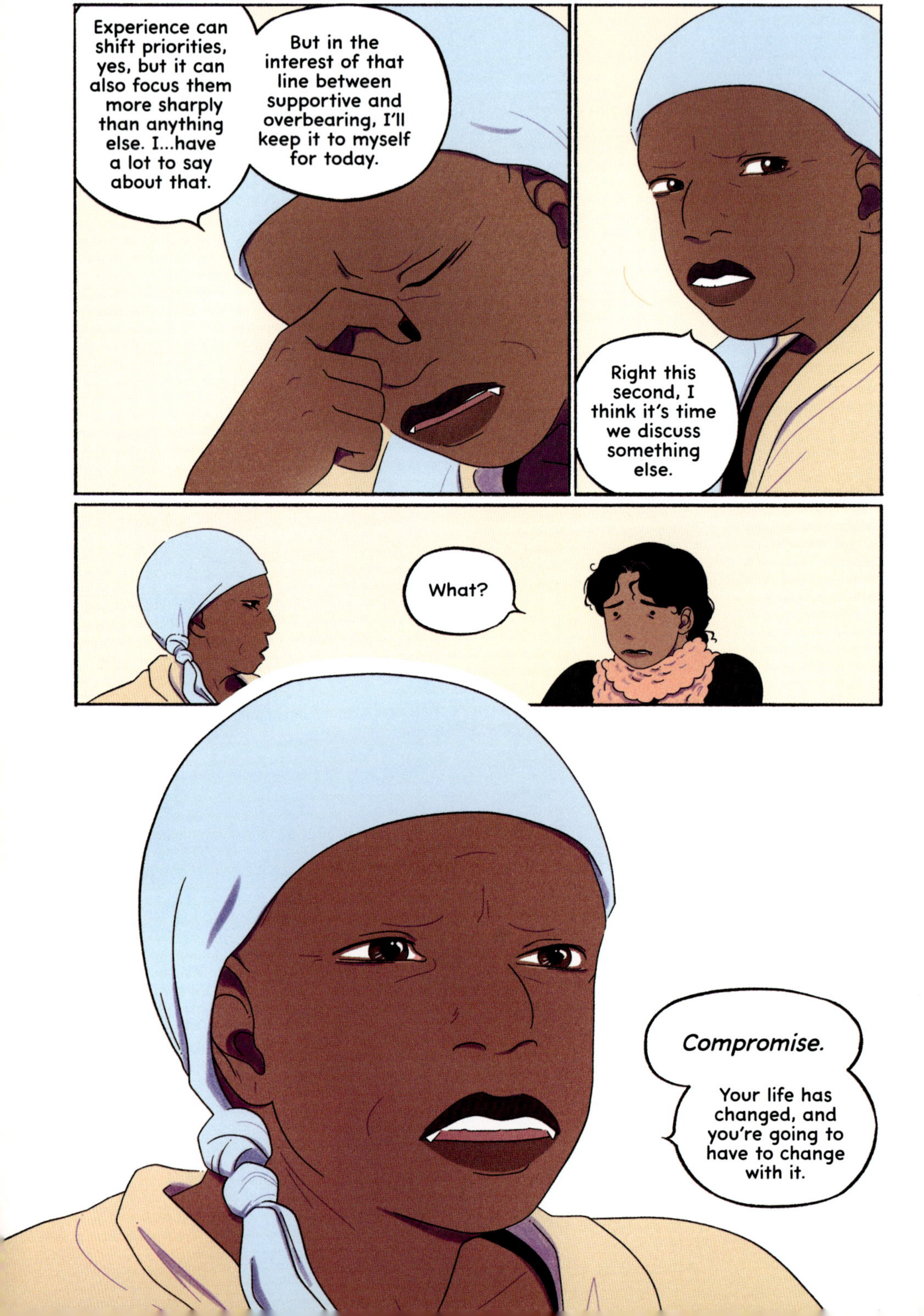
Experience can shift priorities, yes, but it can also focus them more sharply than anything else. I...have a lot to say about that.
But in the interest of that line between supportive and overbearing, I'll keep it to myself for today.
Right this second, I think it's time we discuss something else.
What?
Compromise.
Your life has changed, and you're going to have to change with it.

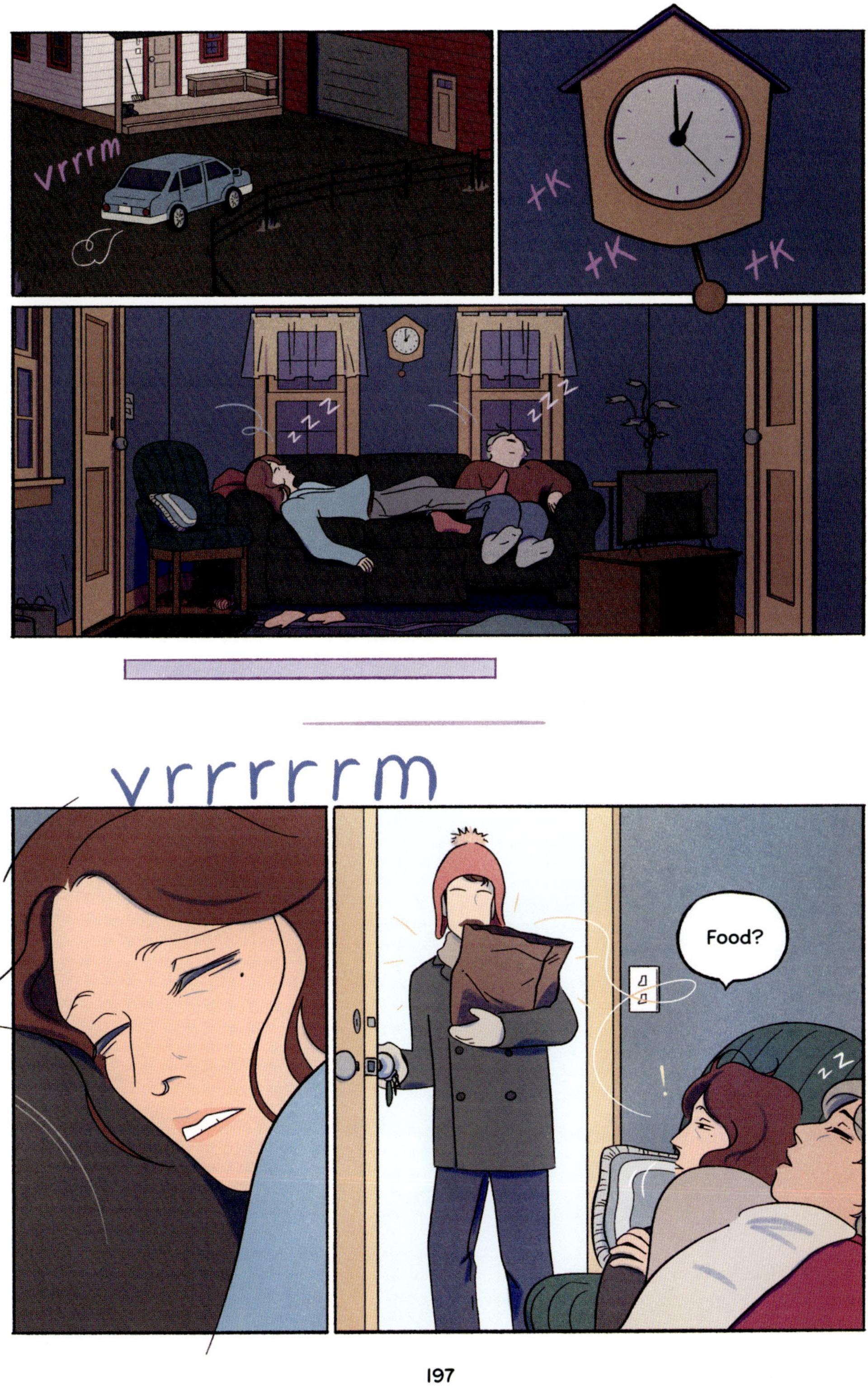

vrrrm
tK
tK
tK
z z z
z z z
vrrrrrm
Food?
!
z z

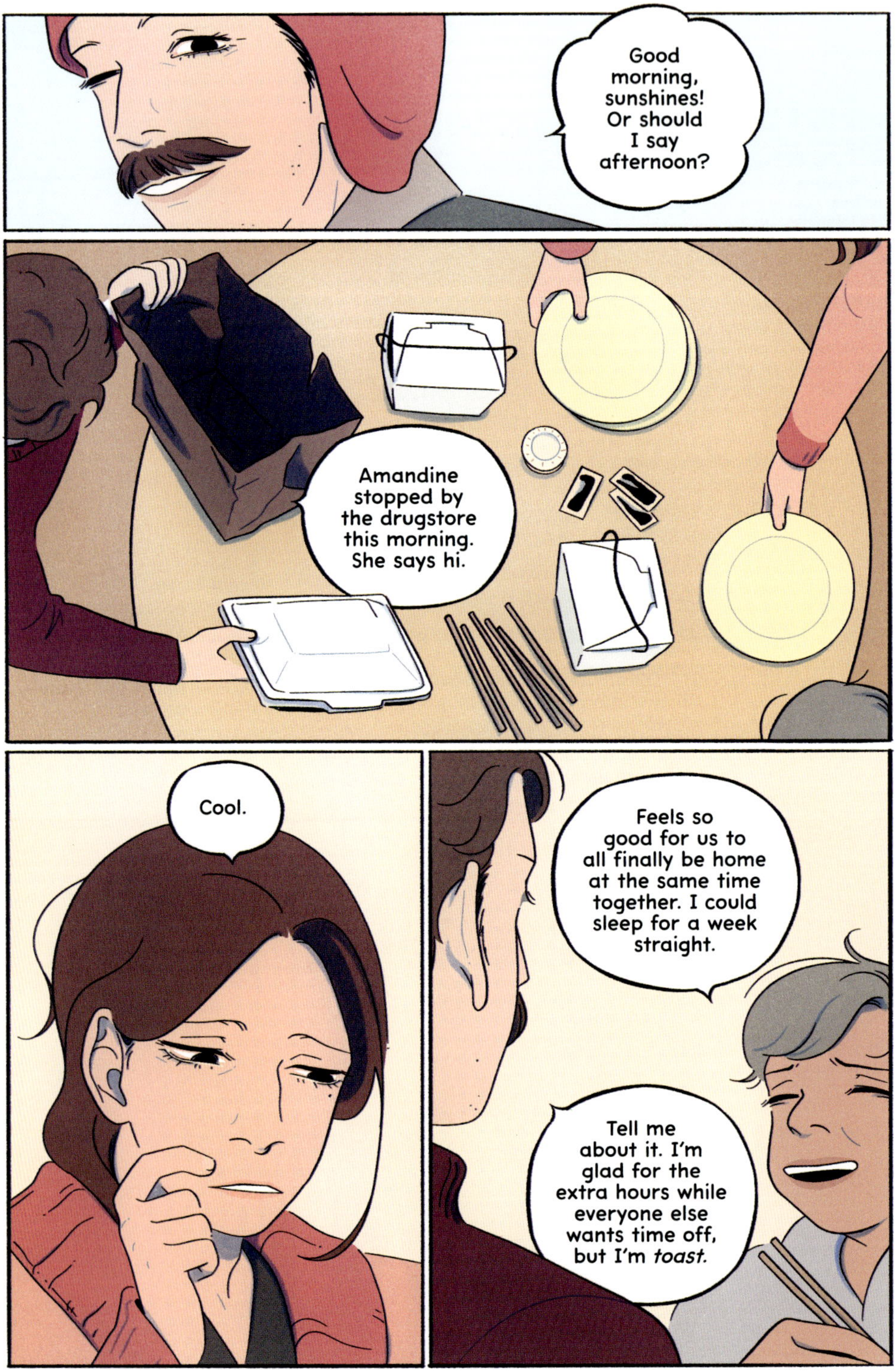
Good morning, sunshines! Or should I say afternoon?
Amandine stopped by the drugstore this morning. She says hi.
Cool.
Feels so good for us to all finally be home at the same time together. I could sleep for a week straight.
Tell me about it. I'm glad for the extra hours while everyone else wants time off, but I'm *toast.*

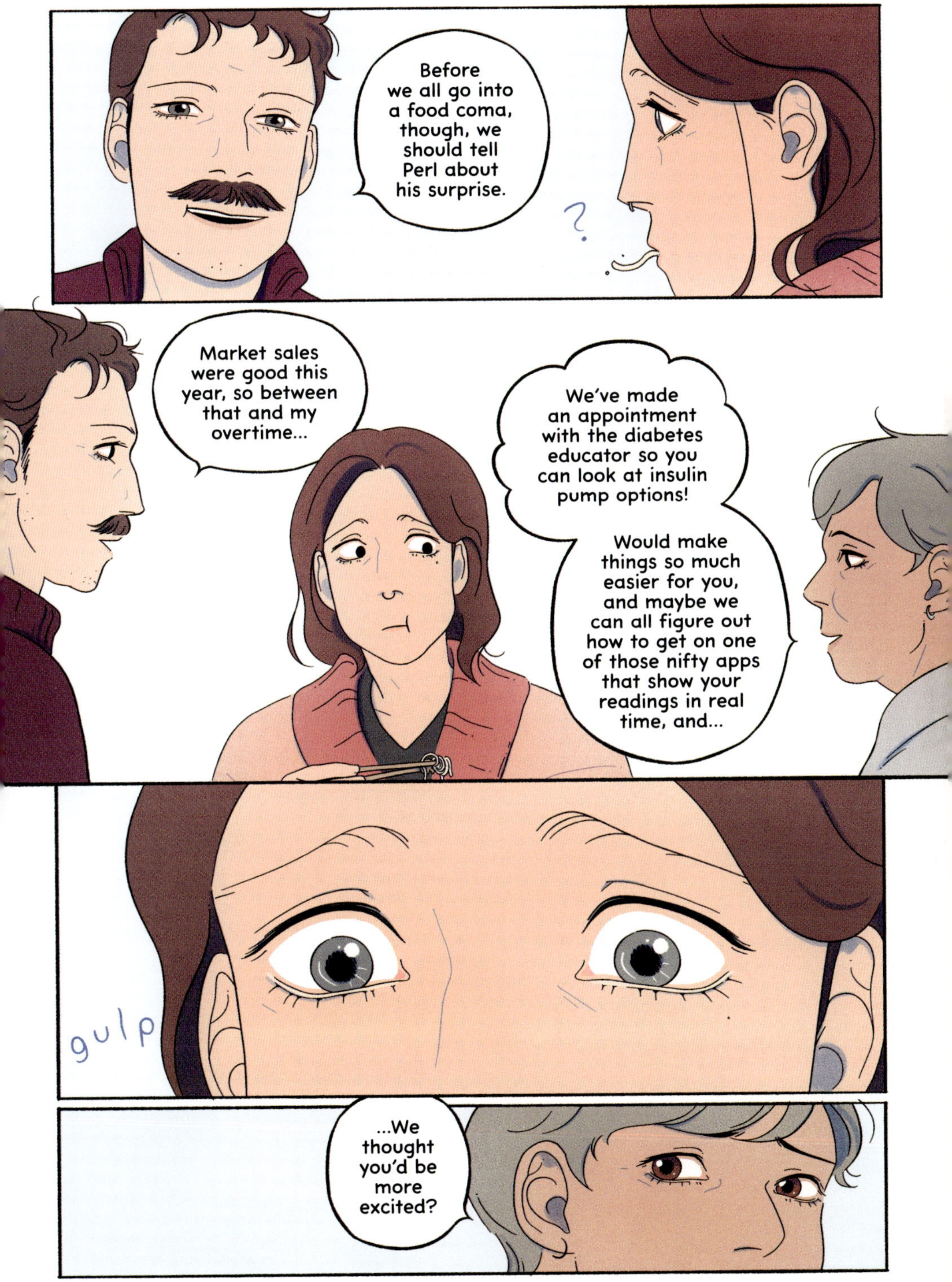
Before we all go into a food coma, though, we should tell Perl about his surprise.
?
Market sales were good this year, so between that and my overtime...
We've made an appointment with the diabetes educator so you can look at insulin pump options!
Would make things so much easier for you, and maybe we can all figure out how to get on one of those nifty apps that show your readings in real time, and...
gulp
...We thought you'd be more excited?

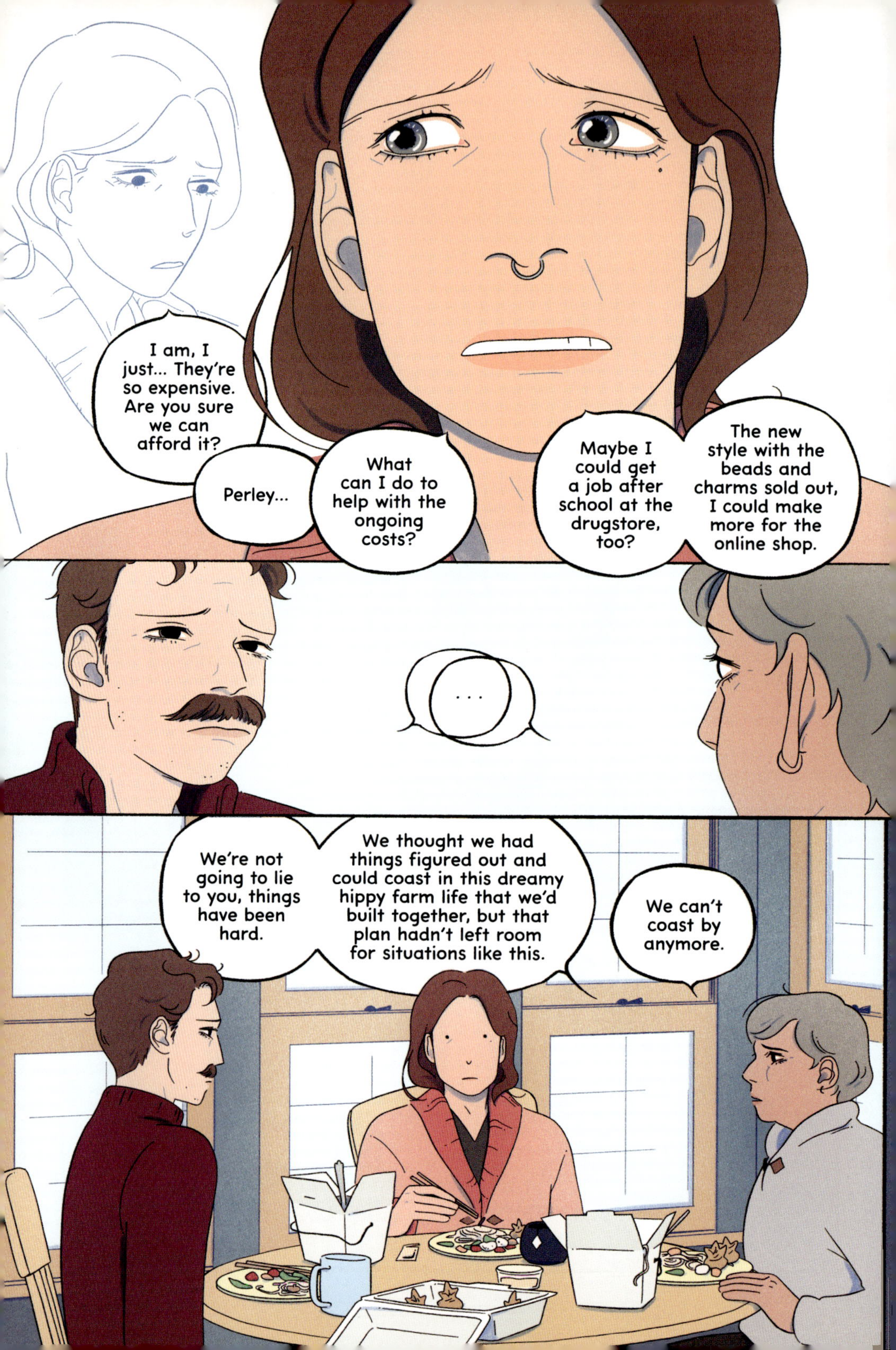
I am, I just... They're so expensive. Are you sure we can afford it?
Perley...
What can I do to help with the ongoing costs?
Maybe I could get a job after school at the drugstore, too?
The new style with the beads and charms sold out, I could make more for the online shop.
...
We're not going to lie to you, things have been hard.
We thought we had things figured out and could coast in this dreamy hippy farm life that we'd built together, but that plan hadn't left room for situations like this.
We can't coast by anymore.

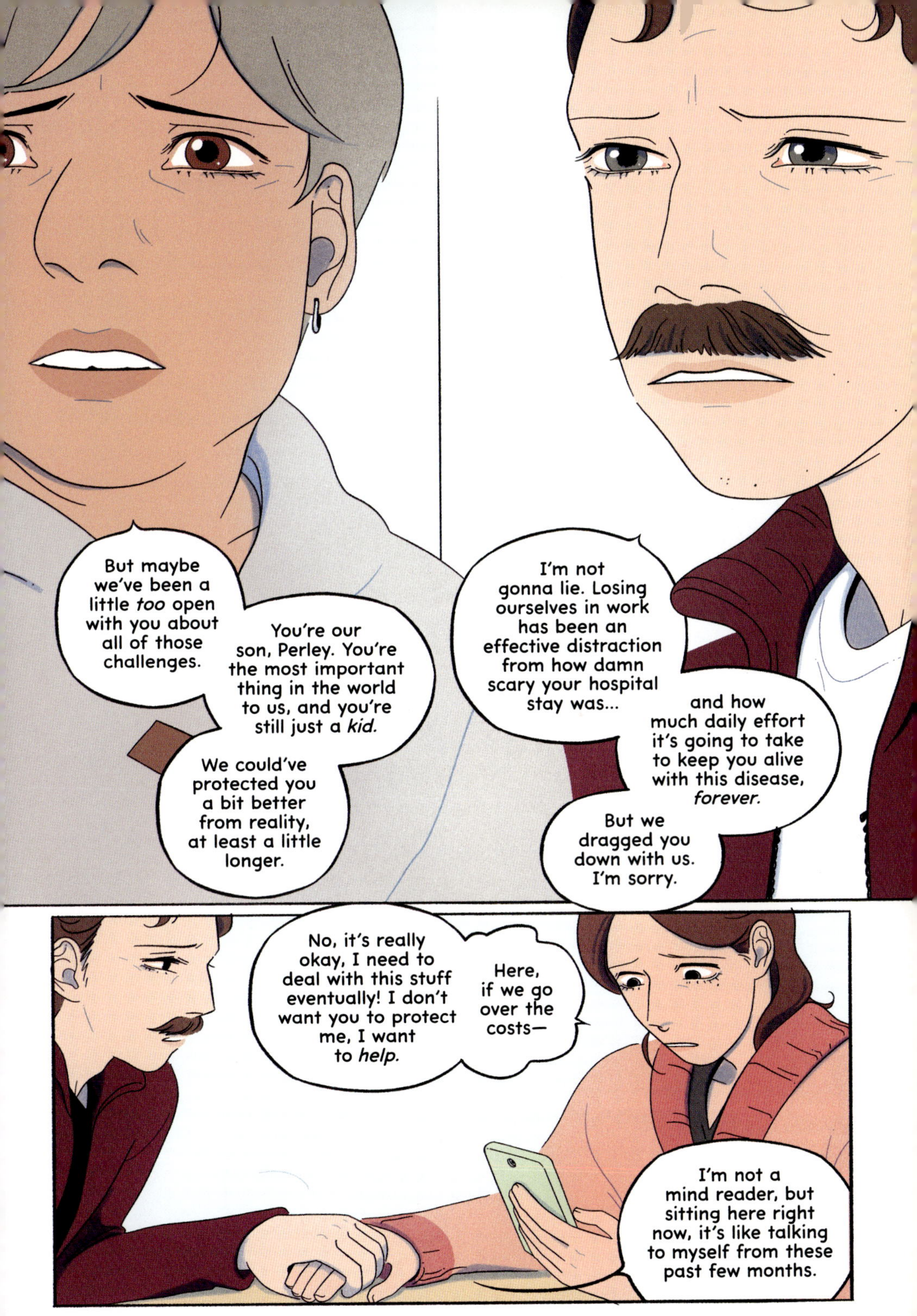

But maybe we've been a little *too* open with you about all of those challenges.
You're our son, Perley. You're the most important thing in the world to us, and you're still just a *kid.*
We could've protected you a bit better from reality, at least a little longer.
I'm not gonna lie. Losing ourselves in work has been an effective distraction from how damn scary your hospital stay was...
and how much daily effort it's going to take to keep you alive with this disease, *forever.*
But we dragged you down with us. I'm sorry.
No, it's really okay, I need to deal with this stuff eventually! I don't want you to protect me, I want to *help.*
Here, if we go over the costs—
I'm not a mind reader, but sitting here right now, it's like talking to myself from these past few months.

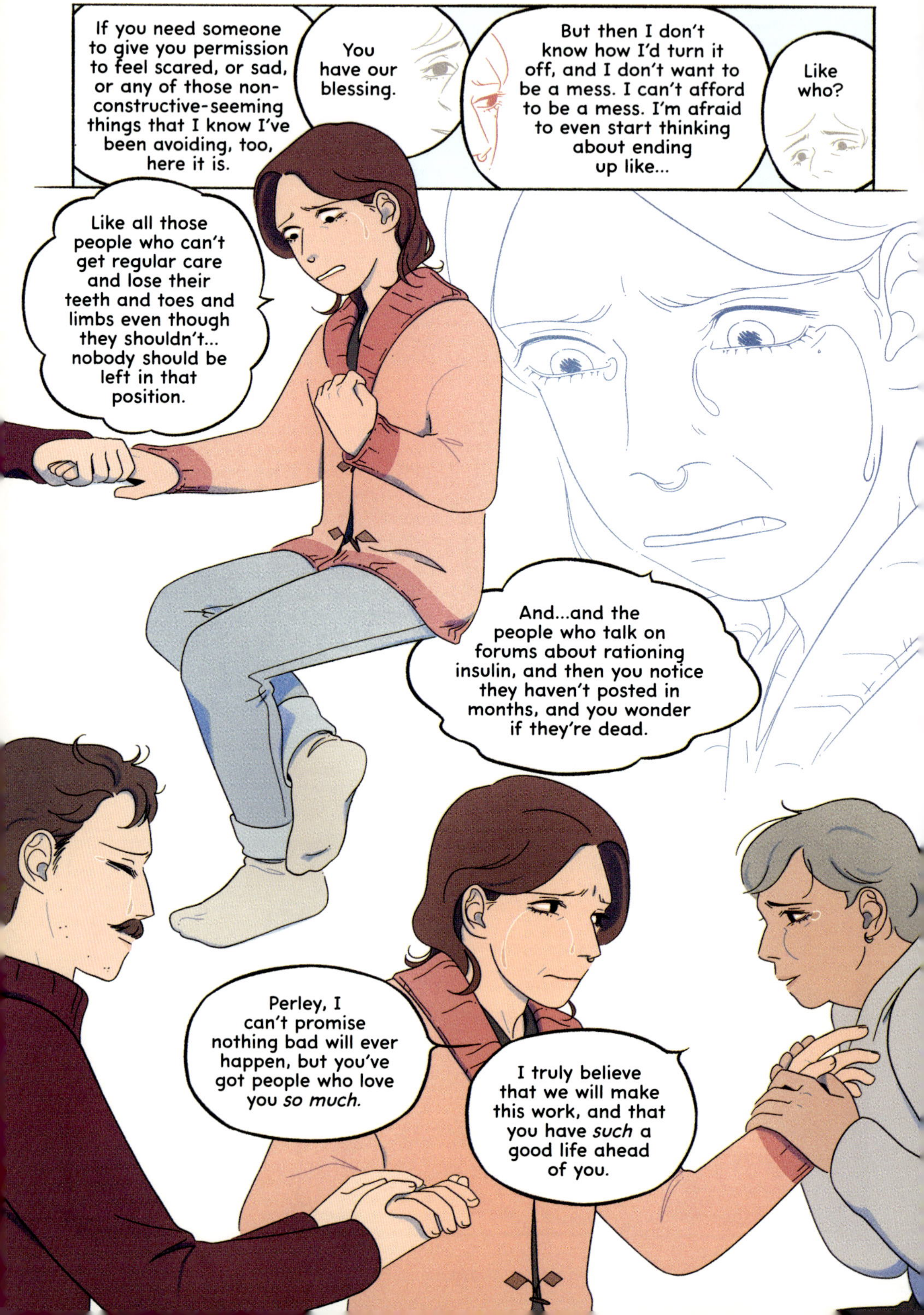
If you need someone to give you permission to feel scared, or sad, or any of those non-constructive-seeming things that I know I've been avoiding, too, here it is.
You have our blessing.
But then I don't know how I'd turn it off, and I don't want to be a mess. I can't afford to be a mess. I'm afraid to even start thinking about ending up like...
Like who?
Like all those people who can't get regular care and lose their teeth and toes and limbs even though they shouldn't... nobody should be left in that position.
And...and the people who talk on forums about rationing insulin, and then you notice they haven't posted in months, and you wonder if they're dead.
Perley, I can't promise nothing bad will ever happen, but you've got people who love you *so much.*
I truly believe that we will make this work, and that you have *such* a good life ahead of you.

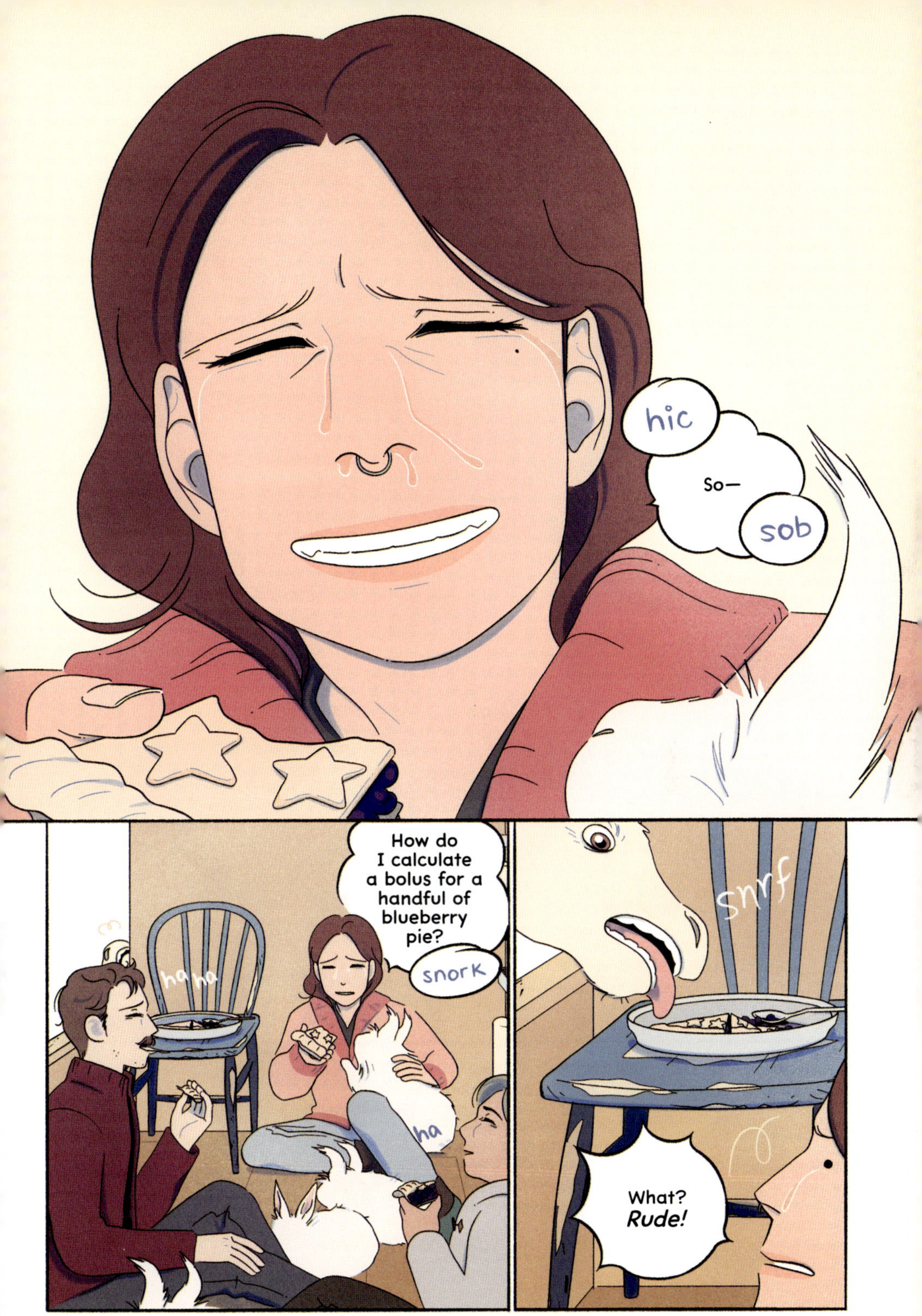
hic
So—
sob
ha ha
How do I calculate a bolus for a handful of blueberry pie?
snork
ha
snrf
What? *Rude!*

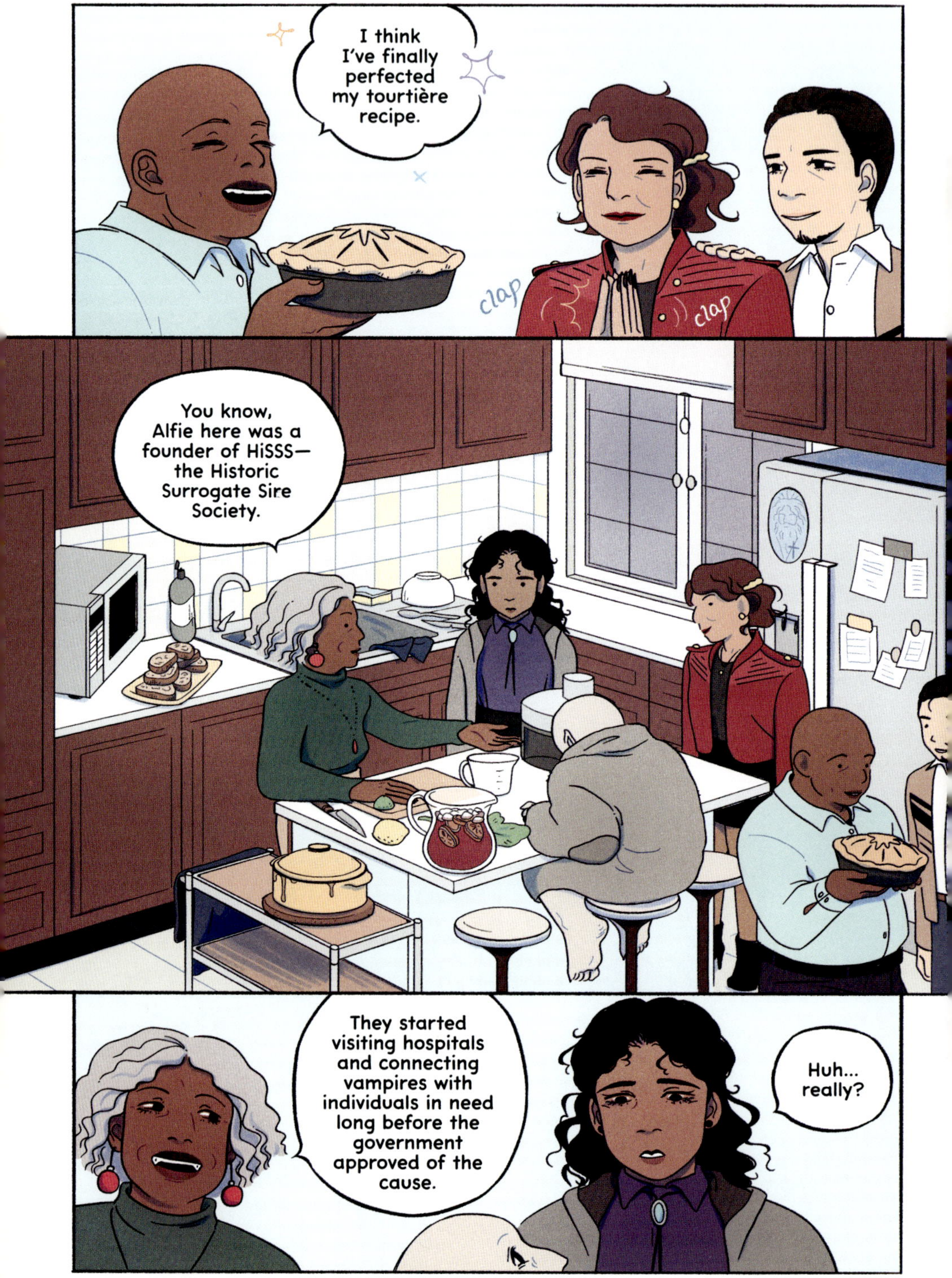

I think I've finally perfected my tourtière recipe.
clap
clap
You know, Alfie here was a founder of HiSSS— the Historic Surrogate Sire Society.
They started visiting hospitals and connecting vampires with individuals in need long before the government approved of the cause.
Huh... really?

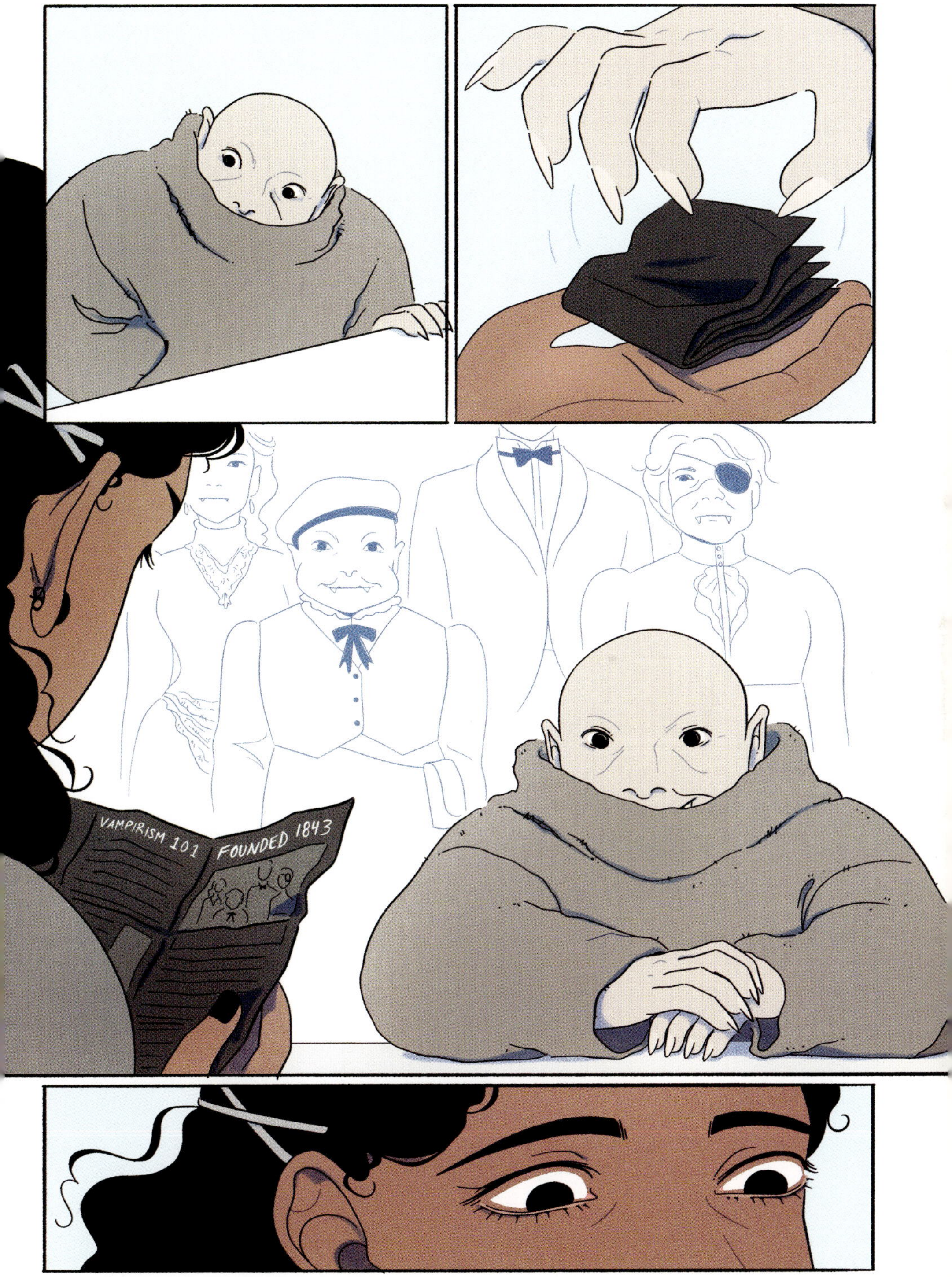
VAMPIRISM 101
FOUNDED 1843

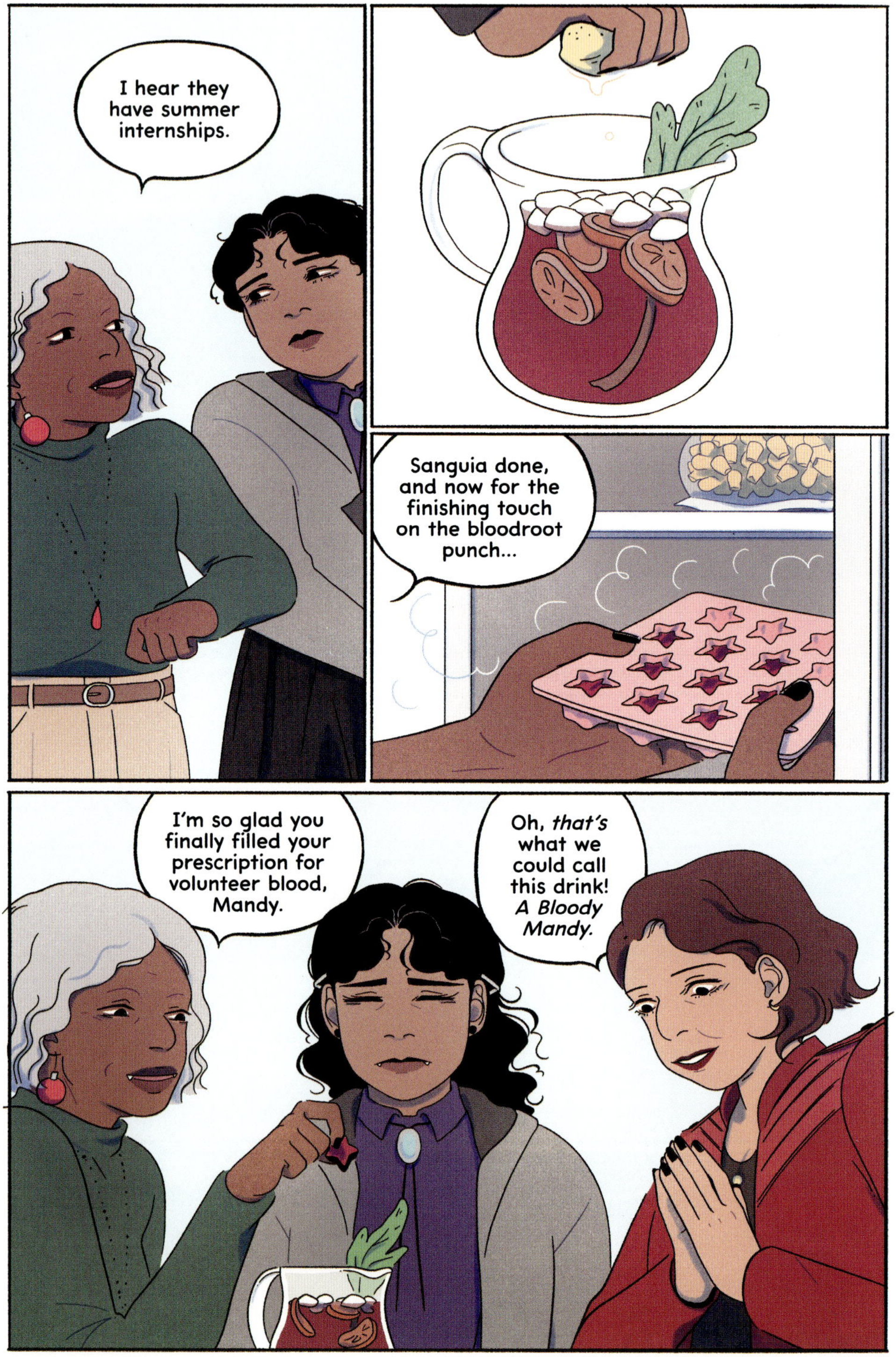
I hear they have summer internships.
Sanguia done, and now for the finishing touch on the bloodroot punch...
I'm so glad you finally filled your prescription for volunteer blood, Mandy.
Oh, *that's* what we could call this drink! *A Bloody Mandy.*

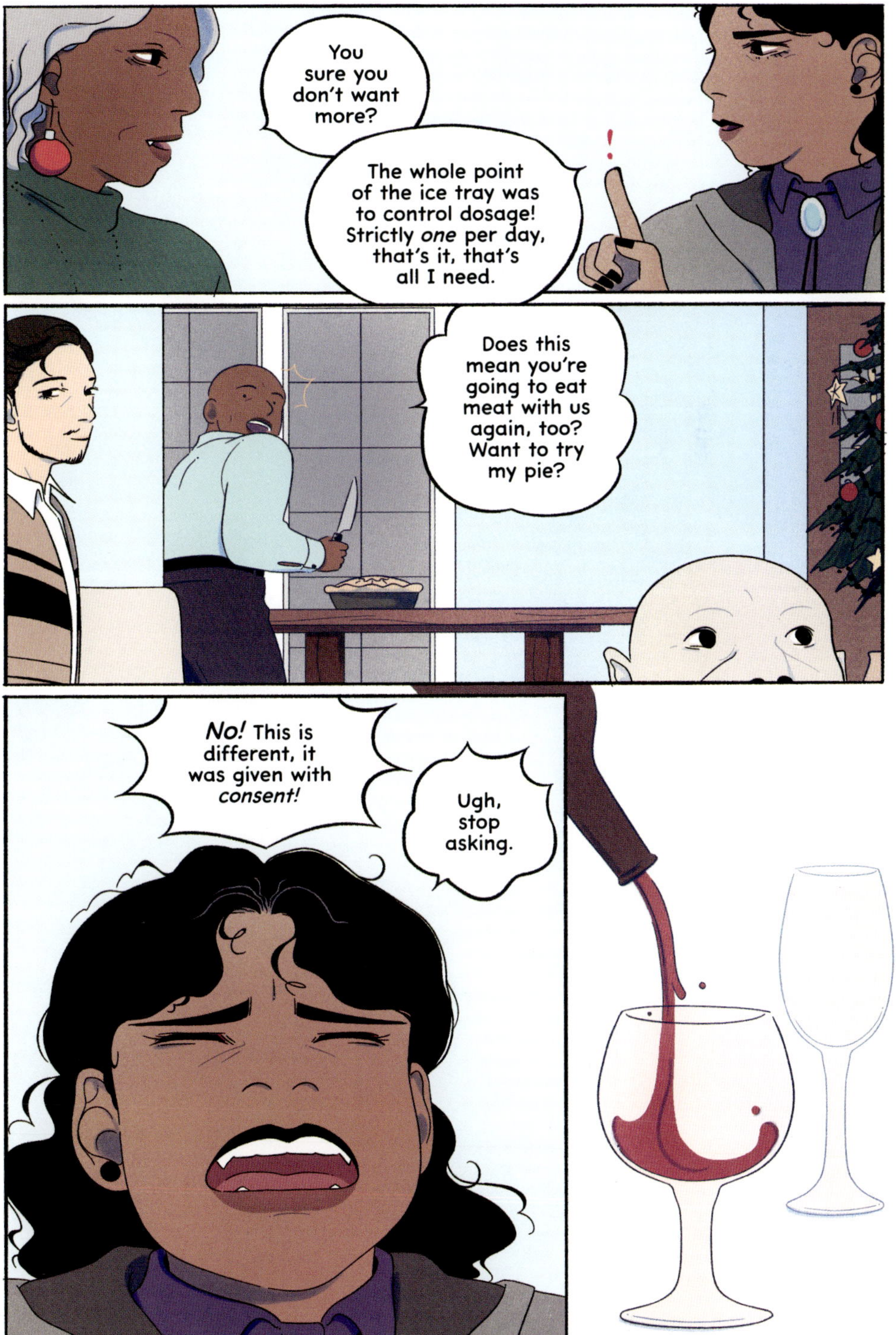
You sure you don't want more?
The whole point of the ice tray was to control dosage! Strictly *one* per day, that's it, that's all I need.
!
Does this mean you're going to eat meat with us again, too? Want to try my pie?
No! This is different, it was given with *consent!*
Ugh, stop asking.

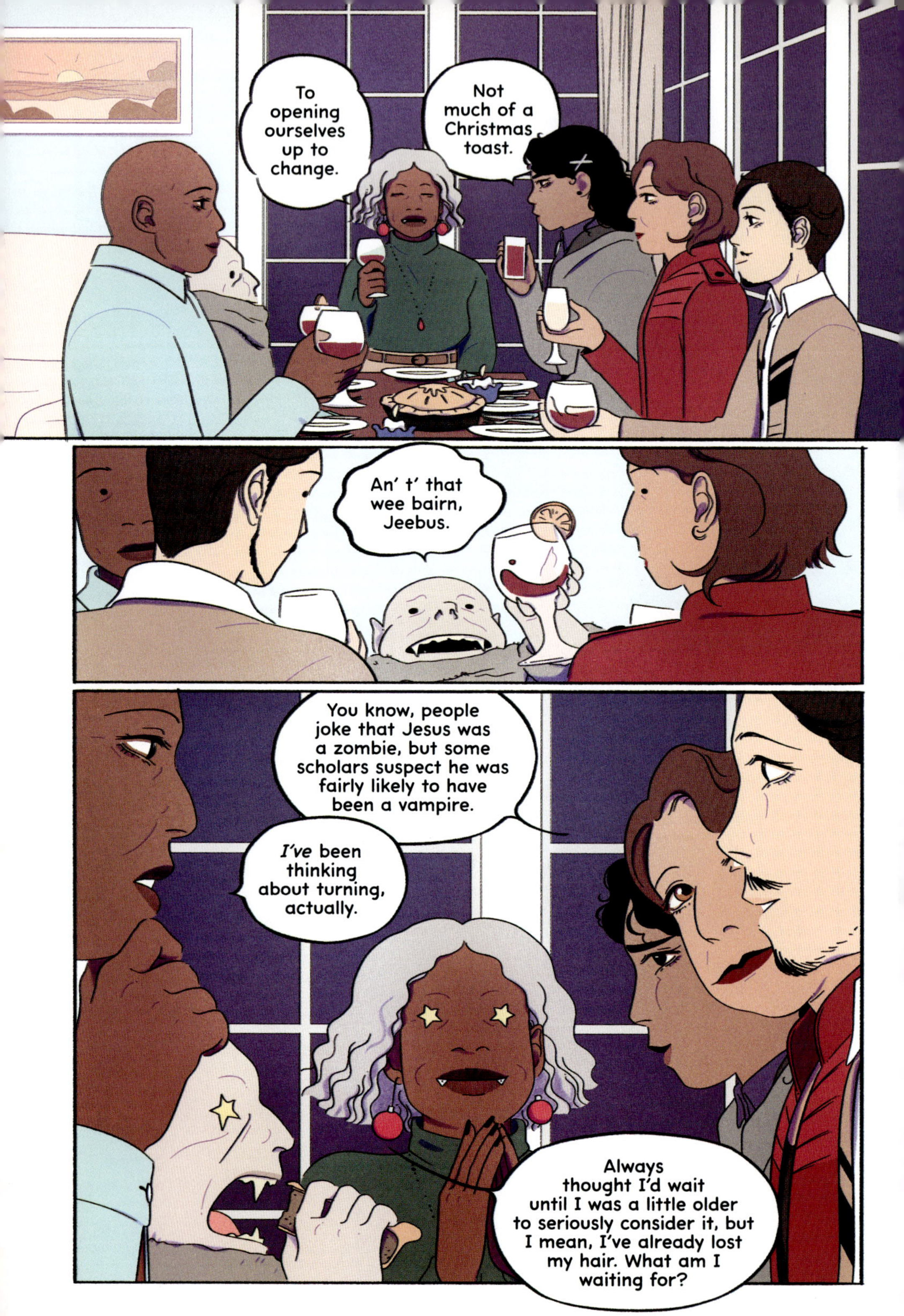
To opening ourselves up to change.
Not much of a Christmas toast.
An' t' that wee bairn, Jeebus.
You know, people joke that Jesus was a zombie, but some scholars suspect he was fairly likely to have been a vampire.
I've been thinking about turning, actually.
Always thought I'd wait until I was a little older to seriously consider it, but I mean, I've already lost my hair. What am I waiting for?

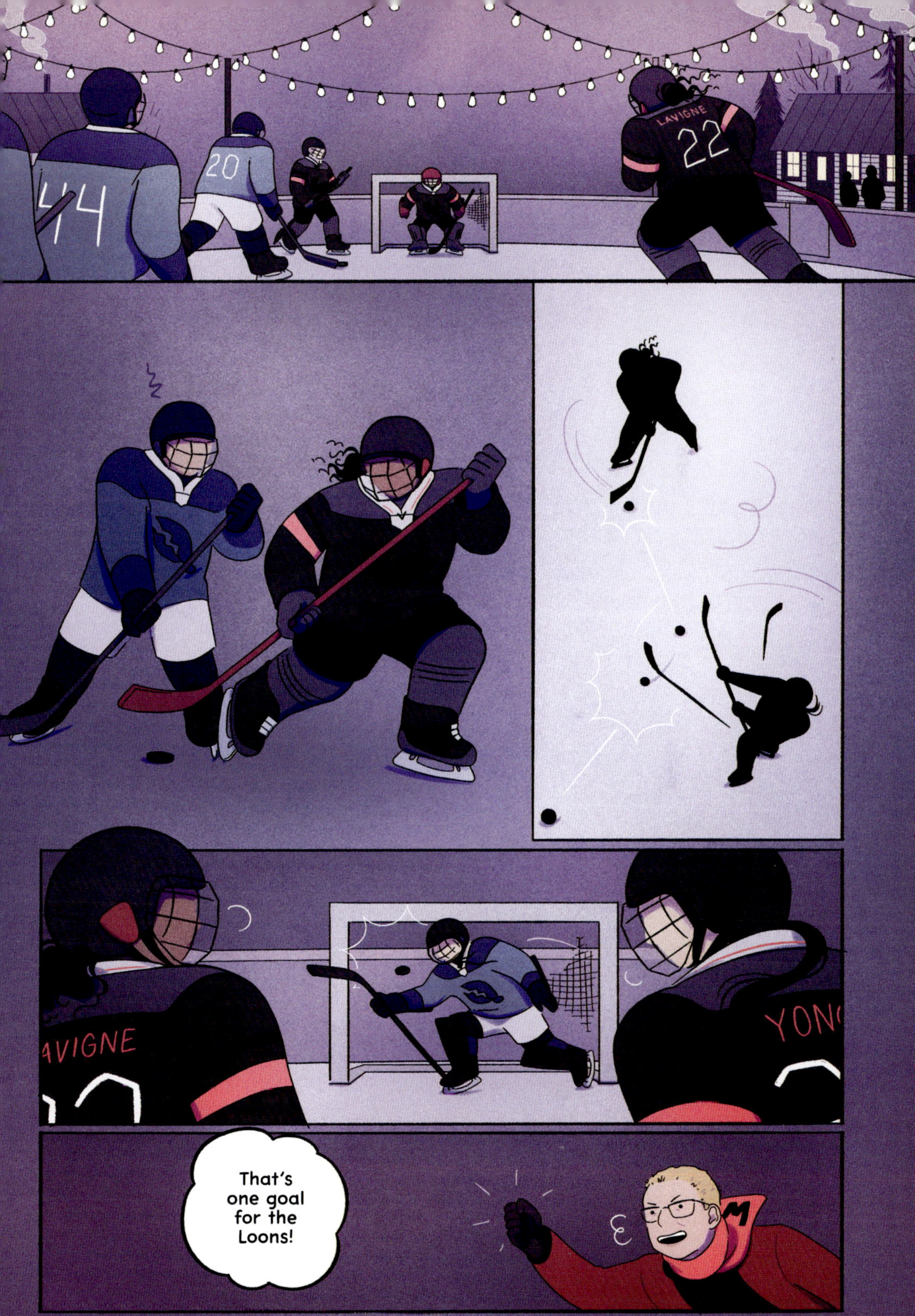
LAVIGNE
22
44
20
AVIGNE
YON
That's one goal for the Loons!

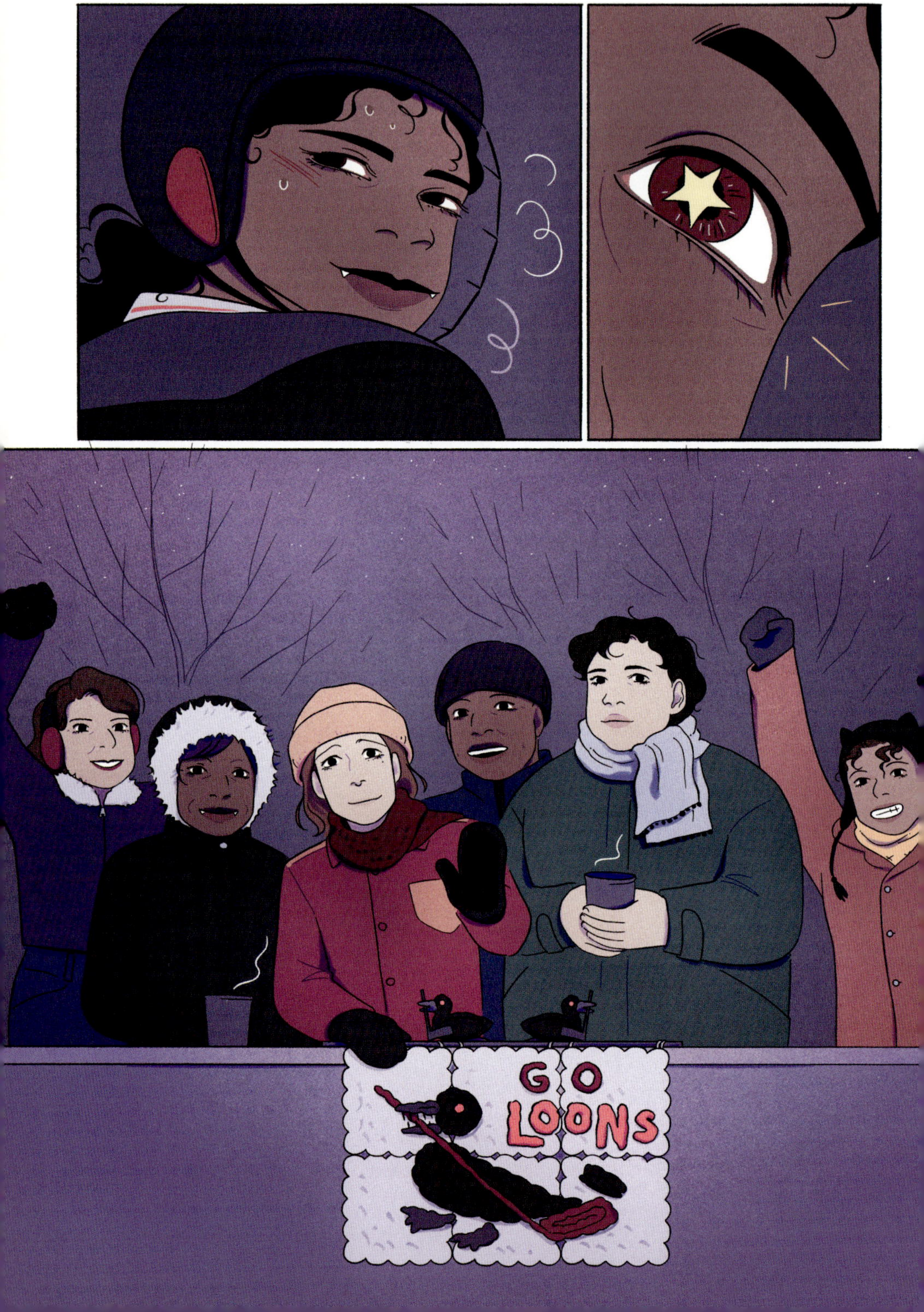
GO
LOONS

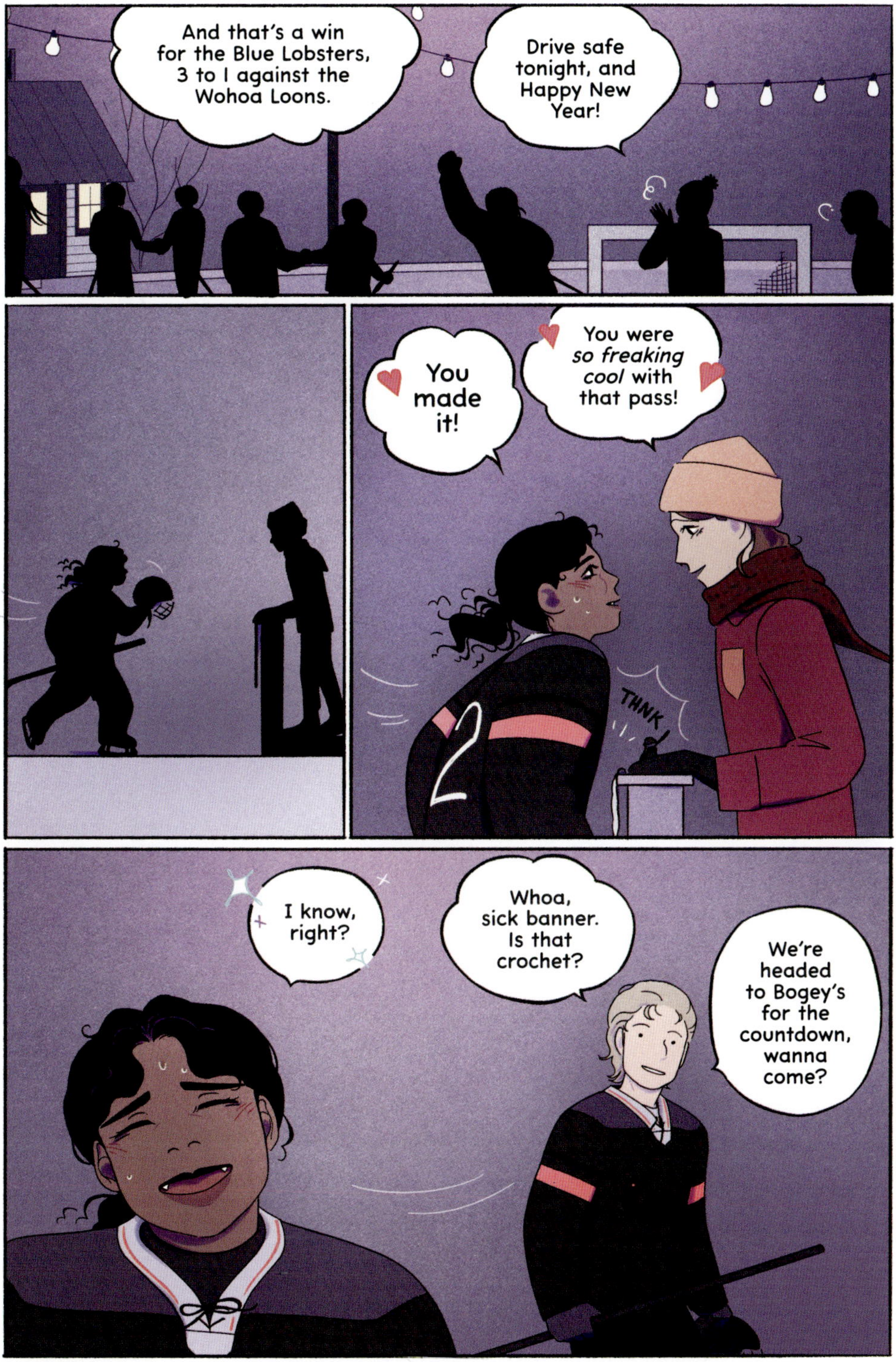

And that's a win for the Blue Lobsters, 3 to 1 against the Wohoa Loons.
Drive safe tonight, and Happy New Year!
You made it!
You were *so freaking cool* with that pass!
THNK
I know, right?
Whoa, sick banner. Is that crochet?
We're headed to Bogey's for the countdown, wanna come?

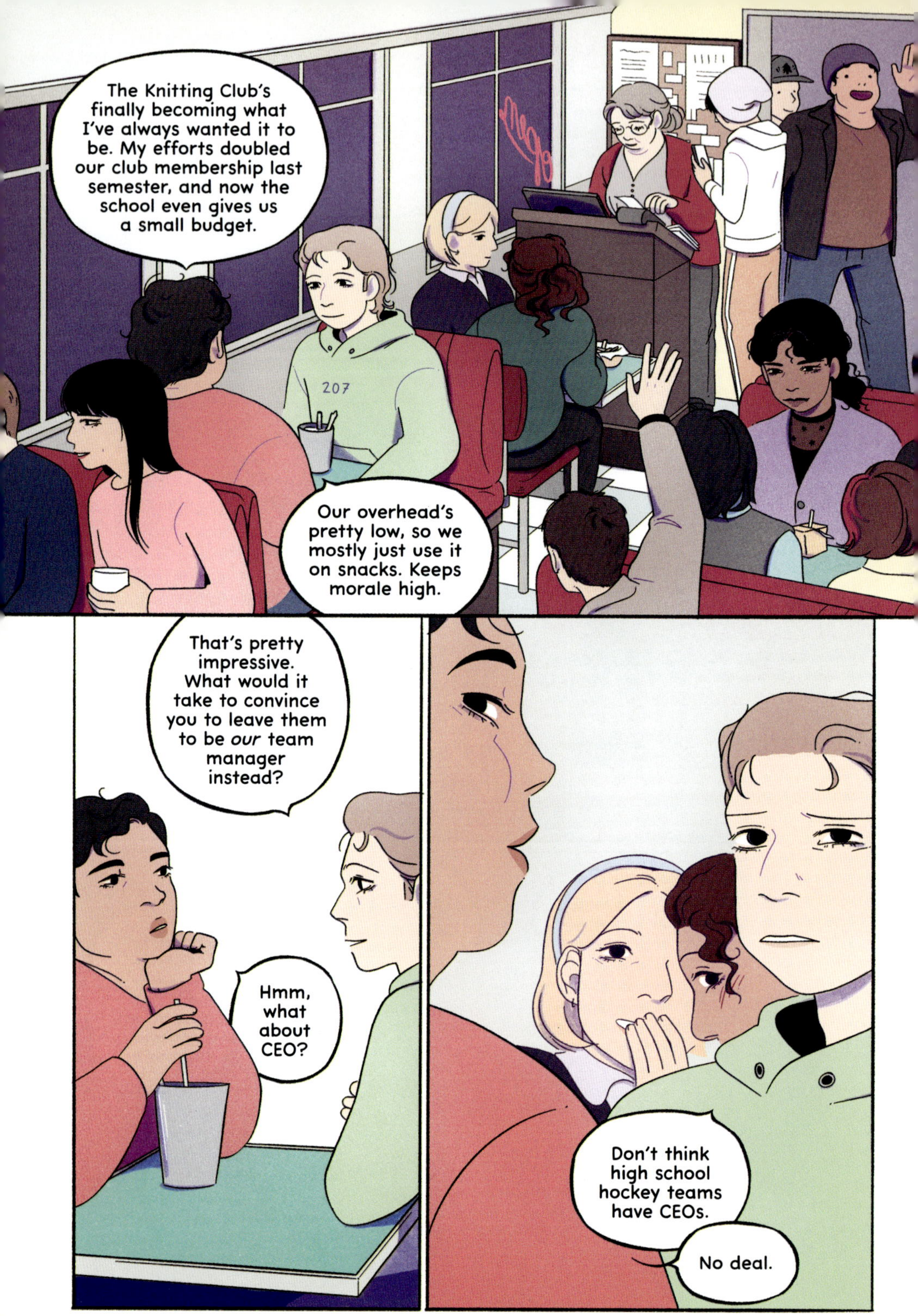
The Knitting Club's finally becoming what I've always wanted it to be. My efforts doubled our club membership last semester, and now the school even gives us a small budget.
Our overhead's pretty low, so we mostly just use it on snacks. Keeps morale high.
That's pretty impressive. What would it take to convince you to leave them to be *our* team manager instead?
Hmm, what about CEO?
Don't think high school hockey teams have CEOs.
No deal.

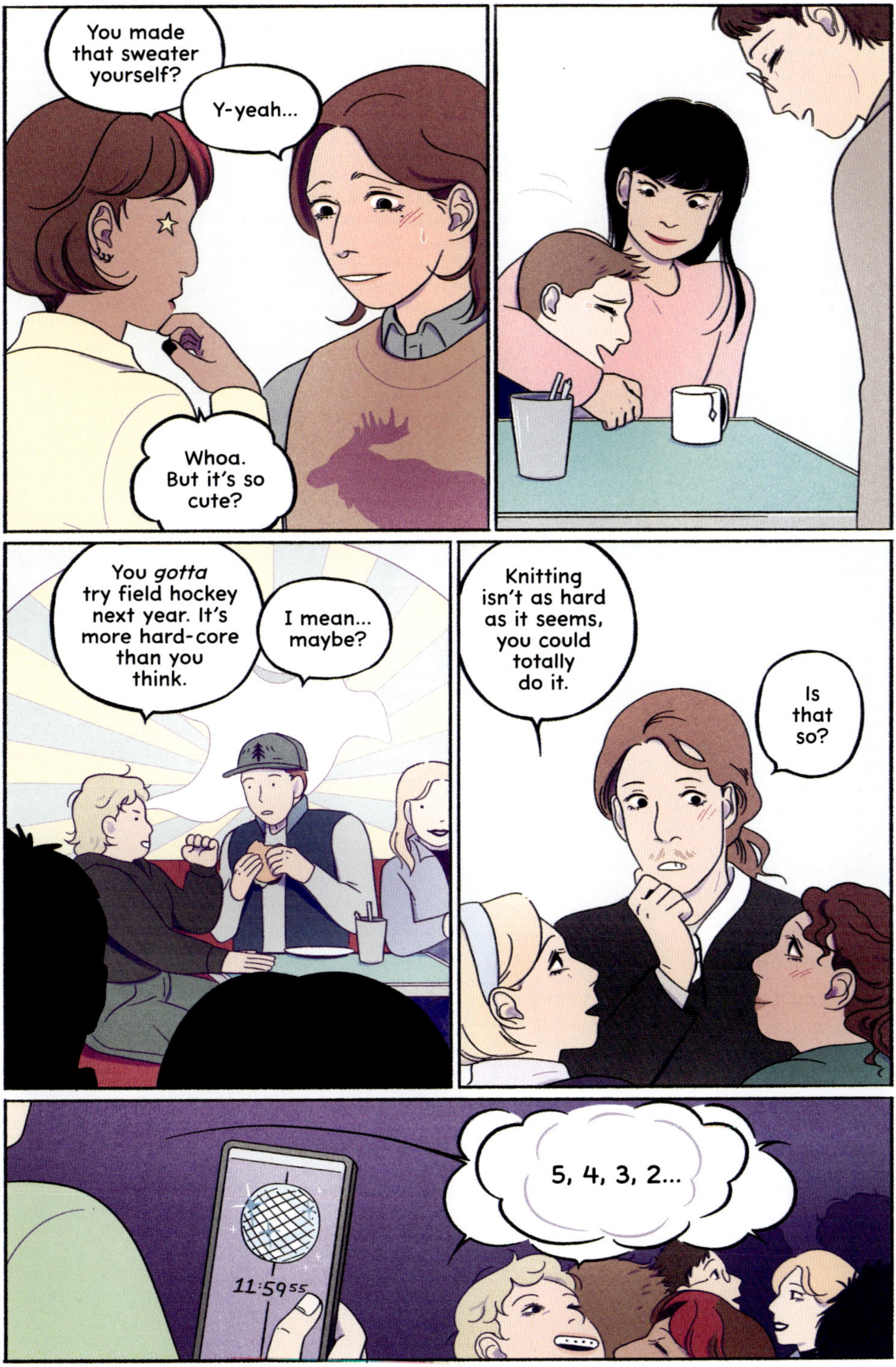
You made that sweater yourself?
Y-yeah...
Whoa. But it's so cute?
You *gotta* try field hockey next year. It's more hard-core than you think.
I mean... maybe?
Knitting isn't as hard as it seems, you could totally do it.
Is that so?
11:59 55
5, 4, 3, 2...

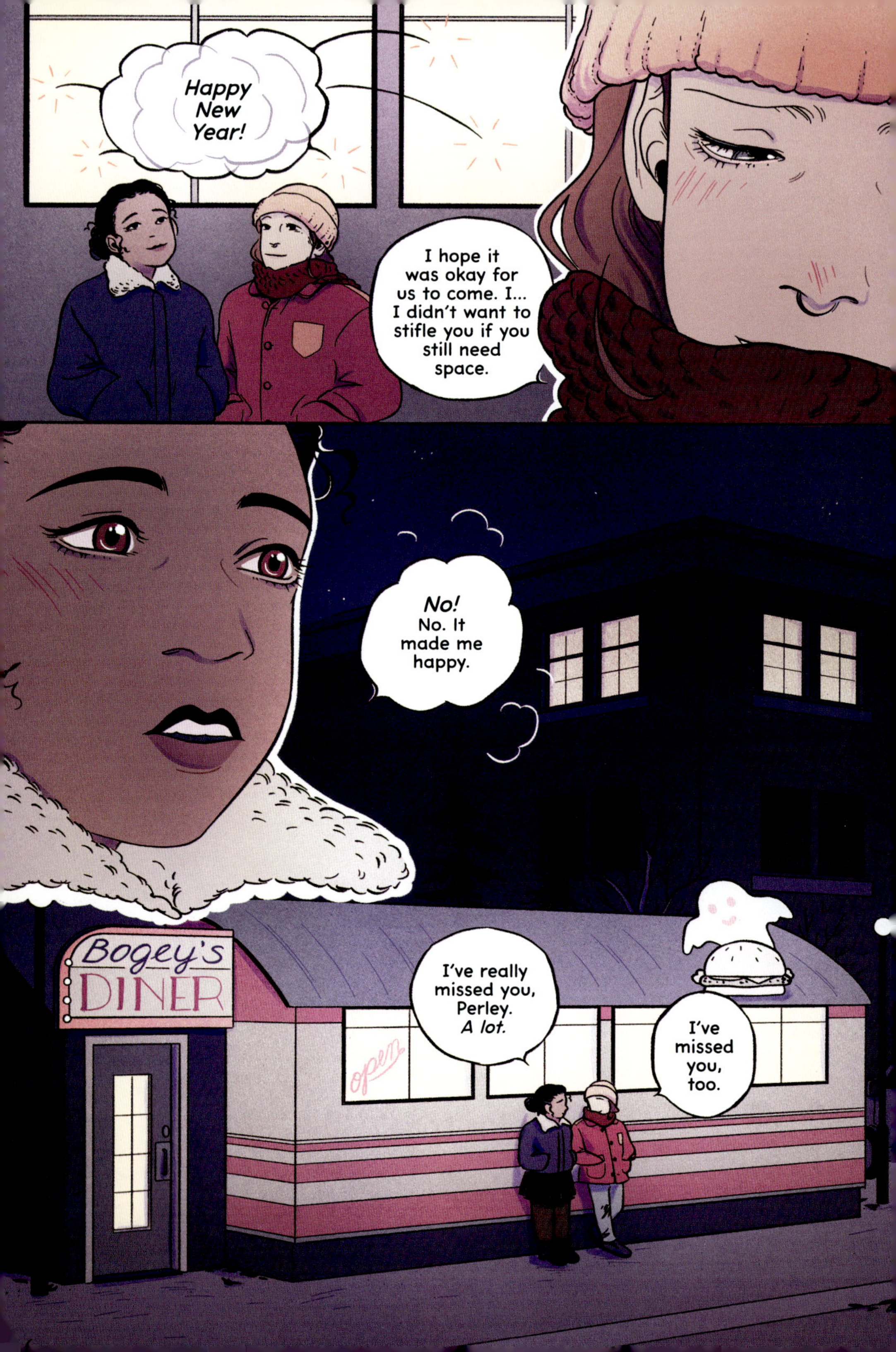
Happy New Year!
I hope it was okay for us to come. I... I didn't want to stifle you if you still need space.
No! No. It made me happy.
Bogey's DINER
open
I've really missed you, Perley. *A lot.*
I've missed you, too.

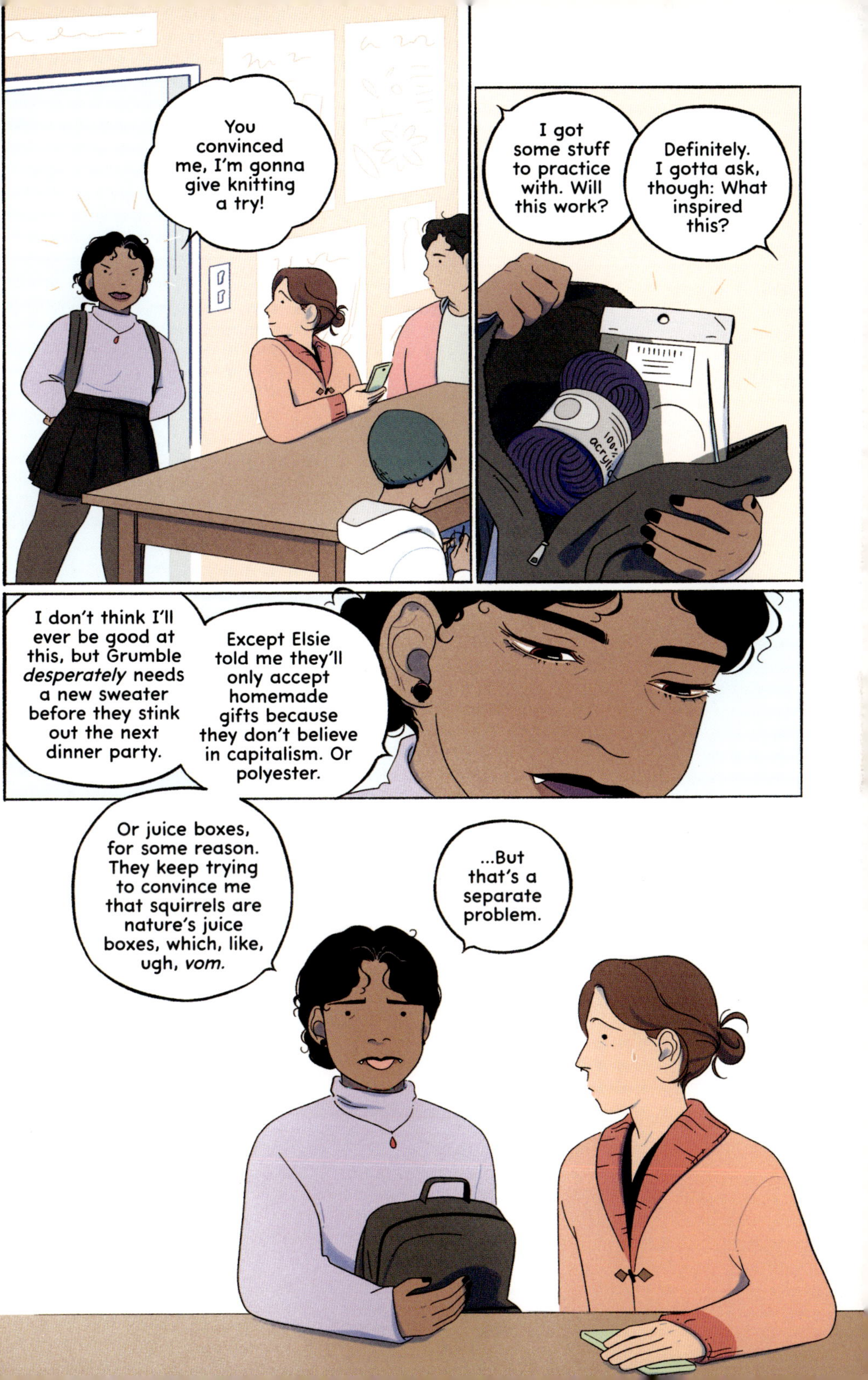
You convinced me, I'm gonna give knitting a try!
I got some stuff to practice with. Will this work?
Definitely. I gotta ask, though: What inspired this?
100% acrylic
I don't think I'll ever be good at this, but Grumble *desperately* needs a new sweater before they stink out the next dinner party.
Except Elsie told me they'll only accept homemade gifts because they don't believe in capitalism. Or polyester.
Or juice boxes, for some reason. They keep trying to convince me that squirrels are nature's juice boxes, which, like, ugh, *vom.*
...But that's a separate problem.

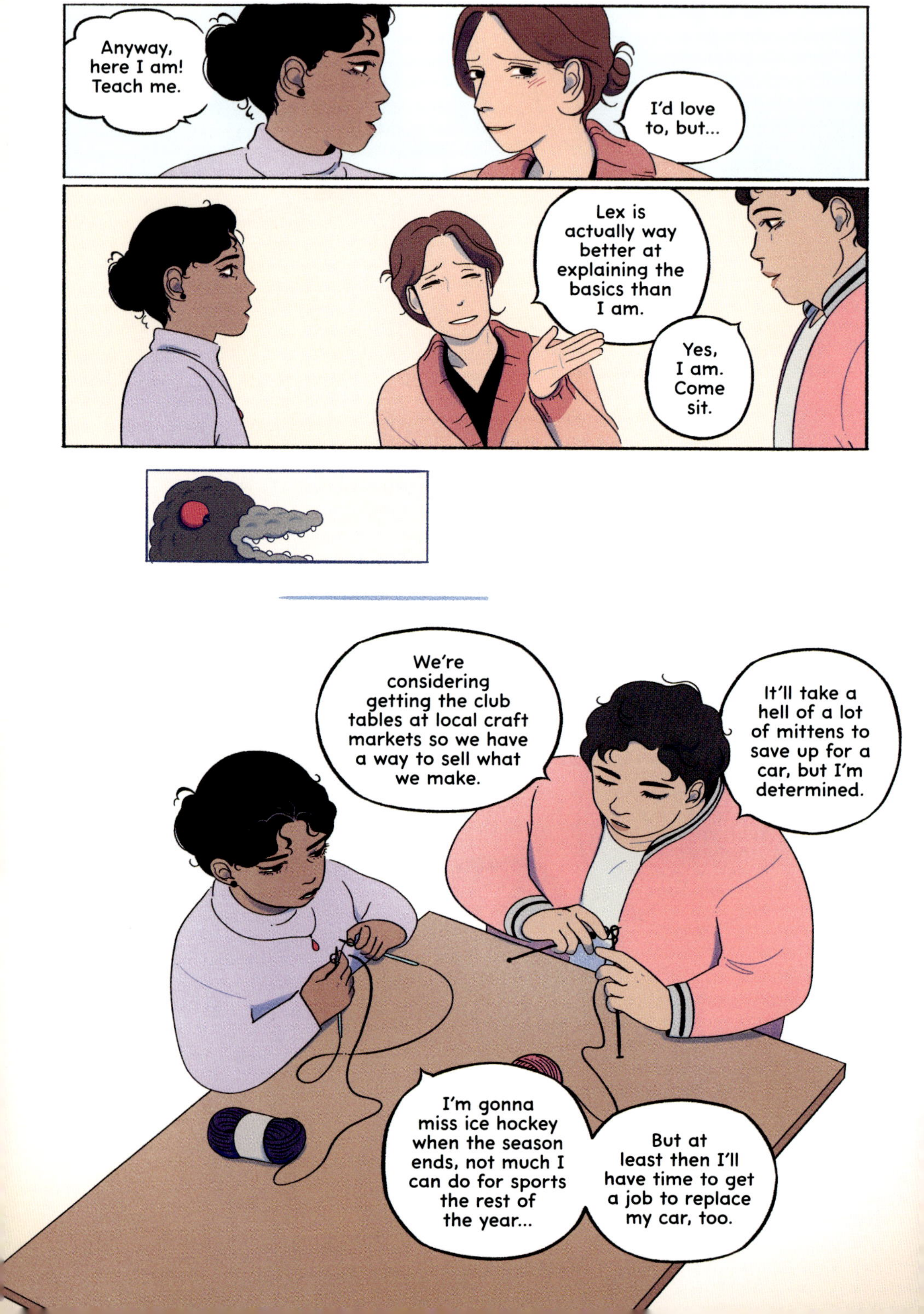
Anyway, here I am! Teach me.
I'd love to, but...
Lex is actually way better at explaining the basics than I am.
Yes, I am. Come sit.
We're considering getting the club tables at local craft markets so we have a way to sell what we make.
It'll take a hell of a lot of mittens to save up for a car, but I'm determined.
I'm gonna miss ice hockey when the season ends, not much I can do for sports the rest of the year...
But at least then I'll have time to get a job to replace my car, too.

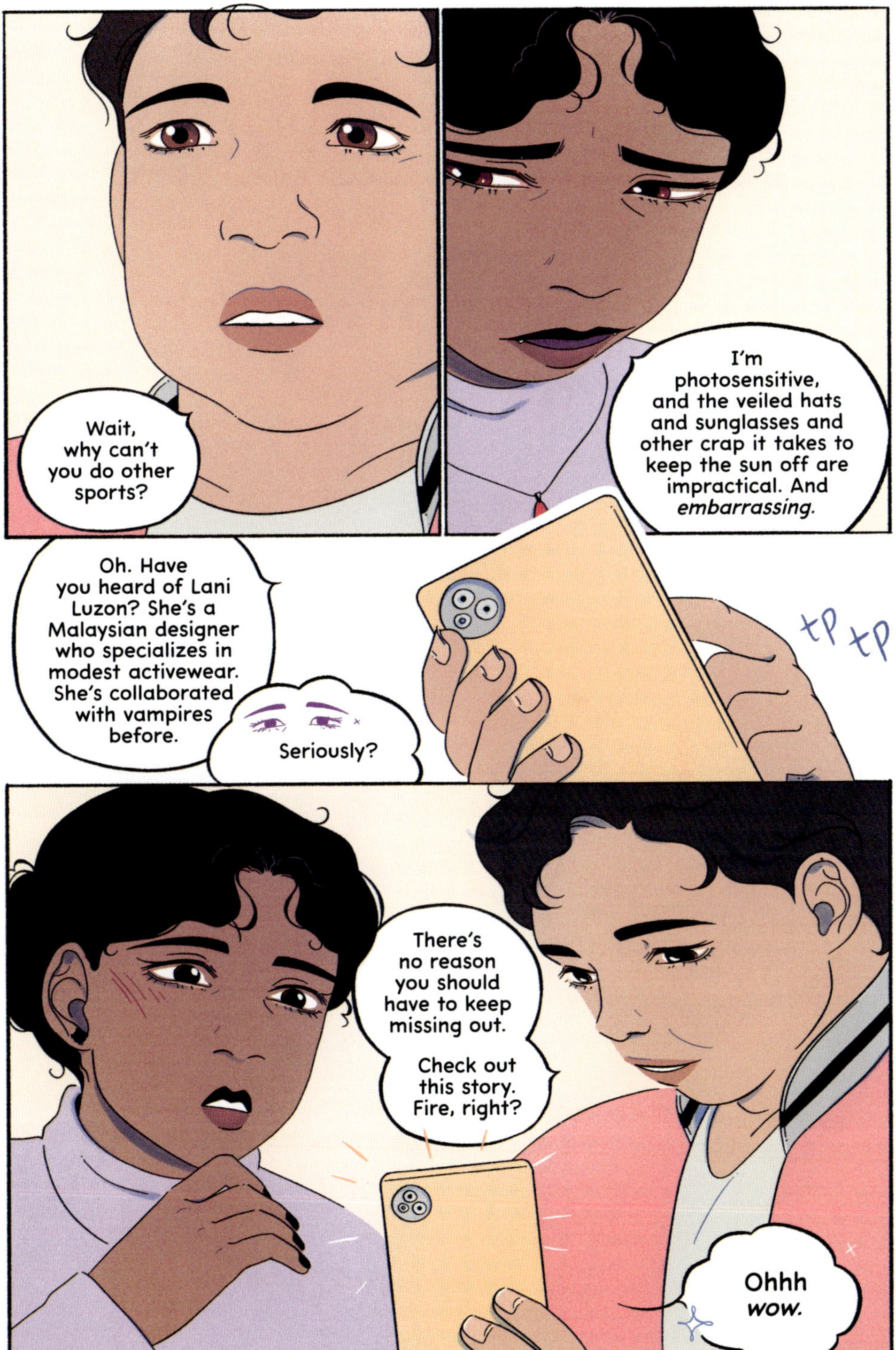
Wait, why can't you do other sports?
I'm photosensitive, and the veiled hats and sunglasses and other crap it takes to keep the sun off are impractical. And *embarrassing.*
Oh. Have you heard of Lani Luzon? She's a Malaysian designer who specializes in modest activewear. She's collaborated with vampires before.
tp tp
Seriously?
There's no reason you should have to keep missing out.
Check out this story. Fire, right?
Ohhh *wow.*

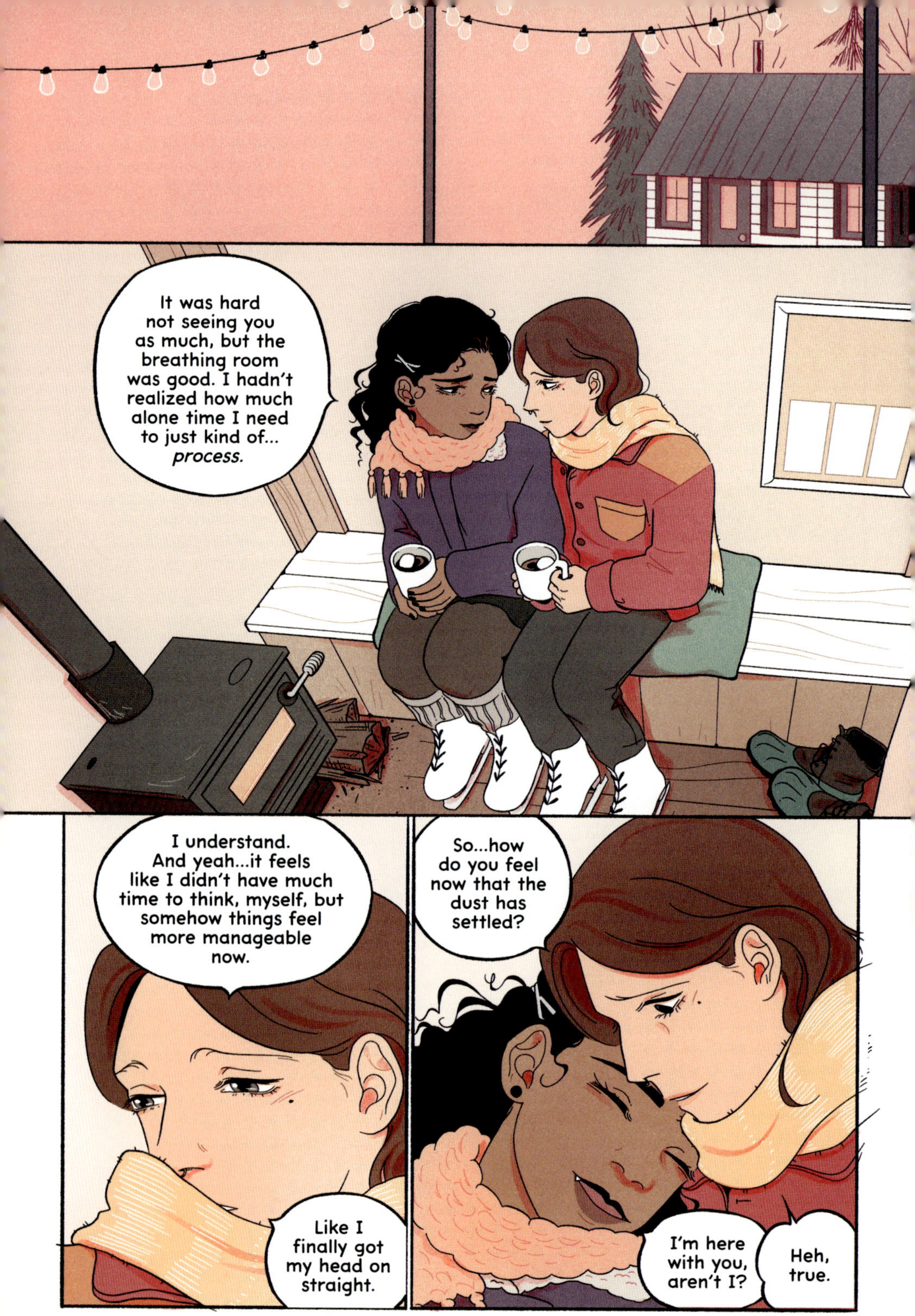
It was hard not seeing you as much, but the breathing room was good. I hadn't realized how much alone time I need to just kind of... *process.*
I understand. And yeah...it feels like I didn't have much time to think, myself, but somehow things feel more manageable now.
Like I finally got my head on straight.
So...how do you feel now that the dust has settled?
I'm here with you, aren't I?
Heh, true.

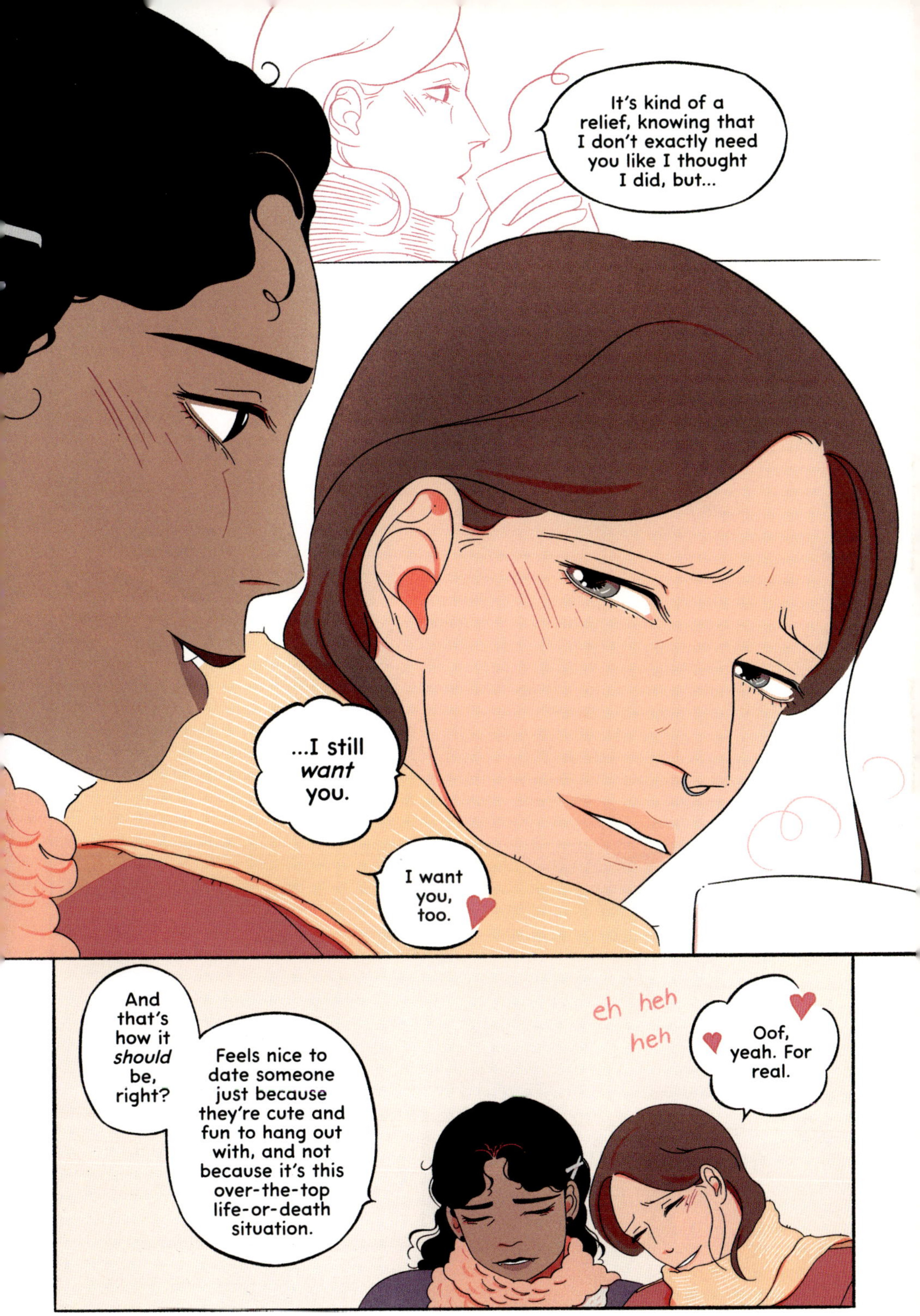
It's kind of a relief, knowing that I don't exactly need you like I thought I did, but...
...I still *want* you.
I want you, too.
And that's how it *should* be, right?
Feels nice to date someone just because they're cute and fun to hang out with, and not because it's this over-the-top life-or-death situation.
eh heh heh
Oof, yeah. For real.

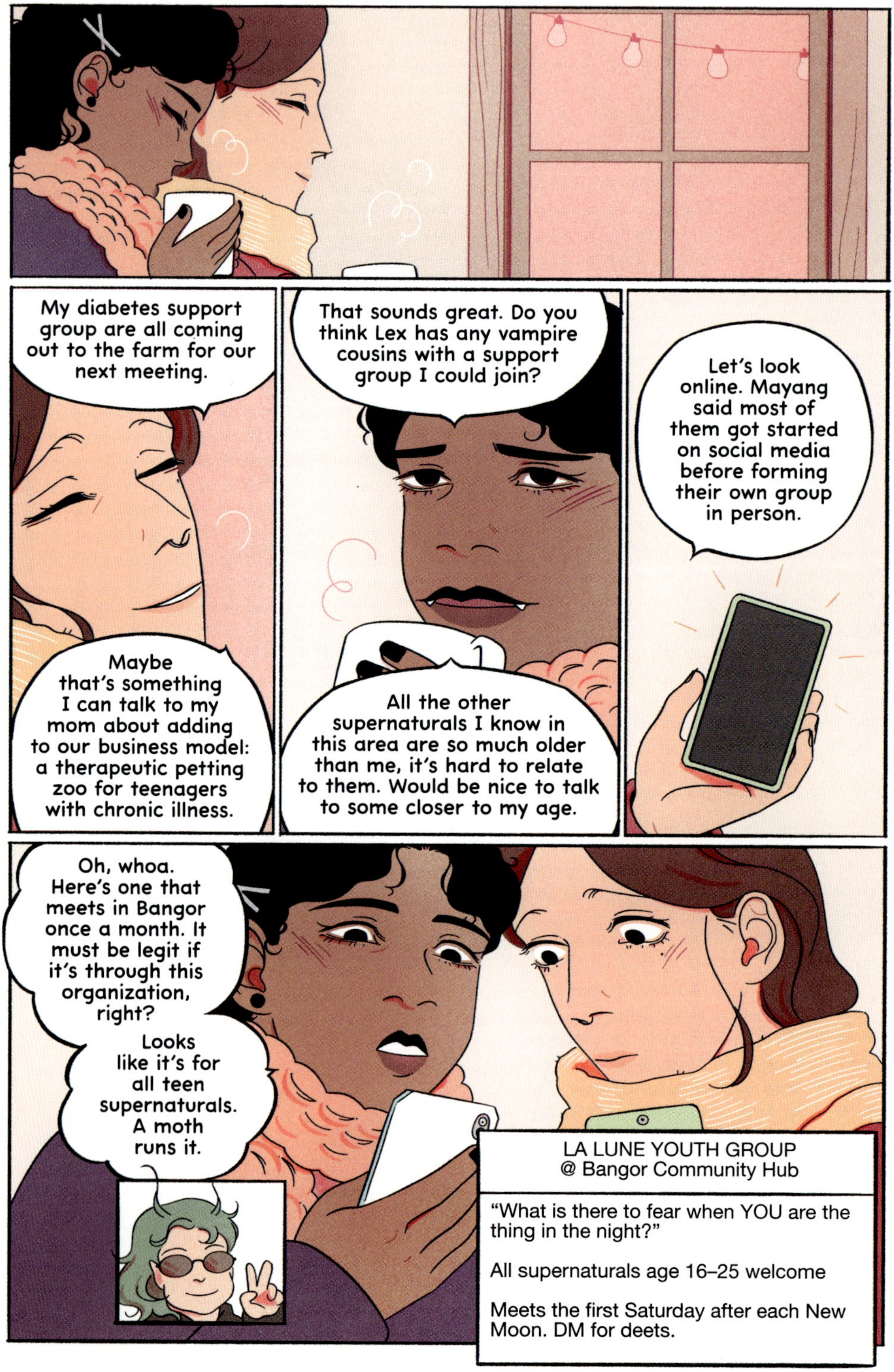

My diabetes support group are all coming out to the farm for our next meeting.
Maybe that's something I can talk to my mom about adding to our business model: a therapeutic petting zoo for teenagers with chronic illness.
That sounds great. Do you think Lex has any vampire cousins with a support group I could join?
All the other supernaturals I know in this area are so much older than me, it's hard to relate to them. Would be nice to talk to some closer to my age.
Let's look online. Mayang said most of them got started on social media before forming their own group in person.
Oh, whoa. Here's one that meets in Bangor once a month. It must be legit if it's through this organization, right?
Looks like it's for all teen supernaturals. A moth runs it.
LA LUNE YOUTH GROUP
@ Bangor Community Hub
"What is there to fear when YOU are the thing in the night?"
All supernaturals age 16–25 welcome
Meets the first Saturday after each New Moon. DM for deets.

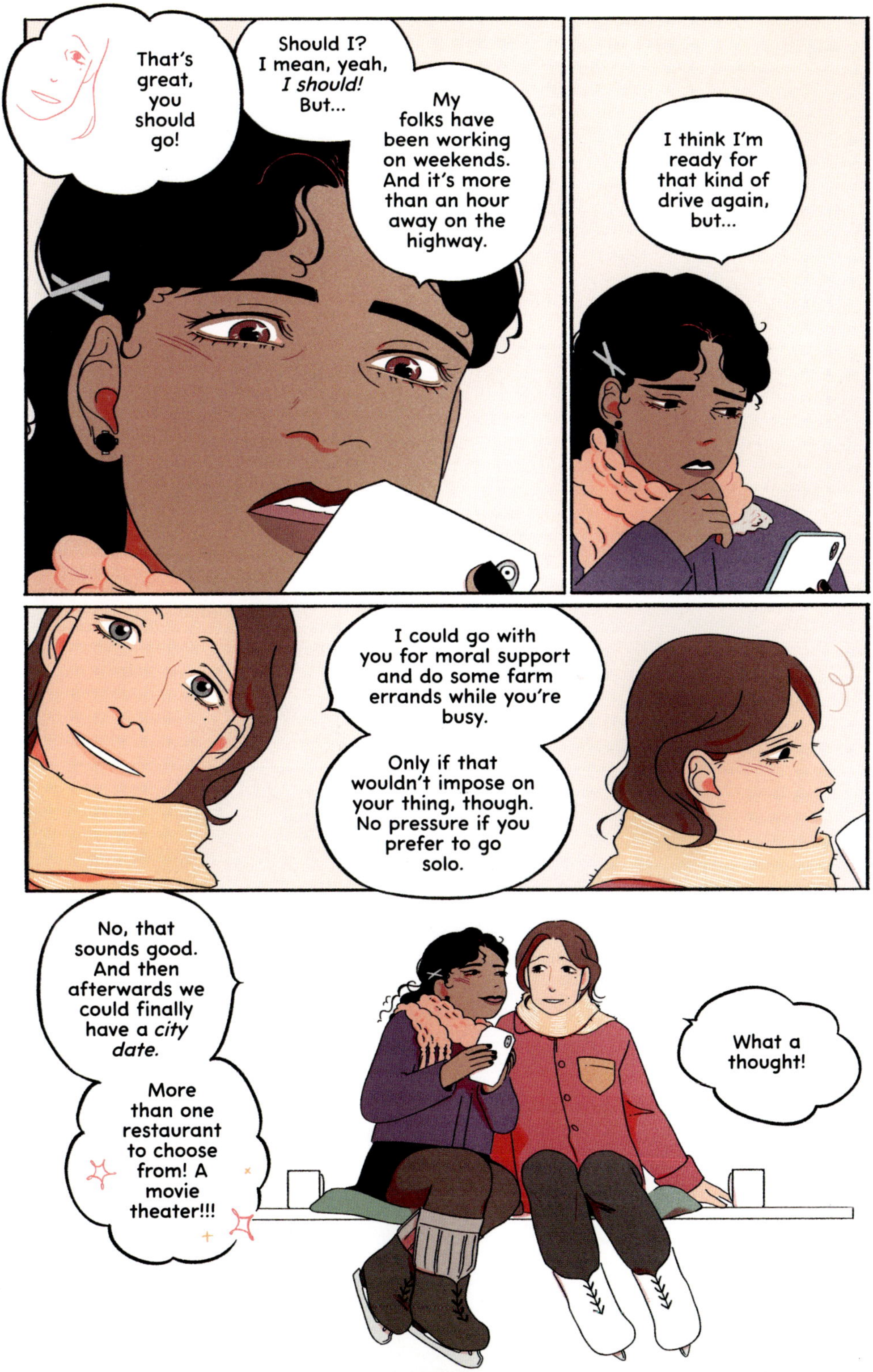
That's great, you should go!
Should I? I mean, yeah, *I should!* But...
My folks have been working on weekends. And it's more than an hour away on the highway.
I think I'm ready for that kind of drive again, but...
I could go with you for moral support and do some farm errands while you're busy.
Only if that wouldn't impose on your thing, though. No pressure if you prefer to go solo.
No, that sounds good. And then afterwards we could finally have a *city date.*
More than one restaurant to choose from! A movie theater!!!
What a thought!

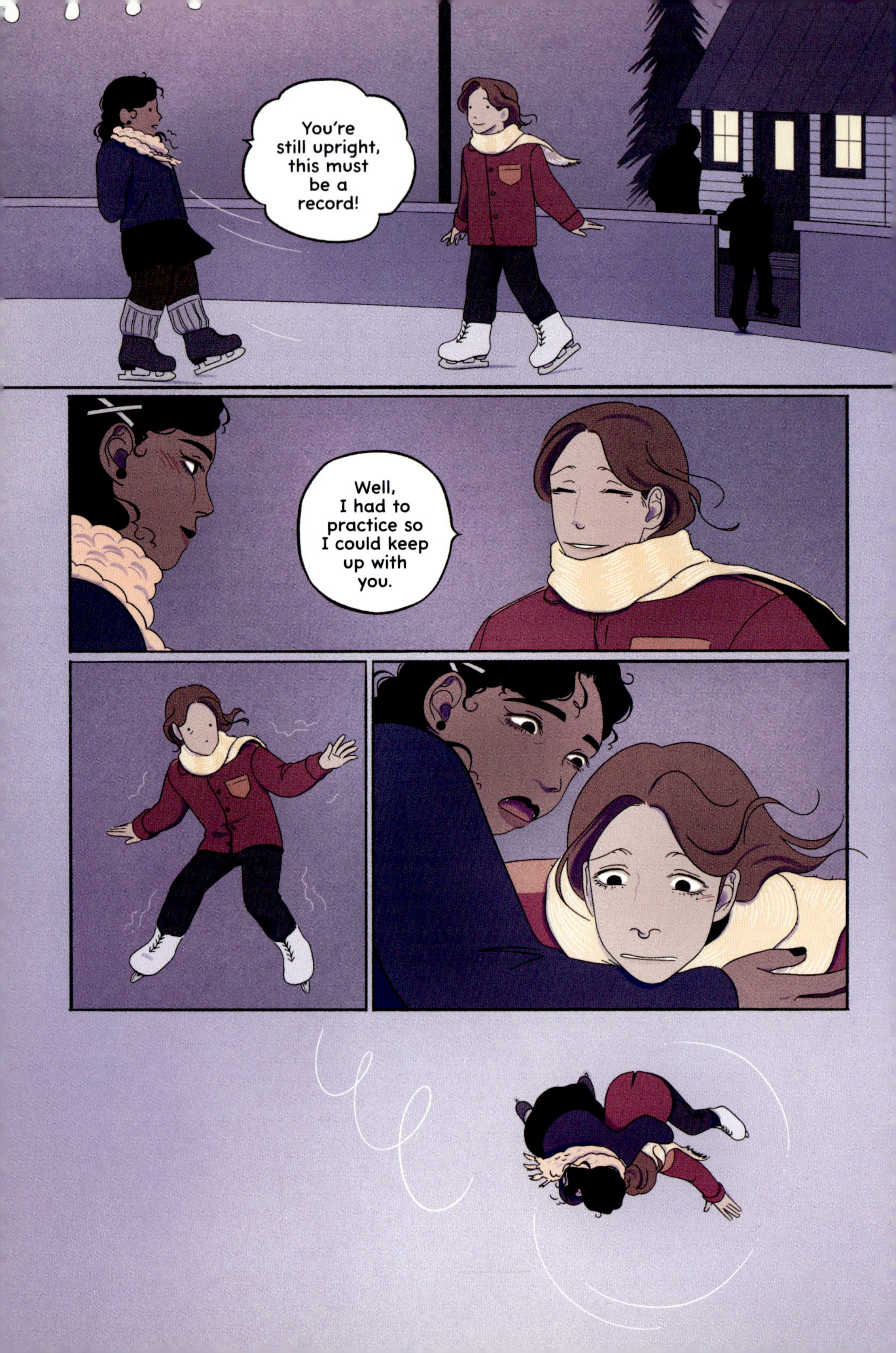
You're still upright, this must be a record!
Well, I had to practice so I could keep up with you.

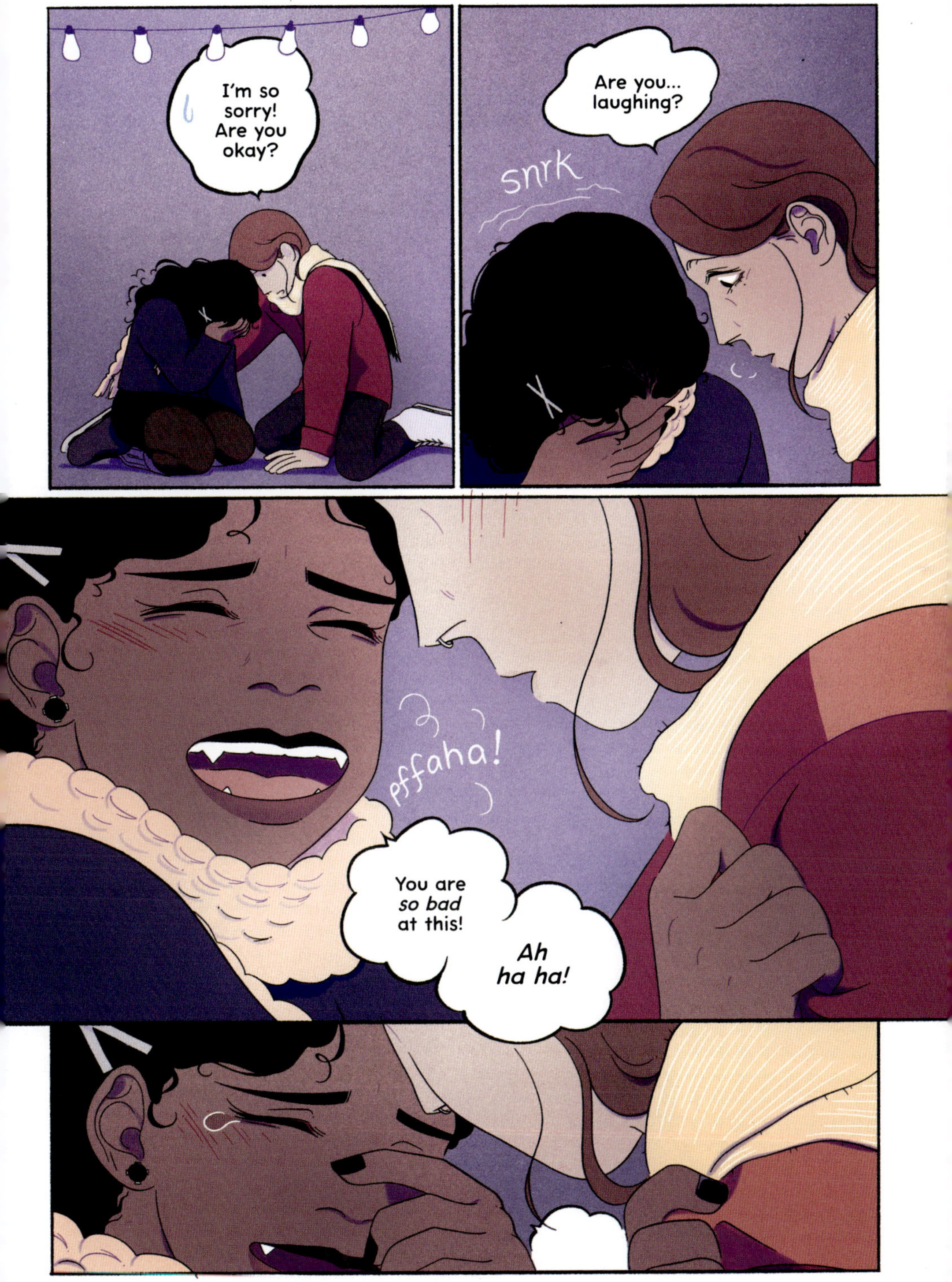
I'm so sorry! Are you okay?
Are you... laughing?
snrk
pffaha!
You are *so bad* at this!
Ah ha ha!

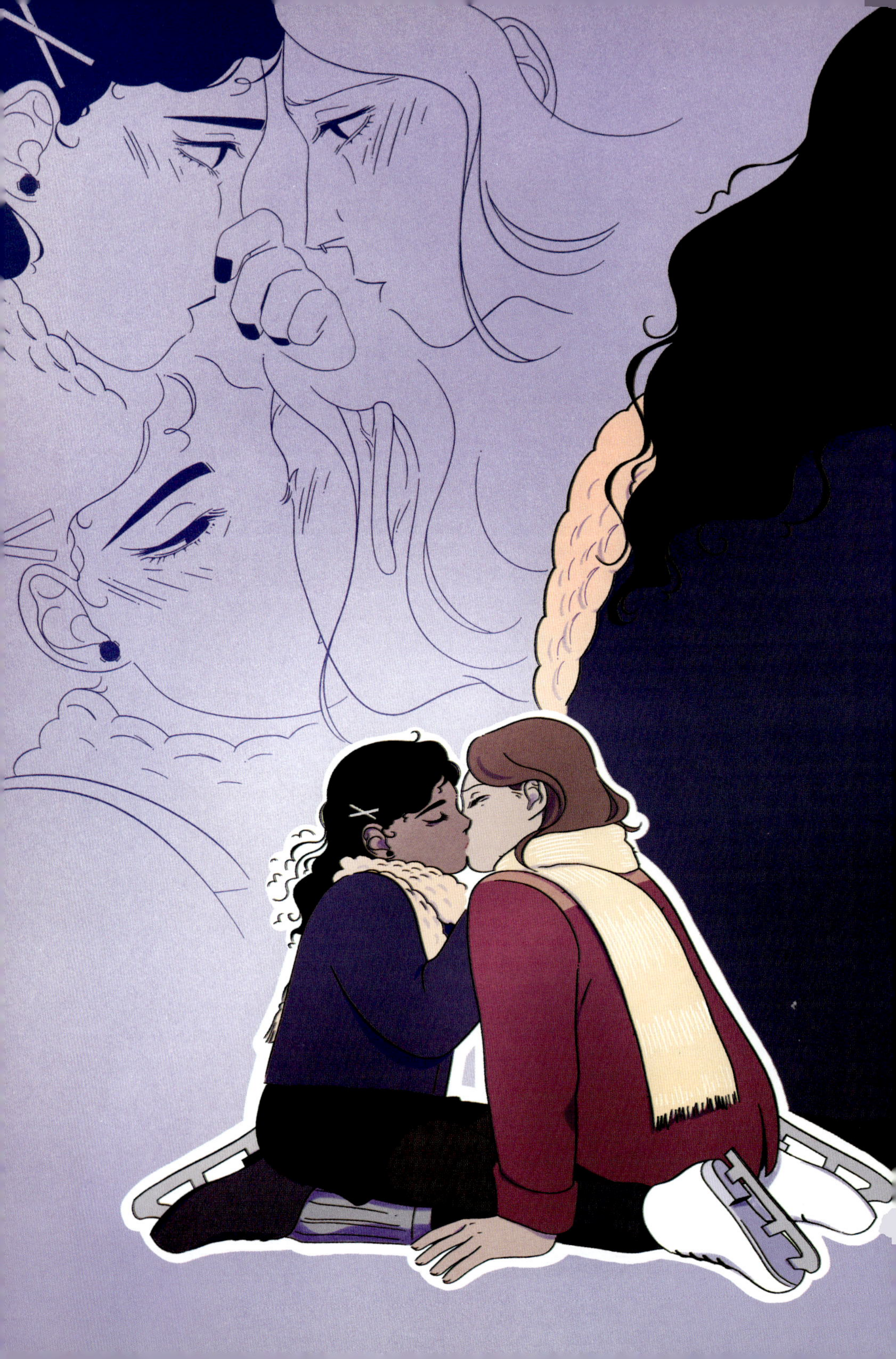

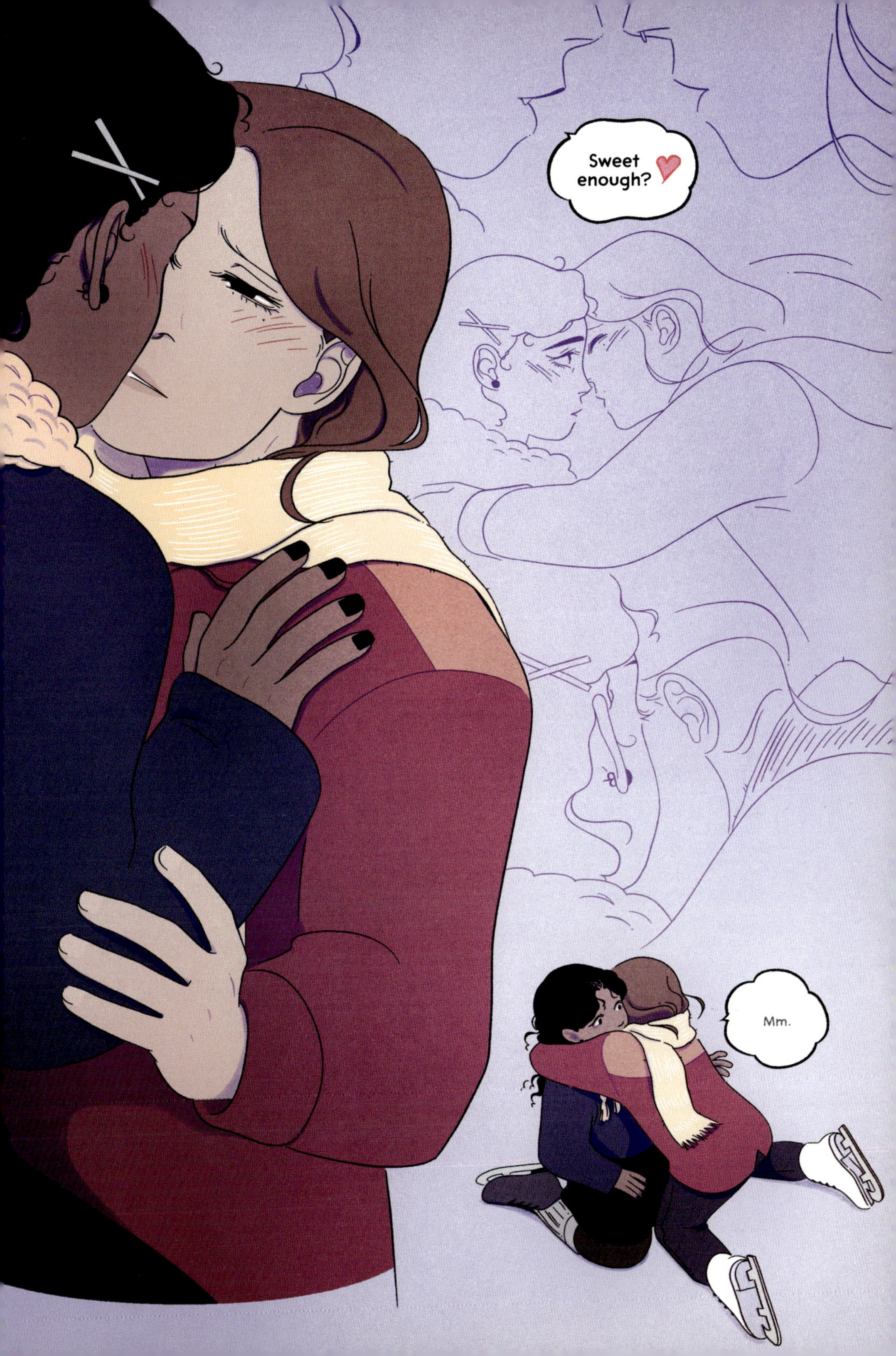
Sweet enough?
Mm.

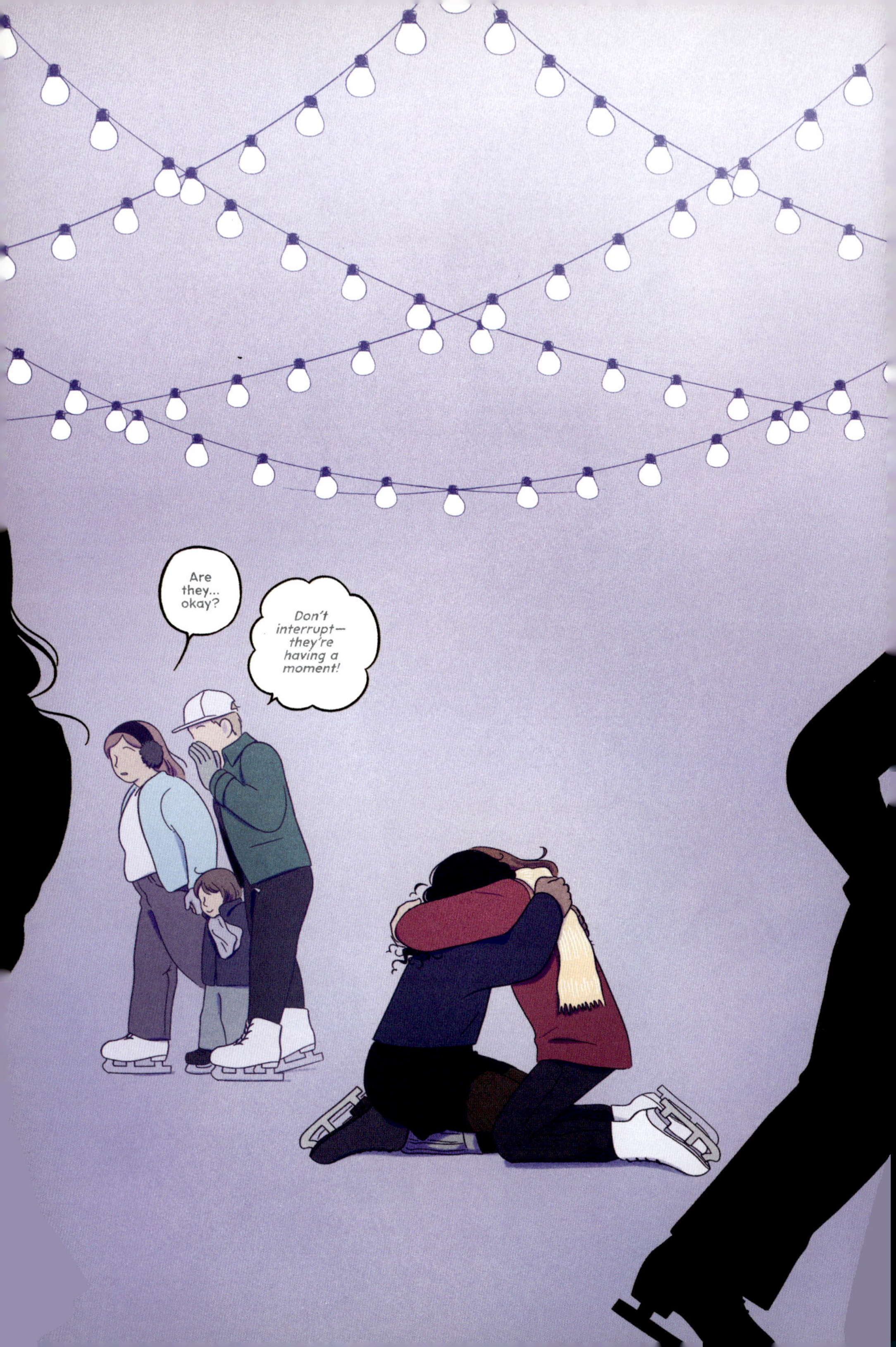
Are they... okay?
Don't interrupt—they're having a moment!

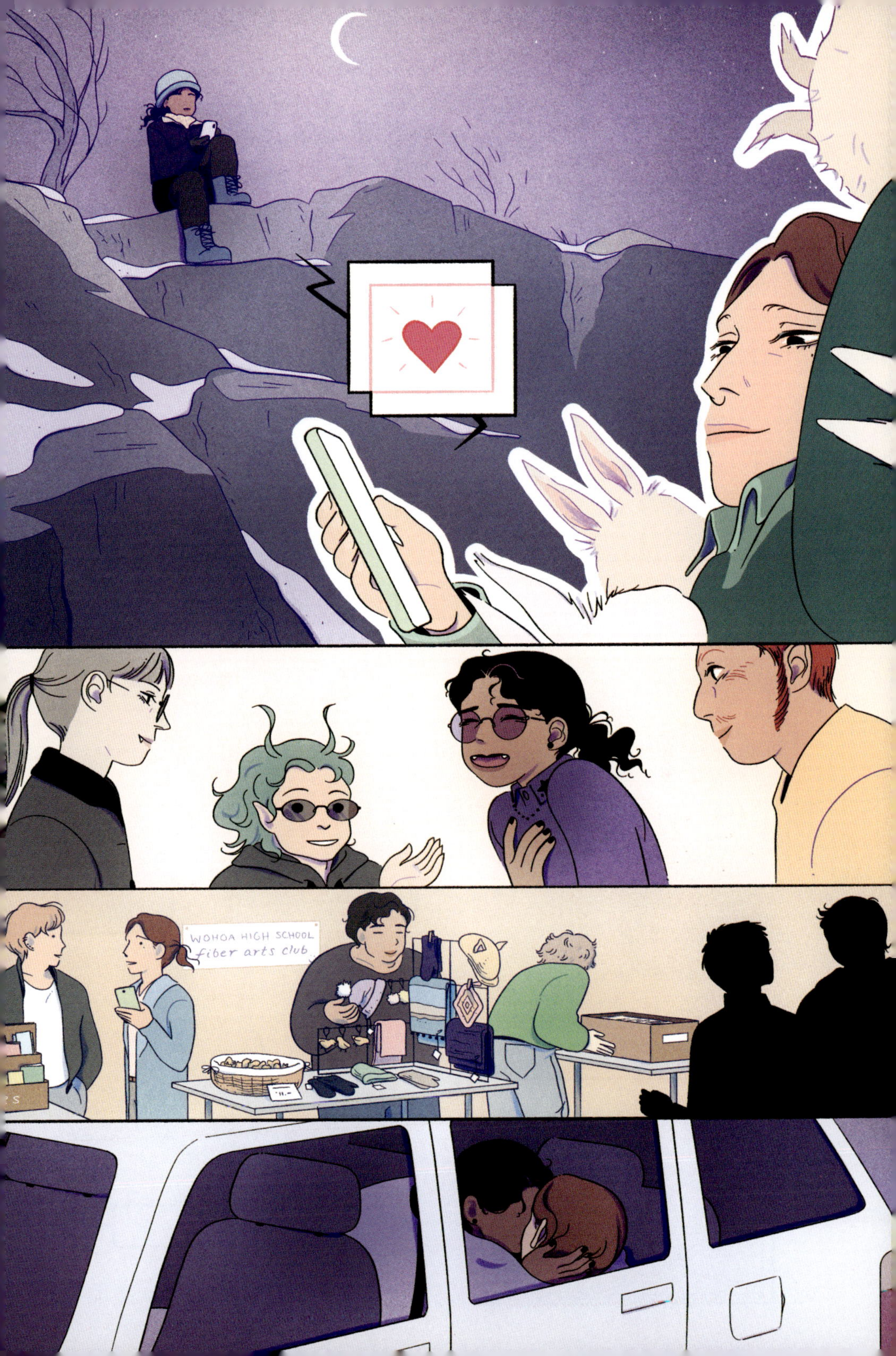
WOHOA HIGH SCHOOL
fiber arts club

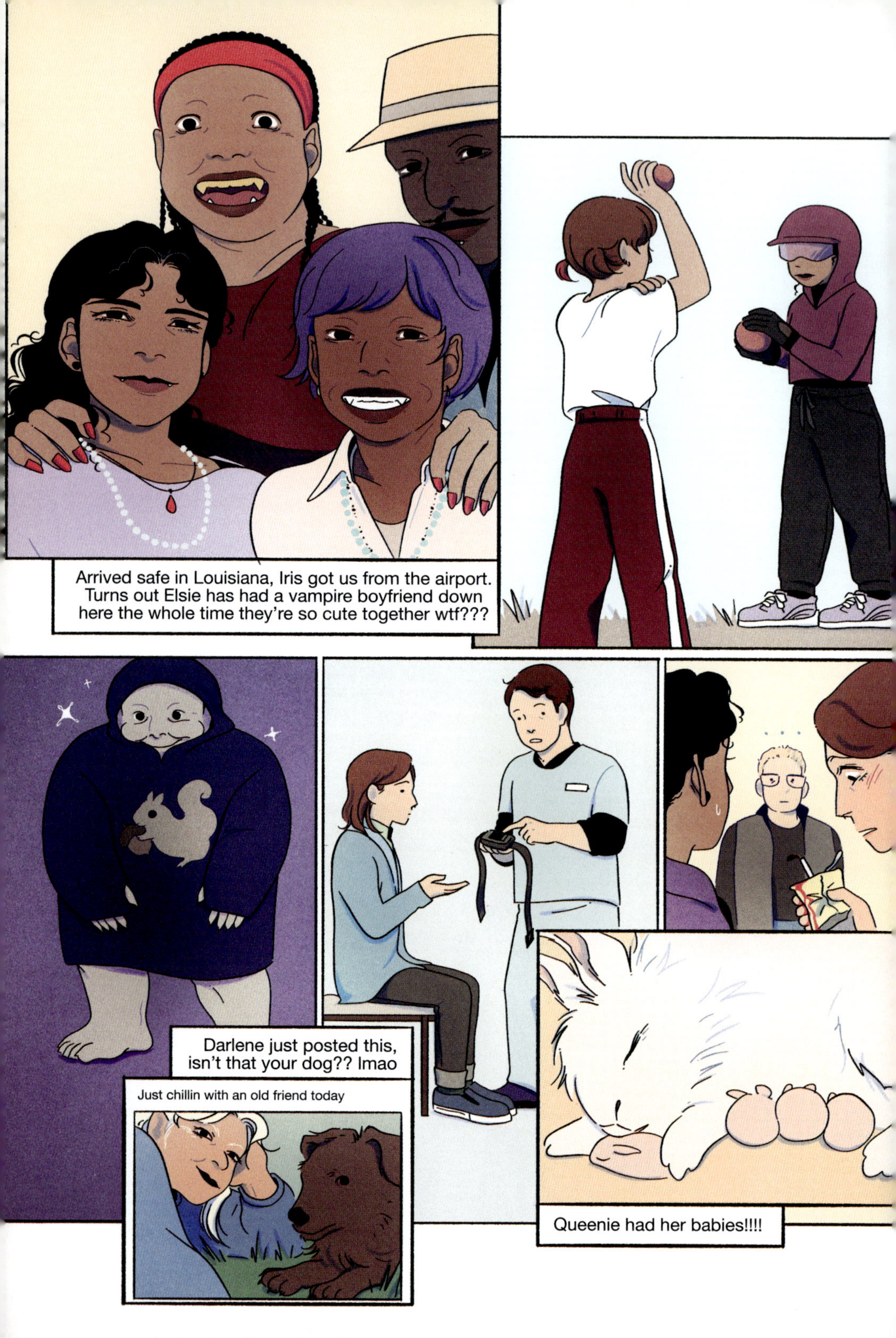
Arrived safe in Louisiana, Iris got us from the airport. Turns out Elsie has had a vampire boyfriend down here the whole time they're so cute together wtf???
Darlene just posted this, isn't that your dog?? lmao
Just chillin with an old friend today
Queenie had her babies!!!!

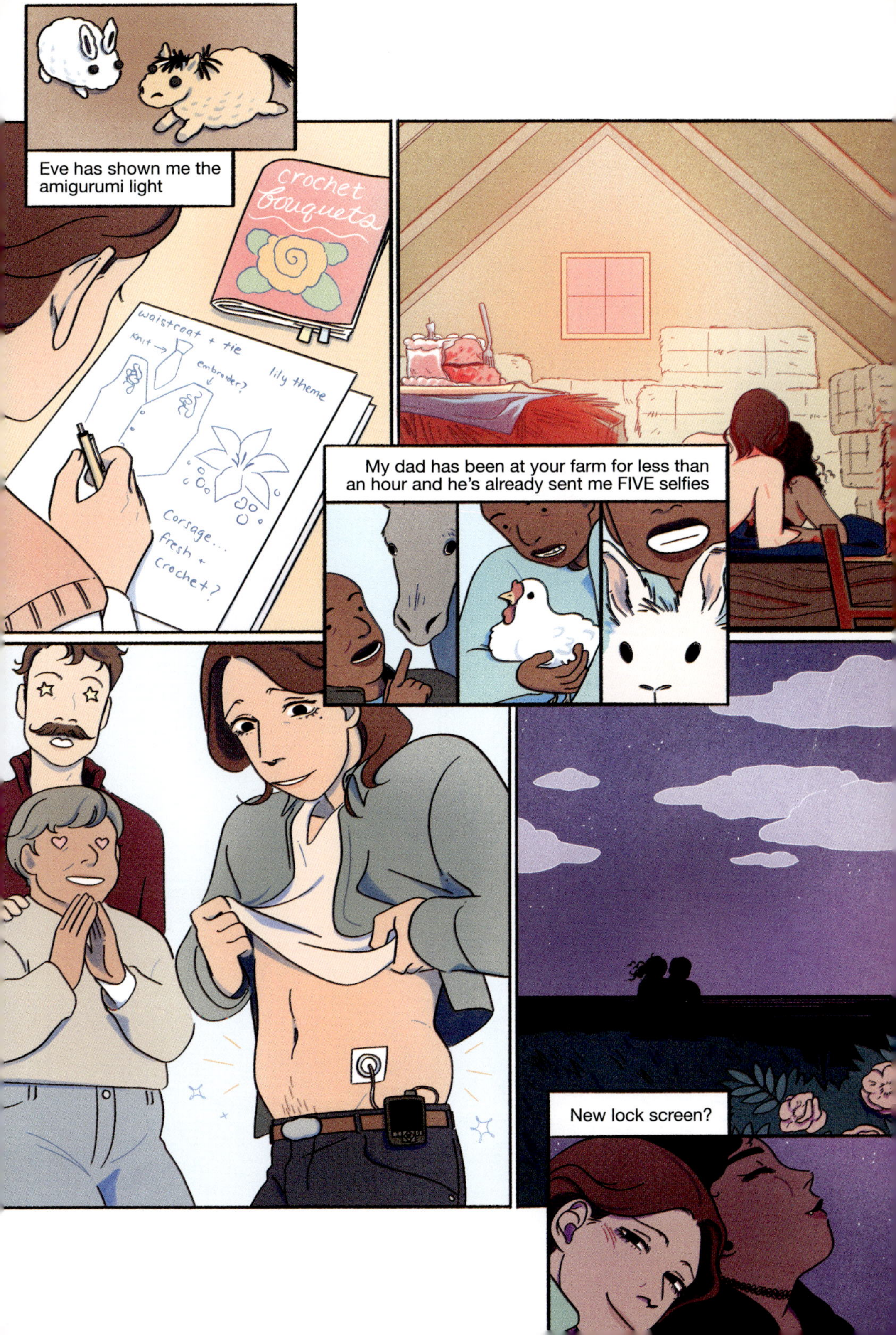
Eve has shown me the amigurumi light
crochet bouquets
waistcoat + tie
knit →
embroider?
lily theme
Corsage... fresh + crochet?
My dad has been at your farm for less than an hour and he's already sent me FIVE selfies
New lock screen?

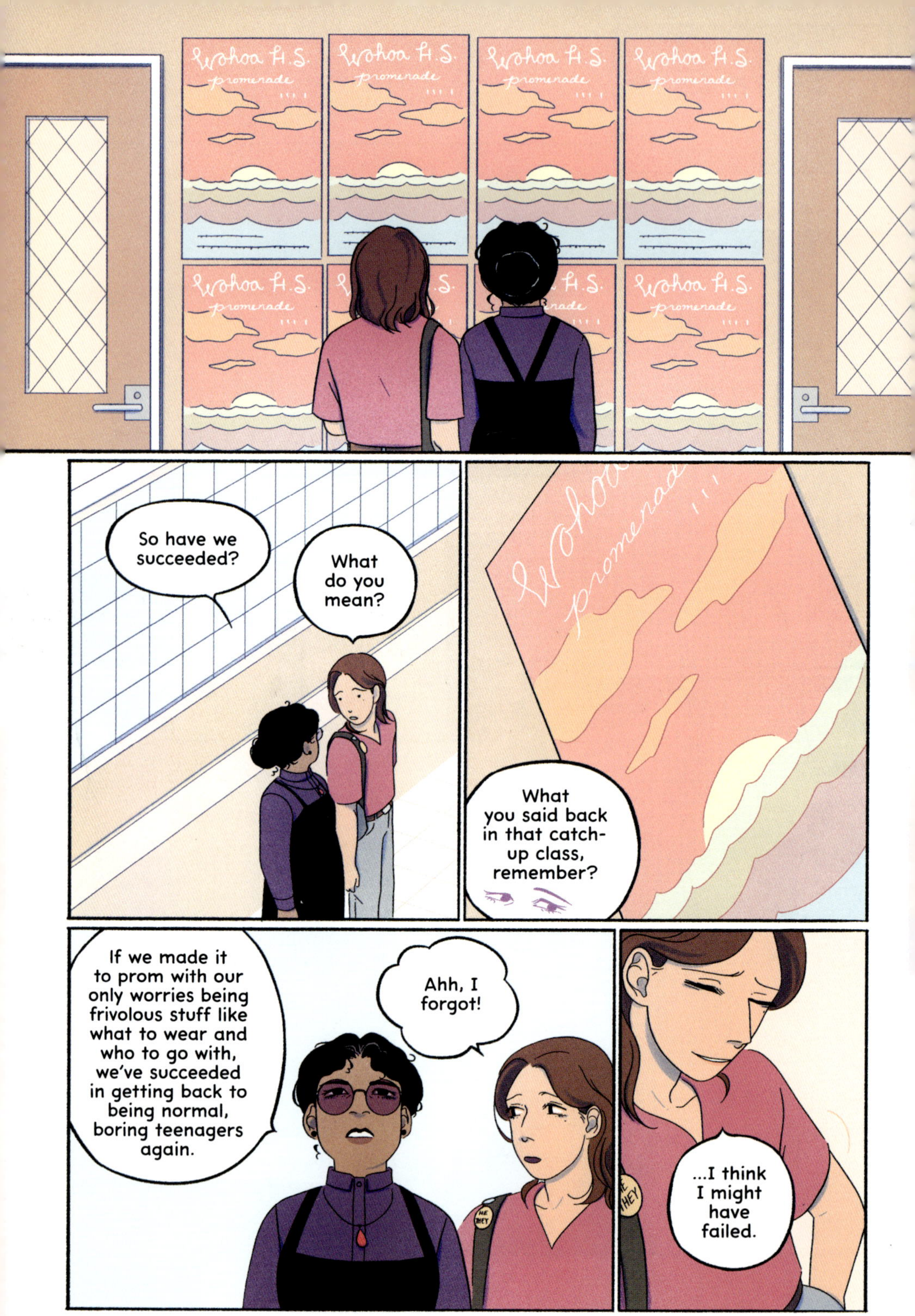
Wohoa H.S. promenade
So have we succeeded?
What do you mean?
What you said back in that catch-up class, remember?
If we made it to prom with our only worries being frivolous stuff like what to wear and who to go with, we've succeeded in getting back to being normal, boring teenagers again.
Ahh, I forgot!
...I think I might have failed.

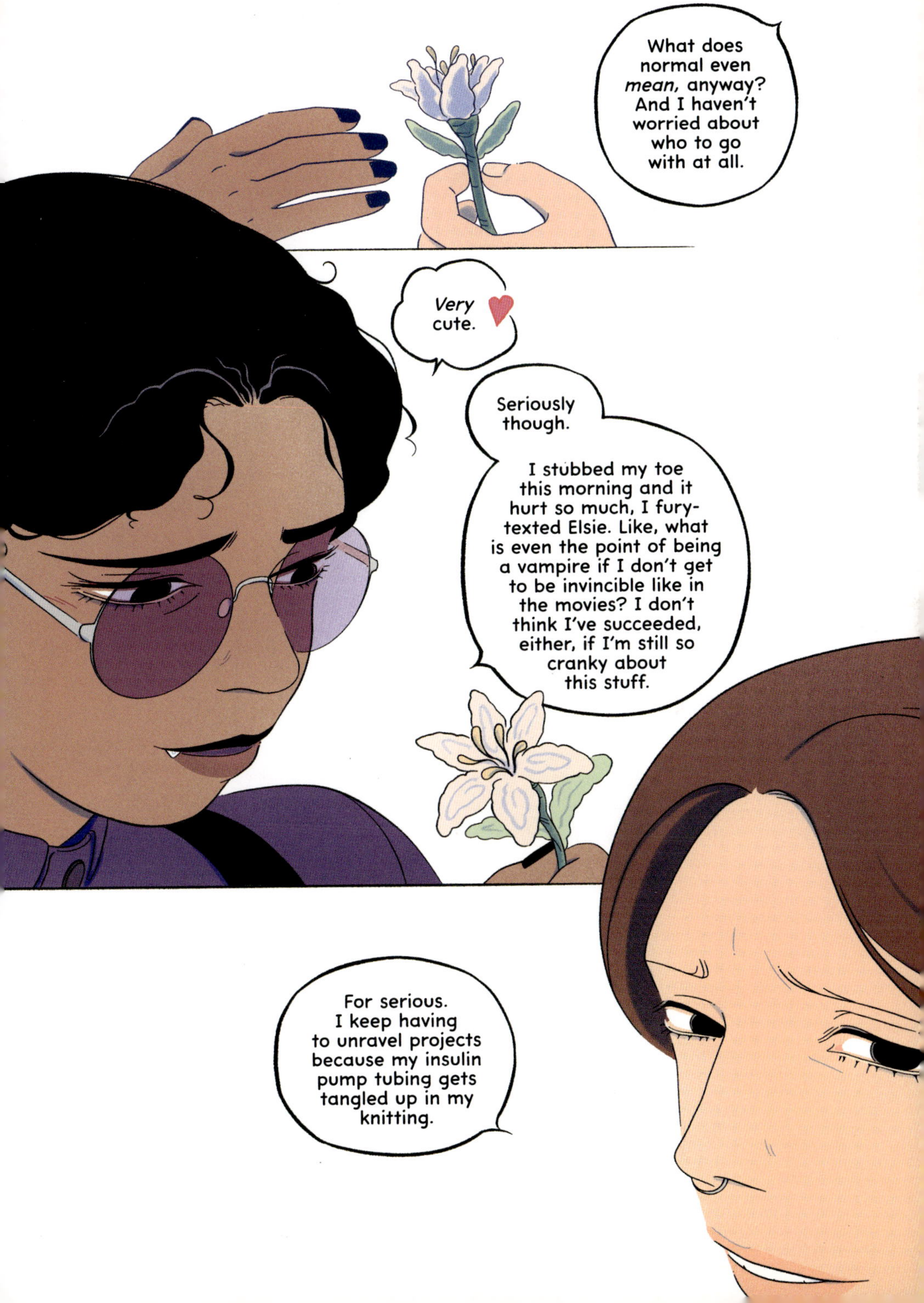
What does normal even *mean,* anyway? And I haven't worried about who to go with at all.
Very cute.
Seriously though.
I stubbed my toe this morning and it hurt so much, I fury-texted Elsie. Like, what is even the point of being a vampire if I don't get to be invincible like in the movies? I don't think I've succeeded, either, if I'm still so cranky about this stuff.
For serious. I keep having to unravel projects because my insulin pump tubing gets tangled up in my knitting.

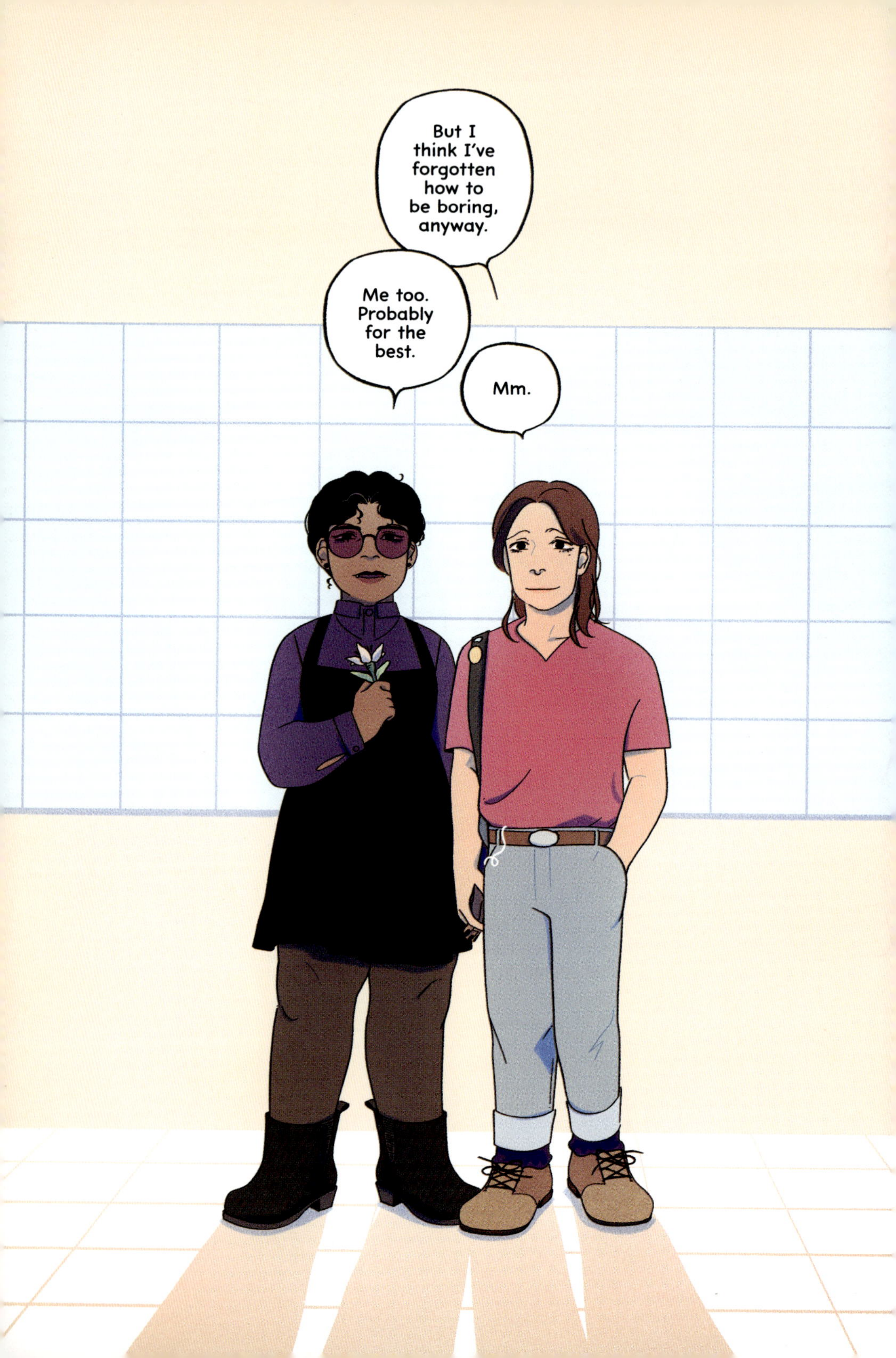
But I think I've forgotten how to be boring, anyway.
Me too. Probably for the best.
Mm.

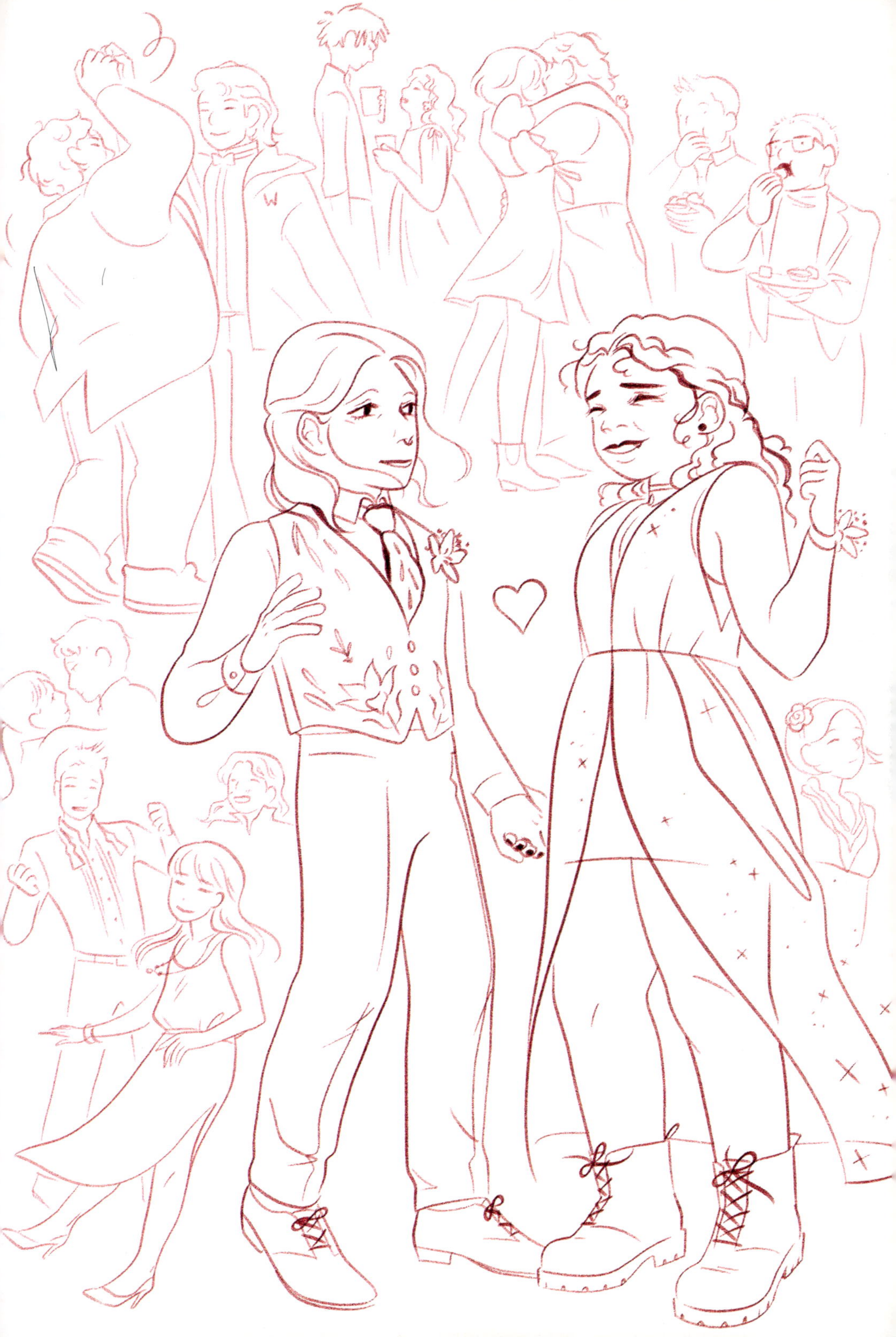

the magic of static

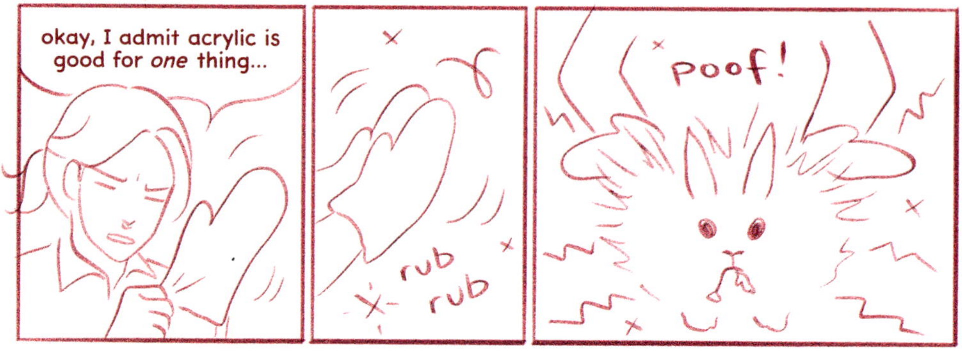
okay, I admit acrylic is good for *one* thing...
rub rub
poof!

small-business dilemmas

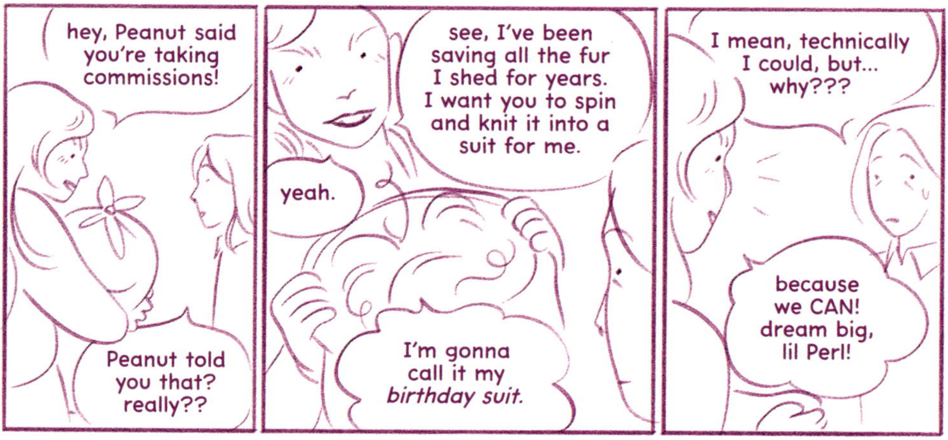
hey, Peanut said you're taking commissions!
Peanut told you that? really??
see, I've been saving all the fur I shed for years. I want you to spin and knit it into a suit for me.
yeah.
I'm gonna call it my *birthday suit.*
I mean, technically I could, but... why???
because we CAN! dream big, lil Perl!

painful memories

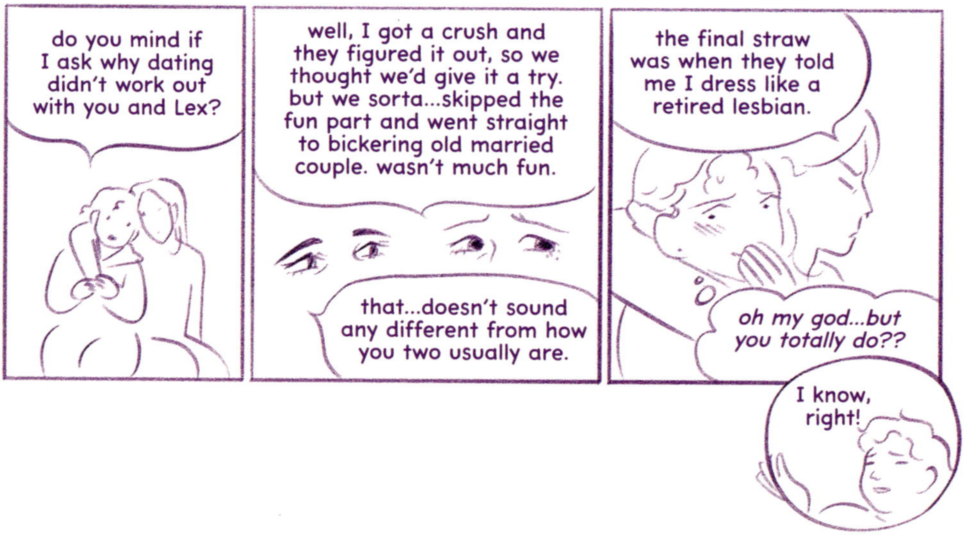
do you mind if I ask why dating didn't work out with you and Lex?
well, I got a crush and they figured it out, so we thought we'd give it a try. but we sorta...skipped the fun part and went straight to bickering old married couple. wasn't much fun.
that...doesn't sound any different from how you two usually are.
the final straw was when they told me I dress like a retired lesbian.
oh my god...but you totally do??
I know, right!

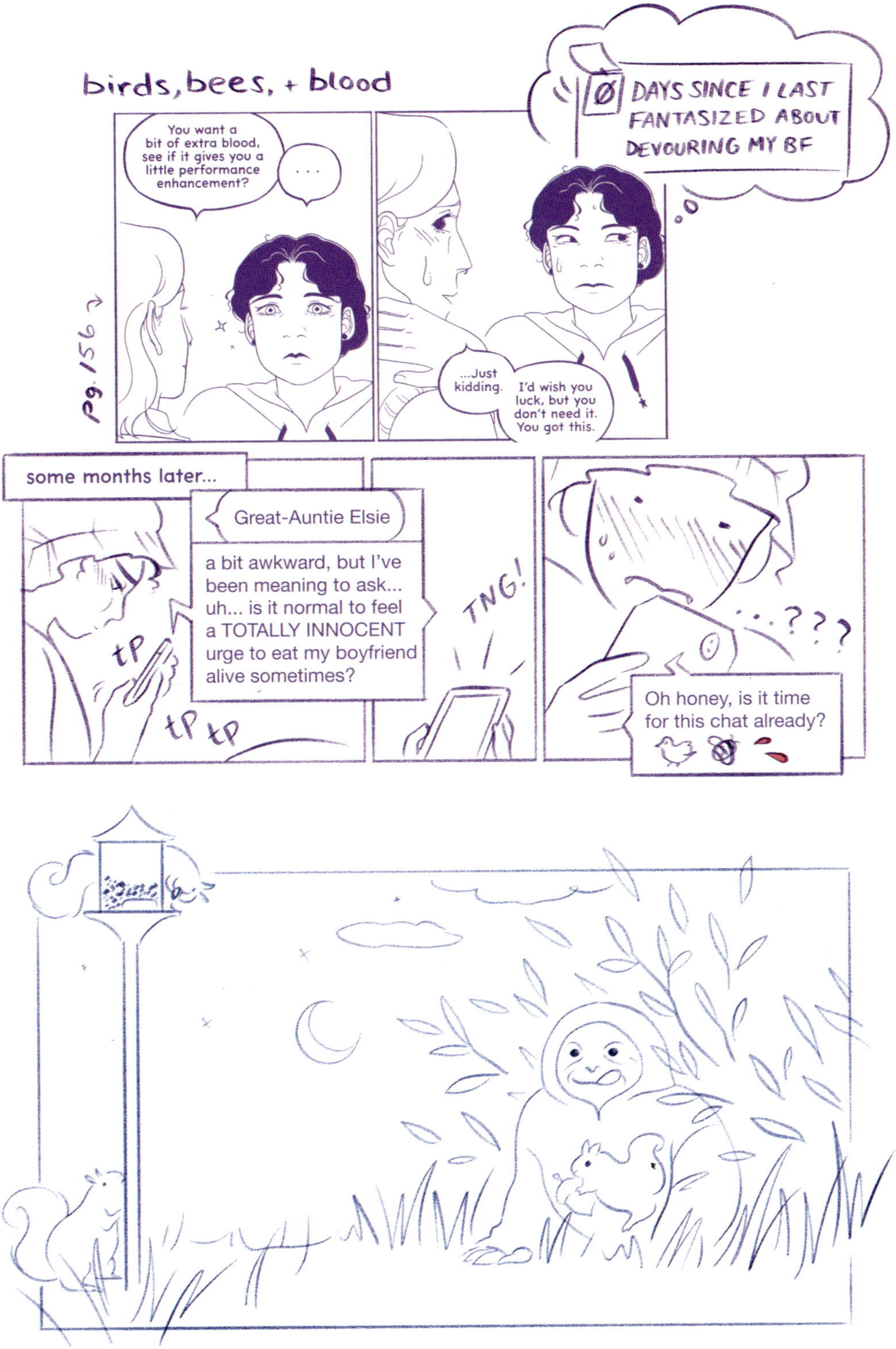
birds, bees, + blood
Ø DAYS SINCE I LAST FANTASIZED ABOUT DEVOURING MY BF
You want a bit of extra blood, see if it gives you a little performance enhancement?
. . .
Pg. 156
...Just kidding.
I'd wish you luck, but you don't need it. You got this.
some months later...
Great-Auntie Elsie
a bit awkward, but I've been meaning to ask... uh... is it normal to feel a TOTALLY INNOCENT urge to eat my boyfriend alive sometimes?
tp
tp tp
TNG!
...???
Oh honey, is it time for this chat already?

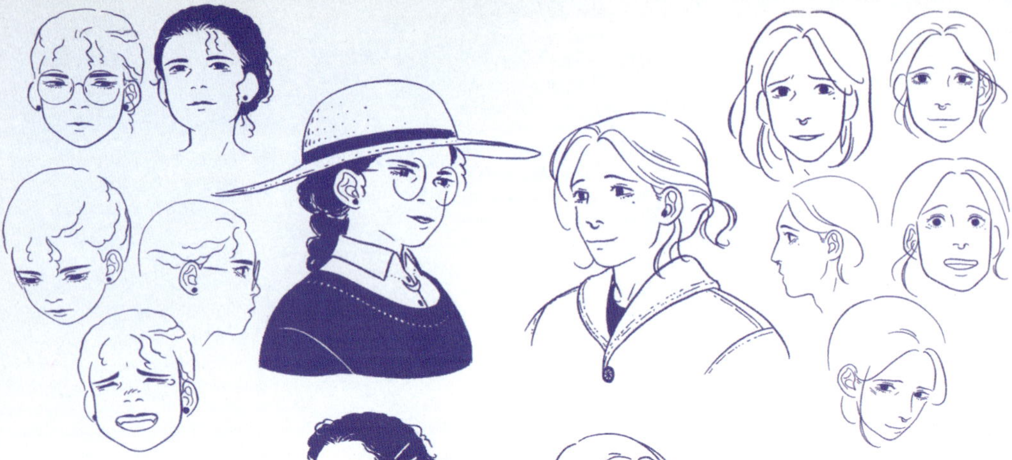

Amandine Lavigne

sixteen years old, 5'7"
fit with chubby hips/legs

jock witch aesthetic:
activewear mixed with
dark femme pieces,
always has her limbs
covered to keep sun off

round glasses
and hats when outside

likes to change up her
hairstyles often

Docs or high-tops

silhouette: crop top,
above knee skirt,
chunky shoes

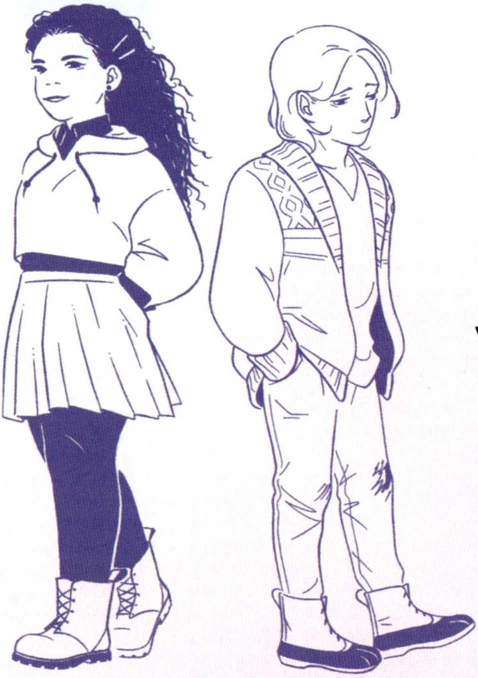

Perley Culpepper

sixteen years old, 5'6"
skinny with loose-fitting
clothes at start from
illness weight loss, gains
love handles back later

Maine farm boy look:
worn-out jeans and tees,
flannel, layers, and all
outfits feature at least
one prominent
home-knit item

simple hair styles

Bean boots or
canvas boat shoes

silhouette:
broad shoulders,
big sweaters, wiry legs

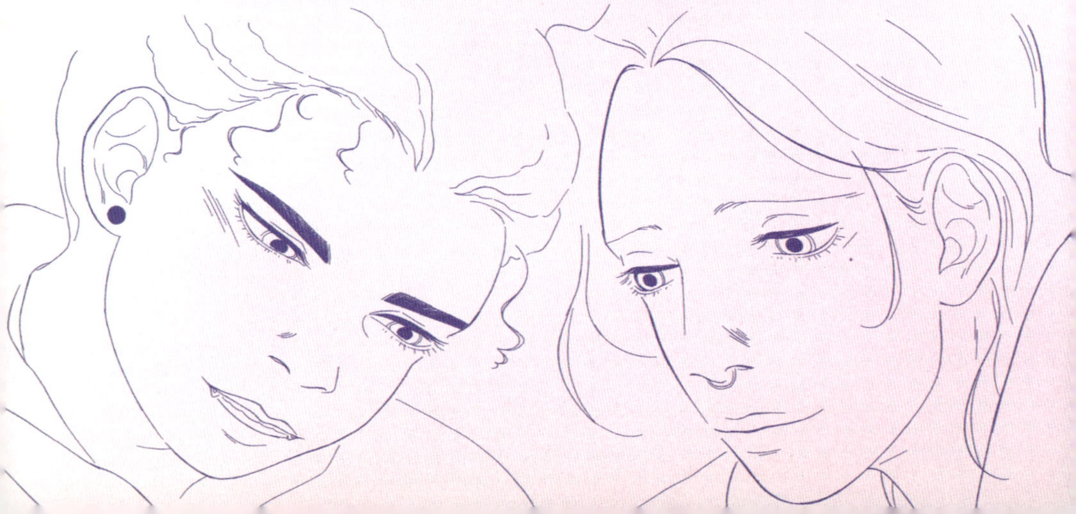

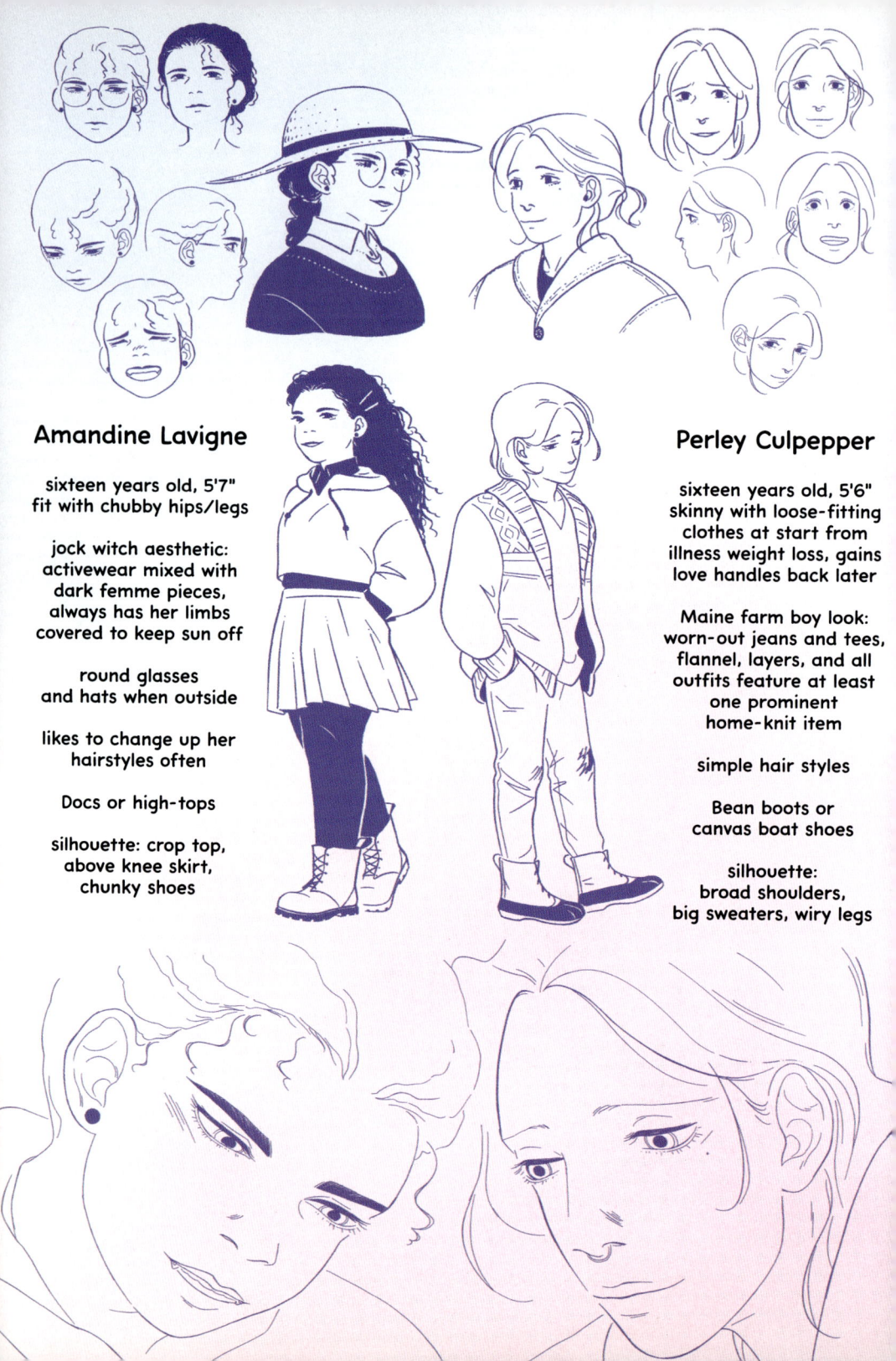

CREDITS

It takes a village to make a book, and I'm so very fortunate
to work with a great one at First Second. Thank you.

- ★ Acquiring editor: Calista Brill
- ★ Development editor: Benjamin A. Wilgus
- ★ Editorial support: Kiara Valdez
- ★ Creative director: Kirk Benshoff
- ★ Book designer: Molly Johanson
- ★ Production editors: Avia Perez and Kelly Markus
- ★ Managing editor: Dawn Ryan
- ★ Production manager: Alexa Blanco
- ★ Editorial intern: Rose Van de Walle
- ★ Copyeditor and proofreader: Kayla Overbey and Nicole Moreno
- ★ Authenticity readers: Autumn Crossman-Serb, Molly Johanson, and Dr. Francesca Lyn
- ★ Literary agent: Jennifer Linnan of Linnan Literary Management
- ★ And so many others, from publicity to printers—you're all amazing!

ACKNOWLEDGMENTS

My love and gratitude to:

Davie, my sweet, for everything;

Jen for your ongoing support and all those amazing knitting
and spinning photo references;

Benji, Niki Smith, Melanie Gillman, and Carey Pietsch
for your invaluable friendship and feedback;

my Perth comics cohort including Campbell, Elizabeth, Kristina, Aśka,
Soolagna, Suzanne, and Andrei for workshopping drafts and cheering me on;

Kori and Peter for the constant stream of photos of
creatures and landscapes I miss so much;

the rest of my beloved family and friends for your patience;

and the state of Maine. The home in my heart will always smell like pine and
salt, no matter how long I am away.

The Sweetness Between Us was written and drawn in Boorloo on unceded Whadjuk Noongar country. The fictional settlement of Wohoa is set on Passamaquoddy territory within the Dawnland, home of the Wabanaki Confederacy. It is a privilege to have lived and worked in these beautiful places.

Published by First Second
First Second is an imprint of Roaring Brook Press,
a division of Holtzbrinck Publishing Holdings Limited Partnership
120 Broadway, New York, NY 10271
firstsecondbooks.com

© 2024 by Sarah Winifred Searle
All rights reserved

Library of Congress Control Number: 2023948818

Our books may be purchased in bulk for promotional, educational, or business use.
Please contact your local bookseller or the Macmillan Corporate and Premium Sales Department
at (800) 221-7945 ext. 5442 or by email at MacmillanSpecialMarkets@macmillan.com.

First edition, 2024
Edited by Calista Brill, Kiara Valdez, and Benjamin A. Wilgus
Cover and interior book design by Molly Johanson
Production editing by Avia Perez and Kelly Markus
Authenticity readers: Autumn Crossman-Serb, Molly Johanson, and Dr. Francesca Lyn

Drawn entirely in Clip Studio Paint on an iPad.

Printed in China

ISBN 978-1-250-86318-8 (paperback)
10 9 8 7 6 5 4 3 2 1

ISBN 978-1-250-86319-5 (hardcover)
10 9 8 7 6 5 4 3 2 1

Don't miss your next favorite book from First Second!
For the latest updates go to firstsecondnewsletter.com and sign up for our enewsletter.